By William Keisling

The Midnight Ride of Jonathan Luna
Not Fade Away
The Meltdown
The Wrong Car
The Sins of Our Fathers
When the Levee Breaks
We All Fall Down
Maybe Four Steps
Helping Hands
Solar Water Heating Systems
Three Mile Island: Turning Point

the Midnight Ride of Jonathan Luna

William Keisling

Yardbird

The Midnight Ride of Jonathan Luna

ISBN 1-882611-18-7
FIRST EDITION, fourth printing (Rev. C)

This book was printed on acid-free paper. Set in Garamond 10/13 with Verdana display faces.

Yardbird Books can be found in any good book store. We encourage our readers to order books directly from us. A single copy can be purchased from us for $20.00, postage included. Pennsylvania residents please add six percent sales tax. Three or more copies of this book can be purchased for $15.00 each, including shipping. Order by calling Yardbird Books at 1-800-810-8770. Or write us at:

Yardbird Books, P.O. Box 5333, Harrisburg, PA 17110.

E-mail orders can also be sent to: info@yardbird.com. Visit our web page at yardbird.com. Digital versions of our books are available.

For document downloads, videos and other materials associated with this book, visit www.yardbird.com/luna.htm

Library of Congress Cataloging-in-Publication Data pending

Dedicated to the memory of
Babe Ruth

Acknowledgments

I'd like to thank Senator Chuck Grassley and Senator Patrick Leahy for their efforts to improve our federal law enforcement agencies. Thanks also to their staffs, for their courteous help with some of the material in this book.

Thanks to all who helped with this project. Steve Edwards and my brother, Craig Keisling, helped editorially. Thanks Dan and John Rivera. Thanks also to Rep. Mark Cohen for his invaluable advice and help.

The front cover photograph was taken by Eric Gerber. Apologies to Edvard Munch.

I'd like again to thank my readers, whose support made this book possible.

— bk

Contents

Part 1

Get your flip on: Warren Grace becomes a double-naught FBI informant

The poet judges not as a judge judges
but as the sun falling around a helpless thing.

— Walt Whitman

1
Ice cold

His car was found idling a short distance from the road, near the trees, in the dark of the night in the heart of Pennsylvania Dutch country. It was just a few minutes drive from the Pennsylvania turnpike. Blood, personal effects, and small sums of money were strewn around the inside of the car.

His body was found outside the idling car, near the front bumper, face down in an icy December stream, water running around him. His throat slashed, his back stabbed, his body pierced and cut dozens of times. His hands were slashed to ribbons, gashed to the bone defending himself. The ultimate barbarity was that his scrotum too had been strangely damaged. Yet all these vicious stab wounds had not finished him. He had been pulled or had crawled terrified from the car, and had drowned in the stream.

It was as if some strange bird of misfortune had fallen here. In older days, people in these parts painted hex signs on their barns to ward from their doorsteps this very sort of bedevilment. Tulips, spinning emblems, and Pennsylvania Dutch birds, meant as talismans of good fortune, still wink from colorful hex signs all around Lancaster County, into Reading, heading north on the "Hex Sign Highway" into Allentown.

But here's an ominous bird of a different feather carried by ill winds from the south. A strange and unsettling crime. A witching murder in Dutchieland, or so it might seem.

The death seemed all the more disquieting and mysterious as the body belonged to a federal prosecutor, thirty-eight-year-old Jonathan Luna. As he lay in the stream, Luna was still dressed in his court clothes, with a Justice Department ID badge hanging from his neck.

Luna was due in court later that morning for a case he was prosecuting. The case was going badly. It involved a hip-hop record producer and an associate who had been accused of selling large amounts of heroin in Baltimore. A little before midnight, facing problems with a plea agreement designed to end the case, Luna had inexplicably gotten up from his desk and walked off the face of the earth. He landed face down in the stream, some seventy miles from his office.

He'd vanished from the U.S. attorney's office in the federal courthouse in Baltimore, of all places. In his office he'd left behind personal effects including his cell phone and his eyeglasses. And he'd left something else behind: an oddly unfinished plea agreement, typed on his office laptop computer, on his desk, by his unseeing eyeglasses and his untalking cell phone.

That morning the prosecutor wouldn't be filing any papers in court. He was dead, his final appeal unheard. He had taken a deeply mysterious and wild midnight run across four states before landing dead in the stream.

There are clues in the stream with him. Or so we'd be told.

In reality, there are clues all around Luna, washing around him like an alluvial deposit. Some of these clues investigators refuse to pick up, lest they lead upstream, back to the investigators, back to a mother lode of political and judicial intrigue, strewn detritus whose trail ultimately leads to the highest reaches of state and federal government.

I've come to see Jonathan Luna as a white-collar canary in a coal mine, his broken body strewn like mining waste in a blackened stream of broken hopes and dashed promises.

On his right hand, in the stream, Luna wears a law school ring depicting scales of justice. I can't help thinking justice had gone down in a cold backwoods field, not very far at all from the place where American government had started.

It was December 4, 2003. Almost Christmas.

2
World War III

In the days before he died, in December 2003, Jonathan Luna, lawman, sat in a raven's perch overlooking unwinding, roiling, boiling Baltimore. He's the red-hot jammaster flash in the middle, scratching the record, naming the tune, wearing his scale of justice bling-bling ring.

You might not realize it to look at his youthful, inquisitive face, but Luna is one of the city's most important, if largely unknown, commanders in an increasingly ugly war against Baltimore's growing legions of free-for-all warring mobs, gangstas and crooked cops.

The office of U.S. Attorney is one of the most powerful in American government. Attorneys in these offices are, at least in theory, the top cops of their jurisdictions. From time to time they even prosecute corrupt local and state cops. Assistant U.S. attorneys such as Luna find themselves playing big roles with small billing, handling much if not all of the unseen workload, making life-and-death decisions as a daily part of their often-obscure jobs.

Many might see Jonathan Luna as a powerful figure. In reality, it's surprising how little power he had over crucial aspects of his job, and his cases. Often, his witnesses were allied with fearful, dark forces over which he had almost no control.

Some of society's worst nightmares cross Jon Luna's desk. In this rough and violent town, Luna handles an endless playbill of some of the country's roughest and most violent cases. These cases involve rough and violent characters. For example, Luna recently prosecuted three men who cracked heads, and sold crack cocaine, throughout Baltimore. Another man planned to burn down a house to rid his neighborhood of six Mexicans. A robber who shot up banks while wearing disguises. A Navy physicist trolling the net to find young girls. And on and on.

It's a tough terrain where it's often hard to tell the good from the bad. Many of Luna's cases rely on a supporting cast of shady, violent, duplicitous government witnesses.

Little recognition, perhaps, but the burden, and the danger, remain.

Luna had reason to fear losing his job. As ever, insecurity lurked behind his outward confidence and coolness. He confided to friends that his boss, U.S. Attorney Thomas DiBiagio, thought he wasn't doing a good job, that DiBiagio was trying to "push him out." So he worked hard, and he worked late.

Even so, Luna was used to working in rocky circumstances. That was his upbringing, and his real secret ride through life.

Still, Luna had to protect his job, and his reputation. His job insecurities had become the fodder of talk with friends and co-workers. One co-worker says he overheard DiBiagio say Luna was "gone." Another co-worker suggested Luna hire a lawyer to represent him in his troubles with DiBiagio. Luna, shortly before his death, retained experienced former federal prosecutor Andrew C. White.

Immediately following his grisly death, Luna's friends confided to reporters that he feared losing his job. When asked, DiBiagio curiously denied it.

"His job was not in jeopardy in any respect," the Baltimore Sun reported DiBiagio as saying.

"Jonathan Luna is remembered by this office as being a wonderful colleague, and his death is a genuine loss to us all," DiBiagio spun in a statement released to the press at Luna's death.

Months would go by before the truth, obscured by DiBiagio, began to emerge. In the summer of 2004, one of Luna's former co-workers, Assistant U.S. Attorney Lisa Griffin, wrote DiBiagio that, "I am deeply embarrassed to hear that you led the press to believe that Jonathan was not in jeopardy of losing his job. That was not so."

Griffin's comments appear in a long missive she composed to DiBiagio on the occasion of her finding another job. She complained that DiBiagio demanded "a dangerous homogeneity of thought," and that, "Good lawyers no longer speak up for fear of having their reputations tarnished."

Caught in a lie, DiBiagio curiously explained he'd merely been trying to protect Luna's family by issuing his earlier, misleading statements.

I would come to see that DiBiagio, withholding the truth, ultimately was protecting himself.

On the last night of his life, Luna was in his office working until almost midnight. He was fearing for his job. He busied himself trying to conclude a troubled plea agreement for two of those he prosecuted, Deon Lionnel Smith, 32, and Walter Oriley Poindexter, 28. Smith operated a fledgling rap music label, Stash House Records. Smith was also an aspiring rap singer who performed under the name Papi Jenkinz.

Luna had spent the week in court prosecuting Smith and Poindexter. He had been having a rough time. The two stood accused of dealing heroin from their Hampden neighborhood recording studio on West 36th Street. Thirty-six is a recurring number in this story.

Smith and Poindexter were charged with multiple counts of heroin distribution and conspiracy to sell heroin. Poindexter faced 60 years in prison for three counts of heroin distribution. Smith was looking at 27 years behind bars. Poindexter also stood accused of killing one Alvin "L" Jones, whom Poindexter suspected had burglarized one of their stash houses.

The government's main witness, Warren Grace, testified he sold and bought heroin with Smith and Poindexter. At trial, Grace's role turned pivotal, and amazing. Grace, it turned out, not only had worked with Poindexter and Smith, he'd also worked as a paid FBI informant.

On the stand, Grace and his principal FBI handler admitted that strange things had happened while he worked for the Justice Department. Though supposedly under house arrest, FBI agents had allowed Grace to come and go as he pleased. Turned loose by his FBI handlers, Grace was soon accused by angry neighbors of shooting up the neighborhood, and dealing heroin. While he worked for the feds Grace distributed heroin, and heroin was even found in Grace's Ford Excursion.

The defense cried foul. They accused a normally fastidious Luna of failing to make proper disclosures before the trial about these strange irregularities involving the government's dealings with Warren Grace. There were more mysteries to uncover. What exactly *was* informant Warren Grace doing with his FBI handlers? What secrets was Luna keeping, and why?

The angered judge agreed to an investigation of Luna and his FBI cohorts. That's when Luna suddenly agreed to a plea deal, stopping the trial, stopping the inquiry of himself and the FBI.

Luna offered a plea agreement that knocked decades off Smith and Poindexter's jail time. In addition, Poindexter wouldn't be charged with Alvin Jones' murder. Trouble was, the agreement wasn't legal.

I came to see that Luna had reasons to be suspicious, even fearful, of the FBI agents working around him. Time would show that certain FBI agents disliked him. Disliked him very much. One or more agents even had reason to want Luna discredited, even gone.

Who was working for whom? Who were the good guys? Who in this dark world of hip-hop, back-stabbing, secret talk money, untrustworthy FBI agents, and hushaboo drug-fueled murder could be trusted? This mix of drugs, violence, informants, duplicity, bad feds and sloppy prosecutions, all were sopping together into a wild, secretive, explosive soup.

Was Luna merely being a good soldier by withholding information from the defense? No. Far from it. He knew his own neck was on the line. This case. Other cases. His career. His deteriorating relations with Grace's FBI handlers. His deteriorating relations with his boss, the U.S. attorney. There was even a matter of large sums of missing money—.

Warren Grace was living the high life while under FBI keep. Luna on the last day of his life found himself paying the price for growing, scandalous problems within the FBI — locally, in Baltimore, Delaware and Philadelphia, and nationally. One malfeasance usually is an indicator of more. Experience trains you to suspect similar problems lurking just out of view.

On this subject of bad-acting FBI agents Luna didn't need to speculate. He had ample reason to know just how bad some of the agents could be.

As prosecuting attorney, Luna had some input concerning the handling of his witness, the FBI informant. *But he didn't have control.* Ultimately, the FBI is in charge of its informant. Informants, and their handling, have become a sacred, secret institution within the FBI.

Lately this has earned the FBI increasing trouble, and unwelcome scrutiny. In next-door Washington DC, throughout much of 2003, in the last months, weeks and days of Luna's life, Congress exposed one horrid scandal after another involving criminal, even murderous behavior involving rogue FBI agents and their unknown legions of informants.

Congress at long last was holding hearings, and uncovering a dark and sinister side to FBI secret operations. The hearings established not only that rogue agents and their informants have long participated in crimes like murder, racketeering and extortion. It also became clear that this wasn't just a problem in the field. Senior FBI administrators were shown to have known about heinous crimes committed by the bureau's informants, and turned a blind eye. Informants who had worked with the bureau for years were suddenly vanishing. A portrait began to emerge of an institution you'd expect to find in a banana republic police state, and not in the United States of America.

These congressional hearings were enough to send shivers down the back of every concerned prosecutor in America. The hearings documented that FBI agents routinely kept crucial information from prosecutors and defense attorneys alike.

Luna, a justice department prosecutor, an avid and close reader of newspapers, a writer of letters to newspapers, would have been professionally remiss not to have known of the storm brewing in Congress.

Luna would have known, merely from reading the papers, of growing signs of nationwide problems within the FBI. Only the week before, on November 22, 2003 (coincidentally the fortieth anniversary of the murder of John F. Kennedy), Luna's hometown newspaper, The New York Times, headlined a story, "FBI let innocents get death sentences: report."

A closely watched congressional committee had, only the week before Luna's disappearance, issued a report exposing what can only he called sinister FBI informant activities in Boston. One retired agent was even charged with arranging a gangland murder, with the help of his longtime informants. One committee witness, a U.S. Attorney, even ominously testified:

"(I)f you go against (the FBI), they will try to get you. They will wage war on you. They will cause major administrative problems for me as a prosecutor.... (It) would have precipitated World War III if I tried to get inside the FBI to deal with informants. That was the holy of holies, inner sanctum. They wouldn't have allowed me to do anything about that."

This amazing report was made public only the week before Luna's death.

At the same time, another report, prepared internally by the FBI, and kept secret even from Congress, detailed criminal behavior perpetrated by scores of FBI agents — from murder, to theft, to rape.

And now, on the day of his death, Luna had obvious problems with Warren Grace, heroin, and the FBI.

In Jonathan Luna we see a young man increasingly caught in rough waters, swamped on both sides of the blurred safety line of the law.

When a federal judge allowed defense questioning of informant Warren Grace, silent alarm bells appear to have gone off in Luna's head. He knew he had trouble with the FBI, and he must have feared his own case would end up a headline.

Many people don't like getting up in the morning to face their jobs.

Jonathan Luna, every morning, had to fear World War III.

One day it came.

3
Welcome to Bawlmer, Hon!

From the fire of the burning city, to the ice cold of the country stream, from his late night office in the federal courthouse in Baltimore, to the icy Pennsylvania creek where his body was found at five thirty the next morning, Jonathan Luna took a mysterious joy ride across four states.

He leaves his desk with all the sudden dispatch of a man fleeing a fire. Leaving his life behind, leaving his cell phone and his eyeglasses behind on his desk, Jonathan Luna inexplicably hurries from his office in the federal courthouse, gets into his car and drives away into the night, leaving few traces and no explanation, no means to call for help, setting himself up as a victim of an almost perfect murder.

The Lombard Street federal building, where Luna worked, and where he was last seen alive, overlooks outwardly placid downtown Baltimore. It's not far from the Oriole's festive Camden Yards stadium. The area is held within the outstretched arms of gusty Inner Harbor, its National Aquarium, touristy shops and restaurants.

It's the Baltimore outsiders see, not the surrounding bombed-out districts of ever-increasing violence and gangland free-for-all. This part of the city — the burning part of the city — is the part that Assistant U.S. Attorney Jonathan Luna knew best.

Baltimore *is* burning these days, at times quite literally. The murder rate is a daily topic. Murder, police say, is often targeted, and focused on the drug trade.

When he ran for the mayor's job in 1999, youthful and photogenic Democrat Martin O'Malley pledged to reduce the yearly murder rate from more than 300, to 175. Since taking office, O'Malley's promise had come to haunt him. In 2002 Baltimore saw 253 murders, just three less than the year before. In 2003, the murder rate climbed to 271. At this writing, in November 2004, there's been 249 killings, and many expect the murder rate to top 2003's total by year's end. So reducing Baltimore's murder rate has been a promise that's proved difficult to keep.

Instead, O'Malley, hoping to raise morale, engaged a PR firm and began pasting the word "Believe" across the city on billboards, banners and ubiquitous bumper stickers.

A high crime rate, at least no doubt partly tied to a poor economy, would seem to be a regional trend. But don't tell that to Baltimoreans. Baltimore's murder rate rose with Philadelphia and New York's. Gangsta violence forced Washington DC officials to declare a "crime emergency" in the summer of 2003. Some of this turf-warring naturally spills over into nearby Baltimore.

Baltimore nonetheless has its own share of problems.

Baltimore's population in the 2000 U.S. census stood at 651,154. Of this, 418,951 (64 percent) are black, with 205,982 (32 percent) listed as white. The U.S. Department of Justice estimates at least 60,000 Baltimoreans are addicted to crack or heroin. (Of these, according to the Justice Department, some 45,000 are heroin junkies.) That's *a full 10 percent* of the city's population. Another 60,000 addict-suburbanites are estimated to come into the Baltimore looking for a fix. That's lots of violence burning in the veins, and the streets, of Baltimore. That's 120,000 drug addicts, to paraphrase Allen Ginsberg, crawling the streets of Baltimore searching for an angry fix.

That's nearly the size of the U.S. occupation force in Iraq in 2004.

"The question is, what are they fighting over?" Duke University sociology professor said Kenneth Land recently mused. "Is it retribution homicides, or turf wars over drugs, or is it protecting turf?"

The sociologists seem to float above the problem with the same lofty detachment an airliner rises from BWI — Baltimore/Washington International Airport. The average Baltimorean will tell you it's about drug warring gangstas and ineffectual (or outright bad) cops, two groups whose allegiances, agencies and activities these days increasingly seem to join, blur, and mix. This official corruption, I'd come to see, festers, always with the help of a well-turned blind eye, on both ends of Jonathan Luna's midnight ride.

As a result, Baltimoreans lately find themselves shocked almost daily by audacious tragedy. Spectacular bank robberies, gangland shootings, cops shot, and cops gone bad.

The low point came with the murders of Angela and Carnell Dawson and their five children on October 16, 2002. The Dawsons had called the cops dozens of times to complain about heroin and crack dealings in front of their home. One Darrell Brooks, 21, retaliated by torching her house late one night, killing Mrs. Dawson and the kids. Her husband, Carnell, somehow managed to jump from the house with burns covering almost 80 percent of his body. Carnell Dawson later died. The house had been firebombed two weeks earlier. Meaningful help seemed out of reach for the Dawsons and their kids.

The police seemed ineffective, if not indirectly (or perhaps directly) complicit. Authorities acknowledged they weren't properly supervising Brooks, who was out on probation at the time. Brooks' in-again, out-again jail career came to be called "revolving door justice." With the deaths of Dawson and her kids the public's trust had been broken. It was the last straw. Some called for vigilante justice.

"Since the police cannot stop these ruthless thugs, it's time for the black community to take the law into their own hands," Noble Johns wrote in a vocal internet broadside, the Black News Weekly, shortly afterward. "Everyone in the black community knows who is selling and using crack, and it's up to us to protect our own communities and take these criminals OUT! We as men must take back our own communities across this country by any means necessary, even if it mean taking vigilante action."

But it's not a vigilante's job to clean up this mess. That job belonged to Jonathan Luna. That is, when he wasn't creating, and trying to cover-up, his own mess.

From his catbird's seat in the Baltimore U.S. attorney's office, our hip-hop lawman Jonathan Luna prosecuted many vicious crimes, that's true. He also observed, and even participated in, official misdeeds, keeping, all the while, a tight-lipped, insider's perspective.

His life became a short thread spun into the sick tapestry of a dirty town. Jonathan Luna would be chewed up and thrown down, and his reputation destroyed, even as Baltimore burns.

4
Unfinished business: Jonathan Luna's last file

Shortly before midnight, when Jonathan Luna walked out of his office in the federal courthouse, he left behind an unfinished plea agreement in the laptop computer on his desk.

That plea agreement, Luna knew, could not be lawfully completed. The plea agreement, Luna knew, would unlawfully cover up a murder he was obligated by law to prosecute: Walter Poindexter's murder of Alvin Jones.

Trouble was, Luna was under tremendous pressure to complete that plea agreement, despite the law.

If he did not find a way to complete the plea agreement, Luna and fellow conspirators working in law enforcement would in a day or two find themselves under investigation in federal court.

The death of Jonathan Luna is an odd mystery, to say the least.

When an assistant U.S. attorney like Luna is found dead in a cold creek, after spending his day in a federal courtroom, there are circumstances not present in the death of an ordinary citizen.

Some of these differences are easy to discern. Some differences are outright curious. Luna's autopsy report, for instance, would be curiously sealed by Luna's co-workers, and mysteriously withheld from the public that he — and they — served. Just as curiously, Luna's reputation and his good name were immediately savaged and destroyed by his co-workers — FBI agents. Also strange, to say the least.

The heroin and murder case Luna worked on at the hour of his disappearance now itself becomes evidence, and provides clues, in Luna's own murder file. I've come to see it as sort of a hall of mirrors.

Luna was working on a legal file that itself is now evidence in a murder investigation file. It's worse than that, really. The people in charge of the investigation are themselves subjects of the investigation.

Look at it like this: If an automobile mechanic suddenly walks out of his garage at midnight, while working on a car, his tools still on his workbench, and is found dead in a stream miles away, we naturally will be interested in the car on which he was working. We'd wonder about his customer, the owner of that car, at the moment of his disappearance. We'd naturally wonder, how well was the repair job going? We'd also want to know if the mechanic was at all involved in some sort of conspiracy with the owner of the car.

If it turned out that the owner of the unfixed car was the proverbial little old lady from Pasadena, that's one thing. If it turned out that the unfixed car was needed by a criminal enterprise as a getaway car, and the mechanic couldn't fix it in a timely fashion, that's a Ford of a different color, isn't it?

It turns out that Jonathan Luna, euphemistically, was working on a very hot car, one that had to be dumped. Worse, Luna screwed up — perhaps even stood in the way of — the dumping.

A good detective will get as much information as possible about the repair job this mechanic was performing at the time of his death. A thorough detective will look at all the written records available about the mechanic's jobs, and more.

Now, imagine, if someone had stood around the deceased mechanic taking accurate, moment-by-moment notes of everything the mechanic, and those around him, said or did in the last working days and hours of his life. That would be invaluable.

Such is the strange case of Jonathan Luna. I would discover over seven hundred pages of transcripts detailing Luna's last curious days and hours on earth.

Shortly after Luna's death in December 2003, I began work on what was to become this book. As chance would have it, this is the fourth book I've written touching on murder and untimely death.

I'm always haunted by the deaths of those I write about. Luna's case is no different.

When I write about someone who has been murdered, or has met with untimely death, I'm writing about someone who has stopped singing in the middle of his or her song. It is an aria broken off into thin air. They are unable to finish their song.

My job, of course, is to try to understand what happened. What was their story? What were they doing, what were they thinking, the moment their voices went quiet? What would they say, if they could? I try to get into their lives, and into their heads. I sometimes feel like I'm walking in the shoes of the dead. The Luna case is no different.

In early 2004 I began researching in earnest the circumstances surrounding Jonathan Luna's mysterious death. I began where Luna started the night of his death: the federal courthouse on Lombard Street, in downtown Baltimore. I arrived one gloomy day in late winter to read the files on the cases on which Luna was working. I also was interested in reading the transcripts of Luna's last day in court, on the last day of his life.

It turns out I was not the only one interested in these court transcripts. With good reason.

The federal courthouse in Baltimore stands, as I mentioned, a few blocks from Inner Harbor. It's across the street from the city's convention center. Still, it's a neighborhood with a strangely abandoned feeling. It's ironically a crime-ridden neighborhood. Employees at the courthouse warn me it's an unsafe neighborhood, particularly after dark. The parking garages warn of the dangers of theft. Be sure to take your cell phone from your car, one sign warns, as cell phones are particularly desirable to thieves.

The main entrance to the courthouse seems hauntingly abandoned. It's a modern building, with lots of glass and steel. Outside, the entranceway embraces an open plaza, with a sculptured seating area in one corner on Lombard Street. In my repeated visits, I seldom if ever saw anyone sit there. No children played there. People seemed to hurry about their business, not lingering in the plaza.

At the other side of the building, at the rear cornerstone of the courthouse facing the convention center on Pratt Street, stands, in isolation, an outdoor statue of late Supreme Court Justice Thurgood Marshall. In his Baltimore days, because of the cases he took, Thurgood Marshall was known as "the little man's lawyer." His statue today fittingly overlooks the corner, facing the convention center. Street urchins shuffle by, under Marshall's owlish gaze. Rather appropriate, I thought. At first you imagine the statue is abandoned by all but the elements and the pigeons. But as the street people of Baltimore saunter by, you realize here is where Thurgood Marshall *always* stood. This is where Marshall, like Franklin and Lincoln before him, always kept his keen eye.

Thurgood Marshall worked as chief counsel for the Baltimore branch of the NAACP, where he championed landmark civil rights cases, including 1954's *Brown v The Board of Education,* which threw out the "separate but equal" doctrine and opened the nation's schools to non-whites. Yet Baltimore wasn't always kind to Thurgood Marshall. He was rejected by the University of Maryland School of Law because of his race. The stone that the builder rejects, the Bible tells us, shall be the new cornerstone.

Today, U of Maryland's law library is named for Thurgood Marshall.

It's paper, scissors, and stone, at the Baltimore federal courthouse, I'd come to see. Thurgood Marshall blazed the trail for many who today work in the glassy, detached Baltimore federal courthouse, and who will figure in this story, including Luna, and federal judge William Quarles. Quarles actually attended the University of Maryland, decades after Marshall was turned away.

Walking quietly into the modern courthouse, finding my way to the clerk's office, I felt vaguely unsettled. These were walls and floors and faces that Jonathan knew, places where he'd walked in life. I felt strangely like the Bruce Willis character in *The Sixth Sense.*

In the clerk of court's office I straightaway asked to see the file on the case on which Luna worked on the last day of his life — Smith and Poindexter case. I had a strange sense that the employee in the office knew that this was prosecutor Luna's last case. It doesn't take long, studying the life of Jonathan Luna, to learn that Luna went out of his way to meet people in the courthouses where he worked. They liked him. I would come to learn that Luna's death was traumatic for many in the Baltimore federal courthouse. In the clerk's office I sensed something else, however intangible. I sensed fear.

And something else. By walking into the clerk's office, and asking for that file, I was walking into a baffling murder investigation.

The clerk handed me a thick manila folder of court papers. I sat at a table in the clerk's office, opened the file, and began to read. I went back for several files. The Smith-Poindexter file. The file on Warren Grace. Related files.

While I read, I noticed, in the corner of my eye, the clerk pick up the phone. She had a brief conversation, then hung up.

A minute or so passed, and then a man dressed in a suit came in and stood at the clerk's window. After a minute or so he turned, and addressed me.

"You look familiar," he said to me. "Don't I know you from somewhere?"

"I don't believe," I responded. He seemed to want me to introduce myself, and to state my business. I did neither. An awkward moment passed. "Is the person I remind you of a good guy or a bad guy?"

"Oh, a good guy," he said. With that he awkwardly left the office.

I thought it a rather strange encounter. My suspicions only grew.

A month or so later I returned to read more of the files. Again, strangely, as I sat reading the court papers, the clerk again picked up the phone and had a brief conversation. No more than a sentence or two. I went out into the hall, turned the corner and stood by the elevators. An elevator opened, and the same man I had encountered on my first visit stepped out. He seemed to recognize me from my previous visit, appeared startled, and muttered something about having gotten off on the wrong floor. He awkwardly hurried away. On the wrong floor.

I began to suspect that someone was watching to see who was coming in off the street to read the Luna files. But why? Certainly, if Luna had been killed in a random act of street violence, I reasoned, his killer wouldn't wander in to study his legal papers.

The Baltimore U.S. Attorney's office, I soon came to realize, had more to worry about here than solving Luna's murder. U.S. Attorney Tom DiBiagio and his staff had to worry that an investigator from the

U.S. Congress, or a major newspaper, or a book writer such as myself, would walk into the clerk's office, and ask to read the Luna files.

They have to worry that the American public will come to read closely these files. They have to worry, as Lincoln Steffens wrote, that the shameful facts in these files, spread out in all their shame, will burn through our civic shamelessness, and set fire to American pride.

Still, I noticed, documents alluded to by other documents were missing from the file. Most glaringly, the transcripts of the court proceedings, the written record of what had been said in court, were not in the folder.

At the conclusion to my first visit to the clerk of court's office, as I returned the files, I asked, in an offhand manner, to see the court transcripts from Luna's last case.

The clerk queried her computer, and told me that court transcripts *hadn't been made in the Smith-Poindexter case.* That was odd, I couldn't help responding. Here supposedly was a murder investigation involving hundreds of FBI agents, scouring the countryside for clues, and there still were no transcripts from Luna's last day in court. Later, I would discover other documents mysteriously missing from Luna's files.

I could order the transcripts from the court reporter, I was told. The court reporter unfortunately was about to retire, the clerk went on, so I'd have to hurry.

I was given the court reporter's office number. By the time I called he'd already retired. I finagled his home number from someone in the court reporter's office.

On the phone, the newly retired court reporter, Ned Richardson, at first expressed reservations about supplying me with the transcripts. He said that they were viewed as "sensitive." By whom? I asked. By the FBI, he replied in a quiet voice. They were part of a criminal investigation, he offered. He said he wasn't sure if they could be released. He explained he'd just finished transcribing them for investigators, a job that had been somewhat delayed due to his retirement, and had just the week before turned them over to the U.S. attorney's office in Baltimore.

I pointed out court transcripts were public documents, and held my breath. There was a pause. He said there were over 700 pages of transcripts. At the federal rate of 83 cents per page, it would cost me a little over $600.

I took directions to his house and left immediately.

The court reporter, Ned Richardson, turned out to be tall and lanky. He has an intense, attentive manner befitting a man who has spent decades listening to, and recording, every word spoken in a federal courtroom.

I expressed wonderment that nearly five months had passed since Luna's death and the government was just now getting around to ordering and studying the transcripts. It was after all early May 2004. I pointed out that the Justice Department had bragged that hundreds of state and federal investigators had been placed on a task force supposedly searching for clues to Luna's death. The transcripts from his last days on the job seemed pertinent to any serious investigation. Perhaps the investigation wasn't serious, I ventured.

Richardson explained that the delay was partly his fault, due to his retirement. He'd had to pack up his office, and finish other pressing tasks, before he could complete the Luna transcripts. Even so, he said, he'd found himself under increasing pressure from the Justice Department to finish the transcripts. He said they'd been calling and asking about the transcripts for weeks, increasingly pressuring him to hurry.

He produced a receipt showing that that Baltimore Assistant U.S. Attorney John F. "Jack" Purcell, one of Luna's former associates, had ordered the transcripts back on February 10, 2004. This two-month delay from Luna's death was really nothing unusual, Richardson tried to assure me. Purcell had finally taken delivery of the transcripts on April 23, a little more than a week before I called, and met, Richardson.

Purcell had requested transcripts of all proceedings, including "any bench conferences." A treasure trove.

Ned Richardson handed me a heavy box containing four thick, bound volumes. Seven hundred and twenty-six pages, in all. I was the only party, aside from the Justice Department, to have the transcripts, he told me. He seemed fascinated by the case, and was naturally upset with Luna's strange and disquieting demise.

As I wrote out a check for the transcripts, the court reporter described Jonathan Luna. "He always wore his glasses in court," Richardson remembers. "He needed them to see." It seems strange, he tells me, that Luna had left his glasses behind on his desk the night he died. And his cell phone.

He describes Jonathan Luna as standing less than six feet tall. "Maybe five-ten." Luna was slight, he says, no more than 165 pounds. While others in the courthouse, particularly prosecutors, characterize Luna as struggling in his job, Richardson remembers Jonathan as a generally bright and articulate young man, with a lot on the ball. That is, until his last case, when Luna seemed to come unglued. Luna, the court reporter says, was obviously fumbling, uncharacteristically so, he said, in his last case. "Jonathan, what are you doing?" he said he asked himself as he watched Luna's last, odd performance.

There were other oddities to the case, Richardson remembers. On the witness stand, FBI Special Agent Steven Skinner, who worked with Luna on the Smith-Poindexter case, "Looked like he didn't want to be there. Which was odd because he spent almost two years on this case. You'd think he'd want to be in court."

Why had Luna agreed to a plea? I wondered. Was it because the judge agreed to investigate Luna's star witness, heroin dealer Warren Grace? I asked.

"That's what it looked like to me," Richardson said. "Go ahead and read for yourself."

He said he believed I would be particularly interested in the workings of Baltimore's heroin shops, as described in the transcripts.

I thanked Richardson, and left with the heavy box tucked beneath an arm.

With growing amazement I discovered a play, and a play within a play. Luna is a real life Hamlet, a fresh of prince of South Bronx, trodding the boards of legal indecision and improvisational deconstruction in Courtroom 3-A, before spinning off the edge of the globe. Trapped in a moral dilemma, Luna must, in the words of critic Ernest Johnson, "disentangle himself from the temptation to wreak justice for the wrong reasons and in evil passion, and to do what he must do at last for the pure sake of justice."

The curtain opens on the day Jonathan Luna met his FBI-sponsored informant, Warren Grace.

5
Meet Warren Grace and get your flip on

Take a long hard look at Warren Grace. What's he doing out of jail? You got him out. What's he doing, of all places, in your office? You brought him here. What's he doing back in his hood? You're going to send him there.

See how he slumps in your chair, his eyes looking furtively back at you, sizing you up. He doesn't seem impressed with your suit and tie. He doesn't know your background, doesn't know you came from surroundings not much different than his own. Ask yourself, why do you think they call him Pug?

His is one of those faces you'll never forget. It will be with you on the night you die.

Dancing like a specter through the neglected tragedy of inner-city Baltimore, paid FBI informant Warren Grace moves like a shadow through the last calamitous days, hours and minutes in the life of Jonathan Luna.

Warren Grace's remarkable career as a paid FBI informant begins in April 2002, shortly after he was caught with heroin and a machine gun in Baltimore. Grace actually had two guns. He's a heroin gangster. At the time, just 21 years old, Warren Grace already was a repeat offender, and had already served nearly five years on heroin and gun charges. Less than eighteen months earlier he had returned to the street from prison. Now it was all but good night for Warren Grace, the cops and the prosecutors would think. Somehow they'd end up writing Grace's own ticket out. Pug, like a mythical mischievous Pan, has a way of turning tables.

He had grown up in inner-city Baltimore with just his mother in the house. There wasn't a family for Warren Grace. There wasn't a village for him either. There was always just himself, Warren Grace, looking out for Warren Grace.

At fourteen he began hustling, selling cocaine and heroin on the street. He was called Pug. He never got past the eleventh grade.

In 1994, just sixteen, Grace was selling crack on the street when he first encountered Walter Poindexter, another lifetime offender three years Grace's senior. Poindexter's street names are equally evocative: Fella and Shorty. As I read the court transcripts I learned the story. Grace recalls, in the transcripts, "I met him beginning in '94, you know, on the strip, on the street corner. He was walking by, (walking) a dog, and we exchanged numbers and just went from there. You know, he was just walking down the street with his dog.

"I was hustling. I was selling drugs," Grace says. "Cocaine. He told me he had a few prices about cocaine." Grace took Poindexter's number. A month or so later, Grace says, "I called him, you know, and we hooked up, you know, and he fronted me some cocaine to sell. It was basically like he would give me the drugs to sell and I would pay him later on after I would finish or whatever. I would keep part of it, and whatever I owed him, I would turn it in."

Under Poindexter's tutelage, Grace would learn the ropes of a heroin organization, or shop. In a shop there was more money, more drugs, than selling alone, but the risks also were higher. Several months after starting with Poindexter, in mid-1994, Grace was arrested for heroin distribution. He also had a gun, which compounded the crime. "I was arrested numerous times during that time, but I didn't have to go to prison until '95, sometime in '95, like around the beginning of '95."

Grace served four years and nine months in the sprawling state prison in Hagerstown, Maryland. Hagerstown has become one of Maryland's main prison towns, its economy increasingly dependent on the big, lucrative business of prisons. Of his family, only his grandfather came to see him, and then only occasionally. In those years behind bars, Grace had only one other visitor. Walter Poindexter.

Poindexter would say he was showing loyalty. But he was also preparing for the future, taking care of Grace for the day when Pug got out.

Grace would call Poindexter from prison. "I would call him and he would come see me occasionally, and send money, something like that." Grace would use the money in the commissary, to buy extra food. Poindexter, Grace says, visited him once or twice a month, for five years.

He was the closest thing that Grace had to family.

Warren Grace can recall the exact day he was released from prison, after his first drug conviction: December 9, 2000. In jail, he'd managed to earn a GED. It was about all he'd take with him from prison.

Following his release, Grace went to live, not surprisingly, with Poindexter, in Poindexter's home on Wellspring Circle, in Owings Mill, Maryland, outside Baltimore.

"I got out and I went to stay with him. It was nothing really said. That's just what it was. That was the only family I had at the time. That's the only family I had, so that's why I went there." He lived with Poindexter, and Poindexter's brother and mother, Nathaniel and Venessa.

At the time, he says, Poindexter was still hustling on the street, selling heroin.

Grace says he did not do much of anything for the first few weeks after his release. Then he began selling heroin with Poindexter. It was still sometime in December 2000. Supplied by Poindexter, he "opened up a shop on the street and just sold drugs there."

Grace describes setting up a shop:

"Basically, you just get some guys together, a group of guys, and come up with a little strategy or whatever. Just call them, or grab them, you know, as you see fit. You find a corner, and you just, you know, you take the drugs there, you advertise the drugs, you package it up, you just go out there and you give some of it to testers or whatever and advertise it, and (the shop) is just where we were stationed at."

Grace says Poindexter already "had a few dudes" working for him. "You had a dude, Dreco. You had a dude, Marcelle. You had me, his brother Nathaniel, and himself, and a few junkies. That was basically it."

Grace sold heroin and coke with Poindexter's dudes. "We sold it together, so I know," Grace says. Poindexter "would package it up and I would package it up and take it out, or he would take it out, he would give it to the dudes. I would give it to the dudes, and I would be with them when we made the transactions."

Only "once or twice," did they package drugs in Poindexter's mother's home. Most times, he says, they did the packaging at Poindexter's "spot," an apartment building in the Willowbrook section of northwest Baltimore.

6
Buckle down and get a curve

They'd buckle down and get a curve, Warren Grace says. That is, they'd stake a claim to a Baltimore street corner, set up a heroin shop, and keep it running.

To do that, they needed to do several things. They had to get a supply, they had to package their heroin, and they had to find a neighborhood to set up their shop.

The supply in December 2000 was plentiful. Poindexter would score the heroin from several suppliers, Grace says, including rap music producer Deon Smith.

Grace and Poindexter were street dealing vials that sold for about ten dollars a piece. They bought their supply from larger distributors, like Smith, who bought kilo bricks from even larger suppliers.

Their heroin came in ten-gram pieces, formed into a "finger." "It's like the form of your finger, like a bullet, basically," Grace explains. "We would break it down into small little rocks. Smash it. Nice little pebble-sized rocks."

Sometimes, Grace says, "The heroin would come in like by the block and we would break it down and chop it up into smaller rocks or mash it into smaller fingers or whatever, and we would make that ready for sale into vials. It's a small little vial. Like a body oil vial or whatever."

They'd buy vials, appropriately, at a vial store. Imagine owning a store and watching hundreds of vials, bought by street hoods, fly out the door.

Different market conditions demand different sized vials. You must compete with rival heroin dealers. "The vials, you have got different sizes," Graces explains. "They have got big vials and smaller. So 3.5 is just a small version of the vial. So you just put less heroin into it and it appears that it's more. You know, it's just a skinnier vial."

Competition often dictates the size of the vial. If you can't get the size vials used by the competition, you can always run the competition off with guns.

"At some point, this other guy used (smaller vials)," Grace says. "So, you know, everybody is in competition, so you might get some guys give bigger vials, so then we would go to bigger vials like that, or run them off.

"I mean, everybody in close proximity sells them, you know. You may have a group of guys on one corner and a group of guys on the other corner." Like any marketer, Grace knows packaging is important. "You knew what was going on because you were out there," he explains. "You knew what the profit margin was for that day," he says, and "if you didn't make your quota," it might be because the competition had better packaging, better-sized vials, not just better heroin.

These problems of supply and packaging aside, there are three other considerations in the opening of any successful heroin shop: location, location and location.

Poindexter, Grace and the other hopeful heroin dealers scouted around and decided to open their shop at Beaufort and Spaulding Streets, in the Park Heights section of northwest Baltimore. "We would go there, you know," Grace says, "and figure out what corner we was going to sell it on."

He explains, "Myself and Mr. Poindexter, and a few other guys, the guys that I named, (we) basically just go out there and we would give away some testers, give away some of the heroin. So that's the way they knew we had it. That's, you know, just giving away free heroin basically, so they can know it's a good product and that's what they want to buy."

They'd further advertise their heroin by giving it a distinctive name. Grace says Walter Poindexter came up with the name "9-1-1."

"It was basically just happenstance, really," Grace recalls. "The name just came up. That was the name we wanted to use, because once they hit it, that's what they was going to need. 9-1-1. They'd have to call an ambulance. It was good shit. So once they hit it, that's what they was going to need. 9-1-1."

It should also be noted that the address of their chief supplier, Deon Smith, was 911 West 36th Street.

A popular misconception is that a heroin dealer is a single guy standing alone on a corner. Rather, Pug explains, it's often a team effort.

"We had a team of guys," Grace says. "We would have a guy that was supposed to look out. We had a guy that would actually serve the pills to the junkies when they came up to purchase it.

"We had the guy that's going to take the money, the money man. We had a gun dude that was going to hold the gun." (Grace explains, that's "the dude that's holding the firearm. Just so someone won't get robbed.")

"And basically my role was just an overseer, just to see if everybody was doing the job," Grace goes on.

"We had (Poindexter's brother) Nathaniel as a lookout." They called him Boo. Boo's job, Grace says, was "just being there and walking around. Just making sure there is no police coming around there."

If Boo spotted a cop, "He would yell, 'Time out!' That was his specific thing. He wasn't set up to do nothing else."

When they heard Boo yell time out, "We would just walk off. We would shut it down. Everybody just walks separate ways."

7
911's a joke: A day in the life at the shop

They kept a stash house in the middle of the block. Pug would open the shop every morning by taking the vials of heroin he'd often had with him from the night before to the nearby stash house. The others in the shop would meet him there.

"We would set up (shop) like 8:30 in the morning," Grace explains. "The guys already know to get there, to be there at nine o'clock or whatever. So I would come down, I would be the first one there, and I would take the drugs to a stash house that we had in the middle of the block. I would take the drugs in there and I wasn't going to open up until everybody got there. (Then) we would open up the shop. Everybody knew what was going on."

Directing operations out on the street, Pug made it a point not to have the vials of heroin on him. It made it harder for the knockers to bust the shop. The knockers were the undercover cops. The knockers would have to know who was holding.

"The longest I had the vials on me was early morning. Like I said, we're open nine to four. I would get there at eight, eight-thirty, and I would have them," he says.

"Mr. Poindexter would drop me off and I would take it to the stash house that we had in the middle of the block, and I would run in there and stash it, and I would just wait until everybody got there before we opened up the shop."

After the team got out on the street they'd take their places and make sure all was clear. Only then would Pug tell Marcelle to fetch the vials from the stash house.

"Everybody knew what their role was. So we had this guy Marcelle. He was the one running the packs. We sectioned off heroin like in packs of twenty-five. You don't want to have big bags. So you would have a baggie with twenty-five vials. Numerous packs with twenty-five (vials) in there. That would be $250 a pack.

"So when we finish one pack, we have a guy that we give the money to. He takes the money, when we finish. He gets another pack (from the stash house). We just keep running it through like that."

"We had this guy Marcelle," Pug goes on, "he would go in the house, get the packs, bring the packs out, give it to the junkies that was going to serve them out. That was just his role for that day."

Junkies working for the shop dispensed the heroin to the other junkies. They worked "hand-to-hand." Pug would hide the dispensing junkies in an alleyway while the others trolled for business. Why junkies?

"Basically because they don't have high expectations, you know," Grace explains. "Plus, they're expendable. So we would use them. And you don't have to pay them much. You just give them a vial. They sniff it, and they're ready to go. And they will pretty much do whatever for that vial."

The junkies "were the ones hand-to-hand. They would actually go hand-to-hand with the other junkies who would just come up to buy. They would serve them."

Pug details the clocklike workings of a shop on the inner-city Baltimore block:

"We are all out there. It's a team effort. We are all yelling the name of the heroin. It was 911. We are all yelling 911 so they know.

"(The customers) know the designated area that we are in so when they come in a certain block this is where we are at. So when they come in, we will point to the alley where the dude is at, the junkie.

"The customers (will be) coming up. (We say) 'How many do you want? Five? Go see him over there.' Some other junkie. So they would go over there in the alley.

"If I was by the customer at that time I would get the money. Whoever was close to them." This would vary, Grace explains, because everybody kept moving on the street, while they were yelling the name of the heroin.

"We never stayed stationary," he reflects. "I mean, you know, we would stay on the block, but we would walk. I would walk to the top of the block. Marcelle was walking around." The gun man, the look out man, the money man. Everybody, he says, "was walking around. Because you don't want to be standing, loitering. The police come around. So, if I'm there, I'll grab it (the money from the customer) and I just let them know I've got it, I've got it. You want five?"

The dispensing junkies were never allowed to take the money from the customers. Pug made sure these "hand-to-hand junkies" who worked for him never saw, nor handled, the money.

Why not? you ask Grace.

"We just didn't do it like that. We just didn't do it like that. No, they wasn't supposed to handle the money at all."

Why not? you ask him.

"They are just not trustworthy," Grace tells you.

8
The night shop

Picture if you would the zombies stumbling in to buy the heroin. The neighborhood overrun with zombies stumbling in for a fix, herded by the shop workers moving up and down the street yelling, "911." Imagine living in a neighborhood like this. Raising kids. Seeing life sucked out of your neighborhood, as the junkies sucked the heroin from the vials.

How much heroin, how much money?

The shop sold about ten or fifteen grams a day, Grace says. That meant about a thousand to fifteen hundred dollars a day. Of that, five hundred dollars was profit, Grace says. And that was just a "bad day."

"On a bad day," Grace says, "it would be from a thousand to fifteen hundred (dollars). And, on a good day, anywhere from three thousand to thirty-five hundred."

Two days a month business would treble, Grace says. These were days when public assistance and other government checks were issued. In these neighborhoods, the government was funding the heroin dealers.

On government check days Grace's shop might sell thirty grams of heroin a day. That's about an ounce. So supply's important.

How often would he sell thirty grams? you ask Grace.

"Twice a month. Like twice a month," Grace says. "On check days, like the 1st and the 15th.... People got money, welfare money or whatever, and it just would be a better time to sell it."

Soon the shop ran like clockwork. It was a real cash box. Pug describes himself as overseeing the day shop. "Just watching to make sure everybody is doing their job." Pug would "walk around and check with people."

After dropping Grace off in the morning, Poindexter would take off to "other places." Poindexter owned both a Mercedes and a '97 white Suburban. He'd usually drive the Suburban for shop work.

He'd return "periodically" throughout the day, "to see how things were on the street, or what we did. He would come out and walk around for a few minutes and then leave. (He'd) pick up money."

Things were going so well that Poindexter soon opened a night shop. After Grace and company left at 4 pm a "guy named Dreco" came in to open the night shop.

"Me and Mr. Poindexter," Grace says, "put together" the night shop. "It wasn't really no conversation about it. It was just that's what he was going to do."

Poindexter decided Dreco should run it.

"I would be there when they come on," Grace says of the night shop. "I mean I would be there when he came on, or whatever drugs that we didn't finish that was left over would get passed over the to next shift."

"I would pick up the money when they finished," the next morning, Grace says. He'd turn the night shop money in to Poindexter, often with the money from the day shop.

The night shop, Grace says, usually brought in "about a thousand to seventeen hundred" dollars a night.

For his cut, Warren Grace says Walter Poindexter gave him fifteen hundred to two thousand dollars a week.

9
Where do they get the heroin?

To buckle down and get a curve, to open a shop and sell heroin regularly, Grace and Poindexter needed a steady supply of heroin. The heroin had to be good, too. If it wasn't good, "people wouldn't buy it," Grace explains. "It wouldn't do anything for them. It wouldn't cure their ills."

So shopping for good heroin was an essential part of the business. They would get the heroin as they needed it, often every day. "I was getting it on an as-needed basis," Grace says.

He, and Poindexter, would get the heroin from a variety of sources. At times they'd get it from "a guy named Fess." They also get it, at different times, from, "A guy named Marty, and a guy named Eddie."

Grace would often go with Poindexter when they'd score the heroin. "We would usually meet (these small-scale suppliers) on the street somewhere," Grace explains. "Might be in the car."

These suppliers usually would sell a few grams at a time, or as much as thirty or forty grams — an ounce or more of heroin.

These still were small amounts from small-time suppliers. Their main supplier of heroin, Grace says, was Deon Smith. It was Smith who operated fledgling rap music label Stash House Records. Poindexter would refer to Deon Smith simply as D.

Smith and several others started Stash House Records in 1997.

By 2003, Stash House Records was located at 911 W. 36th Street, in what's called the Hampden section of central Baltimore. It's a rough neighborhood just west of Johns Hopkins University.

Smith also had a small recording studio in his apartment, Grace says, where he'd sell heroin. At one time, Grace says, "his studio was like in an apartment in the county," and they'd drive out there, sometimes borrowing Poindexter's aunt's car. "It was like a little studio he set up in his apartment."

Throughout the time of his dealings with Grace and Poindexter, Smith was working to produce and independently distribute an eighteen-track hip-hop CD titled "Gumbo." The government would come to allege that Smith was dealing kilos of heroin to finance the CD.

Grace says he'd often see Smith's gun — a nickel-plated 9mm — on conspicuous display at the recording studio.

"I seen him with (his gun) numerous times," Grace says. "I would go up to the studio and sometimes it would be laying on the chair with a shirt over it. Sometimes he would have it on his person." Grace knew the gun well. "At one point I handled it myself. I picked it up and was looking at it."

They would go over to Smith's studio as often as once a day to purchase heroin, Grace says. Sometimes they would procure enough heroin from Smith to last weeks. On at least one occasion, Grace says, they picked up 300 grams — more than ten ounces, or almost three-quarters of a pound of heroin. That's a big chunk of a 2.2-pound kilo brick.

"We would go to the studio every day, just about," Grace says. "Well, we always went to the studio, so it wasn't really talked about or planned," Grace says. "We just got it as needed." He goes on, "We always stopped at the studio at some point in the day, and on a certain day he would just grab some from him."

Often they'd hang out at Smith's studio for an hour or two. Rap music would more often than not be blaring from speakers. Hangers-on, musicians and recording engineers would often be present.

"We would go up to the studio or whatever, and (Poindexter) would go into another room. I didn't see the actual exchange, but he had heroin."

The day they picked up the 300 grams was a case in point.

They got to the studio and spent "like a couple hours, like two hours or so... just listening to tracks."

That day, Grace says, those present included, "Floss, myself, Dana," and "the engineer." There were others present. "The foreign dudes."

"Later that day we had heroin," Grace says. Poindexter, he says, "showed it to me. I said did he get it from some of the other dudes and he said no, he got it from D."

The 300 grams, Grace says, lasted two or three weeks.

When it was gone, they got more.

10
NYC connection: Bricks and bricks from foreign dudes up top

True to form for a rap artist, Deon Smith bragged about the amounts of heroin he'd sell. He'd just about rap the story. He'd brag, "I done sold bricks and bricks." Smith would look down on lower-level dealers like Walter Poindexter, Warren Grace says. "I don't ride around with fifty grams in my pocket," like Poindexter, Smith would sneer.

Where did Deon Smith get bricks and bricks of heroin? To whom did Smith pass along his great quantities of cash in exchange for heroin?

Heroin is big, lucrative business. The local Salvation Army isn't cashing in. It's run by organized crime. In the past, traditional Mafioso out of places like New York, New Jersey and Philadelphia controlled the heroin smuggling trade. They had connections to the Mideast, where the opium poppy was grown. In the last decades newer South American and Caribbean mobs, vicious, and violent, have elbowed their way to the table. These days, the government says, most of Baltimore's heroin is grown and processed in South America. To this spicy Mediterranean and Latino mix sprinkle in those upstarts who previously terrorized the Eastern Bloc before going multi-national, the Russians.

Warren Grace talks about the time he and Poindexter scored the 300 grams from Deon Smith. They were at Smith's studio with a few other people, the recording engineer, and "the foreign dudes."

Grace isn't sure which country they were from.

Another time, Smith told Grace that he wanted "to go to New York to buy some drugs, so he wanted me to put some money together with his money so he could get more."

At the time, Grace says, the local connections for heroin, in Baltimore or Washington DC, weren't available. They had to go "up top," to New York, where bulk amounts of heroin were readily available. *Up top* is street slang for New York, he says.

Smith "was saying there was a spot he knew he could get it from in bulk," Grace says. There was no availability in "DC" or Baltimore. "You couldn't really get your hands on it. But he was saying there was a spot in New York where you could get it in bulk."

"He is saying he has some dudes from Greece," Grace says. There were other "foreign dudes" at Smith's studio. Poindexter, he says, told him Deon Smith "had some people coming down every three months. Every three months they would come down and he would get his big package."

Later, Grace would buy heroin from a Dominican, named Eddie, who he says taught him how to cut the heroin with manitol, an inert and tasteless powder sold as baby laxative.

The U.S. Department of Justice reports, "Dominican and Colombian criminal groups based in New York City, Philadelphia, and Baltimore and Maryland-based local independent dealers dominate the wholesale distribution of heroin in Maryland. Some Dominican criminals have established part-time residency in the Maryland cities where they distribute heroin."

Dominicans, foreign dudes, New York suppliers, and Greeks bearing big packages.

The DOJ continues, "Baltimore serves as the primary distribution city for heroin in Maryland. Salisbury, located along major smuggling route US 13, serves as a secondary distribution city for eastern Maryland. Law enforcement officials have identified a link between Latin Kings gang members from New York City and retail distributors of heroin in Salisbury. Salisbury officials have seized bags of heroin bearing stamps that resemble those sold by Latin Kings in New York City."

This is organized crime, making big money pumping heroin into Baltimore.

Like Jonathan Luna, the heroin came from New York City.

11
Domestic disturbance

As a rule, Walter Poindexter liked to stay out of day-to-day street operations. He told Pug only to call if there was a problem, such as those delicate situations requiring him to bring over his gun.

Sometimes, Grace explains, they wouldn't have a gun at the shop, and they'd have to call Poindexter.

Sometimes they'd have to beat people up just to keep them in line. Sometimes they'd beat people up for the hell of it.

"Somebody might say something out of line," Warren Grace says, "and, you know, we both would beat them up.

"You know, it was like on one occasion a guy said something out of line like, 'I came up now,' (meaning, he was grown, and now) 'things are going to be different.'

"Poindexter asked him, 'Yes, you came up, you are grown?'

"And he said like, 'Yeah, I am grown.'"

Poindexter "went and got the gun and came back and slapped him upside the head with it. So, you know, after he slammed him up, and he had the gun, he said, 'Are you still grown?'

"And he said, 'No, I ain't grown.'"

Pug says he had to use a gun "like twenty" times in the course of running the shop with Poindexter. If he needed a gun, and the gun dude wasn't working, "I would call Mr. Poindexter."

One day at the shop, in December 2000, Grace says, a couple began arguing in the middle of the street near W. Garrison Avenue. It grew into a loud domestic dispute. Grace worried that someone might call the police. He tried to drive the couple away, but they wouldn't budge. He yelled threats at the man, who told him to mind his own business. While the couple still argued in the background, Pug called Poindexter.

Poindexter came with his gun. The couple still yelled in the street. Grace and Poindexter chased after them. Poindexter fired some shots, and chased them off.

12
Lumpin' it

Not long afterward, there was the Lump incident.

Lump was one of the street workers selling heroin for Poindexter and Grace. His real name was Steven Ford, Grace says.

"Well, Lump was getting some heroin or whatever," Grace says, and "when he finished he was supposed to give some of the money — he was supposed to call Walter and give him some money or whatever. He never made that call because he claimed his phone went off or whatever.

About this time Walter Poindexter gets arrested, Grace says. As with everyone else in this story, there is a revolving door to jail, and back out into the community, that Poindexter keeps passing through. It's the spring of 2001.

"He gets arrested," Grace continues. "Mr. Poindexter gets arrested for a house raid or whatever. He get out.

"The dude still ain't called us, Lump, and so at that point we proceeded just to track him down or whatever to locate him, to find out if he had the money or not."

Poindexter and Grace went over to Lump's place, a Baltimore tenement apartment building.

"We knocked on the door. A female answered the door, saying he didn't live there. So we started asking questions about, you know, 'We know he live there,' and 'Tell him to come out.'

"And she said, he don't live there. We leave and we come back again, just trying different tactics to try to get her to disclose his whereabouts or whatever. To no avail. And so we just kept trying and trying and trying, making threats or whatever."

They go to leave the apartment building. On their way out Poindexter's cell phone rings. It's Lump. "He go on rambling, you know, 'What's going on?' He said he had the money but he ain't coming outside. (We told him) 'Just slide the money under the door if you got it."

Lump told them he wasn't hiding. Wasn't he the one calling?

Poindexter told Lump, "You ain't answering the phone!"

"Blah, blah, blah," Grace recounts. "So we go back into the building."

Over the cell Poindexter tells Lump they're coming back inside. Just come to the door, Poindexter tells him.

Lump says no. He ain't coming to the door.

Poindexter and Pug walk to Lump's door. Pug kicks it open.

Gunfire ripped through the apartment building. Lump was inside, shooting.

It was all Poindexter and Grace could do to run from the building, ducking bullets.

"(We) just ran out of the building. To the front of the building."

When they got outside, Poindexter took out his .45 caliber and started blindly returning fire at the windows of the apartment building.

He never hit Lump. Grace says he doesn't think Walter Poindexter hit anyone.

13
J. Vaughn's .357

Imagine, if you will, what it's like to live in an apartment building like this. Imagine, if you can, what it's like to raise kids in a neighborhood, in a city, like this.

Warren Grace knew he was always in danger of being run out of the neighborhood where he had set up shop. Not in danger, for the most part, from the neighbors, nor from the police. The neighbors and the police seemed impotent. He was in danger of being run out by other gun-toting dealers who wanted the territory.

It was for just such a contingency that J. Vaughn, "another dude who was working for the shop," gave Pug a .357 magnum revolver.

And of course Pug could always call for Poindexter's gun. One time, Pug relates, "like the month that I got out (of prison), around that time," a guy, "I don't remember his name, Voss, or something like that, he come out there where I was selling at, telling me I can't sell right there."

Voss was not an angry neighbor, Pug relates, but another dealer who claimed the block. "I was opening up a strip on the street around the area," when suddenly Voss was "telling me I couldn't sell drugs there."

He was trying to "run me away," Grace says. "I called Mr. Poindexter. I told him to bring (the) gun."

Poindexter showed up with the gun.

Grace asked a man on the street, "Where's the guy telling me I can't sell drugs here?"

But Voss was gone.

"The dude already had left, you know. He had run away."

14
Poindexter commits a drug-related murder

Around this time, January 2001, someone broke into, and burglarized, an apartment used by Walter Poindexter as a drug stash house. Word reached Poindexter that the culprit was a man named Alvin Jones.

One of Poindexter's girlfriends, Maronda Cole, telephoned Alvin Jones to warn him.

Alvin Jones hung up the phone and told his father, whose name was Alphonso Jones, "some bitch is accusing me of robbing some house."

On January 22, 2001, Walter Poindexter hunted down Alvin Jones and shot him dead. At least two people witnessed the drug murder, Jonathan Luna later would write in court papers. Afterward, Poindexter would brag to Warren Grace about the shooting.

Federal prosecutor Jonathan Luna would, in due course, make the obvious case that Jones' death, in retaliation for a break-in at a drug stash house, was drug-related. He'd file court document after court document, saying as much, going so far as to threaten Poindexter with the death penalty for Jones' murder. It does not take too much imagination to see why Luna, a judge, or a jury, would make this connection. It would take even more imagination for these same prosecutors to back-peddle and deny that Jones' death had anything to do with the drug trade.

This would turn out to be no small distinction. Almost three years after Walter Poindexter murdered Alvin Jones, on the night of December 3, 2003, the problem of Jones' murder would amazingly resurface and threaten to expose dark secrets in the Baltimore field office of the Federal Bureau of Investigation. It would threaten to expose the FBI's dark world of collaborating informants.

In order to bury the case, after things fell apart and Grace's FBI handlers were threatened with investigation, prosecutors would have to make an about-face. In order to stop an investigation of the FBI, and the U.S. Attorney's office, Poindexter would have to be given a sweetheart plea deal by the prosecutors. And that plea deal could not by law be given to anyone who commits a drug-related murder. So suddenly there would be no drug-related murder. The murder charge would be made to disappear, as neatly for prosecutors as Alvin Jones had disappeared for Poindexter.

To protect the FBI and its worst secrets, Jonathan Luna would have to abruptly about-face. Luna would have to suddenly pretend that Jones' murder wasn't drug related. This would turn out to be an insurmountable problem for Luna. He would not, or could not, bring himself to do it.

A few hours later, Jonathan Luna would be dead.

15
Bailin':
Police arrest Walter Poindexter, then let him go

In April 2001, a few months after Walter Poindexter shot and killed Alvin Jones in what was clearly a drug-related murder, Baltimore city cops raided Poindexter's house. They arrested him on drug charges — not for Jones' murder. Going in through the system's revolving door, he would, in a short while, be tossed back out on the street to once again deal heroin. In the next year, like many repeat drug offenders, Poindexter would be repeatedly tossed in and out of prison and halfway houses, going round and round as though in a revolving door.

"Mr. Poindexter gets arrested for a house raid or whatever," Warren Grace remembers. Then, "He get out."

"Here's a little somethin' bout a nigga like me," Ice Cube and Dr. Dre rap in N.W.A.'s Gangsta Gangsta, "never shoulda been let out the penitentiary. ...Cause I'm the type of nigga that's built to last / Fuck wit me, I'll put my foot up your ass / See I don't give a fuck, because I keep bailin'."

For Grace, Poindexter's sporadic incarcerations meant more money. Now Grace ran his own shop, without Poindexter acting as middleman. Instead of making $1,000 or $1,500 a week, Grace found himself making $4,500 weekly. With the drug money he bought a black 2000 Ford Excursion. One day he walked into a car dealership and put down a cash down payment of $18,000.

Warren Grace now had to arrange for his own supply of heroin. He'd get it from a variety of sources, including from Eddie the Dominican. He also dealt directly with Deon Smith at Stash House Records.

On one of these occasions, when Grace was meeting with Deon Smith, Smith reminded the dealer of his loyalty obligations to Poindexter, then in prison.

"Yo, I am telling you, yo," Smith told Grace, "you know, (the) rules, man."

When Grace was jailed, Smith reminded him, Poindexter had visited him in prison and had given him a phone number he could call. Now Poindexter was complaining to Smith that Grace should return the favor. Those were the rules of loyalty, Grace says.

"You know, when I fell, he came to see me and treated me like family," Grace says. "And then, when he fell, I didn't do none of that back."

Deon Smith told Grace, "You were supposed to send over, yo."

"It means," Grace explains, "when I started getting on my feet I was supposed to send him some money orders as he did me. I was supposed to, you know, have a way for him to contact me, as he did with me when I was locked up."

So Grace went to visit Poindexter in the halfway house. It turned out that Poindexter wanted more from Warren Grace than just familiar loyalty and money orders. In the halfway house, Poindexter wanted to sell heroin. He wanted Grace to smuggle it in.

"Well," Grace says, "there was one occasion I made a trip to the halfway house that he was in and we had a conversation about, you know, if I can get some heroin to him or not. I told him I would see if I could try to get some grams to him or whatever. Different dudes would come out on work release or whatever, and I would meet one of the dudes and give them the heroin to take in to him." Deon Smith, he says, told Grace that he sent "some grams over there two times, seven grams he sent him two times."

Grace explains that heroin, in prison, is a valuable commodity.

"Well, basically, in there," Grace says, "you can pretty much quadruple the profit. Like, say, for instance, (heroin that sells for) ten dollars on the street goes for a hundred dollars in prison." Gangsta math: 4 x 10 = 100!

"From my experience, like when I was up in Hagerstown for the four years, different dudes (were) doing stuff. (They were) into stuff like that. And from personal experience that's what it goes for, because it's small and they can't really get their hands on it so, you know, it's in demand. So when you get something like that in there, everybody wants to get it so, you know, you can jack the price up a whole lot. My understanding is that he wanted to sell it to make some money."

Even while in prison, Walter Poindexter sold heroin.

He'd sell heroin in the halfway house, Grace says, with the knowledge and help of the Federal Bureau of Investigation.

16
Real life on Mars

Warren Grace describes the murder, the shootings, the heroin dealings, the bricks and the mob infiltration in one small block in one small neighborhood in Baltimore. Neglect, decay, corruption. Failure.

Multiply that by *hundreds* of blocks and neighborhoods in inner-city Baltimore, *thousands* of heroin dealers, and *tens of millions of dollars* in mob heroin profits, if not more, and you get some idea of the magnitude of the problem in Baltimore, with its estimated 120,000 addicts.

The U.S. Department of Justice reports, "In Baltimore, loosely organized neighborhood gangs, primarily composed of African American members, conduct most of the retail heroin distribution, often in open-air environments. The location of an open-air drug market determines its customer base. Neighborhood residents purchase heroin at drug markets located in housing projects. Suburban residents seeking easy access to the drug and a convenient route out of the city purchase heroin at drug markets located along main corridors."

Profits from this Baltimore drug trade are hard to estimate, though it is surely a multi-million, if not -billion, dollar industry. (One hundred and twenty thousand addicts purchasing just one thousand dollars of heroin a year — a small amount, really — generates one hundred and twenty million dollars annually.)

There are many hidden social costs. Crime. Disease transmission. In 1999, more Baltimoreans died of heroin overdose than homicide. (Sooner or later, society pays for a doctor.) More importantly for society, bad cops bought with these organized crime profits are destroying the police and courts of Maryland.

Imagine, if you can, what it's like to live in a neighborhood, in a city, like this.

Imagine, if you can, what it's like to raise your kids in an environment like this.

Imagine if there was no one to call for help.

Imagine if the police and courts aren't on the side of your family, but on the side of the drug dealers and the murderers, and you can't get a call through for help.

17
Nightmare on Eden Street

Angela Dawson, and her husband, Carnell, didn't have to imagine. They lived it, hour by hour, day after day.

The facts surrounding the destruction of the Dawson family are legend to Baltimoreans. Memories of Angela Dawson walking with her children through her neighborhood, and their preventable deaths, have come to haunt Baltimore.

They still can see her walking with her children to their tiny corner park. She took a lot of pride in her family, her house, and her block. Every Saturday, she and her kids would clean the tiny park across Eden Street from their corner row house.

Carnell and Angela Dawson lived with their children at East Preston and Eden Streets, in a neighborhood called Oliver, northeast of Inner Harbor, a few miles from the heroin shop run by Warren Grace and Walter Poindexter. Other dealers ran shops on the Dawsons' block, even on their front stoop, in plain view of the Dawson kids.

The Dawsons lived in a sprawling, century old, working-class section of the city, long ago abandoned by fleeing factory and waterfront workers. Oliver today is a grid of low-slung, stone houses, churches, and storefronts, many empty and boarded-up. It still has a bright, working class, if ghostly, feel to it. It's block after block of two- and three-story houses, porches and stairs.

The Dawsons came to Preston and Eden streets in the 1990s, after Angela and Carnell met in Severn, Maryland, a southeast suburb of Baltimore. Carnell had recently arrived from Bristow, Oklahoma, to stay with his sister. He'd been footloose before he met Angela, fathering two daughters by two women. He was known for an almost happy-go-lucky, easy-going nature.

He'd come to Severn after his brother was gunned down and

killed. He hoped to change the course of his life. Carnell himself had been shot years earlier. He's been driving a car. Some friends were fooling around with a sawed-off shotgun in the backseat. It went off, blasting him through the driver's seat.

Angela had three children by two other men by the time she met Carnell in Severn. Lakeesha, Lawanda and Juan. She'd dropped out of high school.

Before long Angel and Car, as the Dawsons called each other, had moved to Preston and Eden streets with the kids, renting a three-story corner house with four bedrooms. The rent was a couple hundred dollars a month. Soon, along came Carnell, Jr., and twins Kevin and Keith.

The Dawsons were married on New Years Eve, 1998.

Neighbors still talk of their vivid memories of Car and Angel walking down the street together. Everyone says it was plain to see the love they had for each other. They cut a vivid sight, coming down the street with their ever-present kids. He was a lanky five-foot-six inches tall, and 160 pounds. She was five-foot-four, and weighed more than 200.

People remember Angela Dawson mostly for the pride she took in her children and her home. How she laid carpet down in her kitchen. The way she insisted her kids say, "No, Ma'am," and "Yes, sir." When passing you on the street, the kids would say, "Hello, Mister." Or, "Hello, Miss."

The neighbors remember them walking together across Eden every Saturday to clean the twenty-foot vacant green lot they thought of as a park.

Carnell for years worked odd jobs, if he was lucky to have a job at all. Angela mostly liked to stay at home with her kids. Times could be tough. Sometimes the phone was shut off.

By the summer of 2001, the neighborhood began its descent into drug shop hell. Angela and Carnell Dawson increasingly found themselves chasing drug dealers off their front stoop.

Those times the phone bill was paid, and the phone was working, the Dawsons got the idea to call 911 for help.

The other end of the phone line wasn't working, they'd learn. Oh, they could get some one to answer, but they couldn't get anyone to provide meaningful help.

The Dawsons' story concerns the nightmare that comes with the disconnect at the other end of the phone line.

The Dawsons, in life, had no connection with the principals of this story. They lived worlds apart. That's the essence of the scandal. Their increasingly desperate plight would be completely ignored by those in the FBI and the Baltimore U.S. Attorney's office, who were distracted by their own outrageous misadventures.

The preventable deaths of the Dawsons, on the other hand, would come to have a direct, and tremendous, *political* connection with everyone working in law enforcement in this story, particularly Luna, his boss, U.S. Attorney Tom DiBiagio, and the FBI.

18
The mix, the regular scramble, and the tools

Now that Walter Poindexter was dealing heroin while temporarily behind bars, Warren Grace learned some valuable tricks of the heroin trade from one of his new Caribbean suppliers, Eddie the Dominican.

To facilitate its transport and smuggling, heroin often arrives in America compressed into short brown sticks, or fingers.

The first step to maximize profits is to chop these sticks into fine, brown powder.

To double or treble the profits, Eddie taught Pug how to dilute the scramble and recompress it back into fingers. The formula for the dilution agent is called the "mix."

"One of the guys I was dealing with, Eddie, he showed me how to cut it," Grace relates.

First one must procure a supply of the cutting agent of favor, manitol. It's a white powder readily purchased in 22-gram blocks.

"You get it from different convenience stores," Grace says. "It's just a baby laxative, really. That's all it is."

First, pulverize the manitol. Grace explains you cannot simply mix the manitol into the heroin. It contains moisture, which must be driven away before it's mixed with the heroin, less you make a muddy mess and ruin your blow. (Though normally a nickname for cocaine, these dealers called their heroin "blow.")

"After you get the manitol, you put it in a bowl," Grace explains. Then, "You put it in a freezer until it freezes hard. Once you bring it out, you place a blow dryer on it. You position the blow dryer over top of it and bring it back to powder form." The freezing crystallizes the moisture, which the blow dryer evaporates. Now, "You have got the mix. It's dried up now. And now you have got to sift it through a strainer and make sure it's dry.

"After it's dry, you let it sit for a little while. When you are sure it's dry," Grace says, you perform another step to improve your mix. You add other ingredients. "It's like a concoction I came up with to make the heroin a little bit more better. I concocted a whole lot of stuff to put in the mix that would give it a little kick."

These additives include vinegar, kahlua, coffee, even rum.

Each cutting agent has a different purpose. "Manitol is chalk white and that's not how heroin comes. Grace says he would add kahlua, or coffee, "so to give it a little bit of color. It turns it brown. Normally your heroin would be a brownish color so that's how they would never know I was cutting it."

Another cutting agent, vinegar, "gives the heroin a better kick. A lot of heroin addicts like the smell of vinegar on the heroin," Grace advises. "I know just from being out there, you know. They think it makes it better, or whatever, so you put a lot of vinegar in there."

Then there's "151."

"That's Bacardi (rum)," Grace says. "Like I said, I concocted a whole lot of stuff to put in the mix, you know, that would give it a little kick. (Like) putting that 151 liquor in there. Because it was brown. So that would make the mix turn that color. Brown."

Having finished concocting the mix, Grace goes on, "then you (decide) how many grams you want to cut (with) the heroin. If you have 20 grams (of heroin) and you want to make it 60, you take 40 grams of the mix and place it on the heroin."

Once Grace decides the proper proportions of the mix, he passes it, and the heroin, repeatedly through a kitchen strainer.

"It's a regular food strainer that you would put things through to drain the water out of it," he says. "You use that to shift the manitol and the heroin around so you can break it down. So it would be fine powder. You just keep running it through and smashing the rocks out of it."

You now have what Grace calls "the regular scramble."

"Once you get all of that done, you are ready to recompress it,"

Grace explains. Grace had a set of tools he used to recompress the scramble into "fingers" to further disguise heroin he'd cut with manitol. Or, recompression could be skipped, and the heroin simply be sold as "regular scramble."

"The regular scramble," he explains, "you go through that same process with the mix, but you don't recompress it. You just cut the heroin with (however) much manitol you want. (Then) you just leave it in the powder form."

"By recompressing it," Grace says, "you are leading people to think it's still raw (and undiluted), because that's the form that it comes in when it's raw. That's the trick to it. By recompressing it, they don't know you stepped on it, and that's where your profit comes in."

Recompressing the heroin into fingers requires a simple apparatus. "I had some makeshift tools," he said. A form, some wax paper, a screw, a vice grip wrench.

To recompress, Grace would place ten grams of scrambled, powered heroin inside a form lined with wax paper. "You would pack the heroin down inside the paper. Once you did that, the heroin would be inside (the form). Then you close it off at the bottom... so that none of the heroin can fall back out, and you pack it down in there.... You would get a vice grip and you would put this part on there and you would crank it.

"As you crank it, it's going to push it in. Once it's done like that you know it's tight. Then you unscrew that (screw) and you push the heroin out. And that's the form it would be in. And that would be ten grams." The recompressed, scrambled heroin now was in finger form, hopefully indistinguishable from raw heroin fingers.

"Once you made the fingers up, you know, you can break it down, vial it up, take it to the street, or however you are going to use it."

Grace was always mindful not to cut, or dilute, the heroin too much. "You can get somebody mad selling them the heroin (if) they won't even feel it," Grace cautions. "It's basically bullshit. It's no good (if) they can't get high off it. You can't be selling people stuff like that because it's going to cause problems. Not only with your profits. Something could happen to you, because you are essentially burning somebody out of their money, so you can't just do that.

"I mean, somebody who is going to spend money to get 300 grams, or whatever they are going to spend, and it's not what they are paying for, they are not going to like that very much. So, you know, there could be repercussions behind that. If you don't give them their money back, there might be some problems.

"There is going to be some violence involved."

19
Cop bait

Warren Grace must've got on someone's bad side, because on April 7, 2002 the police came rushing into the house where he was staying. They brought a search warrant.

Grace says the house belonged to "a girl I was staying with."

The house was on Fairview Avenue, in northwest Baltimore. In the house police found a scale, some heroin, and packaging material.

Grace says the police found "like two vials and a whole lot of paraphernalia, and I think like 300 grams of manitol."

More problematic for Grace, the cops also found two guns. A .38 caliber pistol and an Intertech 9 millimeter semi-automatic — a Tech 9, a favorite for drive-bys, as it sprays bullets.

Grace was jailed and indicted on three criminal counts: possession of the firearm as a felon; possession with intent to distribute 100 grams or more of heroin; and aiding and abetting. He now faced a maximum of 40 years in jail and a $250,000 fine. Eleven days later, on April 18, Grace would celebrate his twenty-second birthday, behind bars.

When he applies for a public defender on May 13, 2002, Grace lists his line of work as a self-employed rap artist. He claims to have no cash or savings on hand, though he reports he makes $1,000 a month as a rap artist. Now 22 years old, Grace lists as his dependant a *nine*-year-old daughter, Chantile Grace, for whom, he writes, he was responsible for a $300 per month child support payment.

"Mr. Grace had a big problem," Baltimore attorney Arcangelo Tuminelli later would say. Grace had already served five years for drug and gun charges. He had two prior convictions. This was strike three, and he was out. "A real serious problem," Tuminelli says. "It became apparent to Mr. Grace he had a very serious problem. How serious was it? He is what is called in the federal system a career offender, which means that he likely would have received a sentence somewhere between 30 years to life, if he didn't do something, and that 30 years is without parole.

"So that meant Mr. Grace, if he didn't come up with some solution to his problem, was never going to see the streets until he was an old, old man, if at all.

"And so what did he do? He thought about it for a little while and he started talking to the Baltimore city police."

He started talking to city police about the murder of Alvin Jones.

"I was caught up," Grace admits. "I would get life."

Grace began by telling the Baltimore police that Walter Poindexter had murdered Alvin Jones in retaliation for the break-in at the drug stash house. It was a drug-related murder that could put Poindexter away for life.

"He was cooperating with the Baltimore city police on the homicide," Assistant US Attorney Jonathan Luna would later say.

There was, attorney Tuminelli recalls, a "recording of Mr. Grace being interviewed by homicide detectives in Baltimore city."

As the Baltimore police began to investigate Alvin Jones' killing, word spread on the street "that Mr. Grace had talked to the Baltimore city police department," Tuminelli relates.

The drug-related murder of Alvin Jones would later loom large and grow into a big issue, and a big problem, for federal prosecutor Jonathan Luna.

For now, in the spring of 2002, the city police were happy to get whatever information they could from Warren Grace. Grace began to spill the beans, searching for a deal that would mean less time behind bars.

Grace told the Baltimore cops about some of his suppliers. He told them about Donny and Eddie. They are Hispanic, Grace says. Donny's from New Jersey. Eddie runs a little chicken shop on Reisterstown Road. Then there was Marty, "over at Woodland Avenue and Reisterstown Road in the Pimlico area." Then there was Fess, on Park Heights Avenue and Cold Spring.

And Grace kept talking. He told them about other street dealers. Elliot on Belvedere Avenue. Dante and Mann, also in Pimlico.

Since he was already telling police about the murder of Alvin Jones, the names Walter Poindexter and Deon Smith had already come up in conversation.

20
The FBI's 'Safe Streets Task Force': How safe is it?

Stash House Records turned out to be the bait that Warren Grace was looking for. Someone in the Baltimore police department at this juncture alerted their cohorts in the Baltimore field office of the FBI.

The idea of busting rap music producers in their recording studio proved irresistible to the feds, for several reasons. The rap music storefront would prove to be more enticing than attaining justice for the murder of Alvin Jones.

It would be perhaps jurisdictionally correct to say that the local cops "called in" the FBI, or otherwise referred the matter to the feds. Actually, they didn't have to call anyone, as they were already closely working with the federal agents.

The FBI had created what it called the "Safe Streets Program." Baltimore FBI Special Agent Steve Skinner explains: "The Safe Streets Program was put together by the FBI to address what is actually called safe streets. Our goal is to make streets safe, to make neighborhoods safe. By doing that, we investigate violent groups, gangs, and we put together investigations against those groups using drug violation laws."

Skinner goes on to describe the far reach of the FBI into local police forces. Skinner says, "We have a task force, which basically means that, in addition to FBI agents, we also have local police officers who are detailed and deputized to work with us. And they include Baltimore city police detectives. At one point we had Baltimore County police detectives. We have had Maryland state police detectives. We have also had housing authority detectives as well."

Baltimoreans like Angela Dawson learn firsthand there are problems with the task force. At best, it was ineffective. Why were so many dealers running loose on the streets? Worse, embattled city residents like the Dawsons couldn't reach the task force.

At worst, task force members secretly aided and abetted the city's heroin traffic, and let its informants run wild, threatening the lives of innocent people like the Dawsons. Grace would actually be free to deal heroin while working for the task force. Unknown is the extent to which the "Safe Streets Task Force" actually played a role in fueling the heroin trade. At its very worst, task force officers belonged to local police departments which were themselves crippled with systemic internal corruption and were undeserving of public trust.

At the *very* time Warren Grace was selling heroin, December 2001 to April 2002, the newly appointed heads of the Baltimore police department, Commissioner Edward Norris and his lieutenants, were engaged in an amusing scheme to use a secret police benevolant fund to finance romantic interludes in private and public locations from Baltimore to New York City. Ed Norris would go on to head the Maryland State Police as its superintendent. To say these cops had other distractions is itself an amusing understatement.

There are reasons — obvious and not — why the FBI and its "Safe Streets Task Force" would attempt to infiltrate an independent rap music label. The FBI no doubt wants the public to think it has its eye on gangsta rappers. And what better entree into the world of rap than to flip a few rap producers, get them working as informants, and sit back while a world of gangstas stream in to rap their crimes in front of government microphones and running tape machines.

There are other pipers playing here than just the rap musicians. The FBI, it's a safe bet, had grander plans than simply taking down Deon Smith and Walter Poindexter.

The FBI runs bogus storefront operations of every stripe. These can be simple fencing operations to ensnare car thieves. Or the storefronts can be quite technologically sophisticated. The FBI Law Enforcement Bulletin of April 1997, for example, tells of one storefront, set up by Florida law enforcement officials and the U.S. Secret Service, meant to lure cell phone thieves hoping to reprogram, or "clone," hot cell phones with usable numbers. The storefront was ironically called "Cellmate."

"They secured a storefront location, renovated the building, and set up a waiting area in the front lobby," the FBI-published monthly bulletin reports. "A back room was used for cloning, and another room was used for monitoring transactions via hidden microphones and video cameras.... Investigators received training on how to operate the telephone programming equipment and practiced cloning different telephone makes and models.... To keep honest citizens from mistaking the new company for a legitimate phone service provider, investigators operated strictly on a referral basis. They gave business cards to *informants,* who spread the word among drug dealers, prostitutes, burglars, and others engaged in criminal activities. Within days, the first customers began calling to inquire about Cellmate's services." (Emphasis mine.)

But such storefronts have a dark side not generally shared with the public. I've learned that many honest law enforcement officers harbor a gnawing concern about cash storefronts.

One federal investigator, by coincidence, complained to me that Assistant U.S. Attorney James Warwick, of Baltimore (as it happens, one of Luna's colleagues) at times pressured him to start just such cash storefronts. "What's wrong with that?" I asked.

"Warwick was just all the time after me to start a fake storefront," I was told. "When you're running a storefront you have to worry about not just the crooks. If you don't regularly switch out the cops, they can go bad on you. Then you've got a network of bad cops and criminal informants more concerned about protecting themselves than the public." This is precisely what happened, it turns out, in the case of Maryland State Police Superintendent Ed Norris, and his security force, who'd end up spending considerable time covering up the fact that they'd been driving women all around town.

This investigator expressed concern that the cash nature of these storefronts, coupled with essentially non-existent oversight and lack of proper public accountability, can turn these operations into breeding grounds for law enforcement misbehavior and outright corruption. As in the Cellmate example mentioned above, informants often are part of the storefront operation. Bad cops end up going into business with the crooks. In Boston, I was reminded, entrenched FBI agents for decades used underworld informants to commit crimes, including murder. Or they would sit back and allow the crimes to happen.

Abhorrent FBI misbehavior in these secret operations in recent years has finally sparked congressional hearings. When I told the federal investigator about Stash House Records, his first, gut reaction was to stop me and say, "Are you sure *the feds* weren't the owners of Stash House Records? Go and see who owned the buildings or paid the rent."

I responded that I believed, in this case, Deon Smith was the owner.

"Well, don't overlook the possibility that the FBI planned a hostile takeover," I was told. Odds are, they hoped to arrest Smith and Poindexter and "flip" them into working with the FBI. But something went wrong. Very wrong.

"Keep in mind," I was told, "this isn't the only operation the Baltimore FBI and U.S. attorney's offices are running. There are lots of interconnected cases. If you start unraveling one, you'll unravel others. Everything you see is just the tip of the iceberg."

All this by way of explanation for the very sweet ride about to be enjoyed by Baltimore heroin dealer Warren Grace on the expense account of the Federal Bureau of Investigation, at the expense of the people of Baltimore.

21
Agent Skinner and the bank robbery squad

FBI Special Agent Steven Skinner is a relatively young and inexperienced agent. He's only worked for the FBI since November 1998. He was stationed in the Baltimore field office in March 1999. Through 2003 he will have worked, by his own reckoning, on a little more than a dozen investigations with the "Safe Streets Task Force."

"I have primarily worked in the area of violent crime," Skinner explains, "which means I have worked on Safe Streets violations. I have worked the Innocent Images Program, which deals with child pornography. And I have also worked on the Bank Robbery Squad."

Skinner's connection with the Bank Robbery Squad is worthy of mention. The Baltimore FBI Bank Robbery Squad, it so happens, carries its own stain of outrageous corruption, and has a direct connection to Jonathan Luna's murder and its subsequent misinvestigation.

Almost forty thousand untraceable dollars, confiscated from the accomplice of a flamboyant Baltimore bank robber, would inexplicably vanish from the Baltimore federal courthouse sometime in September 2002, about the same time Luna would begin to have real problems with Warren Grace and Grace's FBI handlers.

The day the money was last seen, the cash was under direct care of an FBI agent working for the bank robbery squad, with at least one other FBI agent close at hand.

The money, it should also be noted, went missing under the noses of several assistant U.S. attorneys (including Luna), a federal judge, U.S. marshals, sundry court personnel, and a defense attorney. Even so, at the time of his murder, Luna would be the one left holding the bag.

22
The missing $36,000: 'Vanished into thin air'

Circumstances surrounding the missing money are suitably theatrical, mysterious, even comic. A man named Nacoe Brown stood accused of violently robbing Baltimore banks while dressed in a series of increasingly outlandish disguises. He'd rob banks while wearing elegant suits, fedoras, and hospital scrubs. He also may have been commenting on our legal, medical, and entertainment professions. He stole more than $450,000.

One day the law caught up with Nacoe Brown. The FBI's Baltimore Bank Robbery Squad arrested Brown's partner, Kevin Hilliard, and confiscated a safe containing $63,128. Soon thereafter Brown was arrested. The remainder of the $450,000 was never recovered. Hilliard later confessed that Brown told him he'd received a vision from God that they should rob banks to finance Brown's struggling Gospel dinner theater. Brown, curiously, also recorded a gospel CD titled, "In Love With You Lord," marketed by an independent gospel label in Delaware. Everyone in this story seems to have a CD. On his CD, bank robber Nacoe Brown croons songs like, "Jesus Can."

Jesus can, but Nacoe Brown couldn't. Brown was charged with robbing four banks. His case came to trial in September 2002, and was prosecuted by Luna and his co-counsel, Assistant U.S. Attorney Jacabed Rodriguez-Coss.

In addition to Agent Skinner's connections to the bank robbery squad, this case would have several other notable ties to the Smith-Poindexter investigation involving informant Warren Grace. Nacoe Brown's defense attorney was Kenneth W. Ravenell, the same lawyer who would later defend Deon Smith. And Jacabed Rodriguez-Coss would also, for a time, work as Luna's co-counsel in the prosecution of

Smith and Poindexter.

There were other, less apparent, yet more personal ties to Luna. The judge presiding over Nacoe Brown's bank robbery prosecution was federal district court judge Andre Davis. Judge Davis, and attorney Ravenell, were experienced black barristers who had taken young Luna under wing. Both Davis and Ravenell would later describe themselves as friends and even mentors to Luna. Judge Davis would later speak at Luna's funeral.

After Luna's death, Ravenell would describe Luna as "a good friend." Ravenell would tell the Associated Press, "I was kind of his mentor in many ways. He'd call me often and discuss things outside of what we did on cases."

Shortly after the appearance of the third printing of this book, in late 2006, I received several letters from imprisoned bank robber Nacoe Brown. Brown had read my book, and now asked me to look into the missing money. Soon Brown was telephoning me from federal prison in Virginia and we were talking on the phone. Brown by this time was serving a 25-year sentence for his robberies.

It turned out that Nacoe Brown didn't just believe in old-time religion. Nacoe Brown has old-fashioned sensibilities, believing in honor among thieves and even lawyers. When such a man robs a bank, he naturally expects, when going to trial, the money won't be stolen by someone in the courthouse.

In a word, Nacoe Brown was upset about the missing money.

Nacoe Brown has had plenty of time to think about the prosecutor who put him behind bars.

At trial, which began on September 9, 2002, Jonathan Luna seemed to Brown like an experienced federal court lawyer. Luna "seemed like a professional," with "a college boy-type demeaner," Brown tells me. Luna was "very laid back, friendly."

Did Luna appear to be a competent trial lawyer? I asked.

"Definitely. Definitely. Definitely," Brown repeats.

I asked Nacoe Brown to recount events in the courtroom on the day he last saw the money, the third day of trial, September 16, 2002.

Brown's accomplice, Kevin Hilliard, was on the witness stand telling the jury about the money they'd taken from the bank heists. "The reason why (the money) was brought into the courtroom was that it was confiscated out of my co-defendant's safe," Brown says. "And it had the bank wrap labels on it. And (Hilliard) was testifying that he robbed the banks, and so did I, and this was proof that he actually robbed the banks."

Several others were in the courtroom with the money beside Hilliard, Brown, and the jury. Judge Davis sat presiding at the bench. Also present was a court reporter, Sharon Cook, and court clerk Belinda Arrington; a bailiff; and "a couple" of U.S. marshals, Brown recalls. Brown sat with his attorney, Kenneth Ravenell, on the table to the right.

The prosecution table was to the left. Luna, Rodgriguez-Coss, and FBI Special Agent Anthony Compano sat at the prosecution table. Special Agent Compano, like Steve Skinner, was a relatively inexperienced FBI agent. Like Skinner, he'd only been with the bureau a handful of years.

At the defense table, Ravenell sat to Brown's left, Brown says, between Brown and the prosecutors. A small group of Brown's family sat in the gallery behind.

When Brown was led into the courtroom at the start of the proceedings, he says, the $63,128 in recovered currency was already on an evidence cart in the courtroom at the prosecution table, under care of Agent Compano. At least one other FBI agent, Brett Kirby, court records indicate, also moved about in the courtroom as the evidence was on open display.

The money on the cart was in small denominations, Brown remembers. "Tens, 20s and stuff." The money, he says, "was wrapped in like big, sandwich-type bags." There were several bags of money. Each bag, Brown says, was "sealed, tight sealed. No one really could get into it. So that the jury could look at it in deliberations."

Brown described Luna as competently introducing the money into evidence as Hilliard testified. "They introduced it into evidence," Brown recalls. "Of course you know they just can't put it into evidence. They have to introduce the evidence. They have to introduce it through someone. And they did that through my co-defendant, by asking him to identify it. And he identified it, and they made their statements, and they went ahead and submitted it into evidence."

FBI Agent Compano, Brown says, "More than anyone was responsible for it (the money). He was there at the table with it. He was the one that really was handling the evidence, giving it to the prosecutors as they asked for it."

Brown continues, "I guess we know from watching tv is what he'll (Luna) do is (say), 'This is now people's Exhibit A,'" as he passes the money to the court clerk.

The trial transcripts indicate the bags of money were marked Government Exhibits 52A through 52G. (Even so, both Brown and Ravenell remember there were only three or four bags.) The bags containing the money had been "premarked" before trial by prosecution lawyers, Judge Davis later explained to the jury, "to help the court clerk." As Compano handed the sealed bags of money to Luna, Luna in turn handed them to the court clerk, where they were placed on a table in front of the judge, the jurors and the other onlookers.

The money "was given to the clerk," Brown repeats. "She handles all the evidence." The cash, Brown remembers, sat on the clerk's open table for several hours, through the testimony of two witnesses and over a lunch break.

At some point, in the courtroom, in the hallway, or perhaps even *days* later in the evidence vault, the money vanished. The missing bag of money therefore may even have been taken *in* the courtroom, over the lunch break.

Following Hilliard's testimony, trial transcripts describe Special Agent Brett Kirby taking the stand in the presence of the money to testify about how it, and other evidence, was found and sealed for court.

Under examination by Rodriguez-Coss, Agent Kirby first testifies, among other things, about a photo of the getaway vehicle used to rob the banks. "This is the vehicle that we believed to be the getaway vehicle that the defendant was sitting in, on the passenger's side in the front," Kirby tells the court.

Kirby continues, "We proceeded afterward to execute a search warrant at the residence of the individual who we believed to be the getaway driver and the driver of this vehicle, Mr. Hilliard."

"And what was your role once you arrived at that residence?" Rodriguez-Coss asks.

"Searching the residence with other agents that were present," Kirby says, "to attempt to recover any evidence that might be there, evidence of the previous bank robberies."

"Sir, during the course of that search, did you participate in the opening of a safe located inside that residence?"

"I did," Kirby says. "We found a safe in the bedroom closet. We utilized a tool to open the safe, which contained a considerable amount of money as well as some jewelry."

"I want to bring your attention to the items there in front of you which are marked 52A through 52G," Rodriguez-Coss says. "I want you to examine these items, sir, and can you tell me please, do you recognize these items?"

"I do," Kirby says. "I recognize these items as the money which was present in the safe that we opened at Mr. Hilliard's residence."

Also in the safe, and marked as Government Exhibit 101, were assorted items of jewelery. "There's a watch, a few rings, and a bracelet," Kirby testifies.

"And how is it that you recognize that item?" Rodriguez-Coss asks.

"I sealed it," Kirby explains. "And former (FBI) Supervisory Agent O'Hara, who was my supervisor at the time, witnessed it on that same date as the jewelry that came out of that safe."

"Now bringing your attention to what has been marked Government's Exhibit Number 53, can you tell me if you recognize this document?" Kirby is asked.

"Yes, ma'am, I do."

"Can you tell the members of the jury what that is?"

"This is an FD-302 Report of Investigation that I typed up subsequent to having counted this money," Kirby testifies. "I noted on the 302 that there was a portion of the money that on the straps around the bills was unmarked, had an unknown bank strapping. And then on each one of them, they had a stamp from a particular bank, all the way down, with a total at the end."

"What was that total, sir?"

"$63,128," Kirby replies.

Some of the money was traced to three banks. This cash, presumably, would be returned to those banks after trial. "From the Patapsco Bank, $3,600; from the Mercantile Bank, $6,478; and from the Key Bank, $14,950," Kirby testifies.

"And how much of the money was from an unknown source?"

"$38,100," Kirby says.

This untraceable sum of money, we have reason to believe, is the money that will soon go missing.

"I watched this evidence be introduced into the court through my co-defendant and identified by FBI Agent Kirby," Brown tells me. "I also watched this evidence stay in the courtroom for a long period of time and over the lunch recess."

After an afternoon court session, Brown says, he was led from the courtroom, never to see the money again. As he was led from the courtroom, the cash was still on the courtroom table, "with all the other evidence," Brown recalls.

Nacoe Brown by this time in his trial already had had several serious disagreements with his attorney, Kenneth Ravenell. Ravenell at the start of the case had requested a $30,000 fee, Brown says. But Brown says he'd only been able to give Ravenell $10,000.

So you didn't give him twenty thousand more dollars? I asked.

"He (Ravenell) was complaining about that all through the trial," Brown says. "All through the trial. It's all (in) the court records. And he was complaining to the judge about it. He complained to me about it."

On September 16, 2002, on the third day of the jury trial, the same day the money went missing, court records indicate that Ravenell asked the judge for permission to withdraw as Brown's counsel. The motion was denied. Ravenell's fee wasn't the only disagreement. At the start of the trial Brown, against Ravenell's advice, entered a guilty plea, only to withdraw it and change his plea to not guilty.

"In fact," Ravenell later would write the Maryland State Attorney Grievance Commission, responding to a complaint filed against him by Brown, "Mr. Brown approached the Court three times prior to trial indicating that he wanted to plead guilty. Each time he changed his mind stating to me that God would see that he prevail because God did not want him to be found guilty." Ravenell writes that he "advised Mr. Brown against that strategy."

Rocky as things were between Brown and his attorney, Brown says he was unaware that Luna shared personal friendships with Judge Davis and Ravenell. Whenever Ravenell spoke of Luna, Brown says, Ravenell, "really didn't have anything bad to say about (Luna). I can't say he said anything bad about him. Up until the time of the missing evidence, or the murder, I didn't see any type of inconsistencies, you know?"

How did Luna act around Ravenell? I asked.

"The same," Brown says. "Like he knew him. You know, (they) interact(ed) with one another very well."

And how did Luna and Ravenell interact with Judge Davis?

This question sparked a memory in Brown. He recalled a moment during the trial when the three men stood together at the bench laughing at a comment made by Davis. This moment seemed to betray a closeness between the three men. "So it's like, for you to mention that, that comes back to my mind," Brown says.

The evidence used during trial was kept in a supposedly secure evidence lock-up vault in the courthouse. This is not like a locker in a gym where one keeps one's sneakers. It's a high-security vault, with sign-in and sign-out procedure sheets that detail evidence chains of custody.

At the close of each day's court proceedings, it was FBI Special Agent Anthony Compano's responsibility to oversee the money and other valuable exhibits as they were placed from the courtroom table back onto the evidence cart. By all accounts Agent Compano and Luna then wheeled the money on the cart through the courthouse hallways to the supposedly secure evidence vault.

"Luna and an FBI agent took the bags of money into the evidence vault," one courthouse worker told me, "and — poof — the money just vanished into thin air."

The money was *officially* discovered missing shortly after the last day of trial, on September 26, 2002, not long after both defense and prosecution lawyers signed stipulations that all evidence had been properly returned. Whether the money was *unofficially* known to be missing before that remains an open question.

On the morning of the eighth day of trial, September 25, 2002, the case went to the jury and Judge Davis gave his instructions to the jurors. Davis told the jurors, "The evidence in the case, which you may consider with respect to all charges and consistently with my instructions, consists of the sworn testimony of the witness, *all exhibits received in evidence,* and all the facts which have been stipulated.... A number of exhibits have been admitted into evidence in this case and will be available for your review." (Emphasis mine.)

Davis went on to tell the jurors, "After just a few minutes, after you go into the jury room, we're going to send in *all of the evidence* and copies of my instructions, as well as the verdict sheets."

In fact, Judge Davis wasn't telling the strict truth here.

The jurors began their deliberations at about 10:30 that morning.

Once the jurors left the courtroom, Judge Davis turned to Luna. Please see that the jurors are given all the exhibits, or evidence, the judge tells Luna.

Luna tells Davis, "We are going to meet with Ms. Arrington," the court clerk, to get the exhibits together.

Judge Davis asks Luna to please hurry, noting he'd had a "bad experience recently, where it took over an hour to get the exhibits together."

"We're not going to do that," Luna tells him.

"Frankly, I would prefer that you not wait until you've gone through all of them before you start sending them in," Davis goes on. "Get through as many as you can within the next couple of minutes, and then send those in, and then finish looking at whatever you need to look at, and send those in. They don't have to all go in at the same time."

"Yes, your honor," Luna tells him.

"Please take care of that expeditiously," Judge Davis says.

Trial transcripts reveal that there were other problems with evidence handling, and misplaced evidence, in this case. Ravenell now tells Judge Davis, "Your honor, I was just conferring with (court clerk) Ms. Arrington as to whether the exhibit was found that we couldn't find yesterday and she told me yes."

These assurances to the judge notwithstanding, it soon becomes apparent to the jurors that the prosecutors and the FBI have not given all of the evidence to them.

Certain items, including the money, are obviously missing from the jury room, and the jury sends several notes to Judge Davis asking, quite literally, in one note, to see *all* the evidence. This would turn out to be no small point. The *exact* wording of the notes from the jury — what the jury wanted to see, and when — become center to the controversy that follows.

One afternoon in October 2007, overcome by curiosity, I returned to the clerk's office in the Baltimore federal courthouse and pulled Nacoe Brown's bank robbery file. Inside the manila folder, attached to binders behind some court papers, I came upon a sealed, white envelope. The jury notes. The envelope had a look of unopened crispness to it. A few inches of Scotch tape sealed each side of the flap in the back. I gingerly opened the envelope. The tape, I saw, had never before been pulled from the back of the envelope.

Onto my lap poured an assortment of folded jury notes, written on lined spiral notepaper. Two of the notes spoke directly to the issue at hand.

"Can the jury have a list of all the evidence entered?" reads one note that was sent to Judge Davis at 11:45 AM on the first day of deliberations, September 25, 2002.

Twenty minutes later, at 12:05 PM, the judge was handed a far more specific note. It reads, in part, "Can the jurors have all the evidence presented -- primarily the White Accounting Records?"

This note quite clearly expresses the jury's desire to see *"all the evidence."*

Receiving these two notes on September 25, Judge Davis calls the prosecution and defense lawyers back to the courtroom.

"Did we send in the exhibit lists with the evidence?" Judge Davis asks the prosecutors. No, he's told. There was no list of the evidence *entered.*

The problem, the judge is told, is that the evidence list was prepared before the start of trial and contains items that the prosecutors hadn't used. These items were marked on the evidence list for identification purposes before the trial. No longer an accurate list of evidence *actually entered* at trial, it wasn't sent in to the jury. A new list will have to be typed.

The real problem here, we now know, concerns the whereabouts of the evidence, not just the list.

Where's the evidence? the jurors are clearly asking. They could see that some items introduced at trial, including the cash, were not in front of them in deliberations, and they were asking about this.

"Belinda," Judge Davis tells the clerk, "we need Mr. Brown to be brought down. I'm going to bring the jury back into the courtroom and essentially answer all of these questions in one consolidated response.

"I'm going to tell them that we are preparing a sanitized copy of the exhibit list, that it's going to take a bit of time, but we will get it to them," Judge Davis goes on. "And I'm going to tell them that they cannot have any exhibits that were marked only for identification and that, in fact, *they have all of the exhibits that have been admitted as evidence in the trial.* Is that literally true, by the way?"

"Yes," Rodriguez-Coss tells him. The jury, she says at first, has everything except for a witness statement, which is now being retyped.

"But all the money has gone in, and so forth?" Judge Davis asks.

"No, your honor," Rodriguez-Coss replies, contradicting herself.

"I didn't think you'd send in the money," Judge Davis says. "What money did you not send in?"

"We didn't send in any of the money," Rodriguez-Coss now tells him.

"None of the money," Judge Davis says. "Okay."

"Also, we didn't send in the pellet gun, and we didn't send in the pellets."

"Nor should you," Davis agrees.

Judge Davis calls the jury back into the courtroom. In the second note the jurors had asked to see accounting notes (referred to as the "White Accounting Records") that had been mentioned at trial by FBI Agent Compano. These accounting notes hadn't been introduced into evidence, and so could not be seen by the jury, the judge now tells the jurors.

"We have sent in to you, with a couple of exceptions, all of the evidence that was admitted in this case," Davis tells the jury. "We didn't send in the money, we didn't send in the exhibit which was the pellet gun, and we didn't send in the jewelry that was identified. I think, frankly, the reason we didn't send in those exhibits is pretty obvious. There are certain exhibits that we simply don't, under court procedures, allow out of the possession of the United States Attorney's Office and the FBI." Yuk, yuk.

If jurors want to see any of those exhibits, they can ask to look at them in the courtroom, Davis explains. "If you need to examine any exhibit that was not sent in to you, ...any evidence that was admitted but not sent in, simply send us a note that you want to examine whatever it is, and we will bring you back into the courtroom, as you are now, and ... we will allow you to examine that exhibit, including passing it among yourselves, if that's what you desire to do."

Mollified, the jurors thereafter never again *specifically ask* to see the cash exhibits. Even so, *they have been falsely assured the cash is there,* should they want to see it. The next day, Thursday, September 26, 2002, the jury finds Nacoe Brown guilty on three counts of bank robbery.

Following the guilty verdict, all that's left that day in court is housekeeping chores. The evidence lists used by the prosecution, the defense, and the court are tendered for entering on the docket. The lawyers sign stipulations that all evidence on the lists are accounted for.

Then Judge Davis orders that all exhibits in the case "be returned and retained."

Shortly after this the plastic bag containing the $38,100 in untraceable bills is discovered missing.

Agents in the troubled FBI Baltimore field office react to all this in a rather peculiar way. Bear this in mind: these agents were charged with protecting and guarding the evidence at this trial. They failed. The FBI agents have lost the evidence. Now FBI agents from the same field office are placed in charge of investigating their colleagues and themselves, and everyone else in the courtroom, to determine what happened to the missing cash.

Right off the bat the compromised FBI agents do something rather interesting. They leak the story to the press.

Only one week after Brown's conviction, on October 3, 2002, the Baltimore Sun published an article written by Gail Gibson, titled, "Money stolen, found and missing again," subtitled, "Cash: Up to $38,000 used as evidence in a bank robbery trial has disappeared, officials say."

This article itself is curious, and would later become part of and referred to in the court disciplinary inquiry filed by Brown against his attorney, Kenneth Ravenell.

The Sun article begins:

> *As they wrapped up a two-week bank robbery trial in U.S. District Court in Baltimore, federal authorities discovered another possible crime — some key evidence, more than $36,000 in cash, had disappeared.*

From here out, the missing money would simply be referred to as "the missing $36,000," even though, it seems likely, the actual sum was $38,100. Gibson here also, rather clumsily, reveals her sources for the story to be FBI agents. Her article continues:

> *FBI officials confirmed yesterday that agents are investigating what happened to money used as evidence in the trial of Nacoe Ray Brown, who was convicted last week in a string of violent bank robberies in Baltimore County. Special Agent Barry A. Maddox, an FBI spokeman, declined to discuss the evidence investigation in detail or say how much money is missing. But law enforcement sources said that $36,000 to $38,000 was gone and the FBI agents had interviewed numerous courthouse employees this week.*
>
> *The money was determined to be missing as attorneys*

> *packed up after a jury returned its verdict against Brown last Thursday, said U.S. District Judge Andre M. Davis, who presided over the trial and was astounded by the discovery.*
>
> *Davis said investigators have indicated that the money apparently was not taken from his courtroom, but that it likely was lost somewhere between the courtroom and government storage used to hold sensitive evidence during trials.*
>
> *"My understanding is it wasn't taken out of the courtroom, and that gives me a very narrow measure of relief," Davis said. "The bureau is undergoing a very thorough, professional investigation, and we can just await the outcome."*
>
> *Officials with the U.S. attorney's office did not respond yesterday for comment.*
>
> *Federal prosecutors and the FBI agents assigned to the case would have been directly responsible for the money. Such evidence, along with items such and guns and drugs, typically is kept locked in a secure area except for a brief period when it's introduced at trial.*

This last sentence, stating the money was only displayed for "a brief period," is obviously wrong. It sat in open court through two long testimonies of two important witnesses — Hilliard and Agent Kirby. And Nacoe Brown says it remained in the courtroom over the lunch break. It's also apparent that whoever is leaking this story isn't friendly to Luna. In fact, the article seems designed to put heat — and headlines — on Luna, and perhaps on his self-described "mentor," Ravenell. The Sun article goes on to report:

> *A stipulated agreement that all exhibits in the case had been returned was signed on the last day of the trial by each of the attorneys in the case — Assistant U.S. Attorneys Jonathan P. Luna and Jacobed Rodriguez-Coss and defense attorney Kenneth W. Ravenell.*
>
> *Ravenell said yesterday that at the trial, government lawyers asked Hilliard to identify the cash seized from his safe as coming from the bank robberies. Ravenell said the money was heat-sealed in two or three separate plastic bags and that*

each one was extremely bulky because the denominations were relatively small.

The missing bag of money contained as much as $38,000, apparently in $20 bills, according to law enforcement sources close to the investigation.

"Law enforcement sources close to the investigation." Read: FBI agents who are the Sun's sources for this story.

Next in the article, Ravenell is quoted as making a curious misstatement. For a sharp-eyed attorney like Ravenell, it's a very glaring mistake. He again repeats the false notion that the money was only in the courtroom for a "short period," during Hilliard's testimony. For some reason Ravenell forgets that Agent Kirby also testified in front of the cash exhibits:

Ravenell said the money was in the courtroom for only the short period when it was identified by Hilliard and introduced as evidence. After that, he said the evidence apparently was taken to a secure area by government agents or attorneys, who typically wheel case files and evidence boxes through the courthouse on rolling carts. "These were not like little stacks of ... hundred dollar bills," Ravenell said. "It's not something that, in my opinion, is just going to fall off the cart in the hallway and no one would notice."

Ravenell said he had not been interviewed by FBI agents and learned about the missing evidence during an unrelated appearance in Davis' courtroom this week. He said the evidence probe would not affect his client's case or sentencing, which is scheduled for December 13.

"The money was there during the trial," Ravenell said. "What they did with it afterwards, I have no idea."

This last statement was another curious observation by Ravenell. A close read of the records reveals it's not at all clear that the money was "there during the trial."

Nacoe Brown tells me he incredibly first learned of the missing money, not from his lawyer, but shortly after his trial was over, when his wife sent him a copy of the October 3, 2003 Sun newspaper article. Ravenell, he says, refused to raise the missing evidence as an issue with the court, at his sentencing, or in an appeal. Raising the issue of the missing evidence, Brown says Ravenell told him, would be "frivolous." All this mystifies Brown, now sitting in federal prison in Virginia.

"Ravenell is known on the street as being a defense lawyer who looks for any opportunity to get his client off," Brown tells me. Yet, Brown complains, "Ravenell didn't take advantage of this once-in-a-lifetime opportunity to point out the mishandling, stealing and withholding or (contamination) of exculpatory evidence. Even after I requested him to do so, he went out of his way not to let the record reflect what has taken place."

From Nacoe Brown's perspective, sitting at the defense table between Ravenell and Luna, the entire episode of the missing money smacked of chicanery, and legal slight-of-hand. When exactly *had* the money gone missing? Doesn't the FBI owe the public, and Brown, an explanation of the complete circumstances of its disappearance?

What exactly would the FBI's Baltimore field office do about the missing money? The FBI launched what it described as an exhaustive investigation. Agents even twice interviewed Judge Davis. Davis says he provided trial transcripts to agents in the spring of 2003.

Early on, as we've seen, compromised FBI agents would leak information to the Baltimore Sun's Gail Gibson. And, early on, the FBI agents would curiously do so in a way that attempted to pass blame on to Tom DiBiagio's U.S. Attorney's office in general, and Jonathan Luna in particular.

The "missing $36,000" episode clearly and rightly grew into a major FBI embarrassment. The G-men got their panties in a bunch trying to get to the bottom of the mystery. There'd be lots of posturing, finger pointing, and butt covering, yet the bottom line was the money was gone, taken by someone, or several people, while under FBI guard.

The money didn't just vanish into thin air, whisked away by pixies, insiders know. And not just money was missing: trust had been misplaced.

It would grow into a major bone of contention between the Baltimore FBI field office and the U.S. attorney's office.

This then was the Baltimore FBI's bank robbery squad, mentioned by Agent Skinner. We can only hope they don't have a nuclear protection squad.

Aside from his connection to the FBI's bank robbery squad, Agent Steve Skinner has a burden of name to carry. As chance would have it, he shares the same last name as the fictitious, shadowy FBI Assistant Director Walter Skinner, a central character in the television show The X-Files.

On the Simpsons TV cartoon show, Principal W. Seymour Skinner of Springfield Elementary often finds himself at loggerheads with Bart Simpson. "There's no justice like angry-mob justice," Principal Skinner, whose nickname is Spanky, is fond of warning. It's said that Seymour Skinner was the best principal that Springfield could afford. Principal Seymour Skinner has a metal plate in his butt, and was once feared to have been murdered by Bart Simpson, though he was later found to have been merely trapped under a pile of newspapers.

In real life, Skinners have held trusted posts in government. Samuel K. Skinner, a former U.S. attorney from Illinois, served as Secretary of Transportation, and White House chief of staff, under the presidency of George Herbert Walker Bush. Sam Skinner is said to be a close friend of Barbara Bush, mother of President George W. Bush. Former Secretary Sam Skinner, coincidentally, has a son named Steven.

No relation to Baltimore Special Agent Steve Skinner.

23
Agent Skinner taps Warren Grace for government work

How did FBI agent Steve Skinner come to learn about Warren Grace? he's asked.

"Well, like I said," Skinner says, "we have task force officers on our squad. There are local police officers, and they have connections with different local police departments.

"I myself have been working violent crime for a few years and I have developed relationships with local law enforcement officers, and sometimes they may call you and they will say, hey, we just arrested a person, we have a couple of guns on them, they are backing some previous charges. Essentially they say they are in a bind, and this type of person may be a person that you may want to talk to."

"Backing up charges," Skinner explains, essentially refers to the revolving door which career criminals like Grace keep passing through. In plain language, we begin to see the FBI, as a bureaucracy, *benefits* from criminals passing through the revolving door. The FBI, surprisingly, *profits* from society's worst failures.

Skinner stumbles as he explains, "I guess the court systems, at least in Maryland, are pretty — there is a lot of crimes going on. People get arrested and they can be released on bond. That happens quite frequently. And while they are out, they may violate another crime.

"Sometimes, if people are let out on probation, if they get arrested again, they still have to serve the time that they were let out for from the previous charge."

So by threatening an offender like Warren Grace with added time in prison — or holding out the hope of lessening a sentence — the FBI hopes to swing a career criminal into its paid informant program. Information is their commodity.

Investigations into narcotics trafficking, Skinner says, require informants. "Cooperating witnesses are vital to any FBI investigation, particularly drug investigations. They provide us with information that I myself, Steve Skinner, wouldn't have access to, or other agents of the FBI or task force members.

"I didn't grow up in the neighborhoods in the streets, and I haven't made the relationships that a lot of cooperating witnesses have."

"A confidential informant is basically broken down into two categories by the FBI," Skinner explains.

"There is (sic) different subcategories and things like that but, to basically sum up, there is (sic) two types of confidential informants.

"We refer commonly and generally to all of these informants as sources.... The first type of source is what we call a confidential informant. The confidential informant, to me and to the FBI, is a person that just provides information.

"There is (sic) different ways that you become a source. As far as this first category that I am discussing, sometimes we just have people that call up the FBI and they feel a civic duty. This is typically your confidential informant."

"There is a second type of source (that's) what we call a cooperating witness," Skinner goes on. "This is what Warren Grace is." Before explaining how Warren Grace came to his attention and was signed on by the FBI, Skinner takes a moment to describe the program he had in mind when he recruited Grace.

Warren Grace, he repeats, "is a cooperating witness. He is the second type of source that the FBI has. A cooperating witness does more than just provide information. A cooperating witness acts almost like an agent of the government. They are like an arm of our investigation."

Though Grace would be paid by the FBI, Skinner splits hairs by maintaining an informant like Grace, is "not employed by us, meaning, you know, they don't get benefits and a 401k plan and all that." In other words, they are disposable, and off the books.

In any event, Skinner continues, informants like Grace "do

receive things from us, and I will get to that, but they work as an agent for us. They do proactive things for us. And they are more involved in a case that a confidential informant.

"Usually, cooperating witnesses are people that are placed in a certain position in their life. They are people that are going to be involved pretty deep in an investigation and typically your general person doesn't want to expose themselves that way. Especially when you are dealing with violent investigations. People want to limit their exposure to things.

"So when we deal with cooperating witnesses, they are typically people who are in a bind financially, because we do pay some cooperating witnesses. Or they could be people that have been arrested and they are facing criminal exposure, criminal sentences, and they have a hope that if they work with us, with the FBI and other law enforcement agencies, that their exposure to a criminal sentence will be lessened by a court."

So an informant's loss is the FBI's gain.

"It's very seldom that you can have an investigation without the help and assistance of a cooperating witness," Skinner says. "Typically and usually, an undercover (police officer) is introduced (to the criminal element) by a cooperating witness (like Warren Grace)," Skinner says. "That's usually how it's done."

How is an individual like Warren Grace selected to work as an informant?

"There is a balancing act that we use," Skinner says. "There is no exact method to it. There is no exact formula. All I can say is that, at least when I look at a cooperating or a potential cooperating witness, and what other agents do is, we look at that person and we look at their criminal history and we look at the type of person they are and we have to balance that with the potential that they can provide us with in conducting an investigation and where that investigation will go and who can become part of that investigation." Balance, however, in this case would be sadly lacking.

Skinner says the moral and criminal threshold for its potential informants is pretty low. In fact, about as low as it can get.

"The only crime that I am aware of that the FBI has a problem with is child molesters," Skinner adds. "From what I know, the FBI would not use a child molester as a cooperating witness. It's just something that I personally wouldn't do, and it's just something that—. It's not a written rule. But it would just be too extreme.

"But we use— the FBI historically has used murderers for cooperating witnesses and people who have done violent things. It's just a part of the history of the FBI and it's how we conduct investigations. It provides us with information that can solve crimes that have been unsolved for many, many years. It provides us with access to criminal organizations that, but for their cooperation with us — no matter how dark their past was — but for them working for us, those criminal organizations never would have been brought to justice."

24
Two brothers and an agent named Skinner

Agent Steve Skinner says he first heard of Warren Grace hours after Grace's arrest in April 2002.

"I received a telephone call," Skinner recounts. "It was in the evening. It was about 9 o'clock, and it was from an officer that I knew. He said that they had arrested an individual named Warren Grace, that Warren Grace was arrested after the completion of a Baltimore city search warrant.

"And in that search warrant, the police had found two guns. I believe one was a Tech 9 sub-machine gun and another one, I think, was a .38. It was some sort of a revolver. It could have been a .32.

"This officer told me that Warren Grace was providing information to the Baltimore city police department officials regarding various individuals that Mr. Grace knew."

Agent Skinner would later tell all this to the jury in the Smith-Poindexter case. What he would not tell the jury is this: Warren Grace, when Skinner met him, was busy talking to Baltimore homicide detectives about Poindexter's murder of Alvin Jones.

Skinner couldn't wait to get the flip on with Warren Grace. That night he wasted no time trying to get in to see Grace. But the junior FBI agent seems to have been pushed aside by the Baltimore homicide squad. Baltimore PD's scissors cut him out.

"I tried to get in contact with him that evening, but Baltimore city was talking with him about various different criminal activities, and I didn't get to speak with him that evening," Skinner says.

Agent Skinner knows he has a trump card. He can get an assistant U.S. attorney to file a writ of habeas corpus to bring Grace in for a talk. Paper, scissors, stone. The federal paper beats their cutout scissors.

Skinner knows just the lawyer. Like Agent Steve Skinner, assistant US attorney Jonathan Luna was relatively young and inexperienced.

In theory, FBI agents work for U.S. attorneys. FBI agents are the investigators for the government lawyers. It's the government lawyers who ultimately have the responsibility for weighing the legality of investigations, and who ultimately must prosecute a case. In practice, the tail has come to wag the dog. U.S. attorneys — particularly young and inexperienced assistant U.S. attorneys — increasingly find themselves following the lead of the FBI agents. U.S. attorneys have complained in and out of congressional hearings that they do not have the proper control over FBI agents. Often, some have told congress, they are *fearful* of the FBI. They say they fear reprisals and retaliation both from individual FBI agents, and from the FBI as an institution. As we'll see, judges also are often afraid of bucking the FBI — even in cases of improper or outright illegal FBI behavior. Our constitutional system of checks and balances has broken down, and an increasingly unaccountable American police agency has been left unchecked, with too much power.

An FBI agent will often refer a case to a particular assistant U.S. attorney. Skinner had his own reasons for taking the case to Luna. Some of these reasons are obvious. Luna was young, hip and black. Skinner must have hoped that Luna could reach someone like Warren Grace, that they might talk the same language.

Luna had his own reasons for involving himself with Warren Grace and Steve Skinner. He would come to regret all of them.

25
Meanwhile, back on Eden Street

Meanwhile, back in the real world of Baltimore, in early 2002, Carnell Dawson, on Eden Street, at last found steady work. It looked like the Dawsons' luck might be changing.

Dawson was hired on by Chilmar/RWC to refurbish a Dubdalk, Maryland elementary school. It was good job with benefits. At work, on the 2:30 to 11:30 pm shift, Carnell talked incessantly about his wife, Angela and kids. At work they called him Country.

He was hired at Chilmar about the same time the FBI put Warren Grace on the payroll.

At the same time the Dawsons began to see their little piece of the American dream come true, the nightmare outside their door grew menacing. Drug dealers congregated in greater numbers on the Dawsons' corner, out in the street. The Dawsons would find vials thrown on the sidewalk, and paraphernalia tucked in the cracks of their stairs. They began to call 911. The police would come out, but nothing seemed to change.

Anger began to well up in Angela Dawson. In time it would become an all-consuming rage. She decided to fight back. She decided to take back her home and her neighborhood from the legions of dope dealers and heroin zombies. She would in time demand the police and the courts do their job — to serve, and protect, the innocent. Not just pay lip service, or administer the revolving door.

She resolved not to be run out of her own home. She resolved to clean up her neighborhood, and make her home safe for her children.

It would be a very lonely fight. Now that money was coming in, they could pay their phone bill. There was, they would find, a deadly disconnect at the other end of the line.

The "Safe Streets Task Force" was unreachable. Nowhere in

sight. The feds had more pressing priorities than working with the local police to keep families like the Dawsons and their kids safe.

They were trying to take over a rap music label.

26
Down these mean streets: Something better than this

Who was Jonathan Luna? To those he prosecuted, Luna was The Man. It helps to understand a little bit more about Luna's role and his background, and how he saw himself. The short answer is that Luna saw himself both as a champion, and a product, of the downtrodden and powerless neighborhoods he sought to protect.

In his last case involving Smith and Poindexter, Luna would find himself protecting something altogether different than the innocents of Baltimore. He chiefly finds himself protecting Warren Grace, and Grace's government handlers and employers at the FBI, and in the U.S. Attorney's office.

Who was Jonathan Luna? After his death he'd be reduced to a crude stereotype. Look more closely, over the span of years, and you'll see an accomplished man on a self-driven journey. That his life ended in great tragedy and mystery is only part of the story. I've come to see him as an unsung yet noteworthy American original. His midnight ride spanned decades, not hours.

Early in 2005 I met one of Luna's longtime friends, Dan Rivera. Rivera told me there were things I should know about Luna.

"We never called him Jonathan," Rivera told me straight off, the first time we spoke on the phone. "We always called him Joey."

Rivera invites me to come to the Bronx to learn more. There's a photograph he wants me to see, he says.

When I finally arrive, Rivera meets me in the street, and escorts me into his apartment building.

Rivera's in his thirties. He's a mid-sized man with close-cropped hair and a droll laugh. He's a New York sanitation worker and walks with a hunkered-down, sturdy gate.

Rivera recently moved into a well-kept, high-rise apartment building off 161st Street, twenty blocks north of the projects where he grew up with Luna. "Joey never got to see my apartment," Rivera tells me. "He would have been proud that I got out of the projects and into a nice place like this."

Rivera's apartment is on the twenty-third floor. He takes me out to his balcony. He has a great view of the Bronx and beyond. To the far left you can see slivers of Yankee Stadium and the George Washington Bridge. Far below there's a running track where Jonathan would run laps, he tells me. Ironically, Rivera points out, the balcony also overlooks the Bronx courthouse where Jonathan worked one summer.

A bicycle stored on the balcony draws my eye. It leans against the wall. It's a rusted blue bicycle, without a front tire, resting on its bare front fork. It's an old-fashioned ten-speed racer from the early 80s, with white handlebar tape that's peeling off. This was Jonathan's bicycle, Rivera tells me.

There used to be two of them, he goes on. "We actually bought those bikes about a week apart," Rivera says. "We had the same model as a Ross, which back then was too expensive for us. I was hit by a car, and my bike was demolished. After a while, he wasn't going to use this bike anymore so he gave it to me. I don't use it, but I like to keep it as a memory of him." It's a cold February day and the wind is ripping through the bicycle frame. We don't linger long on the balcony.

Back inside his apartment, Rivera takes out a few books Luna had given him, including *Down These Mean Streets,* by Piri Thomas. It's an autobiography of a young, black, Puerto Rican man coming of age in 1930s Harlem. Thomas wrestles with race, violence, drugs and his place in society. Not surprisingly, the book resonated with young Luna, Rivera says. There's also the biography of Dr. Ben Carson, the Johns Hopkins neurosurgeon. Luna sent this book along with a note.

Dan digs out photo books and stacks of letters, and invites me to sit at a small dining table. There are lots of photos. Photos of Luna as a teenager, looking cool in dark glasses. Photos of an older Luna, more stylishly dressed, well-groomed, grinning, and wearing a trench coat.

Photos of an athletic Luna arriving at law school in North Carolina. A snap shot of a Luna sitting in a federal courtroom. A haunting, close-up photo of Luna at night, in front of our nation's capitol building in Washington DC.

Then there are the letters, written over the years, from Luna to Rivera. Dan spreads them out on the table and begins to speak of his friend.

Luna was a "complex" person, Dan Rivera says. He had a ready sense of humor, and an intellect that didn't always operate "head on, but beneath the surface," Rivera explains. "He was larger than life. You really had to meet him and know him to understand what he was like."

And Dan Rivera knew him well. Rivera grew up in the projects with Jonathan and, years later, served as Luna's best man at his wedding.

Luna, it turned out, was no stranger to poverty, violence and drugs. Growing up, he knew and saw these things at his doorstep.

Joey Luna grew up in a densely packed public housing project called the Patterson Houses, off 141st Street, in what's called the Mott Haven section of the South Bronx. Mott Haven includes those areas below 152nd Street. In a November 1999 article, *Scientific American* reported that, "The Mott Haven section of New York City's South Bronx has long been one of the poorest neighborhoods in the nation. The median household income of its residents, most of whom are African-American or Hispanic, is less than one third of the U.S. median."

I convince Dan Rivera to take me to Mott Haven to visit the projects where he and Luna grew up. It's a quick car ride from Rivera's apartment, but a lifetime's journey.

A rusted orange and white sign hangs out front of the sprawling projects. Fenced in from the littered sidewalk in a strip of grass-speckled dirt, the sign reads, "Welcome to Patterson Houses — Please help to keep it clean."

The complex is composed of innumerable rundown, tall, dark brick buildings, some more than a dozen stories tall, all closely packed together in a grassy common, connected by walkways running between the strips of worn grass. The sounds of the city are inescapable.

Rivera leads me to the building where Luna grew up, and points out the two-bedroom, first floor apartment Luna shared with his parents and his brother, David. "I grew up in the Mitchell projects, about two blocks away, and he grew up here in Patterson projects," Rivera explains.

They'd met when Dan was in the fourth or fifth grade, he tells me. Jonathan was three or four years older. "Either my brother brought him over to the house or we went over to his house. I don't recall exactly how it happened. He was always into a lot of different things. I remember one of the things: he had a skateboard. He was into skateboarding and he had a lot of skateboarding magazines. And then I got into skateboarding. That was one of the things that I found interesting about him. He was always into different things."

Rivera says, "Joey was just part of the family. I mean, we didn't even consider him a friend. He would come over for Thanksgiving. If he wasn't with us, we were with him."

Often Rivera would go over to Luna's home. "We spent a lot of time there, " Dan remembers. "His father would ask me how was school. But then they would pretty much go to their room and let me and Joey talk and listen to music or whatever."

Luna's father, Paul, was Filipino, and worked in city restaurants. His mother, Rosezella, an African-American, was a stay-at-home mom. "His mother was more-- she was shy. She was more to herself. And the father, he was a little more outgoing," Dan says. Jonathan's father was light-skinned, while his mother was dark. Luna was half-Asian, yet, like writer Piri Thomas, thought of himself as black. "I think that, being that he was dark skinned, he related more to being black," Dan says. "If you didn't meet his father you would never know that Joey was part Filipino. I guess his name maybe gave it away: Luna. I know he was definitely aware of racism and how it affected his life and everyone in this country."

Early on, Dan noticed something different about young Joey Luna, traits that made him stand out from most of the other kids growing up in the projects. Luna wanted to learn, and read. The linen closet in the Luna's cramped apartment became a library. "The linen closet was full of books and magazines. Every time he would get a book, he would open the closet, and it was just from top to bottom -- no linen, just books," Dan laughs.

The books provided an escape from the mean streets all around them, and helped Joey Luna reinvent himself.

The violence and the drugs, at times, could be both harrowing and close at hand. In the 1980s, from Luna's apartment window, Rivera says, he and young Jonathan used to look out to a nearby walk cutting between the high-rise project buildings. "You could see outside the window by the fence," Rivera says, "and when the crack epidemic was really rampant, you could see the people lining up to buy drugs off the dealer in broad daylight in middle of the complex. It was really surreal. We would just look out the window and shake our heads like it's crazy. And you know the cops would go by and they wouldn't do anything. I guess the community was so out of control that the cops didn't even want to get involved."

They saw the wreckage caused by the rampant drug peddling, and wanted to stay clear. Rivera explains, "We'd look out the window and we'd see these people ruining their lives. And you would see girls in the building that were attractive, and got into drugs, and they would be just skinny, and then all of a sudden they weren't attractive. So to us it was never a temptation. We were always away from that."

Harder yet would be to steer clear of the violence of the projects, and the South Bronx. On one occasion, when Rivera was about 13 or 14, he says he and Luna were returning from the movies. Getting off the subway, he says, they "cut into his complex and we heard gun fire, gunshots. And there was about four of them, and they started running in our direction. And Joey turned around to run, but I told him not to run, because I didn't want to get confused with the people who are doing the shooting. So I told him, you know, 'Don't run, let's just try to walk, as fast as we can.' The guys actually brushed up against us they were so close, and you could see weapons in their hands. I didn't want them to think, 'Oh these guys are witnesses.' I didn't want them to come shooting at us. It was scary."

Rivera goes on, "There was another time, too. We were in his house. And someone knocked on his neighbor's door, which was right next to Joey's door. You know how the projects are; the doors are back to back. And when the neighbor went to look through the peephole, they shot him, right through the door! And I remember, and it was funny — cause Joey dove for the floor, it was so close, it was just a matter of feet. We were just sitting there talking in the apartment, and all of a sudden you hear gunshots, and Joey just throws himself on the floor! It was weird because I had to leave the house at a certain point. So now I had to leave, and walk outside, knowing that someone had just gotten shot. So even if you didn't look for trouble, you would always wind up caught in the middle of things."

In those days, in their mid-teens in the late 1970s and early 80s, Rivera says, "We were just trying to stay alive."

"You really have to live in that environment to really get a full appreciation for how difficult it is," Rivera tells me. "If you walk through for a day, you figure it's not really that bad around here, especially during the daytime when the kids are in school. You really have to live there and go to the schools. It's a really oppressive environment. There was really nothing for the kids to do. Nowadays the schools have a lot of after school programs and stuff. But back then there really wasn't much to do. And if you hung out outside in front of the building in that area, odds are you were probably going to get into trouble."

To hide from this rough world, Rivera says, and perhaps to one day escape from it, Luna as a teen fell into habits of study and self-betterment. He began to run. "Well he would always tell me, always try to stay active," Rivera says. "He was always physically fit, he ran the marathons, and he was always reading. (He believed) it should be your mind, your body, and your soul. He believed in being well rounded. Not just being educated and being out of shape. Or being physically fit and being ignorant. He felt you had to be a well-rounded person in every facet, and that's why he read so many different things, and so many different topics. So he knew a lot about a lot."

Rivera goes on, "He always seemed to be just exceptionally bright." Luna's reading became voracious, and his linen closet library swelled. "Joey was always well read. He was always reading books and magazines. He would always get the Sunday paper, more than one issue. He would get the Times, and the Daily News. So whenever I had a question about anything, like if I would see news, and there was some conflict going on, and I wasn't sure about it, I would always talk to him. Because it almost seemed he had boundless knowledge. He would know about every topic you could imagine, whether it'd be politics, sports, or whatever, he would know. He was always reading and he just knew pretty much about anything.

"We would do a lot of debating and stuff. At an early age he didn't mention being a lawyer. He just wanted to do well in school. He probably got that towards his senior year in high school. But he knew, if you wanted to be successful, he had to be educated. At that point he didn't know what he wanted to do but he knew that he had to get good grades, and go to good schools, and compete."

"If he wasn't on the track running," Rivera says, "he would always be in his house. We would call him out the window — he lived on the first floor — to come out and play basketball. Or sometimes we played baseball in the yard of the junior high school. And he would tell us he was busy. There were times when you couldn't get him to come out of the house. Or we would go downtown, to go to a movie or something. A lot of time he would say no because he was just so caught up in his schoolwork.

"Actually at the time I felt it was like kind of weird. We didn't know anyone who graduated from college. We were just these kids growing up in the South Bronx so at the time I didn't understand why he was putting so much work into it. I figured, you know, he's losing out on hanging out. That was more important at the time than being cooped up in your house, on a nice summer day. But obviously, later on, as we got older and wiser, I realized that he was doing the right thing.

"It's pretty hard, when you're a kid, when you don't have that example around you, like a parent that went to college or something. But he was always very disciplined, like I said, with the running, and with the school. He seemed to have a game plan early on."

Dan Rivera walked me around the back of the bleak building where Luna had grown up. A beaten metal door led from the back of the building, down a flight of worn concrete steps. Luna would run out this back door, through the complex and across the busy street, to the Paul Robeson Middle School across from the Patterson Houses.

From Luna's books came stories of heroes. Surprising heroes kept him from riding alone. "He was a big fan of John Kennedy's," Rivera tells me. "He had a couple of books. And I guess he molded himself after that. I guess that's maybe where he got the clothing from. I don't know. Being around him sometimes, I was in awe of him, even though he was my friend. It was sort of like being, I guess, around a celebrity. He was just so bright, and the way he dressed."

Nice, stylish clothes soon became Luna's hallmark.

"Even in high school, he would dress preppie," Rivera chuckles. "He would have ties and trench coats. I think he knew early on that if you wanted to be successful, you also have to dress the part. He would have *GQ* magazines in the house. A lot of fashion books and stuff. Like I said, he was well-rounded in everything. It stood out even more, because you're in the South Bronx, and here's this fifteen-year-old kid with a trench coat, and a tie, and penny loafers and everybody else is dressed in jeans, and hip-hop fashions and here's Joey, like a business man. It was kind of funny."

Luna's quest for fashion soon helped lead the boys on adventures from Mott Haven.

"He was always into fashion," Dan says. "We used to go to Bloomingdale's, which was definitely out of our price league, but we would always try to buy whatever we could, whether it was a tie, or shoes, we'd always try to get something. We would go to Barneys New York. I remember the first time I went to Barneys was with him. I was intimidated because they have a doorman in the front. And you almost feel like you can't go in, like they're going to stop you. He always was confident. He would walk into a place. He didn't feel like he didn't belong. So here were these teenagers walking into Barneys New York with forty dollars. At first I would feel really uncomfortable in these places. But being with him, and hanging out with him, I would start shopping on my own, and then it was not a big deal. And he would also go to Macy's. So we would go to these big department stores that I guess we really had no business going to because we couldn't afford it anyway."

Rivera snickers when he thinks back to those days. "And so I started to emulate that," he says. "I started to dress with the slacks. And I remember his father used to cuff our pants for us. We used to buy pleated pants and stuff, and his father would do the cuffing for us so we wouldn't have to take it to the tailor."

As young Joey Luna began to take notice of the world outside Patterson Houses, the world began to notice him. Smart, athletic, good looking, neatly turned out in nice clothing, he turned heads.

"People used to tell him he looked like Michael Jackson. Especially Michael Jackson early on," Rivera laughs. "I mean, Michael Jackson has taken a lot of different forms. But early on, when he was starting, like about the time when Jackson had the Thriller album in the 80s, there was definitely a resemblance."

Rivera goes on, "One time we were going downtown, we were on a subway, and Joey had this resemblance to Michael Jackson. These girls were talking to each other, they were giggling, and we knew that they were talking about Joey. So then the girl sits next to Joey and she says, 'Do you mind if I tell you something?' and Joey says, 'No, sure, go ahead.' And then she says, 'Has anybody ever told you you look like Michael Jackson?' And Joey started laughing and he said, 'Yeah, I hear that quite a bit.' And then she said, 'In fact, I think you look *better* than Michael Jackson,' and then we all just started laughing."

Rivera takes out a photo album and shows me photos of Luna dancing. "He's styling in this one," Rivera says, noting Jonathan's moves with a girl on the dance floor.

After junior high, Luna enrolled in the New York School of Printing, a public trade school. "I believe he chose that school because they had a journalism program. He was into journalism," Rivera says. "He definitely had different facets of his life. You know, as you're developing, they're different things you want to be. I think at a certain point he definitely was interested in journalism."

Photos of Luna in this period, in his late teens to early twenties, show him enjoying the company of attractive young women, sometimes dancing, sometimes just hanging out, having fun. "One of his girlfriends in this period actually went off to join the circus!" Rivera laughs. Later, in his college days, Luna is photographed with co-eds. Rivera points to a group photo including Jonathan and a young woman who vaguely resembled a famous singer.

"This one he'd call Bed Midler," Rivera chuckles.

Women were fun, but Rivera says he and Luna early on decided they'd be better off concentrating on their studies and making something of themselves. Getting tied down with wives and kids in their early twenties, they thought, was a trap. Rivera says he once quipped to Jonathan, "He who lives by the pussy dies by the pussy!" an observation which endlessly amused Luna. They developed a shorthand code when talking with each other. One day, Rivera says, he told Jonathan they must "wage an aggressive campaign" to get what they wanted in life, and this became one of their catch phrases.

Luna, the self-propelled boy from Patterson Houses, set his sights ever higher. By his senior year in high school, Rivera says, Joey Luna resolved to study law. After high school he enrolled in New York's Hunter College, and then transferred to nearby Fordham University. In this period, Rivera says, "He was busy and I would see him from time to time. I went to the Fordham campus a couple of times. We played baseball at Fordham."

In late 1988, when he was still 23 years old, Luna was accepted into the University of North Carolina School of Law. Rivera shared with me Luna's letters from this period. Each letter was neatly written, some carefully typed. The writing style is clear, and the grammar and punctuation, for the most part, faultless. There is an almost boyish quality that runs throughout Luna's writings. Most are signed "Jonathan," though a few were closed simply "Joey."

The letters reveal challenging times for Luna. They mention the difficulty of studying law; they also challenged Danny Rivera to stay in school, to work hard, and to make something of himself.

"Sometimes, I'm in class and I can follow what's happening and other times I'm just totally lost!" Luna wrote on September 7, 1988, shortly after starting law school. "This will happen to the best of students. I've found that the best way to cope with such tension and frustration is just to drop everything and relax. Do things like take a nap, exercise, or write your best friend a letter! For me, it's tennis and jogging. Since I've been here I've been playing lots of tennis, and I've been running about every other day. I'm also biking too!" Then he lectures Danny, "Discipline is the key above all. If you can get yourself in some routine that you can follow, then it will make everything else easier on you!"

The next week, in a typed letter dated September 16, 1988, Luna (perhaps feeling a little homesick), writes Rivera (who himself has followed Luna's footsteps and has started taking college classes at Hunter), "The important thing for both of us to keep in mind is that it is normal to feel a little lost when you first start a new phase in studying. It is quite easy to feel intimidated by your fellow students. I know exactly how you feel. It seems sometimes that you're the only one in the class who seems to have no clue as to what's going on! But let me tell you from experience that it is natural to feel that way. You just have to keep reminding yourself that you have the same potential in you that any of these people have."

Several months go by. On January 14, 1989, Luna writes Rivera, in another neatly typed letter, "How are you? I hope things are fine with you and the family. I'm slowly getting settled into my new house here and just trying to get mentally prepared for the second semester of law school. I guess I am already used to being back in Chapel Hill. I got three of my five grades back and I'm happy to report that I passed albeit not with flying colors. The verdict so far is two C's and a B. What's weird about my grades is that the courses I worked most at and thought I was grasping the material in I graded marginally in and the course I was least confident in -- torts -- I did fine in! You just can't tell with these law exams. Like most of the returning students, I have promised myself that I will commit myself to working harder this semester. To be totally honest with you Danny I did not work as hard as I should have worked last semester. I think I got caught up in too many social activities and didn't really get into gear until the latter part of the semester!"

Luna continues, "I've also begun my job at the law library. The job basically entails filing and shelving books with some front desk work like checking out reserved books, articles, etc. The job only pays $3.80 an hour (petty cash) but it's better than nothing! I'll probably work about 10 hours a week." He signs the letter, "Yours, Joey."

Now in law school in North Carolina, Luna still couldn't escape racism. One day in the law library, where Jonathan was studying with another black student, Rivera says Luna was approached by a white security guard who asked, "What're you boys doing in here?" The guard placed his hand on his holstered gun. Luna explained to the guard that they were studying for their law degrees. A new code word for racist America began to creep into Luna's lexicon, and his correspondence: "Amerikkka."

In another neatly typed letter to Rivera dated February 5, 1989, twenty-four-year-old Jonathan goes into greater detail of the distractions at school. "My grades on the other hand were not at all good," Luna writes. "I got one B-, two C's and two C-s. The bottom line is that I could have done much better had I not fucked around and waited until the last minute to really start studying. To be perfectly honest with you I really had fears that I would flunk out of this place! I definitely did not practice what I preached about being disciplined and balanced about studying. Once again, a female was a key factor in distracting me from my studies. Last semester I was dating a graduate student who lived in the same dorm as I did and I spent a lot of time with her instead of keeping on top of my work. It seems to me that law school is just like anything else in life; if you put out hard work, you will get results. My attitude about law school was really bad. It was really hard to get myself motivated to study the law which is at times certainly not the most interesting of subjects, especially in the first year! Even now in the second semester I'm having problems motivating myself to work hard. I've got to keep reminding myself that I am here for a reason, namely to get a legal education which will enable me to practice law and improve myself! Better to sacrifice and work hard now than have to pay the price and suffer later!

"I'm not seeing the graduate student this semester so I don't have that relationship anymore as a distraction. I have been getting to know some of the other law students which is something that I really did not do last semester because I was hanging out with a lot of the graduate students.

"Last week my roommate Kojo and I threw a housewarming party which was a great success! We invited law students and other friends of ours. We must have had close to 100 people here throughout the night. The party got out of hand at about 2:30 in the morning because people were singing and dancing to the loud music and one of our neighbors summoned the police who told us that we had to pump down the volume!" This letter is signed, "Your friend, Jonathan."

A year later, on February 4, 1990, a quintessential twenty-five-year-old Luna writes to Rivera of law school, and of a cross-country trip Luna made:

"Dear Danny,

"Sorry I have not written you in such a long time, but as you can probably guess I am buried in so much work for law school.

"California was really fun; I had a great time in San Francisco visiting Lisa. When I got back to the East Coast, I drove up to Boston to see Traci and I had a wonderful time with her as well! Traci is doing really well too! In fact, she just came down to visit me in Chapel Hill just last weekend!

"Basically law school is the same as it ever was: lots of work and seemingly little time for much else! I am trying to carry a low profile this time around at school! I am trying to stay focused with my studies and not get distracted by any females! As you said, 'Live by the pussy, die by the pussy!'"

Luna, ever the city boy, misses the metropolis of New York. He ends this letter by asking Rivera to, "Please write me as soon as you can find time. You must tell me what's going on with you and our city as well! I am just so out of touch with the happenings in New York down here. I rarely get a chance to buy the New York Times!" He closes the letter, "Yours, Jonathan," and adds, in quotes, "'Take care homey.'"

Dan Rivera, his brothers and friends occasionally made the long drive down to Chapel Hill, North Carolina to visit Jonathan. "We went down a couple of times," Dan says. In this period Jonathan's dad became gravely ill, and Jonathan had to abandon his studies for a year to help care for him.

It's notable there's no mention or complaining by Jonathan about his father's illness in his letters to Dan. Jonathan kept a happy face to the world.

Luna still had the ability to laugh at his surroundings. "The time his father was sick and he had to come up," Rivera recounts. "He had left most of his stuff behind. So he had to pick up his belongings. So we rented a K car. I remember because it was so uncomfortable it had a bench seat in the front. It was just a bare bones car so we were just laughing all the way down. Then he picked up his stuff."

While caring for his father, Luna worked in the Bronx DA's office. When his father finally recovered, he re-enrolled at North Carolina to finish his law degree.

Dan Rivera says he once visited Luna at UNC, "just to visit him," he says. "Well actually I even sat in on one of the law classes, because he asked the professor if I could sit in. I was just, again, in awe. It was like, I mean, how does this guy pull these things off? Again I don't think I was even in college at the time, and this guy's in law school. It was just unbelievable all the stuff that he would do. It was great for me because he would always expose me to different things. And, again, places that I probably would've never seen if it wasn't for him. Definitely not the inside of a law school classroom.

"I tell you I was in awe of him, but I think he was in awe of the situation," Rivera goes on. "Again, you're coming from Bronx, New York, and then you're meeting up with people who have all this money, you know, the kids are in law school running around in BMWs, and he had a bicycle. So it could be a bit intimidating I guess for him, but after a while he got over it, and he felt like he fit in. That's probably one of his driving forces. He felt, 'Fine, I came from where I came from, but that doesn't mean that it should hold me back.'"

In his first weeks away at law school, in September 1988, Luna wrote to Rivera, "Here at law school I was a little awed by some of the students. Many of them have distinguished academic records and many have had other careers before coming to law school. There are many students who have their masters and Ph.D. degrees. There is even one student in the first year who is only 19 years of age! He just finished college last year! What I try to keep in mind is that these people are just people no more or less than myself.

"Remember that you have everything going for you!" Luna continues. He reflects back on their earliest day in the projects. "You are young, bright, healthy, single and the world is at your feet. You are in command and you alone can determine your destiny. All we have to do is remind ourselves of people that we know who really don't have many avenues open to them! Just think that if you and I had fallen into that trap of marriage and parenthood at an early age we would be regretting the fact that we didn't get a chance to go on to school! You and I both are quite fortunate to have had the opportunity and insight to improve ourselves. All you have to do is look out the window and see what the alternative is if we don't try to improve ourselves!"

Now re-enrolled in school, Luna succeeded in gathering himself. He finished law school with a flourish in 1992. "His outgoing manner and winning personality led to his being elected president of his third-year graduating school class," his family later wrote of him. President of his class, he'd proudly wear his class ring till the day he died.

After graduation Luna won a clerkship with U.S. District Judge William L. Osteen, in Greensboro, North Carolina. Osteen would later tell the press he was instantly impressed with young Luna. Luna seemed to exude confidence, charisma, and an unusual capacity to care about other people. He could see things around him that other people missed, and he would try to right things that other people didn't care about.

Within a week of Luna's going to work as a clerk at the Greensboro, North Carolina, federal courthouse, Osteen recalls, Luna seemed to know everyone in the building, from janitors to the judges. Luna had a penetrating-oil personality.

About this period, on February 24, 1993, Luna wrote Rivera, in a letter marked, "Greensboro, N.C.," that, "Lately, I have been busy with work here at the court. I will be in Asheville, North Carolina (Middle Amerikkka) soon for a week of criminal court. As you can imagine, Asheville is not the most exciting place. No doubt Chapel Hill in comparison is like New York City. However, it will be a change of scenery."

Jonathan had no deep pockets to fall back on. He'd graduated, and now was clerking for a small stipend. He was finding it difficult to get by. Rivera had sent him $300 the previous December, as a loan, which prompted Jonathan to tell Dan in a note at the time that the loan, "is helping me out very much! I'll be sure to pay you back when I get my next paycheck at the end of the month." A few months later, in the late February 1993 letter, Luna writes his friend, "I also must apologize for failing to pay back the $300.00 I borrowed from you. I have experienced problems with the Volkswagen and recently had to sink another $300.00 for an exhaust and mufflers." Luna promises to repay the money "next month," with interest. "If you find that you are in immediate need of the $300.00, please let me know and I will make arrangements to get it to you!" Luna concludes the letter. "Unfortunately, my plans for coming to New York City this month had to be scrapped because of both my car problems and work. I have, however, plans to take off a week from work and go up to NYC in April. I am really anxious to get out of 'North Cakalakka' for a while! It is really boring down here!"

He signs this letter, "Jonathan (Joey- not so prestigious) Luna." He adds a slightly humorous postscript, a touchstone of the 1980s and early 90s: "P.S. -Have you looked into getting an HIV test?"

Luna didn't always tackle things so head on, Rivera says. Often, "he'd work beneath the surface." Rivera cited several examples.

"There was one conversation that sticks out because he was playing devil's advocate," Rivera says. "I remember one time he came to the house, and we were watching the news, and they were talking about drugs, and he was telling me, 'I think they should legalize drugs.' And I remember I got really upset cause, he and I, we were very similar in our ways, and the way we thought. And I was like, 'How can you say that they should legalize drugs?' And he goes, 'What do you think about this?' So I spent about a half an hour giving my opinion. Like I said, I was really annoyed, I was talking to him in an aggressive tone, because I couldn't believe that he would say something like that. And at the end of the conversation he starts laughing, and he says, 'No I don't think they should legalize drugs. I just wanted to get your opinion on it.' So sometimes he would work under the surface. So once I realized what he was doing then I started to laugh. And I said, 'Why did you do that?' And he was like, 'I was just playing devil's advocate. I wanted to see where your mind was at.' So that's the type of individual he was."

As Luna began to establish himself, he found himself in ever more impressive surroundings. He'd often invite Rivera along.

Courtrooms where Luna argued cases. A party in a New York mansion. Get togethers in upscale restaurants. Luna now had entré into places that he and Dan Rivera could once have scarcely hoped to see, let alone get through the door.

One time, Rivera says, they met some of Jonathan's friends at an upscale Manhattan eatery. When the bill came, Rivera says he was reaching for his wallet when he felt Jonathan give him a kick. Luna whispered to him that these guys had money, and Rivera should let them pick up the tab. "He didn't always tackle things head on," Rivera says.

As a young man in his mid-twenties, Luna could be carefree about romance.

But, nearing thirty, he met his future wife, Angela, then a medical student at Chapel Hill. Angela came from a fashionable, upscale black family. He seemed to know right away that she was "the one," Rivera says.

"During that period, he met Angela Hopkins, during her last year of medical school," Angela and her family later would write. "Angela was the love of his life."

Jonathan and Angela made a cute couple. The Lunas married on August 29, 1993. Luna asked Dan Rivera to be his best man. Thumbing through the photos, Rivera takes special pride in the wedding pictures. Rivera stands to the left of a beaming Luna (both wearing top-flight suits), while a demure and pretty Angela stands to Jonathan's right.

By now, September 1993, Luna had hired on as an associate at Arnold and Porter, a prestigious Washington DC law firm. It was a long, long way from the Patterson Houses. In a letter dated September 11, 1993, written on a yellow legal pad, a week before he started working at the firm, Luna told Dan, "I could not imagine getting married without having you as my best man." He goes on, "Our honeymoon went very well. It was nice to be in New York City for a couple of days. We basically did a lot of tourist stuff - ferry boat ride, lunch in Chinatown - and lots of shopping. Niagara Falls was great. It was hard to believe that we were still in The State of New York. The country up there is so beautiful. I would recommend you take a trip up to visit. Hope you received my post-card from the Canadian side of the Falls.

"Since returning home to Baltimore, I have been relaxing as much as I can and (am) working out for the marathon. I am really behind the recommended training schedule. Getting married and our honeymoon has put me behind! My previous goal was to finish the marathon in under 4 hours. Now, I have since revised that goal to just finish the course. I have been running everyday since returning. Fortunately, cool weather has been setting in here in Baltimore making my long runs alot more easy to complete."

At Arnold and Porter, Jonathan was one of only a few blacks in the firm. In 1994 he told the Washington Legal Times, "I can't say personally that there's been any overt racism here. However, black attorneys feel a little more isolated than their white counterparts." Danny Rivera remembers seeing this article, and cautioning Luna that it might not be such a good idea to talk like that to newspapers, and to perhaps burn his bridges. Luna just shrugged it off. "That's the way Joey was," Rivera says. *"That* was Joey."

Luna left the firm later the same year. By now Luna was used to carrying a burden of skin that no white American ever understands.

From 1994 to 1997 Luna worked as staff attorney in the Federal Trade Commission's general counsel's office. But he felt drawn to prosecution. He wanted to help people stuck in the same situation he'd been in at the Patterson Houses.

In 1997 he took a job as an assistant district attorney in the Brooklyn DA's office. By 1999 he applied, and was hired, as an assistant U.S. attorney in the Maryland U.S. Attorney's office. He moved his family back to Baltimore, so his wife could be near her family. His mother-in-law lived with them in a room in the basement. He moved his own parents into an apartment a few miles away, and helped with the payments. He drove his parents around in his car. He had weight on his shoulders.

Still, Luna was given to writing letters to newspapers. He was concerned about the problems of others. In 1991 he wrote The New York Times to complain about an article critical of his old Mott Haven neighborhood. "You and your readers should know that there are decent hard-working people like my parents who are struggling every day to make a life for themselves and their families in Mott Haven," he wrote.

"My dad struggled in the restaurant business, while my mom stayed at home to raise my brother and me. Despite all the obstacles they had to contend with, I managed to make my way to Fordham University and the University of North Carolina School of Law."

Later, he'd become known around the office for letters he wrote championing the disadvantaged and impoverished. He'd feel the need to prick the conscience of larger society about the subtleties of racism and powerlessness.

He wrote a letter to the Baltimore Sun in 1995, praising a column criticizing the "racist logos of the Atlanta Braves and Cleveland Indians." Luna wrote, "The difference between Native Americans and African Americans or Jews is that (Native Americans) make up barely 1 percent of the U.S. population, and compared with the other two groups have virtually no political power. Should population or political clout determine the level of tolerance we are willing to give to racist imagery?"

Years later, I sit with Dan Rivera at his table. Spread out before us are the photos, newspaper clippings and the letters. Years after the death of his friend, he still carries a sharp pain, and still has dreams of his pal Joey.

"Here's the photo I wanted to show you," Rivera tells me. "It's a picture I took of Joey driving his car. He's wearing glasses."

The photo is taken from the back seat of Luna's Honda Accord. Luna's at the wheel, wearing eyeglasses.

"He needed his glasses to see to drive," Rivera tells me. "This picture was taken years ago, I'd say in the late 1990s. Like everybody else, his eyes naturally got worse as he aged. The night he died, why would he leave his glasses behind on his desk? Strange, isn't it?"

I closely studied the photo. A poster child for self-achievement, Luna empathized with, and cared about other people. Particularly those he saw as powerless. This was the side he was on. This was the side in which he had grown up.

27
Skinned:
or, paper, scissors, stone

Jonathan Luna was by nature high profile and public, the very opposite of his all-but-invisible cohort, FBI Special Agent Steve Skinner. Luna, practicing in front of a jury, with a natural politician's flair, instinctively understood how things look to an average juror, or voter. Skinner would prove to be remarkably devoid of this crucial instinct. Young Assistant U.S. Attorney Luna would make a fatal mistake of trusting Steve Skinner and Warren Grace. It began like this:

Having heard about Warren Grace, Agent Skinner wastes no time telling Jonathan Luna about Warren Grace.

Rebuffed by the Baltimore police on the night he had first heard about Grace, Agent Skinner says, "I then contacted... Mr. Luna, and I said there is a person that I think, you know, maybe we could talk to. So what we did was we writted Mr. Grace out of jail and brought him to the U.S. attorney's office to talk with him."

Skinner explains that a writ is "a court order essentially saying that if a person is incarcerated in jail... the person can be released into an agent or a law enforcement officer's custody temporarily, and then brought back to prison."

Warren Grace would come to appreciate Skinner and Luna's ability to write all kinds of papers that made his bars go away.

In the coming months Grace would learn that paper beats both stones and nail files.

So Steve Skinner pops Warren Grace. In the revolving door, out the revolving door. One hardly has to imagine Grace's thoughts as Skinner drives him out of jail to the air-conditioned federal courthouse in downtown Baltimore.

The meeting between the three prospective collaborators "was about a week after I first learned about Warren Grace," Skinner says.

Warren Grace, caught with guns and heroin, goes in the revolving door. A week or so later, caught with information, he's out, talking secret deals with Steve Skinner and Jonathan Luna.

Did Luna feel anything extraordinary when he first laid eyes on Warren Grace? Grace was in Luna's office, in Luna's territory. Yet Grace's face would be with Jonathan Luna on the last day of his life.

And what were Grace's thoughts when he first sized up Jonathan Luna? Certainly he was outwardly respectful and compliant. Pug certainly sizes things up. Luna's office. Did he see the photo of Luna standing beside candidate George W. Bush?

Baltimore attorney Arcangelo Tuminelli spins it like this: "Mr. Grace was of the school who thinks the more I give them, the more they are going to give me. So Mr. Grace made a diligent effort to provide as much information as he could," Tuminelli says. Grace, he says, "thought about it for a little while... and said, look, you know, I've got some information, fellows, let me tell you what I can do for you. But, you know, you guys have to do something for me."

"The meeting just consisted of interviewing Mr. Grace to see what he knew about," Agent Skinner says. "To kind of measure his willingness to cooperating with us, and to see potentially if there could be any federal investigations that could result from his cooperating with us." Poindexter's murder of Alvin Jones, for instance.

Grace says the first meeting between himself, Luna and Skinner laid the groundwork for a plea agreement. He agreed to plea guilty to the drug and gun charge, for which he faced twenty and ten years in prison, respectively. The aiding and abetting charge would be dropped. Just by talking to these guys, ten years of his 40-year sentence had been dropped. The revolving door, Warren Grace saw, was beginning to turn.

"Basically, the terms of this plea agreement is that, for these two counts, I am supposed to work with the government and cooperate with the (FBI) agents," he says.

In return, "if I testify truthfully, the government will make a motion for a downward departure" in his sentence.

Luna further promised Grace that the court was "supposed to

take my cooperation into consideration, in working with the officers, or the agents."

Grace also agreed to "follow the rules pursuant to this plea agreement." The rules would be spelled out when Grace formally accepted his plea deal as proposed by Luna and Skinner, on May 31, 2002. On that day he pled guilty to a reduced set of crimes in federal court and was released from prison to a halfway house to work undercover with Agent Skinner and the FBI.

By also signing on that day an "Order Setting Conditions of Release," Grace agreed to, among other conditions, "refrain from possessing a firearm," "refrain from any use of a narcotic drug," and to leave the halfway house, "only with the approval of the Director for official business." Grace, before long, working as an undercover informant for Skinner, would break each of these conditions.

Warren Grace would come to totally disregard the terms of his release back into the community. Often he would do this with the help of Agent Skinner.

The FBI even secretly pays Warren Grace.

Skinner says, "The payments I paid Warren Grace were for expenses. There is two types of ways to pay a source. One is for expenses, and one if for services. Some sources are paid for information that they provide.

"Mr. Grace was paid for services incurred during the investigation such as his cell phone bills, the payments that he needed to make on his Ford Excursion, it may be rent, things like that."

Grace was paid, "Approximately two thousand dollars," Skinner says.

By all accounts, Warren Grace had a talent for telling people what they wanted to hear. He was after all a kind of rap artist.

Warren Grace quickly discerned that Steve Skinner liked most to hear him rap about three little numbers: 9-1-1.

To facilitate Agent Skinner's pursuit of these three little numbers, Jonathan Luna in the coming year and a half would write a file full of legal papers that would send Warren Grace back out the revolving door, back to the streets of Baltimore.

Warren Grace would soon prove to be what he always was: a menace to the innocent people of Baltimore. Agent Steve Skinner would nevertheless continue to insist on letting Grace run free. Jonathan Luna could only hope that that, as usual, nobody would pay much attention.

Time would be unkind. Jonathan Luna would be left in a very bad spot. Luna would spend the last months, days, even hours of his life trying to cut out, cover up, and otherwise suppress, a very troubling paper trail created by Warren Grace and Steve Skinner.

From this we learn that scissors beats paper.

28
Secret agent man: FBI gives Warren Grace a double-naught license to kill

So now Warren Grace was working as an agent for the government of the United States.

Our homeboy enjoyed all the shadowy stealth and protection of a G-Man, as he ran wild and sold heroin on the side. Soon, even complaints that he was shooting at his neighbors with a gun would fall on deaf ears.

From this moment, in the increasingly curious files of the federal court cases associated with Warren Grace, it's not what you see that counts. It's what you don't see that tells the story.

The invisible hands of Agent Steve Skinner and Jonathan Luna become unseen guides, moving Warren Grace through the maze of the federal courts. Though they don't yet realize it, Warren Grace is taking them for a ride of his own. Somewhere in the maze Grace becomes like a minotaur, devouring all.

Soon after he first met Warren Grace, Luna and the U.S. attorney's office assumed federal jurisdiction of Grace's case. This in time comes to include the entire investigation of Walter Poindexter and Deon Smith, including the drug-related murder of Alvin Jones — bumped off for breaking into Poindexter's stash house. Bye bye, city of Baltimore. At least, that's what Luna and Skinner think.

Warren Grace was instructed to apply for a public defender so he would have representation for the plea agreement.

He was bound over in federal court on May 2, 2002, and the next day Luna and his co-counsel, Jacabed Rodriguez-Coss, filed a federal defendant information sheet listing "FBI S/A Steve Skinner" as Grace's arresting officer.

There's deliberately not much paper trail linking Grace to the FBI. Secrecy, as Agent Skinner explains, becomes the watchword.

"We keep cooperating witnesses (and) confidential informants as secret as possible from everyone," Skinner says.

"There is a couple reasons. One is safety.... We do that to protect the source from other people, from other criminals. I instruct the source, if the source is married, or has a girlfriend or a boyfriend, I would say don't even tell your boyfriend or girlfriend that you are working with the FBI, because you could get in a fight with them and they might tell somebody.

"We need to keep our relationships with our sources very private, and that's primarily for the source's benefit, for their safety. But it's also to preserve the secrecy of the investigation."

In recent years, concerned observers have increasingly complained that this secrecy also serves to hide from public scrutiny all sorts of egregious FBI misbehavior involving its "sources." So it would be for Warren Grace.

This secrecy applies even in the "reports that I have written," Skinner says. "In those reports, I never listed Warren Grace's name. I always refer to him as a source. I didn't even refer as to whether he was a he or a she."

A year after Warren Grace's arrest, for example, in May 2003, Skinner would file an affidavit in which he writes of his early interest in Smith, Poindexter and 9-1-1 heroin. The word "source" is used for all references to Grace.

Skinner writes, "in the Spring of 2002, a confidential source (i.e. Warren Grace — ed.) advised that (Grace) was aware of an individual named Deon Smith who was a drug dealer in the City of Baltimore. (Grace) advised that Smith had supplied heroin to a group which called its heroin "911" (pronounced "nine-eleven"). (Grace) advised that Smith owned a recording studio called Stash House Records, which was located at 911 West 36th Street. (Grace) advised that Smith had sold heroin from within Stash House Records. (Grace) advised that Smith operated vehicles to include a Mercedes Benz and a large sport utility vehicle, like a Yukon, which (Grace) would later identify...."

At Warren Grace's first detention hearing, on May 13, 2002, Jonathan Luna is listed as prosecutor. At this hearing public defender Joe Balter was assigned to defend Grace.

On May 31, 2002, Warren Grace pleaded guilty to two charges, as part of the deal. He was released on personal recognizance pending sentencing, with several important provisos, as mentioned earlier. He was assigned to a work release program, Hope Village, in Washington DC. He was only allowed out of Hope Village to meet with the FBI or his attorney. In work release, he had a job: working as an FBI informant. Still the rap artist.

Also, as mentioned, there were several other conditions for Grace's release. He wasn't allowed to have a weapon. He couldn't use drugs — let alone sell or possess them. He had to refrain from "excessive use of alcohol." Violation of any of these conditions, our honorable court assured the community, meant Grace would return to prison. That was the deal, the contract between Grace and our government, and blessed by our federal court.

Grace was nominally placed under the supervision of U.S. Probation and Pretrial Services, the court's monitoring agency. But that's not really the case. In fact, the staff of Pretrial Services opposed the deal. Pretrial Services, on May 21, 2002, wrote U.S. Magistrate Judge Susan K. Gauvey, Luna would later say, "expressing Pretrial Service's concerns about releasing Mr. Grace." The staff of Pretrial Services thought he was a risk to the community.

Pretrial Services thought Grace should remain locked up. With good reason.

But Pretrial Services had little say. The FBI, and Tom DiBiagio's U.S. Attorney's office, represented by Jonathan Luna, wanted Warren Grace turned loose, out the revolving door, to run free in the streets. This is not as exaggerated as it sounds.

The feds wanted to use Grace to bust Smith and Poindexter. Poindexter already had heard "street rumors" that Grace was cooperating with police on their investigation of the murder of Alvin Jones.

Grace would say he had to run free in the streets to rebuild his "credibility," in order to give Smith and Poindexter the false impression that he was not working with police.

Warren Grace now was the FBI's boy. Or so everyone thought.

In reality, it was the other way around. The FBI would become Warren Grace's bitch.

More accurately, he was Agent Skinner's responsibility.

The placement of Warren Grace in Washington DC's Hope Village halfway house has its share of irony. With Grace we have someone who is well versed in bending the rules of halfway houses. Here's a guy who knows how to smuggle heroin into a halfway house to greatly increase profits.

Other ironies abound. At this time, in 2002, Walter Poindexter remained behind bars. What essentially was Agent Skinner's half-baked plan? Skinner and his "Safe Streets Task Force" were waiting for Poindexter to *exit* the revolving door back into the streets, so that they could use Grace to deal heroin with Poindexter and Smith and send them *back through* the revolving door. They had hopes of infiltrating, if not owning, Stash House Records.

These days everybody wants to rap. Even funny white boys. From this story we learn the FBI aspires to open a hip-hop division.

Picture that.

Agent Skinner and Jonathan Luna may have been adept at working the system. But they were no match for Warren Grace.

Quite predictably, Grace almost immediately ran into problems upon his release to Hope Village. The only hope Warren Grace took from Hope Village was the hope to get his ass out of there and back on the streets as soon as possible. Agent Skinner had just lectured Grace on the importance of keeping their undercover work secret. Now, only a few days after he got to Hope Village, Grace complained that someone had blown his cover. Grace seems to have known the only recourse would be home detention.

On June 7, 2002, Luna's co-counsel, Jacabed Rodriguez-Coss, filed a motion removing Grace from Hope Village.

"...(I)n light of the fact that the defendant is cooperating with the government," Ms. Rodriguez-Coss writes, "the Court permitted defendant's release to the custody of Hope Village." The problem was, Grace said, one of the counselors at Hope Village smelled a rat.

"The Director of Hope Village was made aware of the fact that the defendant was cooperating with the FBI but was told to maintain this information (as) confidential," Rodriguez-Coss relates. "However, on Tuesday, June 4, 2002, defendant was confronted by one of the counselors of Hope Village, Mr. Davis, and asked directly about his cooperation with the FBI. Defendant denied the allegations. Yesterday, Thursday, June 6, 2002, defendant was informed by Mr. Davis, within hearing distance of other inmates, that the FBI would be picking him up the next day."

We see how quickly the FBI moves to protect its informants, when matters of an FBI investigation are at stake.

"Both the United States and defense counsel agree that defendant's security at Hope Village has been compromised," Rodriguez-Coss tells the court. "Therefore, both parties agree that defendant should be moved out of Hope Village."

Agent Skinner's solution was to place Grace under *house arrest* at the apartment of Grace's girlfriend, on Edgecombe Circle North, in Baltimore. During home confinement, Grace was supposed to wear a 24-hour monitoring bracelet around his ankle.

Pretrial Services opposed home confinement for Grace, seeing him as a risk to the community.

The U.S. attorney's office handled the public relations problem with the court. Luna and Rodriguez-Coss went along with the FBI and papered over the danger with sweet-smelling words in court documents. "Both the government and defense counsel understand that (home release and bracelet monitoring) would ensure both the safety of the community and his presence at trial, as well as safeguard the safety of the defendant," Rodriguez-Coss glossed.

This assurance about the "safety of the community" would turn out not only to be wrong and misleading. It would be dangerously wrong and misleading. It's interesting to note that Rodriguez-Coss wrote this motion, and not Jonathan Luna.

In U.S. Attorney Tom DiBiagio's office, they knew how to talk the talk.

Pretrial Services, with good cause, at first had serious misgivings about returning a known gun offender and heroin dealer to his home in the hood.

Rodriguez-Coss writes that prosecutors "informed Pre-Trial Services Officer Randy Cannal of this motion. Mr. Cannal stated that the position of the Pre-Trial Services Office remains that defendant should be detained pending trial."

There were other curious issues. Home release is only available, obviously, to defendants who have no outstanding arrest warrants. New warrants, of course, would cause a defendant to be re-arrested for additional offenses. No one bothered to check, or cared, that Grace had *two* outstanding warrants, for failure to pay child support, and traffic offenses.

The risks, and the law, notwithstanding, Chief U.S. District Judge Frederic N. Smalkin approved this motion for home release on June 7, 2002.

29

Dawsons try calling 911

While the FBI's Steve Skinner and federal Judge Frederic Smalkin busied themselves sending Warren Grace home to his neighbors, Angela and Carnell Dawson felt inundated with a rising flood of drug dealers in their own neighborhood.

The dealers loitered in front of the Dawsons' home, or sat on the Dawsons' stairs, yelling out the names of the drugs they were selling. They were rowdy, foul-mouthed, and aggressive.

By June 2002, Carnell and Angela had begun trying to actively chase the dealers away.

If they left at all, the drug dealers would always come back, each day more belligerent than the last.

On June 26, 2002, the Dawsons called 911 for emergency help. It did not do much good. The cops coming out only seemed to irritate the dealers.

In the next three and a half months, the Dawsons would call for help at least *thirty-five more times.* Twenty of these calls would be placed from mid-September to mid-October.

Neither Skinner nor Judge Smalkin would be around to pick up the phone.

30
Warren Grace mysteriously escapes home detention, shoots up the hood

At home, monitoring anklet affixed to his leg, quick-eyed Warren Grace had lots of time to think about things. Think about getting loose, bending rules. It's an open question whether he was doing the thinking on his own, or whether parties unknown were instructing him.

Two months of home detention in mid-summer passes with apparently little or no recorded incident. Troubling events nonetheless, predictably, soon transpire.

"At this point," Skinner says, his interaction with informant Warren Grace was "fairly regular. It wasn't every day. It could have ranged from twice a week, three times a week. It's hard to say. This would have been the beginning of summer to the end of August."

In this period, Skinner says, "We were talking with Mr. Grace. We had a few interviews with him. Just to talk with him. Get specific facts from him. See if we could, you know, corroborate and verify some of the things he was telling us." (A short while later Skinner will contradict himself and say that, other than just "talking with" Grace, the task force in this period, as early as June 2002, was actually placing a body recorder on Grace and sending him into Stash House Records to record conversations with Deon Smith.)

Skinner continues, "And, like I said, the local charges from Baltimore city were... made into federal charges which Mr. Grace ultimately pled guilty to."

So the local cops no longer are involved. In fact, as far as Warren Grace was concerned, the local cops were supposed to bugger off. Agent Skinner had taken the local cops off Warren Grace's back.

That's because government agent Warren Grace is now slipping out of home confinement and is back on the streets, selling heroin with an FBI seal of approval. All the while he's on the FBI payroll.

The record indicates Agent Skinner isn't telling the truth about his interactions with Grace in this period. That's too kind. Skinner is lying, and covering-up. With good reason. His interactions with Grace are troubling and scandalous. Starsky and Hutch, move over. Skinner and Grace are defying court orders, breaking the law and endangering innocent neighbors.

In fact, in August 2002, Grace is running free and dealing heroin. This is also the rough time frame when secret government agent Warren Grace is distributing heroin to Walter Poindexter inside a halfway house, among other secret, FBI-recorded activities.

Rather than merely "talking with" Warren Grace in July 2002, Skinner was wiring Grace for sound and sending him to Stash House Records to talk with Deon Smith.

This was the period in which Smith chided Grace for not visiting Poindexter in the halfway house, where Poindexter was still residing in July 2002.

It wasn't all smooth sailing. Sitting in the halfway house, Poindexter knew Grace had been arrested and smelled a rat. He's heard talk that Grace was working with the police. He's heard Grace was singing to police about the murder of Alvin Jones.

Poindexter fears he's being set-up. Poindexter isn't stupid. But he's also greedy. And the lure of the government's trap is strong.

"Right before he got out," Grace says, "I would go to the halfway house where he was at and tried to talk to him and he wouldn't really talk to me. You know, there was a rumor out that I had been working with the police or whatever, so it was kind of hard, but I kept going with him and then, when he finally got out, you know, we discussed a few things about the situation, about the rumors and everything else." He adds, "At that time I let him know I could double the heroin," by scrambling and recompressing the narcotic. "At that point I discussed with him the different ways I could double the heroin."

Deon Smith also wanted Grace to teach him the secrets of the step-on trade. If Pug would teach him how to recompress the heroin, Smith promised to sell directly to Grace, cutting out the middleman and at wholesale cost — $85 a gram.

"And we started talking about it," Grace says. "If I keep cutting it, he will be my regular supplier. He will get the stuff for me at a cheaper price. The same price he get it for. Eighty-five a gram. Something like that. And it just went from there."

On one occasion Grace would give $4,000 of FBI money to Deon Smith to buy some heroin in a FBI-recorded sting. This proved to be a complicated transaction.

"He told me he had it," Grace says. He says Smith first wanted to learn how to recompress. Smith asked him, "Did I have a mix ready? Because he wanted me to have some manitol already made up so he could step on his heroin and have my part for me too. I told him, you know, the tools weren't really ready yet, because I wanted to draw that out so I could make the buy because I knew that once I had showed him how to make the mix the whole plan was to cut me out of the picture. As soon as they figured out how to recompress it, they would no longer need me, so I had to make the buy first."

Grace paints himself as having to call the shots as part of his work with the FBI. A day or two after he gave Smith the FBI's four grand, he says he returned to Smith's studio to pick up the heroin.

"I didn't leave right away," Grace says. "I continued to talk with him and then I got up a little afterwards and left, went back to my vehicle, drive off, called the agents like I would normally do, which was right across the street from me, and we went to the meeting spot and I turned over the drugs."

As for rumors that he was working with the police, Grace says he tried to reassure Poindexter. "I told him it wasn't true."

It's clear from the record that paid FBI informant Grace supplied heroin to Poindexter while Poindexter completed his sentence in a halfway house.

It also starts to look like paid FBI informant Grace and Agent Skinner were conspiring to break laws — including court-ordered release stipulations designed to protect members of the community — and to conceal this lawbreaking from others, including Pretrial

Services, which was nominally in charge of Grace. By the time Poindexter was released, in August 2002, Grace had already been actively working with FBI Agent Skinner for several months.

This, Grace says, was all part of a plan he concocted with Agent Skinner. While working with Steve Skinner, Grace says, "me and him (Skinner) got together and came up with a plan." Two or more individuals, working together to break laws and conceal their crimes. Lawyers call it a conspiracy.

In order to keep his undercover work secret, Grace says Agent Skinner allowed him the freedom to come and go as he pleased, and to even consort with heroin dealers and users without wearing a recording device, and without supervision. All this while Grace was supposedly under "monitored house arrest."

Skinner permitted Grace to come and go as he pleased, Grace says, because, "You know, well, they wouldn't be there all the time so I had to make it so like I was still on the street so I had to be out there and call them and show up as if I would have if I never got arrested."

"So that was part of the plan that you talked about that you had to appear that you were still on the street?" Grace was later asked.

"Correct," Grace says. And, "Being on the street, I had to make it appear like I was constantly on the street. So I would always be in the neighborhood. I had different guys in and out of the vehicle. Some old guys, friends or whatever, so that they could see I was there. So there wouldn't be no question whether or not I was in the street or not. Because there was already a rumor that I was working with the police. I had to build my credibility back up, so I had people in and out of my vehicle during these times."

How strange were these car rides with Pug? On one of the single worst days in the history of the city of Baltimore, while he worked as an unsupervised, paid FBI informant, heroin would be found hidden in Warren Grace's Ford Excursion.

31
FBI informant Warren Grace terrorizes neighborhood 'innocents'

By mid-August 2002, things slid from bad to dangerous back in the hood with Warren Grace.

On August 22, 2002, Todd Stokes, whose title is Home Confinement Specialist with U.S. Pretrial Services, writes a memorandum addressed to Luna's co-counsel, assistant U.S. attorney Jacabed Rodriguez-Coss noting, "Apparent Violation" of Warren Grace's conditions of home release. The memo is cc'd to Jonathan Luna and Judge Smalkin.

Grace's monitoring equipment consists of an ankle bracelet-transmitter and a receiving device connected to the phone line. By August 14 Grace would report that the phone line had been disconnected. Amazingly, no one does anything about it for a week. For at least a week Grace ran free in his neighborhood — buying and selling heroin, shooting guns at innocent neighbors — much to the alarm of these neighbors, who couldn't seem to get anyone to do anything about it.

The neighbors too began to smell a rat. A bureau full of them. They began to angrily suspect that Grace was working as an FBI informant, and that Grace had been issued the neighborhood equivalent of a government double-naught license to terrorize and kill.

Pretrial Services' Todd Stokes, in his August 22, 2002 memo, summarizes the deep, dark mystery. Stokes reports:

"On August 14, 2002, Mr. Grace called me to advise that his phone service had been disconnected. Due to a delinquent bill, but that his girlfriend, Robin Summers, was calling her service provider to arrange payment. Securicor Electronic Monitoring Services, Inc. advised me the monitoring unit in the defendant's residence was unable to report.

"On August 15, 2002, I spoke to the defendant on an alternate telephone in the residence. He confirmed his girlfriend paid the telephone bill and advised customer service was attempting to determine why her service had not been restored.

"On August 16, 2002, Ms. Summers advised me there was a wiring problem in the phone line and a technician would have to come to the residence."

Four days pass. Incredibly, still no home monitoring,, no follow up, no one in contact with the phone company. Stokes' memo continues:

"On August 20, 2002, at approximately 12:20 p.m., I spoke with Ms. Summers who stated she expected a technician from Cavalier to come to her residence either August 21 or 22, 2002 to repair the telephone line. I asked to speak to the defendant and she advised me he was taking a shower. Ten minutes later, the defendant called me back. I told him the telephone issue had to be resolved today. I asked him why the alternate telephone line (which belongs to Ms. Summer's minor daughter) could not be used for monitoring purposes. Mr. Grace initially stated he was uncomfortable using that telephone line, but then agreed. The monitoring equipment was immediately placed on the daughter's telephone line."

But that wasn't the end of this embarrassing episode. Far from it. Stokes' odd memo continues:

"On August 20, 2002, I received a call from Special Agent Jeremy Gates of the Drug Enforcement Administration advising me that an anonymous caller informed him that Mr. Grace had drugs and guns in his residence and that he allegedly shot at someone at Park Heights and Wiley Avenues in Baltimore on *August 17, 2002.* He related should the individual call him again he would give the person my name and number." (Emphasis mine.)

Note that Stokes does not detail the chronology of the amazing events this day, and whether this call prompted him to telephone Grace with his belated demand to attach the monitoring equipment. Stokes' memo simply continues:

"Later that same day, I received a call from an unidentified male essentially conveying to me what Agent Gates told me. He further advised me the defendant was outside of his residence, that he manipulated the monitoring equipment, and he was 'hurting innocent people.' Another individual got on the phone and indicated since nothing was being done to the defendant, he must be an informant."

As we see, the neighbors don't have much trust for the FBI.

The neighbors suspect an unseen, dark hand at the center of these curious events. DEA agent Jeremy Gates, and home monitor specialist Todd Stokes, know this unseen hand belongs to the FBI. Specifically, the hand belongs to FBI Agent Steve Skinner, headquartered somewhere on Mars.

This memo then is a warning to the FBI and assistant U.S. attorney Jonathan Luna. Stokes is covering his butt in this memo, in the event that Warren Grace kills someone supposedly under his supervision. In reality, he has little or no control over events, or the FBI. The FBI is calling the shots, and is doing a bad job of it.

This memo is a cry for help, an SOS sent adrift to Rodriguez-Coss and Luna, and the federal judge. An unsupervised, untrustworthy, drug-crazed dope dealer with a gun and an FBI license to secretly kill is victimizing the "innocent people" of the neighborhood.

In this memo, Stokes, curiously yet predictably, is not telling all he knows, or all he has done. The chronology also seems disordered. The next day the angry neighbor calls back. Stokes reports:

"On August 21, 2002, I received another call from the unidentified male who again expressed his concerns about the defendant, and stated that since nothing has been done to Mr. Grace, he would contact 'Internal Affairs.' I was able to identify the telephone number of the individual (s) through the use of my caller I.D. feature, and I provided Special Agent Steve Skinner of the Federal Bureau of Investigation with the number. I also apprised him of my discussion with Agent Gates and the anonymous callers.

"Agent Skinner went to the defendant's residence on August 20, 2002 at approximately 5:00 p.m., and advised me that defendant was not present. However, Securicor Electronic Monitoring Services, Inc. indicated he was in the residence. At approximately 10:35 p.m. Mr. Grace called me to advise he returned to his residence after working out. He acknowledged that he slipped off the ankle transmitter by saturating his leg with Vaseline. He related he was wrong for removing the bracelet, and that was the first time he had done it."

This obviously was not the first time Warren Grace had slipped out of his monitoring bracelet. He's not telling the truth. What a shock! He's also violating the court-ordered terms of his home detention. It won't be the last time. He's gone through the revolving door, and is back terrorizing his innocent neighbors.

The monitoring service was seeing a ghost. There are several odd things about what Stokes relates. First, it's all but impossible to slip a monitoring bracelet off a leg. Second, the bracelet incorporates a motion detector, and presumably should have noticed it was not being worn.

Next we learn, from Stokes' memo, that Grace *already has spoken* with Agent Skinner.

Stokes' memo continues, "The defendant stated that Agent Skinner would transport him to the U.S. Attorney's office in the morning. I told Mr. Grace to remain at his residence and I would meet with him in the morning as well."

Stokes curiously adds, "It should be noted when the electronic monitoring equipment was installed on the alternate telephone line August 20, 2002, all events/alerts were retrieved from the time frame when service was first interrupted, and there was no indication that he left his residence during that period."

As the anonymous caller suggests, Warren Grace somehow has learned to manipulate his home monitoring equipment. That's not all that's being manipulated. Somehow, Stokes learns, outstanding warrants against Warren Grace have been suppressed, and ignored.

Stoke relates, "An automated inquiry of the Maryland Criminal Justice Information System conducted on August 21, 2002 revealed no new arrests or outstanding warrants. However, on August 14, 2002, I received a call from Deputy U.S. Marshal Robert Johnson who advised me that he received a telephone call from the Baltimore City Sheriff's Office indicating the defendant had two warrants outstanding for non-payment of child support and for motor vehicle offenses.

"On August 21, 2002, Agent Skinner took the defendant to the Baltimore City Sheriff's Office to surrender relative to the warrants. At this time, Mr. Grace is in local custody awaiting an appearance before a commissioner." Once again, in the revolving door.

Home Monitoring Specialist Todd Stokes concludes his memo with a recommendation: "I recommend a warrant be issued, and that the defendant's bond be revoked."

That didn't happen. Instead, a few weeks later, Warren Grace would, incredibly, again be set loose on the streets, this time *removed from home monitoring altogether.* Once again, out the revolving door.

Grace was now given the ultimate government benefit. He would be free to come and go as he pleased. To deal heroin. Shoot his gun. Fight gangsta wars with a secret agent's badge of immunity.

Pug was now working for The Man. Soon The Man would be working for Pug.

32
Agent Skinner's Rules # 1 and # 2: Cover thy butt and shift thy blame

Baltimore FBI Special Agent Steve Skinner waits a week, until late August, before he bothers to commit to writing his own report on events relating to his mysteriously wayward paid informant, Warren Grace. There's a lot about Grace's handling that doesn't make sense, and which Skinner naturally wants to keep secret, and which you too would want to keep secret, if you were Skinner and were responsible for all this.

Agent Skinner finally writes a memo that belatedly attempts to square stories with the memo of Pretrial Services officer Todd Stokes. Agent Skinner appears to have Stokes' memo in front of him as he writes, as some of terms are used identically. Still there are discrepancies. This is what is called a CYA report: Skinner is covering his ass. It won't be the last time Steve Skinner will have secrets to keep, and can't be relied on to tell the truth. In fact, Skinner can be relied on to lie, cover-up, threaten and intimidate.

Agent Skinner's report was written on FBI form FD-302. Hence it's called a "302." It's dated August 28, 2002. It's a deceptive, self-serving piece of work. It reads:

"On August 20, 2002, at approximately 2:15 p.m., writer spoke with an anonymous telephonic caller, who advised writer that an individual, who is an FBI source, had drugs and guns in the apartment which the source was living. The caller said that although source is on electronic home monitoring, source frequently leaves the apartment. Specifically, the caller said that source removes the electronic home monitoring bracelet from source's ankle, before leaving the residence, and that the source will either place the bracelet on another individual or leave it in the apartment. The caller advised that source was involved in a shooting the Sunday night before in the area of Wiley and Park Heights. The caller also spoke with TODD STOKES, a Home Confinement Specialist with United States Pretrial Services.

"On August 20, 2002, a Federal Bureau of Investigation (FBI) Consent to Search Form (FD-26) was executed *with source at the residence,* and source's vehicle. No drugs, firearms, or contraband were found during the course of the search. The electronic bracelet was found in source's dresser." (Emphasis mine.)

"Participating in the search were the following FBI Baltimore, Safe Streets Task Force Members:

"Detective TODD A. MOODY, Baltimore City Police Department

"Detective GLENN HESTER, Baltimore City Police Department

"Detective KAYTEE TYSON, Baltimore City Police Department."

Baltimore police detective Todd Moody, like Skinner, would increasingly play a curious role in all to follow.

Skinner says he telephoned the concerned, anonymous caller, at the phone number supplied by Todd Stokes, while Detective Moody listened in the background. Skinner asked threateningly, "What is this about?" Skinner seems to have trouble understanding anyone's problems but his own. Skinner asked to meet the anonymous caller in an isolated parking lot. The caller, streetwise and obviously intimidated, never shows up.

In his evasively worded, ambiguous memo, Agent Skinner says that Warren Grace was home when they came for him. It's clearly dishonest and deceptive. The search "was executed with source at residence." This clearly contradicts Stokes' memo: "Agent Skinner... advised me the defendant was not present."

From this we can glean several interesting facts. Someone's getting good at manipulating electronic bleeps. Someone in the FBI — Agent Skinner — is unethically manipulating the words to report all this. Note also that Skinner here demonstrates just how quickly an FBI agent can call in Baltimore police officers, if desired.

Agent Skinner is withholding the truth here. Among other notable omissions, Skinner doesn't mention the monitoring device has been inoperable since August 14. He makes no attempt to explain the odd events of this missing week — other than the most glaring, the reported shooting — nor why it took so long to respond to community complaints. He's looking out for Number One, and he's looking out for Warren Grace, so that he's not thrown out of the informant pool.

Agent Skinner, careless, heedless and cavalier, now must cover his ass. It won't be enough. He'll need Jonathan Luna's help.

Skinner's not troubling himself about the law, the court order, the safety, or the opinions, of the innocent people of Baltimore. Hell, the innocent ain't even in the line of command; the innocent don't even have a phone number connected to the "Safe Street Task Force." Luna would be left holding the bag to worry about all these things.

On August 29, 2002, prosecutors in Luna's office wrote a letter to Pretrial Services "acknowledging Mr. Grace's violations and why they were opposed to him being taken off the streets," Baltimore attorney Kenneth Ravenell later would say.

Luna, in this period, would shortly have more problems with the Baltimore FBI. A week later, in September 2002, Luna would be prosecuting the case against bank robber Nacoe Brown.

Sometime during that trial, under FBI supervision, the $38,100 in untraceable cash would go missing.

33
The Dawsons take a bite out of crime, and crime bites back

In these last hot days of August 2002, while the "Safe Streets Task Force" fiddled with covering up their paid informant's various transgressions (and tacitly threatening a concerned citizen who managed to get through on the phone to complain to officials about Pug), the Dawson family found themselves brow-deep in drug dealers, with no one to call for meaningful help.

It was no secret who was causing the Dawsons' trouble, or even where the trouble lived. Trouble lived just on the other side of Eden Street.

Among those that the Dawsons suspected of selling drugs on their corner was eighteen-year-old John Henry. John Henry lived in a row house facing the Dawsons on the other side of Eden.

The nickel-and-dime, commercial problem was that the Dawsons' corner house, on busy Preston and Eden, commanded a better location for selling drugs than the middle of the block on sleepy Eden, where Henry lived.

By this time the Dawsons, particularly Angela, had taken to fairly regularly chasing the dealers from their corner. Angela, neighbors say, began to loudly yell at the dealers and assorted neighbors, yelling that she knew they were selling drugs, and she didn't want it around her home. She'd also called the cops, by this time, more than a dozen times. The cops would come out and the dealers would scatter, only to return later. It was turning into a very annoying game for all concerned.

By late August, John Henry and perhaps others began to retaliate for these inconveniences of the trade.

On August 23, Angela Dawson found the word "Bitch" written

on the side of her house. She did what she had been doing all along. She tried to clean it up.

A child by her side, she stood in front of her house trying to clean off the word. She later reported that John Henry came across Eden taunting her, bragging he'd written the word and laughing that now she had to clean it up because she was a bitch. She cursed back at him. That's when, she said, Henry hit her, knocking her down. She called the police, who promised to do something. No one at 911 dispatch appears to have called the FBI "Safe Streets Task Force," who, at any rate, had their hands full with Warren Grace and the 9-1-1 hip-hop gig.

Within days bricks flew through the Dawsons' windows.

Angela Dawson would later file a court report that read, in part, "The defendant John L. Henry wrote on my wall bitch.... I stayed out with my child until I could get the words off the wall. John Henry came across the street bragging about he wrote the word Bitch on the wall, and he said bitch that's why you got to clean the wall and I did it bitch. I said (expletive).... That's when John Henry cold-cocked me...."

Two days later, on August 25, Dawson reports, "My husband and sons were cooking in the kitchen. A brick was thrown through the kitchen window. The glass flew and some went in my older son's eye."

On September 4, she complained, "My husband had just come home from work. We sat down to talk about our day & then decided to pop a VCR tape in, when a brick came through the front living room window. The brick struck me in the back. I watched John L. Henry running across the street."

John Henry was finally arrested and jailed. Into the revolving door went John Henry for thirty days, to get his hand slapped.

The Dawsons didn't get much peace from Henry's arrest.

On September 9, John Henry's next-door neighbor, twenty-one-year-old Darrell Brooks, a known crack dealer, was released from jail, where he had been held since June. Brooks had been released from jail even though his latest offense constituted a violation of a previous probation. The spinning revolving door had taken away John Henry, only to deposit Darrell Brooks on the other side of Eden Street.

In the coming month, the Dawsons would call 911 for help *more than twenty times.*

34
Do U really wanna know about some gangsta sh't?

FBI Agent Steve Skinner, when pressed, goes into more detail than he bothers to offer in his official, written report. So he's an untrustworthy reporter; curious in itself. Moreover, he plays down his contacts with Warren Grace in these crucial, mysterious weeks.

Skinner says that in this period in 2002 — the beginning of summer to the end of August — he wasn't working with Warren Grace every day. "It could have ranged from twice a week, three times a week. It's hard to say."

He says, "Pretrial Services was to make sure that Mr. Grace would remain in the apartment that he was staying in when he was not working with myself or another task force officer from my squad." So he blames Pretrial Services, which all along had opposed Skinner's ill-conceived plan.

Skinner continues, "As I said, he was under home monitoring, so what I would do is call Mr. Stokes, the Pretrial officer, beforehand, before a day that I would be working with Mr. Grace, and I would tell Mr. Stokes if he could turn off the home monitoring system on a particular day."

One day, Skinner says, "Well, Todd — Mr. Stokes — advised me that he received an anonymous telephone call from a male who said that Warren Grace was leaving the apartment that he was supposed to be staying in by taking off the ankle home monitoring bracelet without telling anyone. He was leaving when he was not working with myself or other people from my task force."

He and Baltimore police detective Todd Moody, Skinner says, called the anonymous tipster and asked for his name. He asked the concerned citizen to meet up with the officers in a secluded parking lot. As I say, Moody plays an increasingly curious role in all this.

"I got the telephone number from Mr. Stokes. Mr. Stokes saw the telephone number, I guess, on his caller ID of the anonymous male that called him," Skinner says, "I got that telephone number from Mr. Stokes and I called this male.

"I believe I was with Detective Moody.

"I spoke with the male. He said that — he actually said that he — now that I remember, he said that he spoke with a Drug Enforcement Agency agent, a DEA agent, before talking with Mr. Stokes. And I said, well, you know, what is this about?"

Skinner doesn't understand concerned citizens. He resents anyone in his way.

Heard of The Untouchables?

Meet The Unreachables.

Skinner gets down to cases. What the hell did this guy want?

"He said he identified Warren Grace," Skinner continues. "He said the name Warren Grace. He didn't use Warren Grace's street name. He said Warren Grace was leaving the apartment.

"He identified the particular apartment that Mr. Grace was staying in. The address. And he also identified the type of vehicle that Mr. Grace drove. He said that Mr. Grace had been regularly leaving the apartment.

"He also advised me that Mr. Grace had been involved in a shooting at — I believe it was the intersection of Wiley and I want to say Park Heights, but I am not — I don't know the exact intersection. I know it was Wiley.

"He also said that Mr. Grace had been selling drugs. So, you know, I asked the male, I could keep this confidential, you know, could you provide me with your name?

"He said he did not want to. I asked him well, could I meet you just to, you know, talk to you a little more about this. At first, the male agreed, and he said he would meet me at the parking lot near Sinai Hospital.

"We didn't meet. He didn't show. I then called him again, and he said he didn't want to meet me." He's an intuitively smart man.

Skinner says he doesn't know the identity of the concerned tipster. Afterwards, he says, he had a conversation with Grace about the tipster's information.

Lacking grace, Skinner keeps working with Warren Grace.

35
Moody is as Moody does

On August 28, 2002, Special Agent Steve Skinner writes his dishonest report about Warren Grace's breaches of his conditions of release. It's a busy and momentous day for the "Safe Streets Task Force."

The task force for months has had Warren Grace wired for sound. They've already recorded Deon Smith telling Grace he should supply Walter Poindexter with heroin in the halfway house.

The same day Skinner lies and omits facts in his official report, on August 28, 2002, Baltimore police detective Todd Moody videotapes informant Grace standing in front of Stash House Records with Walter Poindexter.

Poindexter, by this date, in late August 2002, has at last gone through the revolving door and has been released from the halfway house. Now he's back on the streets of Baltimore, ready and unsuspecting for the misdeeds that Skinner and Grace have planned for him.

Before Poindexter's release, the task force had been busy recording conversations between Grace and Deon Smith. The recordings, Skinner says, were accomplished with a digital body recorder planted on Grace.

"In general detail," Skinner explains, "the recorder is a— it's a covert body recorder that a person would wear. It records digitally. There is no tape involved, and it's worn by a cooperating witness."

"When we do a body recording," Skinner says, "the recorder is a digital recording device. There is no tape that's ever created. The recording is downloaded onto a computer hard drive which is then transferred into a CD ROM."

Another option, which Skinner passed over, he says, for several reasons, involves a radio transmitter.

"A transmitter is also a covert device that we can use. It lets us listen real time as to what's going on. It works over radio waves," Skinner says.

"They don't work as well as you think they would. If there is a tall building in the way, or if cars are moving, the quality is not that good. But the primary reason why we didn't use a transmitter in this case was that most of the recordings that we did, a substantial amount of the recordings that we did, were done at a studio. A music recording studio. I was afraid that this transmitter, there might be some sort of backfeed. Or, you might be able to hear it through speakers, or any other type of thing."

Skinner says he feared a transmitter planted on Grace might broadcast through Stash House Records recording equipment.

"I know," he says, "through experience that some criminals know about FBI transmitters. You can actually buy some equipment that, and people—. I know investigations where criminals have put these devices in doorways and, when a source walks through a doorway, this light will go on because the transmitter radio waves are going through the device that the criminal bought."

Warren Grace began using this digital recorder, Skinner at last says, "probably in June of 2002. It was either the end of June or the early part of July 2002." This contradicts another Skinner assertion that, in this period between April and late summer 2002, the task force was merely "talking with" Grace. (Skinner earlier had said, "We had a few interviews with him, just to talk with him.")

It's not a small matter, since in this period Poindexter was still in the halfway house. Keep in mind that Grace now worked for the FBI as a paid informant, and Grace says he was supplying heroin to Poindexter in the court-approved halfway house. "Different dudes would come out on work release or whatever, and I would meet one of the dudes and give them the heroin to take in to him." These arrangements were even recorded by Skinner and the FBI. So the FBI knew its paid informant was dealing heroin. This is part of what Skinner is attempting to keep secret.

This important discrepancy aside, Skinner goes on to explain the procedure used to wire Grace for sound.

"Well," Skinner says, "the way we would handle Mr. Grace would be we would meet with Mr. Grace. We might discuss, you know, what might happen, where we might meet, that sort of thing.

"I would activate the body recorder, and I would put what we call the FBI preamble on the recorder. (I say), 'This is Special Agent Skinner," and I give the date and time and then, in this investigation, either Mr. Grace would be sitting with me in the car and I would provide it to him or we would have met real close to the studio and I would have just given it to him.

"We would do our best to see where Mr. Grace was going. Myself, and other law enforcement officers like our task force.... It depended on what we were doing. If we were just doing a recording, meaning we were just going to talk with somebody, it could be one, two or three task force officers.

"If we were doing a buy, or a purchase, rather, of drugs, we would want more people out there, hopefully. Sometimes people have other things going on and you don't have the occasion to do that, but generally we hope to have more people.

"Typically, I would be in a parked car making observations," Skinner says. "Most of the time," he says, he could see where Grace had entered the studio.

So August 28, 2002, was a red-letter day. Poindexter had just returned to the street. The task force planned to entrap him anew.

It's the day Detective Moody videotaped Grace meeting Poindexter in front of Stash House Records.

"He was always still kind of leery about me," Grace would say. Word had gotten back to Poindexter that Grace was cooperating with Baltimore homicide police on the murder of Alvin Jones.

36
Special agent man

When you read the files to see what happens next with our master FBI informant Warren Grace, you don't get the full story. Instead, you detect a shadow moving through the files. That shadow continues to be the FBI, and Special Agent Steve Skinner.

By late August and early September 2002, Special Agent Skinner finds himself in yet another predicament. He's badly mishandled his paid informant. Just one of many predicaments created by Skinner's careless mismanagement of Grace.

It's obvious, to some degree, what's going on behind the scenes. Agent Steve Skinner wants to use Warren Grace to bust Stash House Records. He is possessed with a ruthless abandon to get Deon Smith and Walter Poindexter, who has just been released to the street. Skinner and Jonathan Luna already know that Walter Poindexter shot and killed a man for robbing a stash house.

No doubt, Smith and Poindexter are bad characters and should be taken off the street. Often the ends don't justify the means. That's a lesson, in its long history, the FBI has never been quick to grasp.

Despite his mysterious transgressions while supposedly under home confinement, Warren Grace is not punished. Instead, incredibly, he's *rewarded.* Only three weeks after Warren Grace grievously violated his home confinement and was taken in for new warrants, Todd Stokes of U.S. Pretrial Services suddenly changed his tune.

By August 29, 2002, prosecutors in Luna's office had written Pretrial Services "acknowledging Mr. Grace's violations and why they were opposed to him being taken off the streets," as Baltimore attorney Kenneth Ravenell would later describe the letter.

Agent Skinner has smoothed things out with just about everyone. Everyone but the people of Baltimore — their roar will be heard soon.

Even the new warrants, the child support, are made to go bye-

bye. (We can safely assume the FBI is giving Grace money for the child support.) Instead of demanding Warren Grace's imprisonment and the revoking of his bond, Stokes of Pretrial Services wants off the case and agrees to turn Warren Grace loose on the city of Baltimore.

On September 12, 2002, Stokes, buckling under pressure from Luna and the FBI, files a motion of consent to modify Warren Grace's conditions of release. Grace will now be turned loose on the community, without home monitoring. On the face of things, Stokes' approval of this change is all the more curious since only two weeks before, on August 28, Stokes had written a damning and damaging memo requesting a warrant for Grace "be issued, and that the defendant's bond be revoked."

Again, it's what we *don't* see that's at play here. Stokes' new motion of September 12, reads:

"U.S. Pretrial Services recommends the following modifications of the above named defendant's conditions of release:

"that Mr. Grace be removed from home confinement with electronic monitoring and Pretrial Services supervision.

"Except as modified above, all other release conditions previously imposed shall remain in full force and effect.

"Assistant U.S. Attorney Jacabed Rodriguez-Coss and Defense Counsel have no objection to this modification."

More than a year would pass before the extensive behind-the-scenes wrangling involving this modification would come to light.

After home monitoring specialist Stokes wrote his blistering (and embarrassing) August 22 memo, Agent Skinner and the U.S. attorneys successfully pressured Stokes and Pretrial Services to get off the case.

What caused Pretrial Services to recommend Warren Grace's release from home confinement?

Skinner and Luna's co-counsel, Assistant U.S. Attorney Rodriguez-Coss, told Pretrial Services' Stokes, and Judge Smalkin, that the government opposed ending Warren Grace's bail. The court was told Skinner's investigation would be damaged if Grace "was taken off the streets."

Pretrial Services' Stokes would say, "the comments about damaging their case was an oral communication between he and Ms. Rodriquez-Coss."

A few days after the oral communication, "there was a letter written by the prosecutors in this case dated August 29 of 2002, acknowledging Mr. Grace's violations and why they were opposed to him being taken off the streets," attorney Kenneth Ravenell would say. That August 29, 2002 letter, Ravenell reports, "says it would damage their case in the future" to take Warren Grace off the streets.

This suppressed memo — and hidden FBI pressure — caused Todd Stokes to about-face. On September 12, 2002, Stokes, on behalf of Pretrial Services, filed a court document captioned, "Consent to Modify Conditions of Release." Stokes here tells the court that Warren Grace should be "removed from home confinement... and Pretrial Services supervision."

Judge Smalkin signed this order on September 13, 2002. He contributes to all that is to come. Here's another American judge based on planet Mars. Send Frederic Smalkin fan mail care of the Judicial La La Land Spaceport and Gospel Supper Theater, at the Baltimore federal courthouse. It's a popular judicial retreat. Smalkin's actions should be examined and he should be disciplined. Unfortunately, these days, careless or bad judges are better protected than innocent children in our neighborhoods.

Meanwhile, very much back on earth, Warren Grace now is free to roam the streets of Baltimore and threaten anyone he pleases.

Jonathan Luna would suppress information about this strange "modification" for more than a year. Luna could only hope that nobody in Baltimore was paying attention — as usually was the case.

Todd Stokes' of Pretrial Services, performing his job to protect the innocent people of Baltimore, embarrassed Agent Steve Skinner by writing a memo documenting Warren Grace's August 2002 shooting spree at Park Heights and Wiley Avenue. Grace, Stokes wrote, was "hurting innocent people." Grace, Stokes further noted, had "drugs and guns in his residence." Guns, drugs, and violence: sounds like Standard Operating Procedure for Pug.

This could not have sat well with Assistant US Attorney Jonathan

Luna, who saw himself as the protector of these neighborhoods. Life takes us down strange paths, doesn't it, Jonathan?

Thanks to Agent Skinner, Luna had helped put Warren Grace through the revolving door, back to the streets, risking the lives of innocent people.

Now, with every new step they'd take, Skinner and Grace would take Luna further down a path he was not happy to travel.

The FBI's Steve Skinner would push aside home confinement specialist Todd Stokes, Pretrial Services, the Baltimore police department, the federal court, and just about every other established — and publicly scrutinized — community safeguard.

The Park Heights shooting episode, the record shows, was caused by Agent Skinner's failure to act with sound judgment, complicated by his failure to properly oversee Pug. What if someone's child had been killed?

Agent Skinner, behind the scenes, shifts the blame and knocks Todd Stokes and Pretrial Services off the case. He does this, as usual, in the name of protecting future FBI investigations.

Skinner will be quick to shift blame from himself, and let others take the fall for his mess.

Jonathan Luna would learn this in spades.

In a responsible, professional police force, Steve Skinner would certainly face investigation for his negligent mismanagement of Warren Grace. At the very least Skinner should have been removed from the case, certainly disciplined, and possibly fired.

Instead, working in a troubled FBI, Steve Skinner is left to call the shots. He's ordering a federal judge around, making everyone dance to the faux-rap tune he's calling. What's wrong with this picture?

And what about Skinner's supervisors in the FBI and the Justice Department? Where were they?

In the Baltimore FBI field office, in the autumn weeks surrounding the 2002 DC sniper shootings, Skinner's bosses would themselves be spinning round in a revolving door, coming and going to new assignments.

We know about one Justice Department official involved in all this: Jonathan Luna. Rather than putting the brakes on Skinner, Luna goes into cover-up mode while Skinner's dangerous bumbling continues.

It's interesting, and curious, that Jonathan Luna's opinions about Pug's excellent adventure through the revolving door aren't mentioned anywhere on the record. But that's totally in keeping with this strange story.

Warren Grace, while working as a paid FBI agent, would soon be caught concealing heroin, in further violation of his terms of release. This troubling fact would also be suppressed for more than a year.

None other than Jonathan Luna would suppress these facts.

In fact, cleaning up after Steve Skinner's mess would come to occupy the very last hours of Jonathan Luna's life on earth.

37
Ophelia in the rearview

What's it like to get stabbed in the back by Warren Grace? Better look in the rearview mirror.

Let's take the example of Walter Poindexter who, just back on the street a few weeks, takes a ride with the man he had helped out so much in the past. The date is September 11, 2002 — that's 9/11. It's the day before Pretrial Services would bug off the case, under FBI pressure, and write Judge Smalkin that Grace should no longer be subjected to home monitoring.

Warren Grace is wearing an FBI wire.

Later, Grace would cry crocodile tears, saying, "It's difficult" to stab an old friend in the back. "He was like family to me, and my brother." After all, when a young Warren Grace was abandoned by the world to prison in Hagerstown, Poindexter hadn't forgotten him. "When I was locked up, and they took care of me, he would come see me and send me money and stuff like that."

Now he was going to stab his brother in the back.

Why betray Poindexter? By way of explanation, Grace says only, "We had a falling out over a female." Enter Ophelia, daughter of Bolognaius.

That can't be the whole story. Warren Grace no doubt was thinking about someone's ass; surely, as usual, it was his own. With Warren Grace, it was always about Warren Grace. Going back to his earliest days as a boy, when he had no one else to look after him, it was always Warren Grace looking out for Warren Grace.

Wearing the wire, Grace set up the man he says was his brother, Walter Poindexter, just out of prison.

Poindexter, Grace says, "was a little apprehensive talking to me because of the rumors that was out, so it was kind of hard getting him to conversate with me. I mean, you know, I would meet him and he was constantly looking around, you know. And I, you know, would be talking to him and ask him different stuff. And he would say, 'No. I don't know about you. Some people might be on you.'

"You know, the police was on me. The feds was watching me. So he was really leery about talking to me."

The day before, Grace had met with "the agents" of the "Safe Streets Task Force."

"We were going to make a buy," Grace says. "We met up and discussed how we was going to make the buy with Mr. Poindexter that day. I met the agents, you know. They gave me a certain amount of cash. (Eleven hundred dollars — ed.) (We discussed) how many grams we was going to buy from Mr. Poindexter. I would go there. (The agents) would check the vehicle, they would get the recording, and then I would be on my way to the Stash House studio."

For a variety of reasons, the agents were obliged to check Grace's vehicle for contraband. They had to certify that Grace had no other drugs that day, less Poindexter could claim the heroin had already been in Grace's possession.

His vehicle searched and the FBI's recorder running, Grace phoned Poindexter. "At that point I made a call first to let him know I was coming, or, if he wasn't there, I'd meet him somewhere else," Grace says.

"I told him I had a block (of manitol) and I had run out (of heroin) and I was trying to get some heroin and the people I was trying to buy from didn't have any, so I needed to get some.

"Plus at that point I was trying to get some heroin from Mr. Smith, but he didn't have any at that time. So (Poindexter) said he knew some people that he could get it from." So he met with Smith and Poindexter at Stash House Records and turned over the FBI's eleven hundred dollars.

At the studio, Grace says, he dealt with Poindexter. "Basically I pulled him to the side, and he said he was going to highlight the dude. He was waiting for him to call him back. I told him how many grams I needed. And he asked me for some money too. So some of the money that I had, I told him he could keep most of that and just give me some heroin with the rest of it.... I had to leave the money with him and I came back and got it (the heroin) the next day."

"You know, he was looking out for me, so I just gave it to him."

After months of harebrained planning and nitwit execution, several weeks after the right hand let him out of jail, the left hand once again had the goods on Walter Poindexter in the rap studio. Not exactly Tupac, and not exactly a surprise.

The "next day," when Pug picked up the FBI's first heroin in this operation, happened to be September 11, 2002. *9/11/02.* It coincidentally was, of course, the first anniversary of the attack on the World Trade Center in New York, the anniversary of another monumental FBI failure.

For all these strange 9-1-1 connections, we should focus on the *disconnect* involving the most important 9-1-1. The emergency telephone number.

Innocent victims like the Dawson family couldn't reach the FBI's "Safe Streets Task Force" by dialing 9-1-1 if their lives depended on it. And their lives depended on it.

Instead, the FBI's "Safe Streets Task Force" was too busy keeping its paid informant, Warren Grace, in the heroin and gun business, and covering its bureaucratic butt, to pick up the damn phone, much less actually *protect* a family like the Dawsons.

Anyone, who, by some miracle, did reach the FBI "Safe Streets Task Force" by phone, such as the concerned citizen who tried in vain for days to complain that Grace was loose and shooting up the neighborhood, found themselves threatened by Special Agent Skinner. "What's this about?"

Then they were asked to meet Skinner in a desolate city parking lot.

So on 9/11/02, again wearing a FBI recorder, Grace met Poindexter to pick up the FBI's heroin. "I met him on a parking lot like a couple of blocks away from the studio," Grace says.

"Well, as I told you," Grace says, "from the start, he was always still kind of leery about me, so I was supposed to meet him at one spot and when I come to that spot he switched it right then and there for me to meet him at another spot. So when we got to the parking lot he had to look around and then he finally got into the vehicle and we made the exchange."

After months of planning, the FBI now had the goods on Walter Poindexter.

Poindexter of course had reason to be leery of Grace.

FBI agents were watching the transaction in the parking lot.

"They were in the parking lot too," Grace says. "They followed me. I could see them in the rearview." After the transaction, Poindexter left. So did Grace and his trailing agents.

"After getting the heroin," Grace says, "I would drive over like I normally do and call the agents on the phone. We had a certain spot that we would meet. And then I would hand over the drugs."

38
Amazing Grace

By this time, mid-September 2002, Warren Grace worked full tilt as an FBI informant, pumping thousands of dollars of government money into the local economy.

In the following weeks, on at least three occasions in September 2002, Warren Grace gave a total of $5,880 of FBI money to Walter Poindexter in exchange for heroin.

These *recorded* drug buys with the Safe Streets Task Force continued into the next month.

On October 13, 2002, Warren Grace, wired for sound, walked into Stash House Records, asked for heroin, and handed $4,000 of FBI money to Deon Smith. At the time, Smith was packing a 9-millimeter Ruger pistol. The music playing in the background wasn't Brahms. The tracks were hip-hop.

Secretly overhearing this transaction was FBI agent Skinner and Baltimore police detective Todd A. Moody. Moody was the same cop who, in mid-August, had gone to Grace's apartment with Agent Skinner in search of a missing Grace and his contraband.

How do we know about these drug transactions involving Warren Grace? These FBI intrigues with revolving door beneficiary Warren Grace were the last sentences Jonathan Luna wrote about on the night of his midnight ride, in the last few hours before he died.

Luna could only hope the whole story involving Grace, Skinner and the "Safe Streets Task Force" could be kept from the public.

He could only hope that, as usual, no one would be paying attention.

39
FBI's 'Safe Street Task Force' fiddles with rap music while Dawsons' house burns, Part 1

In any community there is a misery index that can suddenly, in a flash, hit the intolerable. That day often is long in coming. October 16, 2002 became the intolerable day in Baltimore.

The month opened with the DC-area snipers terrorizing the region. Beginning on October 2, in Montgomery County, Maryland, military veteran John Mohammad, and his teen-aged protégé, John Lee Malvo, opened fire from a sniper's nest concealed in the back of a car. Before they were caught on October 24, they would end the lives of ten men and women who had picked the wrong place and time for the most mundane of activities: stopping for gas, mowing the lawn, or shopping.

A growing sense of helplessness turned to rage on October 16, when Baltimore woke up to the tragedy of the Dawson family.

Having served less than a month in jail for vandalizing the Dawsons' wall and smacking Angela Dawson, John Henry was released from jail on October 2. His charges were moved to the inactive docket, on condition he'd keep away from the Dawsons and pay $275 in restitution. The Dawsons supposedly agreed to this. With that, John Henry was out the revolving door.

Early the next morning, John Henry's next door neighbor, probation violator Darrell Brooks, similarly out the revolving door, tossed two Molotov cocktails into the Dawsons' kitchen window.

It was all the Dawsons could do to get their children out alive.

"My husband and I gathered up our babies and led them to safety," Angela later told authorities. "Before getting out we experienced choking from the smoke and could hardly see how to get out the door. The heat was very intense.... I got water trying to put out the fire. Everytime I threw water on the fire it flared up even more. I finally got the fire under control and went outside with my family."

Angela Dawson pointed out that the firebombing appeared to be "set up to kill everyone in the home. To blow my family up."

Darrell Brooks, believed to have thrown the firebomb on October 3, was a lanky twenty-one year old. He had come from a broken home. He was a victim of child abuse. When he was five he was taken from his mother, who was charged with abusing him, and placed in the custody of his father. His father didn't care for him, and soon he was back with his abusive mother. In 1993, when he was twelve, his brother was murdered. In school he was enrolled in special education classes, where he struggled. A concerned Baltimore city councilman found Brooks a part-time clerk's job with the city. But in time Brooks didn't show up punctually and was soon back on the streets.

Brooks had a long history of run-ins with the law, going back at least to 1998. Armed robbery. (At seventeen he took another child's mountain bike at gun point.) Assault. Drug charges. Car theft. A complete list is difficult because, as a minor, his violations were handled by juvenile court, where records are sealed.

In April 2002 Brooks was placed on two years of probation, following a three-year suspended sentence for unauthorized use of a motor vehicle. At that hearing, six other charges, including theft and drug possession, were dropped.

Brooks was supposed to report to a probation officer, but he never showed up. The probation officer — with his own long list of bureaucratic infractions — never bothered to track Brooks down, nor report his probation violations. Brooks was supposed to report twice a month. Because Darrell Brooks never bothered to show up at the probation office, neither his probation nor his probation violations were entered into the appropriate computer system. On June 23, 2002, Brooks was jailed on new charges. Because his probation had never been entered into the computer system, Brooks was released from jail on September 9, and was back on Eden Street.

Turned back to the streets, Darrell Brooks, like FBI informant Warren Grace, was without supervision. Like Warren Grace, *and* John

Henry, Brooks was terrorizing the streets of Baltimore. The authorities either knew about it, or should have known about it.

After tossing the Molotov cocktails on October 3 and seeing his victims escape, Brooks supposedly told his neighbor John Henry that the Dawsons wouldn't be so lucky next time.

Police and prosecutors say they tried to help the Dawsons. They say they offered the family a new home under the witness protection program. The Dawsons, at least at first, refused. "I'm not going to let drug dealers run me from my neighborhood," Carnell told a co-worker.

The Dawsons hunkered down, fearful in their own home. The kids were afraid to play on the street with their friends. Psychologists were dispatched to talk with the frightened Dawson kids, and they all hunkered together on the sofa talking to the shrink. Jung would be shocked.

The Dawsons' house was placed on a "special attention" list, city police say. That meant increased patrols, but only when police were available. Manpower problems.

The obvious question: Where were the feds? Where was the "Safe Streets Task Force?" Where was Jonathan Luna, protector of the innocents?

By mid-October the Dawsons had called 911 at least *three dozen times,* seeking help.

Why weren't the resources of the FBI 's "Safe Streets Task Force" made available to stake out the Dawsons' corner? Later, it would turn out, Skinner's task force was tied down producing almost *one hundred hours* of surveillance tapes proving that Warren Grace and Walter Poindexter and Deon Smith sold heroin. Talk about overkill.

Why the great disconnect? In this story, there doesn't seem to be too much communicating going on between the various local and federal law enforcement offices, except to put an offender in the FBI informant program.

Sadly, while the FBI fiddled with Warren Grace, the Dawsons' house would burn. Had someone in U.S. Attorney Tom DiBiagio's office cared to, they could easily have nabbed several dangerous offenders. They could have truly made the streets safe. They could have saved truly innocent lives.

Instead, the feds were too busy keeping tabs on Warren Grace, who *clearly was making the streets unsafe with federal help,* while Agent Skinner and company attempted to take over an obscure rap music recording studio.

Behold: Operation Hip-Hop Freedom.

They had to hope no one would notice. If they thought about it at all. The record shows there truly doesn't seem to be all that much thinking going on.

40
FBI's 'Safe Street Task Force' fiddles with rap music while Dawsons' house burns once again, Part 2

The last time the Dawsons would need to call 911, on October 16, they wouldn't be able to make it to the phone.

In the early morning hours of October 16, 2002, while the Dawsons slept, Darrell Brooks kicked down the door of the Dawsons' home and threw gasoline on the floor and stairway. It was the only way out of the house.

He lit a fire in the little tinder-box house. The fire this time was all-consuming. Brooks then went up on to his roof, on the other side of Eden Street, and watched the flames lick at the Dawsons' little yellow house. Soon he would hear the screams.

For all their expensive technology, neither FBI's "Safe Streets Task Force," nor the 911 operators, heard the last futile calls for help emanating from the Dawson household on Preston and Eden.

The neighbors are haunted by the memory of the last screams of help from Angela Dawson. Her last pleas were now directed at God:

"God, please help me. Help me get my children out!"

Fire burst through the windows and roof. Someone called 911. Three minutes later the fire trucks pulled up, but Carnell, Sr already lay dying on the sidewalk. Burns covering most of his body, Carnell managed to escape the conflagration by throwing himself from an upstairs window. He broke his pelvis when he hit the street. He was the only one who made it out. A few days later, never regaining consciousness, he died.

Inside his house his wife and kids were burning to death.

Angela and her five children.

Lawanda, fourteen years old, who liked to draw, and said he wanted to study art.

Juan, age twelve, who was a good reader and a good student.

Carnell, Jr., ten, agile and quick.

Keith, nine, always joking.

His twin, Kevin, affectionate, and a great reader. His school's reading room would be named in his honor.

They lived like stones that the builder refused.

Now they are all gone.

The Dawson family had finally been wiped out.

On the day I visited the burned out remnants of the Dawsons' house, a little girl and her sister came up and led me by the hand across the street to the Dawsons' park. It was a small corner lot, no more than fifteen or twenty feet deep. The girls remembered the children.

"Look there are stones," the older girl said. She and her sister fluttered like butterflies across the tiny lot.

Engraved memorial stones were embedded in the grass.

A stone for each of the kids, Angela and Carnell.

Seven stones, I counted.

41
Atomic shock:
No justice like angry mob justice

It's hard to overstate the size of the civic explosion in Baltimore that followed the deaths of the Dawsons. Suddenly everyone was paying attention. Now careers were being destroyed. Any public official who did not want to be destroyed in the blast had to seek cover.

For days, hundreds of outraged citizens gathered at the bombed-out shell of the Dawsons' home. The house still stood, a sore thumb stuck in the sore eye of the city, smoke stains above the knocked-out windows, the roof charred and caved in. It stood like a warning. The meaning of the warning takes moments, yet years, to comprehend. Mementos were left around the burnt-out wreckage. At one rally the childrens' grandmother sobbed inconsolably, and had to be helped into a nearby church.

Speakers demanded an end to what they called a revolving door justice system. Some voiced suspicions that there was more to the arson than met the eye, that Brooks had acted on behalf of darker higher-ups who profit from the drug trade.

Angry residents flooded city hall meetings. Suitably hostile newspaper editorials poured in from around the country, castigating Baltimore's criminal justice system as out-of-control and corrupt.

Baltimore city councilwoman Pamela V. Carter, herself a neighbor of the Dawsons, told the Black News, "All they get is a slap on the wrist and come out the revolving door."

Politicians, prosecutors and police alike postured to escape the torrent of public wrath. Any Maryland public official who had anything to do with law enforcement — from Gov. Parris Glendening on down — felt the heat.

The two officials apparently nearest the epicenter — Mayor

Martin O'Malley, and his police commissioner, Ed Norris — faced the most heat, and scrambled to deflect it.

When a community radio station broadcast diatribes against O'Malley, the mayor arrived uninvited at the station's doorstep demanding equal time.

Mayor Martin O'Malley could only look to the state, and its coffers, for help in the wake of the Dawson tragedy. O'Malley asked outgoing Democrat Governor Glendening for an additional one hundred state police troopers. The mayor said the state had promised to hire seventy-five more probation officers. It was Darrell Brooks' probation lapse that supposedly had allowed the tragedy.

"This is our moment of crisis," Mayor O'Malley told the Washington Post.

Someone meanwhile stuck a Believe sticker on the burned-out steps of the Dawsons' home.

Believe this.

Many blamed the local police. Baltimore Police Commissioner Ed Norris' response to all this is noteworthy. Norris was an import from the New York City police department.

"I've never seen anything like this in my entire career," Norris told the Washington Post. Reporter David Montgomery filed a long article in the Sunday paper a month after the arson, on November 17, 2002, compiled with the help of researcher Bobbye Pratt. In many ways the article exemplifies the best and worst of today's newspapers.

"For two generations at least, neighborhoods like Oliver have been dying, but too many stopped noticing," Montgomery writes. "Now some are hoping that the atomic shock of the Dawson case can be harnessed to accomplish change, finally."

What does The Post notice, and what changes are they talking about?

The most ridiculous fallacy in the article is Montgomery's assertion that Angela Dawson simply had been too harsh, that she should have spoken nicely to her neighborhood drug dealers and none of this would have happened.

"Another woman who lived in the same block of Preston said it's a matter of how you talk to the drug dealers," the Post quotes a neighbor saying.

That's right, whip up a batch of brownies, pat them on their behinds, and ask your friendly neighborhood skag dealers to run along, and kindly move their shop. A reading of Warren Grace's case shows this is not true, that the dealers routinely shoot anyone in the way of profits.

As a large daily newspaper is prone to do these days, the Post then marshals its resources to burrow through public records and trash the Dawsons. We read that the cops, at times in the past, had been called to the Dawsons' for domestic disputes: "Twice Angela was arrested for assaulting Carnell, in 1996 and in May 2001, according to court records. Carnell was charged with assaulting Angela in 1997."

We even learn that Carnell Dawson was arrested for buying a vial of crack in December 2001, at an "'infamous' drug corner a few blocks away from the Dawsons' corner."

Titillating, for sure. Yet there are questions more worthy of the Washington Post. Where are the cops? Where was the FBI? (We know the answer to that one, don't we?) What about the effects of drug profits on police corruption? What about the failed drug policies? These are some of the issues an institution like The Post should champion, investigate, and analyze.

The Post would have been better off assigning a young couple with kids to live in the Dawsons' block for a few months. Interestingly, it's worth remembering that it was this kind of vital reporting that landed the Post in hot water in the past. The Post's infamous "Jimmy's World" series in the late 1970s depicted the supposed life of an under-privileged Washington DC boy. Only after the series was awarded the Pulitzer Prize did editors discover the young reporter had fabricated both Jimmy *and* his world. This presaged similar, recent scandals at The New York Times and USA Today, where at least two reporters were discovered to have for years been rewriting reports from other newspaper articles, without attribution, or making things up whole cloth, including coverage of the 2002 DC Beltway sniper story. Let's call it, in the vernacular of hip-hop, sampling.

Hoping to atone for its sins of isolation, the NY Times appointed an "ombudsman." An ombudsman writes articles employing the same tone used by the psychiatrist in the Terminator movies ("I'm here because something really bad has happened....”). The newspapers would have us believe this is some sort of public service.

In reality, an ombudsman is the hack they hire when the other hacks are too lazy or out-of-touch to do their jobs.

Newspaper staffs today have largely forgotten, or do not know, that the great calling of our Fourth Estate is to succor the powerless, and make the powerful uncomfortable. Instead they get it backwards. The powerful are made comfortable, while the powerless are further insulted.

In the case of the Dawsons, those whose actions (or inactions) should be examined and criticized for not doing the job of protecting the public include the Baltimore police, the FBI, and the U.S. attorney's office. Not the Dawsons.

In the days following the Dawson tragedy, the Baltimore Sun spilled some ink about Baltimore Police Commissioner Ed Norris's weathering of the fiasco.

In the days after the blaze, the Sun reported, “members of the City Council and the state House and Senate delegations criticized the (probation) system in a closed-door meeting with Norris yesterday morning at police headquarters, participants said. Yelling and cursing at times, they called for drastic action, including calling in state police and even the National Guard.”

Norris through it all insisted law enforcement had done everything it could to help the family.

A family member told the Sun, “The police weren't trying to help the way they're claiming.”

The Sun reported, “While the community's anger is understandable, Norris said, that anger should be directed at those responsible for the crime, not at the government.”

“‘It's about time we get the outrage focused in the right direction,’ he said.”

The Sun did not properly follow through.

At the time, Ed Norris had his own distractions. In the very months the Dawsons had called police thirty-six times, Police Commissioner Norris was busy covering-up the fact that, for *two years,* he'd been using a policeman's benevolent fund to finance sexual encounters with more than a dozen women.

Ed Norris had his own problems.

Norris's supporting role in the Dawson story is interesting. But it's not *the* most interesting role of these political players.

The deaths of the Dawsons reverberated to the highest levels of Maryland state politics. In recent years the two political parties have been engaged in a particularly acrimonious fight in the state capitol, Annapolis. Running to replace Gov. Glendening in 2002, Lt. Gov. Kathleen Kennedy Townsend publicly asked Glendening to lift a hiring freeze in the state's probation and parole division. This curiously presaged U.S. Attorney Tom DiBiagio's investigation into Kennedy Townsend's office for what DiBiagio said were unlawful circumventions of hiring freezes in the area of law enforcement. Kennedy Townsend is the eldest child of Ethel and Robert F. Kennedy, the former U.S. attorney general.

Kennedy Townsend's opponent, Bob Ehrlich, stayed cagily mum on the Dawson catastrophe. "I just don't want to politicize the fire bombing, I really don't,' Ehrlich told the Baltimore Sun. Without comment, The Sun noted that Ehrlich said this on his way to a political appearance at a Dawson rally. When a professional politician such as Ehrlich says he does not want to "politicize" some scandal, it usually means he's vulnerable to attack for a similar scandal.

Politics, clearly, already were afoot. Ehrlich's ally in the U.S. Attorney's Office, Tom DiBiagio, was positioning himself for upcoming, high profile political prosecutions. Some of these prosecutions involved powerful opponents of Ehrlich's.

With the deaths of the Dawsons, their house still smoldering in the bonfire of town vanities, DiBiagio positioned himself as detached from all that had happened. He decried the revolving door mishandling of Dawsons' killer, Darrell Brooks, who should never have been out on the street. DiBiagio held himself as above all that. But it was all just meretricious posturing.

DiBiagio quickly moved to bring federal arson charges against Darrell Brooks. Of course, DiBiagio could have brought those charges after the first firebombing on October 3.

Before a year would pass, in August 2003, Brooks would plead guilty to the Dawsons' murders in federal court, prosecuted by DiBiagio's office. Brooks was sentenced to life in prison without parole.

"He's got another fifty or sixty years to think about what he did every day he sits in jail," DiBiagio told reporters. "What a colossal waste. Seven people are murdered by this drug punk."

DiBiagio didn't mention the rampaging drug punks under care of his own office. Few people knew about that. Jonathan Luna was one of the few who did.

In the days and weeks following the Dawsons' losing battle with druggies in their hood, DiBiagio's office would launch an investigation of heroin and crack dealers in Baltimore's nearby Parks Heights area. This Park Heights investigation would be kept under wraps for eighteen months, until the spring of 2004.

Park Heights was the area where FBI paid informant Warren Grace was documented on secret memos as terrorizing helpless neighbors.

Jonathan Luna would be kept busy suppressing these Park Heights memos until the last hours of his life.

42
Savonarola on Lombard Street

So, you see, in the Dawson fiasco, the most interesting high-profile actor was U.S. Attorney Tom DiBiagio.

DiBiagio soon found himself increasingly criticized in Maryland and Washington DC as a politically motivated prosecutor.

The job of U.S. attorney is a political appointment. The top man in any U.S. attorney's office comes and goes. The real continuity in the office rests in the hands of scores of often anonymous assistant U.S. attorneys working there. DiBiagio had a foot planted in both worlds. Before his appointment as U.S. attorney by the Bush administration, DiBiagio worked in the Maryland office as an assistant U.S. attorney from 1991 to 2000. So he was a longtime internal operative. He's a graduate of Dickinson College, in Carlisle, Pennsylvania, and the University of Richmond, where he earned his law degree.

From the earliest days since his elevation as U.S. Attorney in 2001, Republican DiBiagio emphasized prosecution of cases involving public corruption and white-collar crime. In a state historically dominated by Democrats, that means prosecuting Democrats. Early on, U.S. Attorney DiBiagio found himself at odds with the Baltimore office of the FBI, notably former Agent in Charge Gary Bald, who soon left to oversee FBI counterterrorism efforts. In 2002 DiBiagio wrote a memo scolding the Baltimore FBI field office for failing to investigate white-collar crime.

Before long, DiBiagio launched a probe of the Democratically controlled Baltimore city council. He subpoenaed the financial records of every council member. In his sights, everyone understood, was Democratic Mayor Martin O'Malley. O'Malley was seen as Gov. Ehrlich's chief threat and rival.

U.S. Attorney DiBiagio would soon reveal a penchant for writing embarrassingly ill-conceived and revealing letters, memos and e-mails, many of which were leaked to the press.

A written agenda for a May 2004 staff meeting detailed several goals DiBiagio set for his staff to achieve by November 6, 2004 — four days after the general election. The Baltimore Sun reported that DiBiagio's goals included obtaining, "Three 'Front-Page' White Collar/Public Corruption Indictments." Talk about cops with quotas. It would be funny, if it wasn't so dangerous to democracy. In any country where elections determine who goes to jail, bullets soon fly.

Another stated goal of DiBiagio's was to improve his office's relations with the FBI. For the purposes of this story, that's revealing.

The nadir came on July 1, 2004, when DiBiagio sent his assistant prosecutors an e-mail calling attention to high-profile federal indictments of Democratic city officials in Philadelphia. The handling of the Philadelphia case, involving associates of Mayor John Street, in fact caused embarrassment for the U.S. Justice Department in late 2003. Philadelphians came to see the investigation as a politically motivated Republican witch hunt launched against an incumbent black Democrat. In what had once been a tight race for re-election, Street won handily in a campaign suddenly re-energized as Mayor Street vs. The Man.

The lesson was lost on DiBiagio. "Why aren't we doing cases like this?" DiBiagio complained to his staff, citing the headlines in Philadelphia. "Am I the only one embarrassed by the fact that this Office has not convicted an elected official of corruption since 1988?" Two days later, DiBiagio sent an e-mail saying this was the wrong message to have sent, that he simply was frustrated and wanted action.

The damage, unfortunately, was done. Two weeks later, on July 16, Deputy U.S. Attorney General James B. Comey reprimanded DiBiagio for risking the "credibility" of his office by pushing the pelt-seeking, quota agenda and writing the e-mails. Comey wrote DiBiagio that the U.S. attorney was "directed, until further notice, to submit to me for review any proposed indictment in a public corruption matter. You may not bring such cases without my personal approval." DiBiagio was also warned to make no attempt to learn the identity of the party or parties responsible for leaking the memos and other internal documents. Fear of retaliation exists in DiBiagio's office.

The Justice Department in Washington released Comey's letter of rebuke to reporters. They were hanging DiBiagio out to twist in the wind. "Md. Prosecutor Accused of Playing Politics," read one Washington Post headline. The Post quoted former Maryland U.S. Attorney Stephen H. Sachs as saying DiBiagio's e-mails were "a woefully inartful and stupid way of expressing his desire to do as much as he can to establish his legacy." And an increasingly troubled legacy it is.

So DiBiagio was put on a short leash by his overseers in Washington. Speculation flew in the press that DiBiagio wouldn't be reappointed should George W. Bush win reelection. "If Bush is reelected," the Post noted, "he will decide whether DiBiagio is reappointed, though presidents frequently defer to the top elected official of their party in the state — in this case, Gov. Robert L. Ehrlich, Jr. Ehrlich's spokesman said the governor would not comment on this controversy."

That's the realpolitik: DiBiagio was soon seen as Ehrlich's catspaw. Republican Ehrlich wanted, and needed, Democrat O'Malley gone. For this, Ehrlich needed DiBiagio to prosecute O'Malley, or people close to O'Malley. These days, it's inconsequential whether O'Malley had broken any laws. Ask Philadelphia Mayor John Street. They're prosecuting O'Malley already, leaving the trifle of finding any offenses for later. That's the dangerous and cancerous form of "justice," and government, we've allowed to fester and spread in early twenty-first century America.

DiBiagio's office would not only prosecute where there was no crime. He'd stoop lower than that. When DiBiagio's neck was on the line, his office would *protect* lawbreakers, even murderers, to protect DiBiagio and, by extension, Ehrlich.

On the night of Jonathan Luna's death, DiBiagio's office would protect Walter Poindexter from prosecution for the murder of Alvin Jones, which would serve to protect DiBiagio.

Jonathan Luna, the unlawful plea agreement left undone on his laptop at the stroke of midnight, also found himself in the way.

DiBiagio, it turns out, had a terrible secret of his own. DiBiagio's own office gave kid-glove, revolving door treatment to a heroin dealer every bit as threatening to innocent Baltimoreans as Darrell Brooks, the murderer of the Dawsons.

The dealer's name was Warren Grace.

Grace was not just shooting up his neighborhood, nor was he merely escaping home confinement. While receiving money from the FBI, under supervision of Tom DiBiagio's office, Warren Grace was *dealing heroin.*

The fickle finger of fate was about to come crashing down.

On the *very day* the Dawsons died, October 16, 2002, FBI Special Agent Steve Skinner and his unreachable "Safe Streets Task Force" sent Warren Grace into Stash House Records to buy heroin.

Afterwards, as planned, Warren Grace met the task force at the rendezvous spot. Grace's vehicle was searched.

While the Dawsons' house still smoldered, a package of heroin was found hidden in Grace's SUV, in a storage compartment.

Paid FBI informant Warren Grace, on the very day of the Dawsons' mass murder, was caught with a heroin stash. For months he'd been secretly marketing heroin on the side, while under FBI employ and supervision.

Suddenly people were paying attention. Very close attention. Hundreds of people screamed for official accountability at neighborhood rallies and town council meetings.

An unsupervised, paid FBI informant caught dealing heroin in the hood would not have looked very good. In fact, had the truth been made public in that incendiary moment, U.S. Attorney Tom DiBiagio would certainly have found himself under attack, if not driven from office. He would have had his head handed to him in a Fell's Point picnic basket.

A young assistant U.S. attorney in DiBiagio's office, responsible for Warren Grace, suddenly found himself sitting on a political scandal of the first magnitude. He would now have to cover it all up. To protect himself. To protect his boss. To protect the FBI.

The young assistant U.S. attorney's name was Jonathan Luna.

Part 2

Buckle down and get a curve: Luna dances at trial with secrets up his sleeve

1
In a catbird's seat

What now of our champion of the poor and downtrodden, our protector of innocents, Jonathan Luna?

Raised in the South Bronx, the birthplace of rap music, Luna now ironically finds himself overseeing a smelly, incompetent criminal investigation of hip-hop record label Stash House Records. The investigation, he sees, is a threat to the same innocents he'd once hoped to protect.

Luna would remain true to his school. Wearing his scales of justice college ring on his finger, Luna's school was now the law, not his boyhood school of the forgotten projects. Was his school true to him? Absolutely not. In time, he'd figuratively be stabbed in the back, by colleagues and supervisors in the Justice Department, and the FBI, all of whom Luna now found himself haplessly trying to protect.

In time, someone would literally stab him in the back.

Luna was swimming in deep water, in over his head, with no one to toss a life ring. And the sharks were circling.

U.S. Attorney Tom DiBiagio's office, where Luna worked, was left badly exposed by the Dawson fiasco. Few could have understood this better than Jonathan Luna, sitting in his shaky catbird's seat in DiBiagio's office, reading the memos crossing his desk about the FBI's revolving door screw-ups involving Warren Grace, and God knows who else.

Jonathan Luna could not have liked what he saw happening with the FBI, and the bureau's mishandling of informants. At the same time, as if things weren't bad enough, in Washington DC, Congress was holding hearings on the very subject of the FBI and its long troubled history with informants. Luna must have feared being made a fall guy.

Consider the incongruities. In Jonathan Luna we have a protector of the poor. A protector of the victimized neighborhoods of the powerless. In the handling of Warren Grace, Luna sees outright dangerous bumbling in the Justice Department. His own office is the bringer of indifferent misery to these same poor neighborhoods he wants to protect.

Luna, our restaurant worker's son from the Mott Haven section of the Bronx, has risen to a station in life where he begins to see something else. He has a view into the topmost levels of state, and national, politics.

From his post, what can he see? What does he know?

He certainly saw the mechanizations and hypocrisy in Tom DiBiagio's office. He saw DiBiagio's political interplay with Republican gubernatorial candidate Bob Ehrlich. Ehrlich, it turned out, was elected governor of Maryland a few weeks after the Dawson fiasco. He would be the first Republican governor of Maryland in thirty-six years.

Luna certainly understood DiBiagio and Ehrlich's overriding desire to divert attention from their own scandals, to sweep them under the carpet.

Jonathan Luna, it turns out, knew enough to badly damage some of the biggest Republicans in Maryland. At a critical political moment, when Republicans finally recaptured the state house after three and a half decades, and were reaching for the legislature, our lawman from the projects, Jonathan Luna, arguably knew enough to bring down the Maryland Republican party. And they knew enough to bring him down.

Following the Dawson debacle, Luna knows he's sitting on a bad headline, and he could be left holding the bag. As Flavor Flav of the rap group Public Enemy sings, "That's a body bag in disguise, ya betcha."

If he wasn't careful, Luna himself could be that bad headline.

2
Smith and Poindexter refuse to dance

Armed with the hours and hours and hours of undercover evidence attained with the paid help of Warren Grace, the FBI on May 13, 2003, finally raided Stash House Records. Deon Smith and Walter Poindexter were arrested and jailed. More than $50,000 in cash was confiscated from Smith's apartment.

Leading up to the arrests, on May 12, 2003, FBI special agent Steve Skinner filed an affidavit of probable cause requesting a search warrant for the rap studio at 911 West 36th Street. The government affidavit reads that "a confidential source (Warren Grace — ed.) advised that (Grace) was aware of an individual named Deon Smith who was a drug dealer in the city of Baltimore. (Grace) advised that Smith had supplied heroin to a group which called its heroin '911' (pronounced 'nine-eleven')." Skinner describes Grace as "a source who is generally reliable, but whose information should be corroborated."

Skinner writes, "For instance, in October of 2002, (Grace) made a controlled purchase of a quantity of suspected heroin from Deon Lionnel Smith at the studio located at 911 West 36th Street."

It wasn't exactly a "controlled" purchase on October 16, was it, Steve? Skinner makes no mention of the stash of heroin found hidden in Grace's Ford Excursion. Another secret.

"(Myself) and Detective Moody, either together or separately, have conducted of fifty (50) surveillances... during the course of this investigation," Skinner writes. What were they doing? We know they weren't watching Warren Grace too closely.

Too bad they also weren't watching the Dawsons' house, when the family called *911* thirty-six times for help over three months.

If Skinner, Moody and Jonathan Luna expected to flip Smith and Poindexter, and take control of Stash House Records, they were sorely disappointed. The only rap the feds would be directing would be their rap sheets.

Smith and Poindexter weren't dancing. Instead, they hired two of the best, and busiest, defense lawyers in Baltimore. Poindexter retained Arcangelo Tuminelli, while Smith hired Kenneth Ravenell. Both were experienced trial lawyers. Leave these two an opening, and they'll drive a tank through. Ravenell, it so happens, worked opposite Luna on other cases, and was somewhat a mentor and confidant of Luna's.

3
Papering the file

Jonathan Luna, meanwhile, already finds himself way in over his head. And the waters are rising. He begins to look like a sorcerer's apprentice, trying in vain to still the waters by waving his seemingly powerful wand while the deluge, and the brooms, rise up around him. It would only add to the deluge, and the brooms, to come.

In May 2003, Luna filed a sealed indictment jointly charging Smith and Poindexter with heroin distribution and related violent drug crimes. "Members of the conspiracy," the indictment reads, "...utilized physical force against members of the conspiracy and against members of rival drug conspiracies to maintain their reputation in the community, to preserve their own territory, to punish members of the conspiracy who cheated or stole from the conspiracy, and to defend and maintain the loyalty of the members of their own organization."

In a key paragraph, the indictment goes on to explain, "On January 22, 2001, Walter Oriley Poindexter, a/k/a 'Fella,' shot and killed Alvin Jones, a/k/a 'L,' because Poindexter believed that Jones was responsible for burglarizing the stash house where conspirators stored their heroin, money and firearms."

The murder of Alvin Jones would turn out to be no laughing matter. Luna was making the point — as he was obligated to do — that Jones' murder was clearly drug-related. This meant that federal prosecutors — having assumed jurisdiction of the case from the local Baltimore cops — not only had a civic duty to prosecute Poindexter for murder. Under federal law, they now had a *legal obligation* to seek justice, to prosecute Walter Poindexter for a murder committed in the course of his drug dealings.

Walter Poindexter now faced the possibility of a death sentence.

On July 3, 2003, Luna and the defense attorneys held a telephone conference call with federal District Judge William D. Quarles, Jr., who had been assigned to try Smith and Poindexter.

Quarles was an interesting selection for this case. Born in Baltimore in 1948, Quarles was a black Republican (unlike Luna, who was a Democrat). But like Luna, Quarles, early in his career, from 1982 to 1986, worked as an assistant U.S. Attorney in Baltimore. There's another rather startling coincidence. One day, I'm told, while he worked in the U.S. attorney's office, a young William Quarles walked out of the courthouse in downtown Baltimore and was accosted on the street by an unknown assailant.

"Quarles got his head split open and was badly hurt," one courthouse worker told me. "He was laid up for months. We thought he might die."

Now, as federal judge, presiding over the conference call, Quarles was told by Jonathan Luna that the government planned to file a new indictment against Poindexter. The new indictment would charge Poindexter with the murder of Alvin Jones.

On July 10, 2003, in court document titled a "Motion to Sever," Ravenell tells the court Smith should now be tried separately from Poindexter. "The Government has indicated that it will file a superseding indictment against Mr. Poindexter charging him with murder and possibly the death penalty," Ravenell writes. "Severance is required when 'there is a serious risk that a joint trial would compromise a specific trial right of one of the defendants, or prevent the jury from making a reliable judgment about guilt or innocence.' That risk is present in this case. Wherefore the Defendant respectfully requests that the Court grant a severance."

Judge Quarles set a hearing date of November 10, 2003 to discuss the issue.

In the months that follow, Luna acts like an inexperienced prosecutor. He at first acts predictably: he acts like a prick. By the end, he'll be giving away the store.

Lawyers like to add documents to a court file to help make and bolster a case. They call it "papering the file." (Not to be confused with "papering a bird cage.")

I've come to see the Smith-Poindexter file as stuffed with some of the most interesting documents in American prosecutorial history. The file itself, we must always bear in mind, is itself evidence in a murder investigation. Luna's murder.

Luna begins filing court papers that he must have believed were nails in Poindexter's coffin. They would instead turn out to be nails in *Luna's* coffin. With every paper he files explaining the strength of the government's case against Poindexter for the murder of Alvin Jones, Luna is hoisted by his own petard.

Here Luna's inexperience shows. He begins to do two things consistently: first, he time and again attempts to conceal the law-breaking of the FBI's paid informant, Warren Grace, and the scandalous parallels to the Dawson fiasco. Second, he lays out strong evidence that the murder of Alvin Jones is drug related.

If Luna had been a good chess player, thinking more than one move ahead, he perhaps would have foreseen the inevitable outcomes of these two conflicting stratagems.

Luna, instead, keeps on keeping on. He keeps papering the file to ensnare Poindexter in murder.

In response to Smith's request for a separate trial from Poindexter, Luna writes, signs and files a court document titled, "Government's Response in Opposition to Severance of Defendants." It's received and stamped by the court clerk's office on October 30, 2003.

"The government's evidence will establish that Poindexter and Smith conducted a heroin distribution network in which Smith was the primary supplier of heroin," Luna writes. "Poindexter in turn employed a group of street dealers, including Warren Grace, who sold heroin under the street name '911.' The profits from the street sales of 911 heroin were shared by Poindexter and Smith."

Luna lays out the case against Poindexter for the drug murder of Alvin Jones. "During the course of the conspiracy," he tells the court, "Poindexter was advised that Alvin Jones had burglarized one of Poindexter's stash houses. Believing Jones had burglarized the stash house, the government's *evidence will show* that upon finding Jones, Poindexter shot and killed Jones on January 22, 2001." (Emphasis mine.)

How strong was the government's evidence? Pretty strong, Luna goes on to write. There were *at least two* eyewitnesses ready to testify about having seen Poindexter shoot Jones in the drug murder.

"A joint trial in this case is uniquely compelling," Luna writes, arguing against separate trials. "...Another compelling reason for a joint trial is the avoidance of inconvenience and trauma for the witnesses. In this case, that is particularly true. At least two of the witnesses in this case were involuntary witnesses to the murder of Alvin Jones. Two separate trials will require these witnesses to relive horrific experiences of witnessing the murder of a human being ... (joint trials avoid imposing 'trauma' of having victims repeat their testimony). Moreover, the emotional burdens from testifying just once may cause some of these witnesses to avoid testifying a second time, thus unfairly causing prejudice to the Government's case and the victims' interest in justice."

In the end, in a rush to cover-up the government's problems with Warren Grace, *neither* of these witnesses would be called to testify against Walter Poindexter.

When he filed this court paper, Jonathan Luna had less than forty days to live.

4
'A stressful and startling event'

In the coming weeks still more was placed into the file concerning the murder of Alvin Jones. These additions strengthen the government's case that Jones' murder had obvious connections to drugs and violence.

This is not just flailing a dead horse, as it were. Jones' murder, and the cause of the murder, turn out to be central to our story.

"Defendants, Walter Poindexter and Deon Lionnel Smith, have been charged with conspiracy to distribute in excess of one kilogram of heroin from 2000 to May 2003," reads one document entered into the record, in Jonathan Luna's name, on November 3, 2003. "The government's evidence at trial will prove that during the course of the conspiracy, Walter Poindexter used violence to further the heroin distribution network. The government's evidence will further establish that sometime during January 2001, an apartment used by Walter Poindexter as a 'stash house' to store firearms, heroin, and money was burglarized. The government's evidence will show that Mr. Poindexter believed that Alvin Jones committed the burglary of the apartment and subsequently shot and killed Alvin Jones.

"Warren Grace, a government cooperator, will testify at trial that Mr. Poindexter advised him that Mr. Poindexter shot and killed Alvin Jones because of Mr. Poindexter's belief that Jones committed the burglary. Alfonso Jones, the father of Alvin Jones, will testify that approximately a week before his son was murdered, Alvin Jones received a telephone call and became very agitated. Alfonso Jones will testify that he was present and observed and heard his son engaged in the telephone conversation. He will further testify that his son, Alvin Jones, explained to him immediately after the telephone conversation that he was upset as a result of the accusation leveled by the caller.

"Alvin explained, 'Some bitch is accusing me of robbing some house,' or words to that effect."

A footnote reads, "Alfonso Jones will not be able to testify who called his son; he could not hear the other party's voice during the conversation. The government anticipates developing circumstantial evidence at trial that the person who called Alvin Jones in January 2001 was Maronda Cole, the girlfriend of Walter Poindexter and an acquaintance of Alvin Jones. The government's evidence will also show that, at the time of the call, Maronda Cole was a part of the conspiracy."

"Alfonso Jones perceived the telephone conversation his son had with both his eyes and his ears," the motion continues. "While his son was on the phone, Mr. Jones saw that his son was agitated by the call. He heard his son was agitated by the call. He heard his son engaged in the conversation, and immediately after hanging up, Alvin Jones related the substance of the call, *to wit:* the accusation of burglarizing the house. He expressed to his father how the conversation made him feel."

The motion makes the obvious, understated observation that, "Certainly an angry accusation of burglary — particularly when delivered by a known associate of a drug kingpin — is a stressful and startling event. Alvin 'perceived' the 'event' — the phone call — personally, he was agitated by what he had heard, and he told his father why he was upset. There was no time for conscious reflection, and neither motive nor opportunity for fabrication."

The issues of Alvin Jones' murder, and whether Walter Poindexter should be tried separately from Deon Smith, would be addressed by a stipulation, or agreement, between Luna and the defense attorneys.

In the end, court records show, Judge William Quarles would instruct the parties that Jones' murder would not be discussed at the upcoming trial. In exchange, Smith and Poindexter would be tried at the same time for drug offenses. This could mean a mistrial for Smith in the event someone slipped up and mentioned Jones' murder at trial.

The government reserved the right — indeed, had a *legal obliga-*

tion — to prosecute Poindexter for the Jones' murder at a later date, under a separate trial, if need be.

At the time of this November 3, 2003, motion bearing his name, Jonathan Luna had just one month to live.

5
Warren Grace suffers pangs of conscience

These preliminary wranglings resolved, Jonathan Luna set about the business of preparing for the joint trial of Deon Smith and Walter Poindexter. That largely meant preparing his case with his main government witness, our double-naught FBI informant, Warren Grace.

Supposedly to ensure his safety, and to isolate him from the influence of the Baltimore drug trade, Grace had been removed from the Baltimore prison system. By means of a separation order, Grace was jailed at the federal detention facility in Philadelphia.

Luna, accompanied by task force members, specifically FBI Special Agent Steve Skinner, began regularly traveling to Philadelphia to meet with Grace at the detention center.

By this time Grace had already milked the feds for thousands of dollars in secret cash payments and other perks, all of which Luna continued to willfully and consciously neglect to disclose to the defense team.

Months earlier, on May 27, 2003, Luna had written defense attorneys, "to set forth the conditions on which the government is willing to make discovery in this case." Luna represented he would comply with all lawfully required discovery obligations, including Rule 16 of the Federal Rules of Criminal Procedure, as well as case law known by trial attorneys as *Brady, Giglio* and *Jencks.* These discovery rules, which Luna now conspired with the FBI to disobey, guarantee a defendant access to various government-held information that may help in his defense. This requires not only disclosure of information that might outright prove innocence, but that otherwise may impeach the trustworthiness of witnesses or evidence. *Conspiracy* is the operative word here. Luna already had conspired with Skinner to act dangerously with Warren Grace, with disastrous consequences. Now he continues to conspire with Skinner, and others, to cover it all up.

Luna blatantly and systematically violated his promise, and the law, by withholding key information about Grace's swashbuckling double-naught antics with Steve Skinner and The Unreachables of the "Safe Streets Task Force." No use letting the people of Baltimore know that U.S. Attorney Tom DiBiagio's office had incompetently fiddled with hip-hop while the Dawson family burned.

The secrets they failed to disclose included the heroin they had found in Grace's black Ford Excursion on the day of the Dawsons' murder. Luna and the FBI, before the start of trial, would actually host a meeting at the FBI office with attorney Ravenell. Ravenell was shown evidence, which Luna would later say included the heroin found in Grace's Excursion. But Ravenell would insist he was never told the circumstances of the seizure of the heroin.

Luna also kept secret, among other things, the payments Grace took from the FBI, and, we're forced to consider, payments from other sources, not the least of which most likely included heroin sales on the side, indirectly subsidized and enabled by the feds.

Disclosure of the FBI's misbehavior with Grace undoubtedly would have helped the defense undermine Grace's — and Agent Skinner's — credibility with any jury.

Evidence withheld by Luna might also be exculpatory, proving the men innocent. Usually we learn about these things only when the government turns over the information.

Only weeks and days from trial, Luna finds himself in a deepeningly difficult position. He badly needs Warren Grace's help, and cooperation. The stakes are ever higher. Luna needed Grace not only to testify against Smith and Poindexter. He has to worry that Grace, on the witness stand, might spill the beans about his government undercover work. He also had to worry that Grace, when testifying, might blurt out Poindexter's murder of Alvin Jones, which could cause a mistrial.

As if all this isn't bad enough, darker clouds now float menacingly on the horizon. Committees in both the U.S. Senate and the House have begun investigating the FBI and its handling of informants. As Luna's bad luck would have it, Warren Grace's misadventures with the G-Men were precisely the sort of thing that Congress was investigating.

Luna had to worry about far more than losing the Smith-Poindexter case. He had to worry about bad headlines. Careers and livelihoods could be destroyed — his, DiBiagio's, Skinner's.

So it's an understatement to say that Luna needed Warren Grace's cooperation and discretion. *Luna's career depended on it.*

Luna's problem was that Warren Grace, as always, only cared about one thing: Warren Grace. Hardened in the streets to look out for himself, and play all sides against each other, Grace saw no reason to stop now.

Grace knew that all roads still led to Warren Grace. In Grace's mind, they were all toll roads, with a shop set up on every corner to take payment, while the junkie passed out dope in the alleyway.

Once again Luna finds himself sitting across table from Warren Grace. This time Grace sits in a chair in the detention facility, coolly pretending not to be sizing up Jonathan Luna.

Grace mumbled his conscience bothered him. He just couldn't bring himself to rat out Walter Poindexter. Poindexter after all was the closest thing Grace had to family, to a brother. Poindexter had been the only one beside his grandfather to visit Grace in prison, and now Grace was expected to repay all the favors by sending Shorty away.

He just didn't know if he could do it.

Luna and Skinner found themselves working on Pug. Good cop, bad cop. Luna held the stick to play the bad cop. Skinner had the perks and playthings of good cop.

The trial was only days away, yet Luna and Skinner couldn't be sure of their star witness. Luna threatened to revoke Grace's plea agreement and send Pug away for decades if he didn't testify.

Skinner knew that Pug had his price, and that all this guilty conscious stuff was bullshit. Why didn't Grace just name his price, and the FBI would pay?

The day before the trial began, on Sunday, November 30, 2003, Special Agent Skinner took Warren Grace out of jail and back home to Grace's Baltimore apartment, for a secret four-hour conjugal visit with Grace's wife.

We must therefore consider the very real probability that Grace as well continued to receive other largess. Perhaps including secret payments of cash.

By the Sunday before the trial, on the day the FBI agents allowed Grace a secret visit with his wife at home, Joey Luna had little more than seventy-five hours to live.

6
Trial Day 1: December 1, 2003

The courtroom trial of Deon Smith and Walter Poindexter began the next day, Monday morning, December 1, 2003, in the Baltimore Federal Courthouse, Courtroom 3-A, before Judge William D. Quarles.

Quarles, like most judges, has no shortage of his own peculiar set of quirks. At his swearing-in ceremony in March 2003, when he was elevated to the federal bench from Baltimore city court, Quarles, a Catholic, wanted officials in the archdiocese of Cardinal William Keeler of Baltimore to participate, one courthouse worker complained to me. (Cardinal Keeler, a former bishop of the Harrisburg diocese, is fondly thought of in Pennsylvania.) Quarles is active in the church. In the mid-1990s, Quarles served as a board member of the Loyola-Notre Dame Library Corporation. He also serves as a lector at St. Michael's Roman Catholic Church.

The courthouse worker says Quarles brushed away concerns about having church officials participate at his elevation to the federal bench.

"He said, 'I'm a black Republican so no one will mess with me,'" the observer recounted.

Quarles has led an accomplished life. He earned his BS at the University of Maryland in 1976, and his law degree at the Catholic University of America School of Law in 1979. Following his stint in the U.S. Attorney's office in the mid-1980s, where I'm told he was injured by a street attacker, Quarles became a litigator and partner for several years in a private law firm. He's the co-author of the 1991 book, *Summary Adjudication: Dispositive Motions and Summary Trials,* making him an expert on quick, extemporaneous legal proceedings. That expertise will come in handy in this trial.

Quarles is known to be a stickler for punctuality. A clock on

Quarles' courtroom wall is set to atomic time, one associate told me with a chuckle.

"I need you to be prompt," Quarles told the jury at the start of the trial. "As I have told you, that this is a sacrifice for you, so we will be respectful of your time. So I will ask you if you would be prompt with us."

At the prescribed moment the court was called to order.

In the morning session, a jury was selected and sworn in. It was a jury that was "almost all caucasians," attorney Ravenell would soon complain, "and it troubles me that that we have a jury of almost all caucasians sitting in this courtroom trying to make a decision about these two young men sitting here."

"For those of you who were not selected," Judge Quarles said, "please return to the jury room. Please leave quietly and quickly. Please try to hide your disappointment at not being chosen."

Judge Quarles then adjourned for lunch, until 2pm. At precisely 2pm, Quarles reconvened, and asked, "Folks, may we send for the jury?"

Luna saw that Kenneth Ravenell, Deon Smith's attorney, was missing from the defense table.

"I think Mr. Ravenell is missing, your honor."

"Where did he go?"

"Judge," a clerk said, "he is walking slowly up the hallway. I motioned for him to come. He is on his way."

The courtroom waited in awkward silence until Ravenell entered.

"Mr. Ravenell, you timely presence will be expected," Quarles admonished the lawyer.

"I thought I was, judge," Ravenell countered. "I thought we said two o'clock." His wristwatch, obviously, was not set to the atomic clock.

The defendants sat at the defense table. Poindexter wore a pink shirt.

Jonathan Luna, meanwhile, sat, by all appearances ready, at the prosecution table with his co-counsel, Vivien Cockburn. Luna, as always, nattily dressed, wore, as usual, his eyeglasses in court.

"He always had his eyeglasses with him when he was in court," the court reporter later told me. "He needed them to see."

Luna's performance at the Smith-Poindexter trial would be one of the most amazing in the history of American jurisprudence.

It would be improvisational. There's improvisational jazz, unplanned and alive in the moment, as performed by Charlie Parker and Dizzy Gillespie. In literature, improvisational writers like Jack Kerouac and Allen Ginsberg revolutionized American letters.

Now Jonathan Luna sets off to launch the most amazing improv performance ever seen in an American courtroom. Improvisational criminal prosecution. To the end, Luna would be jammaster flash.

Flying by the seat of his pants, having committed almost nothing by way of agreements or discovery to paper, Jonathan Luna begins his case. Quarles asks Luna to present his opening argument, limited to an hour in length.

Rising to address the jury, Luna begins, "Ladies and gentlemen, good afternoon. Again, to reintroduce myself, my name is Jonathan Luna. My colleague and co-counsel is Vivien Cockburn.

"We are attorneys for the government. We have been assigned this criminal case to prosecute on behalf of the United States of America.

"To get you situated, I should also introduce Steven Skinner. He is a special agent with the Federal Bureau of Investigation. He is what we call the case agent.

Skinner, sitting in the courtroom, appeared not to be looking forward to a day in court. He looked unhappy.

Luna continued, "Mr. Skinner will be in the court throughout the trial. He will be coming in and out of the courtroom assisting Ms. Cockburn and I (sic) with the presentation of evidence in this case, so if you ever wonder why he leaves the courtroom and comes back, that's what he is doing. He is helping us with the presentation of evidence and witnesses and such.

"I want to give you, as Judge Quarles has already said, a prediction, an outline, of what the government's evidence will consist of." The evidence, Luna explained, would chiefly be presented in the witness stand.

"I think you generally know that this case involves drugs," he went on. "Illegal narcotics. Let me tell you a little bit more about the case. The case involves a conspiracy between the defendants, Walter Poindexter and Deon Lionnel Smith. A conspiracy to distribute at least a kilogram or more of heroin during a particular time period here in Baltimore."

"What is a conspiracy?" Luna interesting asks the jury. "Well, you are going to hear from Judge Quarles during jury instructions at the close of evidence that conspiracy is really a simple thing. It's nothing more than an agreement between two or more persons to do something. That's all a conspiracy is. It's an agreement. An understanding. It is a common goal that is shared by two or more people. That's all it is."

Luna here was ironically describing the conspiratorial relationship he shared with Steve Skinner, and their conspiracy to keep secret the government's surprising handling of Warren Grace.

Using, of all things, the local newspaper as an example, Luna next launches into a curious explanation of the nature of conspiracies. From his table he picks up a copy of the Baltimore Sun.

"One of the ways that I have dealt with explaining to jurors the notion of conspiracies is to talk about a very common sort of item, if you will, that we deal with almost on a regular basis, and that's a newspaper. And when I use this newspaper, I want you to suspend reality for a moment and just imagine that newspapers, let's take this newspaper, the Baltimore Sun, is illegal."

Luna has to worry that the local paper will expose *his* conspiracy. In his mind, he projects a scenario involving the newspaper in conspiracy. The newspaper, he imagines, should be illegal.

"Imagine that to possess the Baltimore Sun and to produce it and to distribute it was a crime," Luna posits. "And then I want you to imagine that, if that were the case, imagine the number of people who would be part of the conspiracy to distribute and produce and possess newspapers.

"I would submit to you, ladies and gentlemen, it would be an infinite number of persons, beginning with the usual suspects, such as the editor of the Baltimore Sun. He or she — I don't know if it's a he or she — is the person responsible for the editorial content of the paper.

"The writers, they would be part of that conspiracy. Sports writers, feature writers, movie critics. The distribution network of the Baltimore Sun, the people who drive those big trucks to deliver large packs of the Baltimore Sun at the Giant, at the Safeway, they would all be guilty.

"Hecht's Department Store, and Best Buy, who place ads in the Baltimore Sun, they would be guilty. And, in fact, the teenager in your neighborhood who delivers the Baltimore Sun at your doorstep every morning before taking off for school, he would be guilty.

"Now, consider that agreement between the people who put together the Baltimore Sun. Consider a moment and ask yourselves does the editor of the Baltimore Sun, does he know the name of the teenager who delivers the Baltimore Sun in your neighborhood?

"Does the paper company in Canada that supplies the paper stock to produce the Baltimore Sun, do they necessarily know all the names or even one name of the sports writers that work for the Baltimore Sun?

"I would suggest to you that they do not, and would not. But, nevertheless, they would all be part of the same conspiracy, the same agreement, the same understanding. Sharing the same common goal to produce and distribute the Baltimore Sun."

Spooky, isn't it?

"Now, with that in mind," Luna continues, standing before the jury, "let's talk about this case, which doesn't involve the Baltimore Sun or newspapers. It involves, as Judges Quarles says, a very serious matter: narcotics.

"The evidence will show, ladies and gentlemen, that these two defendants had an agreement, had an understanding between themselves and other people, to distribute drugs in Baltimore city."

Luna explains, "You are going to learn that this conspiracy, Mr. Poindexter and Mr. Smith, they each had their specific roles.... Mr. Poindexter, who was previously heading this heroin shop, is no longer on the streets. The evidence will show that the framework of this conspiracy that was set up by Walter Poindexter was still in place and it was taken by the horns of Warren Grace, who you are going to meet during the course of this trial.

"Warren Grace will tell you that he continued to operate this heroin shop, this conspiracy. Now, one more word about Mr. Poindexter's involvement in this conspiracy. Specifically, selling and distributing heroin in Baltimore city.

"The evidence is going to show that not only did Mr. Poindexter sell heroin, at least a kilogram of heroin, during the period of the conspiracy, but the evidence will also show that he committed very violent acts in carrying out this conspiracy." Luna here mentions the shootout between Poindexter and Steven Ford, aka Lump, that occurred at Lump's apartment building. Already, due to his inexperience, Luna has tied his own hands. He is bound by stipulation not to mention the murder of Alvin Jones.

"You are going to learn that part of the way they sold heroin is that they used violence and firearms and intimidation as a way to distribute that heroin. So, for example, if some junkie stole drugs, they would punish that junkie. Or, if there was a rival drug dealer who threatened their turf, they would respond with violence. Or, if there were people on the street who were, let's say, just having a domestic dispute, but they happened to be doing it right in the middle of the heroin shop, and Mr. Grace and Mr. Poindexter didn't like it, they would try to drive those people away.

"And if those people wouldn't go away, they would threaten them with firearms. And, in fact, they would shoot their firearms at those people. That, essentially, is Mr. Poindexter's role. And you are going to hear evidence about that shop, and how the heroin was distributed.

"Now, let's talk about the co-defendant, Deon Lionnel Smith," Luna continues. "What was his role in this conspiracy? The evidence will show that Mr. Smith was not a street-level dealer of heroin. In fact, I don't think there is going to be any evidence that will show that Mr. Smith actually was on a corner trying to sell heroin. But he nonetheless had a very important role. His role was that of supplier to the Poindexter heroin shop.

"In fact, the evidence will show that Deon Smith not only supplied Mr. Poindexter for his heroin operation in Baltimore city, but he also supplied heroin amounts or gram amounts of heroin to other organizations here in Baltimore and throughout Maryland. Mr. Smith, evidence will show, is a wholesaler of heroin. He is someone who supplies the heroin, and it's up to Mr. Poindexter and Mr. Grace and others to package the heroin, to market that heroin, and sell that heroin on the streets.

"Mr. Smith, I would submit to you, is like the paper supplier that might be located in Canada: has no idea how the Baltimore Sun is laid out, has no idea how many copies of the Baltimore Sun are printed every day, but is nonetheless a part of that operation because they supply the paper that goes to print and publish and distribute the Baltimore Sun. So that was Mr. Deon Smith's role, as a supplier. That's what the evidence is going to show."

Luna goes on, "Now, let me talk about what the evidence will consist of. You are going to hear from Warren Grace. In fact, you will probably hear from him later this afternoon. Mr. Grace will come in here and testify that he distributed heroin with Mr. Poindexter and Mr. Smith during the period in question. You are going to learn a lot of things about Mr. Grace. Quite frankly, you are going to learn a lot of things about him that will disturb you.

"You are going to learn that Warren Grace is essentially a career criminal, and has spent the majority of his adult life in and out of prisons. You are going to learn that Mr. Grace has virtually never been gainfully employed other than through illegal activity, specifically, selling heroin." Luna here does not bother to mention that there is reason to suspect that Grace was selling heroin while he was being paid by the FBI and the Justice Department.

"He is going to come into this courtroom, and he is going to testify about the things that he did," Luna does bother to warn. "A lot of those things are going to be disturbing things. Things like shooting at people. Like beating people up. Like threatening people. Like selling heroin to addicts here in Baltimore city."

Luna tells the jury that Grace has signed a plea agreement, "and that agreement provides for him to testify and to have done other things in connection with this criminal investigation." Yet Luna doesn't mention that Grace has repeatedly violated the terms of his agreement, by selling heroin, using guns, and defeating his home detention.

"Now, one of the things that I am sure my colleagues on the defense side will not hesitate to point out is Mr. Grace is a criminal. How can you trust him? He is just trying to help himself out. You shouldn't believe him.

"Well, you know what? The government agrees with that notion. Particularly the FBI."

Luna tells the jury that the FBI, when working with informants like Grace, conducts "a process of verification and corroboration, and you are going to learn that process when Special Agent Skinner testifies. He is going to talk about handling cooperators like Mr. Grace."

You bet he is.

Not.

Luna concludes his opening statement by mentioning the many, *many* tapes (approximately eighty), and transcripts, recorded by the FBI with the help of Warren Grace. "I'm going to ask for your patience when we play the tapes. We are going to play the tapes through (the testimony of) Warren Grace." The problem was, there were lots of tapes. *Lots.* You'd have thought the FBI was documenting a foreign attack, like the bombing of Pearl Harbor, while they let the Dawsons' house burn, and not the hip-hop antics of double-naught informant Warren Grace.

"Mr. Grace will be the first witness in this case," Luna continues. "I also want you to keep in mind that him coming to court will not be an easy thing, because the evidence will show that Mr. Grace had a close personal relationship with both of the defendants, including Walter Poindexter."

The unreliability of Warren Grace is Luna's big problem. As he will continue to do throughout the trial, Luna slyly begins to describe Grace as if Grace is the *jury's* problem, everyone's problem but his, and that he's sympathetic to their plight. You'll soon notice that this is how, time and again, Luna imagines he covers his ass. He's a clever young lawyer, with less than three days to live. Someone, whose ass Luna didn't bother to cover, soon wants him dead.

Luna continues, "The evidence will show that, when Mr. Grace was in prison, Mr. Poindexter visited him, sent him money, corresponded with him, spoke to him on the telephone and, in fact, when Mr. Grace was released from prison in early December of 2000, he went to live with Mr. Poindexter.

"And he joined Walter Poindexter's heroin operation. That's what the evidence will show, ladies and gentlemen." He concludes, "I would suggest to you, ladies and gentlemen, that at the end of the government's case, the evidence will be overwhelming that Mr. Smith and Mr. Poindexter conspired with each other to distribute at least one kilogram of heroin in Baltimore City during the period in question. Thank you for your patience."

Luna sits. Poindexter's attorney, Arcangelo Tuminelli, rises for his opening statement.

"Why do we have the opportunity to stand up here and talk to you?" Tuminelli asks the jury. "Well, the reason is we have some idea, Mr. Luna, Ms. Cockburn, Mr. Ravenell, and I, as to what's going to happen in this courtroom in terms of evidence, and how the evidence will flow." Tuminelli, blindsided by Luna, is in for a rude awakening. "And the reason we have that opportunity is because they, on their side, the government, have had an opportunity to speak to their agent, Special Agent Skinner, review the reports that he prepared, and other law enforcement officers prepared, but they also have to give those reports to Mr. Ravenell and to me as attorneys for Mr. Poindexter in my case and Mr. Smith in Mr. Ravenell's case."

Tuminelli promises he has "some idea of what is going to develop in this courtroom in terms of what the witnesses will say."

He should guess again. In reality, both defendants and their counsel have been deceived. They cannot guess what is about to happen.

Preliminaries aside, Tuminelli first turns to the subject of, as he says, "Warren Grace. The reason Walter Poindexter is here is Warren Grace. Now, Mr. Grace, as Mr. Luna told you, is a drug dealer, and he has been a drug dealer. He has been convicted of selling drugs on at least two occasions before."

"Unfortunately for Mr. Poindexter," Tuminelli continues, "Mr. Grace is an old acquaintance, and what Mr. Poindexter thought was an old and good friend."

"Now, on April 7, 2002, what occurred was Mr. Grace was sitting in a house on Fairview Avenue, over in northwest Baltimore, and the police came rushing in, because they had a search warrant — a judge had authorized them to go in and search — and what they found in that house was heroin. They found packaging material to package the heroin for street sales. They found a scale. They found other types of paraphernalia, and they found a .38 caliber pistol and something called an Intertech nine-millimeter semi-automatic weapon, the type of gun that permits the shooter to spray bullets."

"Now Mr. Grace has a big problem. A real serious problem. ...Two prior convictions.... It became apparent to Mr. Grace he had a very serious problem. And how serious was it? Well, he is what's called in the federal system a career offender, which means that he likely would have received a sentence somewhere between 30 years to life, if he didn't do something, and that 30 years is without parole. So that meant Mr. Grace, if he didn't come up with some solution to his problem, was never going to see the streets until he was an old, old man, if at all.

"And so what did he do? Well, he thought about it for a while and he started talking to the Baltimore city police and he eventually spoke to Special Agent Skinner from the FBI and said, Look, you know, I've got some information, fellows. Let me tell you what I can do for you but, you know, you guys have to do something for me."

Tuminelli lucidly sums up the priorities of Warren Grace: "Mr. Grace was of that school who thinks the more I give them, the more they are going to give me."

Looking out for Numero Uno.

Poindexter, Tuminelli says, was merely selling drug paraphernalia, not heroin. "It was Pug, Warren Grace, that was running the heroin operation in 2000."

"Again, Mr. Grace is from that school (who thinks) the more I do for you, the more you are going to do for me."

"He says — and it's a clever idea, a brilliant idea — Mr. Grace knows he was running something called the 911 drug operation on Buford Avenue and Garrison Boulevard, and how easy it is for Mr.

Grace to say well, you know what, my supplier for that heroin was Walter Poindexter."

"He thought that that would fly," Tuminelli goes on, "because Walter, you are going to hear, worked in a business called Stash House Records. And what they did at Stash House Records is they — it was a recording studio for rap singers, or rappers, but the problem with that business, and for Mr. Poindexter, (is) that he didn't make much money at it. A lot of flash. Little money.

"So what did Walter do? Well, Walter, on the streets of Baltimore, is what's called a hustler. Walter was always looking to hustle to make some money. And here is how he made money, ladies and gentlemen: he sold paraphernalia. He sold cutting agents, dilutents for cutting heroin, for cutting cocaine. He sold implements." Poindexter did not sell drugs, Tuminelli told the jury. "Unfortunately for Walter Poindexter, the truth is that people who sell drug paraphernalia associate with drug dealers. Yes, he associated with Warren Grace. Yes, he associated with other drug dealers, because that's what people who sell paraphernalia to drug dealers do."

Not exactly the best defense in the world, but Poindexter was sticking to it.

Next, Deon Smith's attorney, Kenneth Ravenell, stood. In his opening statement, Ravenell wasted no words ripping into Warren Grace.

"You heard about Mr. Grace," Ravenell tells the jury. "I will tell you a few things about him. He is a liar. He is deceitful. He is a violent individual. He is a man who would do anything he can to get what he wants. It doesn't matter who he hurts, what it takes to get there, as long as Warren Grace satisfies Warren Grace. That's the kind of person he is." Sounds like Grace could have been a Maryland politician.

"So Mr. Grace," Ravenell continues, "the unscrupulous individual that he is, thought that he could snare Mr. Smith in his way, and that Mr. Smith would become one other person that he could bring down along the way of getting a reduction in his sentence and saving himself a long jail sentence."

"My client certainly grew up in the neighborhoods of Baltimore city," Ravenell tells the jury about Deon Smith. "Back in 1994 he, in fact, strayed into criminal activity and was convicted.... And while he strayed into criminal activity, he also did some very positive things when he was released from prison. Many people around him in his neighborhood got involved in criminal activity as well, but later on my client realized, and those around him realized, that he had talent, a talent that had nothing to do with illegal activity, nothing to do with drug dealing.

"As it turns out, and it was recognized by many around him, he was a very good lyricist, (a) very good rap artist. In fact, not only did those around him, those friends and family members recognize it, but people in the music industry did. Sony Records, Def Jam Records, they all recognized this man had talent. And they came to him, looking to sign him.

"You will hear that my client, though, had a vision. He wanted to become and wanted to stay independent. He wanted to found his own company. In fact, with some legitimate friends, he founded a company called Stash House Records. You will find that he surrounded himself (with) positive young men in the community who were working hard jobs, at the same time trying to get the company off the ground."

"Now, the young men around him, they were working towards producing their first CD. They had put out some music, and all of those were singles. In fact, those musics were being played on the local radio, we will be talking about that in this trial as well, so they were on their way. But they wanted to get their first CD out. It was entitled Gumbo. You will hear some comments about that. They had eighteen songs they were going to produce on this first CD. And, if that CD had made it, it would have put them on the map and they thought they were going to take off from that.

"So there was a lot of time and effort being put into that music industry by Mr. Smith and those around him.

"Now, while Mr. Smith surrounded himself with these positive young men I told you about, one of the things that happened to a lot of men like Mr. Smith, people in the record industry, music industry, and people in sports, often, they get the tagalongs, people from the neighborhood who are still around them. They don't cut their ties, they don't sever those ties, because they think it's important not to forget those whom they knew when they were coming along, that you shouldn't leave anyone behind.

"Well, that is one of the reasons Mr. Smith sits here today. Because he does not know how to cut his ties with those in the community. Now, while he, Mr. Smith, got away from illegal activity, some of those in the neighborhood did not. People that he knew from his past did not get away from illegal activity.

"And one of those persons you heard about was this person, Warren Grace. Not to belabor Mr. Grace, because Mr. Tuminelli has already told you about Mr. Grace, and Mr. Luna himself did. I guess Mr. Luna didn't have much choice to tell you how this person is because if he didn't tell you we would have produced evidence about what kind of person Mr. Grace is. So sometimes it's called the 'preemptive strike.'

"He wanted to tell you about how bad Mr. Grace is and what kind of person he is. Because, smart move. But it doesn't change the kind of person Mr. Grace is that you are going to hear about."

7
Judge complains about Grace's control of prosecution

The opening statements out of the way, Judge William Quarles asks Jonathan Luna, "Who is your first witness, Mr. Luna?"

"I'm sorry?" Luna stumbles. Already, Luna appeared unusually distracted.

"Your first witness."

"Oh, Warren Grace, your honor," Luna says.

"Where is he?" Quarles asks.

"He is right next door. Shall we get him?"

"Yes. Get him."

Baltimore Detective Todd Moody, of the "Safe Streets Task Force," brings Pug into the courtroom.

The jury, meanwhile, having enjoyed a recess, is led back in. Some of the jurors remain standing, waiting for the lawyers to sit. "Please be seated," Quarles tells the jury. He feels obligated to initiate the jurors in some of the courtroom pomposity. "Ladies and gentlemen, you have noticed when you come in, that the lawyers stand for you. That's because, at one point in this trial, you will actually become judges. You will be the judges of the facts of this case, so they accord you the customary courtesy that's shown a judge. That is why they stand when you come in. So don't wait for them to be seated. They are waiting for you to be seated.

"Mr. Luna," Quarles continues, "please call your first witness."

"Yes, your honor. At this time, the United States calls Warren Grace."

Grace, fresh from yesterday's secret, FBI-sponsored pipe-cleaning visit home to his wife, saunters up to the witness stand and, all the while casually chewing gum, raises his hand, and is sworn in.

"Please speak directly into that microphone," the clerk asks him.

"State your name for the record."

"Warren Grace." He speaks quietly, looking away.

Judge Quarles asks the clerk, "Would you give Mr. Grace a sheet of paper, perhaps, for his gum?"

Pug, having already sized up Judge Quarles, lets everyone know who is boss of Pug.

"I swallowed it," Pug says.

"You swallowed it?" the clerk asks.

"Okay, very good sir," Judge Quarles tells him. "If you will talk directly into the microphone. Try to keep your voice up as loud as you can."

Luna begins questioning Grace. Like a lion tamer, cracking his whip of terrible inducements, Luna acts to show the courtroom, and Pug, who's boss. He straightaway asks Grace to summarize his previous two convictions. "What were the charges for?"

"Gun and drug charge. Gun possession and heroin distribution," Grace replies.

Luna holds up a document and introduces it into evidence. It's Grace's plea agreement with the government. He hands it to Pug. He walks Pug through a discourse they've already rehearsed in one of their many pre-trial meetings in the Philadelphia detention facility.

"Do you recognize that document?"

"Yes."

"What is that document, Mr. Grace?"

"A plea agreement."

"What is your understanding, Mr. Grace, of the terms of that plea agreement?"

"I am supposed to work with the government and cooperate with the agents over there," Pug nods at the task force members seated in the courtroom. "You know, and just follow the terms of the agreement." Luna tells him to read aloud the wording of the agreement.

Pug reads, "To testify truthfully and follow the rules pursuant to this plea agreement and work with the agents and government in disclosing any information I know about anything, any crimes that have been committed, and so forth."

"Now, have you pled guilty in federal court?" Luna asks.

"Yes."

"Is it fair to say you are awaiting a sentence in federal court?"

"Yes."

"What parties are bound by this agreement?"

"I am."

"Is the government bound by it?"

"Yes."

"What about the court?" Luna asks. "What is your understanding as to the court's involvement in this plea agreement?"

Pug mumbles.

"Can't hear you, sir," Judge Quarles says.

The court, Grace says in clipped sentences, is, "Supposed to take my cooperation in consideration, in working with the officers, or the agents."

"Have you been made any specific promises, Mr. Grace, about what your sentence will be?"

"No."

"What is your understanding as to the maximum possible prison sentence for the gun charge?" Luna asks.

"The maximum sentence is a ten-year sentence for the gun charge."

"What is your understanding as to the maximum for the narcotics charge?"

"The narcotics charge is a twenty-year max."

"Is there anything in this agreement, Exhibit Number One, that says you won't get the maximum."

"No."

"What is your understanding in terms of your obligation to avoid the maximum sentence in this case?"

"The only obligation I have is to testify truthfully," Grace replies. "Nothing was ever promised."

"In exchange for testifying truthfully, what is your understanding of what the government will do for you?"

"The government, if I testify truthfully, the government will make a motion for a downward departure, and it's still up to Judge Quarles to, you know, take into consideration my cooperation and give me a reduction."

"So it is your understanding that Judge Quarles does not have to accept that recommendation?"

"Correct."

"What's your understanding about what would happen if you violated the terms of this agreement?" Luna goes on to ask.

"That it would be over. I mean, if I violated the terms, then it's just done."

"Who is going to make the determination whether or not the plea agreement has been violated?" Luna asks.

"The government," Pug says. He knows, however, that he has time and again violated the agreement, and the government has only sunk deeper into scandal.

The whip snapping out of the way, Luna tries to have Pug describe his dealings with Walter Poindexter and Deon Smith, and the inner-workings of the "911" heroin shop. Grace, for the most part, when he isn't mumbling, gives short, monosyllable replies.

"Do you see Mr. Poindexter here in court?" Luna asks.

"Yes," Pug replies.

"Would you point him out for the court and jury and for the record?"

Pug points at Shorty. Their eyes meet.

"Is that the person in the pink shirt?"

"Yes."

"How do you know Mr. Poindexter?"

"How do I know him?"

"Yes. When did you first meet Mr. Poindexter?" Luna asks.

"I met him beginning in '94, you know, on the strip, on the street corner. He was walking by, and it was his dog, and we exchanged numbers and just went from there."

"You mentioned a dog. What was that about a dog?"

"You know, he was just walking down the street with his dog."

"And what were you doing?"

"I was hustling."

"When you say hustling, what were you doing?"

"I was selling drugs."

"What kind of drugs were you selling?"

"Cocaine."

Luna has Pug describe how he began getting heroin from Poindexter. But their first business venture, Grace explains, was cut short by his arrest. After hustling with Poindexter only "just a couple months," Grace was sent away to state prison in Hagerstown, Maryland.

How long was Grace imprisoned at Hagerstown in the late 1990s? Luna asks.

"Four years and nine months."

"During that time, did you have any contact of any kind with Walter Poindexter?"

"Yes."

"Can you describe that contact?"

"I would call him and he would come see me occasionally, and send money, something like that." Pug quietly says he would call Poindexter, and Shorty would always be there for him.

"How many times did Mr. Poindexter visit you while you were in prison, approximately?" Luna asks.

"Probably once or twice, every other month, or something like that," Pug mumbles.

"So during a four-year period, Mr. Poindexter visited you about once or twice a month?"

"Yes, around there," Pug says. Luna needs to establish Grace's history with Poindexter, but this line of questioning only makes Pug feel all the more like he's betraying the only man who ever cared for him.

"Yes, around there," Pug says quietly.

"I need you to speak up as loudly as you can, Mr. Grace," Luna tells him. "All right. What was the money for that Mr. Poindexter sent you?"

"For commissary, and stuff like that."

"What's a commissary?" Luna asks. Like any good lawyer, he already knows the answer before he asks the question.

"It's like you can buy food in the prison or stuff like that," Grace answers. Now, with Poindexter gone, Skinner and company took over this role and began giving "considerations" for Pug's cooperation.

Did anyone else ever visit Grace in prison at Hagerstown? Luna asks.

"No," Pug replies, guiltily.

"Anytime during the four-year period?"

"No. My grandfather used to come up there."

"Other than your grandfather, anyone else?"

"No."

Attorney Ravenell breaks this questioning. He asks to speak to the judge at the bench. He sees Baltimore detective Moody sitting in the courtroom, listening to Grace's testimony, despite the judge having ruled all witnesses out of the courtroom, so testimony wouldn't be tainted. This would be the first of many curious breaks in the trial caused by members of the "Safe Streets Task Force." In real life, they were unreachable; at this trial, they hovered thick as flies around the stink pile that was Warren Grace.

"Your honor, may counsel approach?" Ravenell asks.

"Yes. Please come up," Judge Quarles says.

The other lawyers joined Ravenell at the bench.

"Did your honor invoke the rule on witnesses?" Ravenell asks.

"Yes."

"Why is Moody in the courtroom?"

Luna injects, "We will get him out."

"As I told you before, you know the witnesses," Judge Quarles scolds Luna. "I don't. I have to rely on you for enforcement."

Quarles checks to ensure that the jury can't hear this exchange.

"Can you all hear these conferences?" Quarles asks the jury.

"No, we are fine now," a juror tells him.

"Okay," says Quarles.

"The reason why," Luna explains, "(is) Detective Moody brought Mr. Grace into the courtroom. Because Mr. Grace is currently in his custody. What I will do is I will alert the (court's officers) that Detective Moody is going to leave the courtroom."

"Okay, thank you," Judge Quarles agrees. "Thank you."

Luna proceeds with his questioning. Grace testifies, little by little, about setting up the heroin shop with Poindexter. Luna has trouble extracting the story. It's like pulling teeth, with Grace often offering the barest of replies. The going gets slow, proceeding, Luna would say, "in baby steps." At last Luna asks about Deon Smith's recording studio, and whether Pug was present one day when Poindexter claimed he got heroin from Smith.

"Did you even know that Mr. Poindexter was going to get heroin on this particular day?" Luna suddenly and amateurishly asks.

Ravenell objects, and the lawyers again go to the bench to conference with the judge, out of earshot of the jury.

"There has been no evidence from the testimony of the witness that Mr. Smith gave Mr. Poindexter heroin," Ravenell says. "So to phrase that question, 'Did you know that he was getting heroin from Mr. Smith?' there is no such evidence. So I think the phraseology of the question is inappropriate, judge."

Luna already is in trouble. The defense attorneys are sharp, and Grace isn't cooperating.

Judge Quarles says, "Okay. I will overrule the objection and give Mr. Luna the evening to work with his witness and get him to be a little more pointed and answer a little more briskly than he is doing now." Quarles now gives Luna a law lesson, one of many to come. "I will caution Mr. Luna against the use of questions that contain in themselves factual predicates such as the source of the drugs that have not been established," Quarles says. "I am advising Mr. Luna that I will expect a more pointed direct (examination) tomorrow, and that I will also expect that his questions will not jump the gun and contain facts that have not been established."

"Your honor, if I may just say for the record," Luna responds, "the government understands fully what the court is saying. I will say that I am at a point with the cooperator — with this witness — where I have to go in baby steps."

"Well, I don't mind the baby steps," Quarles says. "What I do hope is that eventually we arrive at some location."

"Yes, your honor," Luna says.

"Do it as expeditiously as possible," Quarles says. Quarles now makes the cutting observation that *Warren Grace,* not Luna, appears to be in charge of the questioning. The judge instructs young Mr. Luna how to do his job. "We have a process we used to call horse shedding the witness," Quarles tells Luna. "Spelled for the record H-

O-R-S-E S-H-E-D-D-I-N-G, in the event that my diction is not sufficiently clear. But a hundred years ago, when I was an (assistant U.S.) attorney, I made it clear to witnesses that, you know, there was one person who was in control. *It wasn't the witness, it was the direct examiner.*" (Emphasis mine.)

Quarles now subtly suggests that Luna should threaten Warren Grace to be more cooperative. Quarles says, "And also, by revisiting with that witness his incentives to be cooperative and to recognize one authority in the court — and that is the examiner — and focusing the witness on how much better his life would be if he acknowledged the examiner. That worked wonders with witnesses who had attitudes or who were recalcitrant, didn't want to be there, or didn't particularly like me. It was helpful in focusing them on the job at hand, which was the expeditious presentation of the case. So you might wish to have a counseling session with the witness, if he is being forthcoming with you. So let me urge you to take control of your witness and urge you also to focus and take control of your examination, so that we don't put the carts before the various horse."

"Absolutely," Luna says.

"A little more discipline, perhaps, Mr. Luna," Quarles tells him.

"I understand, your honor," Luna says, "but I have to work with what I have."

"I understand. Thank you."

"Thank you," Luna tells him.

"Step back, please," the judge tells the lawyers.

With that, Judge Quarles adjourns the first day of court and sends the jury home for the evening. Always a stickler for time, Quarles tells the jurors, "I would ask you to be in your jury room tomorrow at 9:25. That will permit me to get started at 9:30. As I said, we will be respectful of your time. Let me thank you for your promptness today and for your attention today."

As the jury files out Quarles asks, "Is there someone here to accompany Mr. Grace?"

"Yes, there is," Luna says. "Detective Moody is here."

Grace thereupon leaves the courtroom with Moody.

8
Judge upbraids Luna for improvisational law practice

At the bench, at the close of the first day of trial, the defense lawyers bring up two matters requiring Judge Quarles attention.

The first issue is the most explosive. Attorney Kenneth Ravenell tells Judge Quarles that he has been informed by Barbara Skidmore, a senior Pretrial Services official, that there were many violations in the government's handling of Warren Grace. Pretrial Services, Skidmore told the lawyer, had prepared a detailed report of the violations to send to the judge.

Ravenell must proceed carefully. He knows that Grace has violated his terms of release. If Grace is untrustworthy (and he is), it would certainly serve to undermine the government's case against Walter Poindexter and Deon Smith. Yet he has to fear the judge might disallow any inquiry. An experienced lawyer, Ravenell skillfully stays on Quarles' good side.

A May 2001 newsletter of the Maryland public defender's office details Skidmore's rise up the ranks of Pretrial Services. "Bill Henry has assumed responsibility as Joint Chief of Pretrial Service and Probation," the newsletter relates. "Bill recently selected Barbara Skidmore to serve as the new Deputy Chief of the Pretrial Services Office. Barbara is a talented public servant who has dedicated her entire federal career to the Pretrial Services Office. The district's Pretrial Services Office has been one of the most creative and aggressive in the nation in exploring alternatives to pretrial detention. Barbara's promotion should insure (sic) that pretrial maintains and builds upon its deserved position as a leader in exploring and utilizing alternatives to pretrial detention."

Now defense attorneys are on the cusp of discovering just how "creative" Pretrial Services can be in "exploring alternatives" in the case of Warren Grace. They creatively sat back while Grace ran loose, slipped off his home detention anklet, shot up his neighborhood and, on the very day the Dawson family was obliterated, stashed heroin under the noses of the FBI.

Having been informed by Skidmore of unknown irregularities in Grace's handling, Ravenell tells the judge he now contemplates sending a subpoena to the officer once supposedly in charge of Warren Grace, Pretrial Services' Todd Stokes. He hopes to question Stokes under oath about Grace's excellent misadventure with the FBI. Ravenell is about to hit pay dirt. He is also about to create a career-threatening development for Jonathan Luna and his co-conspirators in the FBI "Safe Streets Task Force." At this very time, in early December 2003, the nation's press is heralding *several* congressional investigations into the FBI's criminal mishandling of informants.

Quarles grants an ex parte, or private, conference with Ravenell, out of earshot of Luna, but in the presence of the court reporter.

"Mr. Ravenell, if you would approach an *ex parte* matter in this case," Quarles tells Smith's lawyer, "I will make it a matter of record."

"According to Barbara Skidmore," Ravenell tells Quarles, referring to the Pretrial Services administrator, "she wrote you a letter—."

"Yes, she did," Quarles allows.

"Obviously, I wanted to—," Ravenell treads carefully, "I don't know what she wrote you, but I wanted to get a subpoena to Todd Stokes."

Judge Quarles cautions the lawyer about recent changes in federal court rules of evidence which, he says, "appears to prohibit" any attack on Grace's character. "I don't know whether that's what you are attempting to do," Quarles tells Ravenell, "but ... you would certainly be able to question him about violations, which I assume is where you are going?"

Ravenell explains he has no way of knowing about the extent of violations in Grace's handling. Luna has not provided the defense with *any* information.

"The problem is, judge, I don't have the violation report," Ravenell says.

"I will have a summary for you, so that you can question the witness," Quarles agrees. "I will direct them to prepare a summary for you."

This conference was conducted out of earshot of Luna, Special Agent Steven Skinner and Detective Todd Moody.

"Can I get that today, judge?" Ravenell asks. "Because I would question the witness, I would guess, tomorrow."

"If I can't get it today," Quarles says, "I will give you a break before you actually use it."

"Okay. So I will have that summary, and I spoke to Ms. Skidmore about that. She said there was a detailed report that she was going to forward to the court."

"I read that," Quarles admits, "and what I will probably end up doing is just directing one of them to sit with you and summarize the report."

"Summarize it, but first let me read the entire report?" Here we see why Kenneth Ravenell is such a good defense attorney. He doesn't give an inch, yet he plays the judge so delicately.

"I assume you are looking for lack of compliance with pre-trial direction?" Quarles asks.

"Yes."

"I think I can get you—," Quarles begins, "I hope I can get you sufficient material without actually requiring the report to be turned over."

This ex parte discussion ended, Judge Quarles now moves to a second pressing matter. Luna and Ravenell disagree over the admissibility of transcripts of the many hours of audio and videotapes produced by the FBI in its surveillance of Smith and Poindexter.

The FBI in fact had produced a ludicrous amount of tape-recorded evidence, nearly *one hundred hours* of tape recordings in the matter of Stash House Records. Often muffled and hard to understand, these recordings had been transcribed to help the jury understand the words. For weeks, Attorney Ravenell had quibbled with Luna about which of these transcripts were admissible or even relevant.

Judge Quarles had expected Luna to provide a detailed response to defense objections to the proposed transcripts the previous Friday, so Quarles could study and possibly resolve any outstanding issues over the weekend, before the start of trial. But Luna had not filed his response, and now the judge was growing impatient and suspected Luna, in Quarles' words, of "stonewalling."

"I assume you are going to at some point want to play certain conversations," Quarles asks.

"Correct," Luna replies.

"And you will want the jury to read along with the transcripts?" the judge asks.

"That is correct," Luna says.

"Okay, if it is all possible, I would like you to discuss any objections that he has with the transcripts, and see if they can be resolved," Quarles tells Luna. "If they cannot be resolved, I will resolve them."

"I hope I would be right that the court would try to work with the government in terms of getting a final product to the jury," Luna says.

Judge Quarles loses his patience. "Well, see," he lashes out, "one of the problems when you all approach the case in preparation the way you have, which is basically spent a lot of time stonewalling on the transcripts, getting them late, and then getting to me a late representation dated this morning as to the progress of your negotiations with defense attorneys, you put me in the position of having to slow the trial for this. So this is something that I asked you all to work on as soon as possible, looking to get working material over the weekend. I got from you this morning material telling me that you thought you had resolved matters, but there still may be matters unresolved. I lost the weekend for preparation in this matter. Now, if you are asking me to advise you, my advice is that you all get yourselves together and try to resolve it, or I will have to resolve it, and that will take some time away from the jury. I can't create time. I can't go back and re-acquire the weekend that I anticipated having this material when it wasn't available for me to review."

Judge Quarles testily suggested they go through the transcripts that very moment. "If you want to waste a couple hours of my time, I would be delighted to sit here and do it," Quarles tells the lawyers. "Let's pull out the transcripts. Ready, folks?"

"I don't want to do that, your honor," Luna tells Quarles.

"I said I wouldn't be happy about it but I will do that, if it saves wasting the jury's time," Quarles replies. With Quarles, it was all about the jury's precious time.

Ravenell suggests, "I have Mr. Luna's home number. He has mine. We will work tonight to come back with you.... We will work it out."

"I can sit here," Quarles says. "I am willing to work through them, and then I will know at the end of the evening that we have what will go to the jury."

"I don't think that's helpful to the court or to us, to try to go through it this way," Ravenell counters. "I think it would make much more sense, as suggested earlier, for us to try to resolve it among ourselves."

"Yes," Quarles tells Ravenell. "I thought I got your piece in time for the weekend. I didn't get the government's response and, as I said, I lost the weekend. So I can sit here and do it."

Ravenell suggests to the judge, "If you eliminate some of the transcripts ... that I was objecting to, there will be less for us to discuss."

"Okay," Quarles says. "Defendant's Objections to Government's Transcripts.... Transcript Number 6. Smith sales of bricks."

Now, another problem. The judge doesn't have the latest draft of the transcripts. "Your honor," Luna tells him, "I think it would assist you to have a copy of this latest draft. I am not quite sure what you have."

"That's not really going to be helpful when his objections are on the earlier draft," Quarles responds, exasperated. "It would add another element of confusion to the spectacle."

At last they begin reading aloud from the transcripts. It makes for a droll exchange in the courtroom. Ravenell reads aloud for the judge a section of the transcripts where Deon Smith is recorded as saying, *"'I've done sold bricks and bricks of mother fucking blow.'"* (Blow, meaning heroin.) Ravenell objects to this, he says, because "There is no time reference at all as to when Mr. Smith allegedly sold bricks and bricks of blow."

"Yes. I think that works against you," Judge Quarles observes.

"Well, I disagree," Ravenell says, "but you get to make the call."

"The call is it works against you," Quarles rules, "and the objection is overruled."

Now Quarles has another bone to pick with Luna. He can't find a response to Ravenell's next objection to a tape made on July 17, 2002, or "7/17." The tape includes advice that Deon Smith gave to Poindexter: *"Do you know what I am saying and what I am trying to tell you,"* the transcript reads in part. *"Stop trying to live above your means."* This advice, eerily, could perhaps as well have been directed at Luna.

Ravenell objected, writing the tape wasn't relevant, and that it was unknown when the advice was given. In reply, Luna simply filed a generic, two-and-a-half page legal argument in general support of his transcripts, curiously not addressing the specific objections. Was Luna in a pinch for time? Was he merely being sloppy? Didn't he care? Or, as with other striking omissions in this case, was he covering-up?

"I can't find the specific response to that objection," Judge Quarles tells Luna. "Would you direct me to it, Mr. Luna?"

"I don't have a specific—."

"There must have been one," Quarles snaps back, "because you just told me how easy it would have been for me to use your response to his objections, so you must have had a specific response to it. Where is it, Mr. Luna?"

"My response to the court was that the legal argument that I referenced in that letter—," Luna begins.

"Which part, sir?" Quarles cuts him off. Luna's improvisational waffling was now outright confusing and angering the judge, something you don't want to do. Quarles asks, "Direct me to it. It's only two-and-a-half pages. Let's see if you can tell me what part of the two-and-a-half pages you want me to read in response to his objection, Mr. Luna."

"Your honor," Luna replies, "there is no specific objection response in that letter."

"There must have been. You just told me that there was. Now you are telling me that there wasn't. You are telling me there was a response generally and now you are telling me there is not a response," Quarles snaps. "Which is it? Is there a response in the letter?"

"There is not a response in that letter," Luna says.

"But just ten seconds ago you told me there was a response, that it was a general response," Quarles snaps.

"I did not put it in the letter," Luna finally acknowledges. Luna now does something that he will attempt to do throughout the trial:

run the case off the top of his head, improvisationally, leaving little or no paper trail. "I will explain to you the government's position as to Mr. Ravenell's objection to the 7/17 (transcript). I will be glad to do that right now."

Quarles has had enough with Luna's improv legal soliloquies.

"I know it's easier to sort of shoot off the top of your head when someone has gone to the trouble of highlighting a transcript, and raising specific objections," Quarles lashes out in a fascinating description of Luna. "I know it's easy to do this, what you call a response to it, which gives me nothing but a general boilerplate.... And now you wish to take further time as you stand there on your feet and try to come up with a response to it. You wish to waste more of my time and do that throughout, in that sort of festival style, throughout the rest of the evening, you gazing off into the middle distance and thinking of reasons why you object to or respond to his objection, reasons that have not been put in, as you represented to me, were not put in a response. You represented to me that there was a government response to the objections. I failed to find, at least as to the relevancy objection, a response."

"I understand, your honor," Luna tells him.

"So, no, I don't want to hear your oral response to it," Quarles says. "As the government is not responding to it, I then assume that the government concedes it. Accordingly, your objection is sustained."

Luna sees he now must worry that the judge will go on a rampage and discard, wholesale, crucial evidence.

"Your honor," Luna says, "the government does not concede it."

"You must concede it," Quarles baits him. "You can't point to me where you opposed it. I look in your response and don't see one, so you must have. You certainly did not intend to stand there at this time and go off the top of your head, ad-libbing a response. You certainly couldn't have meant that, Mr. Luna."

"Well, your honor—," Luna stutters.

"When I was in the U.S. Attorney's office, when I started 21 years ago in that office," Quarles upbraids Luna, "that wasn't how we did things. Has the U.S. Attorney adopted — Mr. DiBiagio adopted — some new approach to trials that require my discussion with him?"

Quarles unwittingly is not far off mark. Luna certainly doesn't want Judge Quarles talking to DiBiagio. That's the last thing he wants. The judge does not understand, nor even realize, that Luna has been told that DiBiagio wants him "gone." Luna's hired a lawyer to help keep his job. A judge going to DiBiagio with complaints about Luna's performance would certainly be used against Luna by DiBiagio in the pending litigation for which Luna has retained a lawyer.

Luna must, all the while, protect his boss, U.S. Attorney DiBiagio, from the fallout of the "atomic blast" of the Dawson family fiasco, and other scandals brought on the Justice Department by its double-naught paid informant, Warren Grace.

"As far as I know, no," Luna replies.

"Or some new approach to trial preparation that I should discuss with him?" Quarles ventures on. Warmer, warmer, Judge Quarles is getting warmer. This novel method of cover-up — hip-hop mean, improvisational, and paper-trailless legal practice — will be Luna's lasting contribution to his profession. Quarles didn't grasp that he was watching Jonathan dance and spin, breakdancing right out of this world. "Or some new approach to responding to objections to transcripts that I should discuss with him?"

"Your honor, I would like the opportunity—," Luna pipes, alto contrario.

"Is there some other document that I am missing?" Quarles counters, basso profundo. Where, after all, *is* the paperwork for this stink of a case? Judge William Quarles, we should keep in mind, knows about the government's missteps involving Warren Grace; he has received reports from Pretrial Services. He is aware of facts the defense attorneys are only now suspecting. Quarles seems to be upbraiding Luna (and DiBiagio) for the entire conduct of this case, and seems to sense what's going on.

"No, your honor," Luna says.

"I have a document dated December 1, 2003," Quarles reads. "It is a one and one-thirds-page response or something that actually tells me that you culled down 90 to 100 hours of recording to roughly three. But that does not appear to in any sense to be a response to Mr. Ravenell's objections. I have the November 24, 2003 letter to me in which you say, 'as directed by the court, we have reviewed the transcripts of recording with Arcangelo Tuminelli and I have been able to resolve some of our differences. The court need not intervene as far as objections from Walter Poindexter. Ken Ravenell and I were able to agree on some redactions. However, there were a number of recordings where we could not agree. I believe counsels' objections surround two issues discussed below.'" Quarles looks from the letter. "And then, as I said, you were good enough to give me some boilerplate authorities, but they don't appear to respond to the effort, the serious effort that Mr. Ravenell undertook to raise specific objections to the transcript."

Quarles now hits head-on the central problem in this case. Lack of documentation.

"So am I missing a document?" he asks. "Is there something between the November 24, 2003 letter and the December 1, 2003 letter that meets these objectives in some detail?"

"You are not missing anything, your honor," Luna says.

"Well, if that is the government's response, then the government is prepared to live or die on that response," Quarles says. Words of striking irony and prescience.

"If the court wishes to rule on the individual—," Luna begins.

"What I wish for you to do is get your act together," Quarles spits at Luna. "What I wish for you to do is to do what I suggested about a half an hour ago, which is you and Mr. Ravenell sit down this evening—"

"Yes, your honor."

"—without wasting any more of my time in determining which of those things you really want to fight about," Quarles goes on. "In other words, which ones of those you want to discuss with me tomorrow and which ones you can live without. Understood, folks?"

"Yes, your honor," Luna says.

"Okay. This is just completely unacceptable, Mr. Luna," Quarles tells the younger man.

"Yes, your honor."

"This is—." Quarles begins again, then checks himself.

"Yes, your honor."

"We are adjourned," Quarles says.

As he walks from the courtroom that Monday evening, Jonathan Luna has less than sixty hours to live.

9
Second day of trial: Judge jokes about 'slapping around' the witness

At 9:30 the next morning, Judge William Quarles calls the courtroom to order. Looking over at the defense table, Quarles sees that attorney Arcangelo Tuminelli is missing. It's the second day of trial, and the second consecutive day that a lawyer has been late at the start of proceedings, violating Quarles' pet peeve for timeliness.

"Anyone seen Mr. Tuminelli this morning?" Quarles asks.

"I think he is on the way," Jonathan Luna says.

"In fact, he is walking in the door now," attorney Kenneth Ravenell volunteers.

Tuminelli comes into the courtroom and takes his place at the defense table. "Judge, I apologize," he says. "I didn't know. I was talking to the agent."

"Yes," Quarles ruffles. "We try to get started at 9:30."

"I thought we were waiting for Jonathan," Tuminelli explains. "Jonathan— and he is already in the courtroom."

Without delay, Warren Grace, under guard, is brought back into the courtroom to continue his questioning. Luna shows Grace some empty glass vials and asks, "What are those vials used for?"

"Packaging heroin," Pug says.

Luna thereupon continues questioning Grace about the heroin shop Grace ran with Walter Poindexter from December 2000 to June 2001.

Tuminelli suddenly stops the questioning.

"Your honor," Tuminelli says, "maybe this would be the appropriate time for the stipulation that we talked about."

"Ladies and gentlemen," Judge Quarles tells the jury, "you will hear the lawyers from time to time talk about a stipulation. That's a lawyer word that means an agreement between Mr. Poindexter and the government that what they are about to tell you is true, so you don't have to go back into your jury room when you deliberate and say, Gee, is this true or not? They agree it's true. The stipulation?"

Luna, off the top of his head, recites his version of the stipulation. Incredibly, *it has not been written down,* and each lawyer remembers a different version, with different wording.

"Ladies and gentlemen," Luna raps to the jury, "the parties agree and stipulate to the following: that Walter Poindexter was arrested on June 4th of 2001. His arrest and the circumstances for his arrest are not part of the conspiracy. We bring out the arrest just to give the jury a context of the entire conspiracy, to have you understand exactly how the conspiracy was operated and changed over time."

Attorney Ravenell interrupts. "Your honor," Ravenell says, "I will make it real clear that I am not in agreement that there was any such conspiracy, so we are not stipulating that there was a conspiracy."

"I understand that," Quarles says.

Attorney Tuminelli next gives his version of the unwritten stipulation. "Yes, the stipulation, as *I* understand it," Tuminelli says, "if I can just clarify, is that Walter Poindexter was arrested on or about June 4, 2001. The charge for which he was arrested is not related to the charge for which he is presently on trial. That was the stipulation."

Judge Quarles, addressing the unwritten, dueling stipulations, tells the lawyers, "One thing that some lawyers have found useful is actually to reduce the stipulation to writing so that it can then be read to the jury so that there is no question about the extra details such as there was, or was not, a conspiracy."

Quarles now addresses the unusual, unwritten nature of this cover-up trial, and what he describes as Luna's "off-the-top-of-his-head," improvisational approach.

"And again," Quarles tells the lawyers, "counsel are urged and encouraged that they might try some of the more traditional litigation tools such as actual written stated stipulations. Again, that has served us well for several hundred years of Anglo-American judicial history. I know it's not quite the excitement of going off the top of your heads, and then we get to have you all discuss what you think the stipulation does or does not mean. It's not quite as entertaining, perhaps, to do it the old-fashioned way, but it does spare us the extended excursions as to what the agreement actually was."

With that, Luna continues questioning Pug on the workings of the heroin shop he ran with Poindexter at Buford and Spaulding streets. Luna has Grace describe the numerous acts of violence associated with the shop, and how Poindexter would arrive with a gun to settle disputes. Pug testifies in detail about the domestic dispute that erupted in the middle of the heroin shop.

"Like I say, I had an altercation with the guy next door, he was beating up his girlfriend or whatever," Pug tells the courtroom.

"Did you know this guy?" Luna asks.

"No. I told him to take it somewhere else," Grace testifies, "that he was going to bring, you know, some heat around to where I was selling at, which he was going to bring the police around there." Grace continues, "I was ready to fight, you know, and he called some dudes down, and then he wanted to fight when the dudes come down, so I called Mr. Poindexter and he come down and by that time they already had left and then we caught up with them or whatever, you know, and he shot at them."

Luna next asks Grace about the shoot-out between Poindexter and Steven Ford, aka Lump. "Tell the members of the jury about this incident with Lump," Luna asks.

"Well, Lump was getting some heroin or whatever, and he was supposed to — when he finished, he was supposed to give some of the money — he was supposed to call Walter and give him some money or whatever—."

"Who was he supposed to call?"

"Mr. Poindexter.... The dude still ain't called us, Lump, and so at that point we just proceeded just to track him down or whatever to locate him, to find out if he had the money or not."

Grace begins to describe the shoot-out at Lump's apartment, how he and Poindexter went to the apartment asking for Lump.

"A female answered the door, saying he didn't live there," Grace explains. "She said he don't live there. We leave and we come back, just trying different tactics to try to get her to disclose his whereabouts or whatever, to no avail. And so we just kept trying and trying and trying, making threats or whatever, and then the last time we was leaving the apartment building, he called his phone."

"Who called?" Luna asks.

"Lump."

"Lump called who?"

"Mr. Poindexter," Grace says. "He made the call. He go on rambling about, 'You are scamming, you know. What's going on? And you know, the money.' And he said, you know, he had the money but he ain't coming outside. And we let him just slide the money under the door if he got it, and he said well, 'I was calling you, you ain't answering the phone,' blah, blah, blah, so we go back into the building."

"Judge, I object," Tuminelli breaks in. The lawyers go to the bench. Poindexter and Smith, sitting at the defense table, have been given receiving devices so that they can hear the proceedings at the bench, which the jury cannot hear. Judge Quarles tests the transmitter.

"Testing. One, two three. Can you hear? Testing, testing," Quarles says into his microphone. Then, "The defendants indicate that they are able to hear what is happening here at the bench. Yes, Mr. Tuminelli?"

Tuminelli complains that Luna has not laid a proper foundation to question Grace about the phone call. This is first-year law school stuff. "Judge, here is what my objection is, and this has happened frequently," he says. "...What's going on right now is Mr. Luna asked this witness what's going on between Mr. Ford and Mr. Poindexter. He also testified that Mr. Poindexter was speaking to the man on the phone. If Mr. Luna lays a foundation that Mr. Poindexter is telling him, telling Mr. Grace, what is being said, then this is admissible evidence. Or, if he says that the phone was on a speaker, it is admissible evidence. We don't know how it is that he knows that Mr. Ford is saying, 'I have your money,' and my objection is that this has happened and it's happened before.... I don't know how he knows this."

"You are asking him to conduct his direct examination in a more traditional direct examination form?" Quarles asks.

"Yes."

"From which foundational predicates proceed as to a factual

description of what's going on?" Quarles adds.

"Yes, your honor?"

"Interesting," Judge Quarles considers. "Mr. Luna?"

"I will lay the proper foundation, your honor," Luna says.

"Okay. That's a good suggestion," Quarles says, "and the court agrees with it."

Luna proceeds with the questioning. Pug slowly details the more violent episodes involving Poindexter, though Luna carefully steers him away from any discussion of the murder of Alvin Jones. The testimony then turns to Smith's recording studio at Stash House Records.

"Mr. Grace, you testified that you would visit the studio with Mr. Poindexter?" Luna asks. "Is that correct?"

"That is correct," Pug says.

"Would you get heroin at the studio, either you or Mr. Poindexter?"

"Mr. Poindexter got heroin from the studio."

"On these visits?"

"Not every visit."

"Not every visit. All right. Let me ask you, how do you know Mr. Poindexter got heroin from the studio?"

"We would go over to the studio every day. We always stopped at the studio at some point in the day, and on a certain day he would just grab some from him. It may not even be that much, but he would just get something, you know."

Ravenell again objects on grounds of basis of knowledge. How did Grace *know* that Poindexter got the heroin? Quarles overrules, allowing the slow questioning to continue.

"How do you know how much heroin Mr. Poindexter would get at the studio?" Luna asks, laying the foundation.

"He would tell me when we come home."

"So can you give the members of the jury an example of how much heroin you would get, that Mr. Poindexter would get?"

"On occasion, it might be 40 grams. One occasion it might be twenty."

"Let me ask you this: What is the largest amount of heroin that Mr. Poindexter received from Mr. Smith during a single occasion?"

"Maybe three hundred."

"Three hundred what?"

"Grams."

Luna asks when this happened, and Grace says, "I can't remember the date."

Ravenell again objects, and the lawyers return to the bench.

"Judge, this witness has not yet established any basis of knowledge that Mr. Poindexter got drugs from Mr. Smith," Ravenell again complains.

"He said Poindexter told him," Quarles says. "Poindexter said he got it from Smith."

"If you may recall, your honor, I made an objection on this earlier," Ravenell says.

"Uh-huh," Quarles says. "In terms of his knowledge, he said, Poindexter told me he got it from Smith."

"After about eight tries, he said he got it," Ravenell complains.

"It's like pulling teeth, but it's coming," Quarles says.

Luna tells Quarles he'll ask Grace how he knows about the origin of the three hundred grams.

"It *is* like pulling teeth, your honor," Luna agrees with the judge.

The night before, at the close of trial, Quarles suggested Luna threaten Grace to get him to cooperate.

Now Quarles asks Luna, "Didn't get to slap him around last night?" This is said at the bench, out of hearing of the open courtroom. Judge Quarles should be ashamed of himself. This is not what the United States of America is about.

Jonathan Luna is taken aback. He doesn't like the suggestion of mistreatment. What goes around, he must know, comes around.

"Well, you know, woodsheds are not what they used to be, your honor," Luna tells Judge Quarles.

"No, but old prisons are, or federal prisons are," Quarles shamelessly presses on. The judge expresses an awareness, and an acquiesce, of brutal practices the world wouldn't imagine until months later, in 2004, when American torture practices were revealed in Abu Ghraib, the U.S.-run prison outside Baghdad where Iraqis were tortured and humiliated. It's notable that one Abu Ghraib torturer had previously been a state prison guard in Pennsylvania.

"That is true," Luna allows.

"I think they are worse than what they used to be," Ravenell volunteers. Charming stuff, this.

"That is true, your honor," Luna repeats. "But I am doing my best with this witness."

"Well, okay, go back," Quarles instructs.

10
Alvin 'L' Jones rears his deceased head

Back in open court, Jonathan Luna returns to his halting interrogation of Warren Grace. Grace discusses how Eddie the Dominican taught him to cut the heroin with manitol.

"And who is Eddie?" Luna asks.

"The Dominican," Grace says.

"Did he provide you with heroin?"

"Yes."

"And when did he begin providing you with heroin?"

"After Mr. Poindexter was arrested."

"A little after June of 2001?"

"Correct."

"Your honor," Luna asks Judge Quarles, "may I approach?"

Luna, at the bench, explains to the judge that the prosecution must tread carefully here. Luna is fearful that Grace might blurt out details of Alvin Jones' murder, committed by Walter Poindexter in retaliation for the stash house burglary. This could lead to a mistrial. Luna has emphatically coached Grace not to go there — not to mention Jones' murder — so he's hopeful he can avoid a crisis if he carefully "leads" Grace through the minefield. It would be the same minefield that Luna would be navigating only hours before his death.

"Your honor," Luna says, "I'm going to get into the point of Mr. Grace's testimony in which he begins cooperating with law enforcement. I'm going to lead Mr. Grace just as far as his cooperation with the Baltimore police department. I feel like I do need to lead him in this area because I don't want him to open up the fact that he was cooperating with the Baltimore city police on the homicide. We have agreed (that) is not going to be in. And so I just wanted to put you on notice that that's where I'm going.

"You know," Luna goes on, "he is getting a little bit better. But I know he is still nervous and, you know, I have instructed him not to mention the murder, but I would feel comfortable leading him in this area."

Quarles says, at the bench, "So that's what he is displaying, huh? Okay. That's what that is?"

"Lack of brain cells," Luna cracks with the judge. Careful, Jonathan. Pug isn't dumb. Luna himself will be dead before two more sunrises. Who'll be lacking brain cells then?

Attorney Tuminelli also wants to obscure the murder of Alvin Jones. He wants to steer altogether clear of what would turn out to be an increasingly nettlesome subject. Why bring up the Baltimore homicide investigation at all? he asks.

"Judge, may I ask a point of clarification?" Tuminelli asks. "Are you going to go into that he was cooperating with the Baltimore city police initially? Because my concern is that this witness may blurt something out. I know Special Agent Skinner gets involved early on. Is there any reason to go into cooperation with the Baltimore city police?"

"I will say, 'Did there come a time when you began to cooperate with law enforcement?'" Luna suggests.

"Lead him quickly through it," Quarles agrees.

"That's what I will do," Luna says.

"All right," says the judge.

"And then I will refer to Agent Skinner and we will go from there," Luna adds.

"Okay," Tuminelli agrees.

Luna returns to questioning Grace. What follows is truly remarkable. The courtroom is in for a shock. In what can only be called a preemptive strike, Luna, without warning, has Grace describe the violations that Luna has kept secret from the defense for months. Almost a day and a half into trial, Luna feels forced to spill some beans. He obviously knows the defense is seeking the suppressed reports from Pretrial Services, and that the judge already has the reports.

Luna begins, "Mr. Grace, at the time of your arrest, or shortly thereafter, did you make a decision to begin cooperating with the police? I'm going to ask you to say yes or no."

"Yes," Grace replies.

"And did that cooperation involve working with Special Agent Skinner and Detective Moody?"

"Yes."

"Why did you begin to work with the agents?"

"I was caught up," Grace says. "I would get life."

"Probably get a life sentence?"

"Yes."

"What sort of things did you do with the agents, Agent Skinner?"

"Recordings. Undercover work."

Luna asks, "Now, during the time that you were working with the agents, had you pled guilty in any court?"

"Yes."

"In fact, after your arrest, were you incarcerated for a period of time?"

"Yes."

"And when you were released, were there any conditions concerning your release?"

"Yes."

"What was your understanding of the conditions of release for you, Mr. Grace?"

"I was to be placed on home monitoring."

"What is home monitoring?"

"Like a wrist band device that keeps you-- that will monitor you when you are in your home."

"Were you required to wear a wrist band device?"

"Correct."

"And were you required to wear that at all times?"

"Correct."

"And who set these conditions of release for you?"

"The government and the court."

"Which court?"

"The federal court."

"The federal court here?"

"Yes."

"Do you know a Todd Stokes?"

"Yes."

"Okay. Who is Todd Stokes?"

"It's Pretrial."

"Pretrial officer where?"

"In federal court."

"Was he part of these conditions?"

"Yes."

"All right. Did he supervise you?"

"Yes."

"In addition to wearing the band, what other conditions did you have concerning your release?"

"That I wouldn't violate the agreement on the band, I wouldn't catch another charge."

"When you say 'catch another charge,' what are you talking about?"

"I wouldn't get arrested."

"All right. Any other conditions?"

"That I was to work with the agents."

"Right."

"Were there any other conditions concerning what you would be doing or where you would be when you weren't working with agents?"

"I was supposed to be in the house."

"And what house were you supposed to be in?"

"At the house where I was staying at."

"And what house?"

"At my house or my girlfriend's house."

"And that particular house, your girlfriend's house, that was the specific house that you were supposed to remain at when you weren't working with the agents?"

"Right."

"Did there come a time during your work with the agents that you violated your conditions of release?"

"Yes."

This gets Attorney Ravenell's attention. "Excuse me, your honor?" Ravenell breaks in. "Did you say violate his conditions?"

"Yes," Luna acknowledges. Working off the top of his head, improvisationally, Luna mysteriously begins disclosing much of what he has previously suppressed. He's telling the jury about the violations, so it won't look like he's hiding anything when it comes out.

As Ravenell had postulated in his opening statement, "I guess Mr. Luna didn't have much choice to tell you how this person is because if he didn't tell you we would have produced evidence about what kind of person Mr. Grace is. So sometimes it's called the 'preemptive strike.'"

Luna forges ahead with his preemptive questioning of Grace.

"You violated your conditions?" he asks.

"Yes."

"Can you tell the members of the jury how you violated your conditions of release?"

"I took the band off."

"You took the band off. And what did you do?"

"I started going out."

"Where did you go?"

"Outside, to the gym, to eat, ride around," Grace says.

"Did you deal in heroin?"

"No."

Luna goes on, "Was the fact that you removed this band, was that ever discovered?"

"Yes."

"Who discovered it?"

"The agent," Grace says, half truthfully.

"Did you have a meeting with the agents about it?"

"Yes."

"What did you tell the agents?"

"I just wanted to go out. I just wanted to go out to the gym."

Grace goes on to say that, when working with the agents, he used his 2000 Ford Excursion SUV, which he says he'd purchased with $18,000 in cash. "Drug money," Grace says.

"During the period of time that you were selling heroin, Mr. Grace," Luna asks, "can you tell the members of the jury the most amount of money, cash, that you had at one time?"

"Maybe $40,000."

"What happened to that money?"

"It's gone."

After a break for lunch, Luna resumes his examination.

"Mr. Grace, are you nervous?" he asks.

"Yes."

"Why are you nervous?"

"It's difficult," Grace says.

"What's difficult?"

"Testifying."

"Why is it difficult to testify?"

"He was like family to me, and my brother."

"Who was like family to you?"

"Mr. Poindexter."

"Mr. Poindexter?"

Pug nods his head shamefully yes.

"Can you describe how you were able to make purchases of heroin from Mr. Smith and Mr. Poindexter while you were working with Steve Skinner?"

"Well, me and him got together and came up with a plan, and they would give me money to go over there and purchase heroin from them," Grace says. "I would go over there and we would talk about it. How much I wanted to get, and where could I get it from, and we would make the deals like that."

"When you went to the various places to meet either Mr. Smith or Mr. Poindexter, did you carry anything with you?"

"A recorder."

"What was the purpose of the recorder?"

"To record the conversations that we was going to have."

"Did you have any conversations with them that weren't recorded?"

"Yes, I had a few."

"What were those conversations?"

Grace says, "I had to make like I was still on the street so I had to be out there and call them and show up as if I would have if I never got arrested."

"So that was a part of the plan that you talked about that you had to appear that you were still on the street?"

"Correct."

Luna touches on the revolving door nature of the case. Government holds Poindexter in jail, government plots to deal drugs with Poindexter, government releases Poindexter from jail. "At some point — Mr. Poindexter — did he come back on the street (from jail) at some point?" Luna asks.

"Yes."

"When he came out on the street, were you then working with the agents?"

"Yes."

Luna begins to dance around the most explosive aspect of the case. He proceeds with a line of questioning for which he has obviously rehearsed Grace.

"Now," Luna asks, "when you worked with the agents in purchasing heroin, did you use your vehicle?"

"Yes."

"When you used your vehicle, what, if anything, did the agents do with your vehicle?"

"Well, it would be searched. Each time we would meet up, they would search the vehicle."

"Every time that you would use your vehicle, it would be searched?"

"Correct."

"Were you present during the searches?"

"Yes."

"Do you know where they searched in your vehicle?"

"They searched the whole vehicle."

"Did there come a time when the FBI searched your vehicle and they found something?"

"Correct."

"What did they find?"

"They found some heroin."

"Where was the heroin?"

"Like in a flap, a ceiling flap."

"In what part of the vehicle?"

"In the front of the vehicle. A little pull down in the ceiling."

"Was it the driver's side or the passenger side?"

Pug, as usual, splits the difference. He says, "In the middle."

"In the middle?"

"Yes."

"And did you know about that heroin?"

"No," Pug says. With double-naught agent Warren Grace, all knowledge is disavowed.

"Did you have discussions with the FBI about that heroin?"

"Yes."

"What did you tell the FBI?"

Pug explains he was in charge, and he had some calls to make. "Well," he says, shedding light on the unsupervised nature of his operations, "upon my cooperation, now being in the street, I had to make it appear like I was constantly in the street, so I would always be in the neighborhood. I had different guys in and out of the vehicle, some old guys, friends, whatever, so they could see that I was out there so there wouldn't be no question whether or not I was in the street or not, because there was already a rumor out that I was working with the police. I had to build my credibility back up, so I had people in and out of my vehicle during these times."

"Did you know how much heroin was found?"

"No. I was told like less than a gram."

"Were you ever shown it?"

"Yes."

Among his growing list of problems, Luna knows the defense would suggest that Grace simply had pocketed the money given him by the FBI and had turned over his own heroin stash to the agents, and had not acquired the drug from Poindexter or Smith.

So Luna now asks Grace, preemptively, "What did it look to you, in terms of the heroin? Was it ... enough for you to sell 150 vials of heroin?"

"No."

"Well, using the vial as a reference point, how much heroin did it look like to you?"

"Maybe half a vial."

"Did you find out where this heroin came from?"

"Yes, I later found out, yes."

"Do you know where it came from?"

"Yes, it was left in there."

"How did you learn where the heroin came from?"

"A friend of mine told me he left it in there," Grace says. Among the more obvious problems with this story is that it's unlikely a heroin junkie will forget his fix and leave it in a dealer's car. It's more likely that this was Grace's heroin and that he was dealing on the side while under government employ.

"Did you talk to your friend about that?" Luna asks.

"Yes."

"Did you tell the FBI about that conversation?"

"Yes."

"Did you continue to work with the agents after having this conversation?"

"Correct."

Attorney Tuminelli, surprised by this revelation, breaks in. "Judge, can we get a time when this is all occurring?"

Luna acts like he does not know the answer to this most prickly of questions, and remains tight-lipped. The date was October 16, 2002. Paid informant Grace was caught concealing the heroin on the same day the Dawson family burned to death.

"Do you know when this happened, sir?" Judge Quarles asks Grace.

"No, your honor, I can't recall."

Luna then has Grace mislead the court and suggest that the incident occurred, "I think (in) the summer of 2003, something like that, in the summer time," Grace says.

11
More indignation and fumbles

Both defense attorneys break in. "Your honor, may counsel approach?" Attorney Ravenell says.

"I join in that," Tuminelli says.

The lawyers indignantly tell the judge they are shocked and surprised by what they have just learned. They complain they've now caught Luna several times obscuring crucial evidence, to which they are entitled to have by the rulings in *Brady, Giglio* and *Jencks.* First Grace's violations of his release conditions, and now this business of heroin in his Ford Excursion. Luna will respond by outright lying. His strategy becomes obvious. Months earlier he decided the safest course was to violate the discovery rules, and to lie or apologize about it later, if caught.

"Your honor," Ravenell tells Judge Quarles, "the Fourth Circuit and the Supreme Court has made it clear that when there is impeachable evidence such as this, the prosecution has a requirement to turn over to us as *Brady.* For the first time today we have heard about this incident and incidents regarding the violations in the pre-trial orders. This is unacceptable."

Luna chimes in. "I beg to differ on that," Luna says. He outright lies, saying he has turned over to the defense *written reports* on these subjects. "We turned over copies of the *Jencks* and *Giglio* on this," he says.

"Did you in some fashion advise counsel that the FBI had found drugs on the defendant?" Judge Quarles asks Luna.

"I did," Luna lies. "And, in fact—,"

"And in what form was that advice?" Quarles asks.

"The form was at the FBI when Mr. Ravenell was at the FBI and we showed Mr. Ravenell the heroin that was recovered from the vehicle."

"Absolutely not!" Ravenell counters, insisting it never happened.

Quarles says he doesn't want to waste the jury's time getting to the bottom of this growing mystery. They'll deal with it later, he says, "outside of the jury's hearing."

"Judge, two points," Tuminelli presses. "I was not present at the FBI. I know Mr. Ravenell and I talked about it. He may have shown the package, but they never disclosed that heroin was taken out of his vehicle."

"Never happened," Ravenell agrees.

"That's number one," Tuminelli continues. "And the second point is that we were never told about his being out on the street without that electronic monitor. All we received was an FBI 302 that said that they had come to his house and found the bracelet in a dresser."

"That's it," Ravenell agrees.

"That's all," Tuminelli insists. "We were never told he was out on the street without it."

The defense hasn't been given Todd Stokes' detailed memo, only Agent Skinner's calculatedly deceptive 302.

"Never," Ravenell agrees. "Today was the first time we have heard that this man had been out on the street, taken off his bracelet, gone out on the streets doing whatever he was supposedly doing. It's never been disclosed. The 302 is a half a page long that says there was — an anonymous call was received that this man was taking off his bracelet and going out, that the police — the FBI — went to his home, and that he was supposedly in possession of drugs and guns also. And they went to his home and searched. That's it."

Judge Quarles asks what the defense wants him to do about it. "What remedy are you seeking?" he asks.

"Your honor," Tuminelli answers, "right now I think what we would like to do is put on the record factually that we believe there was a *Brady* violation, and let us give some thought to what we do on this." By placing their objection on the record, the defense lawyers are creating issues for an appeal of the case, should they lose.

"The record will note that," Quarles says. "I will wait to hear what, if any, remedy you want."

Luna now changes the subject. Luna says, after lunch, he will be ready to introduce the transcripts. "Mr. Ravenell and I discussed the transcripts," Luna says. "We were able to resolve some, and I am prepared to let the court rule on the objections, and we will abide by whatever ruling it will be."

Ravenell, however, protests. Improvisational Luna *still* hasn't put anything in writing. "I still haven't received from Mr. Luna any objections, judge," he says.

"I assume he is relying on his November 24th letter," Quarles sighs. This is the same vague, boilerplate letter that the judge complained about at yesterday's close of trial.

"Well, I am relying on the November 24th letter," Luna says, "and I am also relying on conversations that I had with Mr. Ravenell yesterday. I know the objections that he has and I believe the court is in a position to rule on the objections."

"I am not sure what conversations we had that you are relying on," Ravenell tells Luna. "So let's be careful in what conversations we had that you are relying on."

Back to square one. Luna continues to want to run the case from memory, refusing to put *anything* on paper. Quarles is clearly frustrated.

"Well, again, gentlemen, and lady, I like to divide trial days into their time and our time. The theory is that I can waste our time as much as possible." Now Quarles returns to his soapbox about not wasting the jury's time. "Our citizens resist jury duty service for, among other reasons, that we are not appreciative of their time. We are not wasting their time. Let us make use of their time."

Citizens also are deeply concerned about deception in their government. Quarles seems less interested in this.

"So can we perhaps resume the trial?" Quarles asks.

"Yes, we can," Luna says.

Luna proceeds to ask Warren Grace whether he has been able to listen to the many hours of recordings the latter produced using the FBI's hidden recording device. Close to one hundred hours of tape. An informant's help is usually needed to transcribe these recordings, and to decipher often-muddled conversations that otherwise might be difficult to hear or to understand.

"Have you had an opportunity to listen to those recordings?" he asks Pug.

"Yes."

"On how many occasions did you listen to the recordings?" Luna's questions shed light on his own recent trips to see Grace in the Philadelphia detention center.

"A few occasions."

"Were they here, that you listened to them? Here in Maryland?" Luna asks.

"No." Grace continues to be a font of information.

"Where did you listen to them?"

"In Philadelphia."

"Is that where you were in prison?"

"Yes."

"And with whom did you listen to the recordings?"

"The agents."

"Anyone else?"

"You," Pug tells Luna. "And my lawyer."

"All right. And were you able to look at transcripts of those recordings?"

"Correct."

"And are the transcripts — are they a fair and accurate reflection of the conversations that you had with Mr. Poindexter and Mr. Smith?"

"Yes," Pug allows.

Luna now turns his attention to the transcripts. But they have not yet been introduced into evidence, and so cannot yet be discussed before the jury. Jonathan fumbles, and throws the courtroom into confusion and disarray.

Luna plans to show Pug a VHS video. He has labeled the tape "Exhibit 35." In legal parlance, he plans to "publish" the contents of the tape to the jury by playing it for them. He however has several incredible problems. Exhibit 35 has yet to be admitted into evidence, and so it can't yet be shown to the jury. Worse, Luna, in his haste, has left the VHS tape back at his desk in his office. This last remarkable oversight is perhaps indicative of Luna's propensity for leaving his desk in an improvisational hurry, and leaving important things behind.

"Your honor," Luna tells the judge, "I'm going to have the witness look at Exhibit 35, your honor, and I'm going to post that on the screen Exhibit 35."

"Let me see if I get this straight," Quarles chokes. "You are going to *publish an unadmitted exhibit?"*

Luna says he'll *later* get Agent Steve Skinner to vouch for the tape.

Quarles tells Luna he must *first* put Skinner on the stand if he wishes to introduce the tape into evidence. "I will permit that," Quarles says.

The judge, at times dripping with sarcasm, now launches into an elementary law school lesson for young Mr. Luna. "As a general rule," Quarles tells Luna, "I don't permit the publication of non-evidence to the jury. It is evidence when it, of course, has been admitted. Up until the time it is admitted, it is not evidence; as a general rule not publishable to the jury."

"Yes, your honor," Luna says. "At this time, I would call Steven Skinner briefly to the stand with respect to Exhibit 35, your honor."

"Okay. Sir, would step down?" Quarles asks Grace. Grace comes off the stand, replaced by the Unreachable Special Agent, Steven Skinner.

12
Mission Impossible meets Amateur Hour and the nebulous nature of conspiracy

Steve Skinner takes the stand, raises his hand, and swears to tell the truth, the whole truth, and nothing but the truth.

"It looked like Steve Skinner didn't want to be there," the court reporter remembers thinking. Skinner seemed uncomfortable, not thrilled at the prospect, and shifted in his seat. After all those months on the case, his body language seemed odd.

Luna has Skinner introduce himself and his videotapes to the jury. Unfortunately, with Skinner now in front of him in the witness box, Luna off the bat slips up again.

"Let me turn your attention to Exhibit 35 for identification," Luna tells Skinner.

"Government's 35," Judge Quarles reads into record.

"Have you seen Government 35?" Luna asks Skinner.

"Can you show it to me?" Skinner requests.

Luna realizes he doesn't have the tape.

So here they were, our dynamic duo, the Unreachable and Jammaster Flash. Skinner and Luna stare at each other, in the middle of the waiting courtroom. Sooner or later, odds would dictate, these two would get something right in this case. If one of them doesn't kill the other first.

"Well—," Luna stalls, searching his desk. "Court's indulgence, your honor."

He cannot find the original videotape, signed sometime before the trial by Agent Skinner to authenticate it in the chain of evidence. Luna instead finds, on his prosecution table, a digital *copy* of the VHS tape, transferred to a CD-ROM disc. Luna has captured the VHS video to his laptop hard drive, back in his office, and burned a CD. He also has some still photos taken from the tape.

Trouble is, as Skinner knows, *the tape* is required, since only the tape has been initialed by Skinner as the original tape made for purposes of evidence. Worse, the file is burned onto a CD-ROM disc that contains *all* the audio and video evidence, none of which has *yet been admitted* into evidence.

"Agent Skinner," Luna fumbles, "have you reviewed the CD-ROM that is here in the courtroom today?"

"If you are referring to what I think you are," Skinner tells him, "Exhibit 35 is a VHS tape, if I am correct, that I initialed. But I don't think you have it here in the courtroom." Skinner will reveal a remarkable knowledge of the items on Luna's desk, back in the U.S. attorney's office. "Would I be incorrect?" Skinner prods Luna.

"That is correct," Luna agrees. Then, "Your honor, may we approach? May I approach?"

At the bench, Luna tells Judge Quarles, "Your honor, I was going to elicit testimony about what Exhibit 35 is. It's a videotape. We have reduced all of the videotapes to a computer file which is stored in the laptop at my desk. And I was going to have him describe the video tape and then have him talk about how it was created and then play or at least post a still of that video so he can identify it on the screen, your honor."

Judge Quarles seems to want to put his head down on the bench.

"Where to begin," he sighs. "You wish to publish to the jury something that is not in evidence. The court won't permit that."

"I was going to *publish to the witness*, I'm sorry, *publish to the witness* through using the computer screen—," Luna invents on his feet.

"I—. You have lost me," Quarles chokes, his head spinning. He tries to gather himself. "Okay. Walk me through what you intend to do."

"I was going to have Agent Skinner describe my Exhibit 35, which is a computer file," Luna spins.

"Exhibit 35 is now a computer file, and not a VHS tape?" Quarles groans.

"Well, it *was* a VHS file," Luna says. "But it's—." He sees it's hopeless. "Your honor, I'm going to have to take a break to get that VHS tape."

Quarles announces he will now give the jury an unusually long, two-hour break, so that Luna can find his tape. During the break, Quarles says, the outstanding objections involving the transcripts will also be resolved.

"Okay," Judge Quarles now lectures Luna at the bench, spreading thick the sarcasm. "Trials are built, you see, by proponents and opponents of facts. Those facts are established through *evidence.* Evidence is something that is admissible to the jury. Either in terms of testimony or physical things themselves. Tangible objects."

The trouble with this case, Quarles complains, is that there seems to be a strange and recurring problem with the tangible objects. Physical things, found in the real world.

"Generally," Quarles continues his lashing of Luna, "to permit the introduction of testimony or physical evidence it is required that there be some form, or foundation, or basis of knowledge. As Mr. Ravenell has talked about. For example, for testimony, or something that would authenticate the physical items themselves that are introduced into evidence." This was true for electronic evidence, as well, he went on. "So I will assume that, when we resume the evidentiary portion of the trial this afternoon, there will be some witness who, on the physical thing, can be sponsored, who will authenticate that thing, and at that point I would anticipate that that thing would be published to the jury. However, I do not anticipate publication until there has been reception of the evidence in some admissible form."

"Yes, your honor. Yes, your honor," Luna assures him.

"And, again, it would be helpful to have some witness who can actually identify and authenticate the evidence."

Judge Quarles sends the jury off to lunch, but keeps the lawyers behind to resolve argument over the transcripts.

"Okay," Quarles launches into the task, "does everyone have defendant Smith's objections to the transcripts and the highlighted transcripts themselves?"

Luna, again, is unprepared, and has left, yet again, something he needs back on his desk.

"Just one second, your honor," Luna asks. There's a pause. Luna confers with his co-counsel, Vivien Cockburn. Then, "Your honor, I believe those are on my desk. I am having Ms. Cockburn go and get those from my desk." Even so, ever willing to proceed off the top of his head, Luna adds, "But, your honor, I can begin."

"Didn't anticipate we would get that far, Mr. Luna?" Quarles asks.

"I did not, your honor. I inadvertently left that file on my desk."

"Ohhh," Quarles says.

"Last night," Luna says.

Much of the dispute involving the transcripts hinged on the alleged conspiracy between Smith and Poindexter, who were not always together. Poindexter also bought drugs from other suppliers. At one point Judge Quarles asks Luna, "Just give me the theory that explains why Poindexter is with another supplier (and that) is evidence of a conspiracy in which Smith is a supplier of Poindexter."

"But the conspiracy does not hinge on Mr. Smith always being the supplier of heroin to Mr. Poindexter," Luna says.

"I suddenly had a moment of insight," Quarles says, "understanding all of those commentators who talk about the nebulous nature of conspiracy. I suddenly understand that. Okay."

One by one, Quarles disposes of the defense objections to the transcripts. There's often a wry humor listening to a judge reading transcripts of a street conversation. Such as when Quarles suggests this redaction in an October 11, 2002 transcript: "Can you remove the 'I got the weed,' so it would read, 'I mean the motherfucker, x, the gun, or I got the gun'? Can you remove the words 'weed and,' so that it would read 'I got the gun'?"

"Okay, I could certainly do that with the transcript," Luna agrees. "I will look at the actual audio for that, and we will have to redact that."

Or as when, while reading the slang in the transcripts, Quarles asks Luna, "What does 'buckle down and get a curve mean?'"

Luna becomes the elder man's street-jive interpreter.

"It means to get a shop and keep it going," Luna explains.

The last objection, Ravenell tells the judge, centers around

Poindexter's murder of Alvin Jones, and the agreement not to tell the jury about the drug shooting. In a transcript of a July 10, 2002, conversation Deon Smith tells Grace that the word on the street is that Grace is cooperating with police on Jones' murder.

"Your honor, this conversation is between Mr. Smith and Mr. Grace," Ravenell tells the judge, "and the majority of what they are talking about in this is about the allegation that Mr. Grace was cooperating against Mr. Poindexter in relation to the murder charge, and this is before Mr. Poindexter is (released from jail). And Mr. Grace started cooperating with the government; there is reference to him and word on the street that he was cooperating, and my concern is that the court has indicated that there will be no evidence regarding this murder, and it may be that the jury would have a question of what was he cooperating with the police about prior to him being involved in this cooperation with the police as of July 10, 2002, and thereon because we know that this cooperation began regarding the murder."

"But the jury does not know that," Quarles says. What they don't know won't hurt 'em, right, judge? In fact, this very issue will play heavily in events leading to the death of Jonathan Luna, in less than two days' time.

"Well, they don't, your honor," Ravenell counters, "and my concern is that, you know, what it points to." What it points to, indeed.

"You don't believe they will intuit that from this, do you?" Quarles asks Ravenell.

"I don't believe from this alone, but that was my concern (in) raising that objection. I have that concern."

"Is the government conceding?" Quarles asks Luna.

"We are not conceding," Luna says.

"Objection is overruled," Quarles rules. "Okay, next one?"

"That was the last one?" Ravenell advises.

"That was it," Luna agrees.

"Okay," says the judge, "see you all at 2:00 pm." After lunch.

Ravenell, however, before lunch has one other piece of business. One other thread to pull. The judge has promised to do something about Luna's failure to disclose timely information about Warren Grace's misbehavior with the FBI. The *Brady* violations, as lawyers call it.

"And last, are we going to deal with the *Brady* issues?" Ravenell asks Judge Quarles.

"Oh, yes," Quarles recalls.

Ravenell naturally wants to begin by getting all the documents in Luna's possession which Luna has previously refused to disclose or turn over, as required by law and his own agreement, before trial.

"We need to at least get this information," Ravenell tells the judge, pulling at the thread. He wonders what more the FBI might know. "If there are any (more) FBI 302s—."

The judge turns to Luna. "Do you have anything further on the non-compliance with the electronic monitoring and the—. What was the other one?"

"The search of the—," Ravenell volunteers.

"Oh, yes, the finding of the heroin in the car," Quarles says.

Thinking, as always, on his feet, Luna coolly tries to keep the thread from further unraveling. He continues to stonewall, and outright lie. Better to stonewall, get caught, apologize and take the heat than to turn everything over. Or, does he hope that if he keeps shoving things under the rug, everything will go away? If so, he's dead wrong.

"I have no further 302s on the heroin that was found," Luna begins. "My records show, and I have a big box that says, 'Turned over to defense counsel,' that we turned over reports concerning the violation, your honor." An outright lie, defense lawyers will say.

"I will show you what we got," Ravenell counters.

Quarles asks to see the documents released to the defense. "Why doesn't someone give me what was given?"

"Yes," Ravenell says. He hands Quarles his only document, Skinner's truncated 302 concerning the mysteries of Pug's excellent adventure while under home confinement.

"Well, you say you are giving me everything." Quarles looks at Ravenell. "You are now aware of the two incidents so at least you can cross examine on them."

Ravenell states the obvious. "Well, I don't want to rely on this guy."

"Huh?" Quarles chortles.

Warren Grace. "I don't want to rely on him," Ravenell repeats. Who in his right mind — with the exception of Jonathan Luna and Steve Skinner — would put his neck on the line for scumbag Warren Grace? "I want to have something else that may show different than what he said."

Quarles for some reason isn't making things easy. He reminds Ravenell of yesterday's private conference. He cites an amendment to a Federal Rule of Evidence (604B) that prohibits, he says, the defense from gaining government information if it's intended to be used solely for the purposes of impeaching the integrity of a scumbag witness such as Grace.

"So you are pretty much stuck now," the judge tells the defense lawyers. All they can do, under the new rule, is question Grace under cross-examination, Quarles says. Tough luck.

Ravenell fights on. "Well, your honor, first, even if that were true, and I don't agree that that's the correct reading,—"

"Well, if you want to read the rule, here, please take it," Quarles tells him, "and show me where I have read it improperly."

"I think that there are other rules that may address the issue as well," Ravenell argues.

"It's a public document," Quarles rattles on, "I am not making this up."

Ravenell slam dunks: "But even if that is an accurate reading, judge, (that) doesn't mean that we don't get to have the information on which to formulate the questions." The trial begins to pivot on this single statement.

"Absolutely," Quarles agrees. "And he has said he has given it to you, and I—."

"I showed you what he gave us."

"Then I will direct the government to tell you anything they know about those two incidents that have not been reduced to writing, so that they have a full understanding of what the pre-trial violation was as well as what the possession of heroin was," Quarles tells Luna. Trouble is, he's told Luna that before.

But the defense has made an opening. Now these two experienced trial lawyers will drive a truck through the opening. Luna says nothing.

Now Tuminelli speaks. He says the 608B evidence rule isn't applicable. "We are not talking about we simply were entitled to this evidence for the purposes of impeaching Mr. Grace," Tuminelli argues. He said it was a matter of guilt and evidence, in the face of an untrustworthy FBI and its witness. "Both Mr. Ravenell and I have addressed the jury and told the jury that our defense in this case, in Mr. Poindexter's case, is that the three alleged purchases of heroin from him (Grace) did not occur."

"Uh-huh," Quarles agrees.

"That Mr. Grace, in fact, manipulated Special Agent Skinner, had the heroin available to him when he went in there, and simply took the United States' money and returned heroin that Mr. Grace had, you know, unrelated to Mr. Poindexter," Tuminelli continues.

"An argument for which you now have a factual basis," Quarles agrees. Here Ravenell and Tuminelli's skills are on full display. This is the point where they turn the trial around. Luna continues to say nothing. Does he even gulp or blink? Remain stone faced? Inside, one imagines him sinking. He must feel he is sinking into a morass from which his case, and his life, will never arise.

"Right," Tuminelli tells Quarles. "So my point, judge, is we don't need this simply to impeach Mr. Grace. It goes to, you know, the defendants' guilt or innocence. If Mr. Grace was in a position, as he was, to have some heroin from other source than the alleged defendants—." The defense, at this point, has yet to be given some of the most damning evidence against Warren Grace: an anonymous caller had told Pretrial Services that Grace, under his loose home confinement, had *drugs in his possession.*

"Which is a matter of record," Quarles agrees. "You have an argument basis. But I don't see how that affects the 608B ruling."

"I will tell you how, your honor," Ravenell breaks in.

"Let me—," Tuminelli begs to continue.

"Tag teaming now?" Quarles asks the defense team.

"Sometimes we need to, Judge," Ravenell says. "You wear the black robe. We need to tag team." It's a mistake for Ravenell to blurt this out, as it makes Quarles testy.

"I try to discourage festival-style arguments, folks," the judge says. "That's when people sort of argue as the spirit moves them."

"I'll wait," Ravenell yields. "I understand."

"This is a courthouse, not a church revival," Quarles tells Ravenell.

"Not like a church, judge," Ravenell agrees. It was far from like a church, or other rare places where truth reins alongside the promise of all-seeing justice. A United State's courthouse is not at all like a church, evidently. Except perhaps when His Eminence the cardinal is present.

"I would like to put on the record," Tuminelli says, "that I think both the failure to give us, until we heard it in the courtroom, evidence that Mr. Grace was free to be outside of his residence without his electronic monitoring system in operation and had deceived the agents, because they didn't know about this, Mr. Stokes and Pretrial Services didn't know about it, the failure to disclose that, clearly, the government knew this."

Tuminelli argues that the outcome of the trial might be different had the defense been properly informed. They could have had their private investigator look into things. "Had we been told that he had been found to have heroin in his car, we could have sent our investigator out," he tells the judge. "We are now in the middle of a trial, you know, (and) our opportunities to investigate are severely impaired."

Quarles tries to brush it off. He says the trial will go on into next week, and they still had time to send out a private eye.

Tuminelli, setting up an appeal issue on the pre-trial discovery violations, replies, "I just wanted the record to be clear that, had we been given this information in due course, we would have had a more reasonable opportunity to gather information about the heroin and about what his activity was when he was supposed to be in his apartment."

"I understand that," Quarles promises. "I will facilitate your investigation in any way that I can." They're both talking for the appellate judge.

Now Tuminelli and Ravenell cleverly drive the truck through the hole they've ripped in the case. They've ripped a new barn door in Luna and Skinner's behinds.

Ravenell said they needed the name and address of the person who supposedly left the heroin in Grace's SUV.

"I will direct the government to supply that information to you. By 2 pm today," Quarles tells Luna.

Luna, totem-silent, says nothing.

"Additionally, we don't know how many days this man was out of compliance," Ravenell rips on. "We need to know that." He still hasn't been informed about Todd Stokes' Pretrial Services memo.

"I will direct them to let you know that." Quarles again nods at Luna. "And I have just done that."

"And we need to know the dates he was out of compliance," Ravenell presses on.

"The government will provide that," Quarles instructs Luna.

Ravenell next cites U.S. Supreme Court case law (*"Alaska v. Davis,* or *Davis v. Alaska,* I always get confused which goes first in that case," he says) that, he argues, allows the defense to gain and introduce evidence involving a witness who may actually have committed the alleged crime, beyond the 608B rule. In this case, the defense theory is that Grace may have supplied the heroin to the FBI, not Smith nor Poindexter. Due to FBI missteps or incompetence, this was no longer just a case of whether Warren Grace was a sleaze ball. Where'd all the heroin come from?

Hearing this, Judge Quarles goes further. "I have directed the government to provide you what they have and to *narrate beyond that,"* Quarles directs, "so that you can fully cross-examine and investigate the cooperating witness's heroin possession as well as his non-compliance with Pretrial."

By saying, "narrate beyond that," Quarles has ordered Luna to tell the defense what was going on, not just provide documents. Now, well into the lunch break, Quarles says, "I hesitate to ask this question, but is there anything else?"

Whereupon Tuminelli asks that the case be thrown out.

"Just for the record," Tuminelli says, "I am moving on behalf of Mr. Poindexter that the charges be dismissed for due process violations. I understand what the court's going to rule, but I wanted to make the record that that is the relief we are looking for."

"We join in that request," Ravenell seconds.

"Okay." Quarles looks to Luna. "Government conceding that?" In other words, did Luna agree the case should be thrown out?

"Not conceding that," Luna says. Maybe he should have. Maybe he'd still be alive, and you wouldn't be reading this book. Luna might be out of a job, and you'd be out of a book, but maybe, if Luna shut it down now, he might still be alive.

"Okay. Then the motions to dismiss are denied," Quarles rules. "See you at 2 pm."

13
Luna, the politician, bobs and weaves

The lunch break ends at precisely 2pm. Judge Quarles is chagrined to see the defense lawyers walk into the courtroom a few seconds late. The judge's atomic clock is ticking, and everyone keeps ignoring his pet peeve about punctuality in the courtroom. Now he threatens to fine the next lawyer who isn't punctual.

"Gentlemen," Quarles tells the defense lawyers, "$25 the next time."

"We are going to do a better job, judge," Ravenell tells him. "And you are right. We were sitting right down the hall in the conference room working."

"And actually, Mr. Ravenell said, 'Oh, my God! It's two o'clock!'" Tuminelli adds.

The jury files in and Luna calls, as his first witness of the afternoon, Agent Skinner. Finally Luna and Skinner have their act together, at least as far as the VHS tape is concerned. Skinner explains to the jury that he supervised all but two of the recordings used for the case.

"Approximately how many minutes or hours are the recordings?" Luna asks.

"It's hard to say, but I would say about a hundred hours of recordings," Skinner estimates. That's more than four full days, if played nonstop, from start to finish. What were they making, *Gone With The Wind?* On one of those days, the entire Dawson family died, unable to get help. *They'd* be gone with the wind.

"And with respect to the complete recordings that you have talked about," Luna asks, "did you review those with Warren Grace?"

"The entire recordings?"

"Yes."

"We only reviewed with him recordings that were pertinent to the investigation," he says, not elaborating. It's hard to get a straight answer from Steve Skinner.

It turns out there's a problem with one of Skinner's videotapes. Exhibit 35, which before lunch had gone missing, was not recorded using the proper date, Skinner now tells the jury. As usual, Skinner doesn't affix blame on himself. The tape was of a meeting between Grace, Smith and Poindexter on September 23, 2002, at Stash House Records.

"This tape, Exhibit 35, was created using a covert video camera which was placed inside a duffel bag," Skinner explains. "Prior to making this recording, Detective Moody set the date and time on that camcorder correctly. However, we didn't know that inside that camcorder the internal battery was no good, so that when we took the external battery off to ensure that we would have a fresh battery when using this, or when using the camera, that the date and time function inside the camcorder reset. So when we sent Mr. Grace in with this covert camera, we didn't know that the date and time function of the camcorder reset."

"What was the date and time that was produced?" Luna asks.

"I am trying to recall," Skinner says. "It was roughly a date that was ten years ago or so. I don't remember the date."

Having introduced the evidence, Skinner steps down and Warren Grace returns to the witness stand. Luna has Grace explain some of what is happening on the tapes. Sometimes Grace has to interpret street lingo to the mostly white jury. Such as when he's recorded, on the tape, talking to Smith about compressing the heroin:

"Did Mr. Smith tell you why he wanted to do this compression?" Luna asks.

"He said he needed to get his flip on," Pug explains. "He needed to flip the heroin and double it."

"When you say he wanted to get his flip on," Luna asks, "what does that mean?"

"It means to double his profit on his heroin," Grace says.

Grace elaborated for the jury some of his undercover work with the FBI. Poindexter's well-known murder of Alvin Jones continued to be a problem for the undercover sting operation. Poindexter, newly released from jail in September 2002, heard rumors that Grace was cooperating with police on Jones' murder. One day, on September 11, 2002, Grace says, "I met him on a parking lot like a couple blocks away from the studio."

Luna, however, must steer Grace away from all mention of Jones' drug murder. "And what happened when you met him at the parking lot?" he asks.

"Well, as I told you, from the start," Grace says, "he was always still kind of leery about me, so I was supposed to meet him at one spot and when I come to that spot he switched it right then and there for me to meet him at another spot. So when we got to the parking lot he had to look around and then he finally got into the vehicle and we made the exchange."

The case continues to have strange coincidences of numbers and dates, all of which Luna seems curiously eager to keep from the minds of the jurors.

"Do you have any specific memory of nine —," Luna begins to say. He nearly says "9/11," but checks himself. This after all was the *911* heroin investigation, centering on Stash House Records, based at *911* West 36th Street in Baltimore. "—of September 11, 2002?" Luna finishes his sentence.

"I mean I don't keep them dates, no," Pug says.

After this rather lengthy introduction to the video and audio tape evidence, Luna tells Judge Quarles that he is ready to pass out binder notebooks containing transcripts so that the jury can follow along.

"We are at the point now where I can begin playing the transcripts," Luna tells Quarles.

"Great," Quarles says.

The transcripts have been freshly edited to include the agreed-upon redactions, and have been bound in binder notebooks. Luna asks for a short break so that the transcripts can be brought down from his office.

"And I wanted to ask if the court would take a break so I can bring down—."

"Are we at that point literally?" the always impatient Quarles asks, "or are we making preparations for doing it?"

"That is correct, your honor," Luna tells him.

"I thought you were getting ready to charge right into it," Quarles says.

"Wishful thinking, your honor," Luna replies. "I have binders being prepared."

"But they are not here now?"

"But they are not here yet," Luna advises. As usual, he's not ready.

"The dog ate them on the way," Quarles guffaws. "Who said that in elementary school? The dog ate my homework. The FBI stole my binders. Okay, we will take a break. How much time do you need? An hour or two?"

"No," Luna says. "How about fifteen minutes?"

After this short break, the transcripts are passed out to the jurors. Ravenell, meanwhile, asks for a few seconds of Judge Quarles' time at the bench. "Mr. Luna has been chopping at the transcripts, back and forth," he tells the judge. "There will be occasions when I may be objecting," he tells Quarles. "Some of these tapes are pretty bad."

"Uh huh," Quarles says.

"You hear how this witness testifies and how he mumbles," Ravenell complains. "Imagine hearing this on a tape. Most of it, I don't understand what the hell he is saying, with all due respect, judge." He goes on, "When it gets real bad, judge, I would ask the court to maybe hear some of these maybe without the jury because you have got to hear it.... There are sixty some— how many do you have now?" he asks Luna.

"About eighty," Luna says, standing before the bench.

"About eighty recordings," Ravenell corrects himself. He adds, "It may be fairer to let these jurors listen to some of these without the transcripts, judge."

"You have your objection," Quarles tells him. "It is overruled."

For the remainder of the afternoon the jurors listen to the tapes, and follow along with the transcripts. Grace too follows along, and attempts explaining to the jury what was going on in the recordings. At times his testimony is strangely droll. Such as when Grace explains the operation of the heroin shop, and how the junkies who passed out the drugs in the alleyways are never allowed near the cash.

"Would the junkies ever get the cash directly from the customers?" Luna asks Pug.

"No."

"Why not?"

"Well, we just didn't do it like that," Pug explains. "We just didn't do it like that."

"Did they have any role in handling the money?"

"No, they wasn't supposed to handle the money at all."

"Do you know why they weren't supposed to handle the money?"

"They are just not trustworthy."

Trustworthiness. A concept the Justice Department, and the FBI, should explore, and learn more about.

As the day in court draws to a close at about 5 pm, Judge Quarles dismisses the jury, and Ravenell asks Quarles for a private word at the judge's bench.

Luna, he says, despite the judge's order, continues to stonewall, and has only turned over one short document. Ravenell complains he *still* hasn't been given information about Grace's FBI house arrest violations.

"I still have not—. No one has contacted me from Pretrial (Services)," he tells Quarles with some frustration. Talk about stonewalling: two full days into the trial, direct orders from the judge ignored, and the government cover-up continues.

"I am going to go and talk with Pretrial," the judge promises Ravenell.

Shortly thereafter, now with Luna present at the bench, the judge asks, "Anything else?"

"Yes, your honor," Ravenell again complains. "This morning you directed the government to turn over certain things by 2 o'clock pm. We didn't receive the majority of those things you had directed the government to turn over to us."

"First of all, what did you receive?" Quarles asks.

Ravenell has, in fact, received a curious, solitary document. In the heat of the trial, he doesn't fully recognize its importance. It's a short FBI 302 report, written by Skinner and dated "10/16/02." The 302 mentions heroin having been found in Grace's vehicle. It's dated the same day the Dawsons' house burned down. It of course makes no mention of the ignored Dawsons, or their murdered children.

Ravenell doesn't realize the significance of the date of the 302. In court, he even misreads the date printed on the memo.

"The only thing we received, judge," he tells Quarles, "was a 302 dated *1/16/02,* and I will tell you, after reviewing this 302, Mr. Tuminelli, and I, and I am sure he will tell you himself, we have never seen this document. This is the document that refers to the heroin being found in Mr. Grace's vehicle. I have read it. I will tell you, if I had seen this, I would have remembered it. So we never received it. We both agree on that."

"Okay," Quarles says.

Still more is being withheld by Luna, Ravenell complains. He can sense something lurking behind the door, but doesn't know what it is. It's Darrell Brooks, with his can of gasoline, and Warren Grace, with his Tech nine, Edgar Allen Poe on his last insane night, and a thousand other incarnations of the devil lurking behind the doors of Baltimore.

"What you also instructed the government to do was to give us the name of the individual who allegedly placed drugs in the vehicle, and address, some way to contact that person. There has been no such information given to us. Additionally, in regards to the (home detention) violations—."

Judge Quarles, now growing impatient, tips his hand. "Have you received the violation notice?" he asks Ravenell. Quarles himself has been given a copy of the Pretrial Services' memo, written by Todd Stokes on August 22, 2002, detailing how an anonymous tipster repeatedly complained about Grace running free, shooting at "innocent" neighbors, and possessing heroin.

"No," Ravenell says.

"Do you have the violation notice?" Quarles asks Luna.

"I do not have the violation notice," Luna tells the judge. *It's an outright lie.* Stokes, at the time he wrote the memo, cc'd a copy to both Luna and federal judge Frederic Smalkin.

Out of patience, Quarles volunteers the defense his own copy of the smoking gun memo.

"Here is a copy of the violation notice," the judge tells Ravenell. "It's my only copy, so—." He asks the clerk to make two copies.

"Obviously, after we review that," Ravenell guesses correctly, "it may answer some other questions I have, which were how long he was out of compliance, et cetera. I don't know after I have seen that if I still have those questions to be answered by the government, if they have further information. Those are the two issues that were a breach that I wanted to bring to the court's attention."

"Okay," Quarles says.

Luna, amazingly, continues to lie, cover-up and talk off the top of his head, spouting glib assurances. Here we see Jonathan Luna, the politician, glossing over the facts, quickly changing the subject. "Your honor, if I can respond," Luna tells Quarles, "first of all, our records indicate—. I am not here to quarrel with Mr. Ravenell and Mr. Tuminelli. We have a very good relationship. They know me very well, as I do them, and I can't explain why they don't have it. I looked at our file and our—."

"Do you have a copy of what you sent?" an increasingly disbelieving Quarles asks.

"Yes, I made a copy of that," Luna tells him. A true politician, Luna keeps mentioning his records, but never discloses much, then changes the subject.

Quarles asks about the FBI 302 dated 10/16/02. "Is the 302 in that copy of what you sent them?"

"Yes. Yes it is," Luna says, disputing both Ravenell and Tuminelli. Again Luna changes the subject. "With respect to the person who gave information to Mr. Grace, I spoke with both Mr. Skinner—."

"Well, that information, Mr. Grace alleges that heroin was placed in his vehicle by someone else," Quarles says.

"Correct," Ravenell says.

"Yes," Luna says.

"And I directed you to identify that person," the judge reminds him.

"Yes," Luna says.

"And provide sufficient information for the defense counsel to contact the person."

"Yes," Luna says, tossing out the smallest of morsels. "This is what I have been able to find out. The person's name was Tony. I spoke to—."

"Tony who?" Quarles asks incredulously.

"I don't have a last name," Luna tells them. Now the sloppy, careless, and lazy work of Skinner and his cohort, Baltimore Detective Todd Moody, becomes more evident. "I spoke to Detective Moody about that. He said that he didn't have a last name. He never spoke to Tony. He said he did speak to Mr. Grace about it, that he didn't have a name, other than Tony, or any identifying information like an address, or date of birth, or anything like that."

"Has anyone inquired of Mr. Grace today for further identifiers about Tony?" Judge Quarles asks.

Once again, Warren Grace finds himself in the driver's seat, this time in federal court. Luna says, "I did, personally, during the break, and he had no identifiers, no way of knowing, other than to say that he was a guy that he knew in the block, in the neighborhood, and he knew him by Tony, your honor.

"Your honor," Luna continues, "what I have instructed Detective Moody to do is to make further inquiries beyond Mr. Grace to see if they can locate a Tony, and the government will certainly act in good faith. And if we can locate that person, I won't hesitate but to turn over that information as soon as possible. And, in fact, if we can locate the person, I can commit that the government will make that person available to defense counsel. But as we speak here, at a little after 5:50, I don't have any further information on this Tony. Other than his name. Tony."

"Mr. Ravenell," Quarles tells the defense lawyer. "Tony did it."

"Tony did it, judge," Ravenell repeats. Now he touches on Skinner and Moody's failure to investigate the matter properly. What *were* these guys of the "Safe Streets Task Force" doing while the Dawsons' house burned? "Obviously, that's a little shocking to me that no efforts were made between now and whenever that was, back in October, to find who Tony was. But just to accept Mr. Grace's word on it! The government may choose to handle their case however they wish. The problem is that it doesn't give us a lot to go on. We will see what they come up with. I can't go out and look for a Tony, last name unknown."

"How many can there be out there?" Quarles asks facetiously.

"I would not even hazard a guess," Ravenell says.

Luna comes to the defense of his co-conspirators in the Grace fiasco. "If I may, your honor," Luna says, defending Skinner and Moody, and contradicting his earlier statement that not much had been done to find "Tony." He also contradicts Skinner's own 302 report, in which no effort to find a Tony is mentioned. "At the time of discovery, Agent Skinner and Detective Moody made efforts to contact Tony and find Tony. They certainly questioned and debriefed Mr. Grace at length."

"Did they write a 302 on that?" Quarles asks.

"That's the 302 I referred to," Luna says, dodging.

"Does the 302 in there reference—," Quarles starts to ask.

"It makes no reference to any efforts to locate Tony, Judge," Ravenell points out. "All it says is that—."

"Do you have a copy of the 302?" Quarles asks Ravenell.

"Yes," Ravenell replies. "Mr. Grace said he didn't do it. That's basically what the 302 said. It weren't his."

The judge points out, almost inanely, that another Tony, a Baltimore city detective, is also involved in the case. "So we may now have two Tonys in the case," Quarles counts. "The detective Tyson, a/k/a/ Tony, as well as the dope-planting son of a gun Tony, huh?"

"Your honor—," Luna begins.

"Two Tony's," Quarles rattles on.

"If I may," Luna continues. "Detective Tyson, who is going to be a witness, uses the term, or nickname, Tony, when he is acting in an undercover capacity."

"So there were two Tonys involved the incident?" Quarles muses.

"Yes," Luna says.

"The good Tony and the bad Tony," Quarles says.

"Evidently," Luna offers.

"Okay. Anything else, folks?" Quarles asks the lawyers at the bench.

Tuminelli returns to a subject evaded by Luna — the government's supposed list of discovery documents sent to the defense. Was Luna inadvertently, or *intentionally,* misleading the defense lawyers, the court, and the public? he wonders. As we've seen, Luna clearly was in a long-running conspiracy with members of the "Safe Streets Task Force" to cover-up the bungled Stash House investigation, and God knows what else. Tuminelli wonders why he wasn't given the brief, October 16, 2002, FBI 302 report on the heroin found in Grace's SUV.

Tuminelli *had* been given, significantly, a copy of a FBI 302 describing Grace's early involvement in the investigation of Poindexter's drug murder of Alvin Jones. Again, we note, the Alvin Jones drug murder was well documented by Luna, and the government. Luna and company freely spoke of the Alvin Jones drug murder, unlike the rest of the Grace business.

"Yes, judge," Tuminelli begins. "I just want to respond to the point that there is a set of documents that track what was sent to the defendants. I wanted to join Mr. Ravenell, and I don't say that this was done intentionally, but that 302 (concerning the heroin in the SUV — ed.), I never saw. There's no way. It fits right into my defense. And had I seen that 302, I certainly would have recognized it." Tuminelli says that he and Ravenell apparently had been given different discovery documents. Ravenell, he says, never got the 302 concerning Grace's cooperation with the Jones murder investigation. This jogs Tuminelli's memory.

"Mr. Ravenell and I had a telephone call one day and I mentioned the (Jones murder) 302, or I made reference to something in a 302," Tuminelli recalls. "And he said, 'What are you talking about?' And I said I have this 302 and it says such and such. And one of the documents that he didn't have that I had was the interview of the recording of Mr. Grace being interviewed by homicide detectives in Baltimore city. So it's not accurate and correct to say that there is a set of discovery (documents) that went out to both attorneys."

This mystery sits uneasy with Judge Quarles. Quarles once held Luna's job, and he recalls the standard procedures when he worked in the U.S. attorney's office. "When I was in that office, a million years ago," he tells Luna, "we would usually photocopy what we sent, so that I assume you still do that?" In the discovery phase of nearly every American criminal trial, a page-numbered, photocopied stack of documents routinely is handed over to defense lawyers by prosecutors.

"We do," Luna assures him, "and that's what I photocopied the copies from."

"Okay," Quarles says. "Well, why don't you tomorrow bring down what you sent to them and at least we have the representation of Mr. Luna that it was in both packages they sent."

Now Ravenell, inadvertently or not, touches on the seeming conspiratorial nature of the entire affair. He focuses on Agent Skinner's deliberate obscuration and omission of facts in the writing of his 302 report concerning Grace's home detention violations. The Alvin Jones murder. The home detention violations. Grace's subsequent release from home detention. Finding heroin in Grace's car. And more. Something clearly is going on here, and continues to go on. It's an ongoing, secretive conspiracy, involving, at the very least, Luna, Skinner and Baltimore Detective Moody. Who else? What else?

Ravenell tells the judge he wants Skinner's FBI 302 concerning Grace's home detention violations admitted as court evidence.

"I will at this time, just for the record, move in this August 28, 2002 302 that I had given the court earlier," Ravenell tells Quarles. They discuss numbering the 302 as Defense Exhibit One. Trouble is, the defense has yet to open its case. "Not in evidence, obviously, for the jury at this point, but I will have this in evidence for the court file," Ravenell says. He wants it before the court, among other reasons, to talk to the judge about it on the record, and as possible grounds for appeal.

"Do you want it to be a court exhibit?" the judge asks. In other words, an exhibit entered by the court, not the defense.

"That would be better, if it's a court exhibit," Ravenell agrees. He says it should be given to the clerk, who has stepped out of the courtroom.

Quarles says to remind him about it, "Before my brain turns off today."

Ravenell now addresses the strange discrepancies between Skinner's 302 and the other violations memo written six days earlier by Todd Stokes of Pretrial Services. Ravenell observes that Agent Skinner, in his 302, obviously appears to be outright lying, and hiding Grace's absence. Ravenell says he detects a deliberate, intentional pattern of government misbehavior and cover-up.

At the bench, speaking quietly, Ravenell tell Quarles, "The concern I have, your honor, if you read the document I showed you earlier, is whether this violation of not telling us about this man being out of compliance was inadvertent or intentional. When I looked at the notice of apparent violation, one of the things that jumped out is that Agent Skinner went to the residence of Mr. Grace on August 20."

Ravenell draws Quarles' attention to the blatant discrepancies between Skinner's account and that written by Todd Stokes. Ravenell thereupon moves Stokes August 22, three-page memo into evidence.

"Court Exhibit Number 2 will be the Pretrial Services notice of violation to Warren Grace, dates August 22, 2002. Yes sir," Quarles agrees.

"What I was indicating," Ravenell continues, "on page three of (Stokes') report, it says Agent Skinner went to the defendant's residence, this is, Mr. Grace's residence, on August 20th at approximately 5pm, and advised ... Mr. Stokes 'that the defendant was not present,'" Ravenell reads Stokes account. "'However, the Securicor Electronic Monitoring Services, Inc., indicated he was in the residence.' So we have an agent going out to the man's home and finding out he was not there, while the system indicated he was present, and that Mr. Grace later returned and admitted that he had taken the bracelet off and left it home."

Skinner's 302 report, on the other hand, leaves out these crucial facts. "(Skinner's) August 28th 302 simply says that the agent went to the home, searched it, and that the electronic bracelet was in the dresser," Ravenell points out. "There is absolutely no reference to this, that indicates this man had left the home. They *knew* he left the home, and that he was gone for some period of time. In addition, as we heard today, he had been doing this for some time. Leaving the home, going out for some periods of time, as he alleges, 'to eat and hang out,' but, of course, not to sell heroin or have any contact with heroin.

"Shockingly," Ravenell continues, "on 10/16, we find out there is heroin — 10/16/02. We find that there was heroin actually in his vehicle, as well.

"Your honor, look at this August 28, 2002, 302. It cannot be reconciled with what the agent and the government had to know back in August. And what they had to know, they should have disclosed to us far in advance of today's date.

"In addition, your honor, in that Court's Exhibit 2, on page two, near the bottom, it says that Mr. Stokes was able to identify the anonymous caller's phone number, and provide that information to Agent Skinner. I don't know what happened with that investigation, if anything; who that person was."

Luna at first volunteers that Skinner doesn't know the identity of the anonymous caller. "The agent doesn't know." Then Luna says that Skinner "believes he spoke to the son of a person named Robin. We can get her last name."

Robin, Luna explains, "is the girlfriend and current wife of Mr. Grace. I can tell you that Robin did have some kids who were not, to say the least, thrilled that Mr. Grace was living with their mother. They wanted him out of the house, and knew that he was under electronic home monitoring."

"And apparently also knew that he was slipping off the bracelet," Quarles observes.

"Your honor," Ravenell says, "the point being that this is *not inadvertent."* It's intentional, very much active, and conspiratorial.

"Well, I don't know whether it's inadvertent or not," Quarles counters, "and I don't have sufficient evidence to make a determination (as) to whether it was intentional or inadvertent."

"I would ask the court to conduct a hearing," Ravenell argues.

Quarles says, at this point, he's simply trying to save the trial, which he sees is now threatened by government misbehavior. "What I am trying to do at the moment, first things first," Quarles says, "is to put you in a better defense posture, so that you can use the information that you have, and so that you can conduct whatever additional discovery is necessary so that we can sort of save the trial, having invested two days in it already. So the government is directed to supply the defendants, that's both of them, through counsel, any document relating to Tony and the heroin seized. The Tony heroin seized. What was the date of the Tony heroin seizure?"

Ravenell says, "10/16/02." Dawson arson day. The Dawsons had been complaining for months. Those concerned about Warren Grace found their complaints fell on equally deaf ears. Neither the judge, nor the defense lawyers, understand the significance of the date.

"Ten-sixteen-oh-two," Quarles repeats. "Any document in the government's possession relating to Mr. Grace's defeat of the electronic monitoring system, any document relating to citizens' complaints about Mr. Grace's defeat of the electronic monitoring, and the identification of the caller who informed Pretrial of Mr. Grace's defeat of the electronic monitoring system. Does the government understand the court's order?"

"The government does, your honor," Luna says.

Ravenell asks that the order be put in writing. Quarles is lazy, and says he's not going to write it down. He says the order will be written down only if the court reporter "feels like reducing it to writing for me. I assume the government knows again the four items?" Quarles repeats his order.

"The four items are: Any document relating to the October 16, 2002, Tony heroin seized from Mr. Grace," Quarles repeats.

"The second item is any document in the government's possession relating to Mr. Grace's defeat of the electronic monitoring system.

"The third document is any document in the government's possession relating to citizen complaints abut Mr. Grace's defeat of the electronic monitoring system. These would include, of course, any complaints made by the children of the person with whom Mr. Grace was living.

"And the fourth item, the government is required to identify the caller who informed Pretrial Services of Mr. Grace's defeat of the electronic monitoring system. Everyone got those four items?"

"Yes, your honor," Luna says.

"Anything else, folks?" Quarles asks. "I'm going to stop asking that question."

With that, Tuminelli speaks up, and requests a mistrial.

"I want to move for a mistrial on the basis of the denial of due process because of these instances," Tuminelli requests, "because I think that we have been placed in a terrible position in terms of preparing for trial because of the government's failure to provide this information which has been in their possession for some time now. So I would like, beyond what Mr. Ravenell has done, to move for a mistrial on that basis."

"Your honor," Ravenell seconds, "I have consulted with my client as well, Mr. Smith, and we also join in that motion."

Judge Quarles says he'll sleep on it. "I have often advised defense attorneys to be careful about making for mistrial because I actually grant them," Quarles says. Mistrials come with their own set of risks for defendants, the judge is saying. The case must be retried, not dismissed, and often under less favorable circumstances for the defendants. It could take a year or more to retry a case and, meanwhile, the defendants remain in jail.

"We are making it seriously, judge," Ravenell says.

"So I am going to think about it overnight," Quarles says. "And I, of course, will give the government a chance to respond in the morning as to whether it agrees that the mistrial should be granted, or its reasons for opposing the mistrial, but I take mistrial motions seriously. As I say, I have, in fact, granted them under the appropriate circumstances, and I take both of these motions seriously."

Quarles now comments on Agent Skinner's unethical and incompetent misbehavior: "It is difficult for me to conceive that the government would *actually seize drugs from a cooperator and then, on the same day, send him in to work a case,"* Quarles says. "That is just—. Well, that is difficult for me to reconcile." (Emphasis mine.)

Ravenell points out that Grace is "the key witness."

"The witness is, by and large, the case," Quarles agrees.

"He is, by and large, the case," Ravenell repeats.

"Yes," Quarles says.

"And his credibility is, by and large, the case for the government," Ravenell says.

"It's not as bleak as you put it, because—," Quarles says.

"Well, they do have tapes," Ravenell agrees. One hundred hours of tapes showing Grace, Poindexter and Smith scratching their asses and their vinyl phonograph records, saying "yo," and dealing heroin.

"They did have him under surveillance," Quarles says. "They did have statements, so it's not quite as bleak as you put it. But I am disturbed by the apparent failure to disclose, inadvertent or otherwise, the significant information relating to Mr. Grace.

"So, as I said, I am not making any judgments or findings at this point with respect to whether the government has done anything wrong here. I am not sure that they have." Government misbehavior, apparently, is harder for some to discern than looking at the tick tock hands of an atomic clock.

With that, Quarles adds, "We are adjourned."

It's about 6 pm, on the evening of December 2, 2003.

As he walks out of the courtroom that evening, Jonathan Luna has less than thirty-five hours to live.

14
Trial Day 3:
Travels with Rosencrantz and Guildenstern

The next morning the courtroom of Judge William Quarles is chock-filled with more surprises.

At the appointed moment struck by the electrons in his atomic clock, at precisely 9:30 am, Quarles looks down from his bench. Our young prosecutor, Jonathan Luna, is absent from the prosecution table. Luna at last arrives, hurrying in several minutes late. Luna explains he has been at the hospital, visiting his ailing infant son. Out of patience, Quarles fines Luna $25.

"Excuse me, your honor," Luna apologizes to Quarles. *"Do not come your tardy son to chide,"* Shakespeare writes in Hamlet.

"That's okay," Quarles tells Luna. "Before the end of trial, make a check in the amount of $25 payable to the clerk of the court."

"Yes, your honor," Luna says.

"Call the case," Quarles tells him.

"Your honor, I am calling the case of United States of America v. Walter Poindexter and Deon Lionnel Smith, under Criminal No. WDQ-030-0213. On behalf of the government, Jonathan P. Luna."

Tuminelli and Ravenell introduce themselves for the record, on behalf of their clients. "Counsel, Mr. Poindexter, Mr. Smith, good morning," Quarles tells them. If it weren't for class-action lawsuits, I suppose, there could be millions of people standing to introduce themselves each morning.

The jury has yet to be summoned from the jury room, and a long, remarkable dialogue ensues between the lawyers and the judge, out of earshot of the jurors.

Overnight there have been several startling developments that now require Judge Quarles immediate attention. After court adjourned the previous evening, Quarles, out of patience with Luna's stonewalling, had arranged a meeting between defense attorneys and officials at Pretrial Services. Pretrial Services at one time had been nominally in charge of Warren Grace's home detention. At the meeting with defense attorneys, Todd Stokes and Barbara Skidmore, of Pretrial, disclosed troubling information about the government's handling of Warren Grace.

Defense lawyers learned that the U.S. attorney's office, and the FBI, had thrown caution in the wind in their dealings with Grace. That's putting it mildly. Time and again the Justice Department ignored well-founded concerns from Pretrial Services that Grace should not be running loose on the street, that he was a clear menace to his neighbors in Baltimore. Once Todd Stokes learned that Grace had defeated his home monitoring device, Stokes, following standard procedure and common sense, asked Judge Frederic Smalkin to issue a warrant for Grace and return him to jail.

Instead of protecting the public, the FBI, backed by DiBiagio's U.S. Attorney's office, intervened to keep Grace on the street. This, despite repeated complaints that Pug was shooting neighbors with guns, and dealing heroin. Defense lawyers learned that Luna's co-counsel at the time, Jacabed Rodriguez-Coss, with Luna's knowledge, had intervened with Judge Smalkin to keep Grace at large on the streets. A warrant shouldn't be issued for Grace, the federal judge was told by the Justice Department, because it would "hurt the government's case down the line," Ravenell and Tuminelli were told. Poindexter had yet to be released from jail, so that Skinner could set him up, and send him back to jail.

"Hurt the government's case down the line." This meant the government knew what it was doing was wrong. It meant the government knew disclosure of these facts would hurt its already strange excursion against Stash House Records, Smith and Poindexter. It also meant, to say the least, a conspiracy to undertake these misdeeds against the public, counter their public trust, and to keep these actions secret.

The murder of the Dawsons brought only more dishonesty. U.S. Attorney Tom DiBiagio's public misstatements against revolving door "drug punks," only solidified Luna's desire to keep close to his lawyer's vest the dirty secrets about Warren Grace. He'd given no information in discovery. And Luna continued to stonewall. He feared two-faced DiBiagio would leave him holding the bag and fire him. DiBiagio wanted Luna "gone."

Tuminelli and Ravenell now thought Luna's misconduct was egregious enough to warrant a new trial. The judge could even throw out the case. They then could argue that their clients should not have to stand trial a second time. They'd made a double jeopardy argument. You can't be tried twice for the same offense. Thanks to the ongoing misdeeds of Luna and the FBI's "Safe Streets Task Force," Poindexter and Smith conceivably could walk free.

Anything to protect Tom DiBiagio from the fallout still blowing from the Dawsons' atomic explosion.

The case was falling apart. Big pieces were dropping off moment by moment. Defense lawyers find themselves dodging the falling wreckage. And now, a new problem, of their own making. Late yesterday afternoon, at close of proceedings, both lawyers had asked Judge Quarles to declare a mistrial. In light of the new information from Pretrial, this actually put Smith and Poindexter at risk. Defendants who ask for a mistrial, and have their request granted, waive their rights to protection against double jeopardy. They could, and would, be tried again.

What seemed like a good idea to defense attorneys last night now seems not so wise. Tuminelli, before the start of court, telephoned Judge Quarles chambers to withdraw Poindexter's motion for mistrial.

Now, in court, at the start of the day's proceedings, Quarles asks, "Mr. Tuminelli, you called chambers this morning indicating that you wanted to withdraw Mr. Poindexter's motion for a mistrial?"

"I want to withdraw the motion, but I would like the court to know that I didn't send the court off on this long goose chase," Tuminelli says. "The reason for my now advising the court that we are withdrawing the motion is because of disclosures that were made last night, after the court session, by Todd Stokes and Barbara Skidmore, primarily Todd Stokes, of Pretrial Services." Tuminelli stammers, "It is my position that the kind of conduct involved in particular with Jacqueline Rodriguez (sic) of the United States Attorney's office in this case, while Mr. Luna may have been present—. There is information available to us that the government took affirmative action to prevent Judge Smalkin from issuing a bench warrant for—."

"That had been requested by Pretrial," Quarles finishes the sentence. The judge has already read some of the suppressed memos. Quarles now surely also knows that the scandal, involving as it does Judge Smalkin, reaches into the federal judiciary.

"That had been requested by Pretrial," Tuminelli repeats. "And the reason given by Ms. Rodriguez and the government for not requesting that a warrant be issued was that it would, quote, 'Hurt the government's case down the line.'"

"Who is Ms. Rodriguez?" Quarles asks.

"She is the former assistant United States attorney who was involved in this case early on," Tuminelli says.

"That is correct, your honor," Luna agrees. Ah, conspiracies. We now see the rough spot Luna finds himself in. Does he want to keep his job, and pay his mortgage? Does he want the FBI angry with him? Does he want a federal judge or two angry with him? He is, literally, in an untenable position, with nowhere to turn for help. His secrets keep spilling out, like the blood of a stabbed man. He can do nothing but stall, spin and weave, as he takes the hits.

Tuminelli says he is now renewing his request "that the case be dismissed on due process grounds." For that reason, Tuminelli says, Poindexter was dropping his motion for mistrial. The reason, he says, "is that we want to preserve the possible claim later that this will constitute a double jeopardy violation. If this case, in fact, gets dismissed, and if we consent, as the court knows, we will essentially waive that claim." Aren't lawyers, and courts, wonderful?

"One of the reasons I was always so happy to grant motions for mistrial and tell counsel to make sure that they were serious about granting them," Quarles says.

Tuminelli adds he's a busy lawyer, and his trial schedule in the coming months prevents a quick retrial. Poindexter, he says, "is the one who will bear the brunt of sitting in prison for another six to nine months because of the government's failure to disclose. I understand the court is willing to give us additional time, you know, to investigate these new matters, but—."

"Including a brief recess in this trial, if necessary," Quarles says.

"I understand. But given the impact on Mr. Poindexter, it's our position that a brief recess is not sufficient," Tuminelli says, "that he has been harmed by this, he has been prejudiced by this. In any event, our position is that we withdraw the motion," for mistrial. "If the court were to declare a mistrial, we would seek to raise a double jeopardy claim on re-prosecution."

Ravenell gets up and says, "We do join in the withdrawal of Mr. Smith's motion for a mistrial as well for the same reasons enunciated by Mr. Tuminelli. In addition, your honor, the court has at times in our telephone conferences in this matter made light of my trial schedule, and—."

"Not made light of," Quarles edits.

"Well, a little levity, actually," Ravenell chuckles.

"Merely pointed out that you're—," Quarles begins.

"With some levity," Ravenell breaks in.

"That you are one of the lawyers here in town that could benefit most from cloning, Mr. Ravenell," Quarles says.

"Maybe I could," Ravenell allows. "If I could do that, judge, I would be better off with my family. But I share the same concern, judge. With my trial calendar, we are talking at least the summer or fall before this matter could be back in for another trial." Ravenell mulls the options before them. Two options: An outright mistrial, delaying things for months; or a recess to investigate Grace and his handlers at the FBI and Justice. "I am also concerned about when the court says, you know, 'a brief recess of the trial,'" (to investigate the FBI's handling of Grace), "because I don't know how long the court would want to recess."

"I would hope any recess we have would not inconvenience the jurors," Quarles says. Quarles is always thinking of those jurors. Forget obvious government corruption, reckless endangerment, court complicity, and whether citizens' rights were trampled, and a life surprisingly hanging in the balance. He imagines jurors don't care about those things. "I wasn't considering a month, or a matter of weeks, because I don't want to lose the jury. But if it's a matter of a day or two in addition to the weekend, I would be certainly willing to do that."

Quarles adds that the issues at hand are relatively narrow: "The defeat of the electronic monitoring system, and the government's apparent involvement in Judge Smalkin's failure to issue a warrant for Mr. Grace." As well, he notes, Warren Grace was then removed from home monitoring altogether, and was free to roam the streets of Baltimore. "And removal of the electronic monitoring condition."

"Well, that's what shocked me," Ravenell says.

"While on Pretrial detention," Quarles notes.

"That's what shocked me, with all due respect," Ravenell says, "that the man gained a benefit by having more freedom in the community."

"Well, I guess one of the reasons was since he defeated the electronic monitoring system, why require him to have it all?" Quarles reasons. This is strange thinking, the defense attorneys note. It's like saying, if a prisoner breaks out of jail, why bother jailing him again?

"Why require any?" Ravenell follows the thought.

"Since it doesn't matter," Quarles muses.

"I guess that's one way of thinking about it," Ravenell says, not wanting to ruffle this Mad Hatter judge. He points out, subtly, that he always thought violations such as these merited *increased* punishment, not less. But this case has already passed through the looking glass and is about to sail over the rainbow.

Quarles says he doesn't think the government's misbehavior warrants a dismissal of the case. The problem for the defendants, he reiterates, is the tape-recorded evidence gathered against them. Quarles tells the lawyers, "Last night and this morning, I reviewed the evidence so far, and, although Mr. Grace is a significant witness, I can't ignore the fact that the government has tapes on which, among other things, Mr. Smith has acknowledged heroin dealing and confirms Mr. Grace's account of being supported in prison by Poindexter and failing to do the same. And both Mr. Poindexter and Mr. Smith are seen and heard receiving the (heroin) compaction instruction, which arguably is evidence of their conspiracy. So, although the Grace testimony is significant, it is not the only basis for prosecution. The larger basis, of course, is the words of the defendants.

"So, obviously, you are entitled, under *Brady* and *Giglio*, to the information that apparently you did not receive. But, whether it was a good faith or bad faith suppression of the evidence, I am not so sure that it requires dismissal to remedy the government's defaults in this case.

"So what I offer you, what I've done, as you know, as I required Pretrial to meet with you, as they did last night, to talk to you."

"That's right," Ravenell agrees.

"And they were more forthcoming perhaps about the government's role in keeping Mr. Grace on the street than the government has been?" Quarles asks.

"A lot more, judge," Ravenell says.

"I also required the government to provide certain information to you," Quarles reminds all. "I don't know whether they have done that."

Despite having promised to do so, Luna, in keeping with his unwritten ground rules of the entire case, has turned precisely nothing over to the defense.

"Of which we have received none, your honor," Ravenell complains.

"Well, that's typical of the government so far," Quarles observes. Quarles says, rather than dismissal, he's offering the defense a brief recess, a continuance, "to do any additional investigation that is required." Two "relatively narrow issues" are open for investigation, he tells the lawyers. The first, "the issue of the government's role in keeping Mr. Grace on the streets of our community." The second, "the Tony supply of heroin, and what efforts the government made to investigate that story," on October 16, 2002. The day the Dawsons died.

Defense attorney Ravenell's mind already has turned to Warren Grace, who every day rides back and forth, from prison to court, alongside characters resembling more and more Shakespeare's Rosencrantz and Guildenstern: Agent Skinner and Detective Moody. Who sent them? Who approved their mission? What exactly *is* their mission? Their movements can only threaten trouble for some overwhelmed, entangled Hamlet.

Now Skinner and Moody find themselves subjects of court investigation. Moment by moment, Ravenell and Tuminelli uncover more troubling facts about Skinner and Moody. Moment by moment, it gets worse. This morning, before court, someone called defense lawyers to pass along startling new information. Now they're even phoning in from the street, like it's Dialing for Dollars. The caller told the lawyers that Skinner and Moody had driven Grace to his wife's house the previous Sunday, to spend a few hours. His keepers obviously hoped to please, and influence, Grace before the start of trial. Grace obviously remains in control. What else would he want from his three bumbling keepers? What else could he take?

As late as three days ago the task force rewarded (or is the word 'bribed'?) Grace for his cooperation. Luna had to be involved as well. It's called an ongoing conspiracy.

Now the defense lawyers wonder how they can question Grace about Skinner, Moody and Luna, when the three daily hold such close sway over the man. A real investigation requires Grace to be isolated from Luna, Skinner and Moody. Ravenell decides to ask that Grace be placed in the custody of U.S. marshals, and kept away from the three mouseketeers.

"If the court were to grant a delay over the weekend," Ravenell ventures to ask, "would the court preclude the government from having any contact with this witness once he is finished (with) direct examination?"

"Once he is finished direct, yes," Quarles says. "Uh-huh." That is, once Luna is done with him, Grace will be isolated.

"I don't see any reason why this man can't be placed in U.S. Marshal custody," Ravenell says, "where he would not have to be transported back and forth by the agents involved in the case."

Quarles, incredibly, doesn't want to do it. "Well, I'm not going to further burden the marshals," Judge Quarles says. "I am not so jaded to believe, although you are pushing me close, that the government would ignore a direct order to insulate the witness from further preparation or discussion. Of course, I am willing to be made a believer." What planet does this judge call home? Luna has so far ignored every order of the court meant to expose government deeds and misdeeds. This single, offhand decision may cost a life.

"Your honor," Ravenell tells him, "we certainly have some concerns about that, about any contact." Ravenell imagines he doesn't have to worry about Luna contacting Grace. This may well be incorrect, and is certainly counter-intuitive. Luna has shown he will do what he must to save his neck. In his mind, Skinner and Moody are another subject. "You know, I certainly feel that there would be no contact by the attorneys in the case. But I am concerned that, just because there would be actual contact between the witness and two other witnesses in the case (Skinner and Moody -ed.), that discussions may occur, even inadvertently, that would further harm our case by letting this man sit before we cross-examine him."

"I understand that," Quarles replies. "But I, as I said, am not inclined to grant that."

The lawyers decide to ask for a private chat, ex parte, with the judge. They want to tell him about the tip they received this morning that Skinner and Moody had allowed Grace to go home over the weekend. These misdeeds are ongoing. Certainly they'll do it again.

"Judge, could we make a presentation ex parte?" Tuminelli asks. "And I will explain why the court ought to reconsider what it is—."

"We have gotten some new information," Ravenell adds.

"At the appropriate time," Quarles promises. Now Quarles falls back on his old saw about not wasting the jurors' time. They're still waiting in the jury room, while this interesting conversation rattles on. Fact is, it's a safe bet the jurors surely would have, and should have, been interested in all that Quarles keeps from them, in their name. "What I would really like to do," he says, "as I said, I like to view trials in terms of my time and their time. At this point, we are wasting their time. I would rather you waste my time. Since they are all here and ready to go, I would like to at least conclude the Grace direct (examination), if we can, and then I will take up matters. But it really is unfair to bring them in to serve and then, you know, sort of fritter their time away while we have lawyer discussions. Jurors hate that, and they are right about hating that. You have no idea what a sacrifice jury duty is for most people. For us to waste their time is— should be criminal." Well spoken, judge. Other things about this case should be criminal, too.

"We can certainly take these matters up after direct, judge," Ravenell agrees.

"Okay," Quarles says.

"Your honor," Luna pipes up, "I do have a response with respect to the items that you asked the government to provide."

"That I *directed* the government to provide," Quarles corrects Luna.

"That is right," Luna says. Each moment he sounds more and more like Bugs Bunny — offhand, almost flip. Kwazy wabbit. Someone, very shortly, will want to kill the wabbit. "And, for the record, that is any information or document identifying Tony, and any information or documents concerning the heroin that was found by the FBI in Mr. Grace's vehicle, any information or documents concerning—."

"Well, I know what the list is," Quarles tells him. "Don't waste time reading the list."

"All right," Luna says.

"What do you have?"

"What I have is, I have instructed FBI Agent Skinner to prepare a 302 supplement, and I have that 302 supplement with me, and I will provide that to counsel right now," Luna says. He hands this unusual "302 supplement" to the defense lawyers. This document is strange, to say the least. FBI agents are instructed to write their 302 reports as soon as possible after an incident, not *fourteen months later.* FBI 302 reports, I'm told, should not be edited or redacted, nor in any way revised, all of which later could serve to raise suspicions about agent behavior and veracity.

"Okay," Quarles accepts.

"Secondly," Luna continues, and I know that we are on the jury's time, but, in light of all the discussions about the government's role in facilitating Mr. Grace's work with the FBI, I also want to inform the government—." Luna curiously forgets that *he* is the government. "Or, the government wants to inform the court and counsel that last night I reviewed documents in the Warren Grace file." Of course, Luna previously told the court he has already done this. "I did not find any documents pertaining specifically to the defeat of the electronic home monitoring system, but I did come across three documents that were not turned over to defense counsel that concern Mr. Grace's Pretrial release conditions."

See Luna dance. See him spin, scratch his own record. He also appears not to be telling the truth. He clearly has in his possession Todd Stokes' August 22, 2002, memo describing how Grace greased his leg with Vaseline to slip off the monitoring anklet, and how no alarms were sounded with the security system. This memo was cc'd to Luna.

Luna glosses over the three new documents that he says he happened to stumble across. Two of them have been sealed, and require the judge to sign an unsealing order. One imagines these aren't minor documents, easily overlooked, in most U.S. attorneys' offices, like dry cleaning receipts. "Let me tell you what they are," he begins, as always, making a presentation, a sale. First, a flash of showmanship, to raise suspense. "Well, first of all, let me just say that two are sealed documents and I have prepared an unsealing order for the court to sign. It's a motion and an order for the court to sign."

"The motion is granted, and I will sign the order," Quarles says. "It's no longer sealed."

The first of the two documents is nothing less than the U.S. attorney's original request to modify Warren Grace's conditions of release, removing him from the halfway house to turn him loose on the good people of Baltimore, leading to his slipping, with Vaseline, his surly bonds of home confinement. This is the motion that placed Grace in home confinement "under electronic monitoring." In her request, Rodriguez-Coss writes that these "conditions of release would ensure both the safety of the community and his presence at trial, as well as safeguard the safety of the defendant." Immortal words.

The second document Luna forks over is Judge Smalkin's rubber-stamped approval of one of these harebrained schemes meant, in final measure, to help our government take over a rap music label.

"All right," Luna says. "I will turn those over right now. (The first) is Jacabed Rodriguez's motion for modification of conditions of release. It was filed in June of 2002. The next document is an order that was signed by Judge Smalkin in the case.

"The (third) document that I have — and I have copies for counsel — is a letter written from Pretrial Services to Magistrate Judge Gauvey, expressing Pretrial Service's concerns about releasing Mr. Grace. This is the period of time when Mr. Grace is still detained. He is not out on the street, and that particular date of that letter is May 21, 2002. So I wanted to put that on the record, and make sure that counsel have that."

These documents, while interesting, are small potatoes.

Luna continues, "With respect to the 302 that was prepared by Agent Skinner, it is essentially a supplement to the October 16th or October 17th 302, reviewing the October 16th events. And it goes into some detail as the to actions that were taken by Special Agent Skinner upon discovery of the heroin. It does not, however, give any identifying information about Tony.

"It does relate efforts and identifies persons that were contacted by the FBI to ascertain what, if any, people may have called Pretrial Services about Mr. Grace. With respect to any other matters concerning the defeat of electronic home monitoring, or identification of any callers who may have informed Pretrial Services of the defeat, we don't have any other additional documents."

Luna has brought along a box. Rather than compiling a list of discovery material, as he has been ordered to do, he now invites defense counsel to root through the box to see which documents they may or may not have.

"I have also brought down the box of discovery that, according to my records, were turned over pursuant to the court's request," he says. "Defense counsel is— I will make that available, and they can go through it and compare what's in that box with what they have."

Luna next addresses the situation involving Grace's transportation arrangements back and forth to prison with Skinner and Moody. He points out there's a "separation order" requiring Grace to be held in a dungeon somewhere, possibly Denmark, but probably in Philadelphia (Luna doesn't say), and that the U.S. Marshals have requested the dynamic duo of Skinner and Moody, normally tucked away in the bat cave, do the driving.

"Also, with respect to Mr. Grace, I have no objection whatsoever making Mr. Grace available to defense counsel and they can interview him one-on-one and question him thoroughly about who Tony is. I have no objection to that, your honor, and will make him available. The only reason why the agents are transporting him is because there is a separation order and the situation with the marshals, they had requested the agents do that, but I am willing to do whatever the court wants to do with respect to that. I just wanted to put that on the record."

"Okay," Quarles tells him. "Can we resume the trial now? Where is Mr. Grace?"

"You know, I don't know, your honor," Luna advises. "Let me check that."

"Okay," Quarles says.

The defense attorneys, meanwhile, have been thrown into disarray by Luna's sudden disclosure of the three documents. They know Luna hasn't coughed up all he's got, let alone all he knows. Ravenell says, "While you are getting Mr. Grace, Mr. Stokes (of Pretrial Services — ed.) told us, your honor, that there was a letter written by the prosecutors in this case dated August 29th of 2002, acknowledging Mr. Grace's violations and why they were opposed to him being taken off the streets. That has not been turned over."

Ravenell and Tuminelli are clearly confused by Luna's piecemeal, impromptu dump of documents, and where the documents fit into the growing puzzle.

"That's the letter that says that it would damage their case in the future," Tuminelli ventures.

Ravenell says that's incorrect. "Well, my understanding of Mr. Stokes is that the comments about damaging their case was an oral communication between he and Ms. Rodriquez, but there was also a subsequent letter that—."

"Uh-huh," Quarles says. In the middle of trial, he's forced to keep track of all this. "Does Pretrial have that letter in its files?" he asks.

"Pretrial said they had it," Ravenell answers, "but I did not ask them to turn it over. I would ask the government to give it to us."

"If the government can't find it," Quarles says, "I will direct Pretrial to turn it over to you."

"There is also a 9/13/02 order from Judge Smalkin taking Mr. Grace off of any Pretrial supervision," Ravenell ventures on. "I thought Mr. Luna was referring to it when he says he has an order, but apparently he is referring to a different order. If we could have that order as well."

This trial's becoming Kafkaesque. What are the documents, who has them, what are they for? Who knows? Our hip-hip impresarios,

Smith and Poindexter, all the while sit watching from their stiff-backed chairs at the defense table.

Ravenell lastly requests that Warren Grace's criminal file be unsealed. Luna's office previously had asked a court to seal the file, so the public can't see it. Luna doesn't object, and Quarles lifts the seal.

15
Again we hear the rattling gold chains of the ghost of Alvin 'L' Jones

The jury at last is led in to the courtroom, and Judge Quarles apologizes to the jurors for the delay. Warren Grace returns to the witness stand, under direct examination of Jonathan Luna.

Grace picks up where he left off yesterday, helping the jury to decipher the audio tapes he covertly made with the FBI. He discusses the big shipments of heroin Deon Smith received from "up top," in New York City, and the foreigners who control the trade. "He was saying there was a spot in New York where you could get it in bulk," Grace at one point tells the jury as a tape of his conversation with Smith is played for the courtroom. He goes on to explain how to use "the tools," and how the heroin is compressed.

At the end of his testimony, Grace's attention is directed to a tape he recorded on January 2, 2003. Tuminelli interrupts the examination, and asks for a conference at the bench. The tape contains a conversation with Deon Smith, concerning Poindexter's murder of Alvin Jones, which the jury isn't supposed to hear.

"Judge," Tuminelli tells him, "this transcript relates to the conversation that Mr. Grace has had with Mr. Smith, and they are discussing... the allegation that Mr. Grace had talked to the Baltimore city police homicide department about the murder."

Tuminelli complains he hadn't been given a copy of this transcript "until yesterday. I would like an opportunity to review it." He worries the jury will hear of Jones' drug-related murder.

"We have removed the reference to the murder and the homicide," Luna assures him. Luna wants it both ways. He wants the jury to hear that Grace was talking to the police, but he promises not to specifically mention that the police are investigating Poindexter's drug murder of Alvin Jones. Luna tells the judge, "And what I would like to offer as a suggestion is that I lead the witness. (I'll say), 'Now were you talking about you talking to the police?' just so there won't be any mention of the murder.

"The reason why we want to get this in is it shows that in 2003 there is still this conversation between Mr. Smith and Grace about Poindexter, and it clearly shows a connection to that. So there is still this connection. That's going to be the last recording that I will play, and I can do it in such a way—."

Quarles wants Grace to make no mention of Alvin Jones, or his murder. "I thought you instructed him also not to make reference to—," Quarles begins.

"I have," Luna assures the judge.

"Why don't the three of you go over there and instruct him again," Judge Quarles tells the lawyers. No use having Grace spill the beans about the murder. They'd have a mistrial on their hands.

The judge instructs one of the lawyers to muzzle the microphone, so none of the jurors can hear what's going on, while the three of them explicitly tell Grace not to mention or in way describe how Walter Poindexter, in premeditated fashion, hunted down and shot Alvin Jones in cold blood, in front of at least two witnesses, in retaliation for the burglary at the drug stash house, in a classic drug murder.

More thought and effort was now going into keeping the jury from hearing even a passing reference to Jones' murder than Poindexter expended thought or energy to blow the guy away.

Alvin Jones wasn't making it easy for these guys. He wouldn't simply be murdered and go away. His ghost has begun to haunt the proceedings, as he will haunt the last hours of our struggling Hamlet, Jonathan Luna.

"Why don't the three of you go over there and instruct him again," Quarles tells the lawyers. "Make sure that someone is holding the microphone and explain to him that he is to answer your literal questions and only those questions and not to volunteer anything."

"Judge," Tuminelli agrees, "I would join in his request. I would prefer that he ask leading questions, to get right to the point."

"Yes," Quarles says.

"They can be answered with yes or no's."

"But I want to make sure he is told specifically not to mention the homicide, and someone cover the microphone and make sure our husher system works," Quarles instructs. "Okay?"

Following the judge's instructions, the lawyers go to the witness stand, cover the microphone, and tell Warren Grace not to mention Poindexter's murder of Alvin Jones, and to answer only yes or no.

Luna then returns to his examination. "Mr. Grace, I want to turn your attention to recording Number 80," Luna says. "And I will play that brief recording."

He plays recording Number 80 for the jury.

"Do you recall this conversation, Mr. Grace?" Luna asks.

"Yes," Grace says.

"Are you talking about the fact that you had been talking to the police?" Luna asks, careful to avoiding mention of Alvin Jones.

"Yes."

"And who are you talking to?"

"Mr. Smith."

"And who are you talking about having spoken to the police about Mr. Poindexter?"

"Yes."

"And, in fact, did that happen?"

"Yes."

"There is a reference to, 'Didn't want to say nothing to you on the phone, but this phone ain't no good,'" Luna says. "Do you remember that?"

"Yes."

"What is that a reference to?" Luna asks. "'This phone ain't no good.'"

"It's not a device you want to be talking over," Grace says.

"Why not?" Luna asks.

"Someone could be listening in," Grace explains.

"Who could be listening in?"

"The police could be listening."

16
Warren Grace placed in protective 'bubble' from FBI and Luna

With that, Warren Grace's testimony comes to an end. "Your honor, I have checked my notes and conferred with my colleagues and at this time I have no further questions for Mr. Grace," Luna says.

It's 11:30 am, Wednesday morning. Quarles gives the jurors a twenty-minute recess. The jurors file out, and Judge Quarles turns his attention to the lawyers, and Warren Grace.

"If I may have your attention folks," Quarles says. Quarles tells Grace that defense lawyers will interview Grace at an undecided time, at an undecided location, "at some point later in the trial." Quarles instructs Grace not to have any conversations with Agent Skinner, the other agents or officers, nor Jonathan Luna.

Judge Quarles tells Warren Grace, "I am ordering you to have no conversations with anyone about your testimony or about your pre-trial detention or about the incidents that we were told by Agent Skinner about, about the drugs that you said were found in your SUV that came from Tony. Do not have any discussions about any of those matters with anyone, with this one exception: there will be, within the next few days, a meeting between you and Mr. Ravenell and Mr. Tuminelli. At that meeting, you may discuss all of those topics. Do you understand? With that exception, you are not to discuss what you testified about with anyone, you are not to discuss your pre-trial detention, your defeating the electronic monitoring system specifically, and the drugs supplied by Tony that were found in your truck. Do you understand?"

"I understand," Grace says.

Quarles next gives the same instruction to Luna, Skinner, and Luna's co-counsel. "Mr. Luna and Ms. Cockburn and Agent Skinner," he says, "I am directing you, that is, I am ordering you to make sure that no one on the government's side has those discussions with Mr. Grace, and I am also directing you to advise other people who may be in a position of transporting Mr. Grace to not have any conversations with him about his testimony, about his pre-trial detention matters that we discussed, or about the Tony heroin."

"Understood," Luna says.

Quarles says he expects Luna to help arrange the defense counsel's questioning of Grace. And he wants no FBI agents present during the questioning. "And I will expect that you and defense counsel will determine a day within the next several days when Mr. Grace will be presented to them at a location to be determined by you, a secure location," Quarles says. "Obviously, you will determine the location. Obviously, that location, during the interview, there will be no government agent in the immediate room where he is taken. I understand because he is in custody that you will want to have agents around to secure him, but the meeting between defense counsel and Mr. Grace is not to be monitored in any fashion. Do you understand that?"

Has Luna screwed up? His handling of the affair, on the surface, has been ill planned and ill considered. Or has it? Due to the openings he's given Ravenell and Tuminelli, there'll now be a full-blown inquiry on the misconduct of the FBI, and the U.S. Attorney's office.

Notice, once again, that Warren Grace is in a strong position. Grace holds the cards, and the information. Quarles tells Grace, "Obviously, it goes without saying—. I guess nothing goes without saying, so I will say it. You are not to discuss with the government or government personnel those matters discussed between you and Mr. Tuminelli and Mr. Ravenell until after they have completed their cross-examination of you. At the completion of the cross examination of you, the government may inquire of Mr. Grace as to what matters were inquired of him by defense counsel. So basically he is in a bubble until after cross-examination is completed.

"*Then* you can talk to him," Quarles warns Luna. "You can interview him about what they discussed *after* his cross-examination has been done. Clear, everybody?"

"Clear, your honor," Ravenell tells him. "Your honor, obviously, the court knows how serious Mr. Tuminelli and I take these matters, and the government did not disclose to us that this man, while cooperating, had drugs in his car, was found to have drugs, and that he defeated the electronic bracelet and was going for some time in and around in the community doing whatever. When we—."

Quarles stops him, and looks at Grace. "Do you want him here for this discussion?" Quarles asks.

"No, we don't need him," Ravenell says.

"Would you please take Mr. Grace away," Quarles instructs. Thereupon, Grace leaves the courtroom.

Quarles tells Grace's lawyer, deputy federal public defender Joseph Balter, "Since he is represented, you may be with him during the conversations with Mr. Ravenell and Mr. Tuminelli."

Ravenell asks, "Your honor, I guess while he is still standing there, one other point. We will be allowed to have an investigator or someone with us, is that correct?" Notice how good Ravenell is? He makes the request in the positive, *"is that correct?"*

Judge Quarles, obviously, knows there's a problem. He's already expressed concern about the government's handling of Grace, and the government's handling of this case, now that the tar ball has landed in his courtroom. Now Luna's going to pay.

Luna, we notice, says nothing. He can't decide what to say, or do. So he keeps doing what he's been doing.

"Yes," Quarles grants.

So now there'll be a private investigator in the room, when the can of whoop ass is opened. Things keep looking worse for Luna and Skinner.

"Thank you," Ravenell says.

Luna says nothing. Does nothing.

What is he thinking?

17
'Government gets into bed with its witness'

There must be a cobbler working in the courthouse, the next floor up, because shoes keep dropping all around Jonathan Luna.

Attorney Tuminelli again asks for a private, or ex parte, meeting with the judge at the bench. He still, very rightly, has concerns about Warren Grace being driven around by Agent Skinner and Detective Moody.

"Judge, I had asked earlier if we could approach ex parte about how he is going to be transported, and the reason I am asking you to do it ex parte is because to do it in open court would disclose part of the defense strategy in cross examining him," Tuminelli says.

"Come up, come up," Quarles tells him. Grace's public defender, Joseph Balter, asks to listen.

"Judge, first, my motion is that he be transported, if at all possible, by the United States Marshal's office," Tuminelli repeats.

Quarles still doesn't get it. Again he says no. He, at least, admits he has trouble doing his own job. And it's showing.

Quarles tells Tuminelli, "And that response again is I have enough trouble doing my own job, I don't tell the other ones how to do theirs, and he will be transported as they determine, given their manpower and other considerations."

Tuminelli drops the bomb.

"Alternatively," he tells Judge Quarles, "I ask, if it's going to be by the FBI or local law enforcement agents, that it not be Detective Moody or Special Agent Skinner, for the following reasons. It could be other FBI agents, if the court will not order the marshals to do this, and here is the reason. We received information this morning and I believe it is the same caller who called Pretrial Services back in August of 2001 and reported to me this morning that Mr. Grace this past Sunday was taken to the home, the apartment of Robin Grace, his wife—."

"Uh-huh," Quarles mumbles.

Tuminelli continues, "(Grace) was taken there by two white law enforcement agents, who I believe to be Moody and Skinner. For approximately a four-hour period, Mr. Grace was out of the observation of both Moody and Skinner. He was left in an apartment room with Mrs. Grace. Now, I don't know. My submission is this, your honor, if the agents are willing to take that kind of risk—."

"Conjugal visit?" Quarles wonders.

"Sure sounds like it," Tuminelli agrees. "And we don't know what happened for the four hours while he was in this room. Did he leave the room through another, you know, was there a way to exit the room and leave and be out on the streets? We don't know, but the point is if they will take that risk, my concern is they are going to respect the court's order not to discuss, while transporting him back and forth, the facts of this case, and I am asking that someone else do it."

Quarles refuses to wake up and smell the coffee. He now says something that illustrates he is not doing his job. Perhaps, we're left to wonder, Quarles isn't up to the job of being a judge. Perhaps, like many judges, he's afraid of our rogue FBI. He may well, at this moment, be unintentionally contributing to all that is to follow.

"Well, again," Quarles says, "I am not going to, on the basis of an anonymous phone call, take any steps that would indicate the court's distrust of a law enforcement officer. I have ordered them not to have those conversations. I have ordered them to advise all other people who would be transporting him not to have those conversations. If the information is true, it is, of course, troubling, but it is a different kind of government misconduct, if it is."

"No," Tuminelli says.

"Obviously, all of these matters raise concern about how the government gets into bed with its witnesses," Quarles observes. He's quick to crack jokes, slow to do his job. His job is to safeguard the rights of all parties, not just bad FBI agents, or troubled U.S. attorneys.

"That's a nice term," Tuminelli agrees.

"And those are troubling concerns," Quarles goes on. "However, as I say, that's how these cases are made, so I take it under advisement. Obviously, you will get a chance to question Agent Skinner about Sunday and other matters when he is called, but I am reluctant to take a step that indicates a distrust that a sworn officer will not follow my order, and especially on the basis of an anonymous telephone call this morning." Quarles seems unable to fathom why a caller might fear blowing the whistle on an FBI agent.

Tuminelli, rightly, isn't satisfied. He asks, "Judge, would you consider, and I know the court is not going to delay the jury any more than necessary, would you consider after the break allowing us to call Agent Skinner for the sole purpose of determining whether this incident occurred this past Sunday? If, in fact, it did, then we would submit—."

Quarles tosses him a bone. "Well, if you want to voir dire him outside of the presence of the jury at the beginning of our lunch break, I will let you do that," he says. Voir dire means to formally question someone, in the strictest sense, about one's qualifications. In this case, Quarles is allowing Skinner to be questioned with the jury not present.

"Okay," Tuminelli says. "And, judge, let me just add one other thing for the record, and thank you for that, for allowing us to do that, this clearly would be a disclosure that would have been necessary under *Giglio*. If they provided this man a conjugal visit or just gave him the freedom for four to five hours to be alone while in custody, that is something we should have been advised of by the United States Attorney's office."

"That's an argument that is part of the consideration for his testimony," Quarles says.

"And we have not gotten such material from the United States," Tuminelli repeats.

"Perhaps attorneys for the government will learn it when Mr. Skinner testifies," Quarles wonders.

The proceedings return to open court. The lawyers look around and notice that Luna has left the courtroom.

"Now we lost Mr. Luna," Ravenell notes.

Luna's co-counsel, Vivien Cockburn, explains that Luna went up to his office. "Your honor," she tells the judge, "Mr. Luna went up to his office because of the change of order of witnesses. And he went to take care of that."

Before long, Luna returns to question his next witness: FBI Special Agent Steve Skinner.

Jonathan Luna has about sixteen hours to live.

18
FBI Agent Skinner testifies he paid Warren Grace

After a brief recess, necessitated by Jonathan Luna's unexpected absence, FBI Special Agent Steve Skinner takes the witness stand. He still doesn't look like he wants to be there. No wonder. As the day wears on, he's going to like it even less.

Skinner's reminded he's still under oath. Luna begins by questioning Skinner about his background and duties with the FBI. Skinner replies he's been employed by the bureau, "Since November 8, 1998."

Skinner tells the jury he's worked on the Safe Streets Program, the Innocent Images Program, and the FBI's bank robbery squad.

"Now, you referenced the Safe Streets Program," Luna queries. "What is the Safe Streets Program?"

"The Safe Streets Program was put together by the FBI to address what is actually called safe streets," Skinner replies. "Our goal is to make streets safe, to make neighborhoods safe. By doing that, we investigate violent groups, gangs, and we put together investigations against those groups using drug violation laws."

Following Luna's line of questioning, Skinner begins to describe the highly secretive, confidential informant system which brought them all in contact with Warren Grace, in their effort to make the streets safe.

"There is (sic) different subcategories and things like that," Skinner tells the court, "but, to basically sum up, there is (sic) two types of confidential informants.

"We refer commonly and generally to all of these informants as sources, so when you heard on the recordings earlier, when I said a source, I meant that generally, and I was referring to Warren Grace, but the first type of source is what we call a confidential informant, and the confidential informant, to me and to the FBI, is a person that just provides information. It could be any type of person. It could be a school teacher, it could be a secretary in a firm, it could be a doctor, it could be anybody; and they provide information to help us conduct any type of investigation that we are conducting."

"And let me just go back," Luna says. "You mentioned the term source. How does one become a source for the FBI?"

"Well, there is (sic) different ways that you become a source," Skinner replies. "As far as this first category that I am discussing, sometimes we just have people that call up the FBI and they feel a civic duty. This is typically your confidential informant. There is a second type of source is what we call a cooperating witness. That is what Warren Grace is. He is a cooperating witness. He is the second type of source that the FBI has. A cooperating witness does more than just provide information. A cooperating witness acts almost like an agent of the government. They are like an arm of our investigation. They are not employed by us, meaning, you know, they don't get benefits and a 401-k plan and all of that. They do receive things from us, and I will get to that, but they work as an agent for us. They do proactive things for us. And they are more involved in a case than a cooperating — a confidential informant, excuse me."

"And with respect to cooperating witnesses, or informants, how does one or how does the FBI find such cooperating witnesses?" Luna asks.

"Usually, cooperating witnesses are people that are placed in a certain position in their life," Skinner opines. "They are people that are going to be involved pretty deep in investigation and typically your general person doesn't want to expose themselves that way, especially when you are dealing with violent investigations, people want to kind of limit their exposure to things, so when we deal with cooperating witnesses, they are typically people that maybe they are in a bind financially, because we do pay some cooperating witnesses, or they could be people that have been arrested and they are facing criminal exposure, criminal sentences, and they have a hope that if they work with us, with the FBI and other law enforcement agencies, that their exposure to a criminal sentence will be lessened by a court."

"And with respect to the latter category of cooperating witnesses that you just talked about, someone that's been arrested, how does the FBI even know about these people?" Luna asks.

"Well, like I said, we have task force officers on our squad," Skinner says. "There are local police officers, and they have connections with different local police departments. I myself have been working violent crime for a few years and I have developed relationships with local law enforcement officers, and sometimes they may call you and they will say hey, we just arrested a person, we have a couple guns on them, they are backing some previous charges, and essentially they say they are in a bind, and this type of person may be a person that you may want to talk to." One wonders why no one called the task force to help the Dawson family.

Luna's examination touches on the revolving door nature of our federal criminal justice system. Skinner's testimony illustrates that even law enforcement officers benefit professionally when career criminals pass through the revolving door. It's a new case, with a new offender as an informant.

"When you say 'backing some previous charges,' what are you referring to?" Luna asks.

"Well," Skinner says, "I guess the court systems, at least in Maryland, are pretty— there is (sic) a lot of crimes going on, and people can get arrested and they can be released on bond, and that happens quite frequently, and while they are out, they may violate another crime."

"And so when you say 'backing some time,' what are you referring to?" Luna asks.

"Well, sometimes if people are let out on probation, if they get arrested again, they still have to serve the time that they were let out for from the previous charge," Skinner says.

Skinner goes on to testify that the FBI's standards for informants are surprisingly low.

Luna asks Skinner, "So are there any crimes that a cooperating witness could have that would cause the FBI not to work with them as a cooperating witness?"

"The only crime that I am aware of that the FBI has a problem with is child molesters," Skinner testifies. "From what I know, the FBI would not use a child molester as a cooperating witness. It's just something that I personally wouldn't do, and it's just something that— it's not a written rule, but it would just be too extreme." Now Skinner touches on some of the reasons often cited by the FBI to defend its largely unsupervised system of informants. "But we use— the FBI historically has used murderers for cooperating witnesses and people who have done violent things, but it's just a part of the history of the FBI and it's how we conduct investigations, and it provides us with information that can solve crimes that have been unsolved for many, many years, and it provides us with access to criminal organizations that, but for their cooperation with us, no matter how, you know, dark their past was, but for them working with us, those criminal organizations never would have been brought to justice."

"Brought to justice" is an interesting phrase to hear spoken in this trial.

Luna and Skinner now recount for the jury how Warren Grace came into their lives:

"Now, you have already mentioned Mr. Grace, Warren Grace. He became a cooperating witness for you?" Luna asks.

"Yes, he did," Skinner says.

"Can you briefly describe for the jury how Mr. Grace became a cooperating witness?"

"I received a telephone call, it was in the evening, it was about 9:00 o'clock, and it was from an officer that I knew," Skinner recounts. "He said that they had arrested an individual named Warren Grace, that Warren Grace was arrested after the completion of a Baltimore city search warrant. And in that search warrant, the police had found two guns. I believe one was a Tech 9 sub-machine gun and another one, I think, was a .38. It was some sort of a revolver; it could have been a .32. This officer told me that Warren Grace was providing information to the Baltimore city police department officials regarding various individuals that Mr. Grace knew."

Skinner touches on the Baltimore city police homicide squad's investigation of Poindexter for the murder of Alvin Jones. He's careful not to mention Jones, or the murder.

"And at some point, did you get in contact with Mr. Grace?" asks Luna.

"I tried to get in contact with him that evening, but Baltimore city was talking with him about various different criminal activities," Skinner explains, skirting the murder of Alvin Jones, "and I didn't get a chance to speak with him that evening. I then contacted you, Mr. Luna, and I said there is a person that I think, you know, maybe we could talk to. So what we did was we writted out Mr. Grace out of jail and brought him to the U.S. Attorney's office to talk with him."

"When you say 'writted out,' what are you referring to?" Luna asks.

"It's a court order essentially saying that if a person is incarcerated in jail, if a judge signs a writ, that he can be-- the person can be released into an agent or a law enforcement officer's custody temporarily and then brought back to prison," Skinner explains.

"Was there a meeting at the U.S. Attorney's office?"

"Yes, there was."

"Can you describe briefly that meeting?" Luna asks. It had to be a red-letter day in the lives of all three.

"The meeting just consisted of interviewing Mr. Grace to see what he knew about, to kind of measure his willingness to cooperate with us, and to see potentially if there could be any federal investigations that could result from his cooperating with us," Skinner recalls.

"Now, at this time, was Mr. Grace charged in federal court?"

"At that time, he was not."

"Where was he charged?"

"He was charged in Baltimore city."

"Do you know what happened to the charges that were lodged against Mr. Grace in Baltimore city?"

"The charges were dropped in Baltimore city and they were adopted into federal court," Skinner relates. He goes on, "The local charges from Baltimore city were made into federal charges which Mr. Grace ultimately pled guilty to."

These federal responsibilities would, importantly, come to include the investigation and prosecution of Walter Poindexter for the retaliatory drug shooting of Alvin Jones.

Luna continues questioning Skinner. Almost in an offhand way, they drop an explosive piece of information on the defense team.

"Now, you talked earlier that oftentimes the FBI pays their sources, is that correct?" Luna asks.

"Yes," Skinner replies.

"Did you pay Warren Grace?" asks Luna, already knowing the answer.

"Yes, I did."

"What did you pay?" Luna asks. "What was the payment for?"

"The payments I paid Warren Grace were for expenses," Skinner relates. "There is (sic) two types of ways to pay a source. One is for expenses, and one is for services. Some sources are paid for the information that they provide. Mr. Grace was paid for services incurred during the investigation, such as his cell phone bills, the payments that he needed to make on his Ford Excursion, it may be rent, things like that." Skinner doesn't explain how Grace managed to pay his child support, and other expenses.

"Why did you have to pay for his phone and his car?" Luna starts to ask. "Why not just provide him—."

"Your honor, may we approach," Ravenell asks.

"Okay," Quarles says. "Come up."

"I just wanted to bring to your attention, your honor, that this is again information that has not been disclosed to us, of the informant being paid. I mean this is just unbelievable," Ravenell says at the bench.

Luna, yet again, lies, and insists he's turned everything over to the defense. He says he's perplexed. He says he's scratching his head. Again, he tries to dance, to rap, to change the subject. He scratches his head like another jammaster might scratch a vinyl record.

"I have turned over FBI 302's to defense counsel, and, you know, your honor, I am scratching my head," Luna tells the judge. "I really am scratching my head, your honor. You know, I haven't gotten off to the best foot here in this trial, but I am telling this court that I have provided this information, and—."

"Well, the record is made," Quarles say. He wants, as always, to be hurrying things along. "Let's resume. Let's resume. Do you have anything further to add?"

"I have something to add," Tuminelli injects, barely able to conceal his anger. He agrees with Ravenell that they never received any FBI 302s on the subject of government money paid to heroin dealer Warren Grace, who was found with heroin in his car on the day of the Dawson massacre. No 302 about any of that. "I didn't get it. I did not get it. We don't believe it was given to us. We don't know why it wasn't given to us," he says. Wonder, wonder.

Tuminelli feels moved to remind Quarles of a day, long ago, when both men had first met, and Quarles had been a young, assistant U.S. attorney.

"I have to say, the very first case I've ever had in this courthouse was with you where you sat as an assistant U.S. Attorney," Tuminelli reminds Quarles. "My experience was that you represented what happens in this courthouse, in the United States Attorney's office. I've had every confidence, until this case, that things are done in this courthouse by the United States attorney's office in the way it should be done, and you were a fine example of that. And, judge, what's happened in this case—.'

"We had open file discovery," Quarles shrugs. "I guess that doesn't happen anymore." Only two days before, at the close of trial Monday, Judge Quarles had told Luna, "This is just completely unacceptable, Mr. Luna." And, "What I wish you to do is get your act together." And, "When I was in the U.S. Attorney's office, when I started twenty-one years ago in that office, that wasn't how we did things. Has the U.S. Attorney adopted — Mr. DiBiagio adopted — some new approach to trials that require my discussion with him?"

Now Quarles seems to know the answer to his question, and seems abandoned to the strange political realities of this case. Now he seems only to have his eye on the clock. And time is running out.

"Well, what's happened in this case is absolutely extraordinary in my twenty years in this courthouse," Tuminelli tells Quarles.

"Let's plow forward," Quarles says.

19
Luna steals thunder, defuses issues, covers butt

Jonathan Luna now launches a pre-emptive strike designed to diffuse the many problems Agent Steve Skinner created with Warren Grace.

Returning to his questioning, Luna asks Agent Skinner, "Now, can you tell the jury whether or not you have encountered problems dealing with sources?"

"Well, generally," Skinner replies, "such as in a safe street investigation, one of the types of cooperating witnesses that we typically use are addicts, typically heroin addicts. I have encountered situations where it was my investigation or another agent's investigation where we sent a cooperating witness who was an addict out to make a purchase from a particular drug organization, and, during, during the course of making that purchase, the addicts would either steal one of the heroin pills or maybe try to snort some of the heroin pill, and we found out about that. That's one example that I could think of a problem with a cooperating witness."

"With respect to Mr. Grace," Luna asks, "did you have any problems with Mr. Grace?"

"Oh, yes, we did," Skinner says.

"Could you describe the problems that you had with Mr. Grace?"

"Well, the first problem that comes to mind," Skinner begins, "was when—. It was towards the beginning of the investigation. Mr. Grace, after he pled guilty, was released by this court, by the federal court, pending sentencing. He was to report to a Pretrial Services officer, who is an officer of the court. And part of those conditions were that Mr. Grace was to be placed on home monitoring."

Tuminelli says, "Judge, we object. May we approach, please?"

"Okay," Quarles says, and the lawyers go to the bench.

The defense attorneys say they feel blind-sided and betrayed. They're getting hot under the collar. They've fought tooth-and-nail to uncover the irregularities involving Skinner and Grace. For the most part they've done it out of earshot of the jury, at bench conferences such as this, so the jury has no idea the prosecution has been concealing this, and more. Now Luna and Skinner are attempting to deceive the jurors into thinking they're forthcoming about these problems.

This creates other problems for the defense. How can they fully cross-examine Skinner about Grace's violations when they have yet to have their promised, private interview with Warren Grace?

"The problem we have with this," Tuminelli tells Quarles, "we have been placed in a position that we have to wait and do further examination to cross-examine Mr. Grace." He says Luna "agreed that we would cross-examine (Skinner) about these kinds of issues when (Skinner) returns after Mr. Grace, and we object to him being questioned about this at this time." Confusing, isn't it? This case is tied up in more knots than Gumby in a yoga convention.

"If I may, your honor," Ravenell intercedes, "one of the things that we should have the ability to do is get this matter before the jury, for us to cross-examine Grace, but not to have our thunder stolen because of errors committed by the government. They have now committed these errors. We can't cross-examine right now, and he gets to clean up with his witness before we even get a chance to cross-examine the witness — the witness being Mr. Grace. That is unfair."

The government, after all, created these serious errors of judgment. Why should the government be able to pretend Warren Grace created them? Ravenell asks. Why should Skinner and Luna now be able to pretend that they are forthcoming when, to the contrary, they've been evasive, and elusive, and publicly irresponsible?

"Okay," Quarles says. "The objection is unfairness?"

"No, your honor," Ravenell says. "The objection is that they should not be allowed to go into the area that he is covering, the particular areas that would deal with Grace's cross-examination, before we cross-examine Grace."

"Okay. To the extent that it's an objection, it's overruled," Quarles says. "To the extent that it's a motion, it is denied."

"Judge, may I just add something?" Tuminelli asks.

"Uh-huh," Quarles allows.

"The basis of the objection is what we submit is a clear, consistent series of *Brady* violation," Tuminelli says. "The court is saying, 'I am not going to dismiss this case under due process *Brady* violations, I'm going to give you the opportunity to do further investigation, I'm going to permit you to call Mr. Grace back.' We agreed to that, and didn't argue any further about that, because that was the court's ruling, and we figured we would have the opportunity to interview Mr. Grace. We have excused Mr. Grace. Had I known this witness was going to take the stand and get into this, I would not have agreed to him being called out of order. And, judge, again, if, in fact, he is going to continue, and Mr. Grace is still in the building, I want to cross-examine him."

"I join in that request, your honor," Ravenell says. "No way would I agree, under any circumstance, to not cross-examine Grace and to have this witness on the stand, basically defusing all of the issues before we get to cross-examine the witness."

Luna at last breaks his silence, and shows signs of life. He acts every bit the immortal, tricky lawyer. He has, in fact, about fifteen hours remaining on earth, before he meets his maker. "Your honor," Luna says, "when I had the discussion with counsel about them deferring their cross-examination, I understood that to mean I would not be limited in questioning Mr. Skinner the way I was going to question him, that necessary areas would have opened up that they would cross-examine him on, and I don't see why the government needs to be precluded from putting on its case with this witness when they are going to have their shot at Mr. Grace and, quite frankly, Mr. Skinner, in due course."

"Not withstanding your allocution, Mr. Luna, the ruling stands," Quarles says.

"We would like to cross-examine Mr. Grace now," Ravenell demands.

"No. We have got the witness on the stand. We will finish his direct (examination). And then, after we finish his direct," Quarles says, "I will then permit you to chose to call Grace or go after him."

After a few more heated arguments along these lines at the bench, Quarles announces, "The ruling stands," and Luna is permitted to continue his questioning of Agent Skinner.

20
To plea or not to plea

"We were discussing the problems that you had with Mr. Grace," Luna resumes questioning Agent Skinner. "Do you recall that?"

"Yes," Skinner replies.

"Can you tell the members of the jury what were some of those problems?"

Skinner recounts discovering that Grace had slipped out of his home monitoring confinement. He glosses over the story, without mentioning the discrepancies between his own 302 report and the report written by Pretrial Services — such as that Grace had removed his monitoring bracelet, and that Skinner had failed to report that Grace wasn't at home when he and Moody went to Grace's apartment.

In his professional life, as on the witness stand, Skinner seems intent on silencing anyone who would report these things, and runs roughshod over anyone — concerned citizen, home monitoring specialists, or federal judge — who gets in his way.

He testifies that Todd Stokes, at Pretrial Services, "advised me that he received an anonymous telephone call from a male who said that Warren Grace was leaving his apartment that he was supposed to be staying in by taking off the ankle home monitoring bracelet without telling anyone. He was leaving when he was not working with other people from the task force."

"Let me just stop you and say, after learning about that, what did you do?" Luna asks.

"I got the telephone number from Mr. Stokes," Skinner says. "Mr. Stokes saw the telephone number, I guess, on his caller ID of the anonymous male that called him, and I got that telephone number from Mr. Stokes and I called this male."

"You called the male?" Luna asks. "Were you alone or with someone?"

"I believe I was with Detective Moody," Skinner says. Rosencrantz says he was with Guildenstern.

"Was Mr. Grace present?" asks Luna, our inquisitive Hamlet.

"No," Skinner replies.

"And, as a result of that call, what happened next?"

Skinner testifies, "I spoke with the male. He said that — he actually said that he — now that I remember, he said that he spoke with a Drug Enforcement Agency agent, a DEA agent, before talking with Mr. Stokes. And I said, well, you know, what is this about? He said he identified Warren Grace. He said the name Warren Grace. He didn't use Warren Grace's street name. He said Warren Grace was leaving the apartment.

"He identified the particular apartment that Mr. Grace was staying in. The address. And he also identified the type of vehicle that Mr. Grace drove. He said that Mr. Grace had been regularly leaving the apartment.

"He also advised me that Mr. Grace had been involved in a shooting at — I believe it was the intersection of Wiley and I want to say Park Heights, but I am not — I don't know the exact intersection. I know it was Wiley.

"He also said that Mr. Grace had been selling drugs. So, you know, I asked the male, I could keep this confidential, you know, could you provide me with your name?

"He said he did not want to. I asked him well, could I meet you just to, you know, talk to you a little more about this. At first, the male agreed, and he said he would meet me at the parking lot near Sinai Hospital.

"We didn't meet. He didn't show. I then called him again, and he said he didn't want to meet me."

"Do you know who that person is?" Luna asks.

"I do not," Skinner says.

"Did you ever physically meet him?"

"No."

"After learning about this information, did you have a conversation with Warren Grace?" Luna asks.

"Yes," Skinner says. Skinner's not at all forthcoming. He's adhering to the best advice given to all who face tough questioning: Answer a simple yes or no. Volunteer nothing.

"After that conversation, did you continue working with Warren Grace?" Luna asks.

"Yes," Skinner repeats.

Skinner, characteristically, presents himself as some sort of victim in all this. He positions himself as trying to investigate Grace's transgressions. So why doesn't he do anything about it? Rather than toss Grace out of the secretive and troubled FBI informant program, Skinner gives him even more freedom, leading to ever-more transgressions.

That's actually too mild: What Skinner doesn't say is that he and Luna weren't much concerned about their informant running around Baltimore, shooting up neighborhoods and dealing drugs.

They, after all, responded to this danger, while others issued warnings, by completely removing Grace from home confinement, and turning him loose on Baltimore.

Luna, understandably, drops the subject. He steers the inquiry to safer ground. He has Skinner testify for the next several minutes about the operations with Grace, and wiring Grace for sound. "Typically, I would be in a parked car making observations," Skinner explains, when asked where he would be while he worked with Grace.

Note that Skinner, by his own admission, is literally a pro at following someone, and arranging "confidential" meetings in out-of-the-way parking lots with people who, after all, endanger his career. He's also shown he's willing to omit crucial pieces of truth from his reports.

It's nearing one in the afternoon in the courtroom. Judge Quarles at last breaks into Luna's questioning, telling the jury, "Ladies and gentlemen, we are going to break for lunch now. Please be back in the jury room at five minutes before two, so that we can get started at 2 pm."

Quarles has in mind using the lunch break to grill Agent Skinner. Grill him, that is, with questions, not a rotisserie. Skinner has already removed himself from the witness stand and mills about the courtroom. He knows trouble's coming. Trouble, in this case, after all, has been coming for a while.

"Agent Skinner, would you resume the stand, please," Judge Quarles tells him. "Mr. Ravenell or Mr. Tuminelli wish to take up the matter we discussed ex parte with Agent Skinner."

The defense lawyers want no part of it. They've justifiably grown distrustful of Skinner. Why tip their hand by questioning him? They fear Skinner, violating court order, will alert, and coach, Warren Grace.

"In light of the court's ruling fifteen minutes ago," Ravenell demurs, "that this witness was going to be permitted to testify in certain areas before we cross-examine Mr. Grace, we now do not wish, because of the risk that we perceive of this information being communicated, we don't want to cross-examine — I mean, we don't want to examine him now on this subject."

"Okay," Quarles says. "Mr. Ravenell?"

"I just want to add we will, at the appropriate time, examine him," Ravenell tells the judge.

"Okay, very good," Quarles says. "Anything else?"

"Your honor," Ravenell asks, "should we take up the scheduling matters now, or at the end of the day?"

"Oh," Quarles muses, "why not take them now? Yes."

Ravenell suggests the defense lawyers hold their private examination of Warren Grace first thing Friday morning, the day after tomorrow. Judge Quarles agrees.

At this auspicious moment, right before lunch break, Ravenell succeeds in formally scheduling an official court inquiry into the irregularities involving FBI informant Warren Grace.

Skinner and Detective Moody's bumbling on the streets, and Luna's strange bumbling in the courtroom, have brought it to this. Rosencrantz and Guildenstern, and our struggling Hamlet, are about to see their shit hit the fan.

Skinner, apparently, still sits on the witness stand, though the court record does not say, only that the judge told him a few moments earlier to have a seat.

The court record, for that matter, doesn't mention Luna's facial expression as he stands in his fine suit before Judge Quarles bench, pondering his diminishing options.

Outwardly, Luna shows no alarm. What's he thinking? Years later, when I meet Dan Rivera, Luna's old friend from the projects, Rivera poses an interesting theory. Did I ever stop to think, Rivera asks me, that Jonathan may have deliberately handled the case in this fashion in order to have Judge Quarles order the investigation of the FBI and DiBiagio's office? "I've been with Jonathan in a courtroom," Rivera says."He was an accomplished trial attorney. In this case, he's acting like he doesn't know how to introduce evidence. He's leaving things back in his office, on his desk. Come on, that's not Joey."

"Joey didn't always tackle things head on," Rivera reminds me. "He operated beneath the surface sometimes. He couldn't have liked what Skinner and Moody and the FBI were doing with Grace. And he sure as hell couldn't have liked what happened to the Dawsons. But what was Joey going to do about it? *How was he going to expose them?"*

The court reporter makes no mention of Luna's facial expression as Quarles orders an investigation into the FBI's handling of Warren Grace. We know, nevertheless, Luna's reaction. It will be immediate, and apparently drastic. About as immediate and drastic as it gets for a prosecutor. He wouldn't do it calmly, either. He'd do it with hot blood, fighting and arguing all the way.

Before lunch is over, before the hour has passed, before the sands of Judge Quarles' atomic clock can drip out sixty minutes, Jonathan Luna will announce a plea agreement with the defense lawyers. He will, *on the surface,* move with all deliberate dispatch to immediately stop the court case, and to halt the court's inquiry into Warren Grace and the FBI. But, *beneath the surface,* Luna already knows there's a problem with a plea deal. The murder of Alvin Jones--. Beneath the surface, Luna knows the plea deal *legally* cannot go forward.

To be the hero of his own story, Luna must *disentangle himself from the temptation to wreak justice for the wrong reasons and in evil passion, and to do what he must do at last for the pure sake of justice.*

Luna knows this: the FBI must, and will, be investigated.

To plea, or not to plea, that was the question. It will be the very last question Luna will ponder in his career.

After lunch, at 2 pm, Jonathan Luna will have little more than fourteen hours to live.

21
Judge schedules investigation into 'government's kid-glove treatment of Mr. Grace'

The increasingly curious events unfold like this:

Ravenell, as I say, asks Judge Quarles, "Your honor, should we take up the scheduling matters now or at the end of the day?"

"Oh, why not take them up now. Yes."

"What we are going to ask the court to do in regards to Mr. Grace is, and (the) investigation that we need to conduct, is not to sit on Friday," Ravenell requests. "What we would like to do is use the first part of Friday to meet with Mr. Grace, hopefully around 10 am, and we communicated that to Mr. Luna and Mr. Balter. At the same time, we would like to obviously pursue the other leads and investigate information that we have learned over the last two days."

Ravenell continues by complaining that Luna *has still not* turned over documents the defense has requested. Each document is another smelly brick heading toward the fan.

"I will still draw your honor's attention to the fact that we have not received the letter that we asked about from the government," Ravenell complains. "The August 29th, 2002 letter, and I am not sure Mr. Luna has had a chance to look for it yet." Ravenell is tired of waiting. He proposes a solution. "If not, we can certainly get that letter from Pretrial Services, and your honor indicated you would look into that matter for us. Hopefully—."

Quarles seems to have reached his limit with Luna and Company.

"What was the date of the letter?" Quarles asks Ravenell.

"August 29th, 2002," Ravenell says.

It's an interesting letter from DiBiagio's U.S. Attorney's office stating they don't want heroin dealer Warren Grace back behind bars following his neighborhood shooting incident; instead, they want him running free and unsupervised on the boiling streets of Baltimore.

This missive wouldn't have looked too good following the outrage of the Dawson murders, which occurred about forty-five days after the business-as-usual letter was written.

"From?" Quarles asks.

"From Ms. Rodriguez-Coss to—. I am not sure if it was directed to (Pretrial Services') Mr. Stokes or to Judge Smalkin," Ravenell says.

"Okay," Quarles agrees.

Ravenell asks for two more interesting and, it goes without saying, sensitive, documents.

"There is also a letter written by Mr. Stokes that he told us about dated September 3 of 2002, I believe to the court or to Ms. Rodriguez-Coss. And then there was the 9/13/02 court order signed by Judge Smalkin, from our understanding, taking Mr. Grace off of any kind of supervision from Pretrial."

"Okay," Quarles says. "Well, again, I will direct the government to provide you with those. And if they haven't by the close of business today, I will take it up with Pretrial."

What follows is a droll and poignant exchange between Ravenell and Judge Quarles. Ravenell tells Quarles they'll interview Grace Friday morning, and requests the judge's phone number in case any unexpected problems arise over the weekend.

"What we would then hope to do, your honor," Ravenell says, "is that, through Friday and the weekend, that we can come back and cross-examine Mr. Grace on Monday. What we would ask the court to do is to let us have a number for the court over the weekend, and we can update you as to where we are."

"Oh, I have no great desire to talk to you over the weekend," Quarles replies. The tough, tough life of a federal judge.

As fate would have it, Judge William Quarles' planned weekend of repose would ironically be ruined, anyway. He'd spend the next few days fielding phone calls from the national press, receiving phone calls from reporters asking for comments about the strange death of Jonathan Luna.

At which time, it would be widely reported in the nation's newspapers, Quarles would break down and cry into the phone.

"Well, you may have no great desire to speak to us," Ravenell presses on, "but we may have a desire to speak to you. But if you choose not to, so be it, judge."

Everyone involved in this case seems to grow testier, and more combative, by the moment.

"I will check my court mail over the weekend," Quarles allows.

"However you wish to do it, judge," Ravenell says, "and we can update the court if we need additional time beyond this Friday and the weekend for investigation. That's what I was thinking. I was hoping we would not inconvenience the jurors if we tell the court we need Monday as well, and you bring jurors in here, you are going to be upset with us when the jurors come in."

"Well, I would just as soon know on Friday whether you want the time or not," Quarles says. Ravenell wisely focuses on Quarles pet idiosyncrasy — the precious time of the jurors and how a juror's time spent in front of the boob tube is more important than government corruption, murder and civil mayhem. "If there is any question, ask for the time, and we will tell the jury that we will begin on Tuesday. If there is any question about your needing Monday, do it that way, rather than clerk's office people scrambling on Sunday evening trying to call the jurors off for Monday."

"Well, there is only sixteen jurors," Ravenell observes. "It can't be that many phone numbers they have to call, judge."

"Well, I try not to take other people's time cavalierly, so—," Quarles says.

"Your honor, I want to make clear to you that this is not a cavalier—," Ravenell counters.

"I have no desire to intrude on clerk's office personnel weekends, either," Quarles says. "Their time with their families is valuable as well."

"I understand," Ravenell tells him. "It's not a cavalier request, judge, I have made."

"No no, I didn't say you were," Quarles says. "I just said that I try not to be cavalier with court employees, especially weekend time. Let me know by Thursday morning whether you want Monday off as well."

This exchange underscores the pressures of time bearing on this case, brought about by this judge's drive to always stick with the clock. Haste, Ben Franklin observed, makes waste.

"We will not have met with Mr. Grace on Thursday morning," Ravenell says. It's Wednesday afternoon.

"Well, I want to tell the jurors before I send them away Thursday afternoon whether they will have Friday and Monday off, or whether they will just have Friday off."

"Can we just tell you that on Friday?" Tuminelli suggests. Lawyers and their calendars — designed to boggle the mind.

"Friday afternoon, after we meet with Mr. Grace," Ravenell seconds.

"Okay," Quarles agrees. "Let me know by mid-day, if you can." World crisis, apparently averted. Unless, we can suppose, like Jonathan Luna, you're perpetually trying to stay one step ahead of fiasco.

"That's fine," Ravenell says.

"Okay, anything else, folks?" Quarles asks.

Whereupon, enter stage left, comes Warren Grace's lawyer, public defender Joe Balter, who requests a word with the judge.

"Your honor, may I approach with defense counsel just briefly?" Balter asks.

"Sure. Come on up," Quarles says. Then, for the court reporter, the judge says, "This is an ex parte and accordingly sealed matter at the bench. Present are Mr. Balter, counsel for the government's cooperating witness, Mr. Grace. Also present are counsel for the defendants, Mr. Ravenell and Mr. Tuminelli. Yes, Mr. Balter."

Now let me get this straight, Balter basically asks the judge. My client Mr. Grace was supposed to say *what* to *whom?*

"Thank you your honor," Balter supplicates. "I just wanted to make sure I understood the parameters of what the informal interview of Mr. Grace was to be." Interesting how he uses the term "informal interview," isn't it? Defense counsel, and the judge, are using stronger words — *investigation* and *inquiry.* "As I understand it, it's to be limited to those matters related to the alleged violation." Balter wants to limit the probe. He's an already over-stretched public defender, with limited time, and limited budget. Warren Grace, on the other hand, is never-ending trouble — the Black Hole of Baltimore. Balter fears there'll be no end, once Grace starts talking. Prosecutors, he must also fear, can always renege on Grace's plea agreement....

Judge Quarles tells him the inquiry is not to be limited. Quarles suspects there may be more to the story than already meets the eye. And that's more bad news for Luna and Skinner. Defense counsel, he says, have a right to learn whether information about Grace has been withheld, and whether Grace was given undisclosed benefits from the government. These are, respectively, the *Brady* and *Giglio* aspects of the case's discovery process.

"No, the purpose is to give defense counsel an opportunity to explore the issues, the *Brady* and *Giglio* issues there," Quarles tells the public defender, "because I am not going to say to them you may only inquire as to the alleged Tony heroin transaction, or you may only inquire as to defeating the electronic monitoring."

Quarles adds that he expects Public Defender Balter to advise Grace "not to testify if any statement that he made would be an admission to a crime for which he has not some form of immunity."

Quarles continues, "But I am not going to restrict it just to the Tony heroin, or just to the electronic monitoring only, because their information that they have recently received have indicated there may be other forms of consideration that he has received from the government. So I want defense counsel to explore consideration *as broadly as possible.* Consideration for his cooperation and his testimony. And it might go beyond just a discussion of the alleged Tony-supplied heroin or defeating the monitoring system." (Emphasis mine.)

Quarles pithily sums it up. The defense counsel, he says, should hear about "arguably the government's kid gloves treatment of Mr. Grace."

Balter points out that Grace only has limited immunity in his plea agreement with the government. In other words, Luna and Skinner still have Grace by the short hairs. Or, does Grace have them? "Of course," Balter says, "without some restrictions, this could go on indefinitely." A public defender's worst nightmare.

"Again," Quarles summarizes for him, "what we are looking for is essentially *undisclosed consideration that he has received from the government.*"

Quarles instructs that he wants "defense counsel to explore consideration as broadly as possible." This instruction cuts to the heart of what can only be called an ongoing conspiracy involving Luna, Skinner, Moody, possibly others, and Warren Grace. What exactly *had* Skinner, Moody and Luna given Grace? And what had he been promised? We know he received money from the FBI. Did Grace also receive money from other sources? We know he received freedom from home confinement. We know he received access to guns and heroin. Heroin sales represent more money. We know he also received a secret visit to his wife's home the day before the trial. So he was also given sex. Warren Grace, then was given money, guns, drugs and sex by the United States Justice Department. Everything but a ticket out of the country.

And surely Pug got more. But, exactly what?

What else did Warren Grace get from our co-conspirators? Before lunch on Wednesday, December 3, 2003, Federal Judge William Quarles schedules an inquiry to answer this question.

This can't have made Jonathan Luna, Steve Skinner (apparently still sitting on the witness stand, listening) and Detective Moody, anything but moody.

With that, the court adjourns for lunch.

Rosencrantz and Guildenstern are about to die. All the while, the ghost of Alvin Jones haunts the courtroom, awaiting justice. Luna has screwed up. Big time. Luna's bumbling Hamlet act has completely backfired, and opened an ugly third act.

"This honorable court now stands in recess until 2 pm," the court clerk cries.

This will be Jonathan Luna's last lunch hour. He spends it trying to cover-up his conspiracy. He spends it furiously trying to shut down this case. He spends it trying to make everything go away.

He doesn't quite succeed. The ghost of Alvin Jones will rise up, and God will stand up for bastards, rap musicians, and heroin dealers.

And someone will make Jonathan Luna go away. Soon, to use U.S. Attorney Tom DiBiagio's blunt word, Jonathan Luna will be "gone."

22
Luna kills inquiry by floating doubtful plea deal: 'You either have a deal, or you don't'

Court reconvenes from lunch at the atomic stroke of 2 pm. Judge Quarles sits at his bench, waiting. Luna requests a moment for counsel to confer, and Ravenell asks to step outside the courtroom.

During the lunch break Luna offered Smith and Poindexter a plea agreement. The agreement would drastically cut the defendants' prison sentence. The deal will mean about ten years in jail for Smith, and maybe fifteen years for Poindexter. They'd each been looking at as much as sixty years in prison — the rest of their lives in jail.

The defense lawyers know they should accept the deal. They do have a leg up on Luna with the discovery issues — the government's suppression of information about Warren Grace. But these are mostly issues for an appeal. Ravenell and Tuminelli know this mostly white jury isn't going to look kindly on the underlying heroin and gun charges facing Smith and Poindexter.

As far as an appeal goes, they may, or may not, have strong grounds. The attorneys would have to advise their clients not to get their hopes up. Federal appellate courts in recent years have shown increasing hostility to civil rights or procedural claims.

Chances that an appellate court will overturn a jury's guilty verdict would be slim, though not unheard of. The Justice Department, in its Criminal Resource Manual, informs its U.S. Attorneys that, in 1998, in a case called *United States v. Singleton,* the Tenth Circuit Court of Appeals reversed a defendant's conviction "based on a finding that the District of Kansas' plea agreement with a cooperator violated 18 U.S.C. § 201(c)(2) (the gratuity statute) and Kansas Rule of Professional Conduct 3.4(b), both of which prohibit offering unlawful inducements to a witness." Grace was permitted, if not offered, sex, guns, heroin, freedom, a blind eye, and more, by Luna and Skinner.

Short of an outright dismissal, a retrial is possible. Even if a retrial were to be granted, the two defendants would only face the same risks, and the same long sentence, with another jury. And, while awaiting the appeal and retrial, they'd certainly be sitting in jail.

Chances are good the lawyers will be able to dig up more damning facts when they grill Warren Grace. Whether it will be enough to have Quarles, or an appeals court, dismiss the case is doubtful. The defendants have other legal problems. Poindexter and the murder of Alvin Jones. Due to prior gun convictions in his younger days, Ravenell fears that Deon Smith could be adjudicated, and sentenced, as an armed career offender, and put away for life. The future is a grim roll of the dice; the plea agreement is a bird in hand.

Ripping open the case with Warren Grace, defense counsel were able to save their clients perhaps fifty years of jail time.

Smith and Poindexter jump at Luna's plea offer. They immediately accept it. It's after all an exceptionally lenient deal.

But there's a catch. And a new problem for Jonathan Luna. It's a big problem, too: Alvin Jones.

Tuminelli demands that the plea agreement resolve *all* outstanding issues. As part of the agreement, Tuminelli wants the government to drop charges against Poindexter for the drug murder of Alvin Jones. Luna knows he can't do that. Luna tells Tuminelli he won't ask the judge to connect Jones' murder to this case. But, by federal rules, Luna *must* prosecute a drug-related murder charge.

Once again, Luna dances between a rock and a hard place. Luna, like the defendants, desperately needs this plea agreement. His neck depends on it. If the judge accepts the plea, the trial will be over, the jury sent home. Most importantly for Luna, Skinner and Moody, and their higher-ups, there will be no examination of Warren Grace. To keep secret the Grace conspiracy, Luna needs the jury sent home, and the case closed.

Luna too late realizes he has placed *too much* in the file about Poindexter's drug murder of Alvin Jones. D'oh! A *lawful* plea agreement forgiving a drug murder is impossible. Luna had been a prick about Alvin Jones' meeting his maker, calling it time and again a drug murder, and now Jones is coming back to haunt everyone.

Or is it Luna's fault? He's like a chess player who can't see more than a move or two ahead.

Less than an hour earlier, before lunch, Judge Quarles permitted "defense counsel to explore consideration as broadly as possible." Now, at the close of the lunch break, Luna straightaway returns to the courtroom and suddenly tells Quarles the government wants the case closed.

"Your honor, could counsel approach?" Luna asks Quarles. The lawyers come to the bench.

"Your honor, counsel can report that we have a resolution of this case," Luna tells the judge. Luna's not being truthful, as already he's fretful about the Jones problem. "We have reached terms for a plea agreement that is both acceptable to the defendants as well as acceptable to the government. We would like to ask that you send the jury home and that we be given an opportunity to take a Rule 11." Federal Rule of Criminal Procedure 11(e) "recognizes and codifies the concept of plea agreements," summarizes the Justice Department's Criminal Resource Manual. "After the plea agreement is disclosed," the manual continues, "the court may either accept it or reject it."

Now Luna, having spent months avoiding putting much of anything in writing, save for Poindexter's murder of Alvin Jones, suggests reducing the terms of the proposed plea agreement to writing.

"If the court pleases," Luna continues, "we could put the terms of the agreement orally but, quite frankly, the government and, I think, also counsel would prefer having it reduced to writing, which is something that I could get started on this afternoon." Luna once more stalls for time.

This time, Quarles isn't biting. Luna, in the course of this trial, has been untrustworthy, to put it mildly. Quarles is not going to send the jury home until the deal is complete, and the ink has dried on paper.

"You have until 3:30 pm to reduce it to writing," Quarles tells Luna.

"Judge, I think we are going to have a potential problem with—," Tuminelli begins, breaching the Alvin Jones dilemma. "Mr. Luna has advised me that he will not at sentencing seek to have the court find that the murder was related to this case. I don't know if he is going to be able to put that in a written agreement, for whatever reason." The reason is, it's unlawful.

"Then we will continue with the trial," Quarles says. The judge puts everyone's nuts in a vice.

"Well, I think that we will be able to take care of that," Luna says. In fact, the Alvin Jones dilemma will be a snowballing problem that will grow to consume the last evening, the last hours of Luna's life.

"You either have a deal, or you don't," Quarles snaps at Luna.

"Right," Luna raps back.

"If you have a deal, paper it, and we will do it at 3:30 pm," Quarles tells him.

"Yes, your honor," Luna stumbles. He knows Alvin Jones will still be dead of a drug murder at 3:30 pm. So the plea agreement will be unlawful and impossible at 3:30 pm. He has to find a way to get rid of the evidence of the drug murder by 3:30 pm, or to disavow the evidence, but he's tied up here in court. Perhaps he can simply say he has no evidence the murder is drug related with this conspiracy case. But what about everything in his files, in the court records, in the files of the Baltimore homicide squad? There's that interrogation of Grace conducted by the city homicide boys. That's evidence, isn't it?

Luna now sees he must find a way to deep-six and negate all the evidence he's shoveled into the record about Alvin Jones for the past months. But what about that the file created by the Baltimore police department's homicide squad—? And what about Jones's family? Would they allow the murder case simply to be dropped, as though Alvin had never lived or died? That's a problem too.

See Jonathan Luna. See Jonathan Luna dance. See him rap, spin, improv and bop.

Ravenell informs Judge Quarles there's another problem, er — issue. There's Deon Smith's past criminal record.

By the moment, the plea agreement looks more questionable, and appears to be falling apart.

"May I inquire on the court just on one issue, before we even go into that?" Ravenell hedges. "One of the things with Mr. Smith would be if he is found to be an armed career offender, or armed career criminal, that we be allowed to withdraw the plea." It's a new wrinkle Ravenell wants incorporated into the plea agreement. If Deon Smith pleads guilty for the purposes of the plea agreement, he wants to be able to withdraw the plea in the event Quarles must dispense a long sentence.

Already the plea is a plate of spaghetti. Best served, no doubt, with fava beans, and a nice chianti.

"For 'tis the sport to have the engineer / Hoist with his own petard," Shakespeare writes in Hamlet, Act III Scene IV, when Hamlet agrees to cast his fate on a boat ride with Rosencrantz and Guildenstern, his "two schoolfellows," who carry a sealed letter to have him killed. A petard was an explosive charge detonated by a slow-burning fuse, set off by a military engineer. To be hoisted by one's own petard, then, means to blow one's self up with one's own ammunition.

This time Agent Skinner, on the wrong end of his own slow-burning fuse, has hoisted himself by his own petard. In an affidavit of probable cause Skinner filed on May 12, 2003, to search Deon Smith's home and Stash House Records, Skinner detailed a long list of Smith's gun and drug offenses dating back to 1988. Smith, Skinner documents, was sentenced for "Handgun violation and Violation of Probation," in 1988; "possession and Violation of Probation" in 1989; "Storehouse breaking" in 1990; "Breaking and entering, Rogue and vagabond and Malicious destruction of property" in 1990; "Handgun on person" in October 1990; controlled substances abuses in 1993; "possession with intent to distribute" in 1994; "possession with intent to distribute" in 1994; "conspiracy, possession - not marijuana," in 1997; "possession of firearms, Handgun on person" in 1998.

Deon Smith sure could be confused for an armed career criminal. By ignoring a record like this, and ignoring Poindexter's drug murder of Alvin Jones, Luna's proposed plea agreement looks, to say the least, questionable.

"Let's call the jury," Quarles snarls. "If he is an armed career criminal, he gets sentenced as an armed career criminal." This sentence encapsulates the problem Luna is having with Quarles. Quarles relentlessly runs the case by the atomic clock, and relentlessly moves things along, and he is not allowing Luna to hide much under the carpet.

"He would not be allowed to withdraw the plea?" Ravenell asks.

"Of course not," Quarles says.

"Well, I don't know that it's of course not, judge," Ravenell presses on.

"Of course not," Quarles repeats. "If he is an armed career criminal, and is found to be such, I am not going to do anything that gives him a lighter sentence."

Tuminelli cites a Federal Rule of Criminal Procedure (Rule 11 [C] [1]) that he says allows Quarles to "wait until the pre-sentence report comes in to decide whether or not you are going to accept it."

"If you can do that—," Ravenell grasps. Now they all sense the agreement is falling apart.

"No, no," Quarles snaps back. "Look, folks, if you have got a deal, you have got a deal. If you don't have a deal, we have trial. We have a jury here. Time is wasting for them." Now Quarles climbs back up on his rocking horse about the jurors' time. "Have any of you ever served on a jury?" he asks.

"Pardon me, your honor?" Tuminelli asks.

"I would love to," Ravenell says. "I would love to, but I never got the opportunity."

"Well, let me tell you, our fellow citizens really get irritated by this stuff with bits and starts at trial," Quarles lectures. "Folks, either you have a deal, up and down, you have got a deal. You have until 3:30 to paper it, and I will take the plea. If you don't have a deal, and if there is more negotiating to be done, then you do the negotiation and that's required on your own time, (or) we get the jury in and we finish the evidence. Now, if you get another trial day in the bag, it doesn't mean we can't take the plea tomorrow. It doesn't mean tonight we can't do the plea. But if this falls through and, again, I hear you don't have a deal, if this falls through, then I am not going to have lost this trial day. Trial days are a diminishing resource. You lose one, you never get it back, you know." The same can ironically be said about assistant United States attorneys. "This trial day happens once. You lose it, and that's it. It's gone."

"All I was asking for us to do, so that we do not waste time," Ravenell presses on about Smith's criminal record, "is whether, if the plea agreement that we reach—."

"He is at risk because of conduct that he has engaged in," Quarles tells Ravenell. "I have no desire to shield him from his past criminal conduct. So if he is an armed career criminal, so be it. He gets sentenced as an armed career criminal. If he is not an armed career criminal, he won't be sentenced that way. And if he has got any doubt about whether this is the right thing to do, we have a jury impaneled. We can finish the trial. Life is real simple, guys. You have got a case. You try the case. If you have got a deal, put the deal on the record. Life ain't difficult. Life is real simple."

"Well it's not that simple, your honor, when you are dealing with people's liberty on this side," Ravenell fights on.

"People's liberty are conditioned upon things that people have done," Quarles replies.

"I understand that," Ravenell says.

"If people have engaged in criminal—," Quarles says.

"It doesn't make it simple though," Ravenell observes.

"—they have got themselves a problem."

"I understand that," Ravenell says. "That may be the way the court sees it, but—."

"That's the way the world is, in this little part of it," Quarles lectures. All the courtroom's a stage, and the lawyers merely litigators on it.

"All right," Ravenell says.

"In Courtroom 3-A, that's the way the world is," Quarles says.

"All right," Ravenell allows. "Well, I guess we will continue with the trial at this point. If we can resolve it later, we will do it."

"Good. Let's call for the jury," Quarles says.

The plea agreement was hardly a sure thing. "If we can resolve it later, we will do it," as Ravenell says.

The jury is led back into the courtroom, and Agent Skinner is recalled to the witness stand. He's reminded he's still under oath. Skinner takes the stand for the remainder of the afternoon to resume his testimony. He's still not looking too happy.

"We were talking this morning about your handling of Mr. Grace," Luna reminds Skinner. He straightaway reminds everyone that it was Skinner who was responsible for Warren Grace.

After this, Skinner mostly fields softball questions from Luna. In general, how did Skinner search Warren Grace and wire him for sound? Luna asks. In general, how did Skinner search Warren Grace's black Ford Excursion?

Skinner describes his surveillance of Stash House Records, and so on. No mention is made of any of Grace's transgressions, or of his wilder exploits with the "Safe Streets Task Force," or of the many secret "considerations" given to Pug by the government.

Luna, with Skinner still on the stand, moves several pieces of evidence into the record. He's about to introduce into evidence some of the cash confiscated from Stash House Records when Ravenell objects and asks for a conference at Judge Quarles' bench.

This is curiously about the same juncture where, the year before, in a bank robbery trial, Luna and an FBI agent introduced confiscated cash into evidence, only to have $36,000 of it disappear, minutes later, in the courthouse's secure evidence vault.

This time, in this case, Ravenell doesn't want the cash evidence introduced, saying there's no proof of any conspiracy in May 2003, when the cash was confiscated. Quarles overrules, and allows Luna to place the confiscated cash into evidence.

"While we are here, judge," Ravenell says, "I have had some additional time to review Mr. Smith's criminal history, judge, and after having some further conversations with him, we will tell you that he is willing to enter the plea that we discussed earlier."

Ravenell thinks Smith's record is clean enough so that Smith won't be classified as an armed career criminal. Ravenell and Tuminelli clearly believe their clients' best bet is the plea agreement.

Judge Quarles says he's now going to send the jurors out for their afternoon recess, and have them return at 4 pm. Quarles instructs Luna, "If you would have the agreements done by 3:45."

Previously, he told Luna to draw up the plea agreements by 3:30 pm.

"I think I can get that done," Luna now tells Quarles.

But Luna is only blowing more smoke. He knows the Alvin Jones murder stands in the way of an agreement with Poindexter.

Jonathan Luna now has about twelve hours to live.

The recess concludes at 4 pm, and Luna still hasn't written down the plea agreements. Poindexter's plea agreement will remain unfinished in Luna's office laptop when he begins his errand shortly before midnight. The jury returns to the courtroom, and Luna continues his questioning of Skinner.

"Now," Luna asks Skinner at one point, "can you tell the members of the jury approximately how many search warrants you have executed in narcotics cases, approximately?"

Skinner, curiously, doesn't seem to know, or want to say. "Numerous. Several. I really can't say," Skinner responds. Is he testy? The record doesn't say.

Luna and Skinner prattle on like this, for a few minutes more, until the end of the afternoon session.

"Would your vehicle be in this area of 911 West 36th Street, during the times that you were working with Mr. Grace?" Luna asks. This will be the last question Jonathan Luna will ever ask a witness in a courtroom. He's talking to Skinner, and he invokes Warren Grace. His question also, fittingly, contains the numbers "911" and "36." Nine-eleven. This cursed 911 heroin investigation. Nine-eleven. The bureaucratically disconnected telephone number the Dawsons kept calling, when help didn't arrive. And 36. The missing $36,000, last seen in the evidence vault with Luna and an FBI agent. Thirty-six. The number of stab wounds that will be found on Jonathan.

"Sometimes," Skinner replies. Skinner seems testy with Luna at the close of his examination. Everywhere you look, a shadow runs through this case. A shadow of a trace of Steve Skinner of the FBI. The undocumented, ghostly hand you don't see, time and again, is Steve Skinner. Where was Steve Skinner? What was he doing? Who knows?

Luna tells Quarles, "Your honor, at this time the government has no further questions for Special Agent Skinner."

Tuminelli and Ravenell elect to postpone their cross-examination of Skinner until they've first questioned Warren Grace.

Quarles tells Luna to call his next witness.

Luna replies that his next witness, Baltimore police detective Kaytee "Tony" Tyson, has left the courthouse. Curious. He must've had more important business than testifying in federal court. Perhaps Tyson went to find the Baltimore police homicide squad's file on the murder of Alvin Jones.

"I have just been advised by Ms. Cockburn that our next witness, Kaytee Tyson, has left the building and is not available," Luna tells Quarles.

"So," Quarles sighs, "in the words of the Moxie Brothers, we have managed to fritter away another day."

"Tomorrow, you won't have to worry about (that)," Ravenell tells the judge. He's presumably talking about the pending plea deals.

"Ladies and gentlemen, we appear to have run out of evidence today, so I will send you home to your families," Quarles tells the jurors. "Thank you. Goodnight, ladies and gentlemen."

The jury files out of the courtroom.

"Your honor, if I may," Luna tells Judge Quarles, "counsel anticipate having written plea agreements." Once again, Luna strings Quarles along. Luna will never finish Walter Poindexter's plea agreement.

"Okay. Have witnesses available, should the pleas fall through," Quarles tells Luna. In fact, Poindexter's deal *will* fall through, due to Poindexter's murder of Alvin Jones.

"Yes, your honor," Luna replies. "May I approach, your honor?"

"Sure," Quarles says.

"And counsel," Luna tells Ravenell and Tuminelli.

At the bench, Luna apologizes for his lateness in court this morning, an offence for which, at the start of proceedings, Quarles fined Luna $25.

Luna says to Judge Quarles, "Your honor, I just wanted to apologize for this morning. I'm sorry I was late. I just wanted to express that, that I meant no disrespect to the court. That's all I wanted to say."

"You have already expressed it well," Quarles tells him. He asks about Luna's hospitalized infant son. "You have given me your check so that does more than anything else to say you are sorry. How is your son, by the way?"

"He is better," Luna says. "I called during the break and he is better, and I appreciate your asking about him."

"Very good. Thank you," Quarles says. "See you tomorrow morning."

"Thank you," Luna says. He takes his bow, wearing his court suit, wearing his scales of justice college ring. He exits, stage left, with Ravenell and Tuminelli, to continue their heated argument over the plea agreements.

In less than twelve hours, Jonathan Luna will be dead, stabbed thirty-six times, lying face down in a stream seventy miles away.

23
After court, Luna argues heatedly with attorneys

Jonathan Luna and defense attorneys Ravenell and Tuminelli exit the courtroom and immediately begin heatedly arguing over the terms of the plea agreements. They can't agree on the agreements. The three walk a brief distance down the hall and continue their heated arguments outside the office of court reporter Ned Richardson, who himself has just returned with the court record.

"My office is near the courtroom," Richardson told me. "I was in my office on my computer working on the trial transcripts. I heard Jonathan, Ravenell and Tuminelli outside in the hall arguing about conditions of the plea agreement." Their disagreement was heated, loud and disruptive, Richardson vividly remembers.

"They were making so much commotion I was afraid I'd make some mistake with my computer and my notes," Richardson says. He says he stuck his head out his office door and told them, "Take it somewhere else, guys."

24
'The federal nexus'

Consumed in argument, the three lawyers walk down the hall, arguing as they go, looking for an office to continue their disagreement over the plea agreements. Luna's state of mind, after a bad day in court, was combative and testy. His state of mind of course is important. Luna did not seem at all depressed. Nor did he act like a man about to throw in the towel, professionally or personally. Rather, he's angry and combative, caught between a rock and a hard place, stuck where he didn't want to be, and fighting.

At the meeting, Smith, through his lawyer, agrees to plead guilty to one count of distribution of heroin and possession of a firearm for purposes of drug trafficking. Poindexter pleads guilty to three counts of heroin distribution. The conspiracy counts against both are dropped. Luna further agrees, Tuminelli says, to reduced sentencing guidelines.

But there's a problem. A serious problem. In his meeting with Ravenell and Tuminelli, Luna finds himself in another deepening dilemma. Tuminelli demands, as part of the deal, that Luna drop all charges against Walter Poindexter for the murder of Alvin Jones.

Problem is, by law, Luna can't do that. The drug-related nature of Jones' killing over the burglary of the stash house creates what's called a "federal nexus" in this drug conspiracy case, *demanding* prosecution by the feds.

Although the word sometimes enjoys slightly different usage by the legal profession, nexus refers to a link, a tie, or a connected series or group.

Luna knows that an abundance of federal statutes demand prosecution and severe penalties for murders committed in the course of drug or other racketeering enterprises. For example, the Violent Crime in Aid of Racketeering Act (VICAR 18 U.S.C. § 1959[a]), often applied in cases like this, demands prosecution when the murderer's "general purpose... (is to) maintain or increase his position in the enterprise." The federal death penalty, moreover, is provided in cases of "murder committed by the use of a firearm during a crime of violence or a drug trafficking crime (18 U.S.C 930)," and, "murder involved in racketeering offense (18 U.S.C. 1959)." These aren't obscure prosecutions, but everyday events in federal courts across the country.

Case after case of homicide prosecutions are routinely brought by the feds against drug traffickers like Poindexter. (To see for yourself, conduct a web search for "drug-related murder federal nexus.") In fact, critics complain that blacks and other minorities are more likely than whites to face the death penalty for these crimes. In this case, Poindexter, a black, career offender, has only one thing going for him: the U.S. attorney's office must now protect *itself* from scandal by dropping a murder case against him. It only creates another scandal, one that amazingly points back to the Dawson tragedy.

Not only does the federal criminal code demand prosecution for drug-related murders, significant government resources, and congressional oversight, are focused on the issue of drug-related murder. This is particularly so in Baltimore, where drug-related murders remain a problem. The Drug Enforcement Administration maintains several High Intensity Drug Trafficking Area (HIDTA) task forces in Baltimore, including "a REDRUM group, whose main focus is to investigate drug trafficking organizations *with a nexus* to drug-related homicides," the DEA's Preston L. Grubbs, Special Agent in Charge of the Baltimore District Office, told a House Government Reform subcommittee in July 2003, following the Dawson tragedy. (Emphasis mine.)

"Unfortunately, the Dawson family tragedy highlights in many ways the problems we face in combating the drug trafficking organizations operating in Baltimore and the violence associated with them," the DEA's Grubbs ironically told Congress. "Following that horrible tragedy, I made all investigative resources of the Baltimore DEA office available to target the perpetrators of this heinous crime as well as to target the drug distribution organizations in the Dawsons' neighborhood."

Only several months after Grubbs tried to reassure Congress, Luna now must entertain granting Poindexter *protection* from a drug-related murder, in order to cover-up the Justice Department's own failures to protect the Dawsons, and others.

As Luna is about to find out, murder can't so be easily swept under a rug. Except, perhaps, his own.

Earlier, in court, Luna expressed doubts to defense attorneys about the plea deal, due to the prickly problem of Poindexter's murder of Alvin Jones. Now, after court, as night descends, Luna's doubts continue to mount. He's so concerned he confers with another, more senior prosecutor in the office.

Luna's contacts within his office become part of the mystery. An assistant U.S. attorney does not have the power to approve, or even authoritively offer, a plea deal. The deal must be approved by higher-ups. In many jurisdictions, the criminal chief approves the deals. In some jurisdictions, plea agrements are approved by the U.S. attorney personally. Therefore, Tom DiBiagio or his chief criminal prosecutor *must* have been part of Luna's interactions on his last night.

Luna and Tuminelli moreover met with Assistant U.S. Attorney James Warwick. Warwick, it turns out, is the same assistant U.S. attorney who a former federal investigator complains applied ceaseless pressure to set-up phony, cash storefronts.

"I had a conversation ... with Mr. Warwick, and Mr. Luna, primarily with Mr. Luna," Tuminelli agrees. "Mr. Warwick sat in and gave some guidance."

Warwick, for his part, says Luna and Tuminelli consulted with him about the problem of the pending murder charges against Poindexter. Warwick recalls that Poindexter's own lawyer, Tuminelli, used the phrase "related conduct" when talking about Jones' murder.

"The concern that Mr. Tuminelli had was the *related conduct* on the homicide," Warwick recalls. Warwick says he questioned both Luna and Tuminelli. "And my questions to both Mr. Tuminelli and to Mr. Luna were essentially it's related conduct if we can establish a federal nexus, specifically that we can establish that the murder was related to a drug crime or a drug transaction."

In other words, was Jones' murder tied to the Stash House drug conspiracy? Certainly it was.

Yet, Warwick says, there came a moment when he flat out asked Luna whether there was any proof, or evidence, that Jones' murder was drug related.

Luna, we know, filed court documents stating that he, and the police, had plenty of proof.

Luna's problem was that Jones' murder clearly was drug related. Poindexter shot Jones because he thought Jones had burglarized his drug stash house.

That Jones' murder should be viewed as drug related is endorsed by no less an authority than the White House. A 2000 White House position paper called "Drug Related Crime," issued by the Executive Office of the President and the Office of National Drug Control Policy defines the crime. A drug-related crime is not just a crime committed while the perpetrator is under the influence of drugs, the paper points out. It includes violence or other crimes committed by those involved in drug trafficking.

In a section titled, "Drugs generate violent crime," the White House paper states, "Trafficking in illicit drugs tends to be associated with the commission of violent crimes. Reasons for the relationship between drug trafficking and violence include the following: ...The tendency toward violence of individuals who participate in drug trafficking." Drug-related offenses include, according to the paper, "offenses connected to drug distribution itself." The paper concludes, "murders related to narcotics still rank as the fourth most documented murder circumstances out of 24 possible categories."

The administration of President George W. Bush publicly advocated prosecuting such drug-related murders. "The best way to prevent crimes with guns," Bush said while campaigning in October 2004, "is to prosecute crimes committed with guns."

So, yes, Poindexter shooting Alvin Jones because he thought Jones had robbed his stash house is a drug-related murder. No one seems to dispute this. But, as Warwick says he asked, did Luna have any evidence — proof — that Poindexter killed Jones in drug-related circumstances?

Certainly he did. By Luna's own admission, submitted in court documents, there was much hard evidence, even *several* witnesses. There were the early interviews of Warren Grace conducted by the Baltimore homicide detectives. Grace "was cooperating with the Baltimore city police on the homicide," Luna told Judge Quarles. There was a recording made of Grace's statements to the Baltimore homicide cops. Tuminelli told Judge Quarles that there even existed a "recording of Mr. Grace being interviewed by homicide detectives in Baltimore city." So transcripts would even be available. That's hard evidence.

There was even a FBI 302 on Jones' murder. Tuminelli told Judge Quarles at a bench conference, "Mr. Ravenell and I had a telephone call one day and I mentioned the (Jones murder) 302, or I made reference to something in a 302," Tuminelli recalls. "And he said, 'What are you talking about?' And I said I have this 302 and it says such and such. And one of the documents that he didn't have that I had was the interview of the recording of Mr. Grace being interviewed by homicide detectives in Baltimore city." The FBI 302 represents more evidence.

Then there are all the references to the murder that Luna *himself* papered into the file, back when he was still threatening Poindexter with the death penalty. It's about the only thing he bothered to commit to writing in the file. The May 2003 indictment of Poindexter reads, "Members of the conspiracy ...utilized physical force against members of the conspiracy and against members of rival drug conspiracies to maintain their reputation in the community, to preserve their own territory, to punish members of the conspiracy who cheated or stole from the conspiracy, and to defend and maintain the loyalty of the members of their own organization." The indictment explains, "On January 22, 2001, Walter Oriley Poindexter, a/k/a 'Fella," shot and killed Alvin Jones, a/k/a 'L,' because Poindexter believed that Jones was responsible for burglarizing the stash house where conspirators stored their heroin, money and firearms."

Luna, four weeks before the trial, specifically told the court there *was evidence* to establish Poindexter's guilt in a drug-related murder. In his October 30, 2003, brief seeking to try Smith and Poindexter together, Luna told the court, "During the course of the conspiracy, Poindexter was advised that Alvin Jones had burglarized one of Poindexter's stash houses. Believing that Jones had burglarized the stash house, the government's *evidence will show* that upon finding Jones, Poindexter shot and killed Jones on January 22, 2001."

The evidence will show, Luna told the court, that Poindexter killed Jones. There were even witnesses. At least two witnesses were ready to testify about the murder, Luna wrote, and he was worried about further traumatizing these witnesses. "At least two of the witnesses in this case were involuntary witnesses to the murder of Alvin Jones," Luna writes. "Two separate trials will require these witnesses to relive horrific experiences of witnessing the murder of a human being.... Moreover, the emotional burdens from testifying just once may cause some of these witnesses to avoid testifying a second time, thus unfairly causing prejudice to the Government's case and the victims' interest in justice."

Merciful heavens, let us not forget, as Luna writes, the victim's interest in justice. There was Jones' father, who overheard the phone conversation Jones had with Poindexter's girlfriend, Maronda Cole, warning him of Poindexter's planned revenge. "Alvin explained, 'Some bitch is accusing me of robbing some house,' or words to that effect."

And on and on. There was even the FBI recording of January 2, 2003, mixed in with the hundred hours of surveillance tapes, which contains, in Tuminelli's words, a "conversation that Mr. Grace has had with Mr. Smith, and they are discussing... the allegation that Mr. Grace had talked to the Baltimore city police homicide department about the murder." Everybody knew that Poindexter killed Jones over the stash house burglary, even Deon Smith, who could now be forced to cooperate under his plea agreement. Instead, Smith, and Poindexter, are let off the hook.

Judge Quarles even went out of his way to instruct the lawyers, when this January 2003 tape was played for the jury, "Why don't the three of you go over there and instruct (Grace) again. Make sure that someone is holding the microphone and explain to him that he is to answer your literal questions and only those questions and not to volunteer anything," about Jones' murder.

Making matters worse, Luna knows, Quarles is a judge who takes this recorded evidence seriously. Quarles refused to dismiss the case on the strength of evidence found on these tapes. This judge, if pressed, Luna must know, will believe the rather copious evidence that Poindexter's murder of Jones was drug related. "People's liberty are conditioned upon what things that people have done," Quarles says. "That's the way the world is, in this little part of it."

In short, there was plenty of evidence, and witnesses, that Poindexter killed Jones in a drug-related murder. There *was* a federal nexus demanding Luna prosecute the murder, in the "victim's interest of justice," in Luna's words.

All this prevented Luna from writing a lawful plea agreement forgiving the murder. This in turn meant the trial must go forward, and Warren Grace would be examined by defense lawyers "as broadly as possible" about the "forms of consideration that he has received from the government." The sex, the freedom, the drugs, money and guns.

Yet, amazingly, when Assistant U.S. Attorney James Warwick asks Luna whether he "can establish that the murder was related to a drug crime or a drug transaction," Warwick says Luna told him *he didn't have any evidence.*

"Mr. Luna represented that he did not have that proof," Warwick says. Note that Warwick uses the lawyer's word, "represented." That's what Luna told me, Warwick is saying. Warwick interestingly isn't himself taking responsibility for this false claim.

If there was no evidence, Warwick says he told Luna, it was possible to issue a plea agreement stating the murder would not be prosecuted. Warwick says he even conferred with others in the U.S. Attorneys office. "And I told him (Luna), in my opinion," Warwick says, "which I have gone through my— other people in the office, is that if we cannot establish a federal nexus, it's not related conduct under the guidelines."

So if Luna doesn't want Skinner's task force and himself investigated for their mishandling of Warren Grace, he must lie about the facts to pull off the plea deal. It's a measure of his desperation to shut down the case that Luna exposes himself like this.

Lawyers may not always have pangs of conscience, but they always weigh exposure to risk. That's their job. And Luna was exposing himself with this agreement. Does he suddenly realize this?

The first rule of legal survival is to do nothing to harm yourself. Luna doesn't need to call another lawyer to tell him this.

By writing this plea agreement Luna's cutting his own throat: suicide by word processor. Luna's an officer of the court. An officer of the court isn't supposed to write false statements on court documents. He's spent most of 2003 papering the file, attesting to ample "evidence" of Poindexter's drug-related murder of Jones. Now, to bury the case, he has to file another set of court documents ignoring evidence. Luna already fears losing his job. He's recently retained a lawyer to help save his job. There are other job-related issues, such as the missing $36,000.

If Luna elects to shut down this case by filing false statements, he ironically risks giving his unfriendly boss, U.S. Attorney Tom DiBiagio, all the ammunition DiBiagio needs to justifiably fire him. Luna might even risk his law license. Or worse. Getting caught writing false court statements damages his credibility in the collateral matters, like the missing thirty-six G's.

Until now, Jonathan Luna has not been a very good chess player. He fails to think more than a move or two ahead. If he were now to stop and think about it like a chess game, Luna's left holding the bag, isn't he?

On the other hand, if he doesn't complete the agreement, and the Grace business comes out, it's largely DiBiagio and Skinner's problem, isn't it? Why now should Luna stick his neck out for his boss, when DiBiagio wants him "gone?" In fact, Luna's hand is strengthened if he resists office pressure exerted on him to file a bad or unlawful plea deal. "And I told him (Luna), in my opinion," Warwick says, "which I have gone through my— *other people in the office,* is that if we cannot establish a federal nexus, it's not related conduct under the guidelines." (Emphasis mine.) These words must linger, and ring, in Jonathan Luna's mind.

Did he suspect or fear he was being set up by the "other people in the office" who now wanted him to contradict his earlier court filings?

To plea or not to plea, Luna must be wondering. Would it be

nobler to take arms against a sea of troubles, Hamlet muses, than to suffer the slings and arrows of outrageous fortune?

It certainly would be wise for Luna to talk to his lawyer before putting his name to any questionable plea deal like this—.

All, some, or none of which may help explain why Luna never completes Poindexter's plea agreement.

Let's see him dance out of this one. Luna responds to all these pressures and dilemmas with one last great improvisational performance. It will be his famous and perplexing midnight ride.

That's right. Luna never completes the plea agreement before he takes off on his ride. The suspect deal remains curiously unfinished, and unsigned, on Luna's computer when he walks out of the courthouse a little before midnight.

Part of the problem no doubt is the complexity of all that has now been set in motion. Behind the scenes, surprising things were happening. Other cascading problems, beyond Luna's control, now confronted the plea deal. Though Luna supposedly pretended the evidence didn't exist about Jones' murder, there was the other problem. Even if DiBiagio's office demurred on prosecuting Poindexter, the Baltimore state's attorney's office could reassume jurisdiction in the case and prosecute Poindexter for killing Jones.

Tuminelli, and Luna, needed the local prosecutor to agree to a deal. That evening, they contacted head Baltimore homicide prosecutor, Assistant State's Attorney Mark Cohen, to ask him to sign off on the questionable deal.

Tuminelli would say he witnessed Luna speaking with Cohen. They were alone at the time.

"I was present when Mr. Luna spoke to Mark Cohen of the Baltimore City State's Attorney's office," Tuminelli recalls, "and am aware that Mr. Cohen advised Mr. Luna.... I just want to make this clear. Mr Cohen did not say this directly to me. He said it to Mr. Luna. And Ms. Cockburn, I believe, can confirm that that's how the negotiation took place."

At some point, Luna's co-counsel, says she returned to the room with Luna and Tuminelli. "I was not present during the phone call," Cockburn says. "However, Mr. Luna did relay that conversation to me in front of Mr. Tuminelli."

Luna says Cohen agreed to drop the murder charges, Cockburn says. Cohen, she says, supposedly sought the permission of Alvin Jones' parents.

It's a play within a play, a file within a file, a murder case within a murder case. Now the city's top homicide investigator comes into the story of Jonathan Luna's last hours. Lt. Columbo, call the office.

Cohen's involvement was so interesting that it would get back to Judge Quarles by early the next morning.

"Someone told me that Mark Cohen had to be consulted," Quarles would tell lawyers at a bench conference the next morning, while Luna lies dead in the Pennsylvania stream.

"Any deal with regard to Mr. Tuminelli's client's state liability is between Mr. Cohen and Mr. Tuminelli," Warwick would say. Tuminelli would dispute this characterization, saying he did not negotiate the deal with Cohen. "Mr Cohen did not say this directly to me. He said it to Mr. Luna."

Luna's co-counsel, Vivien Cockburn, says Baltimore prosecutor Cohen "was consulted." The defendants, and Luna, and the plea agreement, supposedly hinged on Cohen speaking to the parents of Alvin Jones. Cohen "has spoken to the victim's parents," Cockburn would say early the next morning.

There's delicious irony in that phone conversation. Before he was murdered, Jones took a phone call, overheard by his father, from "some bitch" who warned him that Poindexter would kill him for the drug stash house burglary. Now, three years later, the Jones family's phone supposedly rings again, this time to strangely inform the family that there will be no prosecution for their son's drug murder.

Some bitch says they're not going to prosecute Alvin's murder!

So this was hardly a cut-and-dried, run-of-the-mill deal. There were serious problems that ended with the whole matter being sent out of DiBiagio's U.S. attorney's office.

After the strange and telling meeting between Luna, Warwick and Ravenell breaks up, at about 6 pm, Jonathan Luna has about ten hours to live. Between that time, and Luna's strange departure from the courthouse shortly before midnight, an important part of the plea agreement was supposedly in the hands of local prosecutors, and the victim's family.

Luna went home for dinner, promising he'd return to his office that night to "finalize" the plea in time for court in the morning.

With that Luna drives to the Elkridge home he shares with his wife, Angela, an obstetrician, their two young children, and his mother-in-law. Elkridge is a short fifteen minute hop southwest on I-95, toward Washington DC.

About 8:48 pm Luna returns to his office. There seems to be some discrepancy about Luna's movements. Attorney Tuminelli says his caller ID reflects that Luna called him by cell phone at 9:06 pm. Luna told him he again had to go home, but would return to the office to finish up, Tuminelli says. He says Luna told him he'd completed Smith's paperwork but had yet to write Poindexter's, and wanted to make sure he wasn't mistaken about the terms of the agreement.

"He called me at home and said, you know, I just want to make sure we got all the details," Tuminelli recounts. "He went over the details and I said that is correct. He said, 'I left the office but I have got to go back and complete the agreement. And he was supposed to fax the agreement to me sometime last night." Tuminelli adds, "It was not faxed."

The call, Tuminelli remembers, lasted no more than five or ten minutes.

At 9:30 pm, Attorney Ravenell says, Luna left a similar message on the voice mail of Ravenell's cell phone. Luna assures the defense lawyer he's working on the agreement.

Flashing that million-dollar smile, Jonathan Luna is about to come undone. Some not-so-visible wheel in the machine of his life is ready to fly off.

He never faxed over the paperwork for the plea deal.

At 9:30 pm, Jonathan Luna has less than seven hours to live.

25
A false sense of security, and sex, at the Baltimore federal courthouse

Despite what he says to the defense lawyers about going home, Luna appears to have lingered in his office for two hours more, with the paperwork, his phones (office and cell), his eyeglasses, his laptop, and any co-workers or courthouse personnel who may have happened to have been with him in the downtown federal courthouse while he had his doubts about the plea deal. While, we're told, he cynically abandoned the lofty idea of justice for Alvin Jones, and the innocents of Baltimore.

Dark questions start to eclipse the surety of courthouse statements.

Was Luna even alone? No one, surprisingly, can say for sure. Researching this book, I'd hear about security problems aplenty at the courthouse. I'm told Luna could easily have been lured away from his desk by an insider, someone of misplaced trust, who would leave no trace. Or he could have taken himself away, to an arranged rendezvous. Why then leave his cell phone, and his eyeglasses?

About one hundred and seventy-five Justice Department employees, including some fifty attorneys, work out of the federal building office, according a Baltimore business journal, and the U.S. Attorney's own web site. Hundreds of additional employees, working for other agencies, including court personnel, also work in the building.

Security problems in this dodgy neighborhood start at the curb side, and are exacerbated by vain and out-of-touch federal judges. For example, nearly all drivers of delivery trucks — UPS, Fed-Ex and the like — must unload their trucks in the street, at a prescribed distance from the building, and laboriously cart their cargo by hand into the building. Everyone, that is, except the drivers of dry cleaning trucks literally loaded with the judges' dirty laundry. Trucks carrying the judges' dirty laundry are allowed to pull up at the courthouse door, in plain sight of everyone on the street. Drivers hop out and run the judicial clean linen inside, watched by bemused courthouse workers taking breaks outside.

Courthouse security is otherwise lax, particularly for insiders. Security flaws continue, and worsen, as the visitor moves through the courthouse entranceway. At the door there's the obligatory security check and metal detector, and a sign-in sheet for workers, but these are meant for strangers. Courthouse employees tell me it's not unusual, in the crush of getting to court, to be waved past a line, and told to sign-in later. Just as interesting, I'm told, several assistant U.S. attorneys carry guns, which they routinely check in when they enter the courthouse. That is, if they're asked to sign-in.

FBI agents, I'm told, often come and go in the courthouse, unchallenged, without having to sign-in or out, leaving not a trace in their otherwise traceless existence. It's a measure of how the agents rank themselves in the roost. I've come to see it's also a measure of the fear the agents instill in the other employees. No one wants to stand up to Praetorian FBI agents and demand they follow the rules the rest of us live by.

Amazingly, the corrupt and venal Roman Praetorian Guard, which started out protecting emperors and ended up murdering them and auctioning off the throne, was named for the tent of the legate of a field legion — the praetorium. A Praetorian Guard, like a Baltimore FBI agent, enjoyed free access in and out of the tent.

The Romans also passed down a proverb, *Quis custodiet ipsos custodes?* Who is guarding the guards?

In all, I've learned, security in the Baltimore federal courthouse is abysmal. The courthouse accordingly has had its share of scandalously juicy behavior. A mentally impaired cleaning lady once stumbled into a vacant jury room to find a court clerk having sex with a judge's secretary. The cleaning lady became upset, and the behavior came to light, I'm told, when she asked whether she'd be required to clean bodily fluids from the jury table.

An understandable fear. It's the American way. The guy wearing the suit makes the mess, and someone else cleans up.

26
A great reckoning in a little room

The Justice Department will later issue a sketchy timeline of events that follow. At about 11:38 pm, Jonathan Luna's car is recorded leaving the courthouse's secured parking garage.

Leaving no explanation, leaving behind his cell phone and his eyeglasses, walking out of his office, to all appearances walking out of his life, his work incomplete, his life incomplete, Luna drives his silver 2003 Honda Accord from the federal building's underground parking garage.

Set in motion is a truly baffling series of events. Each detail seems a puzzle of its own. Why would Luna leave behind his cell phone? His eyeglasses? Where was he going at this hour, in such a rush? It seems likely he was meeting someone. Who? Where was he going, so late at night, when he had to be in court first thing in the morning?

Has he been called away on urgent business? Does his mission have anything to do with the incomplete plea deal?

Also left behind, most strangely, unfinished on Luna's laptop, and in earlier drafts of hard copy, is Poindexter's plea agreement. In the morning, the draft paperwork of the unfinished plea deal would be quickly slapped together by his former colleagues and introduced in court and filed into record. At this writing, the original document remains in the court file, in the clerk's office, free for public inspection.

Alfred Hitchcock once produced a famous episode of his television series in which a woman beats her husband to death with a frozen leg of lamb. She defrosts the roast and serves it to the baffled homicide detectives, unaware that they are consuming the evidence. (The episode, full of Hitchcock's mordant humor, is called "Lamb to the Slaughter.") And so the court, in this case, consumed the suspect plea deal paperwork.

Luna, by contrast, had completed Smith's paperwork. It's crisply composed and printed. Poindexter's paperwork, on the other hand, contains typos, hand written cross-outs, insertions and amendments lifted directly from a draft of Smith's plea deal, all clearly revealing the document remained uncompleted at the time of Luna's disappearance. Unfinished business owed the people of the United States.

He's walked out of his office in the middle of a typing job. Due in court in the morning, he's already been warned and fined by Judge Quarles for lateness. He's worried about his job. Why risk not completing this paperwork before he leaves his office for the night? Unless he knows the plea deal won't be completed. Unless he knows, as he does, that the plea deal can't be lawfully completed.

There's an explanation for his mysterious behavior. To weigh possible motives, we must ask ourselves, What sort of person was Jonathan Luna? Good Luna, or Bad Luna? Was he acting properly, with integrity; or *improperly,* without integrity? Was he a courageous whistleblower, or a government stooge?

Did Jonathan, as his friend Dan Rivera suggests, intentionally behave as he did in court to slyly expose the FBI and force the judge to order an investigation? A man of integrity, in over his head, with few other options available, might act this way. Or, was Luna all along a willing participant in an ongoing cover-up? A Bad Luna, a stooge, would act another way.

If he was a stooge, a willing participant in an ongoing cover-up, how might he act? This crisis might cause him to improvise a solution to the problem of the faulty plea deal. Perhaps he'd decide to buy some insurance, as it were.

Having scuttled Poindexter's plea deal, Bad Luna would ponder making last-minute arrangements to secretly prep, and ply, Warren Grace for his coming examination. This would involve secretly violating Judge Quarles' order for the prosecution team to have no contact with Warren Grace. It would essentially involve bribing Warren Grace with more perks, even money. That's what they'd been doing all along. These secret "considerations" were an ongoing conspiracy. Such a sensitive mission would have to be conducted with the utmost discretion, out of office hours, and remain untraceable. It would even be wise to make it look like he'd never left the office. It perhaps fits together.

Why leave his cell phone behind? Perhaps he's worried about being traced. Many cell phones today have a tracking feature. The tracking feature supposedly only works when the phone is turned on, but I've heard some people express suspicion of being tracked, and bugged, even when the phone is deactivated. Under court order to have no contact with Warren Grace, Bad Luna wouldn't want to risk having his movements tracked. Better safe than sorry, he simply leaves the phone behind.

But the Bad Luna theory starts to fall apart. Why leave his *glasses* behind? Even Bad Luna needs to see to drive.

The problem with the Bad Luna theory is the growing weight of evidence that Jonathan was a good man, who generally acted with integrity. How would Good Luna act?

Testy and combative, unwilling to complete a bad plea deal, Luna might decide to tell someone to shove it, that he's not going to take the fall for Warren Grace. Like they're trying to make him take the fall for the missing $36,000.

This could certainly spark a sudden and vicious confrontation.

Assistant U.S. Attorney Warwick, for his part, would say he spoke to Luna sometime during the night. "I spoke with Mr. Luna last night," Warwick would say in the morning. What exactly did Luna tell him?

Only this much is certain: when he walks out of his office a little before midnight, Luna has less than five hours to live.

Let's not overlook the central mystery. What of Jonathan Luna?

Jonathan, as Tom DiBiagio had strangely predicted, was gone.

He had begun his famous midnight ride.

Part 3

Night shop: Exit, Luna

1
Lamb to the slaughter

A periodic table of heavy and light elements fuse together in the midnight ride of Jonathan Luna. Murder, rap music, informant money, secrets, undercover ops, crooked cops, sex, violence and mystery. A minority, a lawman, hip and young, smart, tough and tender, a victim, a ghostly nightrider, no longer in control, Jonathan Luna suddenly finds himself embodying all the swirling trouble of Baltimore.

In the middle of the night, in the middle of performing a complicated, important task, with someone supposedly on the other end of a waiting fax machine, with a court appointment a few hours away in the morning, worrying about his boss, worrying about the FBI, leaving personal effects behind, Jonathan Luna gets on I-95 and heads east, out of town, out of state.

The official FBI outline provides the sketchy and beguiling facts of Luna's midnight ride. We can no longer follow Jonathan Luna, so much as we must follow the remaining electronic traces of his life.

At 11:38 pm, the first blip. His car leaves the supposedly well-secured parking garage at the U.S. courthouse. It's where Luna usually parks. It's also the place where FBI agents park their cars, and other government lawyers. The public, strangely, isn't shown video of Luna leaving the courthouse.

We don't know whether he was alone in the car. Rather than heading south and west to home and hearth, his traces veer away north and east into the cold December night, a strange and seemingly inexplicable midnight jigsaw puzzle ride. East into Delaware, skirting around Philadelphia, north into New Jersey, back west into Pennsylvania, to the dark field where he's found lying face down in a stream, stabbed thirty-six times.

Jonathan Luna rides to the city's beltway in his nondescript, late-model Honda Accord. There's a baby seat in the back. He wears his University of North Carolina scales of justice class ring on his finger. He's dressed in business suit and overcoat. He's still wearing his Justice Department ID badge, which swings from a necklace.

In his car Luna has an EZ Pass, allowing him quick passage at tollgates, bridges and tunnels throughout much of the northeast corridor. The next blip of his waning life shows Jonathan Luna using his EZ Pass, north on I-95, at the Fort McHenry Tunnel Toll Plaza, at 11:49 pm. About ten minutes have passed since he left the parking garage. This means Luna is driving with all deliberate speed, past Fort McHenry, not wasting time. He has a purpose.

To reach I-95, Luna must've entered at I-395 North, the city expressway's downtown spillway. Interstate-395 South would have carried him home. It's a crossroads moment in his life.

Riding north, I-395 rises up over the water and city, passing the refineries and smokestacks of the city incinerator, the all-consuming hellfire burning below. It's a futurist smooth ride that carries you up into the clouds above a boiling city below.

Leaving Baltimore, the first set of toll/EZ Pass booths are at the Fort McHenry tunnel. Again, we're told Luna hits here at 11:49 pm, just over ten minutes after leaving the parking garage. He's not wasting time. He's booking.

This fifty-mile stretch of I-95 north of Baltimore to the Delaware line is called the John F. Kennedy Memorial Highway. The highway was begun in 1962, the Maryland Transportation Authority tells us in a publication. "The highway was dedicated at 4 pm on November 14, 1963," the authority's brochure reads. "President John F. Kennedy, with Governor Millard Tawes of Maryland and Governor Carvel of Delaware officiated the ceremony. It was President Kennedy's last public appearance."

That's not quite right, as we know. Less than a week after dedicating this stretch of I-95, Kennedy made an appearance in Dallas, Texas. Not at a toll plaza, but Dealey Plaza, where he lost his life.

"The roadway was renamed the John F. Kennedy Memorial Highway in 1964 to honor the fallen president," the transportation authority tells us.

The Kennedy Highway carries Luna to another set of tollbooths, at Perryville, where I-95 crosses the Susquehanna River. He passes through this toll plaza at 12:28 am. He's traveled almost 40 miles in fifty minutes, including stop lights in downtown Baltimore.

The next blip we have of Jonathan Luna places him in Delaware. He passes through the state line toll booth at 12:46 am, at Elkton, Maryland. When he puts in at Elkton, he's full sail into his midnight American ride. He's traveled now almost sixty miles in a little more than an hour. He's driving the speed limit, but he's not wasting time. Notice — he's not breaking the law, either.

A few miles down the road he reaches the I-95 Newark, Delaware, rest stop. The John F. Kennedy Plaza, it's called. The Kennedy Plaza is a sprawling rest stop, surrounded by a large, unevenly lit ocean of parking lot.

Authorities say that at 12:57 am someone uses Luna's debit card at one of two ATM Wachovia Bank cash machines in the plaza of the rest stop. Two hundred dollars, we're told by way of leakers in the press, is withdrawn from Luna's account. (The timeline officially released by the FBI says only that "12:57 am — Luna's debit card is used at an ATM at JFK Plaza in Newark, Del.")

This withdrawal seems a deliberate act, with not much time wasted. Only eleven minutes have passed from the state line toll booth. He's parked his car in the busy plaza, and someone's walked inside the plaza to the ATM machine. That doesn't leave much time for lollygagging, or jawboning in the parking lot.

Someone needs two hundred dollars for something, and wastes no time getting it. As the money is withdrawn from the ATM, video cameras in the lobby for some reason are unable to capture usable images of the transaction. The security cameras, strangely, aren't working.

Though Luna is in Delaware, jurisdictions within the Justice Department place him closer to home than many might suppose. FBI agents in Delaware work under the agent in charge of the Baltimore office. At the time of Luna's disappearance, acting special agent in charge Jennifer Smith Love had been newly charged with overseeing FBI agents in both Maryland *and* Delaware. So it is not out of the question that Luna may have planned to meet an agent with whom he regularly worked. In Delaware, he had every reason to believe he's still under the protection of the home office.

Look at a map, and you'll notice the Newark, Delaware, rest stop lies about halfway between Baltimore and Philadelphia. Has Luna agreed to split the distance with someone he will meet coming from Philadelphia? For Luna it's not an unknown drive. In the weeks leading to Poindexter-Smith trial, Luna repeatedly drove to the Philadelphia federal detention facility to meet with witness Warren Grace, who remains behind bars, chauffeured, over defense objections, by our Rosencrantz and Guildenstern — Agent Skinner and Detective Moody.

It appears reasonable that, temporarily leaving the office at 11:38 pm, Luna expects to drive no more than an hour to Newark, Delaware, meet someone, then head back to his office or, more likely, home, by 2 am.

He appears to have no desire to finish the paperwork for the stinking plea deal.

Why withdraw two hundred dollars? Maybe he needed the money. Or perhaps someone else made the withdrawl.

There could be other explanations. I keep thinking of Warren Grace, sitting in that cell, on top of the world. Could the two hundred dollars have been meant to go to Warren Grace? Prison canteen money, or perhaps money to a family member. This after all was the role that Poindexter once played in Grace's prison life. Having ratted on Poindexter, Grace now had no one but Luna and Skinner. As Deon Smith once advised Grace, "You were supposed to send over, yo." Now that the plea deal had fallen through, was this Jonathan's last great improvisational fix, "sending over" to Grace to buy Grace's help with the impending defense investigation of the FBI? The problem then would be how to get the money to Warren Grace, without it being traced. Which may have been the object of Luna's midnight ride. Somehow, though, this doesn't make sense. Luna seemed in no mood to do any favors for Grace, Skinner or DiBiagio.

By the time the two hundred dollars is withdrawn from the ATM, Luna has maybe three and a half hours to live.

2
When lilacs last in the truck stop bloomed

About the time the two hundred dollars is withdrawn at the John F. Kennedy rest stop, odds are good something goes bad.

It's seems possible this is the general time and place Luna met someone and was attacked, or at the very least had his movements arrested. We can surmise this for several reasons. The EZ Pass, the timeline.

After this stop, Luna no longer uses his EZ Pass. Tolls will be paid with cash from someone's pocket. At least one turnpike ticket will be taken, and returned. There are several possibilities: Luna is not driving, or he is in no condition to tell whoever is behind the wheel about the EZ Pass. Whoever is driving either is unaware of the EZ Pass, or is playing it safe and is unwilling to drive through the EZ Pass lanes and risk being photographed or pulled over.

Another possibility is that Luna *himself* suddenly grows concerned about his movements being traced by the EZ Pass. As with leaving his cell phone behind, he doesn't want to *at all* risk being traced by the Justice Department, or the court. So Luna himself, perhaps in the company of another, begins to take the toll tickets. Such behavior would again imply Luna's ride is connected with nefarious, work-related activities, and that he has perhaps rendezvoused with someone who is equally protective and stealthy, and who may also work for the Justice Department. They are two invisible blips, meeting under cover of darkness. That means they are *professionals,* knowingly engaged in improper behavior, and literally covering their tracks. Pretty much what Luna has already been doing for the past year and a half with Warren Grace's case.

That said, if Luna did not want his movements traced, why then withdraw the traceable $200 in Newark, Delaware?

This much is obvious: with the sudden silencing of the EZ Pass, we appear to see a deliberate manipulation of evidence, by someone who knows the importance of evidence, and who knows how to manipulate evidence. That will be a common thread in this ride.

In any event, the use of a toll ticket further argues against suicide by Luna. Why would a despondent man about to kill himself first want to pay a cash toll on the Pennsylvania turnpike? If his intent is to kill himself, why not pick a non-toll road?

Most Pennsylvanians will tell you, we'd rather die first, before we pay the toll.

It seems unlikely that Luna met with random violence, perpetrated by a stranger. Too much points to a deliberate, if inexplicable, series of actions leading to some arranged rendezvous in this rest stop's obscure parking lot, or beyond.

That said, Luna at the I-95 rest stop conceivably could have met with an unplanned and violent, Quentin Tarantino-style mishap, on his way to some other, nefarious business. The Kennedy Plaza is not far from the intersection of I-95 and Delaware state route 13. Route 13, law enforcement officials say, happens to be a major heroin trafficking road, carrying skag on its way down to Salisbury, Maryland, on the Delmarva peninsula.

A web page titled Maryland Drug Threat Assessment, published by the National Drug Intelligence Center, states:

> *Maryland-based local independent dealers and Dominican and Colombian criminal groups based in New York City and Philadelphia are the dominant transporters of heroin into Maryland. These independent dealers and criminal groups primarily travel via private or rental vehicles on interstate highways or via public transportation (buses and trains).*
>
> *Couriers primarily transport heroin into and through the state in automobiles and buses traveling on I-95. These couriers sometimes use alternate, less traveled routes to avoid highway interdiction. These couriers travel US 13 to US 50 and then I-97 to Baltimore, or follow US 13 to areas along the Eastern Shore....*
>
> *Baltimore serves as the primary distribution city for heroin*

> *in Maryland. Salisbury, located along major smuggling route US 13, serves as a secondary distribution city for eastern Maryland. Law enforcement officials have identified a link between Latin Kings gang members from New York City and retail distributors of heroin in Salisbury. Salisbury officials have seized bags of heroin bearing stamps that resemble those sold by Latin Kings in New York City....*
>
> *In Salisbury heroin traditionally has been packaged in blue, waxed paper bags, as is heroin sold in Philadelphia, a distribution center for heroin sold in Maryland. Heroin packaged in glass vials also was seized in Salisbury in 2000. The Maryland State Police reported that glass vials of heroin are common in Baltimore, and the emergence of glass vial packaging in Salisbury may indicate a change in the source of Salisbury's heroin supply.*

So, granted, the intersection of Rt. 13 and I-95 isn't exactly the smartest place for a federal drug prosecutor to be standing alone in the middle of the night. Still, we must ask, why was Luna at the rest stop in the first place? Odds are, he was on a prearranged rendezvous, which went bad. Testy and combative, his back to the wall, he fell into an argument. Or, was outright betrayed.

For several months after Luna's death the public could only speculate on the route taken by Luna's car to reach the Pennsylvania turnpike. The most direct route from Delaware (aside from Route 272 North through Lancaster County) would take his car through Philadelphia, either by way of Route 476 or Route 76, which ring the city.

On March 12, 2004, the FBI released a timeline. The scant timeline lists only ten known places and times visited by Luna on his ride. It quizzically shows that Luna's car didn't take either of these direct routes. Instead, at about 2:37 am, Luna's car enters the *New Jersey turnpike* at exit 6A, on the east shore of the Delaware River, entering from Route 130, which runs along the eastern shore of the Delaware.

The time, 2:37 am, offers several clues. It's an hour and forty minutes from the withdrawal at the ATM machine in Delaware. The trip normally may take forty-five minutes. So time is missing. About an hour is unaccounted for. This is probably the hour in which Luna was suppressed. Or, at least, kept busy talking.

There are several remarkable things about the choice of New Jersey Route 130. It certainly appears someone is deliberately trying to skirt Philadelphia. Odd, isn't it? Someone we may suppose did not want to be recognized behind the wheel of Luna's car by a Philadelphia-based policeman or trooper. This again suggests a law enforcement official, perhaps a federal agent, who regularly works with Philly cops, who feared instant recognition, even by night. It also suggests premeditation for the murder to follow.

New Jersey Route 130 itself is an interesting choice. It's a back road that runs parallel to the heavily traveled New Jersey turnpike. It's an industrial road known mostly to homeboys and local cops. Commuters don't take it. Luna, a New Yorker, probably never traveled Rt. 130 before in his life. Does someone here know these roads?

Several toll bridges cross the Delaware River from I-95 to Rt. 130 in New Jersey. The most obscure of these is the Rt. 322 Commodore Barry Bridge to Bridgeport, NJ, just a few miles south of the Philadelphia airport. To the north, in Philadelphia, stretches the Walt Whitman Bridge. When lilacs last in his dooryard bloom'd, did Luna ride Walt's bridge to that Jersey highway in the sky? The Whitman bridge, near downtown Philly, though poetic, even Springsteenesque, is an unlikely choice if you're trying to act inconspicuous while driving around with a stabbed federal prosecutor. But we're talking Philly here, so who knows.

To the south, the New Jersey turnpike connects to the Delaware Memorial toll bridge outside Wilmington at I-295. That's a possibility, but why later get off the Jersey turnpike and get back on at Rt. 130 in Trenton?

The Rt. 322 Commodore Barry Bridge from Chester, PA, into Bridgeport, NJ, however, offers several conveniences. It's just a few miles away from the Philadelphia airport. Several federal law enforcement agencies, including the Drug Enforcement Agency, keep facilities near the Philadelphia airport, I'm told. The airport is surrounded by abandoned, no-man's-land stretches of warehouses and roads which are particularly desolate at night. What would Luna be doing here? Again, the best explanation is meeting a federal agent and/or informant. Sometimes they're the same thing, aren't they?

From here it's a short hop across the Delaware River into New Jersey. An entrance ramp to Rt. 130, incidentally, lies just on the Jersey side of the Commodore Barry Bridge.

Despite the mystery of how he gets into New Jersey, at approximately 2:37 am, Luna's car leaves Rt. 130 and enters the New Jersey turnpike, heading west, *now returning* to the Delaware River into Pennsylvania.

Why take a ticket on the Jersey turnpike? Aside from skirting Philadelphia, or further confusing jurisdictions, the possibly exists that someone is sending a message, leaving a calling card, or intentionally attempting to deflect attention to other parties.

One of America's most-watched television shows conspicuously begins each episode with a character taking a ticket on the New Jersey turnpike.

In any event, just south of Trenton, New Jersey, Luna's car heads west toward the Delaware River, into Pennsylvania.

After a moderately paced, ten-minute drive, Luna's Accord reaches the Delaware River, just south of Trenton, and enters the Pennsylvania turnpike at 2:47 am.

Here it's dark, flat, lonely, and the air smells of the broad river. Jonathan Luna has less than ninety minutes to live.

3
The sun falling around a helpless thing

In the dark of Valley Forge, at 3:20 am, someone uses Jonathan Luna's debit card to buy gas at the Peter J. Camiel rest stop past King of Prussia, on the Pennsylvania turnpike. The security cameras here are grainy, the public's informed. These cameras, like the security cameras at the I-95 rest stop, again curiously fail to capture events.

Several incongruities surround the use of the debit card. If Luna, and/or another party, is attempting to leave no traces of their travels by leaving cell phones behind, and not using a traceable EZ Pass, why then use a debit card? (For that matter, as I point out, if Luna was deliberately trying not to be traced, he would not have earlier withdrawn $200 from the Delaware ATM machine.)

Luna seems to have had cash to buy gas. *Someone* withdrew $200 from the ATM, and small sums of cash later were found in his car. It seems again, as with the circuitous route taken by Luna's car, someone is acting as if irrationally. Or, again, someone is deliberately manipulating, or "randomizing," the crime profile.

Days afterward, employees at the King of Prussia rest stop tell the newspapers a man resembling Luna came into the store and bought two drinks, but the description seems off, and this encounter seems unlikely.

Other sightings seem even more ludicrous. A waitress working in a restaurant somewhere off the PA turnpike told the papers Luna came into her restaurant early that morning, looking all the world like TV host Bryant Gumbel. We're left to suppose, in his last minutes, Luna ordered pancakes and joe. Funny thing is, every disappearance I've ever followed invariably produces a sighting at a pancake house. It's as if, before we Americans walk off the face of the earth, we're expected to grab flapjacks at IHOP. Like NASA's astronauts get steak and eggs before blast off.

In reality, at King of Prussia, Luna may already have been beaten and stabbed, and lay bleeding in his car.

The timeline states Luna's car left the turnpike at Exit 286, at about 4:04 am.

Exit 286 is a rather desolate area of creation. Rolling dark hills. The mysterious heart of Pennsylvania Dutch country. Here the turnpike meets Rt. 222, heading south out of Reading into Lancaster. It's a Pennsylvania netherland, a nexus of mysteries, where the commercial Pennsylvania Dutch of Lancaster County, and the industrious Amish, meet the rough Dutchies of Reading, still speaking Pennsylvania cracker Dutch.

It's about a forty-five minute drive to the Rt. 222 exit from the King of Prussia turnpike plaza. That's driving at a moderate speed, without calling attention to oneself. Forty-four minutes have passed from the time Luna's card is used to buy the gas at King of Prussia, to his car's exit from the turnpike at 4:04 am.

The ticket given the tollbooth collector was later found to carry a small spot of Luna's blood.

Again, splitting differences, turnpike Exit 286 is a spot both halfway between Philadelphia and Harrisburg, as well as between Reading and Lancaster.

Jon Luna's car was abandoned about two miles from the turnpike exit, on state Rt. 897. It's a desolate place, and any killer would have needed a ride out.

Route 222 South, locals know, also provides a direct route south through Lancaster County, back to I-95, to Philadelphia or Baltimore. Rt. 222 S. also carries you to Rt. 30, by way of neighboring York County, then onto I-83 South, to Baltimore.

The end of the midnight ride of Jonathan Luna is as perplexing and disturbing as the beginning and the middle. About five-thirty in the morning — about an hour and twenty minutes after he passed through the nearby turnpike exit — Jonathan is found face down in a stream under the front of his idling car.

He's fully dressed, still wearing his courtroom business suit, shirt and tie, overcoat and court shoes. His magnetic courthouse identification badge hangs from a necklace.

Someone had turned the car off Dry Tavern Road and guided the car up the driveway belonging to the Sensenig and Weaver Well Drilling company. The company operates from a low-slung, warehouse-type building just off the road. A parking lot filled with industrial equipment stretches some distance behind the building.

Ron Weaver, one of the owners of the company, tells me a streetlight had burned out on the back corner of the building, and so the back parking lot, normally lit, was dark. It was a cold morning and the driveway, parking lot and lawn were covered with a thick frost. Tire prints in the frost revealed that Luna's car first was parked behind the building, in the dark. "They were behind the building, doing something," Ron Weaver tells me. The car, and Luna's body, however, would not be found behind the building. The car would be found in the *side yard,* several hundred feet away, its front tires hung up on an embankment alongside a gorged creek.

The sun, meanwhile, had yet to come up. An employee was just arriving to start the day at the well drilling firm. Down the road, in a scattering of houses, neighbors began farm chores and readied themselves for the day.

An employee at the well drilling firm, Daniel Gehman, arrived at work about 5 am. He drove up the dark driveway and at first had noticed nothing unusual or out of place. Perhaps Luna's car was already perched at the creekside, at an angle unlit by Gehman's headlights as he came up the drive. Or, perhaps, Luna and his assailants were at this time still in the back parking lot, and were surprised by the early arrival of Gehman. Perhaps Luna, at this point, mortally wounded, was left for dead in his Accord.

Tire tracks through the thick frost tell a strange story. Tracks through the frost show that Luna's Accord left the rear of the building and headed down the driveway toward the road. The Accord made a sharp left turn, leaving the driveway, and heading into the grass. It seems likely that Luna, left for dead, had managed to get behind the the wheel of his car and tried to get away, disoriented by loss of blood and terrorized. His car suddenly left the driveway, drove a hundred or so feet across the lawn, before getting hung up on the embankment beside the creek. Joey Luna, the marathon runner, was trying to get away. Perhaps he was hoping to hide from his assailants by running into the dark trees on the other side of the creek. Luna apparently stumbled from his car, as blood was found smeared on the driver's side door and front fender. Splashing into the icy creek, unable to make it across, he instead pulled himself under the front of his car, trying to hide. Curled into a fetal position, hiding under his front bumper, he fell unconscious and drowned, face down in the water.

Inside the well drilling firm Gehman made coffee. At about 5:30 am, Gehman went outside, into the back parking lot, to prepare equipment for the day ahead. It was then that Gehman spotted an odd red light glowing in the darkness by the creek. He pointed a drilling truck's headlights on the Accord. The car tottered on the edge of the narrow creek bed. Walking toward the car, Gehman noticed some blood smeared around its exterior. The red light glowed from the dashboard. He saw a baby seat in the back of the car, though he noticed no body. It looked like some kind of traffic accident. He called 911.

Two state troopers arrived at about 5:45 am. The police too at first mistook it for some kind of traffic accident. Then they found the body face down in the creek, below the front of the car. Police summoned Lancaster County Coroner Dr. Barry Walp. The coroner arrived at around 8 am. Dr. Walp noticed a knife wound in Luna's neck, putting to rest the traffic accident theory.

Trooper Douglas Burig, of the Lancaster State Police barracks, wrote out an affidavit to search the car. The violation causing the search, Trooper Burig wrote, was "Criminal Homicide." At about "0539 Hours," Trooper Burig notes, "Daniel Gehman - an adult male, contacted the Pennsylvania State Police Ephrata barracks via telephone.... Gehman related he observed a silver colored vehicle on the company property which was partially in a creek. Gehman related there did not appear to be anyone around the vehicle."

At approximately 5:45 am, Trooper Burig writes, "Patrol Unit Troopers James Fassnacht and Keith Noll from the Pennsylvania State Police- Ephrata Barracks arrived at Sensenig and Weaver Well Drilling. Trooper Fassnacht observed a silver colored Honda Accord with its front wheels and engine compartment over the edge of a creek embankment on the Northern side of the company property. Trooper Fassnacht related the vehicle was bearing Maryland registration plate UNC 0011. Trooper Fassnacht observed what appeared to be blood smeared on the drivers' (sic) side door and left front fender of the vehicle. Trooper Fassnacht also observed numerous bills of United States currency scattered throughout the interior of the vehicle and cell phone equipment. Trooper Fassnacht observed the vehicle was running and had no apparent exterior or interior damage consistent with a vehicle collision.

"Trooper Fassnacht examined the rest of the scene," Burig continues. "Trooper Fassnacht observed the body of a deceased adult African American male lying face down in the creek in close proximity to the front wheels and undercarriage of the Honda Accord. The male was attired in a business suit." The car was registered to Luna care of the federal courthouse in Baltimore, Burig notes.

"At 0805 hours," Burig continues, "Lancaster County Coroner Dr. Barry Walp declared the victim deceased at the scene."

Three hours later, "At approximately 1100 hours," Burig writes, "Lancaster County Forensic Patholgist (sic) Dr. Wayne Ross examined the victim at the scene and observed a traumatic wound to the right side of the victim's head."

The affidavit notes a large pool of blood on the right rear floor of the car, and blood smeared on the driver's side door and left front fender. Cell phone equipment was strewn around the inside of the car. Burig notes, "numerous bills of United States currency (were) scattered throughout the interior of the vehicle." Walp later would say about $30 had been thrown around the car. Luna's wallet was missing, we're told. As well, traces of a second blood type supposedly were found.

Police helped identify that body by removing the University of North Carolina law school ring, decorated with its scales of justice, from Jonathan's finger. His name was engraved on the ring.

Coroner Walp expressed shock over the depravity of the crime. He initially told the press that Luna, "was alive when they put him in the creek. Several deep cuts caused internal hemorrhaging, and the water in his lungs caused the drowning."

The luridness of the discovery, and the inital confusion at the crime scene, seem to have initially caused the coroner to say that "they put him in the creek." Rather than having been carried from the car, it seems more likely that Luna may have been left for dead in the Accord. Still alive, a strong and fit young man, a marathon runner, it seems plausible that Luna tried to drive away; he was disoriented and in shock; the car left the driveway, got hung up on the creekside, where he staggered from the car trying to get away from his assailant or assailants, only to collapse into the creek, where he drowned face down.

Others suggested that someone tried to run over Luna with his car. The press luridly reported that the car had been left in neutral and perhaps pushed several feet toward the creek in an effort to crush Luna. (The police told the owners of the well drilling company that the car was in neutral, and its handbrake set.)

Perhaps because the incident was first viewed as an accident, forensics seem to have been somewhat carelessly conducted, to say the least. Police and other investigators left footprints in the frosty grass leading to the car. No effort was apparently made early on to isolate any footprints which may have been left behind on the frozen ground, either behind the building or at the creekside. Even so, Ron Weaver tells me that the Accord's tire marks clearly could be seen running from behind the well drilling company, veering left from the driveway, across the grass to the edge of the stream.

One news story, incidentally, reported that a woman who lived near the well drilling building told the state police she'd seen headlights of a car parked behind the building about 10:30 pm Wednesday night.

On the back of Luna's car, peering out from the landing in the stream, is a remnant of a past vacation and stroll in the sun — an oval OBX sticker from the Outer Banks of North Carolina.

It's where the Wright Brothers first slipped the surly bonds of earth and took flight, to touch the face of God.

4

'You would think they were perhaps after information from the guy when you see something like this'

By early afternoon Luna's body was officially identified, and U.S. Attorney Tom DiBiagio was notified in Baltimore that one of his prosecutors had been found murdered at a creekside in Pennsylvania.

In Lancaster County, pathologist Dr. Wayne Ross and county coroner Dr. Barry Walp examined Jonathan's body. They found wounds consistent with a sudden and furious attack on the assistant U.S. attorney.

A worker who closely examined Jonathan's body described the wounds to me as follows:

Both of Jonathan's *hands were badly lacerated and "shredded,"* obviously in defense against a sudden flurry of vicious knife slashes. There were deep slashes between each of his fingers, with more cuts to the front and back of both hands. These deep and long slashes peeled away the skin between the fingers, cutting, in places, to the bone. "They were like slicing razor wounds" to his hands.

The wounds to his hands, "were clearly defensive wounds," revealing that Jonathan had been fighting for his life.

Jonathan had been *stabbed in the back* several times. These wounds fell in the *middle of his back,* and near the shoulder blades. Nearly impossible to inflict on oneself.

Jonathan's *neck was slit open* on the right side, and all the way around the throat. The slit to his throat cut deep, several inches in places.

Most disturbing of all: Jonathan's *scrotum had been slashed open.* His genitals were strangely and viciously mutilated.

Luna clearly was the victim of a violent, explosive attack. It was a crime of rare intensity and savagery.

From the looks of things, a first-rate sicko had tortured Jonathan.

Who does things like this? It sure looks like a gangland murder.

Not surprisingly, Coroner Walp ruled the death a homicide. At the time, this ruling surprised no one. In the months ahead, the homicide ruling would for some reason grow into a major problem for the FBI's Baltimore field office.

Luna's body was found to have been pierced thirty-six times by knife, Dr. Walp told the press. No one seemed to have noticed that Luna had been stabbed or slashed once for every thousand dollars missing from the evidence lock-up.

The deadly, *coup de grâce* slash to the throat was deeply placed (and seemingly expertly and coolly delivered). The slash to the throat appeared in places to be about four inches deep, Walp said. Walp noted hemorrhaging on both sides of the neck.

Dr. Walp would say that many of the stab wounds were no more than shallow pricks to the skin, as if a knife was held to Jonathan Luna to inflict pain, or to make him talk.

Walp shared his first impression with the press: "You would think they were perhaps after information from the guy when you see something like this." Or, he thought aloud, "perhaps for kicks."

In keeping with Pennsylvania law, the autopsy report was not made public.

With the autopsy report sealed, wild rumors began to fly, in and out of the press. Already, with the discovery of Jonathan's body, a media storm gathered. The revelation of unspecified savagery would quickly set off a sensation in the media.

Some initial news reports stated that Luna had been shot and stabbed. (No shots were fired; considering the wounds, this murder for some reason was a strangely quiet death.) Soon it was reported worldwide that Luna had been tortured (that's obviously correct), and that his genitals had been mutilated and pummeled. This too was essentially correct, though rumors spread by U.S. marshals in the Baltimore federal courthouse had it that Luna's genitals had been completely severed.

5
Oops, they lynched me again

What followed, initially, was a high-speed get-to-know-you of a young man taken in his prime. A life force cut off before its time now imprinted itself on the mass psyche. Intense press coverage gripped the East Coast. On the web you could read stories posted by all the newspapers. The TV and radio stations, and their web sites, gravitated toward a boogie-man-got-'em kind of story. Black man gets his on mystery road trip. Lots of attention was paid to the rap music aspect of the story.

Luna's personality seems to leap out. Stories of his generosity. Giving away a baseball he caught at a Yankees game. His diverse taste in music, from jazz to classical. His love of entertaining, of making big meals, of making his guests feel comfortable. The photo of Jonathan his father kept on his refrigerator, showing a grinning Joey standing beside George W. Bush in 2000, when Bush was running for president. Endless snapshots.

How Jonathan bounded into his first job interview after law school, before U.S. District Judge William L. Osteen, pluckily telling the Southern judge he was a Yankees and Knicks fan. Coming to his job interview in the Baltimore U.S. attorney's office wearing a bow tie.

Luna's life takes on wide appeal because his reach so far exceeded his grasp. On the surface, his everyday family life seems to ring familiar with many young professionals. Two advanced degrees under one roof. Parties attended by interesting, diverse people. The balancing of time and debt. Those things you always mean to do. Those things you mean to stop doing. Things we never get to say. The precariousness of our lives, the awful hole that's left when there but for the grace of God go I.

These too were some of the snapshots that may also have played through Jonathan's mind on his ride. Thinking about Angela's pretty eyes, their kids' pretty eyes.

Vivid too were the pictures of how badly all these people were crushed by his loss. There would be true Tom Sawyer moments. Presiding Judge Quarles, no longer peeved at his tardy prosecutor, unable to hold back tears when he gets the news, saying Jonathan was a wonderful young man.

Jon's friend and fellow assistant U.S. attorney Andrew Norman reflected, "Everyone I know liked him. Jonathan did not have a mean bone in his body."

Beneath the surface, unknown to the public, and even many of friends, was the story of how Jonathan struggled for years, on his own, to get out of the projects in the South Bronx, to put himself through law school, while caring for his parents.

Even so, someone in some quarter wanted him not just out of his life, they wanted him dead.

It certainly is not hard to find people with good things to say about Jonathan Luna. The people who knew him in their everyday lives gush about him, and mourn him. What's more difficult to find are people who *publicly* say bad things about him, and use their name for attribution.

Others weren't content with a rosy and tragic, first-blush picture of Luna. Others clearly did not like him. This secret quarter, motivated by diverse interests, quickly set about in strange fashion to destroy Luna's reputation.

The second amazing lynching of Jonathan Luna occurs a day or two after his death. It's an unprecedented, electronic lynching, every bit as appalling and ghastly as the first. The electronic lynching of Jonathan Luna also plays out in the mass media. Those behind the trashing of Luna's reputation had a simple message: Luna, they'd have us believe, was living some sort of secret life.

This anonymous character assassination bears consideration. Who's behind it, and what are the motives?

A day or two after Luna's death, events take a surprising turn. Now, Luna not even buried, someone is talking up the missing thirty-six grand. Who's talking up the missing $36,000? None other than Baltimore Sun reporter Gail Gibson, the same reporter who first wrote about the missing money only a week after it went missing in 2002, based on leaks from her FBI sources. This time the same sources are spoon-feeding Gibson their character asssassinations of murdered Luna. And this time Gibson's FBI sources are even quicker to smear Luna.

Only a day after Luna is found dead, on December 5, the Baltimore Sun runs a story, written by Gibson, reporting, "Authorities also were combing through Luna's work files to determine whether the motive behind his killing could be found in any of the cases he was prosecuting.... Late last year, Luna won convictions in a string of violent Baltimore County bank robberies in a curious trial that produced its own mystery: at the end of the trial, authorities discovered that more than $36,000 in cash disappeared somewhere between the courtroom and the government storage area used to hold evidence during trials. That case was never solved."

The clear implication was that Luna was a suspect in the theft of the money. No one else, for some reason, is held accountable, including Gibson's sources. When, in fact, the Baltimore FBI office shares equal blame and suspicion, and obviously leaked these stories.

Who most likely took the money? One day I discussed the mystery with a prominent federal court attorney, while he prepared court papers. "An FBI agent took it," he said, not looking up from his paperwork, without skipping a beat.

No attorney with his name on a court stipulation would be foolish enough take evidence, I'm told again and again. The growing consensus seems to be, on the other hand, that your friendly neighborhood local FBI bureau often shelters a bad actor.

That's when I began hearing the phrase "bad actor." A bad agent. I'd begin to hear the phrase often. If insiders suspect an FBI agent took the $36,000, you'd never hear about it reading the newspapers. Instead, FBI agents are given free reign to trash Luna, and blame him for the mysterious theft.

The next deep cut is delivered by Time magazine, a scant two days after Luna's death. Time even tells us who's behind the story: unnamed FBI sources.

"FBI examination of internet postings found messages on adult sites placed by 'Jonathan Luna' seeking female sex partners," Time's web site declares. "Investigators found he had debt problems, including credit cards his wife did not know about."

The two-paragraph article carries a dateline, "Sunday, Dec. 07, 2003," and begins, "New York – An FBI examination of Internet postings turned up messages on adult sites placed by a Jonathan Luna seeking female sex partners... Someone else may have posted them (a much younger person also called Jonathan Luna is a convicted sex offender.) But Time located two personals that are dated 1997, conform to the prosecutor's age and marital status, and are signed with his three initials backward." We're invited to buy a copy of the magazine, we're told, "on newsstands Monday, Dec. 8, 2003."

We're not even left guessing who's behind this story. We're told: an FBI agent. Agents, who either do not like Luna, or who have their own agenda, or both, are out to get him, even after he's dead.

In true Roman Praetorian fashion, the body's on the floor, and now they've each got to get in their knives.

When you study it, this well-timed hit on Luna's reputation is as professional a job as the betrayal that takes his life.

The next day the FBI-circulated sex story takes on a life of its own. Meat is added to the bones. The Baltimore Sun, on Tuesday, December 9, headlines a story, "Slain prosecutor's relationships with women examined: Investigation focusing on personal life of Luna; possible financial, work troubles."

This story hints at the fact that Luna's genitals had been mutilated. (Genital mutilation, by the way, is very unusual. The practice, culturally and historically, is prevalent in only a few areas of the globe: Africa and the Middle East. It's a form of *emasculation,* intended to deprive a man of his male role or identity.)

"Among Luna's wounds were injuries to his genital area, law enforcement sources have said," the Sun's story reports. This is a pivotal moment. From here on out, Luna's death would, for some odd reason, be treated as a personal matter, not worthy of a true, work-related investigation.

"Investigators believe that Luna's death was the result of a personal relationship that turned violent, not a random crime or in retaliation for his work — reducing the likelihood that his death would be prosecuted as a federal crime," Gibson writes.

For this story the Sun mentions as it source, a "law enforcement official, who spoke on the condition of anonymity." This source, we're led to believe, has insider's knowledge of the federal investigation. Read, FBI agent.

We're told by the Sun, "Over the weekend, federal agents asked Luna's family about other trips he might have taken in recent months to the area where his body was found.

"They also were examining messages posted by someone using the name Jonathan Luna on internet dating sites. The author of the messages, from April 1997, described himself as a discreet, 31-year-old married black man seeking a white female sexual partner and indicated a preference for blondes and redheads."

There's more than a whiff of racism here. It's the old racial slur that a black man with money can't control his impulses when it comes to white women. It's overt racism, the type Luna tries to diplomatically hint about in his Legal Times interview.

As we'll see, nothing approaching this is done to State Police Superintendent Ed Norris and his "romantic-hearted" buddies of the greater-Maryland precincts who, we may suppose, were shopping at Victoria's Secret to donate to the Loyola Sisters of Charity.

On the face of it, this internet date posting under Luna's name is spurious, to say the least. At the time of the posting, Luna would have been working as an assistant prosecutor in the Brooklyn DA's office. It's ridiculous on the face of it. No married man (let alone an attorney, and a prosecutor) in his right mind is going to post an ad like this on the internet, using his own name. Particularly when such postings can be done anonymously.

Time Magazine graciously offers one explanation even as they destroy Luna's reputation: another Jonathan Luna, "a convicted sex offender," may be the poster. There's a third possibility, just as likely, curiously left unmentioned by the all-seeing FBI sources, and their surrogates in the press.

These ads may also have been posted in Luna's name, by someone who did not like him. Someone who perhaps saw, and despised the fact, that women around the office (a blond, a red head?) liked Jonathan. Who could that be? Again, sounds like a lesser-educated, jealous white cop, or FBI agent.

How, incidentally, had the FBI known to go so quickly to these "dating" sites, which aren't all that easy to find. (You simply can't Google them.) And what's the FBI doing trolling the date sites? We've yet to see a story that the G-men have conducted a search of the letters Jonathan wrote on behalf of the impoverished.

I'd bet this vicious story of the sex ad was circulating in some circles for some time, and was the subject of smirks and derision. Had someone been laying an ambush for Luna? Behind his back, perhaps behind a friendly smile, a badge and a gun, lurked someone who hated him.

And Luna probably worked with him.

In the same December 9, 2003, Baltimore Sun article, we're told the "law enforcement official, who spoke on the condition of anonymity, said federal agents also were reviewing adult pornographic files found on Luna's Justice Department computer that appeared unrelated to his caseload, which had included the prosecution of online child pornography and predators."

Don't you love how they word this? They're "reviewing" his "adult pornographic files." Rest assured tonight when you're home cuddled in your fuzzy slippers and nightshirt, sipping your warm milk: J. Edgar's boys and girls have this bird well in hand, and are giving these "adult pornographic files" a good review. By now they've no doubt got them classified into specimen varieties, phylum, sub-phylum, with Latin names, such as *dirkdigglerium.*

It goes without saying that Luna, who prosecuted cases involving kiddie porn and child molesters, is more entitled than most to such files.

"I shall not today attempt to define the kinds of material I understand to be embraced," Justice Potter Stewart famously fumbled in

1964 when trying to define pornography in the landmark *Jacobellis v. Ohio.* "But I know it when I see it." At some point in his personal or professional life, Stewart is telling us, he has viewed pornography, as have most of us, and he seems to expect to view it again. No one called him on the carpet for it, or suggested he's perverted.

To view pornography, or to work with it as part of one's job, Justice Stewart knew, is not to love it or subscribe to it. Stewart would probably be the first to defend Luna's right to these files, as would most sensible newspaper editors, if they thought about it.

To deride Luna for this smacks of another racial slur. Another black man who can't control his passion, these agents are insinuating.

6
Another gentleman's correspondence

Pricklier is the issue of privacy, particularly the privacy of a man who disappears from his office in the middle of the night and who now cannot defend himself.

"A gentlemen does not open another gentleman's mail," was the stern admonition tendered by an American intelligence official who balked at intercepting mail sent between German spies in World War I. How far we've come. These days it would appear there are no gentlemen, and the feds insist they're free to open whatever's not encrypted.

Next came reports that the feds had trouble breaking into all corners of Luna's computer. He'd supposedly *encrypted* parts of his hard drive, the public was told. The news was floated to suggest Luna had something to hide. In fact, many government employees routinely encrypt their computers, often at the directive of their departments. The oddest thing about this is that we're expected to believe the feds can't crack into their own computers. Bet on it, they can. More to the point, whose eyes worried Luna?

The Justice Department certainly has an obligation, as an employer, even as a conflict-ridden investigator of an employee's heinous death, to worry about the contents of Luna's hard drive. Even so, they have no right to leak private information to the press.

Soon the feds would leak that Luna had confessed in e-mail messages to friends that he sometimes felt overwhelmed with debt from his student loans. (Welcome to modern American life; even so, let's remember, Jonathan put *himself* through law school — daddy didn't help.) Even that there were problems in his marriage. (Marriage is another way of spelling problems.) These clearly are shameful breaches of personal confidences.

Jonathan Luna is hanging in there, doing his best. He always wore a smile, his father tells us.

These leaks only backfire and show Luna all the more real and sympathetic a figure. We wonder about the character, integrity, and motives of the people behind the leaks. I don't know, but I suspect, the last thing the wife or husband of a slain FBI agent wants to read in the papers a few days after a loved one is killed in the line of duty is that sometimes the marriage was rocky. Sounds like marriage to me.

These singsong, everyday complaints reveal the *real* secret side of Jonathan Luna, the long-distance runner breathing a sigh before returning the outward mask of confident ambition. (Attorney Ravenell says he was like a mentor to Luna, that often the younger man would call and they would talk about the ropes, or whatever came to mind.)

That Luna may have felt compelled to encrypt his data while working for the Justice Department itself speaks volumes. He obviously suspected he must protect himself from prying eyes. Perhaps he was concerned that someone might alter his hard drive, even log into the internet on his computer.

Whose eyes, whose *hands,* worried him? Who had after-hours access to his office?

Something certain: Luna didn't trust someone.

7
'Not great writers'

In his 1835 book *Democracy in America,* Alexis de Tocqueville writes of American newspapermen, "They certainly are not great writers, but they speak their country's language and they make themselves heard."

For the most part this observation remains true to this day. De Tocqueville, writing in the French, didn't have to worry about his book being reviewed in American newspapers.

De Tocqueville passed through Pennsylvania some fifty years before newspaper denizens Twain and Whitman penned *Huck Finn* and *Leaves of Grass,* ninety years before Hemingway drank his way through de Tocqueville's country, and almost one hundred years before Ring Lardner would leave behind his Chicago Tribune job, check into a hotel, pull down the blinds so no one could see him and write about his gangster acquaintances in the City of Broad Shoulders.

A day after the FBI spoon-fed the Baltimore Sun the story about Jonathan Luna's "relationships with women," the white evidence-room gloves come off and they curiously go after a dead Jonathan hammer and tong about the missing $36,000. The Sun runs a story headlined, "Missing money noted in probe; Cash evidence in '02 case Luna handled vanished."

This December 10 article, written by Gail Gibson and Lynn Anderson, and again attributed to unnamed "law enforcement sources," reports that "investigators... are taking a second look at another mystery: the disappearance of about $36,000 in cash introduced as evidence in a bank robbery trial the lawyer prosecuted last year."

We're told, "FBI agents are reviewing the unsolved case of the missing money as they search for clues...."

In this article, anonymously, FBI agents all but accuse Luna of taking the money. There's a slight and curious disclaimer. "The sources cautioned that nothing links Luna, 38, to the missing cash, or the money to his slaying. But the case stands out among Luna's files, all of which were being closely examined as authorities continued the search for suspects in Thursday's killing." Reading this paragraph the headline could as easily have read, "No links between Luna and missing cash," or even, "Compromised agents pass missing bucks to silenced prosecutor."

The FBI has a conflict on this, and apparently wants to spin the controversy away from its embattled agents. This only raises questions.

The Sun's not being even-handed. Starving for news, the paper allows itself to be used. They don't bother pointing out that the FBI agents and their supervisors have an obvious conflict when it comes to the missing $36,000. One of their own agents may be, and, odds suggests *is,* the culprit. The FBI doesn't want people thinking about that. Certainly the FBI's Baltimore bureau shares blame for sloppy evidence handling, and record keeping. They don't want the Sun's readers thinking about the implications of that, either. Nor lack of oversight, and so on.

They are for some dark reason using Jonathan Luna's death to draw attention away from themselves. In criminology, this is called "deflection." Someone is deflecting attention away from aspects of a criminal case. In this case, it's the FBI that's acting in this suspicious manner.

The missing $36,000 involves a thrice-rehashed, bitter, interdepartmental squabble — between the lawyers and the agents — and now the other team's curiously used it to pollute the Luna investigation. Some agents want the dead stereotype to hold the bag. What does that suggest about the quality of the investigation into Luna's death?

Someone in the Baltimore FBI office starts to look guilty of more than mismanagement. It starts to look unprofessional, unbalanced, even underhanded.

The agents, more than most, should know. Creating a whispering campaign against a defenseless Jonathan Luna to take the blame for the missing thirty-six G's is, after all, not merely highly curious. It makes Luna a fall guy.

It begs the question: was Luna murdered by someone who's happy to see him take the blame for the missing money? That's a motive for murder.

The FBI agents, for the most part, want the detective's glass pointed in one direction. Away from them. As far away from the Baltimore field office as possible, thank you. This continues to hold true.

Too bad for them. Their continued curious bumbling and misconduct invites attention.

It's a distorted, hateful and hurtful picture of Luna they paint, a picture drafted by pros who know how to make society look away, an ugly picture of a fast-and-loose-living hypocrite whose secret life got him iced.

By the time they're done painting their picture of Luna, they'd have us believe someone did society a favor.

As it unfolds in the mass media, it's an ugly picture that shocks and angers his friends and family. And increasingly doesn't ring true.

Dorian Gray grew young as his picture aged. As Luna's portrait worsens, the FBI agents vainly imagine they look better.

Yet they'd been working alongside the guy for years.

The next deep cut is delivered by way of the New York Post, on December 14, in an article titled, "'Double Life' Eyed in Feds Murder." It's written in the breathless Fleet Street, Australian-nightmare-style of a Rupert Murdoch rag.

Reporter Niles Lathem suggests that though Luna's life appeared "picture-perfect ...there were hints that his world was spiraling down in despair.

"There was the beautiful family, his Tiger Woods smile. But there was also the mounting debt and his 'party guy' reputation."

Champaign wishes and caviar dreams are about to hit the shit fan.

Lathem reports, citing unnamed "investigators," that, "it appears that Luna was living at least two lives well before he moved to the Baltimore area four years ago." Though, he writes, "A spokesman for the Brooklyn DA's office called him a 'dedicated and capable attorney,' legal sources in Brooklyn remember Luna as a 'party guy' who kept late hours at bars on Court Street." But is it true?

"No, it's not true," Luna's longtime friend Dan Rivera tells me. "Joey might drink a beer or two, but he certainly wasn't a big drinker." Rivera points out that Luna was a disciplined marathon runner and a devoted family man, not "a party guy."

Even if true, it's again a double standard. Merciful God protect us should any reporter or cop keep late hours in a bar! The New York Post's own Pete Hamill wrote a good book, *A Drinking Life,* about navigating through years of newspaper work while Hamill was three sheets to the wind.

Once again, note we see a difference of opinion between the lawyers and the cops in their estimation of Jonathan Luna. There's a class, as well as a racial element at play. Lathem continues, "These sources said he associated with a group of rogue assistant district attorneys who later were investigated in a scandal that involved throwing cases for bribes. One assistant DA was fired and the rest were cleared as result of the probe."

Here Lathem bothers to tell us, almost as an aside, "Luna was not involved in the case, and *cops* say there is no evidence these links were in any way involved in his murder." (Emphasis mine.) So cops are feeding Lathem this story. For some reason, some cops and agents did not like Jonathan Luna.

The Post next hits an easy infield fly by mentioning the missing thirty-six Gs, and from there tries to slide on a stolen base by implying Luna threw the Smith-Poindexter case.

"Recently, during a case involving two aspiring rappers accused of running a violent drug ring, Luna appeared distracted and stressed out," Lathem writes.

"Luna was later forced to enter a plea agreement favorable to the defendants when it was revealed his star witness had escaped monitoring while under house arrest and was caught with cocaine. (The Post gets this wrong too; it was *heroin.)*

"Luna had failed to mention that in pretrial sessions. The judge gave the defense extra time to prepare for cross-examination. But Luna chose to enter a plea."

Lathem suggests that Luna "threw" the case to protect Smith and Poindexter when, a reading of the record shows, instead, the case was shut down to protect the FBI and Luna's superiors in the Justice Department.

Lathem notes, "The increasingly lurid twists to the Luna murder case have painted a picture of a man his own family did not know."

Well, yeah.

Yes, we're told, he's a man with a secret life. God help Joey Luna's soul. What crimes earn such fate? Not enough that he suffers so unjust and mysterious a death. Now he's manufactured into some sort of fast-living phony, a man whose helpless boss knew too little, a hip-hop Cary Grant in *North by Northwest,* recast as *South by Southeast,* the marathon man who can't run fast enough. What about the Jonathan Luna who *avoided* the hip-hop and drug culture of the South Bronx, who moved his parents into a good neighborhood, who lived with his mother-in-law, and who obviously struggled to make ends meet? These are acts of a good man, a decent guy.

Those closest to Luna somehow had to endure this posthumous drubbing. His family insists it must've been the job that got him killed.

Our society grows more complex, our mass media dumbs down. A Rupert Murdoch publication accuses Luna of sexual impropriety, but no one points out that Murdoch made his fortune by every day publishing photos of topless women (called "Page 3 girls") on the first inside page of his newspapers, and otherwise catering gutter trash.

Fortunately, opinions no longer are shaped solely by a compromised and lazy, corporate mass media. On the day of Luna's murder, on December 4, an old friend posted this touching note on a web log:

> *An assistant US district attorney Jonathan Luna was found murdered today. I lived in the same suite as him our first year at Carolina in Craige Hall, the graduate student dorm. He was a nice guy, very outgoing and charming. He was tall, thin, athletic. A good looking guy who was good with the ladies.*

After our first semester in Craige he wanted to move out and get an apartment. He asked me if I wanted to room with him, but I decided to stay in the dorm another semester. Who knows why, since Craige sucked.

After he moved out, I ran into him a few times. His father was dying during his second year, I think, so he took a semester off. I helped him with some computer / word processing type things later on. After he graduated I never heard from him again. I googled him once and saw that he had clerked with a Federal judge and become a district attorney.

So long Jonathan.

(For months you could view this interesting blog yourself at: http://www.chen.net/~dave/blog/archives/000231.html; the blog has since been taken down —ed.)

There's a silence on this blog as events unfold. Then, in late December, posters begin asking readers not to rush to judgment of Luna. One post in particular caught my eye. Posted by someone calling himself Get Real, on January 12, 2004, it reads:

People are in jail due to the Justice Dept's nappy-headed poster boy's holier-than-thou hypocrisy. Can't say he got what he deserved - no one deserves being murdered like that... but spare us the deifications of the guy! He was a porn downloading, adulterous S.O.B., and he got burned leading his dangerous double life!

An almost an identical posting, curiously, was made on another web page.

Now we're getting somewhere. The "Justice Dept's nappy-headed poster boy." With this we begin to get some hint of what Jonathan Luna was up against from some quarters every day of his professional life.

Simply put, there are people out there who did not like Jonathan Luna because of the color of his skin. That's too mild. They hated him. They hated the success he worked hard to attain, and they hated the idea that his future might be brighter than theirs.

Why don't we get real? To me this sounds like a bad actor — a bad FBI agent — talking. They've got the dope on the phony, and they want to let the world know.

Trouble is, people who know Luna best aren't buying it.

The next poster, Becca, on January 14 replies,

> *Wow! 'Get Real' Now (you're) the one acting like an S.O.B. ....Some hard-hearted, cold blooded people have no remorse. There could be more to Jonathan Luna's death than what the FBI is telling us, (and) you could be his killer for all I know....*

By February 7, 2004, another poster comes to Luna's defense. A woman calling herself Shaina writes:

> *Jonathan Luna had prosecuted my brother a few years back for drug trafficking. I wasn't too familiar with the justice system back then and my brother and I were the only surviving members of our family. Mr. Luna made sure I knew everything that was going on and he was the nicest person to me. Instead of being mad at everyone in that courtroom for making my brother serve time I was happy that they were helpng my brother get on the right track. Mr Luna was really nice to me and kept me smiling even when he knew my brothers case would end up in jail time. On December 9 I was lying in a hospital bed after giving birth to my daughter Janette when I saw on the news about his murder. My brother called me crying asking me had I heard about his death. It was a very hard time for us. Even though some people's cases went wrong while Mr. Luna was prosecuting them his personality left no room for you to hold a grudge. My brother went back on drugs and died of an overdose on January 21st. I think Jonathan Luna's death had an emotional effect on him (he didnt go back on drugs and die of an ovedose because of it — I dont think). Mr Luna was a great guy and he had a very remarkable personality that no one can forget. RIP AUSA Jonathan Luna.*

A few days later, on February 12, 2004, a poster calling herself Rae writes:

> *I also knew Jonathan from law school. While we were not close friends, I always found him pleasant, friendly and interesting to talk to. Ironically, the thing that gave him a special place in my heart was an exceptionally kind note he wrote to me when my husband died suddenly and tragically. I still have that note. My thoughts and prayers go out to his family. Jonathan Luna was a fine man.*

8
FBI seeks sex clues in Luna's murder

The day after Jonathan Luna's death, FBI agents were already telling the Baltimore press that Luna's murder appeared to be the result of a personal relationship that had turned violent, with no connection to his job.

The FBI, significantly, would be telling other things to other people. Luna's father, Paul, told me that FBI agents informed him they suspected Jonathan's murder could be a *hate crime,* and so the family shouldn't talk about it.

Reggie Shuford, a friend of Jonathan's from law school days, is a staff attorney with the ACLU's national office. Several months after Jonathan's death, in May 2004, he was visted by two FBI agents, Shuford told me. "They told me that the results were inconclusive, but that Jonathan may have committed suicide," Shuford says. "Because it was inconclusive, they said, they felt it was 'in everyone's best interest to say it's a suicide.'"

So the FBI was "dialing in" on each person differently, giving a different story to each to get desired results.

This included the media, and the public. In the days after Luna's death, agents increasingly told the media that Luna's death appeared to be the result of a personal relationship that had turned violent, with no connection to his job.

This is no minor distinction. To kill a U.S. attorney in the line of duty is a federal offense, *requiring* FBI involvement. Remember the federal nexus. The FBI seemed overly eager to get off the case, and pass it off to the ridiculously under-funded and under-resourced Lancaster County, Pennsylvania district attorney's office. It seemed apparent to anyone observing these odd developments that the sensational murder would never be solved without FBI involvement, coordination and resources. To pass off the investigation to Lancaster County would be to see the investigation wither and die.

This odd rush to judgment seemed all the more puzzling due to the interstate nature of the case. Luna's wild ride — certainly at times against his will — through parts of Maryland, Delaware, New Jersey and Pennsylvania, is tailor-made for federal jurisdiction and involvement. All the more so since Luna had worked with these guys. Instead, poor Jonathan Luna was being relegated to a legal no-man's land, every bit as isolated and desolate as the place where he died.

FBI officials curiously sent signal after signal not only that they wanted off the case, but that they wanted off the case as soon as possible.

Two days after Luna's murder, on Saturday, December 6, 2003, citing an unnamed "law enforcement official...who spoke on the condition of anonymity," the Baltimore Sun reported, "authorities could announce as early as Monday that the slaying was unconnected to Luna's job and was expected to be handled as a state murder case by the local prosecutor in Lancaster County, Pa — not as a case of federal kidnapping or the killing of a federal law enforcement official."

Lancaster County District Attorney Donald R. Totaro, for his part, sounded less than enthusiastic, and kept referring reporters back to Tom DiBiagio's office in Baltimore.

All this despite the fact that barely enough time had passed for any investigation, let alone a thorough one. The feds were heading for the doors with much the same speed and inexplicable mystery that Luna had driven out of the courthouse on December 3.

Luna's murder was soon repeatedly described by Justice Department leakers as "not related to his work and personal in nature that turned violent." This seems increasingly unlikely, but let's take the leakers at their word and explore the avenues. "Personal in nature" suggests several possibilities.

Certainly a romantic liaison fits within this category, though it's hard to explain why a personal tryst would end with such torturous violence. Another possibility fitting the description of "personal in nature" is prostitution.

It was this thinly veiled second possibility that FBI agents time and again reinforced, in word and deed. Only a few days into the investigation, FBI agents leaked to the press that they were showing Luna's photograph to motel managers in the area near the Pennsylvania turnpike where his body had been found. "Unnamed law enforcement officials" at the same time leaked that the area was a known hotbed for prostitution. (Residents in Lancaster County, and local police, by the way, counter this is not true.)

These assertions were quickly coupled with reports from "unnamed authorities" that Luna lived "a secret life;" that he held credit cards, "unknown to his wife," with tens of thousands of dollars in charges*; that pornography had been found on his work computer; even the report that his genitals had been mutilated. The middle-of-night withdrawal of $200 from an ATM machine suggests dark activities. The questioning of Lancaster motel operators seemed designed to reinforce the public impression that Luna was a sex-crazed trawler who had fallen victim to a prostitute, and so had sealed his own fate. Trouble is, Jonathan had no need to buy women.

It seemed far-fetched for other reasons. Luna was a good-sized, fit young man in the prime of life, a marathon runner. It seems unlikely a woman could overpower him, let alone pull him around the inside of a car. When questioned along these lines, FBI agents in Baltimore went so far as to suggest that Luna may have fallen victim to a jealous husband, boyfriend, even pimp. One reporter was even told that Luna may have been secretly bisexual and perhaps had been killed in a fit of rage by a male lover or hustler. Talk about amateur sleuthing.

I can almost hear Jonathan laughing. Jonathan, you see, liked the ladies, and the ladies liked him. Whoever cut his balls knew that too.

*In a document filed with the Howard County, Maryland, Register of Wills dated October 8, 2004, Angela Luna lists Jonathan's credit card debt as $17,677. This amount, Angela reports, includes charges on four credit cards: $9,034.47 on an American Express account; $8,500 on an MBNA account; $110.69 on a Citicorp account; and $32.44 on a Citibank/Amoco account.

9
Wake interrupted

Meanwhile, what of Jonathan and his family?

In Baltimore, on the morning of Jonathan's death, Angela Luna received a phone call from the federal courthouse inquiring about her husband's whereabouts. Dr. Luna said Jonathan hadn't been home overnight. She hadn't heard from him since the night before, and didn't know where he was.

A neighbor, Rebecca Fields, says Angela came over that morning and exclaimed, "He's missing!" Fields and the Lunas' children play together. Fields would later describe Luna to the Associated Press as follows: "He's the best guy, neighbor, friend, father." Later in the day, a soft snow having fallen, shocked and saddened neighbors shoveled off the Lunas' walk.

Her husband viciously murdered and mutilated, the nightmare only worsened for Angela Luna. FBI agents, through the media, threw everything but the kitchen sink at Jonathan. Soon the newspapers would be filled with innuendo — Jonathan was a thief; Jonathan walked off with the $36,000 right under the nose of a trusting, true-blue FBI agent; Jonathan led a secret life; Jonathan had secret credit card debt; Jonathan's mutilation was the result of an encounter with a prostitute; Jonathan was secretly gay. One has to wonder how a fellow like this ever had time to practice law for the U.S. Government.

Luna's midnight ride was far from over. Some of the worse was yet to come. As those closest to Jonathan gathered to bury him, Jonathan's widow and her family would be treated like common criminals.

On December 14, 2003, the evening before Jonathan's memorial service and funeral, his friends gathered at the suburban Maryland home that he'd shared with his wife, two children, and mother-in-law. It was a snowy night, and several of Luna's New York friends braved bad driving conditions to console Luna's shocked and deeply wounded family.

At the gathering, one of those in attendance recalls, Angela Luna expressed deep puzzlement about her husband's fate, and the motives for his killing. Dan Rivera says he asked her what had happened, and Angela replied, "I don't know, because who would want to kill him?" Angela pointed out that Jonathan was known for maintaining good relationships, and that he seldom ended relationships on a bad note. "He always ended things on a good note," Angela said. Even Jonathan's former girlfriends would stay in touch, she added.

Gathering in the Lunas' living room, the mourning friends and family considered the disparity between the good friend, husband and father they knew so well, and the puzzling accounts apparently leaked by the U.S. Attorney's Office and/or the FBI to the national press, complete with increasingly wild and baseless accusations.

As the shocked mourners tried to console one another and make sense of the unfolding nightmare, the gathering was suddenly interrupted by the appearance of two FBI agents. A cadre of suspicious and clumsy federal agents soon would repeatedly interrupt the mourners.

"It was bizarre," one of those in attendance recounted. "We all got there, it was a snowy night. Jonathan's mother-in-law at one point announced she had to go to the post office, which seemed a little strange. We were in the living room talking when, maybe around 7 o'clock, two female FBI agents came to the door."

Several of those in attendance say they believe the two female FBI agents were FBI Baltimore field office acting assistant Special Agent in Charge Linda B. Hooper, and Special Agent Marina Murphy.

"One woman was kind of heavy set," and exhibited somewhat masculine characteristics, a mourner recalls.

"They were both blonde, and one of them was on the chunky side," another remembers. "The chunky one had short hair to her shoulders. The other one was slimmer, with slightly longer hair. Both had pony tails. Both were wearing all black, and the one on the heavier side was wearing a bright red blouse or something under her blazer."

"We jokingly called them Cagney and Lacey," one of Luna's friends recounted.

Having interrupted the wake, the two female FBI agents, "acted like they were in charge. They pulled Angela aside and spoke with her in the kitchen," one mourner remembers.

"They said that they had to go upstairs and take pictures," another says. "The slimmer one had a small cardboard box. It was open, and the edges were folded inward. The heavy one had a camera to take some pictures, and they just went straight upstairs."

The mourners attempted to ignore this strange interruption when, several minutes later, a *second* party of FBI agents arrived at the Luna home and caused further disruption.

"First the women came in, and then I would say ten or maybe fifteen minutes later three to five men came in," a mourner recalls. "They actually stopped Angela and they asked where the women were. Angela pointed upstairs. One of the agents was I'd say of medium build with brown short hair, wearing a blue blazer, a jacket kind of."

Another recounts, "They went upstairs. They wore latex gloves. They were searching upstairs."

The search of Luna's house during the wake was unsettling. "At a certain point some of us decided to go for a drive to get out of the house," one mourner recalls. "We were all upset. I mean the whole thing was so bizarre, like a bad dream. We went upstairs to get our coats, which were in Joey's bedroom. We saw an agent on his knees, in Angela and Joey's bedroom. He was down on his knees, wearing latex gloves, checking the molding on the wall, kind of like swabbing it for 'evidence.'"

"After the agents were done upstairs," another friend recalls, "the guy (i.e. male agent — ed.) in the blue jacket went into the kitchen and started talking with Angela and her mom. They were just asking questions. Angela had her left arm folded, and her right hand was up by her face, supporting her face."

Another adds, "Then the agents went downstairs and started searching Jonathan's mother-in-law's room. His mother-in-law had her bedroom in the basement. They spent a long time down there.

When they came up they were carrying zip-lock evidence bags.

"When they finally came up from the basement they had odd looks on their faces. This one agent—. How would you describe the expression he had on? He was an older gentlemen and he gave another a tense look, like he was annoyed about something. They were acting odd. Apparently they didn't find anything. It was just a weird, odd feeling."

The disruptive experience at Luna's wake continued, finally forcing the mourners from the sitting room where they tried to comfort one another.

"At one point we had to leave the living room because they said they had to dust that area, or whatever," one mourner says.

"Shortly before we were leaving," another recounts, "Angela's mom came out of the kitchen. She came into the living room and asked us if we could please move into the kitchen area so the agents could search for 'evidence.'"

"The agents didn't speak to us whatsoever. They just gave us a quick glance when they came into the room."

"At no point did the agents speak with us or even introduce themselves," another says. "They didn't even give us a card. Which is odd, if they're conducting an investigation."

That night Luna's friends tried to fathom the nightmare they now inhabited.

"We were asking ourselves as we left the house, How in the hell is it these people are searching the house eleven days after it happened?" one mourner asks. "When we saw them we were kind of chuckling under our breath, saying, you know, Is *this* what the FBI has to offer? Like most people, I grew up thinking the FBI was prestigious. You expect better than this from the FBI."

Those in attendance would end the evening openly wondering about the ethics, competency, professionalism, and lack of basic human civilities of the FBI agents involved.

Despite efforts to keep the true nature of Jonathan's wounds secret, there would be no hiding the naked facts from the undertaker. Jonathan's body was transported, under police escort, to the Witzke funeral home in Ellicott City, Maryland, where undertaker Kim MacLeod embalmed him.

I met and interviewed MacLeod under somewhat remarkable circumstances. In August 2006, I appeared on a Baltimore radio talk show. A listener phoned in to say he was a funeral home employee. He knew the mortician who'd worked on Jonathan's body, he said. Luna had stab marks in the middle of his back, the listener told me, which made reports of a suicide ridiculous and impossible. He said MacLeod had phoned the authorities after she'd seen the body, saying Luna clearly had been murdered, and asking why news reports were making it out to be a suicide.

Late one afternoon I visited MacLeod at the suburban Baltimore funeral home where she now works. A viewing was in progress in the next room. Mourners drifted in and out while I spoke with MacLeod.

MacLeod is a tall woman with mid-length, blonde hair. She spoke animatedly of the condition of Jonathan's body before his burial.

"I've seen lots of murders, but this was definitely the worst one I've ever seen," MacLeod told me. She said she'd been selected to work on Jonathan's body because she knew the pastor of the Lunas' church, and because of her extensive experience working with badly damaged bodies.

"This was no suicide," she smiled. There were stab wounds on his back, she explained. Turning, she placed her finger slightly below the middle of her back, off to one side. "There were stab wounds, here, in the middle of his back, slightly below the shoulder blades, and also around the shoulder blades," she said.

Worse, said MacLeod, Jonathan's hands had been "shredded." "There were long cuts between all the fingers, and cuts to the front and back of each hand." These deep cuts were like slicing razor wounds to his hands, peeling away the skin around his fingers, at places cutting to the bone, indicative of someone having slashed at Jonathan savagely with a knife, she said. To demonstrate, she held her hands up and out as if to block repeated downward stabs from a knife.

"They were clearly defensive wounds," to his hands, she said. Jonathan had been cut savagely trying to fend off his attacker.

"I tried to sew them up as best I could but we had to put gloves on for the viewing," she explained.

She said the federal prosecutor's neck had been slashed open on the right side, and all the way around his throat. She drew her finger along the underside of her neck. She should know, she said. "I was the one who sewed him up."

Had his genitals been cut? I asked.

"It was his scrotum," she said. The U.S. attorney's scrotum had been slashed open, she said, but it didn't appear to be a clean slash. His scrotum looked as if his assailant had been "working on it."

She said it made her "wonder whether this was something a woman might do?" but wasn't sure. As she spoke, I wondered whether Jonathan's hands had been slashed while trying to protect his genitals.

She reiterated this was the worst murder she'd ever seen.

"He lost a lot of blood," she said.

I asked about the number of stabs wounds. She said, interestingly, "There were *thirty-two* stab wounds." This conflicts with the widely reported thirty-six wounds. But who's counting?

MacLeod said the funeral home had been inundated with calls from the tabloid media. America's Most Wanted had even called, she said, rolling her eyes.

When it came time to transport Jonathan's body from Pennsylvania to the Maryland funeral home, they decided to go at night so the media wouldn't trail them, she said. A Maryland State Police trooper escorted the hearse, she said.

"I was going for the body earlier but the trooper called to say they'd found more evidence they had to deal with," she said.

"What evidence?" I asked.

"A knife," she said.

"A knife?" I repeated. Luna's funeral was on December 15, 2003. The authorities would tell the public they found *a* knife some *six weeks after the death,* in mid-January 2004.

"They found *two* knives," MacLeod goes on to tell me. "A penknife, and another knife, I believe," she said. She raised her eyebrows.

If this was the case, that *two* knives had been found, authorities had clearly and deliberately been misleading the public, and the assailants.

MacLeod said she spent a lot of time talking with Luna's widow and mother-in-law before the funeral. They were particularly concerned about the media, she said. "The Luna's were in bad shape," she added. "Jonathan's father had been ill even before this happened, and he looked really bad."

At the viewing, Jonathan's closest friends and family had trouble choking back their emotions as they viewed the body.

In his casket, Jonathan's hands were covered with gloves, obscuring wounds that seemed consistent with his desperately trying to defend himself.

"I know Jonathan, and he would have fought for his life," his old friend, Dan Rivera told me. "And that's what happened."

"The person who worked in the funeral (home) said the reason he was wearing gloves was that his hands were really cut up," Rivera says. "I guess (his hands) must have been really mutilated and I guess they didn't want people to see that and to get upset. They just wanted us to understand why he had on gloves. Obviously, when you go to a funeral, you don't expect to see somebody with gloves."

"It definitely looked like he was beaten up," Rivera goes on. A big gash was visible on the side of Jonathan's neck, partially obscured by the collar of his burial suit. "And I was really upset. I was hysterical because you could see he looked like he had been beat up. Just to see your friend in that condition—."

Dan Rivera's brother John accompanied Jonathan's crushed parents, brother, and widow into the viewing room. John Rivera had last spoken with an upbeat Jonathan over the Thanksgiving holiday, he told me. Jonathan, he said, had been looking forward to taking a trip with his father to the Philippines.

Now Paul and Rosezella Luna's greatest pride, their most wonderful hope, their son Jonathan, lay mutilated before them. So smart, so driven, so optimistic and ambitious. America's best and brightest.

Their Joey was dead.

The next day, Monday, December 15, 2003, Jonathan's body was interned at the Dulaney Valley Memorial Gardens, in Timonium, Maryland, just north of Baltimore. John Rivera was one of the pallbearers.

Leading the list of eight speakers who were asked by the family to pay tribute to Jonathan was Reg Shuford, the American Civil Liberties Union attorney who knew Jonathan from law school. Also speaking were two federal judges: Judge William Osteen, with whom Jonathan clerked after college, and Judge Andre Davis, a black Baltimore judge who presided over the Nacoe Brown case when the $36,000 went missing. Luna tried many cases before Davis and looked to him as a mentor.

"I am just devastated," Davis told the Baltimore Sun. "He is a fine young man, and I had sort of taken him under my wing.... His whole life was ahead of him, and I really liked him. I liked him a lot, and I saw him grow in the years he was here."

Who wasn't asked to say a few words?

U.S. Attorney Tom DiBiagio, Jonathan's boss.

How bad was the damage to Jonathan's body? Documents submitted to the Howard County, Maryland, Register of Wills by Angela Luna, dated September 1, 2004, include an invoice the Witzke Funeral Home. The total charge for Jonathan's funeral was $10,597.

This amount included a $1,995 charge for "professional services," including the sewing of the extensive wounds on Jonathan's body.

These were not shallow, "pin-prick" wounds.

10
Motives for murder: Must be the slush fund

A charismatic young public official, whose star is on the rise, is mysteriously kidnapped and found murdered, his body curiously dumped in the obscure countryside, on a dirt road, off a highway, miles from the city where he worked. The death comes at a sensitive moment, at a time when secret government slush funds are being exposed.

Officials at first maintain the murder is an ordinary crime, without connection to the victim's official duties. They describe it as a "random act of violence." Jurisdictional problems impede an investigation. The matter is allowed to drop.

The name of the young man is not Jonathan Luna, but Celso Daniel, mayor of Santo André, Brazil. Daniel was found murdered in January 2002.

In time, by late 2003, witnesses came forward to detail a carefully calculated and orchestrated murder of Mayor Daniel. Local prosecutors now say the mayor's own head of security, Sérgio Gomes da Silva, also called "Sérgio the Shadow," organized the murder.

Witnesses say Mayor Daniel, a fifty-year-old economist, was murdered in a dispute involving an out-of-control political slush fund. The mayor's own political party had been demanding (somewhat traditional) kickbacks from government service contracts. "Middlemen" were exacting ever-higher percentages of the kickbacks. The mayor had been working to rein in the middlemen, who retaliated by organizing his murder.

In December 2003, the mayor's head of security, "Sérgio the Shadow" da Silva, was arrested for organizing Daniel's murder, with the help of parties as yet unknown. When he wasn't protecting the mayor, Sérgio the Shadow's other responsibilities included administering the citywide kickback system that financed the secret slush fund.

"The mayor was killed because he was trying to dismantle a corruption scheme embedded in his own city hall," one of the local Brazilian prosecutors told the press. "This wasn't a kidnapping, it was a settling of scores in a fit of rage."

Daniel's murder is far from solved. Local Brazilian prosecutors are stymied because they lack jurisdiction to pursue national suspects, who now include two top aides to Brazil's president. Federal jurisdiction protects the alleged conspirators. Witnesses, and traced money from the slush fund, point to the involvement of the chief of staff of the Brazilian president, as well as president's personal secretary. National party officials are accused of working behind the scenes to erect roadblocks to a full investigation.

The president's chief of staff, José Dirceu de Oliveira e Silva, one of the accused, on January 16, 2004 complained about the local prosecutor and the press, and said the country could use a press gag law.

Interesting how things work in banana republics, isn't it?

11
The return of Holmes

Shortly before Jonathan Luna's death, I had by chance made acquaintance with a man who has spent a large part of his professional life in the field of criminal investigations. His specialty is internal investigations. He was a cop the cops sent around when they had to investigate themselves. In his long career, he has worked in the very highest levels of American government. I'll call him Holmes.

Our conversation soon turned to the mysterious death of Jonathan Luna. What was my thinking on the case? the investigator asked me.

Well of course, I replied, it could always have been a random act of violence. By coincidence, I postulated, Luna had bumped into a stranger who killed him.

The investigator shook his head no. "There's no such thing as a coincidence to a criminologist," he told me. A little old lady might be run over by a car in South Succotash, but there's always a *reason* she was crossing the street (perhaps she was on her way to the store), and there's always a *reason* why the car was coming down the street when it hit her. Human beings are not quarks or neutrinos who magically appear and disappear, by quantum mechanics. Neither the woman, nor the car, magically appear on the street to allow the hit-and-run to happen. There's an explanation why each party meets at the moment of death.

The FBI has suggested that perhaps Luna met a lover, or a prostitute, who stabbed him and ferried him around the countryside of four states, I told the investigator.

Again, the investigator shook his head. It's unlikely the murderer was a woman acting alone, he said dismissively. Luna's too big. A woman couldn't pull him around, inside or outside the car.

Maybe he met a gay hooker or a transsexual, I said. It could happen at an interstate rest stop.

I related that a relative of mine has extensively studied hate crimes perpetrated against transsexuals and gays.

"A hate crime is overkill," she told me. "In a hate crime, you don't just kill, you overkill. Someone who stabs a gay or a transsexual kills them many times over."

Slashing his scrotum, his neck and his hands, and stabbing him in the back, fits the bill of overkill. There seems to be an element of hate here, but was sex involved?

I've read accounts of transsexual or gay hookers killed by a guilt-ridden straight man. Why, I asked the hate crime expert, would a gay hooker kill?

"During or after sex, he may suddenly feel guilty about his unresolved sexuality and lash out (at the john)," the hate crime expert told me.

Holmes, my investigator acquaintance, shook his head no. "If Luna had been stabbed by a gay prostitute the killer would have just run from the car to get away. He wouldn't've driven Luna around for hours."

I mentioned that Luna had been wearing his Justice Department identification badge around his neck, making it all the more unlikely he was cruising for sex at truck stops.

Holmes said the spot where the body was dumped was of significance. Normally it would mean the perpetrator lived within ten miles or so of where the body had been found. But not in this case, Holmes said he suspected. The killer or killers almost certainly needed a ride out. Thus the turnpike, or Rt. 222, providing ingress, and egress, for the ride out.

This was not a random murder, Holmes pronounced. This was a pre-meditated, planned and orchestrated murder, done by someone with an insider's knowledge of law enforcement techniques.

Why do you say that? I asked.

Holmes said he was suspicious of the thirty-six stab wounds. One stab wound for each thousand dollars missing from the evidence lock-up. That's not a coincidence, he said.

"That's a calling card to a criminologist," he said. "The murderer's sending a message."

"What's the message?"

"He's warning other FBI agents to stay away. The same thing could happen to you, he's telling them."

Holmes said he had another problem with the stab wounds. The mix of the deep wounds and the little pricks. Reports of these wounds suggested they were "disordered," he told me.

What did he mean?

A typical profile of a murder, he explained, is displayed with building anger and rage. An argument builds to a fight; shallower, skirmish wounds lead to the *coup de grâce* stabbing, in a fit of rage. So the wounds build progressively, in a discernible pattern, to the death wounds. Yet that doesn't appear to be the case here.

He explained how an investigator or a coroner typically counts, charts and describes stab wounds like these on a piece of paper. Early wounds, say, shallow, defensive wounds on the forearms, are listed at the top of the page, noting their depth and damage, building to the deep, killing wounds, farther down the sheet of paper.

Jon Luna was stabbed deeply in the neck, with many additional, slight, prick wounds seemingly sprinkled in, apparently at random. Holmes squinted his eyes. It appeared to him, he said, that someone may be intentionally manipulating the profile, perhaps even adding the prick wounds *after* the deep, killing stabs.

If someone is manipulating the profile, it's an effort to throw investigators off track. In Luna's case, someone may be trying to manufacturer a sex crime or even a suicide profile.

Suicide? I asked.

Sometimes, in a suicide, criminologists find what are called "hesitation wounds," pricks of hesitation leading up to the killing stabs, he explains. In this case, the profile might have been manufactured to make it look like suicide, or a sex crime. That's deflection.

This would point to someone familiar with criminal profiling, and familiar with the profile of a sex crime. An insider.

"I suspect a bad actor," he said.

"A murder is most always very simple, direct and uncomplicated," Holmes went on. "It's usually among the most simple of crimes, committed by someone in the immediate vicinity. A violent murder is most always about someone trying to protect themselves. I was taught a murder is usually about one of three things: wine, women, or song. The song is the money. This is about the missing $36,000. Somebody likely feared Luna would expose them. The calling card is the thirty-six stab wounds. That's probably the last thing Luna heard, while he was being stabbed. 'I'll give you the thirty-six thousand,'" Holmes mocked the murderer, swinging his arm in a stabbing motion. "'Here's a thousand!' (Stab) 'Here's another thousand!' (Stab).

"Luna probably trusted this person, and did not meet him that night with the $36,000 foremost on his mind. It was, however, what was on the murderer's mind."

Often, Holmes explained, an investigator begins by working up a timeline, or storyboard of known places and times leading to the crime. This helps to fill in the blanks, to weigh likelihoods, and probabilities, and not rule anything out.

"Let's play a parlor game," Holmes announced. "Let me show you how an investigator might storyboard this murder."

He produced a large tablet of paper, the kind you place on an easel, and a magic marker. On the tablet Holmes had me draw a small box, which he had me label, "Luna, Baltimore Courthouse, 11:40 pm." The victim, the location and time he was last seen.

Now, he said, we add as much information as we can to our storyboard. We assign a box with all the places and characters leading up to the murder. If we come upon something strange, at all curious, or worthy of a closer look, we'll assign it a star. At the first box, I added a star for the personal effects Luna left behind, his cell phone and his glasses.

What happened leading up to the murder? Holmes asked.

"Thirty-six thousand dollars went missing. The theft was investigated in the months before the murder," I said.

I drew a box labeled, "$36,000 Missing." I drew a star on the box.

Those connected to the missing $36,000 include the FBI agents, and the lawyers who signed the stipulation that the money had been returned, including Luna, and attorney Kenneth Ravenell.

I drew a box labeled "FBI Agents," and drew a star.

The day of Luna's murder, Luna agreed to pleas in the Smith-Poindexter case. Smith's attorney was Kenneth Ravenell, who describes himself as Luna's personal friend, even mentor. Ravenell also was a lawyer involved in the case when the $36,000 went missing.

I drew a box labeled "Attorney Ravenell," and placed a star inside.

There were boxes and stars for each station of the cross of Luna's murder. The $200 withdrawn from Luna's ATM at Newark Delaware at 1 am. The cameras in the lobby of the rest stop were not working, which earns a star.

At about 2:37 am Luna's car entered the New Jersey turnpike, avoiding the EZ Pass, and taking a ticket. A star for the taking of the ticket, instead of using Luna's EZ Pass.

I drew another box and a star for the gas purchased at the Peter Camiel rest stop on the Pennsylvania turnpike at 3:20 am. Again, no usable camera, a curiosity that earns a star.

The Reading turnpike exit where Luna's car passes at 4:04 am merits another box and a star. A spot of blood on turnpike ticket earns a star. Another box and a star for the murder scene behind the well drilling company in Denver, PA, where money was found strewn around the car, even while Luna's wallet was missing.

How many stars do you have? Holmes asked.

"About nine so far," I counted.

Holmes explained, "An investigator would work with a point system. So we'll assign ten points for each star," Holmes said. "Anything above, say, fifty points is usually considered to merit closer investigation, and tends to rule out a random murder, or suicide."

For example, the hypothetical case of the little old lady in South Succotash, run down by a total stranger, or victim of a botched house burglary, would earn few stars.

Luna's case was different, Holmes made me see.

So far we had nine stars and ninety points. Holmes said this suggested pre-meditated murder. But, he said, we weren't finished.

I began adding boxes and stars for each of the known, curious events involving Luna's paid informants, in the months leading to his murder.

A star for Warren Grace, who was allowed out by his FBI handlers while under house arrest. A star for the drugs found in Grace's possession, while under FBI "oversight." A star for Luna's failure to disclose these lapses in pre-trial discovery. Another star for Luna's plea agreement, which served to short-circuit the judge's allowance of a defense investigation of the informant irregularities.

Suddenly before me exploded a galaxy of stars. An unknown number of stars for each irregularity involving Skinner and Luna's questionable informant "considerations" and vouchers. Stars for the FBI agents who worked with these paid informants. Stars for the Maryland and Delaware FBI agents who worked with Luna, and stars for the FBI agents in Philadelphia, whom Luna may not have known so well.

Stars for FBI supervisors who allowed these problems to fester and grow. Stars for the unknown FBI supervisors involved in the missing $36,000 incident.

Holmes pointed to the sudden explosion of stars. A constellation of stars. A black hole of stars, where, no doubt, one could get sucked in and swallowed alive, if one wasn't careful.

"Interesting, isn't it?" he says to me.

"Let me show you another way to chart this murder," Holmes offers. On a fresh sheet of paper, he has me draw a box and label it "Luna." For each of the known parties and events connected with Luna's last days, we draw a box, and a line connects each new box with Luna's box.

To the right of Luna's box, for example, I draw a box for U.S. Attorney Tom DiBiagio, and connect it to Luna's box with a line. (It's interesting to add a U.S. attorney's name to a chart investigating murder, isn't it?)

I add a box for the FBI, and connect it to Luna's box with a line. The line represents the interplay between Luna and FBI agents. Another line connects the FBI agents to DiBiagio. Still more lines connect the FBI to Smith and Poindexter, and the missing $36,000.

Next I draw a box labeled "Sources," representing the FBI's paid informants. This too is connected to the FBI box.

As I draw this chart, it soon becomes apparent that *FBI agents,* and not Luna, are at the center of the web of lines. Many of the puzzling contacts and events flow to Luna, I see, by way of FBI agents.

In the mysterious turning wheel of Jonathan Luna's last days, many of the events revolve around the hub of the Federal Bureau of Investigation.

"Notice how the FBI is at the center of things?" Holmes says. Then he asks me, "Who handles the sources, the paid informants?"

"An FBI agent."

"Who would know the security procedures at the Baltimore courthouse, and how to circumvent them?"

"An FBI agent."

"Who might know which security cameras are defective on I-95 and the Pennsylvania turnpike?"

"An FBI agent."

"Who knows about the criminal profiles of sex crimes or hate crimes, and how they can be manipulated?"

"An FBI agent."

"Who knows the methodology of criminal investigators, and how they can be confounded?"

"An FBI agent."

"Who knows about jurisdictions?"

"An FBI agent."

Here Holmes raises his eyebrows.

"Who leaked the damaging information about Luna?" he asks.

"An FBI agent."

"Who's in charge of this investigation?"

"An FBI agent," I say.

Indeed, shortly after Jonathan Luna's murder, the FBI posted on its web site the most curious wanted poster I've ever seen.

"FBI seeking information — Jonathan Paul Luna," the FBI web page reads. Next comes a boilerplate wanted poster like the ones we've all seen in post offices and the like. There's a naively smiling photo of Jonathan Luna, who's described as "MURDER VICTIM, BALTI-

MORE, MARYLAND, DECEMBER 4, 2003."

Below this, we read a brief description of the victim's physical attributes: Age: 38 years old; Sex: Male; Race: Black; Build: Medium."

Next follows a brief section titled, "The details surrounding the crime."

It begins, "The body of Jonathan Paul Luna, an Assistant United States Attorney for the District of Maryland for the past four years, was found alongside the road near Ephrata, Pennsylvania, on December 4, 2003. He had been stabbed multiple times."

Now comes a truly singular sentence. The FBI advises us, "Luna was last known to be alive working late in the U.S. Courthouse in Baltimore, Maryland, on the evening of December 3, 2003."

(From this perhaps we may glean a hint that those involved in the investigation aren't sure whether Luna was even alive when he left the courthouse, let alone in Newark, Delaware, or while on the Pennsylvania turnpike.)

What grabs my eye is the sheer ridiculous improbability of having lost an assistant U.S. attorney, who happens to be swirling in a storm of trouble with the FBI, while he burns the midnight oil in a federal courthouse. It's really at the heart of our murder mystery.

Here, in the federal courthouse, amid all these sharp-eyed FBI agents and federal marshals, Jonathan Luna drops off the face of the earth, and was murdered.

"There's at least one bad actor in the Baltimore FBI field office," Holmes tells me. "Those are the FBI's own odds. In this case, there may be a network."

12
'Everything Secret Degenerates: The FBI's Use of Murderers as Informants'

Jonathan Luna, it turns out, kept company with a troubled organization that has increasingly acted with lawlessness, deceit and dishonor. This organization has grown into an almost secret society, acting often in an un-American fashion, in the dark, without proper oversight. This organization has been known to intimidate, threaten, and destroy the innocent lives of any who stand up to it. It's an organization that has spent years trying to keep its members' worst deeds — including murder, rape, theft, deceit and child molestation — away from public scrutiny.

In the weeks surrounding Jonathan Luna's disappearance and murder, troubling reports about this organization began dripping into the public consciousness. These steady drips seem to build to a torrent.

Luna's own dealings with this organization, had they come to light, undoubtedly would have sparked more trouble for Luna, the organization, and its agents.

In February 2004, Republican U.S. Senator Charles Grassley, of Iowa, would make public a report detailing what he angrily called the "shocking" activities of this organization.

"The shocking report is a laundry list of horrors," Senator Grassley would write, "with examples of agents who committed rape, sexual crimes against children, other sexual deviance and misconduct, attempted murder of a spouse, and narcotics violations, among many others."

The name of this organization? The Federal Bureau of Investigation, or the FBI. It's a division of the U.S. Justice Department.

Jonathan Luna's murder fell in a period that produced amazing revelations about deep, systemic and enduring scandalous behavior within the FBI and the Justice Department. These revelations serve to detail unimaginably dreadful stories involving FBI agents and their informants. These seem to dovetail with problems Luna was having with his own stable of FBI agents.

Less than two weeks before Luna's murder, in late November 2003, the first in a series of revelations about FBI misconduct was released by the House Committee on Government Reform. The committee would title its report, with a nod to Lord Acton, "Everything Secret Degenerates: The FBI's Use of Murderers as Informants." The report is must reading, not only for those interested in the Luna case, but for all who are concerned for the United States, and concerned with the state of free societies in the world today.

In hearings held into the summer of 2003, the committee gathered evidence of almost unimaginable FBI misconduct in Boston, Massachusetts. The hearings were sparked by revelations that four men were tried and convicted for a murder the FBI knew the men did not commit.

The committee ended up learning the FBI in Boston kept murderers on the payroll as informants for *three decades,* from the mid-1960s into the mid-1990s and beyond. More than twenty people were killed by the FBI informants from 1965 on, often with the help of FBI agents, the government now reports. The FBI clearly knew some of its informants were aspiring murderers. At least one ex-agent planned and carried out a murder with the help of his former informant and the Mafia, in a conspiracy to protect mob skimming activities. This agent was protected from prosecution for twenty years.

Boston FBI agents, the committee's report says, helped their informants commit murder, and stood by silently while innocent men were convicted of the crimes. All this was done to protect the FBI's informant operations, with the approval of Director J. Edgar Hoover.

The FBI's decades-long policy had "disastrous consequences," the congressional report says, and "must be considered one of the greatest failures in the history of federal law enforcement."

The FBI's horror-show in Boston began when then-Director

Hoover belatedly decided to go after the Mafia, after years spent denying the Mafia even existed, the report notes.

Why had Hoover for decades protected the mob? The question really is, why, in the early 1960s, did the FBI suddenly change course? The answer's obvious. Hoover's boss, Attorney General Robert F. Kennedy, made it his department's mission to go after the mob.

The committee relates:

> *For decades, FBI Director J. Edgar Hoover publicly maintained that there was no such thing as organized crime. As Hoover's long-time aide Cartha "Deke" DeLoach pointed out (in his book, Hoover's FBI: The Inside Story):*
>
> *"Despite this now-familiar history of the mob in America, it surprises most people to learn that from the early 1930s until 1957, J. Edgar Hoover had insisted that there was no such thing as La Cosa Nostra—that is, a network of interrelated mobs that coordinated activities and maintained a kind of corporate discipline. . . . His profound contempt of the criminal mind, combined with his enormous faith in the agency he created, persuaded him that no such complex national criminal organization could exist without him knowing about it. He didn't know about it; ergo it did not exist."*

So, comrades, the official version is that Hoover saw himself as a colossus bestriding the world, his profound contempt for the criminal mind unable to fathom the possible existence of the mob.

No one of course buys this. Call it a fairy tale. Politicians knew that Hoover stayed in power by collecting garbage and not-too-subtly blackmailing anyone and everyone in power.

Lyndon Johnson famously appraised the situation by observing it was better to have Hoover inside the tent pissing out, than outside the tent pissing in.

Everybody here had Hoover's knife to his throat — Jack, Martin Luther King, Lyndon and Dick — and just about everyone went down but Hoover. Hoover died in office in 1972. That said, it's interesting to note that, in death, Hoover's reputation has suffered more than the others. He's come to represent the very worst the United States had to offer in the third quarter of the twentieth century. That's J. Edgar Hoover's public legacy.

Hoover's great accomplishment was building an independent law enforcement agency aloof from the political pressures of the White House, Congress, and the Justice Department. That is a worthy goal. Unfortunately it wasn't his lasting legacy.

When Hoover needed to get around political roadblocks, or bolster his or the agency's reputation, he would go to the press. Hoover, in his early years, used the press like no other public figure. He carefully crafted a persona as the untouchable G-Man who'd brought down John Dillinger.

In fact, Dillinger was shot to death in 1934 by a team of G-Men led by field Agent Melvin Purvis. Following Dillinger's death in a hail of bullets in front of a Chicago movie theater, plain-speaking Purvis's popularity eclipsed that of Hoover's.

A jealous and threatened Hoover proceeded to hound Purvis out of the bureau. Hoover assigned Purvis to bad cases and subjected him to intense internal investigations. Purvis left the bureau within the year, and Hoover prevented him from ever again working in law enforcement. Purvis died in 1960, a victim of a bullet fired from a .45 automatic ironically given to him by fellow FBI agents when he resigned from the bureau. Suicide was suspected, though Purvis was later thought to have died trying to remove a stuck tracer bullet from the gun.

"No one employee of this Division can be responsible for the successful termination of any one case... Through cooperative efforts a case is broken," became Hoover's dictum. And so was born the image of the bureau as Borg, the Star Trek machine nemesis who act as one, and dress alike, talk alike, and think alike. Led by an all-seeing, all-connected, Hydra-headed grotesque — Hoover.

The point I'd like to make is that leaking to, and cultivating, the press from the beginning was a potent weapon in Hoover's FBI arsenal.

Hoover taught his agents the importance of going straight to the public.

Hoover is buried a few yards away from his longtime FBI associate director, and inseparable companion, Clyde Tolson, who in 1975 followed John Edgar to the grave. Hoover willed his estate to Tolson, who'd also moved into Hoover's home. Hoover left behind files on everyone from Albert Einstein to Frank Sinatra to Dwight Eisenhower to Louie Armstrong and John Lennon.

While Hoover still lay in state in the Capitol rotunda, President Richard Nixon sent L. Patrick Gray III to the bureau to ask for Hoover's "secret" files. There ensued an angry face-off with bureau employees. Tolson and Hoover's longtime secretary, Helen Gandy, told Gray there were no secret files, and sent Gray away.

Within a few hours Nixon selected Gray to replace Hoover as acting FBI director. Nixon elected to pass over many career FBI men, including Tolson and number three man, W. Mark Felt, a quintessential FBI man. This may have been Nixon's undoing.

Clyde Tolson and secretary Gandy resigned after Hoover's funeral, taking with them, it's said, some of Hoover's files, while the rest went to Felt. (The teamsters probably had to be called in to truck away the file on Nixon.) Felt remained on as Gray's associate director, so was ironically seen within the bureau as Nixon's political pawn.

Over the decades, Felt has risen to the top of many lists (including Nixon's) as a candidate for Watergate double-crossing informant Deep Throat. Washington Post reporter Bob Woodward knew Felt from Woodward's days at Yale, theorists suggested, when Felt was an FBI recruiter on campus. Later, in the Navy, Woodward served in Quantico, Virginia, where Felt also worked as director of an FBI training center.

Woodward for years said he wouldn't reveal the identity of Deep Throat until the world's most famous informant was dead. The way it should be. At this writing, Felt is an octogenarian living in retirement in California.

In 1999, Felt denied to online Slate magazine that he was Deep Throat. Wouldn't he be a hero if he was? Felt was asked.

"That's not my view at all," Felt whistled. "It would be contrary to my responsibility as a loyal employee of the FBI to leak information."

Felt obviously wasn't working on the Luna investigation.

In reality, Felt was known as a careful cultivator of reporters and a deft practitioner of the casually dropped press leak, as taught by Hoover. Felt was regarded by reporters as someone accessible within the bureau. While his personal motives have been called into question, it's known that Felt resented the political pressure applied to the bureau from Nixon's White House to quash the Watergate investigation. It wouldn't have happened under Hoover, Felt knew. It threatened the bureau's independence, and could only lead to the bureau becoming a political enforcement arm of the White House. That is, an all-powerful, national police force under control of the White House, used to punish political enemies.

While the bureau, left to its own devices, certainly wasn't shy to spy domestically, to its credit it resisted some of the worst domestic intelligence-gathering schemes of the Nixon White House. These included the "Huston Plan," designed to expand domestic intelligence gathering using informants, mail openings, buggings and break-ins.

Felt and two other career bureau men famously confronted Gray, and insisted they would interview an attorney who'd deposited money from a secret slush fund into a Watergate burglar's bank account. Nixon had put the CIA up to telling the FBI that this was a matter of national security and should be left alone.

The press, and the public seeing what was going on, turned out to be the only means of ensuring an investigation.

Knowing too much, and suspected of leaking, Associate Director Mark Felt's life was in danger. Another FBI informant was informing on Felt. It's interesting to recall Woodward's description of Deep Throat in *All the President's Men,* looking over his shoulder in parking garages. Had Deep Throat been an FBI agent, J. Edgar Hoover had done something right, and one of the agents he had trained had come forward during one of the deepest crises in American democracy.

The transcript of one Watergate tape, dated October 19, 1972, doesn't leave much to the imagination. Nixon makes a chilling suggestion that aide H.R. Haldeman pretends not to hear. It's six months after Hoover's death and four months after the Watergate break-in:

Nixon: Well, if they've got a leak down at the FBI, why the hell can't Gray tell us what the hell is left? You know what I mean?...

Haldeman: We know what's left, and we know who leaked it.

Nixon: Somebody in the FBI?

Haldeman: Yes, sir. Mark Felt. You can't say anything about this because it will screw up our source and there's a real concern. Mitchell is the only one who knows about this and he feels strongly that we better not do anything because—

Nixon: Do anything? Never.

Haldeman: If we move on him, he'll go out and unload everything. He knows everything that's to be known in the FBI. He has access to absolutely everything ...

Nixon: What would you do with Felt?

Haldeman: Well, I asked Dean ...

Nixon: *You know what I'd do with him, the bastard?* Well that's all I want to hear about it.

(Emphasis mine). This piece of transcript became famous for what immediately follows. Nixon's thoughts for some reason turn to religion. Here we see the darkest corners of Nixon's mind critiquing Hoover's staffing decisions. He inquires about Felt's religious affiliation:

Nixon: Is he Catholic?

Haldeman: (unintelligible) Jewish.

President Nixon: Christ, put a Jew in there?

Haldeman: Well, that could explain it too.

The definitive study of the identity of Deep Throat, incidentally, was widely considered to have been written by Woodward's one-time Post colleague, James Mann, who published in the May 1992 issue of *The Atlantic.* Mann points out that the bureaucratic squabbles between the FBI and Nixon's White House had roots in a corruption scandal in the Washington DC police force.

"Some members of the D.C. vice squad had been found to have been involved in gambling and prostitution, and there were allegations that others had ties to narcotics figures," Mann recalls. Shades of today's Baltimore police woes. In an effort to go around Hoover's FBI, Nixon planned to groom the compromised DC police chief, Jerry V. Wilson, to succeed Hoover as FBI director. Chief Wilson was more pliant to the whims of politicians than Hoover. Hoover's G-men torpedoed that boat, with the help of adroit leaks to the Washington Post, by disclosing grand jury investigations of the DC police force, and casting doubts on Chief Wilson's integrity. Here we see parallels with Maryland's indicted-for-romance Police Superintendent Ed Norris, the politicians' darling. Most interestingly, Mann writes:

> *Wilson's police force was everything the FBI was not: it espoused a belief in the need for more progressive law-enforcement techniques, and it got along well with the Administration. The D.C. police hired minority members, women, and even a handful of "Ivy League cops" — young college graduates who were eager to learn about law enforcement at the street level. These personnel practices were intensely mistrusted by the FBI.*

In the FBI culture, Jonathan Luna — black, well educated, independent — embodied everything the bureau historically despised and mistrusted.

It's worthy to note that the time-honored FBI tradition of the press leak was misused in the death of Jonathan Luna. One seems hard pressed to imagine how a dead Luna could possibly be a threat to the political independence of the agency, and be deserving of such a torrent of leaked attacks. But maybe, due to Warren Grace, that's precisely the case.

Most significantly, leaks in Luna's case weren't used to ensure an investigation. Leaks in the Luna case were used in an attempt to *kill* the investigation.

In May 2005, five months after the first printing of this book, Mark Felt admitted he was Deep Throat.

13
A great reckoning in a little room, Part 2: Informants through history

Thanks to these very curious FBI leaks, much was made in the mass media of a supposed "secret life" lived by Jonathan Luna. Little attention was paid to the very real secret life of Luna's employer, the U.S. Department of Justice.

The Justice Department and the FBI employ a far-flung and largely hidden network of paid informants. This secret network of paid informants has yet to receive the proper national attention it's due, in this, and other, cases.

Within hours of Jonathan Luna's death, FBI agents were going through Luna's personal records. His legal cases were also being reviewed, the FBI let leak.

What about the records, financial and otherwise, of the informants used in Luna's cases?

Jonathan Luna's problems with informant Warren Grace, and his FBI handlers, are indicative of problems the Justice Department has had for decades. Luna swam in dark, shark infested waters.

Informants, we should note, have caused problems throughout history. Due to their inherent secretive nature, and lack of daylight in their oversight, informants have always caused intrigues, and not only in modern America. History is well-stocked with colorful stories involving shadowy paid informants.

In Shakespeare's time, Queen Elizabeth I reined over an army of paid informants, mostly employed against Papal loyalists. Shakespeare's friend and fellow playwright, Christopher Marlowe, worked as a paid informant, and was probably killed as a result.

Marlowe is considered the founder of English drama and the great innovator of blank verse. Some say he was forced into the informant trade under threat of not being allowed to continue his studies. "In all his actions he had behaved himself orderly and discreetly whereby he had done Her Majesty good service, and deserved to be rewarded for his faithful dealing," the Queen's Privy Council wrote of Marlowe, when it allowed him back into Cambridge.

Christopher Marlowe was stabbed to death under mysterious circumstances in 1593. Government disinformation about Marlowe's death obscures events surrounding his curtain call to this day. Jonathan Luna has something in common with Christopher Marlowe. Immediately after his stabbing, Marlow's murder was portrayed as a matter involving his allegedly wild private life, unrelated to any secret government work. A story was concocted that Marlow had been killed in a barroom brawl in an argument over the bill.

It's generally held today that Marlowe was stabbed to death with his own knife by another paid informant in a boardinghouse. Marlowe's murderer was an agent known to have worked for Sir Walter Raleigh. Marlowe had been called to give evidence to the queen's council of ministers in the Star Chamber. Speculation has it that Marlowe was about to divulge secrets about Raleigh. Raleigh's agent killed him with a stab delivered above his eye.

Shakespeare's line in As You Like It (Act III, Scene 3), "it strikes a man more dead than a great reckoning in a little room," is thought to refer to Marlowe's murder.

The paid informant system is as old as the Bible. For example, Chiapas gives Judas of Iscariot thirty pieces of silver for information leading to the arrest of some reform-minded Galileans; well, you know the story. The transaction is marked down, not only in God's ledger in the sky, but on an earthly ledger, in the form of payment vouchers. At the end of the day, if there's an audit, there better be a Judas running around Iscariot to account for the thirty pieces of silver missing from the state coffer.

14
Helping informants murder: The case of Whitey Bulger

Everyone from Einstein to Eisenhower found himself the subject of J. Edgar Hoover's files. Even Pops Armstrong, the greatest musical innovator of the twentieth century, had a dossier. Most, if not all, of these nefarious files were built with the help of informants.

Why then had J. Edgar Hoover *really* given the mob a pass? Popular, and rather entertaining, theories persist. For example, on the web site,. The Secret Life of J. Edgar Hoover [http://www.geocities.com/northstarzone/HOOVER.html], we read:

> *Rumors of Hoover's homosexuality were rampant but suppressed during his lifetime. A favorite story is that Mob-friendly lawyer (and deep closet case) Roy Cohn possessed a photograph of Hoover in drag, which he used to blackmail the FBI director into denying the existence of the Mafia. In 1993, (BBC investigative reporter) Anthony Summers, in his book Official and Confidential: The Secret Life of J. Edgar Hoover, also claimed that Hoover did not pursue organized crime because the Mafia had blackmail material on him. In support of that, Summers quoted Susan L. Rosenstiel, a former wife of Lewis S. Rosenstiel, chairman of Schenley Industries Inc., as saying that in 1958, she was at a party at the Plaza Hotel where Hoover engaged in cross-dressing in front of her then-husband and Roy Cohn, former counsel to Senator Joe McCarthy.*
>
> *"He (Hoover) was wearing a fluffy black dress, very fluffy, with flounces and lace stockings and high heels, and a black curly wig," Summers quoted Susan as saying. "He had makeup on and false eyelashes." Susan claimed Cohn introduced Hoover to her as "Mary." Hoover allegedly responded, "Good evening."*

She said she saw Hoover go into a bedroom and take off his skirt. There, "young blond boys" worked on him in bed. Later, as Hoover and Cohn watched, Lewis Rosenstiel had sex with the young boys.

It could just as likely be that Hoover repressed his sexuality, locking it away in some bureau dungeon, which might help explain some of his abhorrent behavior. But, we digress. Pink taffeta dress or not, Hoover increasingly found it more difficult to deny the existence of the Mafia.

In 1957, New York state troopers and two federal treasury agents raided a peculiar gathering of "soft drink executives" held at Joseph Barbara's Apalachin, New York home. Barbara owned a local Canada Dry distributorship, and his son had been overheard by two state troopers arranging for rooms at a local motel, telling the clerk, "We have a convention of soft drink people." The cops knew it was a ruse (some say they had a vendetta for Barbara). Those attending the soda pop convention included, among scores of other notables, Santo Trafficante, Carlo Gambino, Joseph Bonnano, Joseph Profaci, Carmine Lombardozzi, James Montana, Vito Genovese, and Harrisburg, Pennsylvania's own Aldo Magnelli, with his boss, Russell Bufalino, who was just driving in behind the wheel of his Chrysler Imperial as the cops came busting through the gate.

So after 1957, under pressure, no doubt, to get the bottom of the cola wars, Hoover finally acknowledged the mob. In the early 1960s Hoover began recruiting mobster informants. His boss at the time was mob-busting U.S. Attorney General Robert Kennedy. Ironically, under President Lyndon Johnson, Hoover greatly broadened his contacts with the Boston mob. LBJ apparently wanted Hoover to dig up skeletons in Bobby Kennedy's own family closet.

Soon, Boston FBI agent Paul Rico recruited Jimmy Flemmi and Joseph "The Animal" Barboza to work as FBI informants.

The 2003 congressional report reveals that the FBI agents and supervisors as high as J. Edgar Hoover knew the men were killers. FBI agents for example listened in on an unauthorized wiretap of Flemmi's phone when he spoke with New England mob boss Raymond

Patriarca. "An FBI agent who prepared a memorandum about the microphone surveillance noted that Flemmi and Barboza requested permission to kill Deegan," the report notes. Deegan was shot dead a few days later.

The FBI had been so anxious to *protect their informants that they allowed the murder* of Deegan to proceed. They likewise refused to bring Patriarca to trial for the murder. And this wasn't an isolated instance:

"The Committee received testimony and other evidence that major homicide and criminal investigations in a number of states — including Massachusetts, Connecticut, Oklahoma, California, Nevada, Florida and Rhode Island — were frustrated or compromised by federal law enforcement officials intent on protecting informants," the report relates. "It appears that federal law enforcement actively worked to prevent homicide cases from being resolved."

So the FBI actively worked to frustrate the solving of murders. The entire bureau was involved in these decisions, directed by J. Edgar Hoover's office.

"Senior FBI staff —and possibly FBI Director J. Edgar Hoover — appear to have been personally involved in decisions relating to the development of Jimmy Flemmi as an informant," the report reads. "Notwithstanding the fact that those officials had received reports by memorandum that Flemmi wanted 'to become recognized as the No. One "hit man" in this area as a contract killer' and that Flemmi had committed seven murders, 'and, from all indications, he is going to continue to commit murder,' the FBI continued its efforts to develop and keep Flemmi as a Top Echelon criminal informant. There was no evidence that anyone expressed concern that Jimmy Flemmi would kill people while serving as a government informant. This is consistent with what happened later when agents in the FBI's Boston office used Stephen Flemmi and James Bulger — who appear to have been involved in at least nineteen homicides — as informants for nearly a quarter of a century."

The congressional report's curt summation: "Stephen Flemmi served as an FBI informant for thirty years. During that time, the FBI promised him protection. (T)he FBI made good on this promise, protecting him from a long list of crimes, including murder, attempted murder, and even gun smuggling to a foreign country."

Astonishingly, in the organization that worked alongside Jonathan Luna, there existed a mentality to protect informants, even when they are involved in murder. Just as in the case of Warren Grace. Most significantly, the criminal activities of informants were protected even at the expense of misleading and threatening prosecutors.

The committee's 2003 report goes on to say that the FBI misled prosecutors and allowed four men the agency knew were unconnected to the murder of Edward Deegan to stand trial. Two innocent men were sentenced to death for Deegan's killing, while two more were given life sentences. Two died in prison, while the other two had their sentences commuted and were released after thirty years in prison. No FBI agents were ever disciplined, the congressional report notes. These revelations sparked the congressional hearings.

The report reads:

"The lead prosecutor in the Deegan case testified that if he had the information available to the FBI, he not only would have refrained from seeking the death penalty, he never would have indicted the defendants. He said:

"'I must tell you this, that I was outraged — outraged — at the fact that if [the exculpatory documents] had ever been shown to me, we wouldn't be sitting here . . . I certainly would never have allowed myself to prosecute this case having that knowledge. No way. . . . That information should have been in my hands. It should have been in the hands of the defense attorneys. It is outrageous, it's terrible, and that trial shouldn't have gone forward.' He further testified that he now believes that Barboza's FBI handlers 'knew from the beginning that Joe Barboza was lying. . . . They have a witness that they knew was lying to me, and they never told me he was lying.' He concluded: '[The FBI] figured, well, let's flip Joe, and let Joe know that we're not going to push him on his friend Jimmy Flemmi. So they let Joe go on and tell the story, leaving out Jimmy Flemmi; and then Jimmy Flemmi is allowed to go on and be their informer.'"

Once again, the report explains, these weren't simply the decisions of an agent or two in Boston.

"Senior staff close to FBI Director J. Edgar Hoover were kept personally informed of steps taken to develop Joseph Barboza as a cooperating witness," the report states. "Hoover or other senior law enforcement officials were in possession of information that could have led them to the conclusion that Barboza was committing perjury in a capital murder case. If Barboza had not been permitted to lie at trial, those indicted would not have been convicted. Furthermore, when Barboza was part of the Witness Protection Program, affirmative steps were taken to help him escape the consequences of a murder he committed in California. Director Hoover's office was aware of these initiatives."

As for the subject of this book, Jonathan Luna, and his problems with the FBI and its informants, the report describes an alarming dynamic in the relationships between prosecutors and FBI agents. We begin to understand the squeeze that a tight-lipped Luna must have felt his last day of life, in court, when the explosive issues of Warren Grace, the FBI and its informants, ticked away.

The report relates:

"Former U.S. Attorney Jeremiah O'Sullivan testified that there were fundamental problems between federal prosecutors and FBI investigators. O'Sullivan stated, for example, '[I]f you go against [the FBI], they will try to get you. They will wage war on you. They will cause major administrative problems for me as a prosecutor.' O'Sullivan also testified that it 'would have precipitated World War III if I tried to get inside the FBI to deal with informants. That was the holy of holies, inner sanctum. They wouldn't have allowed me to do anything about that.' O'Sullivan had so little confidence in the FBI that he recommended that federal agencies other than the FBI participate in a state investigation of Bulger and Flemmi. Upon learning that O'Sullivan circumvented the FBI, the head of the Boston FBI office berated O'Sullivan for targeting bureau informants for investigation."

In time, the congressional report says, more than twenty people would be murdered by FBI's Boston informants, often with the help of agents. *This went on into the mid-1990s, at least.*

It's just as startling that Congress took almost forty years to disclose this to the American public.

The 2003 report of the House Committee on Government Reform followed hearings in June 2003, in which William Bulger, former president of the Massachusetts state senate, and later president of the University of Massachusetts, was quizzed concerning the whereabouts of his gangster brother, James "Whitey" Bulger. While William ran the state senate, his brother Whitey ran the Winter Hill Gang in Boston, with considerable help, it now turns out, from FBI agents. The Bulger brothers, walking as they do on both sides of the street, continue to fascinate Bostonians.

The committee's November 2003 report reveals that Whitey Bulger was working as a star FBI informant until he fled in 1995 to parts unknown. The information between the informant and his FBI handlers ran in both directions. The report says Bulger was tipped off by an FBI agent that a secret indictment had been handed down against him, causing Bulger to flee.

The report of the Government Reform Committee finds, "The use of James 'Whitey' Bulger as an informant specifically undermined public confidence in the integrity of state government by raising serious questions about whether the FBI used its authority to protect former Massachusetts State Senate President William Bulger from scrutiny by law enforcement or to advance his political career and whether he, in turn, used his authority improperly and with impunity to punish those who investigated his brother."

Parts of William Bulger's testimony before the committee centered on a phone call between the brothers while Whitey was on the lam. Why hadn't William Bulger notified the FBI of the phone call with his fugitive brother? the committee wanted to know.

William testified that brother Whitey had become the Man Who Knew Too Much. William Bulger told Congress he was convinced the FBI wanted to kill his brother. To keep the informant from talking. To keep the informant from informing.

No man, no problem, as Joseph Stalin used to say.

William Bulger had good reason to smell a rat, it turns out. Rather, a rat's nest.

On October 9, 2003, less than two months before Luna's death, Whitey Bulger's handler in the FBI, former agent Paul Rico, was himself arrested for murder.

Ex-agent Paul Rico, by 2003, was 78 years old and living in retirement in Florida. He was charged with arranging the 1981 murder of Tulsa, Oklahoma businessman Roger Wheeler. Wheeler had been chairman of Telex Corporation, and owned the World Jai Alai, a gambling establishment in Florida, where Rico had worked as head of security, after he retired from the FBI.

Even in retirement, Agent Rico remained in business with his mob informants. Wheeler came to suspect that Boston mobsters were skimming money from World Jai Alai, the FBI now ventures to guess. Shades of Brazilian Mayor Daniel: Wheeler's head of security, former agent Rico, arranged his murder. One day after a round of golf in Tulsa, Wheeler was shot in the head.

Some twenty years later, in March 2001, Boston Winter Hill Gang members Whitey Bulger, Stephen "The Rifleman" Flemmi and John Martorano were charged with Wheeler's killing. Bulger by now was long missing in action. Martorano pleaded guilty to second-degree murder for executing the hit. He received a fifteen-year sentence. In October 2003, Flemmi pleaded guilty to racketeering charges connected to ten murders, Wheeler's included. That's when the informants started spilling the beans on ex-FBI agent Rico.

Thanks in part to the pressure of the congressional hearings, they finally arrested ex-agent Rico. Rico was extradited to Tulsa in his wheelchair, where his lawyer charged he had been beaten while held in Florida. In the tradition of Uncle Junior Soprano, Rico, saying nothing, wordlessly moaned before the judge. His lawyer told the court, "I am telling you this man is sick, extremely sick." The judge agreed to a competency hearing. On January 16, 2004, Paul Rico died, *while under guard.* It's not immediately known whether agents drew lots to guard him.

In 2006, a second retired FBI agent was accused of "acting in concert" with mob informants, this time to kill four people.

On March 30, 2006, Brooklyn, New York, District Attorney Charles J. Hynes announced the arrest and indictment of retired FBI Agent Roy Lindley DeVecchio and two other men, Craig Sobel and John Sinagra, associated with the Colombo crime family, who have all been implicated in mafia murders from 1987 to 1992.

DA Hynes announced, "The murders all took place when DeVecchio was assigned to work with FBI 'top echelon informant' and Colombo Family kingpin Greg 'The Grim Reaper' Scarpa, in Brooklyn. Sobel and Sinagra are charged with being triggermen in two mob hits, and DeVecchio is charged with acting in concert in four mob-related killings.

"This is the most stunning example of official corruption that I have ever seen," said District Attorney Hynes. "Four people were murdered with the help of a federal law enforcement agent who was charged with keeping them safe. Lindley DeVecchio deserves the maximum sentence of 25 years to life for each of these killings."

In one of the murders, the indictment charges, "DeVecchio told (The Grim Reaper) Scarpa that (another mobster's beautiful girlfriend) had been speaking to federal authorities and should be taken care of. On September 25, 1984, she was shot and killed in a Brooklyn social club by Scarpa and other members of the Colombo crime family."

From all this we learn that dead informants, and fugitive informants, do very little informing.

The former head of the Massachusetts senate, William Bulger, told the investigating committee the FBI didn't seem overly concerned that his brother couldn't be found. One must wonder, in this milieu, if Whitey Bulger is even alive.

Whitey Bulger today can be found only on the FBI's most wanted list. In curious company. The FBI's Ten Most Wanted Fugitives web page boasts Whitey Bulger's photo, just below that of Osama Bin Laden.

It's just a few clicks away from the FBI web page seeking information on the courthouse disappearance of Jonathan Luna.

15
World War III: The terror within

It would be reassuring to write that the FBI in 2004 has changed its ways, and turned a page from its outlaw past, but that's clearly not the case. The bureau for some reason continues to thumb its nose at the law, at our Congress, and at the American people. What we have here is an organization lacking proper oversight that brooks no interference or dissent. It's intolerable in a free society. We will either have a free society, with the people and our Congress informed and in charge, or we will have an outlaw, secret police state. We cannot have both.

The House Government Reform Committee's conclusions state the obvious:

"Democracy succeeds in the United States when the rule of law is respected. When the government strays from the rule of law, the harm outweighs the benefit." No shit, Sherlock.

Throughout the 2003 House Government Reform Committee report we read that the FBI continues to resist reform as well as lawful and necessary oversight that is the hallmark of a free society. The committee's report concludes with ten pages decrying the FBI's failure to submit to proper congressional oversight in this and other instances, including a section titled the FBI's "Institutional Reluctance to Accept Oversight."

This report hints at the difficulties we face getting to the bottom of the Luna case.

"It is hard to understand why it was so difficult to conduct a thorough investigation of the FBI's use of informants in New England," the report states. "In hindsight, a statement made by a senior FBI official provides a glimpse of what may have been happening. In early 2001, just as the Committee was beginning to focus on the FBI's use of informants in New England, Charles Prouty—then the Special Agent in Charge of the Boston office—made the following statements about the Deegan case: 'The FBI was forthcoming. We didn't conceal the information. We didn't attempt to frame anyone.' In retrospect, Prouty's assertion appears ill-considered. Indeed, its contrast with a statement made by FBI Director Louis Freeh just a few months later is stark. Freeh stated that the case is 'obviously a great travesty, a great failure, disgraceful to the extent that my agency or any other law enforcement agency contributed to that.'"

In other words, it's an attitude problem. A bad attitude problem, at that. The FBI's response to the House report is telling, and consistent. It came in November 2003, coincidentally a few weeks before Luna's disappearance.

"While the FBI recognizes there have been instances of misconduct by a few FBI employees, it also recognizes the importance of human source information in terrorism, criminal and counterintelligence investigations," FBI Director Robert Mueller's bureau said in a statement. The problem is, the FBI here brushes aside whole cloth the fact that everyone from Hoover on down was involved in these outrages, and ignores the ingrained institutional problems. In this regard, the agency is still involved in cover-up, and hopes the public remains tuned-out to what's going on. It's only paying lip service. As usual, the agency blames "a few FBI employees." And, as usual, they go on to stir the fear of "terrorists," avoiding the deeper problem at hand involving the very real terrorists working within the American public's own bureaucracy, criminals who threaten, as President Eisenhower often cryptically warned, to destroy a free society from within.

At issue is not just whether the FBI is protecting "a few" rogue killers and outlaws within its ranks, or in its employ as informants. The question is whether the FBI, institutionally and secretly, is encouraging or turning a blind eye on unlawful, even murderous activities.

Say it ain't so, Director Mueller, and *mean it.*

The FBI statement continues, "the FBI has taken significant steps in recent years regarding the management and oversight of human sources of intelligence."

The House committee report acknowledges several supposed

changes undertaken by the FBI in its informant, or "human resource" program, but recommends further review. The report sheds light into the belly of the beast and the FBI's internal workings:

"The Committee also recommends further review of the FBI's human source program. The Committee has been informed by the FBI that following the revelations regarding the misuse of informants, FBI Director Robert Mueller has undertaken re-engineering the administration and operation of human sources. This effort includes the centralization of the administration of all human sources, development of a 'Risk Factor Model,' and, for certain categories of human sources, implementation of a validation process. Each FBI Field office has at least one human source coordinator, and 34 offices have two coordinators. Inspections and on-site assessments are conducted. Files are reviewed by Supervisory Special Agents and Assistant Special Agents in Charge at least every 60 days, and in some cases every 90 days. The FBI has implemented significant new training requirements in connection with its informant program.

"Other measures have been undertaken that may also prevent FBI misuse of informants. Director Mueller has undertaken a review of the Office of Professional Responsibility to ensure that the system of internal discipline is effective. The FBI is also seeking to enhance oversight and accountability of human source management in the wake of the revelations as a result of undertaking a new internal security program following the allegations against former Agent James Smith and his source Katrina Leung regarding the loss of classified information. In January 2001, the Department of Justice revised its Confidential Informant Guidelines that, among other things, established a Criminal Informant Review Committee consisting of senior FBI and Department officials. Finally, the Department of Justice's Inspector General now also has authority to investigate allegations of misconduct against employees of the FBI.

"The Committee will examine these reforms to ensure that they are being implemented and to ensure that, as implemented, they are effective."

Trouble is, it's obviously not enough, and these "reforms" obviously are not entirely effective. This report was adopted by the committee on *November 20, 2003.* Two weeks before Luna's disappearance.

None of these supposed "measures" prevented the problems with Jonathan Luna's FBI-supplied government informant Warren Grace. Required is an attitude to make it right, not just another system.

As was the case in Boston, defense attorneys were not informed of these irregularities involving informant Grace. We must wonder if Jonathan Luna himself suspected the full severity of the problems with Grace until he was in court on the very day Luna was killed, when the judge allowed a defense investigation.

We also can reasonably wonder whether Luna, back in his office that evening, balked about the informant problem.

Had this, in the words of former U.S. Attorney Jeremiah O'Sullivan, precipitated "World War III" with one or more of the agents?

16
Bad actors: A laundry list of horrors

In the weeks immediately preceeding Jonathan Luna's death, the issue of FBI misconduct and cover-up had come under intense congressional scrutiny. Both houses of Congress, driven by concerned members of both parties, were beginning to wake up and smell the bad coffee.

The alarming report of the House Committee on Government Reform was just an appetizer for a shocking report delivered to the chambers of the U.S. Senate Finance and Judiciary committees.

It took two years for members of the U.S. Senate to learn that the FBI in 2000 conducted its own internal study on agent misconduct. The FBI then stonewalled for months to keep its report from the Senate. Known as the Behavioral and Ethical Trends Analysis, or BETA, the report details a study conducted by the FBI's Behavioral Sciences and Law Enforcement Ethics units. The Ethics Unit has since been starved of funds by the FBI.

The report focused on seventy-seven agents who had been caught, investigated and fired by the FBI from 1986 to 1999. The study helps us to profile bad acting FBI agents. Bad actors aren't newbies, the report finds. On average they'd been with the FBI for more than ten years before they were caught, and seventy percent had received bureau commendations. These, then, are agents who know the ropes. They'd also had a history of misconduct problems.

The bad actors engaged in everything from child abuse, sexual fetishism to murder. More to the point of this book, one agent had stolen $400,000 from the informants' fund, while another killed his informant, after carrying on an affair with her for years.

Senator Charles Grassley, the Iowa Republican who chairs the Senate Finance Committee, and Senator Patrick Leahy, a Democrat from Vermont on the Judiciary Committee, got wind of the BETA report in 2002. In November 2002, a year before Jonathan Luna's death, and about the same time the $36,000 went missing from the evidence vault, Grassley and Leahy wrote the FBI for a copy of the BETA report. It was easier to get the money out of the evidence vault. The senior senators didn't receive the report until *July 2003,* shortly after William Bulger was grilled by the House on his brother Whitey's disappearance.

With this secret, internal FBI report came a letter from the Justice Department stating the report contained "sensitive data" and "should not be publicly disclosed." On February 18, 2004 Grassley wrote FBI Director Robert Mueller about the report and the claims of secrecy surrounding it.

The senator posted a press release to his web site titled, "Grassley says FBI must address internal misconduct." The letter describes portions of the BETA report, which Grassley describes as a "laundry list of horrors."

Grassley wrote Director Mueller that he had "concerns about the Behavioral and Ethical Trends Analysis (BETA) report, its alarming findings, a lack of response to the findings and recommendations, a general lack of support for the project and even efforts to prevent its completion, and attempts to withhold the report from Congress and the public.

"The BETA report analyzed the worst of the worst at the FBI - agents whose actions were so egregious that they were fired and oftentimes prosecuted. Authored by the Behavioral Sciences Unit, with the aid of the Law Enforcement Ethics Unit, the shocking report is a laundry list of horrors, with examples of agents who committed rape, sexual crimes against children, other sexual deviance and misconduct, attempted murder of a spouse, and narcotics violations, among many others. For example:

- An agent "was calling sex hotlines with Bureau phones while on duty."
- An agent "engaged in egregious conduct engaging in a non-consensual sexual acts with a subordinate employee (rape)..."
- An agent ... "used his Bureau weapon to shoot his spouse

resulting in criminal attempted homicide charges."

- "A former agent engaged in interpersonal violence, such as sexual abuse of minor children, physically assault of an adult female, and long-term misconduct."
- "A former agent had a severe gambling/alcohol problem and engaged in theft of informant funds to the excess of $400,000 resulting in an indictment, arrest, and imprisonment."
- "This agent was dismissed for admission of unauthorized disclosures of classified information to individuals representing a foreign intelligence agency... SA acknowledged disclosing a substantial amount of classified information about the FBI to others..."
- "Former agent pled guilty to manslaughter after killing his informant, after years of an inappropriate emotional and sexual relationship with her. He covered up the murder ..."
- This agent was fired for criminal, sexual offenses involving numerous incidents of sexual behavior in public, including public masturbation and frequent assault on his victims.

"Overall, the report indicated that these fired agents often exhibited warning signs, such as a history of misconduct, before they committed the act that warranted their termination. The majority (63%) of fired agents had been engaged in long-term misconduct, and almost half (45%) had a history of previous disciplinary action. While it's laudable that the FBI does fire agents who commit such terrible acts, these findings raise concerns about whether the FBI was dealing with problem agents soon enough and rigorously enough, possibly because of a reluctance to impose severe discipline. The report states, "There were some 'markers' identified in dismissed FBI Agents that included Agents hired with a checkered past, Agents with an established history of long-term misconduct ... Agents with a history of severe emotional, psychological, family problems, substance abuse problems, or clear indicators of such." By identifying whether there are common traits among agents who commit such wrongdoing, as the BETA report suggests, the FBI might be better able to screen out potentially troubling applicants, more closely monitor agents who commit misconduct and react more quickly to severe and repeated misconduct....

"Another alarming finding in the report was that the FBI failed to conduct a thorough background check on some of the agents in the study, or it hired them despite knowing they had problems: 'Despite a negative recommendation or "no hire" from employers, the individual was hired.' The report recommended that the FBI keep statistics on fired agents in the future to identify other trends in behavior."

Grassley wrote that he was particularly concerned that the FBI had suppressed the report and cut funding to its authors.

"This is unfortunate because it sends a signal to the public, as well as to other law enforcement agencies in this country and around the world, that ethics is not important to the FBI," Grassley wrote. "The specific role and mission of the ethics unit - to teach ethics to new agents and other agencies; and to cast a critical eye on the operations of the FBI and raise concerns about unethical practices - is now essentially gone, and the FBI is the worse for it. The ethics unit's useful and important projects such as the BETA report, or the 1999 report on the double standard in discipline, will be no more."

Grassley points out, "The BETA report almost never saw the light of day. Preliminary work began in 1996, but approval did not come until January of 1998. However, as the report states on page 80, 'Funding was again delayed by FBI HQ in the fall of 1998.' I understand there were other obstacles as well, but the report was finally completed in June 2000 and then presented to senior FBI officials. It was not released publicly, nor was its existence even announced.

"There were other efforts to cover up the BETA report. Sen. Patrick Leahy — in his capacity as Chairman of the Senate Judiciary Committee at the time — and I requested the BETA report in a letter dated November 26, 2002. We did not receive the report until July 2003. Along with the report came a letter from the Justice Department that stated, in part: 'The Bureau has advised that this document consists of a compilation of sensitive data concerning FBI disciplinary matters and should not be publicly disclosed.' The letter gives no other justification for the statement that the BETA report should be suppressed. Privacy concerns cannot be an issue, since the fired agents in the study are not named, and even names of agents who worked on the report are redacted. Essentially, the Department letter states the FBI's position is that the BETA report is embarrassing, so the public, who paid for the report with tax dollars, should not know about it. I find this to be a novel approach to suppressing embarrassing information. Usually when agencies seek to suppress information, they invoke reasons such as 'classified information' or the 'privacy' of bureaucrats who commit wrongdoing."

In other words, the FBI was developing tools to help identify and profile bad actors. It turns out FBI directors think profiling is a useful tool to catch criminals; all criminals, that is, except those who work for the bureau.

Director Mueller's FBI responded predictably to Grassley's release of the report. FBI Assistant Director Cassandra Chandler issued a press release describing the FBI's BETA 2000 report as old and containing "anecdotal evidence." Mueller and Chandler know that's not honest. If the report was old, it was only because the FBI sat on it for four years. And "anecdotal" is a lawyer's phrase that seems misapplied to a scientific study involving almost eighty known wrongdoers.

"It is important that the American public understand that the Bureau has gone to great lengths to improve its internal disciplinary process and bolster confidence in its effectiveness and impartiality," Chandler wrote.

As for bad acting agents, Chandler wrote, "Any allegation of wrongdoing or impropriety by FBI employees is taken seriously and aggressively investigated. Nothing better ensures this standard than a fair and equitable disciplinary process that applies to all employees."

Yet it was neither fair nor equitable, two months earlier, when leaking FBI agents summarily destroyed the reputation of their colleague, Jonathan Luna. They demand a better standard of treatment for themselves than they offer others.

The men and women of the FBI are undoubtedly intelligent. Many of its 11,000 employees undoubtedly rank among the finest law enforcement professionals in the world. They're vested with the best technology history has ever seen. Arguably, too much technology, not enough plain old common horse sense and honesty.

Why then does the FBI fail to understand that the American public, and our representatives in Congress, increasingly do not trust the agency to act with integrity, independence, professionalism, and lawfulness?

The public, simply put, no longer trusts the FBI. The once-great bureau, once the most respected law enforcement agency in the world, has fallen from grace to find itself feared, despised, suspected and reviled. Think Gestapo, with a frilly pink dress hidden in a rather foul-smelling closet.

Why doesn't the FBI get it? It's time that the FBI is renewed as a law enforcement agency that keeps faith with the better principles of American justice.

It's time J. Edgar Hoover's name is removed from FBI headquarters in Washington DC. It should be renamed for Martin Luther King, Jr.

When the day arrives that our agents come to work in the King Building, they'll be reminded, every day forward, of the true triumphs of American justice, not its most shameful failures.

17
Bad actor specimen file: FBI's own suppressed case studies

For those of you who savor casual moments of horror reading, this chapter reproduces actual case summaries documented in the FBI's own suppressed Behavior and Ethical Trends Analysis (BETA) study.

You don't think an FBI agent is capable of murder, voucher fraud, or unholy alliances with informants? Think again.

The BETA report documents instances of FBI agents committing murder, fraternizing with informants, and misappropriating informant voucher money. The entire report documents about 80 instances of criminal behavior perpetrated by bad-acting FBI agents. Some of this criminal behavior went undetected for years.

For space considerations, in this chapter I've reproduced only the 26 instances of criminal misconduct most germane to our story. Misconduct, you'll note, includes leaking information to the media. All these forms of misbehavior are indicated in the Luna case.

These summaries speak for themselves. While FBI administrators have oddly called this study "anecdotal," a shocking lack of oversight and accountability is clearly evident. The FBI has truly become America's problem agency.

The following are some case examples of FBI Agents removed from the rolls as defined by the Office of Professional Responsibility (OPR's) final disposition:

- Former Agent pled guilty to manslaughter after killing his informant, after years of an inappropriate emotional and sexual·relationship with her. He covered up the murder and failed to advise FBI HQ that he was interviewed by the state police in the whereabouts of his victim. He was sentenced to prison.

- An Agent engaged in reckless endangerment of others; was emotionally and physically abusive to family; used his Bureau weapon to shoot his spouse resulting in criminal attempted homicide charges.
- An Agent engaged in egregious conduct engaging in a non-consensual sexual acts with a subordinate employee (rape); increased alcohol abuse and became unfit for duty.
- A former Agent engaged in interpersonal violence, such as sexual abuse of minor children, physically assault of an adult female, and long-term misconduct.
- Former Agents' office was notified that an Agent was arrested for felony sexual abuse charges alleging rape, child abuse, and second degree sex offenses charges. Former Agent was indicted in excess of 20 sex abuse charges and eventually was sent to prison.
- This Agent was dismissed for misuse of a Bureau vehicle; unauthorized passengers in a Bureau vehicle; improper association with informants and their families; improper handling of informant payments; and falsification of an administrative subpoena.
- This Agent was fired for criminal, sexual offenses involving numerous incidents of sexual behavior in public, including public masturbation and frequent assault on his victims. Agent was a paraphiliac engaging in "fetishism."
- An Agent was arrested for public exposure/masturbation during work hours; misuse of Bureau position requesting professional courtesy; lack of candor during inquiry.
- A former Agent lacked candor during administrative inquiry; falsified Bureau forms regarding his recent arrest for performing a sex act in public; and failed to report a law enforcement contact to authorities.
- An Agent submitted fraudulent vouchers to FBI; fabricated receipts to support vouchers amounting to excess of $5,000; falsified T&A cards; admitting lied to superiors on many occasions.
- An Agent took money from a citizen through false pretenses;

falsified voucher records and made false claims against the government; took loans from informants; and willingly failed to cooperate in an administrative inquiry.

- A former Agent had a severe gambling/alcohol problem and engaged in theft of informant funds to the excess of $400,000 resulting in indictment, arrest, and imprisonment.
- An Agent misused a Bureau vehicle; improperly claimed expenses on a voucher....
- This former Agent was initially investigated for allegedly dealing drugs. Internal investigation resulted in former Agent selling cocaine to Undercover FBI Agent. Former Agent received a prison sentence.
- This former Agent was dismissed for submitting fraudulent vouchers during transfer and was overpaid thousands of dollars. (He stayed with relatives when claiming transportation and relocation expenses.) Former Agent pled guilty to criminal charges.
- This Agent, with a history of previous misconduct, was dismissed for willfully engaged in a sex act with a prostitute; misuse of a Bureau vehicle; an unauthorized passenger in his vehicle; filing a false police report. Former FBI Agent was dismissed for misuse of a government credit card and lack of candor during the signed, sworn statement. Agent had an extensive history of misconduct for obstruction and insubordination.
- Former Agent engaged in criminal misconduct and series of violations of rules and regulations; Agent was engaging in unprofessional conduct and depositing Bureau money into his personal accounts.
- This former employee had a history of misconduct involving vehicles and Bureau equipment. Agent was dismissed for voucher fraud, improperly charging personal calls to the Bureau for more than one year while he was engaged in romantic relationship with another employee.
- A former Agent engaged in sexual relationship with a prostitute dozens of times, misused a Bureau vehicle with the same, utilized an apartment for same purposes knowing illegal activ-

ities would occur, and insubordination.

- This Agent provided false information to the FBI to obtain more money from vouchers; made false statements to OPR during inquiry, fraudulently claimed thousands of dollars during an elaborate financial real estate scam; failed to satisfy financial obligations; insubordination; and misused Bureau telephones.
- Agent submitted numerous fraudulent vouchers, filing repeated false trips while, supposedly, on official duty. Agent pled guilty, was sentenced to fines. and probation with restitution ordered.
- This former Agent engaged in inappropriate relationship with a subordinate employee, extending favors to an employee; used sexually explicit language in the workplace; lacked candor during the inquiry; misused a Bureau vehicle; committed voucher fraud; and displayed poor judgement.
- Former Agent, willfully, solicited a prostitute and engaged in sexual acts in an FBI vehicle, attempted to obstruct his investigation by the police; former employee was already under investigation for threats towards others and misusing a government credit card.
- Former Agent had a history of misconduct for misrepresentation to government witnesses, and substandard performance as an Agent. Agent disclosed sensitive material to unauthorized persons, including a well-known media person.
- An Agent made false statements on government forms; lacked candor in sworn, signed statements; misappropriated FBI property and converted it to own use; unauthorized disclosure of information to non-FBI employees; unauthorized disclosure of undercover operation to non-FBI employees.
- An Agent engaged in numerous unauthorized disclosures of sensitive information to unauthorized individuals regarding FBI investigations and lied to OPR under oath during administrative inquiry.

18
Letter from Detroit FBI informant charges lawbreaking: 'My life has been destroyed'

Scandals involving paid FBI informants, their shady handling and payment procedures, now explode north, south, east and west on the national radar, not limited to Baltimore, Philadelphia and Boston.

An informant scandal rocked the FBI's Detroit field office early in 2004. Similarities to problems in Baltimore — systemic breakdowns of safeguards, misuse of informants by FBI agents, mysterious payment arrangements, informants used to break the law, information kept from defense lawyers, and retribution against prosecutors who speak out against wrongdoing — are striking.

On January 21, 2004, FBI informant Marwan Farhat wrote a good-bye letter at the airport before he fled the country for parts unknown, with the curious blessing of the Bush Administration. His letter was addressed to his handler, FBI special agent Robert Pertuso. He handed the letter to immigration officials before getting on his plane.

Farhat was running because senior Justice Department officials had blown his cover in leaks to the media. The informant, in this case, was expendable. He was small change in a battle the Bush administration was raging against an out-of-favor prosecutor who had dared to testify before Congress.

Informant Farhat wrote in his six-page letter that Agent Pertuso and others ordered him to spy on Arab Muslims. Farhat wrote he was ordered by FBI handlers to break the law by stealing mail, among other activities. The informer felt betrayed. The FBI, he complained, had failed to make good on its promise to award Farhat 25 percent of any money confiscated from alleged terrorists.

Jesus on the cross! You can't trust anybody in this paid informant business.

"I was ordered by the United States attorney, Rick Convertino, to assist you (Pertuso) and (FBI Special Agent) Kevin Tyus by all means," Farhat wrote.

"I followed his orders and I assisted the FBI in giving information about ... Arab Muslims who are criminals, radicals and extremists."

Farhat wrote, "I worked around the clock helping and assisting the government of the United States to put Muslims in jail." He noted he'd passed along information on scores of Arabs.

"I risked my life for the sake of the FBI," Farhat complained. "I worked very loyally to you. You sent me places around the city to do jobs and find out information." Yet he hadn't received his 25 percent cut. Farhat's letter describes a payment arrangement pegged to a sliding scale of misdeeds.

Now, his cover blown, he feared for his life, and felt compelled to flee the U.S.

He told the FBI, "My life has been destroyed, abused and used to benefit your interests."

Informant Farhat found himself caught up in a growing fracas involving fumbles in some of the Justice Department's most prominent anti-terrorist prosecutions following the 2001 attacks on the World Trade Center in New York.

Arrested for conspiracy to sell cocaine in 2001, Farhat writes he was ordered by Detroit Assistant U.S. Attorney Richard Convertino to spy on suspected terrorists in return for leniency.

Assistant U.S. Attorney Convertino was a seasoned federal prosecutor with fifteen years experience. In 2003 he won convictions against several men accused of having formed a "terror sleeper cell" in Detroit.

Several months later, in July 2003, he was asked to testify before Senator Charles Grassley's Finance Committee on identity fraud in terrorism. He complained to the committee about a lack of resources. Shortly thereafter, Convertino charges, an enraged Bush administration removed him from the terror cases and launched an internal investigation of him.

Convertino currently remains subject of an internal Justice Department investigation, accused of a laundry list of improprieties in what amounts to overzealous or downright dishonest handling of his terrorist prosecutions. Grassley penned a letter to Attorney General Ashcroft expressing concern over the treatment shown Convertino. Convertino's cases meanwhile have floundered, along with a host of other Justice Department cases brought after 9/11. Some of these government cases, including the holding of Americans without access to lawyers, amount to un-American activities.

A judge meanwhile threatened to throw out Convertino's most prominent terror case. Crucial information was withheld from defense attorneys. Prosecutors failed to disclose a letter from a jailed drug kingpin who says the government's main witness lied. More shades of Warren Grace and the last days of Jonathan Luna.

All this stewed behind the scenes in December 2003, the very time of Luna's death. In mid-January 2004, the Justice Department leaked documents to the press confirming the internal investigation of Convertino. The documents contained informant Farhat's name, which quickly was published in the Detroit Free Press.

Exposed, Farhat hastily departed the country, with the blessings of the Justice Department. No congressional hearings on this any time soon.

Appalled observers say they cannot remember another instance of an informant being exposed and thrown to the wolves. This, from the same administration whose central players are currently under investigation for leaking the name of a CIA analyst after her husband questioned the existence of weapons of mass destruction in Iraq. For these leaks, American writers are now being threatened with jail.

Here we see the Justice Department, the FBI and the CIA all misused for political ends. The ultimate no-no of J. Edgar Hoover.

He'd be turning in his grave, if he hadn't been screwed into the ground.

Hours after informant Farhat's letter hit the newsstands the Justice Department pretended to take action. The head of the Detroit

FBI field office, Special Agent in Charge Willie Hulon, found himself temporarily removed from his post and reassigned to headquarters in Washington for, we fear, cranial reconditioning at Borg Central. An out-of-state agent replaced him. The Justice Department meanwhile sent in its embattled Office of Professional Responsibility staff, the see-no-evil-hear-no evil team which couldn't find a lunch bag in a bureau icebox. The OPR supposedly launched an investigation of Hulon's agents' use of confidential informants. Hulon is a black man.

One Detroit agent abruptly resigned as questions arose concerning his handling of paid informants.

Also reassigned were two of Hulon's FBI agents. Husband and wife FBI agents Robert and Karen Pertuso, Farhat's handlers, were removed from their posts on the anti-terrorism task force. The two were placed under investigation for breaching any number of departmental rules regarding the handling of informants, including guidelines that prohibit a husband and wife team from supervising paid informants. These breaches of course call into question the quality of supervision by the agent's superiors. Thus, Agent in Charge Hulon was removed. What about *his* supervisors?

Assistant U.S. Attorney Convertino, meanwhile, in a surprise move in mid-February 2004, sued Ashcroft, the Detroit U.S. Attorney, and three others, including Marshall Jarrett, head of the Office of Professional Responsibility, charging Convertino's rights had been violated in all this. This supposedly is only one of many similar problems in the Detroit office. Stay tuned.

Convertino's law suit says the Bush administration is primarily concerned with looking good in the media. It doesn't really care about fighting terrorism, Convertino says. All hat, no cattle.

But get along, the little doggies still do. Several days later, the Justice Department's inspector general's office revealed that thirteen FBI agents had been caught removing debris, mementos and valuables from the rubble of the World Trade Center.

Relatives of the three thousand victims immediately complained the agents appeared more interested in decorating their bookshelves with mementos from America's worst tragedy than solving the crime.

"Our investigation found that memento-taking at recovery sites has been a longstanding practice with F.B.I. agents," an inspector general's report explained. Places where most people work, it's called stealing. Trouble was, the report says, there were no written rules against taking "mementos" from crime scenes.

Henceforth, the inspector general's office says, there's a *written* policy prohibiting memento removal. Perhaps an agent considered the $36,000 in the Baltimore courthouse evidence lockup a memento from the Nacoe Brown costumed-bank robbery caper.

One wonders if there's yet a written policy prohibiting agents from engaging in murder with informants.

What's the big story here? It's amateur hour at the United States Department of Justice. Instead of sending in the cover-up experts and the study hall monitors, it's time we send in the grown-ups, the *real* lawmen, and clean up this mess. But where are the real law men?

It should go without saying: we need a Justice Department Americans can look up to, trust, and respect.

19
T-1000:
FBI informant sets himself on fire at White House

Yet another FBI informant scandal burst, quite literally, into the American consciousness in late 2004.

FBI informant Mohamed Alanssi, 52, of Yeman, set himself on fire in front of the White House on November 15, 2004, as a protest, he wrote, against his mistreatment by the FBI in its informant program.

Alanssi had volunteered with the FBI shortly after the 9/11 attacks on the World Trade Center, saying he loved America and Americans and wanted to help. Soon he was recruited for several prominent sting operations involving alleged financiers of al Qaeda. Court papers filed by one of his FBI handlers described Alanssi as a Yemeni citizen who had "contributed, in part, to the arrests of 20 individuals and the seizure of over $1 million." In 2003, Alanssi's name was leaked to the press, and he was featured in a series of Washington Post articles, as well as a subject of press reports back home in Yeman.

In 2003, the FBI paid him $100,000 for his services. But the bureau wouldn't allow him to leave the country or to see his family, he complained.

"I must travel to Yemen to see my sick wife (stomac [sic] cancer) and my family before I testify at the court or any other places," Alanssi wrote the FBI agent handling his case, Robert Fuller, in New York. "Why you don't care about my life and my family's life? Once I testify my family will be killed in Yemen, me too I will be dead man."

"It was my big mistake that I have cooperated with the FBI," Alanssi told the Washington Post. "The FBI have already destroyed my life and my family's life and made us in a very danger position... I am not crazy to destroy my life and my family's life to get $100,000." Another glowing testimonial. In several letters to the FBI, Alannsi complained the bureau cared neither for him nor his fate.

The New York Times, meanwhile, identified one of Alanssi's FBI handlers as Agent Brian Murphy, who the paper reported had shipped off to Iraq on reservist duty. Agent Murphy is "a fit man with close-cropped brown hair," the Times reported. "Inside the FBI, he is sometimes called 'T-1000,' for a robot-like persistence, people who know him say."

Feeling betrayed, used and ignored, and unable to get help, informant Alanssi notified the Washington Post that he would "burn my body at unexpected place." The newspaper's reporters, taking the threat more seriously than had the FBI, tried to notify Alanssi's FBI handlers, but it was too late.

The FBI informant approached the gate of the White House and asked a guard to pass a note to President Bush. The guard refused, Alanssi stepped back and lit his gasoline-soaked coat, lighting himself afire. Shocked Secret Service agents threw him to the ground and extinguished the flames with fire extinguishers. Alanssi was admitted to Washington Hospital Center in critical condition with burns over 30 percent of his body.

In a letter he faxed to the Washington Post, Alanssi wrote, "I would like to tell all American people that I love them and I am proud to be a good friend for all American People, and I am asking them: Do you think what FBI did to me is it FARE or UNFAIR?"

The FBI, as usual, declined comment. "We don't have a policy on revealing who is a cooperator or informing witness," Joe Valiquette, an FBI spokesman in New York, told the Washington Post.

This presumably includes, to their way of thinking, informants who have been flambéed, fricasseed, shot, stabbed, folded, spindled, mutilated, or otherwise transported by Mr. Scott or Commander Data to the planet Romulus 3.

20
Maryland State Police Superintendent Ed Norris's sex slush fund

Murder is often a very simple and direct crime. The murderer is usually someone close at hand, and known, to the victim. Jonathan Luna's case *may* be different. For several reasons.

Working in a federal prosecutor's office, Luna lived in an environment of heightened danger. He was endangered not only by those he prosecuted. The fact is, staggering and shameful levels of corruption exist in the law enforcement communities of Maryland and Pennsylvania, on both ends of Luna's midnight ride.

Much of this police and court corruption bears the unmistakable fingerprints of organized crime. Mob connections are hard-wired into the highest levels of the police, and the courts, in both states.

As it happens, Maryland's top state policeman faced corruption prosecution by the office where Luna worked in the very hours of Luna's disappearance.

In the months, weeks, and days leading to Luna's death, the big show in Baltimore, and all of Maryland, for that matter, involved a secret fund in the Baltimore police department. Luna's boss, U.S. Attorney Tom DiBiagio, alleged that the state's highest ranking boys in blue ran a sex ring financed by the secret police account.

In early December, in the days leading up to Jonathan Luna's death, DiBiagio's office was only days away from handing down an indictment against Maryland's top cop, State Police Superintendent Edward Norris, and Norris's former chief of staff, John Stendrini, for broad-based corruption and fraud in the handling of police accounts. They were caught running a sex ring out of Baltimore police HQ. The investigation had begun while Norris had worked as Baltimore city police commissioner under Democrat Mayor O'Malley. Norris left the Baltimore police department in December 2002, when newly elected Governor Bob Ehrlich appointed Norris superintendent of the Maryland State Police.

A series of federal subpoenas — some involving Superintendent Norris's father — came noisily crashing down in the Norris case around Thanksgiving 2003, a week or so before Luna's disappearance. The town and the state — particularly law enforcement circles — buzzed about how and where the case might bounce. Insider information obviously was at a premium.

The scandal developed slowly. Several months after Ed Norris was sworn in as the state's top cop, Tom DiBiagio's office requested an audit of an obscure, supplemental Baltimore police account. The audit yielded a $7,700 discrepancy of funds misused for Norris's personal expenses, which Norris was ordered to repay. "I wrote a check before I left the Baltimore police department and paid it all back," Norris later told me. Nevertheless, the investigation quickly broadened, focusing on the home Norris bought, Norris's father, Norris's travels and acquaintances.

Just the tip of the nightstick. Soon Norris, Stendrini and a wide network of cops stood accused of using the police accounts to finance sexual favors; fund sexual encounters in luxury hotel suites; buy lingerie in Victoria's Secret, and other offenses. Police officers drove women to encounters with the city's finest, and waited around while the deeds were done. Norris and Stendrini were further accused of using other officers to cover up all this, and incurring bogus overtime expenses to help fund all this.

Talk about stepping on big, flat-footed toes.

On December 10, 2003, not even a week after Jonathan Luna was found murdered in Pennsylvania, U.S. Attorney DiBiagio announced the indictment of Maryland State Police Superintendent Edward Norris, 43, and Norris's chief-of-staff, John Stendrini, 60. The two were specifically charged with misusing a secret police fund for personal use and "romantic" encounters. The indictment, as written by DiBiagio's office, implies the involvement of sinister forces. It says the Baltimore cops were caught using a secret slush fund, and an elite cadre of Baltimore policemen, to finance and operate a far-reaching sex ring out of Baltimore city police headquarters, with tentacles spreading as far as New York City. It was inter-state. Norris, on the other hand, tells me all this was nonsense, that the "romantic encounters" involved women who were simply his friends.

Even so, "A decision was made not to look the other way," DiBiagio announced.

The morning of his indictment, State Police Superintendent Norris telephoned Governor Bob Ehrlich with the bad news and resigned. Governor Ehrlich said Norris could have his job back if he was cleared.

Norris and Stendrini at first pled not guilty. At a hearing, when asked by a television reporter whether the indictments were political in nature, Norris replied, "What do you think?"

Would he go after anyone in Mayor O'Malley's office? DiBiagio was asked. The U.S. attorney said he intended to get to the bottom of the secret fund, and pursue anything having to do with it.

"We're looking at everyone involved in the spending of this fund," DiBiagio promised. To the contrary, there's every indication DiBiagio did the opposite. DiBiagio was good at filing complaints, not so good at shedding light.

Like Jonathan Luna, and others in this story, Ed Norris had come to Baltimore from New York City. Norris had been NYPD's deputy commissioner for crime control strategies. He previously had worked in New York's 17th Precinct, as commander of the detective's squad.

Norris was Baltimore police commissioner from May 2000 to December 2002, when he was promoted to Maryland state police superintendent by Gov. Bob Ehrlich.

When top cop Ed Norris first came to Baltimore from New York he brought with him a much-praised computer system designed to track trends in crime. Norris also brought with him officers from NYPD. Among these was retired deputy inspector John Stendrini, whom Norris made his chief of staff. Norris hired Baltimore policeman Tom Tobin as his driver. Tobin also was a native of New Yorker. As well, "certain officers of the Baltimore Police Department were assigned to an Executive Protection Unit (EPU) that was responsible for providing security for Norris," DiBiagio's indictment would say.

Before long Commissioner Norris discovered an obscure police fund with origins in Depression-era charities established to help indigent police officers. These included an "Athletic Fund" established 1929; an "Unemployed and Emergency Fund," from 1931; and a "Christmas Basket Fund," begun in 1936. These accounts, in 1983, were rolled into a newly created "Baltimore Police Supplemental Account."

Norris and his underlings, DiBiagio alleged, soon were using funds in this account for personal perks, including stays in luxury hotels in New York, and expensive dinners at the Smith & Wollensky steak house in Norris's old 17th Precinct. The funds were also used, DiBiagio would say, "to finance romantic encounters with several different women."

Tom Tobin, hired as Norris's driver at $58,000 per year, chauffeured women to encounters with Norris and other officers. Tobin soon ran up $80,000 in overtime. Some of Tobin's overtime pay was expected to be plowed back into illegal activities, the government charged.

Norris bought a house with a $10,950 down payment. On his mortgage application submitted to the municipal credit union, Norris listed the down payment as a gift from his father. Norris's father, Ed Norris Sr., is a retired NYPD captain who recently worked as chief-of-staff for New York Public Advocate Betsy Gotbaum. Ed Norris Sr., gave his son the $10,950 down payment, investigators say, but only after driver Tom Tobin had given young Norris a check for the same amount, and young Norris had given the money to his father. That's called money laundering.

Tobin would tell friends he loaned additional money to Norris, which was never repaid. Tobin began cooperating with the feds.

Two weeks before Jonathan Luna's death, the week before Thanksgiving 2003, Norris's father was subpoenaed to testify before a federal grand jury. Ed Norris, his marriage, and his father all risked going down. While Superintendent Norris was quick to blame DiBiagio and "politics" for his predicament, Ed Norris did this to himself. With the help and loyal cooperation of a lot of cops.

Less than a week after Luna's death, on December 10, Norris and his top co-conspirators were indicted by Luna's former boss, Tom DiBiagio.

Norris's December 10, 2003 indictment alleged that between May 2000 and August 2002, Norris and Stendrini, while running the Baltimore police department, misused more than $20,000 from the hidden account. So much for the policeman's benevolent fund.

The twenty-three-page indictment specifically mentions "romantic" encounters involving Norris and at least eight women in Baltimore and New York. Reading between the lines, it's clear there were more than eight women. At least a dozen women, if not more, were apparently involved. There were fancy dinners. Norris's financial books, DiBiagio says, were also fancifully cooked. Policemen, he says, drove the women around on the public dime.

Norris also stood accused of lying on his mortgage application about the source of the money he used for his home's down payment.

Announcing Norris's indictment, U.S. Attorney DiBiagio said the cops used the secret fund, "as if it were their own ATM ... financing romantic encounters with several different women." He said money from the fund was used to stock Norris's home with alcohol, was applied to his mortgage payments, and spent at Victoria's Secret.

We're beginning to guess Victoria's secret.

Mixed up with the mishandling of the supplemental police fund were several alleged money laundering schemes, here and elsewhere.

The cops went so far as to write, or cause to have written, more than forty fraudulent authorization letters to obscure the nefarious purposes of the withdrawals from the Supplemental Account. These letters, the indictment alleges, served to hide other, secret activities.

"Because Norris and Stendrini knew that funds from the Supplemental Account were to be used for the benefit of the Baltimore Police Department," the indictment reads, "Norris and Stendrini signed and caused to have signed letters to the Fiscal Section authorizing the disbursement of funds from the Supplemental Account that gave the false impression that the funds were to be used or had been used for legitimate business expenditures.... Norris and Stendrini directed member of the EPU (Executive Protection Unit) to take the authorization letters to the Fiscal Section to obtain monies from the Supplemental Account.

"In response to the authorization letters, employees of the Fiscal Section caused checks to be issued from the Supplemental Account, usually made payable to the EPU (Executive Protection Unit) member who delivered the authorization letter. Norris and Stendrini then caused EPU members to cash the checks. Norris and Stendrini then caused EPU members to hold the cash for Norris and to give the cash to Norris at his direction."

What was the money, cashed and carried by this elite police unit, used for? DiBiagio's court filings allege:

"Norris and Stendrini routinely caused EPU members to transport Norris and female companions, including Female #1, Female #2, Female #3, Female #4, Female #5, and Female #6 in connection with romantic encounters at private residences and other locations in the Baltimore City area, including Stendrini's apartment in Baltimore City, and in New York City and elsewhere."

"Numerous EPU members and several women would have testified that Mr. Stendrini allowed Mr. Norris to use his apartment at the Redwood apartment building for romantic encounters — referred to by Mr. Norris as 'naps' — often during the workday, and sometimes several times per day."

"Norris and Stendrini routinely caused EPU members to earn overtime pay while waiting for Norris at residences and other locations during these romantic encounters."

The boys in blue in were really going to town, literally and figuratively. You have to wonder what else was going on. And the people of Maryland are left to wonder, because Tom DiBiagio curiously wasn't telling the whole story.

In gentlemanly fashion, DiBiagio described these sexual improprieties by Norris, who is a married man in his forties, and his badge-toting accomplices, as "romantic encounters." Maybe that's not totally disingenuous, as Republicans often have strange and mercenary ideas of romance.

DiBiagio, as if he's suddenly a student of diplomacy, curiously calls the festivities "romantic encounters." The cops, DiBiagio says, for some years used their slush fund to finance "romantic encounters," with the help of shadowy players unknown.

What we're talking about here is a slush fund used to pay for encounters with women. Encounters arranged, organized, paid for and obscured, no less, by police officers.

Keep in mind that not even elite, top cops can run a sex ring by themselves, not when they also have everyday, mundane distractions to occupy their time, like running the police department and upholding the law. That's why it's always helpful to have associates to assist with the women.

In next-door Pennsylvania there exist strikingly similar arrangements. There are ongoing allegations of a sex ring run from a county courthouse, not far from where Jonathan Luna was found dead. (See Appendix.) One of those drawn into the controversy provides security for the Pennsylvania turnpike, near where Luna's body was found. The Pennsylvania sex ring is protected by officials in the highest offices of state government. In the Pennsylvania sex ring, investigators say state police officers have recieved sexual favors from the women involved.

In 2004, Ed Norris would plead guilty and the mess would be swept under a carpet in the U.S. attorney's office. By now there were some fairly sizable lumps under that carpet. Before that could happen, DiBiagio's office filed at least eighteen pages of court papers documenting episode after episode of the "romantic encounters" involving Maryland's top cops. The shameful filings are enough to curl anyone's stomach. It's enough to make you wonder about the future of our country. For example, we read:

"On or about October 16, 2000, Norris traveled to New York City for a romantic encounter with Female #1 and paid for and caused to be paid lodging expenses at the Best Western Seaport Inn in the amount of $274.67, travel expenses, including an Amtrak train ticket in the amount of $116.00, and dining expenses with money from the Supplemental Account....

"On or about February 13, 2001, Norris purchased and caused to have purchased lingerie and other personal items from Victoria's Secret at Towson Town Center for Female #1, Female #2, and Female

#3 with money from the Supplemental Account.

"From on or about Friday, February 23, 2001 through on or about Saturday, February 24, 2001, Norris traveled to New York City for a romantic encounter with Female #2 and paid for and caused to be paid lodging expenses a the Wall Street Inn in the amount of approximately $170.75 and dining expenses with money from the Supplemental Account....

"From on or about July 11, 2001 through on or about July 13, 2001, Norris traveled to New York City for a romantic encounter with Female #1 and paid for and caused to be paid lodging expenses at the W Hotel in the amount of approximately $918.70 and dining expenses with money from the Supplemental Account."

An amusing encounter is described, giving a whole new meaning to "Internal Affairs": "EPU Member #1 would have testified that he, Mr. Norris, a female companion of Mr. Norris's, and a fourth person shared a personal meal at Smith & Wollensky in New York City on August 13, 2000. EPU Member #1 would have testified that while in the restaurant, Mr. Norris ran into an old NYPD friend who would later join the Internal Affairs Section of the Baltimore Police Department. EPU Member #1 would have testified that because of this unplanned meeting, Mr. Norris decided to change seats with the female in order to make it appear that the female was with EPU Member #1. The BPD Internal Affairs employee would have testified that she ran into Mr. Norris at Smith & Wollensky just a few days before she entered duty at the Baltimore Police Department on August 16, 2000. She would have testified that at the time, Mr. Norris was with an unidentified female. The United States would have also introduced the receipt for this dinner, which cost $225.00."

In the above story we see cops playing musical chairs so another cop can't see what's going on.

It should be noted that Norris and Company's extracurricular activities continued through the summer of 2002, when the Supplemental Account scandal was uncovered by the Baltimore Sun. Norris continued his trips through June 2002, DiBiagio notes. After that, Norris and his top cops went into full cover-up mode, lying about, and obscuring, their misdeeds with the Supplemental Account. This fell in the same time frame when the Dawson family began calling police for help. When the ignored Dawson family was finally wiped out, Norris told outraged Baltimoreans that their anger was misplaced by questioning police conduct. That's not quite right, is it, Ed? Their *trust* had been misplaced. It turns out Ed Norris and his officers had been too busy with "romantic encounters," and covering their tracks, to fully focus on the Dawsons and their children. Corruption has real-world implications. It often hurts children.

The full implications of this horrendous scandal have yet to set in. For the purposes of this story, DiBiagio documents a most interesting series of events occurring almost two years to the day before Jonathan Luna's disappearance:

"On or about December 6, 2001, Norris had a romantic encounter with Female #6 at the Hyatt Regency Hotel in Baltimore, Maryland and paid for or caused to be paid lodging expenses in the amount of approximately $123.75 with money from the Supplemental Account."

That day also produced a bar bill for $210.00, from the Pisces Bar in the Baltimore Hyatt. The most startling revelation concerns what happened about two weeks later, a few days before Christmas. Police Commissioner Norris intimated to his chief of staff Stendrini that he feared his romp with woman #6 had been caught on the Hyatt's video security cameras. The cops returned to the crime scene to case for cameras.

What happens next? Stendrini and another Baltimore Police Department employee went to the Hyatt to look for security cameras. We read DiBiagio's account, filed at the time of Norris's plea deal:

"A BPD (Baltimore Police Department) employee would have testified that Mr. Stendrini told this employee, around December 23, 2001, that Mr. Norris was concerned that Mr. Norris had been videotaped with a woman going into a room at the at the Hyatt Hotel in early December. At Mr. Stendrini's direction, the employee went with Mr. Stendrini to the Hyatt to look for video cameras.

"Female #6 would have testified that she went to the Pisces Bar, met up with Mr. Norris, and stayed with him that night in a room at the Hyatt Hotel."

So here we have top-ranking cops snooping around for video

cameras that may or may not work.

What about those video cameras at the I-95 Kennedy Plaza, and the Pennsylvania turnpike rest stop, that didn't work, and which strangely did not capture events from Jonathan Luna's last minutes of life? It turns out Maryland's highest ranking cops were keeping tabs on security cameras. What about other cops?

Was Jonathan Luna intentionally lured to places where no eyes could see? The possibility can't be ruled out. I keep thinking about the words of the Lancaster County coroner, Dr. Barry Walp, following Luna's autopsy. "You would think they were perhaps after information from the guy when you see something like this," Walp said.

Ed Norris, facing a possible 30-year jail sentence for the mortgage fraud charge, accepted a plea deal in May 2004, and served six months in prison. He was given an additional six months of home detention, and 500 hours of community service. Upon completion of his sentence, in 2005, Norris was hired by Baltimore radio station WHFS, a CBS affiliate, as a talk show host. He remains popular in Baltimore.

As luck would strangely have it, I was contacted by Norris's staff in August 2006, and invited onto his radio show to talk about *The Midnight Ride of Jonathan Luna.*

It was one of the most interesting encounters I have ever had, on or off the air. Ed Norris turned out to be charismatic, humbled, and very well-informed. He seemed genuinely concerned about Luna's last case, and his death. Norris told me he had been the subject of political prosecution by Luna's boss. U.S. Attorney Tom DiBiagio had indicted him, he said, due to critical testimony Norris had offered before the 9/11 Commission. Norris told me the women mentioned in his indictment had been his personal friends, and that several of the women mentioned in the indictment merely had been passing acquaintances.

Norris said FBI agents asked him to lie about corruption in Mayor Martin O'Malley's administration, hoping to falsely indict O'Malley. Norris said he refused to do it.

And DiBiagio? Norris says Gov. Ehrlich refused to talk to the U.S. Attorney the entire last year DiBiagio was in office.

21
Under Old Nick's family tree

Who left the body of Jonathan Luna near the trees, with the winter birds sipping from the freezing creek?

We should ask a reasonable question: did the mob have a hand in the death of Jonathan Luna?

In the old days, if a policeman or a federal prosecutor turned up dead nearby, mobsters would be quaking in their wingtips, as they knew, their fault or not, retribution from The Man would come swift and severe.

That's why a don would keep such things from happening in his territory. That's why a don doesn't hang out a sign that says, "Dead prosecutor drop off." It draws too much attention, and heat.

In the Luna case, all this becomes an interesting subject.

One would imagine, had the mob been involved in Luna's death, that his body would not have been found, let alone in one piece, off Exit 286 of the Pennsylvania turnpike. He would simply have disappeared. Unless, of course, the murder was botched. Or somebody felt they were protected. Or someone was sending a message.

The mob loves to send messages. You'd think they work for Western Union. In *The Godfather,* when Vito Corleone's henchman, Luca Brasi, goes missing, his vest arrives wrapped around fish. It means Luca Brasi sleeps with the fishes, Sonny is told. It was a message, and a warning.

After Sam Giancana was subpoenaed to appear before the Church committee on assassinations in 1975, he was found murdered at home, killed by someone he trusted, a wound to the back of his head, and five bullet holes around his mouth. It was a message, and a warning, to others not to talk.

Precisely because the body was found off the Pennsylvania turnpike, Luna's body was left strangely on the doorstep of the Pennsylvania mob. In recent years the turnpike has had peculiar contacts with organized crime families, and not just in its security operations. In Pennsylvania, amazingly, in more ways than one, The Man has been married to The Mob.

There are three organized crime territories in Pennsylvania, not counting Philadelphia: east, middle, and western Pennsylvania. It's an open secret in law enforcement circles who controls these territories, yet for some reason no one does much, if anything, about it. In fact, the Pennsylvania Crime Commission was disassembled in the 1990s by state politicians angered at the agency's successful pursuit of mob infiltration of the state attorney general's office.

The mob payroll includes attorneys general, judges, agents and cops. Philadelphia is in a class by itself. Philadelphia municipal corruption investigations are neverending. Genovese family ally Nicky Scarfo rose to prominence in the early 1980s, in part because he'd been exiled, after a barroom brawl, to Atlantic City in the early 1970s. When casino gambling was approved in 1976, Scarfo had learned the ropes of the Atlantic City construction business well enough to control the unions. The mob threatened strikes if the casino developers didn't pay them off. Scarfo also owned his own construction company, and would later murder his own partner, Vincent Falcone.

The web site Organized Crime and Political Corruption (www.ipsn.org/scarfo.html), reports, "Vincent Falcone was a partner with Scarfo in his construction company. Scarfo believed that Falcone was ripping him off, but his only real crime was to criticize Scarfo's quality of workmanship in the construction business. Scarfo and (Scarfo's nephew Philip) Leonetti invited Falcone to a hideaway where they had dinner. After they ate and drank, Leonetti shot Falcone in the back of the head. Scarfo celebrated by drinking more, putting his hand on Falcone's still body to feel for his heart beat, ordering his nephew, Leonetti to shoot him one more time in the heart. With them at the time was another Bruno family member, Joe Salerno, who feared he, too, would be killed."

In the 1980s, in Philadelphia, the feds inadvertently caught leaders of a rackets-influenced Roofers Union handing envelopes stuffed with cash to more than a dozen city judges at Christmas time. When the dust settled, RICO violations were filed against fourteen judges, a Department of Labor official, and thirty-six city and state officials. The Labor Department demanded a trusteeship of the union, "to prevent the union from being managed as a racketeering enterprise in the future." No such probation was placed on Pennsylvania courts. Instead, worthy of note here, several of the collared judges were made into "cooperating witnesses" by the FBI. The corruption of Pennsylvania courts finally threatened judicial independence. Judges presiding over cases while wearing FBI wires found their rulings thrown out by shocked appellate courts forced to uphold the notion that defendants should not be tried by agents of the government.

Several recent Pennsylvania attorneys general had close ties to organized crime, including Ernie Preate, who went to prison for fixing gambling cases while taking unreported money from gamblers. In the last two decades, every state row office but the governorship has seen an officeholder successfully prosecuted for corruption. There's obviously a deep and enduring problem in Pennsylvania.

Pennsylvania courts, which often condone organized crime activity, as we'll see, remain the laughingstock of the nation, and historically have ties to organized crime.

It's worth mentioning that, at the time of Jonathan Luna's disappearance, slot machine gambling was being hotly debated in Maryland and Pennsylvania. Gambling's a cash cow for the mob, as Nicky Scarfo demonstrated. In Maryland, Republican Gov. Bob Ehrlich was the main proponent of slot machines. If Ehrlich and his Republicans were damaged due to scandals, the prospects for slot machines in Maryland, and mob profits, dimmed.

In early March 2007, Luna's boss, former U.S. Attorney Tom DiBiagio, in fact called in a New York Times reporter to say he believed he'd been forced from his job because he'd been investigating alleged ties between gambling proponents and staff members working for former Maryland Republican Gov. Bob Ehrlich. DiBiagio said he felt his life at one point was threatened during the curtailed investigation, but that the FBI refused to protect him.

"There was direct pressure not to pursue these investigations," the Times quoted DiBiagio. "The practical impact was to intimidate my office and shut down these investigations."

In Pennsylvania, at the same time, under governor Ed Rendell, a convicted felon with known ties to organized crime was successfully seeking a casino license by giving office holders in both political parties large campaign contributions.

The mob and Pennsylvania state government go together like, well, beer and sausage. It may be hard for outsiders to believe, but the mob has for a long time been a not-so-silent partner of Pennsylvania state government. Examples are flagrant, and always humorous to Pennsylvanians.

In his 1994 book, *Here's Morgan,* old-time radio personality Henry Morgan talks about attending school in Harrisburg, the state capitol, in 1929 and 1930. Morgan writes:

> *The way we got drunk on Saturday nights was this. (These were Prohibition years, mind you.) Downtown, there was a small saloon in the basement of the State Capitol. The Building that housed the Government of the State of Pennsylvania. The saloon had an inside entrance which I never saw, and an outside entrance lit by a single, naked bulb. (My schoolmates) and I were the only teens allowed in ("'Sall right, they're Academy kids") and that's where we drank needle beer. This is ordinary beer which is amplified by advancing the tap all the way, thus allowing a "needle" of real ether to shoot into the glass.*

Who supplied the beer? Who supplies the women? Not the Amish. In Pennsylvania, the mob is a service provider.

The Pennsylvania Turnpike Commission, whose highway hosted Jonathan Luna in the last minutes of his life, is Pennsylvania's bipartisan patronage dumping ground. Organized crime is a family trade at the turnpike. Until early in 2003, the executive director of the Pennsylvania turnpike was John Durbin, Jr. Durbin was appointed to head the turnpike in 1995 by Gov. Tom Ridge, the once and future homeland security director.

Turnpike Executive Director Durbin's uncle was Aldo Magnelli, the Russell Bufalino capo who was caught with his boss at the

Apalachin soda pop convention in 1957. Durbin's father, John Durbin, Sr., of Windber, married Romilda Magnelli, sister of Aldo Magnelli.

John Durbin, Sr.'s lasting political legacy was a political action committee, or PAC, which he formed. He bequeathed the PAC to his son, John Durbin, Jr. God only knows how and for what services the funds in the PAC were raised by the father; it's well known what the son did with the PAC. He raised even more money, and donated most of it — tens of thousands of dollars — to Tom Ridge, when Ridge was running for governor of Pennsylvania in 1994. At the time, Durbin, Jr. was a lower-level functionary at the turnpike commission.

In return for the PAC money, upon his election, Gov. Tom Ridge appointed Durbin, Jr. executive director of the turnpike commission.

Ridge's appointment of Durbin to head the turnpike is only one example of cash and carry government that today makes careless spoils of our government. It was during the administration of Tom Ridge that Schaad Detective Agency began providing security for the Pennsylvania Department of Transportation. In Harrisburg in 2003, bank robbers were found with extremely well-made Pennsylvania drivers licenses. PA drivers licenses, I'm told, are offered on the street for several hundred dollars a piece. "You wouldn't believe how real they look. They looked better than the real ones," I've was told by someone who was offered a fake ID in a bar.

The Pennsylvania turnpike headquarters, like the Pennsylvania transportation building, where drivers licenses are made and issued, is guarded by employees of the Schaad Detective Agency. A Pennsylvania newspaper publisher and a city police commissioner passed along allegations to the federal government that the owner of the Schaad Detective Agency enjoys a not-so-secret involvement with a courthouse sex ring. (See Appendix.) The feds to date have done nothing.

Tom Ridge's turnpike director, John Durbin, Jr., was replaced in early 2003 by a new executive director, Joseph Brimmeier, of Pittsburgh. Democrat Mitchell Rubin, of Philadelphia, became the new turnpike chairman. These and other changes came with the election of Democrat Governor Ed Rendell.

Jobs, and unbelievably lucrative turnpike business contracts, rolled to different people with the turning of the parties after eight years of Republican control.

The Democrats have their own interesting familial bonds. A long-time turnpike bond underwriter and a recently retired state supreme court chief justice are immediate family to late Pittsburgh mobster John Bazzano. Bazzano married into the Zappala family of Pittsburgh.

Zappalas are principals in the firm Russell, Rea, Zappala and Gomulka, which through much of the 1980s and 90s controversially underwrote, in a no-bid fashion, most of the financing bonds for the turnpike. True family bonds.

Newly retired Pennsylvania state Supreme Court Chief Justice Stephen Zappala, a brother to one of the bond underwriters, found himself, in the mid-1990s, at the center of the first impeachment proceedings of a state supreme court justice in a century. Zappala and fellow justice Ralph Cappy stood accused by a brethren justice of fixing cases involving the interests of Zappala's brothers' bonding firm. Chief Justice Zappala retired at the end of 2002, having reached mandatory retirement age. He was succeeded as chief justice by his protégé, Ralph Cappy.

Cappy kept his mentor working for the court in an emeritus role. Chief Justice Cappy decried in early 2003 that Zappala would oversee the state judiciary's computer upgrades. Cappy, who presided over a recent legal case allowing slot machine gambling in Pennsylvania, in September 2007 announced he was retiring early from the bench, to spend more time with his family.

Justice Zappala's son, Stephen, Jr., now sits as district attorney in Pittsburgh, Allegheny County. In Pittsburgh, murder rates are at an all-time high, even though the population is declining.

Family patriarch, the late Frank J. Zappala, Sr., came to prominence as a Pittsburgh attorney, magistrate and state representative. He would father the state supreme court chief justice and the bond underwriter. Frank, Sr., had something in common with John Durbin, Sr. For years it was one of the closest held secrets in Pennsylvania politics.

"Frank Zappala's sister was married to gangster John Bazzano," I was told one day, when a reader learned I was working on a book about Jonathan Luna. "Look into what happened to John Bazzano," I was told. Though Bazzano is stuff of legend in Pittsburgh, I'd never heard of him.

Bazzano, it turns out, died in a curious fashion in 1932. For the purposes of this story, very curious. He died not in a hail of bullets, but a hail of ice picks.

Twenty-two tiny pricks to the skin, to be precise.

I was referred to an interesting article titled, "Mafia has long history here, growing from bootlegging," published on November 6, 2000, by the Pittsburgh Post-Gazette. The article is interesting not only for what it reports, but for what it omits. In it, reporter Torsten Ove writes colorfully of Bazzano:

> *John Bazzano, whose son John Bazzano, Jr. is one of the few remaining Pittsburgh mob members, became the new boss.*
>
> *An unimposing Sicilian who immigrated to the United States in the 1890s, John Sr. worked as a theater manager, then built an empire by controlling sugar and yeast for beer makers. He lived with his wife and five children in a palatial Mt. Lebanon home where the lawn was "as smooth as golf links."*

It's notable Ove's story doesn't mention who Bazzano's wife was: the aunt of the then-current chief justice of the state supreme court. The story continues:

> *In 1932, he (Bazzano) tried to consolidate his power by ordering the most spectacular gang murder in the city's history: the Volpe killings....*
>
> *The eight Volpe brothers were racketeers in the Turtle Creek Valley who claimed royal Italian blood and virtually owned police and politicians in Wilmerding. One of them, James, served on Wilmerding Council...*
>
> *John Volpe drove a 16-cylinder Cadillac with bulletproof windows and a license plate that read "J.V.8." — the 8 stood for the eight brothers. He also wore a watch fob studded with*

> *25 diamonds arranged to form his initials....*
>
> *But when the brothers expanded their territory into East Liberty and the North Side, Bazzano ordered them rubbed out....*
>
> *On the morning of July 29, 1932, gunmen pulled up to the coffee shop and opened fire. John was shot four times on the sidewalk. Inside the shop, a spray of bullets struck Arthur Volpe as he ate a bowl of corn flakes. James Volpe died trying to hide behind the counter....*

Bazzano's brother, Santo, meanwhile, managed to hide behind the steel-protected counter in the coffee shop as the three hired gunmen pulled up to serve the Volpes a triple mocha. That day the Volpe brothers got their cappuccino frothed.

And you thought the price of coffee was steep at Starbucks. The Volpe brothers spent their time at Bazzano's coffee shop, a 1932 Post-Gazette article relates, "not because it was their headquarters, but because of business dealings with Bazzano." The August 12, 1932 Post-Gazette, page 5, article further explains,

> *Bazzano... was the real power in the booze racket in the Hill district and a large part of the downtown when the Volpes, extending their activities from the Turtle Creek Valley, came into Pittsburgh to set up as "big shots" in the liquor traffic here.*
>
> *Many of Bazzano's customers, it was said in this whispered story, began to slip away from him when the Volpes arrived, and when he investigated, he learned that it was because the Volpes were able in some way to obtain liquor at $24 a case, much less than he could get it for.*
>
> *Considering it was much more advantageous to put them out of business by shrewdness than by force. Bazzano conferred with the Volpes, the underworld story goes on, and suggested that, since they could buy at so low a price, they sell to him, take their profit and abandon the small selling. The idea of selling in such quantity appealed to the Volpes, it is said, and they began to act as a kind of super-wholesaler, bringing liquor in from Brooklyn and selling it to Bazzano.*

But suddenly, according to the underworld story, Bazzano found his customers dropping off once again. Once more he investigated and learned he was being undersold. Further inquiry revealed, say the underworld gossipers, that it was the Volpes who were underselling him — going to see his customers, offering them the same liquor for less money and leaving Bazzano, with the large store they had sold him, "holding the bag."

Under these circumstances, it was only natural that Bazzano should be interested in seeing those he considered double-crossers "rubbed out," says the underworld — and when the Volpe's finally were "rubbed out," they pointed out, it also was entirely in order that Bazzano should be the next one to die at the hands of the Volpe's friends.

All this sounds remarkably prototypical of today's sometimes cooperative, sometimes cut-throat non-competitive bond business in Pennsylvania state government. The writer of the 2000 Pittsburgh Post-Gazette reminiscence naturally seems to have been, well, in the morgue, reading the articles from the newspaper's 1932 articles. "Gaudy splendor Marks Burial of Three Volpes," ran the August 2, 1932 headline. "More than 250 autos in procession." Torsten Ove, in the 2000 article, writes it like this:

On the weekend of the funeral, an estimated 50,000 people visited the Volpe home to pay their respects — including judges, prosecutors, police and politicians.

By paying off police, judges and politicians, gangsters had the power to keep the peace, convey favors, sell jobs and take care of neighborhood problems.

Sometimes, of course, killing was also necessary.

Is this what Jonathan Luna discovered? Even then, mobsters had more responsive redress of grievances than most Americans have access to responsive courts. The remaining Volpe brothers filed a complaint to the same mobster commission that J. Edgar Hoover took twenty-five years to admit existed.

Ove relates:

> *After the Volpe hit, two of the surviving brothers, Louis and Joseph, complained to the La Cosa Nostra Commission in New York, which had been recently formed to oversee Mafia disputes. Because the hit had not been sanctioned, the hierarchy decided to make an example of Bazzano.*
>
> *In an often-used mob trick, he was lured to a dinner in New York and set upon by almost everyone in attendance.*
>
> *On Aug. 8, 1932, his body turned up in the middle of a street in Brooklyn, N.Y., wrapped in a burlap sack. He had been stabbed 22 times in the chest with ice picks and strangled with a rope. His tongue had also been cut out and his lips sealed with tape.*

There's something today's readers of the Post-Gazette weren't being told by their newspaper about this fascinating chapter in Pittsburgh lore, I'd learn. And it wasn't because the Post-Gazette didn't know about it. Readers weren't being told the surprising role Zappala family members played in events surrounding the murders of the Volpe brothers and the retaliatory killing of John Bazzano.

A search of public records in the Allegheny County Courthouse reveals only a few clues. Yellowed records disclose that Frank Zappala, Sr., the father of the future state supreme court chief justice, and grandfather of today's Pittsburgh DA, handled the estate of John Bazzano following his mob killing, and represented Bazzano's widow in probate.

But what exactly *was* Frank Zappala's relationship to racketeer John Bazzano, and his widow? Looking at the courthouse records, it's hard to say. Bazzano's marriage records aren't to be found in the Allegheny County courthouse; perhaps they're filed in another county, the clerk suggested to me.

I finally got the answer from none other than the Pittsburgh Post-Gazette. In the State Library of Pennsylvania, in Harrisburg, I dug through the back issues of the Post-Gazette. I unearthed the Zappala-Bazzano family relationship on no less than the front page of the Friday August 12, 1932, edition, in an article announcing the gangland murder of John Bazzano. The article reports that Pittsburgh homicide detective Frank Ferris traveled to Brooklyn to identify Bazzano's ice pick-stabbed body.

"Ferris had gone to New York with Andrew Zappala, *brother-in-law of Bazzano,* and had stood beside the body of the slain Pittsburgher in a Brooklyn morgue while Zappala definitely identified the body as that of the man at whose Wylie avenue establishment, the Roma Coffee House, the murders of 'Prince Johnny' Volpe, and his two brothers, Arthur and Jimmy, occurred two weeks ago." (Emphasis mine.)

It takes a tough man to brew a murderous cup of joe, but a rather stupid one to serve it up in his own coffee house. Uncle Andrew Zappala was the dead cappuccino brewer's brother-in-law.

What about Frank Zappala, Sr., the family patriarch? The same article, continued to page 5, relates that before Bazzano was murdered, he was questioned by police about the Volpes' coffee house creaming.

"Bazzano, questioned by homicide detectives in the presence of another *brother-in-law, Attorney Frank Zappala,* declared that when the Volpe killings occurred he had been in Midland, where he said he operated a restaurant." (Emphasis mine.)

So Frank Zappala, Sr., wasn't only the probate lawyer. He was John Bazzano's brother-in-law and personal attorney. One could say he was Bazzano's counselor, his *consigliere.* Frank Zappala, Sr., screwed up that job, didn't he?

This dark family secret was carried by Chief Justice Stephen Zappala all the years he sat on the bench, a secret his brothers carried all those years they'd held a strangle-hold (no pun intended) on the lucrative Pennsylvania turnpike bond business. One Pennsylvanian tells me of once asking Supreme Court Justice Zappala about his rumored Bazzano family relationship, only to have Justice Zappala stop the questioner and admonish that this subject never be brought up again. This Pennsylvanian expressed some surprise when I explained that John Bazzano was Justice Zappala's uncle.

We can only speculate the extent to which Frank Zappala, Sr., may have known of Bazzano's business dealings. He certainly knew of the mob's retaliation.

The Post-Gazette reported in 1932, "Quiet grief reigned in Bazzano's palatial home at 1287 Washington Road, Mt. Lebanon, last night following the first outburst of emotion among Mrs. Bazzano and her five children when the news of Bazzano's violent death was brought to them."

John Bazzano had overreached, and *La Cosa Nostra* had slapped him back down.

The Post Gazette, in the same 1932 article mentioning Frank and Andrew Zappala, describes the wounds on the body of John Bazzano:

> *Bazzano's body, trussed up like that of a slain animal, with the head and arms drawn down between his legs, with 22 tiny stab wounds in his chest and the other end of the rope with which he was tied drawn tight about his neck, was found before dawn Monday morning in the middle of Center street, Brooklyn, in the heart of the notorious Red Hook underworld district.*
>
> *The maimed body, the hands and feet also securely bound, had been thrust into a burlap sack, and from the position in the street where it had been found, New York police believed that Bazzano had been murdered elsewhere and thrown from a speeding automobile in Center street. The face of the murdered man, swollen by strangulation, still was distorted by the anguish of his torturous death.... The New York police representative, who was first at the scene when Bazanno's body was found, denied the story told here that Bazzano's tongue had been severed, and a strip of adhesive plaster stuck across his lips.*

The "22 tiny stab wounds" seems eerily similar to the circumstances in which Jonathan Luna was found off the turnpike, slashed violently, but also stabbed by dozens of smaller prick marks, and left face down in the stream.

The fury and number of wounds inflicted on Bazzano clearly expressed mob displeasure with a double-crosser. The motives behind Luna's death appear similar. His death, it seems, was not the result of a chance encounter, or a random act of violence committed on a stranger.

Had Jonathan Luna double-crossed or betrayed someone, as the fury of his wounds perhaps suggest? That night he had failed to complete a plea agreement. By failing to complete this plea deal, he not only left Smith and Poindexter exposed. By not shutting down the case, he left exposed U.S. Attorney Tom DiBiagio, and members of the FBI's "Safe Streets Task Force."

That very evening, hours before his death, Luna had double-crossed several dangerous foes.

Organized crime is what the Pennsylvania turnpike in recent years has been all about. Both political parties flagrantly break the law at the turnpike, with no cop or U.S. attorney in sight. Political patronage was outlawed by a 1991 U.S. Supreme Court decision, but you'd never know it to look at the turnpike's employment roster. Children, family members and friends of turnpike commissioners and legislators bloat the turnpike's staff to this day, flaunting the law, ignored by the FBI. They thumb their noses at the law. It's organized crime of a highly perfected nature.

Did we hear the FBI say sex may have played a hand in Luna's death off the turnpike?

Well, sex and organized crime Share-A-Ride at the Pennsylvania turnpike. Concerned citizens are curiously unable to do anything about it. They are curiously unable to do anything about the allegations dogging the owner of the turnpike's security service, I'd learn. For reasons of politics, the U.S. Justice Department, and the FBI, don't care.

"The Pennsylvania Turnpike Commission has a history of public scandal and corruption dating to the 1950s," sums up the Allentown Morning Call in an April 18, 2004 article. In its Hall of Shame, the paper lists a 1999 incident involving the wife of the then-president of the state senate and a future lieutenant governor.

In 1999, the paper recalls, "State Sen. Robert Jubelirer files for divorce after nude pictures of his wife, a turnpike employee, are discovered on a computer at work. The employee responsible for the camera used to take the pictures was fired. Jubelirer's wife resigned.

Her hiring five years earlier had prompted a lawsuit that was settled for $250,000. The plaintiff also was hired by the turnpike."

What's the wife of a top state senator doing with a turnpike job? Today, Jubelirer has remarried, this time to a judge. He was also recently thrown out of office by voters.

At the Pennsylvania turnpike, at the time of Luna's death in late 2003, different factions, shall we say, were in, while other factions were out. In Pennsylvania government, it's the old in/out.

Did a mob faction dump Jonathan Luna's body near the turnpike to send a not-too-subtle message to Gov. Ed Rendell, the former Philadelphia DA and mayor, that they expect a cut of slot machine casino revenues in Pennsylvania? Or because they're upset at being cut out of turnpike contracts and jobs? What about the many, tiny prick marks on Luna's body, and their remarkable resemblance to the "22 tiny stab wounds" on the body of John Bazzano? Was someone sending an instantly understandable message to Chief Justice Zappala and Cappy's family factions, whose grip so dominated the turnpike and strate courts for so many years?

Perhaps it's just a bizarre coincidence. It could also be a deflection by someone in law enforcement, someone well versed in state lore, meant to frame the mob.

If the mob is behind Luna's strange murder, the message sent would be this: they are powerful, their reach is everywhere, they are masters even of the police, and they want to wet their beaks.

Is that why Jonathan was found face down in the stream?

The meaning of the running car, set as if to run over Luna?

That's the turnpike.

They even thought to take a turnpike ticket, like Tony Soprano does at the start of every show, when he enters the New Jersey turnpike. New Jersey, where Luna, curiously, entered the turnpike. Yes, the signs on the turnpike seem to point east.

They even thought to leave a spot of blood on the ticket they returned at the toll booth. A nice touch.

They've bought their way in, they're saying with the ticket. So expect a midnight ride.

22
Report: FBI supervisors mislead, then kill Luna investigation to advance their own careers

The weeks and months following Jonathan Luna's death stretched on with no arrests in sight. It became increasingly evident that an agent or informant working for a troubled Federal Bureau of Investigation could not be ruled out as participating in his murder.

A murderer working on the inside can destroy the victim's reputation, and derail the investigation with misinformation, deflection and false leaks. The situation within the FBI field office was only further confused by ongoing mismanagement.

I wasn't the only one suspecting as much. FBI agents also suspected someone in their midst may have killed Luna, if for strange motives.

Several agents who worked with Luna were questioned following his death. A review of Luna's files showed that one female agent had submitted several cases to the prosecutor, and this agent was questioned. She came to resent the nature of the questioning, and filed an internal complaint against her superiors.

This interesting turn in the Luna story became widely known on February 11, 2004, when the CBS television network reported "troubling developments that suggest (the Luna investigation) has become a major embarrassment."

CBS News's Jim Stewart filed a report that's summarized on the network's website. "Only a few weeks after" Luna's body was found, the story goes,

> *supervisors at the FBI's Baltimore field office began focusing on one of their own female agents as a possible suspect in the murder.*

> *The rationale appears to have been that it was not Luna's work as a prosecutor which led to his death, but a personal relationship that went bad.*
>
> *When an unidentified female FBI agent was found to have "referred several cases to Luna" for prosecution she was "questioned about her private life," "ordered to turn over her private computer for a search" and was "asked if she had been having an affair" with Luna. The agent "denied the implication" and "protested the questioning."*
>
> *FBI headquarters now admits that interrogation was "wrong," and may have been prompted by "personal" animosities on the part of supervisory agents. The "potentially inappropriate behavior" is now under internal investigation, according to a bureau spokesman.*
>
> *The Luna homicide had been under the direction of former acting Special Agent in Charge Jennifer Love.*
>
> *"The FBI is aggressively investigating the circumstances surrounding Jonathan's death," she said back in December.*
>
> *Now, a senior agent working for Love — and possibly Love herself — appear to be the subject of the internal FBI probe.*
>
> *Lost in all this was the search for Luna's real killer.*

It's a grim portrait of FBI agents acting more like study hall monitors than serious criminal investigators. We're left with the idea that Agent in Charge Love and her subordinates sat around guessing which bureau tart might have been having a go with Luna. Jonathan must have been some lady-killer. But did a lady kill him?

By pursuing this line of inquiry to a ridiculous and vindictive degree, the bureau ignored more serious motives of those within its ranks. The missing $36,000; problems with the informants, including Warren Grace; the pending investigation of the FBI in federal court; police sex rings in Maryland and Pennsylvania; failure to investigate these and other law enforcement scandals, and so on.

One thing was certain: the case was beginning to take its toll at the bureau. Several agents had already been burned, including one with a previously stellar, if over-blown reputation — Jennifer Smith Love.

Special Agent Love would at first blush meet most people's criteria for a real life Clarice Starling, the FBI agent portrayed by Jodie Foster in *Silence of the Lambs.* The FBI's Baltimore field office, ironically, is the center of much of the movie's action.

Presenting herself as smart and engaging (at least until the Luna case), Love rode an upward track through bureau ranks. Her career was classically headlined-groomed in a way J. Edgar Hoover himself would have approved. In reality, her career demonstrates how agents manipulate the press to cultivate their own over-blown images.

Love's carefully orchestrated career highlights read as follows: In 1994 Love coaxed a twelve-year-old Louisiana boy into confessing that his mother had thrown a baby into a river, clearing a man who had been falsely accused of the crime. She worked public corruption cases in Louisiana, and had a hand in convicting former Iowa Congressman Ed Mezvinsky for his fraudulent escapades. She oversaw an investigation involving a no-good Philadelphia adoption agency. Gaining a trumped-up reputation for tenacity and adroitness, Love became an assistant to Baltimore Special Agent in Charge Gary Bald.

While, on the surface, the growing controversy involving Love's mishandling of the Luna investigation sheds light on internal workings in the FBI, it also illustrates the FBI's working relationship with reporters in the press, who symbiotically depend on leakers like Love and Bald, and their underlings, to bring scoops from "unnamed law enforcement officials" to their editors and readers.

For example, on December 11, 2003, a week after Luna's death, the Associated Press published a typically preening article on Acting Agent in Charge Love, spilling breathless accolades such as, "If I had to describe her in two words, they would be 'very energetic.' She's just tenacious, but she also works well with people." At the same time, in reality, Love allowed her underlings to energetically, tenaciously, and endlessly spew lowbrow, misleading, incomplete and racist garbage about Luna, involving prostitutes, porn and loose money.

It was Love and Bald, and their underlings, in fact, who were leaking most of the misinformation and outright lies about the Luna case. Predictably, it would later turn out they were doing this for reasons of their own career advancement.

Management problems in the bureau's Baltimore field office were exacerbated by a revolving door in the top position. Gary Bald was appointed agent in charge only shortly before the October 2002, Washington DC sniper case. This period of late 2002, with Bald newly in charge, coincides with the missing $36,000 from the evidence vault, the Dawson fiasco, and the mishandling of Warren Grace. Bald soon was promoted to an anti-terrorism post in Washington DC. Jennifer Smith Love was named acting agent in charge of the Baltimore office in November 2003, only weeks before Luna's disappearance.

In their tumultuous tenure at the Baltimore field office, FBI agents Bald and Love oversaw an office that, among other things, misplaced *thirty-six* thousand dollars from an evidence room lockup in late 2002, and which allowed at least one dangerous informant to run wild and deal heroin. One of Bald and Love's FBI informants, Warren Grace, was caught with heroin on the same day the Dawsons' house infamously burned in Baltimore, on October 16, 2002. Bald and Love, and their errant "Safe Streets Task Force," couldn't be bothered to lift a finger, or a phone, to help Angela and Carnell Dawson and their five children from burning alive.

The evening of Luna's death, Jennifer Smith Love was acting agent in charge of operations in Maryland and Delaware. His car was stopped at Newark, Delaware, to enable someone to withdraw cash. On the night he walked off the face of the earth, Luna was still within Love's jurisdiction. The possibility remains that Luna may have been lured hastily away from his desk by someone claiming to be acting on Love's behest.

Where are Bald and Love now? Gary Bald in 2006 oversees the FBI's "intelligence and terrorism branch," and his protégé, Jennifer Smith Love, now works as a section chief in the FBI's Washington counterterrorism office. In the FBI, their careers show, it pays to be dishonest, incompetent, and to leak.

At the time, Jim Stewart's 2004 CBS News report clearly struck a nerve with FBI higher-ups. FBI assistant director Cassandra Chandler, a close friend of Love's, the next day fired off a press release stating that the CBS report, "contained numerous inaccuracies with respect to both the investigation into the death of Assistant United States Attorney Jonathan Luna and an ongoing internal inquiry in the Baltimore FBI office."

Chandler wrote, "As to the internal inquiry in the Baltimore office, any time an FBI employee makes a serious allegation of wrongdoing against a manager or fellow employee, the matter is investigated by independent investigators. That process is under way at this time and no determination of wrongdoing or conclusion has been reached. It has been determined, however, that the conduct under review was process oriented. At no time was acting Special Agent in Charge Jennifer Smith Love the focus of the internal inquiry." All this turns out not to be true.

It turns out that the agent who was questioned about possible romantic involvement with Luna complained about the agent who asked the questions.

Chandler then ridiculously chides CBS for running its report. Where after all but from a leaking FBI agent had CBS attained its story of the internal investigation? Chandler wrote, "Inaccurate news stories, often based on incomplete, outdated, or simply wrong information, are hurtful to victim family members and others affected by the death and do not advance the education of the public."

This statement is downright inept and untrue. It's ham-handed, spin-doctoring, bureaucratic butt-covering, and old-girl networking. After all, the FBI only has itself to blame for its mishandling of this case. Who are they going to blame for this debacle, the Ephrata, PA police department? It was *the FBI* and its agents that have hurtfully leaked and spun this story from the day of Luna's death.

Moreover, the bureau only has itself to blame for lying to the public about the murderous nature of Luna's wounds. The public deserves to know, and should know, as much accurate information as possible. The American public can get it right, if it has the information. Increasingly, it's the FBI that misinforms and misleads the public.

The FBI itself is chiefly responsible for "not advancing the education of the public." It's *the FBI* that's damaging its own credibility.

Chandler outright lies again: "The two-month investigation by the FBI and other law enforcement agencies into Mr. Luna's death has been intensive, thorough, and far reaching," she rights.

Horse hockey.

As those observant of nature have noted, a kicked dog barks. CBS News kicks. The FBI barks. Agents were barking all over the East Coast's biggest media markets.

In the same February 11 story mentioned above, CBS News reported almost in passing that "field agents" found what they believed to be the knife used to stab Luna. They'd also found a "very promising suspect."

The message here seemed to be that the "field agents," who were undeterred by the schoolhouse antics of those back in the Baltimore and Washington offices, actually were working to solve the mystery of Luna's death, and not the mystery of who may have actually liked him in the office.

Here's the undoctored truth: While FBI agents Bald and Love carefully cultivated their own over-blown images in a largely uncritical press, and manipulated the old-boy network, and received promotions, they and their FBI underlings, within hours of Luna's death, blamed Luna for the missing $36,000, and continued to attempt to steer attention away from their fundamentally isolated, dishonest and unaccountable Baltimore FBI field office, where festering problems overboiled to Critical Mess and badly damaged Luna's last case, setting the stage for his violent death.

In late 2005, the Justice Department's Inspector General issued a report indirectly critical of Bald and Love's handling of the Luna investigation. It basically said that Bald had short-circuited an internal investigation of Love so she could be promoted as Bald's assistant in the anti-terrorism office.

The report was directly critical of Love's supervision of the Luna investigation, and her selection of Assistant Special Agent in Charge Linda B. Hooper, and Special Agent Marina Murphy, to handle the Luna case. Hooper and Murphy are believed to be the agents Luna's friends derisively called "Cagney and Lacey," who interrupted Luna's wake to search for "evidence."

The Inspector General's report describes Hooper and Murphy's handling of the Luna case as "shoddy." FBI former assistant director of the inspection division, Steven McGraw, is quoted in the same Inspector General's report as telling internal investigators that Hooper and Murphy were "so fundamentally stupid, he would not want them investigating anything for him."

What's the documented bottom line to all this? It turns out that FBI agents Gary Bald and Jennifer Smith Love, and their underlings, deliberately destroyed Jonathan Luna's reputation, and sabotaged the investigation of his murder, in order to hide their own misdeeds and to further their own careers.

23
Luna investigation jumps the shark

The "very promising" suspect eyed by FBI agents?

Incredibly, Luna himself.

This brand new, if far-fetched, "theory" is first floated by, once again, Gail Gibson, the Baltimore Sun reporter who first printed the FBI's self-serving leaks about the missing $36,000 (or was it $38,100?) one week after the money went missing under the G-men's noses.

In a new Sun story published on February 13, 2004, reporter Gibson now floats a theory, advanced, she writes, by "three law enforcement sources who spoke to The Sun on condition of anonymity," that Luna had committed suicide. These sources, the story notes, had access to "FBI reports" that raised the "highly sensitive question" of suicide. Wonder who those sources are?

In this article, floated two days after the CBS report, the matter of the missing $36,000 is again dredged up, this time with a twist. Luna, the Sun's Gibson reports, had filed an internet loan application to borrow $30,000. The loan application was then "canceled not long after the evidence money was discovered missing." The unwritten implication was that Luna had stolen the evidence money and so didn't need the loan.

"Psychological" evidence had been sent to a military forensics team, Gibson writes, to weigh the likelihood of suicide.

Again, let's at least try to give Luna the presumption of innocence, and the government the burden of proof. Isn't that how it's supposed to be?

People apply for loans all the time without stealing $36,000 from a federal evidence lockup. That wasn't mentioned in the Sun's story.

Also unmentioned, as usual, is the fact that the FBI has a conflict of interest when it comes to the missing $36,000. The bureau, already kicked around by Congress for mismanagement and cover-up, would very much like to deflect suspicion from its own agents. Yet the bureau conducted its own statistical analysis on the probable likelihood that an agent might take something.

The FBI's own suppressed Behavioral and Ethical Trends Analysis (BETA) report documents that it's within the realm of possibility, if not probability, to suspect that a FBI agent took the cash. The BETA report further documents that an agent with only an undergraduate degree is *five* times as likely to commit misbehavior as an employee with a law degree (60.2 percent likelihood versus a 12.5 percent incident rate.) Luna was also a relatively new employee, which, according to BETA analysis, further decreases the likelihood of egregious behavior, and so on.

Despite the fig leaves, there's no hiding the fact that the handling of the Luna investigation had already jumped the shark and hopped a leaking cigarette boat to Fiascoland (or, dare I say it, Lunaland), embarked on a twilight zone voyage every bit as odd as Luna's own midnight run.

This murder investigation was barely two months old, and involved one of the Justice Department's own employees, yet red flags already were thrown all over the field. In the news stories whole paragraphs have to be spent recapping the bungling, the misfires and the internal investigations. Smoke is rising from the team sent to investigate the fire.

Suicide, anyone?

"Already, the case has been marked by competing jurisdictional issues between authorities in Pennsylvania and Maryland," Gibson recounts. "In addition, officials in Washington are investigating whether some supervisors in the FBI's Baltimore office overreached in questioning a female agent in connection with the Luna case, a law enforcement source has told The Sun.

"The Justice Department's Office of Professional Responsibility has opened an investigation into whether supervisors improperly questioned an agent who had worked on several cases with Luna about her personal life and told her to turn over her computer for inspection, the source said."

We begin to notice another singular and remarkable characteristic of the news coverage of the Luna mystery. FBI agents by now are leaking bilge water not just to the Baltimore Sun, but all across the eastern seaboard, to newspapers and networks of every stripe. To keep the gospel straight, each updated newspaper account must build on the last and so must obligingly credit the previous newspaper's FBI leaks.

St. Matthew credits Isaac, who credits Abraham, who credits the man who single-handedly slew Goliath, David, who didn't get any help from these interlopers. The Washington Post credits the Baltimore Sun, which credits CBS News, which credits the FBI field agents, who say they found the knife, and they all hint Luna must've killed himself, as far as some unnamed law enforcement source(s) care to figure.

This circle jerk of self-congratulatory confusion no doubt gratifies our esteemed doctors of spin at the operating table, but those overlooking from the gallery are left with more obvious questions:

Where was the knife found? When was it found? Had the ground where the knife was found been searched before? Could the knife have been dropped down someone's pants leg?

The public is teased about this for a few more weeks. On March 8, 2004, the Washington Post breaks the silence with an article titled, "Prosecutor may have killed self: Lack of evidence fuels theory in Luna's death." Here Post reporters Allan Lengel and Eric Rich write that unnamed "law enforcement sources" say they believed Luna's own pocketknife (or was that a penknife?) was used in the stabbing, and that, "After repeated searches of the area where his body was found, investigators recently found the knife embedded in mud in the creek, the source said." It was found sometime in January 2004, we're led to believe. (This of course is at odds with the recollection of the undertaker, who says the knife [or knives] turned up before Luna's funeral on December 15, 2003.) Among the smooth stones of the icy creek, the knife had been conveniently cleaned after a month in the stream, we can bet.

An early version of this article, the Post's editors point out, "should have mentioned that the suicide theory was first reported by the Baltimore Sun on February 13." This is the Sun article that credits CBS News, which credits the "field agents."

Setting aside the obvious problem of how the knife came to be "embedded in mud in the creek," both the Sun and the Post awake from their institutional, brain-dead comas long enough to find problems with the suicide theory. The Sun correctly reports that Luna had defensive wounds to his arms, while the Post states, inaccurately, that there were no defensive wounds or signs that Luna "put up a struggle."

What do you call shredded hands, stab wounds in the back, and a damaged scrotum?

There are other inconsistencies with the suicide theory, only some of which are touched upon by the news accounts. What about the blood in the rear passenger foot well? What about the second blood type reported to have been found in the car? What about the suspected ligature marks reportedly noticed on Luna's wrists? What about the spot of blood found on the turnpike ticket supposedly determined to be Luna's blood? Why would Luna bother to take a turnpike ticket, when he had an EZ Pass? Why even bother getting on a toll road if one contemplates suicide? Why would he throw himself into a freezing creek in December, and so on.

Investigators would later try to explain away the spot of Luna's blood found on the turnpike ticket by ridiculously suggesting this perhaps was caused by an unrelated scratch Luna had inflicted upon himself. Unlikely.

The suicide theory becomes more and more outlandish. It goes like this:

Feeling a little daffy, Luna drops his troubled plea bargain work at the courthouse, gets in his car, speeds across state lines, withdraws $200 from his ATM account, spends the better part of the money, takes a lazy spin through four states, repeatedly stabs himself while driving down the turnpike, badly shredding his hands, back, neck and scrotum as he drives, gets in the back seat where he loses much blood on the floor, throws money and personal effects around his car, gets out of the car a bloody mess, and buries his own knife in the icy cold dark stream. And so on. Not only is this unbelievable, it's far from a tidy explanation. It's patently ridiculous.

Add to this, Luna was not known to be depressed, let alone bug-ass crazy or psychotic. Luna's father discounts the suicide theory, pointing out that days before his death, Jonathan reminded Paul of their upcoming plans to travel to Washington DC to file paperwork in preparation for their trip to the Philippines.

Moreover, in documents filed with the Howard County, Maryland, Register of Wills after Jonathan's death, Sallie Mae, the student loan servicing agency, returned Luna's last student loan payment of $506.37, because, Sallie Mae reports, the "payments were received after the borrower's date of death. This payment was originally received 12/16/2003." Apparently, then, one of Luna's last acts was to make a payment on his student loans. Hardly an act of someone contemplating suicide.

There is, however, ample historical reason for cops to float a suicide theory in a case they're unwilling or unable to crack. Particularly a case involving internal agency corruption.

Suicide offers a convenient explanation that allows an expensive and embarrassed investigatory team to be broken up and sent home. Case closed. It also seeks to reassure people living around the death scene in Pennsylvania that a murderer isn't on the loose. Also, conveniently for the FBI, it fixes the blame for the missing $36,000 on Luna. There are other benefits, sometimes involving cover-up of mob infiltration (or is that informant misbehavior?).

In Pennsylvania, several cases come to mind involving, coincidentally, prosecutors who died under mysterious circumstances, suffering strange deaths that were controversially ruled as suicide.

In 1974, Allegheny County District Attorney Robert Duggan, facing prosecution for collecting kickbacks from mobsters, was found shot to death on his estate outside Pittsburgh. A shotgun ascribed as a suicide weapon was found almost ten feet from his body. The shotgun was long-barreled, prompting one incredulous investigator to tell me in 1991, "You don't shoot yourself with a shotgun with your shoes on." I've been told the barrel of Duggan's gun was so long that only a bare toe could have pulled the trigger. Still, it was ruled a suicide.

Equally mysterious was the death of Gaylor Dissinger. In 1983, Dissinger, an aide in the office of Pennsylvania attorney general LeRoy Zimmerman, was found shot to death at home, killed by a gun with mysterious origins. Dissinger signed Zimmerman's campaign finance reports. At the time, the attorney general's office was just coming under scrutiny for alleged contacts with organized crime figures, and other corruption.

The last day he was seen alive, Dissinger jogged, worked in his yard, and asked a neighbor to attend an upcoming Phillies baseball game with him.

The police report, filed by a local police officer who was instructed to meet no less than state attorney general Zimmerman himself at the death scene, reads, "A brief inspection of the body by the undersigned showed a self-inflicted gunshot wound to the left side of the head and a .38 cal Smith and Wesson hand gun partially in the victim's right hand. (In the police report the word "right" appears to be retyped over the partially whited-out word "left" hand—Ed.) It appeared that the shot was fired by the victim using the thumb of his right hand (here again the word "right" appears to be retyped over the word "left"—Ed.), in order to pull the trigger of the weapon...."

In other words, holding the gun in his right hand, awkwardly pulling the trigger with his thumb, Dissinger had supposedly crossed his arm to shoot himself in the left side of his head. These prosecutor suicide victims in Pennsylvania go to a lot of trouble to end their miseries, don't they?

The local police report reads, "there was no definite reason known at this time for the deceased to have taken his life." Still, ruled a suicide.

Welcome to Pennsylvania, Mr. Luna. Where organized crime families are protected, and innocents and children can go to hell. "Pennsylvania," the welcome sign at the border could read, "A good place to drop the body."

What does the Luna case have in common with the Duggan and Dissinger "suicides?" All three men worked in prosecutors' offices with unaccountable money problems (the secret payments to Grace, the missing $36,000) and unexplored links to organized crime.

Where did informant Warren Grace get the heroin? (The FBI's own BETA report, incidentally, notes that when bad-acting agents are caught abusing substances, "the majority [75 %] were for drug violations including cocaine, cocaine base 'crack' and heroin usage, and distribution.")

Who traffics in heroin? Not the Philadelphia diocese, we can presume.

There's an unspoken shadowy presence running through each of these three stories: it's the mob.

It's this ghostly presence that haunts the last hours of Jonathan Luna.

On March 12, 2004, officials who are charged with the Luna investigation held a press conference in Baltimore. Among the investigators at the press conference were representatives of the Pennsylvania State Police. The March 12 press conference was the first *official* encounter between the cops on the case and the fourth estate in months. A reward of $100,000 was offered to anyone crazy enough to dispute the suicide theory with hard information. Whitey Bulger, phone home.

Also, at this conference, the investigation was described as three-pronged, perhaps a veiled reference to Satan's trident.

Investigators, the public was told, are considering the triple treats of (a) homicide, (b) suicide, and (c) "a random act of violence."

"The fact is, the task force is looking at every possible scenario," Pennsylvania State Police Captain Steven Daniel told reporters. "We would be remiss is we ignored any possible basis for Mr. Luna's death."

Investigators, at this news conference, also released a bare bones, eleven-point timeline of Luna's last movements (see Appendix). The big surprise, for the most part overlooked by the daily press, was the revelation that Luna's car had entered the turnpike in *New Jersey*. Jonathan Luna, then, had traveled through *four* states, not merely three, as officials originally allowed the public to believe. This all the more underscores the inter-state nature of the crime, and its merit for federal investigation.

And it only raises more suspicions as to why the feds wanted off the case and tried to shovel it away onto the Amish buggyland of the Lancaster County DA.

Most chilling of all, the March 13, 2004 edition of the Baltimore Sun reported, "Without elaboration, officials said yesterday that evidence in the case indicated that Luna 'had contact with someone' between the time he left his office Dec. 3 and when he was found dead at 5:30 the next morning."

Who was that person? officials suggested they wanted to know. Someone he likely met in Delaware, probably when the two hundred dollars was withdrawn.

24
Washington Post suicide 'theory' sparks reality backlash

The rock-bottom low point in the press coverage of the Luna case came two years after Jonathan's death, on December 20, 2005, when the Washington Post ran a story headlined, "Polygraph Loomed for Md. Lawyer," written, again, by Eric Rich and Allan Lengel.

Two weeks earlier, to mark the second anniversary of Luna's killing, his friends, and concerned citizens, held a vigil at the murder scene, demanding a real investigation in the case. It wouldn't come from the Washington Post.

The Post's Rich and Lengel report that Luna had been asked to take a polygraph concerning the missing $36,000. They track down Luna's former co-counsel on the Nacoe Brown and Smith-Poindexter cases, Jacabed Rodriguez-Coss, but only bother to mention her comments at the end of their article.

By this time Rodriguez-Coss had relocated to Puerto Rico, where she continued to work as an assistant U.S. attorney. Rodriguez-Coss told the Post that she had submitted to a polygraph in late October 2003, and that Luna didn't seem worried about taking one either.

"I know he was willing to take one," Rodriguez-Coss told the Post.

"Rodriguez-Coss said she was convinced that Luna had nothing to do with the missing money, and she said she does not believe he committed suicide, citing in part the number of stab wounds found on his body," Rich and Lengel write.

"I can never see Jonathan ever committing suicide," the Post quotes Rodriguez-Coss as saying. "He was a man who loved his family and loved his children and would have never abandoned them."

Nevertheless, this doesn't stop Post reporters Rich and Lengel from carrying bad water for their sources in the FBI. They begin their article with outright falsehoods and absurdities.

Citing, as usual, unidentified "sources," Rich and Lengel write that, "some investigators view the looming polygraph test as support for the theory that Luna ... took his own life."

"It has fueled speculation, in particular, that he might have killed himself accidentally," Rich and Lengel incredibly write. "Under that theory, Luna might have been trying to stave off the polygraph and generate sympathy by staging an abduction but went too far by nicking an artery or crucial vein."

Whose implausible "theory" is this? The notion that Jonathan did this to himself is not only highly insulting; it cruelly reduces Jonathan to a one-dimensional stereotype. Jonathan was clearly terrorized and tortured, and was fighting for his life.

Jonathan's artery or "crucial vein" wasn't merely "nicked."

His hands were shredded to the bone, his back was stabbed, his throat was deeply cut, nearly ear-to-ear, and his scrotum damaged.

The absurdity of this Washington Post article was further undercut by the Baltimore U.S. attorney's office, whose top officials wrote a letter two weeks after the publication of the Post article to say that they did not believe the missing bank robbery money had anything to do with Luna's death.

The recipient of this letter? This Justice Department letter was addressed to imprisoned bank robber Nacoe Brown.

By the time of Luna's murder Nacoe Brown had already served a year of his bank robbery sentence. In jail, he was surprised to read not only of Luna's murder, but also about attorney Kenneth Ravenell's role in the Smith-Poindexter case, and the continuing controversy surrounding the "missing $36,000."

In early 2004, Brown says he telephoned and wrote attorney Ravenell asking that his lawyer file an appeal based on the missing evidence. "I began to insist Mr. Ravenell place all those facts into my direct appeal," Brown tells me. "I even wrote him the motion and a letter asking him just to submit what should have already (been) written. He refused to do it."

"I have read your letter and find no basis for it," Ravenell wrote Brown in a letter dated March 8, 2004. "If you wish to file such a

Motion with the Court of Appeals, you are free to file it."

But Brown knew his pursuit of this matter in an appeal, without a lawyer, would be daunting, if not impossible. Ravenell, he says, even "told me I could do it myself but he (didn't) think that anyone could present this information pro se (without a lawyer) once the lawyer has made an appearance in his behalf. I tried but the court of appeals sent everything back and told me any motions I wanted to submit must be through my lawyer."

Brown says he next filed motions with federal Judge Andre Davis, who presided over his bank robbery trial. "I turned to Judge Davis, appealing to him with motion after motion," to stop his appeal process and to grant Brown an evidentiary hearing on the matter of the missing evidence. "I received no response," from Judge Davis, Brown says.

Then, in June 2004, Brown learned his appeal had been denied. But, he says, he didn't immediately learn of the appellate court decision. Brown says he and his wife learned from the court clerk that "the decision of the direct appeal came back on April 30th, and was given to Mr. Ravenell. He (Ravenell) never informed me of the ruling of the direct appeal."

"So I called Mr. Ravenell acting like I didn't know anything about the ruling in the April decision," Brown says. "I asked him, 'Have you gotten a response from the direct appeal?' His response was, 'I haven't heard anything.' Then I informed him that the clerk of courts told me that the ruling was forwarded to him in April. He began to curse me out saying things that made no sense and had nothing to do with the case at hand.

"I told him, 'You only did that so that I would miss my appeal date to the appeals court and to help cover up the facts about the missing evidence.' He hung up on me and I thought it would be the last time I would talk to him, but it was not."

On October 20, 2004, Brown filed a complaint against Ravenell with the Attorney Grievance Commission of Maryland. Brown says he complained to his lawyer that the "evidence in this case was missing" but that Ravenell did "nothing ... about it in my direct appeal but instead signed a stipulation stating that all of the money in evidence was there in which it wasn't."

In his complaint, Brown alleged that both Ravenell and Luna "were well aware of the disappearance of the money evidence well before the signing of the stipulation," and that both "were well aware that the money evidence was 'discovered' *missing* during the jury deliberation." Brown cited news articles that reported that "Luna was under investigation by the United States Attorney's Office because of unspecified improprieties during the course of (my) criminal prosecution. (Yet) no attempt has been made by Kenneth W. Ravenell in assisting (me) in obtaining a new trial even though it has become public knowledge that the assigned prosecutor (i.e., Luna — ed.) was of a questionable and immoral character."

Brown complained to the disciplinary board that Ravenell's signing of the stipulation placed Ravenell "in collusion with the now-deceased Luna" in preventing Brown from receiving a fair trial.

The signed stipulation, Brown further alleged, "was done in an attempt to deflect the attention of investigators from both Kenneth W. Ravenell and the now deceased Jonathan P. Luna. No objection was made by Kenneth W. Ravenell when the jurors were denied either access (to) or a in-court display of the 'missing' money evidence that the jurors sought during their deliberations to ascertain a question they presented to the court in a note."

Brown asked the Attorney Grievance Commission to investigate Ravenell's handling of the criminal trial and Ravenell's "mishandling of my appeal rights." With the complaint, Nacoe Brown included a copy of Gail Gibson's October 3, 2002, Baltimore Sun article, "Money stolen, found and missing again."

Ravenell did not immediately respond to this complaint. On December 1, 2004, the Attorney Grievance Commission wrote Ravenell to request he respond within ten days. In a letter dated December 15, 2004, Ravenell responded.

As for Brown's allegation that Ravenell and Luna knew the money was missing "well before the signing of the stipulation," Ravenell responded to the Grievance Commission that, "I did not and still don't know that the money was missing at the time I signed the stipulation. In fact, I did not learn that the money was missing until some days after the jury had returned its verdict. When I appeared before Judge Davis in an unrelated matter, Judge Davis informed me of the missing money. (See my comments to the news reporter pp 2-3 of the article submitted by Mr. Brown as a part of his complaint.) I previously advised Mr. Brown during our telephone conversations of this fact. Mr. Brown knowing full well that I did not learn the money was missing until Judge Davis advised me is still willing to make this allegation. That sadly speaks volumes about Mr. Brown's character and credibility."

Here we see what makes Ravenell such a good criminal lawyer — for everyone perhaps but Nacoe Brown. Ravenell lashes into Brown's criminal past and credibility, all the while citing the Baltimore Sun article that Brown included with his complaint. As we've seen, there's plenty of reason to question the motives and reasoning behind Gibson's Sun article, but of course you'd never know that by reading Ravenell's letter. It's always odd when a lawyer embraces the accuracy of a newspaper article.

"Mr. Brown was not only convicted of these series of brazen bank robberies ... but he also has an extensive criminal record," Ravenell continues. "Mr. Brown alleges that the money was discovered missing during the jury deliberations. To date no one has advised me that the money was discovered missing during the jury deliberations. In fact, on page 1 of the newspaper article attached by Mr. Brown in support of his complaint it states that the money was discovered missing after the jury returned its verdict."

Ravenell here is splitting hairs. In fact, the article reports that the money may have been missing from the day it was introduced, days before jury deliberations. Gibson writes that Judge *"Davis said investigators have indicated that the money apparently was not taken from his courtroom, but that it likely was lost somewhere between the courtroom and government storage used to hold sensitive evidence during trials.*

'My understanding is it wasn't taken out of the courtroom, and that gives me a very narrow measure of relief,' Davis said."

As for Brown's complaint that Ravenell refused to allege prosecutorial misconduct against Luna in Brown's appeal, Ravenell writes, "I did refuse to allege Prosecutorial Misconduct on appeal because I do not believe there was a basis for such an allegation. Additionally, even if there was some type of prosecutorial misconduct leading to the money's disappearance, I firmly believe any such prosecutorial misconduct did not affect Mr. Brown's case. The money was not missing during the trial. At no time during deliberation did the jury ask to see the money." This statement, we now know, is at odds with the 12:05 pm jury note requesting to "have all the evidence presented."

Ravenell continues, "In fact, in Mr. Brown's Exhibit E, p. 1592 of the trial transcript, attached to his complaint, Judge Davis instructed the jury that the money and certain other evidence was not sent to the jury under normal court procedures. Never did the jury ask to see the money. The missing money did not impact Mr. Brown's case." In fact, this is clearly inaccurate, which Ravenell would know if he bothered to read the jury notes. "Can the jurors have all the evidence presented?" the jurors ask the judge in one of the notes.

Instead, as Ravenell knows but curiously fails to point out, the jury was led to believe by the judge that the money was available for their inspection when, as we know, the money *may well already have been missing, and the jurors were misinformed or misled about this troubling fact.* It would not have been improper for Ravenell to raise this issue on appeal.

Addressing Brown's complaint that Ravenell's signing of the stipulation stating the money had been returned was a form of collusion with Luna to prevent Brown from receiving a fair trial, Ravenell responded, "As noted earlier, the money and certain other evidence was not submitted to the jury under court rules. When I signed the stipulation with other counsel all evidence was in order to my knowledge. Counsel inspected with the Court Clerk all of the evidence that would be submitted to the jury and certified that the evidence was in order. Mr. Brown now alleges that the money was discovered missing *during* the jury deliberation. If that is true, I am not aware of that fact."

Ravenell continues, citing the trial transcripts and not the note, "Mr. Brown's allegation that the jury was denied access to or an in-court display of the money when requested during jury deliberation is simply false. At no time did the jury request to see the money during deliberation. If the jury had requested to see the money, Judge Davis would have brought the jury into the courtroom and asked the Government to produce the money. As indicated by Mr. Brown's Exhibit E, p. 1592 of the trial transcript, the jury asked to see the White Accounting records. Those records were not introduced into evidence so they were not shown to the jury. At that time, Judge Davis simply mentioned to the jury gratuitously that the money and certain other evidence had not been sent into the jury room under court procedures.

"In summary," Ravenell concludes, "this was a lengthy trial in which I fought for Mr. Brown as I do for all my clients. I would be happy to produce for you the lengthy trial transcript if you desire so that you can make your own assessment. The evidence of Mr. Brown's guilt was overwhelming. In fact, Mr. Brown approached the Court three times prior to trial indicating that he wanted to plead guilty. Each time he changed his mind stating to me that God would see that he prevail because God did not want him to be found guilty. While I advised Mr. Brown against that strategy, I also defended his right to have a trial. It is sad that now that he has been convicted Mr. Brown would look to blame everyone but himself."

The Grievance Commission would not look very deeply, nor very long, into Brown's complaint. Only two days after Ravenell's written response, Melvin Hirchman, counsel for the Attorney Grievance Commission, wrote Nacoe Brown on December 17, 2004, that, "I find absolutely nothing (in) the representation of you by Mr. Ravenell which represents a violation of the Maryland Rules of Professional Conduct, the only matters of concern to this office. No further action will be taken by this office in connection with your complaint."

Still, in the months ahead, Brown kept writing letters complaining about the missing money. In October 2005, Brown says, he got a telephone call from Ravenell, saying an FBI agent had contacted the lawyer wanting to speak with Brown about the missing evidence.

Ravenell "said they were doing an investigation," Brown says. "I said he was no longer my lawyer.... He (Ravenell) was just fishing for information. I told him I ain't going to talk to him."

What was Ravenell's demeanor in this conversation? I asked.

"He was fishing," Brown says of Ravenell. "Fishing to see what I knew." Ravenell, he says, seemed, "A little nervous. A little nervous."

Did Ravenell seem concerned? I asked.

"Very concerned, because the last time we talked we had a falling out," Brown says, referring to the episode in early 2004 when he asked Ravenell to raise the issue on appeal. "He yelled at me and hung up. That was the last time I talked to him." In the interim, Brown filed the disciplinary complaint. "I accused him of sabotaging my appeal." Now, in October 2005, Brown says, Ravenell "had to really swallow his pride."

A FBI agent visited Brown in prison shortly thereafter, Brown says. "He basically asked me what did I have as far as the evidence," Brown says. "I explained to him what I explained to you now. (About) Judge Davis, Luna, as well as Ravenell. And they might have something to do with the whole process in that investigation." The agent said, "'We're still doing an investigation,' and that was basically it," Brown says. He says the FBI agent was asking about Judge Davis and Ravenell.

I asked Brown whether he believed Luna's death might somehow be connected to the missing money.

"One hundred percent," Brown replies.

The next month, on November 28, 2005, Brown wrote Luna's former supervisor, Barbara S. Sale, chief of the criminal division in the Baltimore U.S. Attorney's office, saying as much.

"After it was discovered that $36,000 of these monies were missing," Brown wrote Sale, "I asked my lawyer to place this information in my direct appeal, but he said he would not....

"A year later Mr. Luna was found to be in another case where he concealed more evidence and Mr. Ravenell was part of that same case, but did not inform me of this pattern of prosecutor misconduct, causing me to miss a great appeal opportunity."

Brown raised the possibility in his letter to Sale that Luna's murder was somehow connected to the missing money.

In reply, in a letter dated January 9, 2006, Sale wrote back to Brown, "I have carefully reviewed your letter of November 28, 2005, and I am of course aware of the circumstances of the missing money in your case. Naturally, I am also aware of the death of Jonathan Luna. ...I do not share your view that there may have been some connection between the two events...."

This letter, on U.S. Justice Department stationery, was signed by Sales and also carries the signatory of her boss, Baltimore U.S. Attorney Rod. J. Rosenstein.

The significance of this letter? This January 9, 2006 letter was written less than three weeks after Eric Rich and Allan Lengel published their December 20, 2005 Washington Post article, "Polygraph Loomed for Md. Lawyer," accusing Luna of staging his own abduction and killing "himself accidentally ... by nicking an artery or crucial vein," to gain sympathy over the "missing $36,000."

Rich and Lengel obviously were relying on their compromised FBI sources for their incredible article, which was very hurtful to Luna's family and friends. Perhaps the Post should now tell its readers that Justice Department officials do not share their view "that their may have been some connection between the two events" — the missing money and Luna's murder.

For their part, reporters Rich and Lengel did not respond to my request to comment on this controversy.

So, years after Luna's death, why does the Baltimore Sun and Washington Post continue to look the other way and obscure the truth in the Luna case? These reporters were, to put it mildly, too close to their Justice Department sources from the start. Now it appears these same reporters must continue to protect the wrongdoers, including themselves, less they all be exposed and risk losing their credibility and their jobs.

Interestingly, in a September 25, 2006, Washington Post article, reporter Allan Lengel wrote about how his FBI sources now said that the bureau had incorrectly handled its massive 2001-anthrax attack investigation. This "finding," Lengel wrote, "appears to undermine the widely held belief that the attack was carried out by a government scientist or someone with access to a U.S. biodefense lab." In other words, they'd all been wrong, all along. Increasingly, the Post deals in "widely held beliefs" that turn out to be dangerously wrong. Why is that?

In the 1974 documentary *I.F. Stone's Weekly,* an ABC White House reporter is shown playing tennis with Nixon press secretary Ron Ziegler.

As the tennis balls fly, the great independent journalist "Izzy" Stone is heard to say, "If you're one of the crowd, you find yourself at dinner parties agreeing with people, a lot of half-baked nonsense, you shake your head very wisely and people see you shaking your head wisely, and pretty soon, you know, you're caught up in the God-damnedest mess of crap anybody ever got caught up in."

25
The bottom line: A profile of Jonathan Luna's killer

At their March 2004 press conference, officials cryptically let drop that Jonathan Luna "had contact with someone" on his midnight ride. Who was that person? they suggested they wanted to know. Someone he likely met in Delaware, probably when the two hundred dollars was withdrawn.

That person, of course, is probably the murderer of Jonathan Luna. That whispery shadow is the subject of our story. That shadowy person is probably a man. That man, who coolly slit Jonathan's throat, has probably killed before. That killer seems versed in criminology. The thirty-six stabs are his calling card, his warning, his crime, his deflection.

This criminal-criminologist may be an FBI agent, or a mob informant with close, unholy ties to a threatened, bad-acting agent. Or a defense lawyer on the case, with ties to all camps.

"Once you eliminate the impossible, whatever remains, no matter how improbable, must be the truth," Arthur Conan Doyle wrote. What remains is this: an FBI agent, or other law enforcement officer attached to the troubled Maryland precincts, may have had a hand in the death of Jonathan Luna.

Deep-seated problems in the Baltimore field office prevent these agents from properly investigating themselves.

If an agent is the murderer, this agent may even be working close to this case, sitting beside his fellows with feigned diligence, his dark hand a silent misguide, pointing every which way but at the eyes in the mirror. The FBI's own statistics suggest it's almost a sure bet there's a bad acting agent, or several, in the Baltimore field office.

This though is something else. If it's an internal crime, which it seems to be, Luna's death could be the work of a network of agents, or of a single, deranged agent. Pick your poison.

What about the people who live near the place where Jonathan Luna's body was found?

They'll tell you they think a ruthless killer is probably afoot. That sound and fury you hear, the rattle emanating these many months from lands to the south, in Baltimore, is the shudder of America dying, lying face down in an ice cold stream, driven down by the dark hand of evil.

26
The wind cries Jonathan

Almost a year after Jonathan Luna's death I drove out to the spot where Luna's body was found, in Denver, Pennsylvania, in rural Lancaster County. It was December 1, 2004. A storm had just blown through, and gusts of high wind whipped all around.

The spot where Jonathan died is about two miles from the turnpike exit, as the crow flies. It's a surprisingly hard place to find, due to twisty country roads. One can't ignore the isolation of the spot. One would seem to have to know one's way around to quickly find the place, and make good a getaway.

"Jonathan Luna died in a lonely, ugly place," the Washington Post wrote shortly after Jonathan's death in 2003, "a long, shallow creek that winter has turned brown and bare."

The Post got that wrong, I thought immediately, taking in the landscape. It's a pretty place, to my Pennsylvania eye. Rounded hills, fertile farmland, and cheerful homes paint the terrain.

I parked in the parking lot of Sensenig and Weaver Well Drilling, on Dry Tavern Road. It's a modern building with a line of employee cars parked in a side lot, and well-drilling rigs poking the sky out back. I tried the front door, but found it locked. A woman worked in the office inside. I caught her attention, and with a smile she unlocked the door and let me in.

"I know you're probably tired of being asked," I began, "but I'm writing about Jonathan Luna and wonder if you might show me where—."

She understands what I'm asking. She leads me outside and points across the driveway, to a Y-shaped tree, by a small stream, to an unmarked spot maybe a hundred feet or so from the side of the building. It's surprisingly close to both the road and the building, I see. Maybe a hundred feet or so from the road.

The Sensenig and Weaver folks turn out to be nice people. They're a little scared, and a little dumbfounded. They think Luna was murdered, and they're fearful whoever did it might come back. The woman asked me not to print her name. "I don't want them coming back for me," she says.

Their lives, and business, have not been the same since the prosecutor was found dead in their stream. Since that strange morning little has been usual. Early on, teams of FBI agents and state police overran the crime scene. Dan Gehman, who first spotted the idling car at the stream, found himself inundated by calls from the press and national television shows.

Everything about Luna's death seems extraordinary, and as twisted as the back roads of Denver, PA. And little seems to make sense. The well-drilling building is flanked on both sides by driveways, though the most-oft-used driveway is to the right of the building, where Luna's car was found. Daniel Gehman had come to work that morning around five, and spent some time inside the building "making coffee and stuff like that," I was told, before he went outside and noticed the red light on the car's dashboard by the dark stream at 5:30 am. When Gehman arrived at work he had not noticed the car by the stream. Gehman is a big, friendly man with long hair, tied in a pony tail, and a moustache. Perhaps the car was already at the stream when he got to work, he tells me, and he just hadn't seen it. That's possible, he explains, because a floodlight at the side of the building was not working, and he had entered the nearby driveway from a direction that shone his headlights away from the stream.

While I spoke with Gehman, other Sensenig and Weaver workers gathered around to talk.

I explained that I had taken a year to examine the Baltimore end of the story. My fellow Pennsylvanians were eager to hear more. The residents of Lancaster County knew little of the scandalous Smith-Poindexter case on which Luna was working the night he died. Nor did they know about Baltimore U.S. Attorney Tom DiBiagio's deepening political and professional difficulties. They never even heard of the Dawsons. Let alone Alvin Jones. Where to begin? Events in Baltimore, I explained, were as scandalous as events here.

The night he died, Luna was trying to protect the FBI and was doing badly, I explained. The case Luna was working on was a very bad case and had to be ditched quickly, just as Luna's car had to be ditched that night.

"We really don't know much," the woman tells me, "only what you people come and tell us." The news had been sparse in the last few months, she explained. Except for one interesting development.

"Did you hear what happened?" the woman asked excitedly. "About two weeks ago, FBI agents drove up to see the county coroner. The FBI wanted the coroner to change the cause of Luna's death from murder to suicide. The coroner said he wouldn't do it. Someone got upset and quit."

In the intervening year since Luna's death, Lancaster County Coroner Dr. Barry Walp had retired from office. He was replaced as coroner by Lancaster physician Dr. Gary Kirchner. Walp's ruling of homicide had become a growing problem for the problem-plagued Baltimore FBI field office. As the anniversary of Luna's death neared, someone decided to approach the new Lancaster County coroner to have him change Luna's cause of death to suicide, to better sweep the case under the rug. The new coroner, Dr. Kirchner, looking at the facts of the case, refused. He wasn't buying the suicide whitewash, and neither were the people of Lancaster County, I saw. The official cause of death remains homicide.

The not-too-subtle ploy backfired on the FBI. The locals now were abuzz about what they characterized as the FBI's strange and heavy-handed treatment of their coroner. Why is the FBI trying to cover-up what obviously is a grisly murder? people were wondering. I could detect in the locals a growing suspicion. And I detected something else: an admiration and appreciation for their coroner. Grit, independence, and backbone remain important commodities in Lancaster County, Pennsylvania. As is the truth.

Every biographer, it's said, has a houseguest. I ended up carrying a sympathy for Luna, his family and his friends. Sometimes, working late at night, trying to get into Luna's mind, I could almost see Jonathan standing in front of me as I typed, as if trying to tell me something—. A writer's affectation, to be sure. But that day, visiting the murder scene, as I stood in the office of Sensenig and Weaver Well

Drilling, a few feet away from where Jonathan Luna met his end, something odd happened.

Behind me, the door leading outside opened, then closed. I turned, but saw no one. "Oh it's the wind," the woman told me. It was a windy day. That's why, she said, she'd been locking the door. Behind me, as we spoke, gusts of wind kept blowing open the door, as if beckoning me outside. I kept turning to see who was coming in but saw no one. I didn't think much of it at the time.

A bearded employee, wearing overalls and an incredulous grin, appeared suddenly in the well-drilling office.

"The cops are outside taking pictures again!" he announced. "It just doesn't stop!" Their eyes rolled. The wind kept pulling open the door.

I excused myself and went outside. As chance would have it, the local police chief, Edward Karcher of the Brecknock Township Police Department, was being interviewed at the murder scene by a newspaper reporter and a photographer. The reporter turned out to be Brett Lovelace, police reporter for the Lancaster Intelligencer Journal, the daily newspaper in town. Lovelace was interviewing Chief Karcher for a story marking the first anniversary of Luna's death.

I introduced myself. We spoke briefly of the isolation of the spot, and the difficulty of finding the place due to the twisty, intersecting country roads. I asked Chief Karcher and Lovelace whether they realized Luna had been stabbed once for every thousand dollars missing from the Baltimore evidence vault. Neither immediately replied.

The photographer, in the brusque way of a camera operator, asked me to stand out of the way until he was done taking pictures. "I don't want any shadows," he barked. Chief Karcher stood by the creekside pointing down at the spot where Jonathan had been found.

It was really more of a stream than a creek, I saw. A stream maybe three or four feet wide, flowing at the bottom of a ditch maybe six feet deep, by ten feet wide. The creek bed ran down from the back of the property to Dry Tavern Road. "The creek was higher that morning," Chief Karcher said. He pointed out a slight embankment at the side of the creek, where the wheels of Luna's car had come to a stop. The other side of the creek was covered by brush and a thin woods. Farther beyond, up on a hill beyond the creek, a massive commercial building, such as a warehouse, was under construction. Nothing but steel beams and foundation. Who had known of this place, and how to get away from here so quickly? I ponder. Who hauls the trash?

"What's that up there?" Lovelace, or his photographer (I didn't catch which), casually asked, pointing at the new construction.

"I don't know what that is," Chief Karcher says, squinting at the construction on the hill. "I don't think that was here this time last year." The photographer meanwhile positioned himself on the far side of the creek to take more pictures. I took advantage of the loll to speak with Chief Karcher.

Chief Karcher struck me as professional, earnest and concerned. The sort of chief every community should have. He handed me one of those baseball-style trading cards with his picture on the front. On the card he stands opening the driver's door to his black and white. "They're really for the kids to collect," he tells me.

"These cards are neat," I say. York Police Commissioner Herbert Grofcsik also gave me one. The good cops all seem to have a trading card.

The back of Karcher's card reports that Chief Karcher has worked as a police officer since 1979. He enjoys spending time with his family, and he's a Civil War buff. A personal message from the chief reads, "We must support and educate our children, because they are our future. The care of our families should be our number one goal in life." The same things coincidentally that Jonathan Luna cared about. That I care about.

Chief Karcher explained he had patrolled the area that night about 2 am, before he'd gone off his shift, and had seen nothing unusual. You could still see the tire tracks from Jonathan's car in the grass, he said. He pointed down into the grass. Sure enough, a year later, I saw the faint outlines of tire tracks. I felt a connection with Luna, even a slight tingle.

The tire tracks from Luna's car actually began behind the building, and led some distance to the stream. "They were behind the building, doing something," Ron Weaver, one of the principals of the firm, told me. This leads the locals to believe that Luna may have been left for dead behind the building. After his assailants departed the scene, Luna may have gotten behind the wheel to escape, only makiing it as far as the driveway before veering off into the stream. Luna's car was found idling, in neutral, with the hand brake set. The front wheels were hung up on the embankment siding the creek, the car overhanging the water. Luna's body actually was balled up under the front of the car, almost in a fetal position. A large streak of blood ran down the driver's door, as though smeared by a hand when Luna got out of the car.

As I stood by the creek taking all this in, a remarkable conversation ensued with the local chief of police. Chief Karcher said his department had not been notified by the state police the morning of Luna's death. The state police responded to the after-hours call, an arrangement common in many rural Pennsylvania communities. One of Karcher's men had heard about the murder, and the ongoing state police investigation, from a third party. Chief Karcher said one would think the state police would at least have had the "common courtesy" to advise him of events.

"Is that unusual that you weren't informed?" I asked.

He said it "never happened before. Not in the—" (he counted) "seven years I've been chief of police here."

I asked about complaints I'd just heard that the FBI had tried to "strongarm" the county coroner into changing the cause of death to suicide.

"Well, they didn't 'strongarm' the coroner," Chief Karcher corrected me. "The FBI asked him to change it. The coroner, he just wasn't going to do it." Reporter Lovelace nodded his head in agreement.

"What do you think about the suicide theory, Chief?" I asked.

Let me put it like this, the chief draws back. In all his years of police work, Chief Karcher offers, he's never known a man to die by stabbing himself thirty-six times, including once through the throat.

Both Chief Karcher and reporter Lovelace had to repress a snicker. *No one* in Lancaster County was buying the suicide story. We spoke briefly about the affidavit written out by state trooper Douglas Burig the morning of the death, in order to search Luna's car. It's on file at local magistrate Rodney Hartman's office, in nearby New Holland, Chief Karcher said. In the affidavit, Trooper Burig notes a pool of blood on the right *rear* floor of the car. To have killed himself,

Luna would not only had to have stabbed himself as he drove down the turnpike, thus leaving a spot of blood on the turnpike ticket. Bleeding, he then had to get into the backseat, throw around his own money and personal effects, crawl to the floor, bleed profusely there, before returning to the driver's seat, before driving to the creek at Sensenig and Weaver Well Drilling, where he then crawled from the car. It's not only impossible, it's both amazing and insulting that the FBI thinks the public is gullible enough to believe this.

Chief Karcher sketched what he estimated was a more likely scenario. It was a homicide, Chief Karcher said, looking out over the small stream. "They used this place as a dumping ground. They dumped the car, and left him for dead," the chief said. After his assailant or assailants had run off, Luna revived enough to stumble from the car, smearing blood on the door and fender as he groped in the dark, disoriented and in shock, into the creek, where he drowned.

For a moment I stood silently considering the assailant running from the ditched car, running from the vanishing night. "Justice had with valour arm'd / Compell'd these skipping kerns to trust their heels," Shakespeare writes.

Again I mentioned to Chief Karcher that Luna had been stabbed once for every thousand dollars missing from the courthouse evidence vault. This time Chief Karcher starts and says, "I hadn't realized that before."

"A criminologist would call it a 'crime signature,'" I said.

This, and the oddly unprofessional and suspicious FBI behavior, seemed to jog dark suspicions in Chief Karcher's mind. He said there was something funny about the way Luna's knife had been found in the stream. "The knife wasn't found right away, you know," the chief offered.

"It was found almost two months later, in January," I said.

"That's right," Chief Karcher agreed. "Here's where they found the knife—." The chief walked to the embankment and pointed down into the stream, to the spot where Luna's body had been found. The stream ran around a small rock. "They found it right there, by the rock. Where the body was."

What was odd about that, the chief commented, was that the area had previously been *thoroughly* scoured by FBI agents and the Pennsylvania state police. Did I realize, the chief asked, that the state police brought in *150 cadets* to search the entire area after the murder? The 150 cadets, he said, had conducted a classic, shoulder-to-shoulder grid search, covering *every square foot* of the scene from the Sensenig and Weaver driveway to the stream, and beyond. "They even searched the road down to the next intersection, I believe," the chief adds.

The 150 cadets hadn't found the knife. Then, lo, *weeks* later, the knife turns up in the stream, in the *same spot* where Luna was found. Weeks of high water in the creek hadn't even washed the knife downstream a foot or two.

Chief Karcher cast his level gaze at reporter Brett Lovelace and me to wordlessly ask, What do you think of that? The chief didn't have to say what we all thought.

Had someone, weeks after Jonathan's death, returned to the murder scene and placed the knife in the stream?

I had only one more place to visit. I said goodbye to Chief Karcher, and reporter Lovelace, and drove down to Baltimore, back to the federal courthouse on Lombard Street. I went to the U.S. Marshals' office, on the sixth floor. It's next to the U.S. attorney's office, where Jonathan Luna once worked.

I asked to see the transport records for FBI informant Warren Grace. Was Grace still in the Philadelphia Detention Center on the morning of December 4, 2004? Other questions pop to mind. What time had untrustworthy, self-serving, and duplicitous Agent Steve Skinner and Detective Todd Moody returned Grace to incarceration on the evening of December 3, the night Luna left the courthouse and headed toward Philadelphia? What *exactly* were the movements of Skinner and Moody? What are their alibis? Who are their informants? Do they have contact with other task forces? Have they taken a polygraph? What questions have they been asked by investigators? Had they picked up Warren Grace in Philadelphia on the morning of December 4, 2004, to transport him to Baltimore, and if so, what time? Have your witnessses ready in case the deal falls through, the judge told the prosecution. If they had not brought Grace from Philadelphia, why not?

And who are you? one marshal asked me, swaggering. I was gruffly told by several representatives in the U.S. Marshals' office that it was the agency's policy to release no information on prisoners, even ones who had been moved a year ago. They told me, as they'd tell any member of the public, to take a hike. They pointed next door, to the U.S. attorney's office. I should ask the U.S. attorney's office for that information, I was told.

I took in the dark door leading into the U.S. attorney's office. One of those security punch boxes guarded the door. Lots of good it did Luna. I didn't expect to get any truth, or honesty, out of Tom DiBiagio's office. Why waste my time? So I left the courthouse, taking the elevator past Courtroom 3-A, walking outside past the statue of Thurgood Marshall.

Two days later, on December 3, 2004, U.S. Attorney Thomas DiBiagio, forty-four years old, announced he was resigning. Exactly one full year had passed since the death of Jonathan Luna, and the sun had played all houses of the sky.

Shakespeare believed in ultimate justice. "In these cases we still have judgment here," he has Macbeth say. "That we but teach bloody instructions, which, being taught, return to plague the inventor: this even-handed justice commends the ingredients of our poisoned chalice to our own lips." When Shylock seeks heartless justice, without mercy, in The Merchant of Venice (as Tom DiBiagio had ruthlessly pursued his political opponents in Baltimore), Portia warns Shylock, "none of us / should see salvation."

Tom DiBiagio, then, would be the first to take a hike.

Some justice, after all, for Jonathan Luna.

Part 4

The midnight ride of Jonathan Luna

1
The midnight ride of Jonathan Luna

As Jonathan Luna leaves his office and drives out of Baltimore at the mournful stroke of midnight, gliding up the freeway beside gleaming Inner Harbor, he takes an amazing ride steeped in two centuries of American history, even as he rides the highway out of the burning town.

This isn't the Baltimore that H. L. Mencken knew. Mencken would surely say today they're dumbing down the boob-oisie, and further diluting the gene pool of what he studiously identified as our ruling class, the *boobus americanus.* (Baltimore film director John Waters, and his memorable actor, Divine, built smart careers on the *boobus baltimoron.)* The Baltimore Sun's great newspaperman and pontificator supreme cut his teeth in the 1904 Baltimore fire. At the outbreak of the fire, seeing no point in standing around and shooting the breeze with other newspapermen, Mencken took it upon himself to assign other reporters to every corner of the burning city. It would be pleasant to say that Mencken saw the fabric of his town held together by the unfissionable atoms of its families, their down-to-earth language, their solid work ethic, and their strong neighborhoods.

Truth is, even in Mencken's time there were crumbling families, and tumbling neighborhoods. About the time of the great 1904 fire, a young boy, only seven years old, was brought to a Baltimore orphanage, the St. Mary's Industrial School for boys, not that far at all from the courthouse where Jonathan Luna begins his midnight ride. This was one hundred years before the Dawsons would burn in their forgotten home.

The unruly young boy in 1904 was all but abandoned by his parents, who ran a tavern. They casually walked into the orphanage and signed custody of their son over to the Xaverian brothers, the Catholic missionaries who ran the school. For twelve years the boy barely saw his family; they didn't come to visit him on Christmas or other holidays, or on the one Sunday per month when families were allowed a visit. They tossed him off and cast him away like a refused stone.

From this we again see that the stone that the builders refuse will be the new cornerstone. The "incorrigible" boy fell under the wing of a large and burly, but caring priest, Brother Mattias. The brother encouraged the boy to swing a bat straightaway, like it was the only way to swing a bat, and to hurl a ball like cannon fire, as God pitches His own balls and strikes. People say the crack of his bat as he hit the ball was unlike any other sound they would ever hear, in or out of baseball.

In time the boy made the St. Mary's varsity baseball team. At 19, the castaway was spotted by Jack Dunn, owner and manager of the Baltimore Orioles, who signed him. The other players called their new teammate, "Jack's newest babe."

The castaway boy's name was of course George Herman Ruth, Jr. From then on he'd always be known as Babe Ruth.

After just five months Babe was traded to the Boston Red Sox. They kept tossing away Babe Ruth, like a bad penny, some say cursing themselves as they did. From the Red Sox, of course, he was traded to the New York Yankees. History records that Red Sox owner and Broadway producer Harry Frazee traded Ruth to the Yankees for $125,000 in cash and a loan of $300,000. Frazee used the money to open the musical "No, No, Nannette" on Broadway. Opening in 1925, the show ran for 321 performances and was the longest lasting musical hit of the 1920s. In his first two seasons for the Yankees, meanwhile, Ruth would slug 109 home runs. By 1930 Ruth would be paid a higher salary than President Herbert Hoover, prompting Ruth to famously laugh, "I know, but I had a better year than Hoover."

"Took a look at the mercury, forty below. No life for a lady, to be dragging her feathers around in the snow, leaving me blue, off she flew," goes the haunting Hoagy Carmichael song, Baltimore Oriole. *"Messed around with that big guy, till he singed her wings."*

Who says nothing good flies from Baltimore? An indomitable spirit pulsed through 20th Century America, and its beat was laid down by Brother Mattias's abandoned boy, Babe Ruth. He turned baseball from a pitcher's game into a slugger's game. No other sports figure, possibly excepting Muhammad Ali, so transcended the sport of his day, and set the tone for broad American culture. Ali may have set the tone for his *time;* Ruth set the tone for his century.

Babe Ruth swings his bat in the center of the golden moment of the golden age of baseball. And so he swings at the center of the golden age of America. On a fateful day in the 1932 World Series, playing against the Chicago Cubs, in the depths of the great Depression, Ruth stood at bat with two strikes against him. "Never let the fear of striking out get in your way," Ruth once advised the youth of America. As Cubs fans heckled, Ruth pointed to the center field bleachers. With the next pitch he slammed the ball out of the park, above the spot where he had pointed. It was the longest home run ever to be hit out of Wrigley Field.

In that one mythic moment of instant prophesy, determination, and straightaway action, Babe Ruth embodies the American century, and the spirit of unstoppable American accomplishment. The Wright brothers pointing to the sky. Jack Kennedy pointing to the moon. Eisenhower pointing his men to the beaches of Normandy. FDR pointing our way out of the Great Depression, despair and darkness. As we point, in our new century, to an American renewal.

Where have you gone, Babe, and Boog, and Frank, and Brooks? A nation turns its longing eyes to you.

As Jonathan Luna rides that highway out of town on his last night, Baltimore is ablaze. But it's not the great 1904 fire witnessed by Mencken. This time, it's a different sort of fire. It's more like the Fall of the House of Usher. Perhaps there's a holdover curse from the last tormented days of Edgar Allen Poe, who capped off his unfortunate career on earth while passing through Baltimore in 1849. Poe, appropriate for invocation here, is considered the inventor of the detective story.

Near a Baltimore saloon in late 1849, not far from where Luna begins his midnight ride, Edgar Allen Poe was found in a semi-conscious state. He lies dying in the street, wrapped in strange clothing, suffering a famously mysterious delirium on election day. A sheriff's election, no less. Perhaps, historians have speculated, local election press gangs plied an alcoholic Poe with bad liquor, disguising him in the strange clothes to cast multiple votes. This practice was called "cooping." Bystanders were kidnapped and held in a room called "the coop," before being dragged off to vote. In those days, "suppressing the vote" had a different meaning.

Others note that Poe had been on a lecture tour to raise money for the launching of a magazine. He may have been traveling with as much as $1,500, which was not found on him in Baltimore. One witness said two men appeared to be following Poe on the train into town. In a mix-up, at the start of his trip, Poe had hastily set off, mistakenly taking the walking stick of a friend, leaving behind his own. Poe's own walking stick, which he left behind, was later discovered by friends to have contained a hidden saber.

This much is certain: Edgar Allen Poe had his own nightmare midnight ride in Baltimore. Poe's strange death strangely seems to share eerie foreshadowings to Jonathan Luna's midnight ride. Poe had been on a circuitous journey to New York City, by way of Philadelphia. He had the week before written his landlady in New York, "*possibly* on Thursday I may start for N. York...." Poe inexplicably adds, "It will be better for me not to go to Fordham — don't you think so?"

Fordham, in New York City, would be Jonathan Luna's alma mater.

Poe's bones and spirit must still rest uneasy in Baltimore. As if in search of appeasement, every January 19 since 1949, the centenary of Poe's death, his grave at the Westminster Burying Ground has been visited by a mysterious, black-cloaked Baltimorean, who walks with a silver-tipped cane. In the early, dark hours of Poe's birthday, the cloaked one arrives to kneel at the grave and drink a toast of Martell cognac. He leaves the half-empty bottle and three red roses at the grave. In recent years, the tradition has been passed to a new generation. A younger man who affects a limp now places the placating roses and brandy at Poe's graveside. Some dark corner of God's raven eye witnesses this, and the fall of other sparrows and helpless things. One of the few American poets worthy of comparison with Whitman reminds us, somewhere beats a telltale heart, stirring in a secret wall, its noise rising up, till drowning all.

The allusion to the Fall of the House of Usher seems appropriate here. The story is after all a symbolic account of the destruction of an individual's personality, and the end of his broader family.

And so would Jonathan Luna's reputation be destroyed, even as Baltimore burns.

So fly, Baltimore oriole, singe your wings, your EZ Pass marking the trail. The first blip of his waning life shows Jonathan Luna using his EZ Pass north on I-95, flying through the Fort McHenry Tunnel Toll Plaza, at 11:49 pm.

As chance would have it, it's only a few miles from the spot where another young lawyer, held prisoner on the deck of a British sloop, saw our star-spangled flag still flying on the morning of September 14, 1813, after witnessing twenty-five hours of what was described as a "grotesque" British bombardment. This was almost a year before the British, in 1814, torched the White House and the Capitol in Washington DC. Americans have often in the past been attacked on our soil. No one but our enemies spoke of limiting American freedoms following these attacks.

Instead, inspired, Francis Scott Key began writing a defiant poem on the back of an envelope. Sailing back to his hotel in Baltimore, he wrote lines about faith in the resoluteness of freedom, honor and justice, in the face of despotic terror, impressment, great odds, and adversity.

O say can you see, at the start of his midnight ride, Jonathan Luna is driving with all deliberate speed, past Fort McHenry, not wasting time? He has a purpose.

He gets on the John F. Kennedy Memorial Highway, where JFK made his last public appearance before Dallas.

The next blip we have of Jonathan Luna is where the road enters Delaware. He passes through the state line tollbooth at 12:46 am, at Elkton, Maryland. Now he's set full sail into his midnight American ride. He now flies across Delaware, into New Jersey, not all that far from where Walt Whitman, in Camden, lived and sang his body electric. Here Luna enters the New Jersey turnpike, and someone takes a ticket.

Now, having circumnavigated Philadelphia, Luna's car soon

heads back west toward the Delaware River, into Pennsylvania. After a moderately paced, ten-minute drive, Luna's Accord reaches the Delaware River, just south of Trenton, and enters the Pennsylvania Turnpike at 2:47 am.

Today the drive across the Delaware River takes less than a minute. It's easy to forget, though it's our responsibility never to forget, the sacrifices made for that one-minute drive.

It's a cold December night. One bitterly cold December night, long ago, the same crossing took four hours. This turnpike lane where Luna rides is less than ten miles from the spot where another man once crossed the same river on another perilous midnight ride, ironically, with the help of a double-crossing informant.

Like Luna, General George Washington had been defeated in New York, humiliated, and retreated south. If they caught him, he would be hanged. The British by this time had offered New Jersians amnesty for their pledge of loyalty to the crown, and had begun setting up a wide network of spies and paid informants, soon to include such notables as spymaster John André and itinerant peddler Ann Bates.

André was a second lieutenant in the Royal Welsh Fusiliers in Quebec when he was captured by American forces in late 1775. Taken to Lancaster County, Pennsylvania (not very far from where Luna died), André was held captive in rough circumstances until he was freed as part of a prisoner exchange in 1776. André later became head of British intelligence, overseeing a vast network of deserters and American turncoats.

André's greatest conquest, Benedict Arnold, by 1780 would pledge to deliver West Point and its 3,000 defenders to the British crown, for 20,000 pounds sterling.

By December 1776, George Washington's troops had dwindled from thirty thousand to three thousand men. Washington wrote his family and advised them to take shelter in the mountains. The situation was desperate, the Cause all but lost.

While Washington did employ his own spies, most noted among these Nathan Hale, he was drastically outnumbered and outfinanced by the British. Early on he recognized he must use the British informant system against its own masters. Washington's masterstroke was a disinformation apparatus designed to provide false information to British informants.

On Christmas night, 1776, hunkered down in a flat-bottomed boat, Washington led his men across the Delaware River just north of Trenton, on a surprise attack on Hessian forces. The Hessians were lulled into a false sense of security by a Washington plant, a former British soldier named John Honeyman. Washington knew how to keep a backfield in motion.

Honeyman convinced the Hessian commander in Trenton that American forces were under-equipped and starving, and in no condition for winter battle. Believing this misinformation, the Hessians proceeded with their traditional Christmas Day bouts of feasting and drinking.

Washington began his crossing at about 11 pm. The same dark hour Luna began his ride. For Washington, and America, it was a midnight ride of great danger and historical import, made possible by a double-dealing informant.

With Washington on the crossing that night were about twenty-four hundred men in a flotilla of leaky, groaning boats, among them future presidents James Madison and James Monroe. Future supreme court justice James Marshall came along, as did future duelists Alexander Hamilton and Aaron Burr. No jovial duck hunt, this, quack, quack.

Most of his men could not swim and some fell overboard. For four hours they braved a blinding storm of snow and sleet as they perilously crossed the ice-choked Delaware. When they finally reached the other side, his half-frozen men ripped fence posts from the ground and built fires to stay alive.

Daylight fast approaching, fearful of having lost the element of surprise, Washington sat down on a bee hive and wondered if they could go on.

Washington wasn't a perfect man. He lost most of his battles. As a young officer he was accused of bumbling and even of single-handedly starting the French and Indian War. All his life he struggled with a horrific temper. He once knocked down an aide. Jefferson describes an enraged Washington throwing down his hat and stomping on it. As president, he stood by while cabinet members Jefferson and Hamilton bitterly feuded, splitting the nation into factions that would become our modern political parties.

Washington fought loyally for a cause that had barely been defined. Would there be a federal government? Would there be slaves or no? Who would get to vote? These outcomes hardly were addressed, yet Washington fought on. He believed in his country and his countrymen. A just cause, he simply felt, could not lose.

Sitting on his bee hive at 3 am on the night he crossed the Delaware with his men, Washington saw there was no turning back. The risks of retreat outweighed those of advance. Moving across the river that night with them was a spirit that had not visited the earth for thousands of years, since the age of Pericles. These men did not move about the battlefield on the orders of kings or dukes, bishops or mullahs. They were driven by their own free will. On an inhospitable frozen river, on this continent, democratic government took root.

One of Washington's men wrote an account that surely would have been Exhibit A in British treason court: "It was broad daylight when we came to a house where a man was chopping wood. He was very much surprised when he saw us. 'Can you tell me where the Hessian picket is?' Washington asked. The man hesitated, but I said, 'You need not be frightened, it is General Washington who asks the question.' His face brightened and he pointed toward the house of Mr. Howell."

It was now the morning after Christmas, 1776. Before crossing the Delaware, the soldier wrote, "They make a great deal of Christmas in Germany, and no doubt the Hessians will drink a great deal of beer and have a dance to-night. They will be sleepy tomorrow morning. Washington will set the tune for them about daybreak."

This was about twenty months after Paul Revere's midnight ride of April 18 and 19, 1775, which also began about 11 pm. Revere rode as an informant. Setting out on his ride to Lexington to inform John Hancock and Samuel Adams of their impending arrest, Revere luckily spotted two British officers, probably themselves tipped off by an informant, concealing themselves in the shade of a moonlit tree, and barely made his escape.

Washington's midnight crossing of the Delaware River is a pivotal moment in history. Jonathan Luna, on his midnight ride, as I say, coincidentally crossed the Delaware about ten miles from the spot where Washington landed. There are other little coinkeydinks.

Luna crossed the Delaware River at about 2:47 am. Washington's men also finished their crossing shortly before 3 am.

At daybreak, upon reaching the New Jersey shore, on their way to surprise the Hessians and change the course of history, Washington's men forged inland to reach *Bear Tavern Road.* They had before them another five brutal years of struggle and sacrifice before Washington, aided by the French fleet, would, with great courage, sagacity and planning, defeat Cornwallis at Yorktown. Washington would then reject a crown, resign his commission, and return to Mount Vernon, the modern Cincinnatus. Most implausible to European crowns was that Washington would *twice* walk away from power. When Washington left the presidency to retire, King George III famously remarked that Washington's stand-down placed him "in a light the most distinguished of any living man," making him "the greatest character of the age."

In December 2003, almost 227 years after Washington's crossing, at 2:47 am, three hours after he had inexplicably walked away from his own office, Jonathan Luna crossed the Delaware. He had about two hours of life remaining on this planet.

In Lancaster County, Pennsylvania, near daybreak, Jon Luna gave his last full measure of devotion at *Dry Tavern Road.*

There's another Yankee Doodle coincidence. At 3:20 am, someone once more used Luna's debit card, this time purchasing gas at a Sunoco station on the Pennsylvania turnpike at King of Prussia, near Valley Forge. Luna by this time may have been suppressed, and without his freedom.

Many Decembers before, of course, George Washington had slept and suffered here too. What was freedom worth to Washington's men? The Marquis de Lafayette visited and wrote about our forefathers at Valley Forge: "The unfortunate soldiers were in want of everything; they had neither coats nor hats, nor shirts, nor shoes. Their feet and their legs froze until they were black, and it was often necessary to amputate them."

Military historians tell us Washington had to worry ceaselessly about disease at Valley Forge. He allowed medical vaccinations — feared and highly experimental at the time. He was obliged to order latrines built as far as possible from water sources, and in the end had to threaten the lash to any man who persisted in relieving himself too near camp.

At Valley Forge, Washington continued to brilliantly foil British informants with his disinformation effort. Among other activities, Washington's aide, Major John Clark, adroitly allowed false muster lists to fall into the hands of British informants. These lists suggested a continental army five times the actual size of the force.

Washington found himself encamped at Valley Forge in December 1777. The British had taken Philadelphia. Slothful British commander Maj. Gen. William Howe had hoped that by occupying Philadelphia, our most populous city and erstwhile capitol, the back of the resistance could be broken and the war ended. By this time the Continental Congress had turned tail and was sponsoring a debating society in backwater York, Pennsylvania. The Continental Congress, much to Washington's exasperation, was not doing much to support the men at Valley Forge. Congress in York, appropriately enough, had before it such questions as whether, for taxation purposes, the feeding of slaves should be considered the same as the feeding of cattle.

In August 1777, British General Howe had set sail from New York City with more than 15,000 troops. Some 250 vessels weathered three choppy weeks at sea, before turning up the Chesapeake and landing, coincidentally, at *Elkton, Maryland.* Howe landed not far from the spot where, more than two centuries later, Jonathan Luna's EZ Pass records show he crossed the Maryland-Delaware line with all deliberate dispatch on his midnight ride.

Unlike Luna, General Howe, in 1777, easily marched onto Philadelphia, repelling Washington's attacks. Washington's men, meanwhile, were foraging and starving in a way that had not been seen by Europeans or Africans on the American continent since Cabeza de Vaca, in the days of the Spanish conquistadors, walked for weeks to find a prickly pear, as de Vaca vividly recounts in his *Relacion.* Mass starvation has been here before, and Washington, more than any man, knew that wrong circumstances could bring hunger here again.

Once encamped in Philadelphia, Maj. Gen. Howe was given the bogus muster lists Washington had cunningly supplied to unsuspecting British informants. Recognizing Washington's handwriting, Howe accepted the overblown roster lists as genuine, and delayed attack.

When told his home city had fallen, Ben Franklin, in Paris to court support for the American Cause, scoffed and cryptically quipped, "No Sir, Philadelphia has taken the British."

Ben would manage nicely in Philadelphia today.

While unraveling a dark mystery like the midnight ride of Jonathan Luna, it's necessary to look for patterns. It's also important to filter out patterns that mislead, red herrings that do not apply, that may even have been deliberately left by a perpetrator to mislead. It's equally important not to overlook clues because they are politically or socially uncomfortable to consider.

The mysterious death of a public official offers clues to the health of a society to which he belonged. Again, canary in a coal mine.

With the death of Jonathan Luna, a public servant under pressures professional and personal, one naturally begins thinking of the health of our American democracy. As I've written, there are fascinating coincidences involving Luna's midnight ride and movements of others dating to the American revolution, hundreds of years in the past.

For the purposes of this story it's a nice literary device. There are nonetheless remarkable coincidences. Meaningful coincidences, you'd call them. Psychoanalyst Carl Jung called meaningful coincidences like these, sometimes involving great measures of distance and time, "synchronicity."

Jung wrote about a patient describing a dream in which she was given a golden scarab. Jung famously writes, "While she was telling me this dream I sat with my back to the closed window. Suddenly I heard a noise behind me, like a gentle tapping. I turned round and saw a flying insect knocking against the window-pane from outside. I opened the window and caught the creature in the air as it flew in. It was the nearest analogy to the golden scarab that one finds in our latitudes, a scarabaeid beetle, the common rose-chafer *(Cetoaia urata)* which contrary to its usual habits had evidently felt an urge to get into a dark room at this particular moment. I must admit that nothing like it ever happened to me before or since, and that the dream of the patient has remained unique in my experience."

Jung came to believe that synchronicity allowed access to archetypes, or patterns, in our collective unconscious. These archetypes provide opportunity for insight, even healing. His patient, dreaming of the scarab, an Egyptian symbol of rebirth, actually dreamed of healing, and rebirth, and needed to be liberated from excessive rationalism, Jung wrote. She, and society, had lost their religion, Jung came to suggest.

Mythology, Jung wrote he believed, was based on powerful archetypes such as these. Jung's system of archetypes and the collective unconscious have proved influential in our time, even in our popular culture, though many may not always realize it. Joseph Campbell, with his explorations of the power of myth and archetypes, and mythic tales involving characters of good and evil, helped George Lucas plot out *Star Wars.* Michael Stipe, and R.E.M., sing that we are losing our religion.

Robert Todd Carroll, in his entertaining *Skeptics Dictionary,* writes, "Dreams and psychological crises, fevers and derangement, chance encounters resonating with 'meaningful coincidences,' all are gateways to the collective unconscious, which is ready to restore the individual psyche to health with its insights."

In his theories of synchronicity, Jung was influenced by modern science, particularly physics, and newly discovered quantum mechanics. Today science tells us of such oddly behaving particles as quarks and neutrinos, which mysteriously influence other particles over unlikely distances of space and time.

Sigmund Freud would have nothing to do with synchronicity. He thought Jung was nuts. One psychiatrist and author, Anthony Storr, even goes so far as to suggest Jung was mentally ill in this period, 1913 to 1917. Jung himself said he was confronting his unconscious, and called his work in this time a "creative illness." Ill or not, Jung's work is arguably more influential today than is Freud's.

In psychiatry, *apophenia* is described as perceiving connections and meaningfulness in unrelated phenomena. So a mentally ill patient, for example, might see randomly arranged sticks on the ground as evidence of witches and warlocks. Another patient might see an oven as Dante's Inferno, and so on. Researchers suggest that high levels of dopamine in the brain might cause one to find meaning, patterns and significance where none exist.

This compares with *pareidolia,* in which often obscure stimulus is perceived in clear and distinct form. And so the face of Jesus is seen on a burrito, or the Virgin Mary is seen in a tree, or a window pane. Sometimes psychologists encourage pareidolia, such as when patients view Rorschach ink blots.

All this said, and not merely for literary device, as I say, I came to notice, quite by accident, while studying the life of George Washington, meaningful coincidence between the movements of Jonathan Luna, and the movements of our Continental Congress in the 1770s.

Consider this: the seats of our 2nd Continental Congress are as follows:

Philadelphia, PA: May 10, 1775 - December 12, 1776
Baltimore, MD: December 20, 1776 - March 4, 1777
Philadelphia, PA: March 5, 1777 - September 18, 1777
Lancaster, PA: September 27, 1777
York, PA: September 30, 1777 - June 27, 1778

Jonathan Luna, unknowingly, in the last days and hours of his life, retraced the movements of the infant government for which he worked.

Consulting with informant Warren Grace in preparation for the Smith-Poindexter trial, Luna traveled between Philadelphia and Baltimore, as did our Congress. On the last night of his life, seemingly caught in a cat and mouse run, Luna too traveled from Baltimore, around Philadelphia, to Lancaster, where he died, on his way toward

York. Add to this Luna's pass-through in Elkton, Maryland, the Delaware River, even Valley Forge, and it's downright spooky. He's on a mad, Yankee Doodle gallop through the dark heart of the American night.

More tongue-in-cheek, Congress sought an accord with the British; an Accord, after all, was the model of the car that Luna drove.

Finally, and curiously, in 1831, Alexis de Tocqueville selected a route remarkably similar to that followed by Jonathan Luna on his midnight ride one and three quarter centuries later.

De Tocqueville, on one leg of his trip to write about our new democracy, in October 1831, traveled from New York City, to Philadelphia, to Baltimore. From Baltimore, de Tocqueville journeyed back in Philadelphia on November 6. From Philadelphia, de Tocqueville's trip even more amazingly traces the midnight ride of Jonathan Luna. De Tocqueville set out from Philadelphia, through Lancaster County, crossing the Allegheny Mountains into Pittsburgh on November 22 (the day that JFK coincidentally died, centuries later). De Tocqueville's trip over the Alleghenies closely matches the route taken by today's Pennsylvania turnpike, where Luna's ride ran out. The turnpike was carved from ancient Indian trails that ran over the mountains.

What was de Tocqueville doing in Philadelphia?

He was visiting the prison there, on official business.

Just like Jonathan Luna.

As I write this, word comes that the Red Sox of Boston have defeated the Yankees of New York, and the Sox have gone to win the World Series, for the first time since 1918, when Babe Ruth played for the team, and since the Sox traded him to the Yankees.

The afternoon bells have sounded, and some angel has got his wings. In this fresh century, the Curse of the Bambino at last has been lifted.

2
No man, no problem

We have one place yet to revisit. On the morning of Jonathan Luna's death, on December 4, 2003, at precisely 9:30 am, Judge William Quarles calls Courtroom 3-A to order.

Jonathan Luna is not seated at the prosecution table. He's late, two days in a row! Quarles must think. Unknown to Judge Quarles, Luna is dead, his body slumped in the cold stream in Lancaster County, as yet unidentified by police. It will take several hours before Luna's body is identified and his former boss, U.S. Attorney Tom DiBiagio, notified of the death.

In the Baltimore federal courthouse, meanwhile, Smith and Poindexter, Ravenell and Tuminelli, sit waiting at the defense table for court to begin.

The court reporter, Ned Richardson, sits at his stenographer's machine, ready to take down what we are about to read. Richardson is about to take down a very curious end to a very curious case. Richardson will unknowingly be a stenographer for a murder investigation.

At the prosecution table now sits assistant U.S. attorney James Warwick, Luna's former colleague. Warwick, we'll recall, had conferred with Luna the night before about whether it would be prudent to allow Poindexter off the hook for murder, in order to bury this case.

Warwick was also the assistant U.S. attorney who one investigator complained to me was always pressuring him to open phony cash storefronts in his investigations. The investigator expressed concern that Warwick's pet cash storefronts, run as they were by a network of unaccountable agents and informants, were troubling to him. "It *breeds* corruption," I was told. Warwick has handled a number of drug cases, including an early 2004 case involving a shipment of 154 kilos of cocaine seized from a Jamaica, New York man.

"Good morning, your honor," Warwick now tells Judge Quarles. "I do apologize for, I guess, my sudden appearance before the court."

"Always a pleasure to see you, Mr. Warwick," Quarles says.

"Thank you very much, judge," Warwick continues. "Yesterday, I became involved in some discussions with Mr. Tuminelli relative to his client and so I have obtained at least a limited degree of knowledge of what the issues are. I do believe that we do have something worked out with Mr. Tuminelli. Mr. Luna was finalizing the agreement. I spoke with Mr. Luna last night. I don't know where he is at the moment. We are trying to locate him, and trying to locate the final agreement."

The uncompleted plea agreement, in fact, was up in Luna's office, in his laptop.

"Uh huh," Quarles mutters.

Several months later, I show the transcripts of this extraordinary court proceeding to Holmes, the internal investigations expert. "Warwick?" Holmes says. "What's *he* doing here?"

Holmes expressed astonishment that DiBiagio even allowed the plea agreement to move forward while Luna remained unaccounted for. What's the rush? "You're telling me, here's a violent heroin case and the AUSA (assistant U.S. attorney) is missing, and they push ahead with a plea agreement he was having trouble with? DiBiagio should have gone down to the courtroom and told the judge Luna was missing and hold everything until he can be located."

In a hurry they nonetheless were, and proceed with the plea agreement Warwick and DiBiagio did. The lawyers go to the bench and confer with the judge.

They speak to Quarles about the conditions of the plea deal. Tuminelli explains that he and Luna consulted with Warwick the might before. "Mr. Warwick sat in and gave some guidance," Tuminelli says, "and I understood that we had a plea agreement."

"Someone told me that Mark Cohen had to be consulted," Quarles says. Cohen is Baltimore's assistant state's attorney for homicide prosecutions.

"He was consulted," Tuminelli says.

"He was consulted, your honor," Luna's former co-counsel, Vivien Cockburn, agrees. "And he has spoken to the victim's parents. And they are— as part of the plea agreement, the state will not proceed in any manner—."

"On the murder?" Quarles asks. "The alleged murder?"

"Well, actually, the murder or any charges in state court that resulted out of the conduct that was the basis for this indictment," Tuminelli says.

"By the way, give Mr. Cohen my regards, if you would," Quarles says.

"I will," Cockburn says.

"With regard to Mr. Poindexter," Tuminelli continues, "I believe that we did work out the terms of the plea agreement. I spoke with Mr. Luna at 9:00 pm last night."

"Uh huh," Quarles says.

"He called me at home and said, you know, 'I just want to make sure that we got all the details,' he went over the details and I said that is correct. He said 'I left the office but I have to go back and complete the agreement.'"

"Okay," Quarles says.

"And he was supposed to fax the agreement to me sometime last night," Tuminelli says.

"Have you seen the paper yet?" Quarles asks.

"No, because he was supposed to fax it during the evening. It was not faxed," Tuminelli says.

"Generally, what's the deal?" Quarles asks.

"Generally, the deal—," Tuminelli begins.

"I'm sorry," Warwick interrupts. "The deal, as I understand it, is that he will plead to the drug charge. The concern that Mr. Tuminelli had was the related conduct of the homicide, and my question to both Mr. Tuminelli and Mr. Luna (was) essentially it's related conduct if we can establish a federal nexus, specifically that we can establish that the murder was related to a drug crime or a drug transaction. Mr. Luna represented that he did not have that proof, and I told him, in my opinion, which I have gone through my— other people in the office, is that if we cannot establish the federal nexus, it's not related conduct under the guidelines."

Again, here Warwick used the lawyer's word "represented." That's what Luna told him, he's saying.

"Okay," Quarles says.

"And any deal with regard to Mr. Tuminelli's client's state liability is between Mr. Cohen and Mr. Tuminelli, and that has been resolved," Warwick says. He's incorrect about this, Tuminelli would say.

"Okay," Quarles says.

Warwick now says something odd. He says he knows discussion of the murder has previously entered into the case. This is fairly in-depth knowledge for an attorney who says he was just "consulted" for a short period the previous evening. "But I felt it important," Warwick adds, "to bring to the court's attention that despite the fact that the homicide had been referenced in earlier discussions, it needed to be clear that, absent the federal nexus, which we did not have, it's out of the case for our purposes."

The murder of Alvin Jones now conveniently swept under the carpet, like Luna himself, the lawyers discuss with the judge the fine points of the plea agreement, including the reduction of the sentences of the two defendants. Reading this transcript, Holmes choked, "My God, they're giving away the store!"

"I do apologize for not being more versed in the facts," Warwick tells the judge. Funny the things he is versed in.

"Mr. Warwick, I appreciate your infusion of sanity here on the government's side," Judge Quarles tells him. "No offense to defense attorneys." He's talking openly about his displeasure with Luna. Who else may have been even more displeased?

"I think we have been relatively sane," Tuminelli says.

With that, Warwick asks for a fifteen minutes recess to find the plea agreement Luna walked away from when he began his mystery ride.

"May I ask for the court's indulgence in giving me fifteen minutes to finalize any changes with Mr. Ravenell and to find out where the heck that other document is?" Warwick asks.

"Very good," Quarles tells him.

"Thank you very much," Warwick says.

With that Warwick exits the courtroom to search Luna's office for Poindexter's incomplete plea agreement.

It remains unfinished, in Luna's laptop, on his desk, in his office. Beside his cell phone. And his glasses.

Quarles calls a recess. Afterwards, back at the bench, he asks Tuminelli, "Any progress?"

Tuminelli reports, "Mr. Warwick left with Ms. Cockburn and told me to advise the court, if the court needed information, that he was going upstairs, and I think he is trying to put together these documents, and—,"

"Have we found chief trial counsel yet?" Quarles asks. At last he's addressing the elephant in the room. Rather, the elephant *not* in the room.

"No," Tuminelli says.

"No luck," Ravenell says. "My understanding—."

"Has anyone called his home?" Quarles asks.

"May we approach with the agents?" Ravenell asks.

"Yes, come up."

The lawyers go to the bench with several FBI agents, including Steve Skinner.

Tuminelli tells Quarles, "Apparently, judge, no one has heard from him since 9:00 o'clock last night."

Agent Skinner speaks up, curiously contradicting Tuminelli.

"Your honor," Skinner says, "we called his house and we didn't get an answer. We called his wife at work and (the) last she said that she saw him (was) last night at midnight and he left again."

Angela Luna later would say she had been mistaken, that her husband had left home earlier that evening, earlier than midnight.

Skinner, most oddly of all, is talking as if he already knows a tragedy is at hand. Rather than the hip-hop comedy that has been playing in Courtroom 3-A all week. Skinner is the guy who took, by his own written reckoning, a week to figure out Warren Grace was leaving his apartment and shooting up the hood. Even with everyone's phone ringing off the hook about it, Skinner couldn't deduce whether Grace was even in his apartment, even after Skinner finally paid a visit there. This morning, displaying remarkable deductive foresight, Skinner speaks as if he already knows Luna may be in some sort of dire trouble. He already knows about things left behind on Luna's desk and in his computer. He knows what Luna was *supposed* to be doing: finishing the smelly plea deal designed to protect DiBiagio and the "Safe Streets Task Force" from investigation in open court. He even knows that Luna, for some reason, never completed that task demanded of him.

Skinner's the guy who didn't know or care whether Warren Grace was at home. He didn't seem to care much for anyone's safety then. For all Steve Skinner should know this morning, at this moment, Luna may simply have stepped out to get a cup of coffee, to shine his shoes, or to visit his sick son, as was his reason for tardiness only the day before.

"Mr. Tuminelli spoke with him last night and he was supposed to fax down the plea agreement," Skinner continues. "It was still in his computer up in his office, and we have paged him, and his cell phone is on his desk, his glasses are in his office. We are probably going to go over to the parking garage where he— where *we* park and just look for his car." (Emphasis mine.)

Ned Richardson here takes careful dictation. Skinner starts to say this is where Luna parks, but then stops to say it's where "we" park. From this we glean not only that the agents park where Luna parks, but also that they know the car Luna is driving. They were going to "look for his car."

Ravenell interjects, "Your honor, I was going to ask the court just to take a recess until we find out what's going on. You know, as much as we're concerned obviously about the jury, and about the defendants, I mean all of us are personally concerned about Mr. Luna. I think that we need to try to let the agents focus on trying to find him."

"Well, we don't need the agents for the—," Quarles begins, speaking of the plea agreement.

"No, no, Mr. Warwick is still working on that," Ravenell says.

"So if you guys want to take off and look for him, please do," Quarles tells the agents. It's not clear from the record whether Baltimore's Detective Moody is among them.

The agents exit the courtroom.

"As soon as Mr. Warwick comes, we will let you know," Ravenell tells the judge.

"Well, I will sit here," Quarles says.

Luna's former co-counsel, Vivien Cockburn, re-enters the courtroom. "Mr. Warwick has finished one agreement and would ask the court's indulgence. He is quickly doing the second one, he wants to look at it, and then he will be right down."

Quarles thanks her, and Cockburn asks to "be excused for a moment," and exits the courtroom.

In his rush to facilitate this suspicious, and probably unlawful plea deal, that was left undone by the missing assistant U.S. attorney, Warwick is actually altering evidence in what in only the matter of an hour or two will become a murder investigation. He better hurry, before Luna's office is roped off and swarming with investigators. Gotta get that phony plea agreement filed! Not only are Warwick and DiBiagio not asking for a halt in the trial until they can learn what has happened to Luna, they are quickly forging ahead and *altering,* after all, the document Luna was stumbling on at the time of his disappearance.

If they're so damn concerned about Luna, as Ravenell and Skinner have us believe, why doesn't Warwick, the seasoned criminal prosecutor that he is, close down the crime scene, and immediately freeze everything in Luna's office? Instead he acts like a busy Chinese cook, throwing dishes together in a hot kitchen. Why isn't he asked to preserve the scene by the agents, if they're so damn worried about Luna? Instead, he's changing Luna's stalled document. The agents felt the need to "look for his car." The agents talk and act like they're aware they may be investigating a crime, while Warwick curiously and feverishly works on incomplete documents found on Luna's curiously left-behind laptop. It doesn't add up.

Warwick at last enters the courtroom with the two amazing plea agreements, most of which were written in heaven, while other parts were scribbled in hell. They are ready for the signatures of defendants Smith and Poindexter, and their counsel, Warwick announces. It's taken him a half hour, maybe forty-five minutes, since he left Courtroom 3-A, "to find out where the heck that other document is."

Luna, we should consider, could have completed the same task in as much, or less, time, the night before. If he had wanted. We must conclude that Luna did not *want* to finish the paperwork for the phony deal. He certainly had the time to do it. *Before* he was killed.

It's rather suspicious that Warwick and DiBiagio did not step in to freeze the case. Either it's an outrageous oversight or it's a serious breach of professional standards. Take your pick. At this moment they could easily be calling in the best forensic teams in the world, who could be on the scene in minutes. That call never seems to have been made, even to this day.

Instead, their man's dead, and they're altering evidence.

No hombre, no problemo.

Why? From all of the above we can deduce two facts:

DiBiagio's office obviously badly wanted, or needed, this questionable plea agreement completed and filed. Luna just as obviously didn't want to do it.

Now Luna was dead. Draw your own conclusions. The hard copies of the plea agreements, as I've pointed out, are truly remarkable documents. For the most part they were drafted and typed by Luna. Only the finishing touches have been added by Warwick.

The documents had been written on a word processor. Luna, true to what he told defense lawyers the night before, completed the paperwork for Smith's plea deal. It's neatly typed, and completed, with no cross-outs.

Poindexter's plea is altogether different. Many of the sections of Poindexter's deal were written in boilerplate court language, sharing identical language with Smith's agreement, and a thousand other plea deals. In Poindexter's deal, paragraphs specific to Poindexter have been added. A short paragraph, for example, has been inserted in Poindexter's deal letting him off the hook for the murder of Alvin Jones.

The paragraph, "Agreement with State's Attorney's Office," reads:

> *The Baltimore City State's Attorney's Office has authorized this Office to be bound by this agreement in the following manner: the Baltimore City State's Attorney's Office will not charge Walter Poindexter for any conduct that formed the basis of this federal prosecution, including a shooting incident that occurred on or about January 22, 2001, in Baltimore City, Maryland.*

Another section, titled "Factual Stipulations," dealing specifically with Poindexter's drug offenses, was sloppily (if not hurriedly) typed. The three paragraphs in this section were slapped together, and include an extra period at the end of one of the sentences, and an uninitialed cross out. The date of one of the drug buys, originally typed as "September *23,* 2002," has been altered to read September "24," by someone who had hand-drawn a 4 over the 3. It looks at first glance sloppy. But a closer consideration of the dates September 23 and 24, 2002, reveals a time period when Luna was gravely distracted by outrageous FBI misdeeds. It is after all only a few weeks after Luna has been cc'd by Pretrial Services that Grace had removed his ankle bracelet, which quickly led to Grace's being cut loose from home confinement. And it is only two or three days before Luna would discover, on September 26, 2002, that someone had stolen the $36,000 from the courthouse evidence safe. It's also a few weeks before the Dawsons would burn alive. It's a strange nexus of catastrophe for Luna, who certainly appears to be squeezed by circumstances. Luna, we know, certainly was also squeezed by FBI agents.

Sloppiest of all, an entire page from Smith's plea deal, Page 5, has simply been copied over, complete with the page header for Smith's case, which has been crossed out. "Amendment to Plea Letter of 12/3/03 to Walter Poindexter," is instead scribbled in pen on the top of this page to mark its insertion in the deal. The slapped-together page is simply stapled onto the back of Poindexter's plea. Most of the page has been crossed out by pen, except for a single boilerplate section, "Waiver of Appeal," forbidding the defendant the right of appeal should he sign the deal. Warwick didn't even take the time to have it retyped, or to even cut and paste it into the document. In this sloppy way, the moment he signed this deal, Poindexter was prohibited by the government from ever appealing the case.

"What I am going to do in making part of Mr. Poindexter's agreement," Warwick will tell Quarles, "I have just cannibalized a page with the waiver of appeal on it, which has been initialed by all parties and, Ron, I will just staple that on to the end of it," he tells the clerk. "It's part of the Poindexter agreement." It might be dirty, but it's quick.

Warwick hands the plea documents to the defendants to sign, and then he asks to step out of the courtroom.

"Your honor, while counsel is finalizing these agreement with their clients, may I just use the facility?" he asks the judge.

"Sure," Quarles says. Warwick exits the courtroom.

When Warwick returns, they begin the business of finalizing the plea agreements. Quarles asks first Smith, and then Poindexter, to stand and say whether they comprehend what they are agreeing to. They say they do.

"Did anybody use any threat or force or violence to get you to plead guilty?" Quarles asks Poindexter.

"No, they didn't," Poindexter tells the judge.

"Other than what's inside the plea agreement itself," Quarles asks, "has anyone made any promise or prediction about the sentence that I am going to impose in this case?"

"No, sir," Poindexter answers.

Tuminelli now says, "Judge, there is two matters with regard to this agreement."

"Okay," Quarles says.

Tuminelli has some concerns. He says he wants to clarify the deal not to prosecute Poindexter for the murder of Alvin Jones. He contradicts something that Warwick, a few minutes earlier, had told the judge.

"Mr. Warwick advised the court that I was in negotiations with the Baltimore City State's Attorney's office," Tuminelli says. What Warwick has said about this is not exactly the truth, the way it happened, Tuminelli feels the need to say. In his careless haste, Warwick has strangely got this wrong, too. "I was present when Mr. Luna spoke to Mark Cohen of the Baltimore City State's Attorney's office, and am aware that Mr. Cohen advised Mr. Luna that what's contained in that paragraph is Baltimore City's position. I just want to make this clear. Mr. Cohen did not say this directly to me. *He said it to Mr. Luna.* And Ms. Cockburn, I believe, can confirm that that's how the negotiation took place."

Luna was now dead, unable to confirm anything on this earth. They all turned to his former co-counsel, Vivien Cockburn.

"Is that correct, Ms. Cockburn?" Quarles asks her.

"Your honor, I was not present during the phone call," Cockburn says. "However, Mr. Luna did relay that conversation to me in front of Mr. Tuminelli."

"Thank you very much," Quarles says. It's amazing that Quarles, at this moment, does not stop the proceedings.

Now Warwick asks Cockburn, "And do I understand that Mr. Cohen was head of the homicide bureau in the State's Attorney's office, and did confer with the victim's family?"

"It is my understanding," Cockburn replies. But no one seems quite sure. Luna sure isn't saying.

"And, based upon those conversations," Warwick now quizzes Cockburn for the record, putting the responsibility on her, "and his evaluation of the situation, he made those representations, which Ms. Cockburn has signed onto this agreement."

Cockburn is a signatory to Poindexter's plea agreement, as completed by Warwick. She signs it as "Assistant States Attorney Baltimore City." Her signature does not appear on Smith's plea deal, only Poindexter's. Warwick, for his part, signs both agreements as "Jonathan P. Luna," and adds his own initials after he signs Luna's name.

"The other point, your honor, is something that was addressed at the bench. It's not part of the agreement because it doesn't need to be part of the formal agreement, but the United States has represented to Mr. Poindexter that the shooting, the fatal shooting, on January 22, 2001, which this court has previously heard about, is not, for the purposes of this federal proceeding for federal sentencing, relevant conduct in this case. And the government's position is, and I would ask Mr. Warwick to confirm this—. Because it is not relevant conduct, it will not be communicated to probation. Nor will the government contend at sentencing that it in any way is related or is relevant conduct, or is in any way relevant to the sentencing that this court will impose."

Now that Poindexter won't be prosecuted for murder, Tuminelli wants to make sure his client won't be *sentenced* for murder.

"That is correct, your honor," Warwick strangely guarantees. "As I explained at the bench, in my discussions with Mr. Luna yesterday, and Mr. Tuminelli, it is my understanding that the evidence regarding the fatal shooting indicates that it was not related to any narcotics distribution activity."

Now Warwick again has changed his story. At first he told the judge there was no evidence, and now he's saying that the *"evidence... indicates"* the murder had nothing to do with drugs. In fact, as we know, he's incorrect on both counts. Jones was murdered because he was suspected of burglarizing Poindexter's drug stash house, and for interfering with Poindexter's drug sales. That's a drug-related murder.

"Therefore," Warwick goes on, "there was no federal jurisdictional nexus between that shooting and any of the crimes that are charged in this indictment, so there would not be any federal jurisdiction over that homicide.

"That's why Mr. Cohen from the State's Attorney's office was involved in the discussions," Warwick curiously goes on. *"In that it was not related to the drug activity,* there is no federal jurisdiction, and it is my position and my understanding that it should not be part of the sentencing equation in terms of the pre-sentencing investigation."

With that, Warwick sweeps the murder of Alvin Jones under the rug. Luna is gone, and cannot comment.

"Okay, that's the agreement," Quarles says, content.

Those in the courtroom still have not received word that Luna has been stabbed thirty-six times and now lies dead, by a stream, miles away in the countryside. Judge Quarles, concluding the proceedings, exchanges pleasantries with the lawyers.

Judge Quarles tells Ravenell and Tuminelli, "Let me again express my pleasure. I have always enjoyed our trials and other things. It was — the word, I don't like to apply it here — but it was fun. I enjoyed it. You are both extraordinarily good lawyers."

"Thank you, judge," Tuminelli says.

"And it's always a pleasure to have you," Quarles adds. "Please tell Marion that I did surrender you in time for the trip to Hawaii, so I hope you enjoy the time in Hawaii."

"Thank you," Tuminelli tells him.

"Thank you, judge," Ravenell says.

Quarles now turns to the prosecutors left standing. "Mr. Warwick, it's always a pleasure," he says. "Ms. Cockburn, I seem to see you under unusual circumstances."

"I was looking forward to it very, very much," Cockburn tells Quarles.

Quarles concludes, "It's always a pleasure to see you and please advise me when — and I will be optimistic — when Mr. Luna shows up, could you tell him I would like to see him? Tell him I'm not going to yell at him or chew him out. But I do have perhaps some fatherly advice for him."

"I will tell him that you have some concern for his welfare, and that you would like to see him," Warwick says.

"Tell him, you know, no yelling, no problem, just concern," Quarles says.

The time for fatherly advice and concern has come and gone. Skylarking Luna lies dead in a stream, the police going through his pockets, his reputation soon picked apart by the jaybirds in the FBI, and the buzzards in the press. While some all-seeing dove, or raven, wings home, to tell a tale to God.

The time for sensible, fatherly advice had been yesterday. Soon a soft snow will be falling outside the courthouse, swirling around the statue of Thurgood Marshall, dusting the pavement on Pratt and Lombard streets.

Take a look at the mercury, it's forty below. No use for a man to be dragging his feathers around in the snow. He's messed around with the big guys, and singed his wings....

Upstairs, in Jonathan Luna's quiet office, his eyeglasses, his cell phone, his laptop, his photographs, soon will be caged behind a police line. The paper trail leading out of his office, leading down to the courtroom below, admitted into evidence, flies home to roost.

Last night had been a night of wild mystery, and a sudden fall to earth. Today will be a day of mourning and tears.

Maybe now he'll fly back home, that Baltimore oriole.

Appendix

The official timeline

Here's the timeline of stops made by Jonathan Luna in the hours before his death, as released by the FBI:

Dec. 3, 2003:

- 11:38 pm - Luna's vehicle departs the U.S. Courthouse in Baltimore
- 11:49 pm - Luna's vehicle passes through Fort McHenry Tunnel Toll Plaza in Baltimore, northbound on Interstate 95

Dec. 4, 2003:

- 12:28 am - Luna's vehicle continues northbound and passes through the Perryville Toll Plaza in Maryland
- 12:46 am - Luna's vehicle passes through the Delaware Line Toll Plaza
- 12:57 am - Luna's debit card is used at an ATM at JFK Plaza in Newark, Del.
- 2:37 am (approximate time) - Luna's vehicle gets on the New Jersey turnpike at Exit 6A, from Route 130
- 2:47 am - Luna's vehicle enters the Pennsylvania turnpike at Exit 359, the Delaware River Bridge
- 3:20 am - Luna's debit card is used at a Sunoco gasoline station, King of Prussia, Pa., to purchase gas
- 4:04 am - Luna's vehicle exits the Pennsylvania turnpike at Exit 286, the Reading/Lancaster interchange
- 5:30 am - Luna's body is discovered off Dry Tavern Road in Denver, Pennsylvania

The Pennsylvania corruption chapters

These chapters, addressing security concerns at the Pennsylvania Turnpike, where Jonathan Luna last traveled, originally appeared in Part 3 of the book, as Chapters 21 through 26.

1
Town fathers try to fight alleged deep-rooted sex ring

To hear the FBI tell it, Jonathan Luna's death was not work related. With leaks to the press they point to sex, and search for lurid clues at the hotels surrounding the Pennsylvania turnpike.

To have been work related, this line of reasoning goes, Luna would have to have been involved in a deep-rooted prostitution ring run by other law enforcement officials with a working familiarity with the Pennsylvania turnpike, where his body was found.

U.S. Attorney Thomas DiBiagio, and the Baltimore office of the FBI, nonetheless promised the public no stone would be unturned in finding Jonathan Luna's killer. The acting FBI Agent in Charge for Maryland and Delaware, Jennifer Smith Love, at the same time asked the public for tips. Love promised the FBI was "aggressively investigating the circumstances surrounding Jonathan's death."

Should we take Agent Smith Love at her word?

If DiBiagio and Agent Smith Love had bothered to take an hour's drive north from Baltimore — not far from the area where Jonathan Luna was found dead — they'd have gotten an earful from some of the most respected and prominent citizens in south central Pennsylvania.

It turns out, these Pennsylvanians say, law enforcement personnel are running a deep-rooted prostitution ring out of a Pennsylvania county courthouse, not far from where Luna was murdered. They fear this not-too-secret sex ring has ties both to Baltimore organized crime figures, and a secret law enforcement fund. Concerned citizens have been trying to close down this sex ring for several years, with no help from state or federal law enforcement. In fact, they alleged, local and state officials are keeping the sex ring in business.

One of the alleged suspects in this Pennsylvania/Maryland prostitution ring holds a contract to provide security for the Pennsylvania turnpike.

At the time of Jonathan Luna's death I was at work on a book concerning the amazing degrees of systemic corruption in the communities of south central Pennsylvania, specifically York County, and to a lesser extent, neighboring Lancaster County, where Jonathan Luna's body was found.

Community members for some time in York County have been coming to me with any number of stories involving official corruption, prostitution, even murder. They complain the county, and state, legal establishment won't lift a finger to investigate, much less shut down, the prostitution rings.

South central Pennsylvania remains a hotbed for illicit sex. As most travelers know, or can readily deduce, Pennsylvania's highway truck stops are crawling with hookers and pimps. A central Pennsylvania sex trade also flourishes on the internet. Wife swapping, sex clubs, you name it, you can find it, without looking far or hard.

Did Jonathan Luna die meeting a prostitute, as FBI leakers intimate? It seems far-fetched, due to his personal history, the time of his disappearance, and his unfinished business for the next day. Yet the FBI seems unwilling, or unable, to follow its own assertion to its logical conclusion.

If Luna were to have sought a hooker in Pennsylvania, it's unlikely he was cruising the many truck stops and street bazaars where sex is for sale. It's much more likely he would have been lured into, and involved with, one of the sex rings run by law enforcement personnel, such as the one run by the police in Baltimore, or the sex ring run out of the county courthouse in York, Pennsylvania. The Pennsylvania sex ring, allegedly run by security personnel with close ties to law enforcement, at this writing in 2004 enjoys the de facto protection of a district attorney, county judges and their overseers in the state capitol. Just like in Prohibition.

It helps to understand regional influences in southern

Pennsylvania. Lancaster County, where Luna's body was found, historically has been a satellite community of Philadelphia. Going back to the days of Quaker founding, Lancastrian merchants and farmers brought their wares to Philadelphia to sell.

Cross the Susquehanna River west into York County, and it's a different story. York County, adjoining Lancaster County on its western boarder, has historically seen itself as a satellite of *Baltimore.*

Look at a map and you'll see why. Baltimore is closer. The old rail lines and roads tie York to Baltimore.

Many southerners have immigrated to southern York County. Both Baltimore and York County held broad-based southern sympathies during the Civil War. Several times in Pennsylvania history, in the nineteenth and early twentieth centuries, York County and points west threatened to fully throw in with Baltimore's expanding railroad and canal system. This risked the viability of Pennsylvania's own routes to westward expansion, including the Pennsylvania Rail Road.

In my history of political patronage on the Pennsylvania turnpike, *When the Levee Breaks,* published in 1993, I point out, "Many western Pennsylvanians feverishly advocated tying Pittsburgh into the growing Baltimore B & O canal and rail system, on into Ohio, completely bypassing Philadelphia and the eastern part of the state. This scheme had the potential to tear the state in half and permanently damage state-wide development." The very real threat of Baltimore connecting to Pittsburgh finally spurred Philadelphians in 1847 into backing a three million dollar stock offering to finance the Pennsylvania Rail Road's northern route across Pennsylvania. The PRR effectively cut Baltimore out of the loop. Philadelphia's railroad came too late to stop the growing influence of New York City to the north, and Governor De Witt Clinton's Erie Canal.

To this day there's a rivalry between Philadelphia and Baltimore. One cannot overstate the cultural influence and gravitational pull of Baltimore on southern Pennsylvania communities, particularly York County.

From some sections of York, Pennsylvania, it's a quick, forty-five minute drive south on I-83 to Baltimore. It was widely noted at the time of Jonathan Luna's death that this drive through York is the most direct route from Baltimore to the spot where Luna's body was found.

Yet, for some reason, this direct route wasn't taken.

This combination of factors — convenience to Baltimore's crime emporiums, the obscurity of backwoods south-central Pennsylvania, and inter-state jurisdictional difficulties — made York County a garden spot for a sex ring operated and protected by law enforcement officials.

Moreover, Pennsylvania organized crime families — the Bufalinos and their successors — have long claimed a piece of Baltimore's mean streets.

When individuals close to the York County district attorney's office decided to set up a prostitution ring in the York County courthouse, connections with Baltimore organized crime played a role, the town newspaper, the York Dispatch, learned.

By all accounts, the sex trade in York County was booming before it was made a semi-official and none-too-secret business in the county courthouse. Massage parlors, escort services, and sex clubs have thrived in York, Pennsylvania for decades. An industrial town, York long tolerated streetwalkers as a service for the factory workers. Sex and hard drinking are time-honored traditions there.

These ingrained practices, among others, in turn deeply corrupted the police and courts of York. York cops for years were serviced by hookers in a bicycle shop downtown, among other places. Judges for years looked the other way, and even refused to treat oral sex as prostitution. In the 1990s, prominent York businessmen affiliated with the Chamber of Commerce — and other political donators — formed a group called the Reciprocity Club to facilitate the sex trade, with the blessing, even the participation, of some town fathers. Many members of the club are the top businessmen in their fields, active in the country club set. They include real estate developers, printers, and car dealers. Picture, if you would, a backwoods secret sex society. Stanley Kubrick's *Eyes Wide Shut* meets Hee Haw.

This arrangement remains to this day. The York County courthouse prostitution ring is deep-rooted, well-financed, all-corrupting, and, involving as it does law enforcement officials, self-protecting.

At the heart of it, observers allege, is a secret fund in the office of

York County District Attorney Stanley Rebert.

In the late-1990s, the arrangement exploded into full-fledged scandal when a young, up-and-coming Pennsylvania lawmaker, state senator Dan Delp, found himself lured into the prostitution ring by associates of the DA's office.

The scandal became newspaper fodder in Pennsylvania. In the end, it would cost Senator Delp his political career, and the curious deaths of two men connected with the prostitution ring, and thought to have mob connections.

At the center of the ongoing controversy are two York private investigators with close ties to the district attorney's office: Richard Parks and Russell Wantz.

Parks would be found dead in 1997, an apparent victim of suicide under mysterious circumstances.

Wantz remains protected by District Attorney Rebert, York countians connected to the scandal allege. More colloquially, they're protecting each other. Wantz for years owned a York County car dealership. Wantz's other business, the Schaad Detective Agency, at this writing in 2004, provides security for the York County courthouse, and sundry state agencies, including the Pennsylvania turnpike, the Pennsylvania Department of Transportation, and the Pennsylvania Liquor Control Board.

It's not at all clear who's protecting the public.

I touched on the York County courthouse prostitution ring in my 2002 book, *The Wrong Car.* The book concerns the 1969 murder of Lillie Belle Allen, a young, black, minister's daughter, and the murder's subsequent cover-up. Allen was brutally murdered under the watching eyes of racist York policemen. At a trial in 2002, witnesses placed the current county sheriff, William Hose, his deputy sheriff, James Vangreen, and other former policemen, at a white-power police rally preceding Allen's murder.

The man convicted of pulling the trigger on Lillie Belle Allen, Robert Messersmith, testified in late 2002 that he was encouraged to shoot blacks by the racist policemen, including Sheriff Bill Hose. Messersmith testified, "(Jim) Vangreen, the police commissioner

William Hose, Jim Brown, Mike Brown, Newt Brown, Willard Dinges and two or three other officers were there at least."

Yet Hose, Vangreen and other Republicans go unprosecuted by the Republican district attorney, who instead curiously prosecuted the Democratic mayor for the same murder of Ms. Allen. Fortunately, there is no statute of limitations on murder, and the York City Council has requested the currently unreceptive U.S. Justice Department to reopen the case, which presumably could lead to charges of murder filed against Hose, Vangreen and others.

Allen's murder seems to grow more famous with the passage of time. Hose, Vangreen and the others who may have attended the white-power rally leading to Allen's murder can't rest too easy.

In York County, Pennsylvania, a stone's throw from where Jonathan Luna died, corrupt and racist police have no bones about killing a defenseless black in organized, premeditated fashion, and covering up the murder for years. They're still doing it. Ask Lillie Belle Allen.

Better yet, ask Sheriff Bill Hose, or his deputy, Jim Vangreen.

The transparently appalling, endemic levels of corruption in York County, Pennsylvania, and the refusal of the U.S. Justice Department to take action, sparked my interest. This, after all, was the community that hosted the drafting of our federal Articles of Confederation in 1777. It's where America started. How far had we fallen, from hope and honor, to hookers and whores, and why?

In *The Wrong Car,* touching on the ongoing and highly curious sex-in-the-courthouse scandal in York, PA, I noted:

"The most socially prominent of these secret sex clubs calls itself, interestingly enough, The Reciprocity Club.... Activities of The Reciprocity Club include greased pig events attended by strippers and call girls. A local restaurant was once booked after hours for the greased pig night, featuring a slippery pig running wild through the establishment, chased by the girls, themselves chased by club members. They wrecked the place. The restaurant never had the club back. Other sex activities included golf games where the winner of each hole was awarded a blowjob from a hooker."

In 2004 a shocked worker in the food service industry described to me what happened when catering staff arrived at a Reciprocity Club dinner at Ski Roundtop, outside Harrisburg, in northern York County. It gives new meaning to ski lifts. The caterers found a surprise menu item. A roomful of wealthy and prominent York County businessmen and others passed strippers and hookers around the dinner table. "As they sat eating their dinner they'd pass the women around from place-setting to place-setting and perform oral sex on them," I was told. "There was no bathroom on the floor where they were eating, so they took the hookers to a men's room downstairs. At the end of the night there were used condoms all over the men's room floor."

The women on the Ski Roundtop menu were supplied by caterers of a different stripe.

I noted in *The Wrong Car,* "Sex clubs need 'girls.' For a steady stream of fresh girls, the clubs relied on several York-area 'escort services.'"

David Ness and Richard "Dicky" Parks ran one of these escort services, a venture called Platinum Escorts.

Richard Parks was a York County private investigator with deep, varied, and long-lasting ties to DA Rebert's office. Witnesses would say that Parks used to flash a special DA's office badge. When he wasn't passing himself off as one of the DA's associates, Parks was a partner in Platinum Escorts. He had other activities on the fringe of the law. He also used to run midnight "sex club" parties at a bar in town.

Dicky Parks regularly socialized and golfed with Assistant District Attorney William H. Graff, the county drug prosecutor.

William Graff kept popping up in the story. Graff remains, in 2004, a high-profile, deputy district attorney in the York County DA's office. Graff was a close friend of Parks, and helped Parks get his private investigator's license. Graff also administers a shadowy drug fund in the DA's office.

I note in *The Wrong Car,* "When Parks applied for a private investigator's license in 1994, deputy DA Graff paid the $200 fee; Graff's name is on a receipt in the clerk of court's office. When Parks was granted his license in a court hearing in April 1994, Graff's wife,

Leah B. Graff, represented Parks in this proceeding. DA Stanley Rebert himself, raising no objections, represented the commonwealth."

Dicky Parks, when he wasn't hanging around the DA's office and passing himself off as a private eye, concentrated his talents running Platinum Escorts. "We started it to make money," his escort service partner, David Ness, told me.

Another York-area escort service was operated by Larry Keeney, Keeney's wife, and a silent partner. Keeney would end up committing suicide under mysterious circumstances, on the eve of forced testimony before a grand jury.

The public of south central Pennsylvania would only learn some of the facts surrounding Keeney and his enterprises. The most startling facts were withheld by the town's newspaper company, concerned citizens say, under pressure from District Attorney Rebert.

The town's afternoon daily newspaper, the York Dispatch, hired a private investigator to get to the bottom, as it were, of the sex club. The editor and publisher of the newspaper ended up taking his concerns to the city police commissioner. The newspaper's hired detective, its publisher, and, later, York's police commissioner, ended up hearing allegations that Russell Wantz, owner of the Schaad Detective Agency, was Keeney's not-so-secret partner. The newspaper's publisher and the city police commissioner officially asked an agent of the U.S. Justice Department to investigate.

The Justice Department did nothing, locals complain. For some reason the Justice Department doesn't care that a sex club is run from a county courthouse down the street from the spot where our Articles of Confederation were drafted.

The late escort provider Larry Keeney operated several massage parlors, including one on Queen Street in York, and one in Wrightsville. The Wrightsville establishment, near the Susquehanna River, provided easy access across the Columbia bridge to Lancaster County. Keeney is dead, and his establishment is gone, but I'm told another well-heeled sex club operates quite openly in Wrightsville in 2004.

Wrightsville is about thirty miles from the place where Jonathan Luna lost his life.

Investigators looking into the Pennsylvania courthouse sex ring over time would come to suspect that payments to the various escort services also served as a money-laundering scheme enabling broader criminal activities. Observers came to suspect that at least some of this cash flowed from the district attorney's office.

Again, as with the Baltimore police sex scandal, we see sex and slush funds.

York County ranks high in drug confiscation money doled out by the state. The late Dicky Parks' friend and sponsor, William Graff, the county drug prosecutor, administers these funds. The money coming into the district attorney's office is well documented. The money flowing out has never been properly accounted for, the newspaper publisher learned, leading to suspicions it's been used for dark purposes, needful of laundering. Hence the sex clubs and the escort services.

Also undisclosed is the amount of federal money flowing into the York County district attorney's office. All federal funds for police activity in the county flow through the district attorney's office, one concerned official told me. It's a substantial sum of federal money, I'm told, well over $10,000. If they had a desire, the federal government could also claim jurisdiction in any investigation. (It was a $10,000 threshold of federal funds that, by law, allowed the Baltimore U.S. attorney to investigate Maryland state police Superintendent Ed Norris.)

Now we get to another telling part: how and why Parks and company used sex to lure astray a promising young public official, a protégé of the district attorney.

One day, near Labor Day in 1996, Pennsylvania state Senator Dan Delp asked his friend Dicky Parks for a girl, "an escort."

Dan Delp was the young son of a wealthy York industrialist. The young Delp parlayed his family's fortune into a state senate seat. Delp quickly became the darling and rising star of the Republican leadership in York and at the state capitol in Harrisburg. He was a close friend and favorite of Rebert's, and county Republican chairman John

Thompson. Rebert and Delp used to share campaign funds. Rebert in many ways was a mentor.

David Ness remembers the fateful day in 1996 when he spoke with Dicky Parks about getting a girl for state Senator Delp. "Dick said can I get two girls to go on a boat ride with Dan Delp? I said yeah I'd be able to," Ness remembers. "I talked to two girls and they said they'd do it."

The girls traveled to Harrisburg to meet Delp and one of his legislative aides. They were taken for an outing on a boat. Afterwards Delp and his aide took the young women to a Harrisburg sports bar. The bar and restaurant was a popular hangout for the late Aldo Magnelli, the Bufalino family capo of central and southern Pennsylvania, and his associates.

The bill at this mob hangout was charged to Delp's state expense account. One of the girls the senator took to the bar was just nineteen years old.

From there it was back to Delp's place, where the escorts spent the night, and had sex with the state senator and his aide.

In the morning the young women were sent on their way with fifty dollars each. They were mad about it, and complained to David Ness. Ness in turn passed on the complaint to Dicky Parks and the legislative aide. The aide quickly produced one hundred and fifty for each girl, in cash, given by way of Parks, Ness says. Parks kicked in another hundred dollars for each girl.

In 1996 and 1997, the Pennsylvania state police began a crackdown of York County escort services and massage parlors. The cops booked their own undercover sex event at a local motel. When the girls showed up at the motel with the escort service driver they were busted. They began to talk, angrily saying they had important clients. Before long one of the girls complained she'd been with state senator Dan Delp.

Escort service provider Larry Keeney by and by was arrested, and his bank accounts frozen. Stashed away in the bank accounts, I'm told, investigators found $1.3 to $1.4 million. People wondered about the origin of the unaccountable cash deposits, about the identities of those who may have helped with the untraceable cash sums. At one point, an observer told me, criminal charges mysteriously were withdrawn against Keeney by DA Rebert.

State Senator Delp soon was prosecuted by the state attorney general for misappropriation of state funds, procuring a nineteen-year-old prostitute and providing alcohol to an under-aged drinker. Before long, Delp would give up his senate seat; two men would kill themselves (or were helped, some say); and DA Stan Rebert's office was shown to have connections to prostitution and mob operatives.

"The district attorney or some members of his staff had been called 'clients' or friends of Ness," the town's morning paper, the York Daily Record, reported. "Rebert has described the accusations as 'baseless.'"

David Ness tells me that he and Parks never sent girls to Rebert or his staff, or other country club types, just Senator Delp. There may have been, he allows, "bachelor parties where police were present."

The real provider of girls for the country club set, Ness says, was Larry Keeney, and Keeney's silent partner. "He had a lot of people high up in the country club circle," Ness told me.

Ness says one of his girls also worked for Keeney. This girl told him that Russell Wantz, the owner of the Schaad Detective Agency, was involved with Keeney's operation, Ness alleges.

The state attorney general's office soon convened a grand jury on the Delp-escort service affair.

Escort service operators Larry Keeney, Dicky Parks and Dave Ness, Senator Delp, drug prosecutor William Graff and DA Stan Rebert all found themselves in trouble. Other escort service providers began to come under the spotlight. Many more upper-crust York countians involved in the secret sex clubs might soon find themselves exposed.

Many prominent York countians were beginning to squirm. That's when the bodies started turning up.

In January 1997, while traveling in Moosic, Pennsylvania to offer court testimony, escort provider Larry Keeney, age forty-nine, was found dead in his locked room, stabbed a single time in the chest. The police suspected foul play, but the coroner ruled suicide.

By this time Keeney and his wife had been charged by the state with promoting prostitution, criminal conspiracy and *money laundering.*

"It's a locked-room mystery," an observer says. Stabbing one's self in the chest seems like a curious way to commit suicide. But if not by his own hand, how had the room been locked? Whatever happened, it killed a man as dead as a great reckoning in a little room, as the bard writes.

Many suspect a professional job. Perhaps someone made threats against Keeney's loved ones, and forced him to do the job himself. Not far from Moosic lives one of the state's top bosses, a businessman with mysterious legal immunities, a successor to the Russell Bufalino crime family, which for years controlled the state's underworld. The legal immunities of the boss aren't so mysterious, one investigator tells me. Local police, Pennsylvania state troopers, judges, magistrates and politicians, and all level of functionaries, are on his payroll.

Jonathan Luna was dumped in his territory. When someone dumps a federal prosecutor in your territory it means one of three things. You're losing your hold on the territory; someone's very foolish; or someone's sending you a message.

Back in 1997, one of the main suppliers of prostitutes to The Reciprocity Club was dead under mysterious circumstances. Leaving a wife, a silent partner tucked away in York County law enforcement circles, and bank accounts filled with large, untraceable sums.

Dicky Parks, with ties to the DA's office, not only was involved in prostitution, but also the servicing of video poker machines, gambling, and money laundering. "Dick Parks was a collection guy for poker machines, and he used to take the money to Butler, Pennsylvania," one investigator told me. Butler has figured in recent mob escapades in Pennsylvania. A gambling center, its denizens had links to former Lackawanna County DA and state Attorney General Ernie Preate. Preate in the 1990s was prosecuted for links to underworld gambling. The mob likes vending businesses, as endless streams of coins are perfect for money laundering.

So with Dicky Parks, we had prostitution, gambling, money laundering. Investigators began to suspect the mob had infiltrated the York County district attorney's office and its courts.

"We started to see lots of flags," I was told. Flags involving not only the DA, but also York County judges.

A York County judge strangely ruled oral sex for money wasn't prostitution. "For a number of years you could get a blowjob in York County without fear of arrest," I'm told. This very accommodating court ruling immeasurably helped the sex trade, until a higher court overruled the county judge.

A York bar openly known as a house of prostitution and gambling remains open and goes unprosecuted to this day, seemingly untouchable. One of the escort service providers told investigators the bar has links to the Baltimore mob.

"We started wondering which mob controlled York," I was told by a newspaper employee. Baltimore? Butler? Northeast Pennsylvania? It was starting to look like one big happy family, helped in no small part by corrupt York law enforcement and courts.

On June 16, 1997, at the height of the unfolding sex, money laundering, and political scandal, Dicky Parks, the friend of the county drug prosecutor, shot himself in the head with a 9mm. He died the next day. He was now the second man connected to the sex scandal to die under mysterious circumstances.

"Dick just wanted this thing to end," his partner in Platinum Escorts, David Ness, says.

Others aren't sure it's so simple. State prosecutors and others wondered whether Parks had been pushed.

"In the back of my mind I can't stop thinking that Dicky was threatened," one observer says. "Some very big people were about to get drawn in. I can't help thinking someone came to Dick and said this better stop now, or one of his family members would die. So he killed himself to stop it."

Upon Parks' untimely death, York's morning newspaper, the Daily Record, ran a story with this fascinating sentence, which, in any healthy community, would set alarm bells ringing: "Parks' name has been linked to York's Republican state Sen. Dan Delp, the county district attorney's office and several accused prostitutes."

York community members remain disturbed by reports that the courthouse prostitution ring retains connections to Baltimore and/or Pennsylvania organized crime figures. The DA's office was actively looking the other way, and obviously was in no position to weed out any corruption. Worse, concerned citizens didn't know where to turn for help. (Now we begin to see the importance of legislation enabling federal government involvement in entrenched corruption cases like this.)

Equally disturbing were reports of unaccountable funds and allegations of money laundering in the DA's office, a secret cash flow allegedly used to help finance the sex ring, and Deputy DA drug prosecutor William Graff's recurring and conspicuous role in all this.

And what about the late Larry Keeney's silent partner? Most disturbing of all were open and unchallenged allegations of a security contractor's alleged ongoing involvement in the sex ring. Because of his close association with the beleaguered district attorney, the community came to view the security contractor as protected. So who's protecting the public?

The York sex clubs, meanwhile, roll on in 2004, responsible for several deaths and untold corruption in a people's courthouse in south central Pennsylvania.

The influence of the Baltimore sex trade continues to spread north. In late 2003, even the Pennsylvania State Police complained about open prostitution at a truck stop on I-78, north of Harrisburg. The state police said pimps were running women in from Baltimore and Ohio, and complained there wasn't much they could do about it. Truckers, they said, were protecting the women. In fact, in April 2008, *Pennsylvania State Police Trooper Kevin Coleman pleaded guilty to tipping off pimps and prostitutes at the truck stop in exchange for money and sex.*

Meanwhile, incredibly, Russell Wantz's Schaad Detective Agency, alleged to have ties to the sex ring, won contracts to provide security for the Pennsylvania Department of Transportation, and the Pennsylvania turnpike.

2
'We didn't know who the good guys were'

Shortly after Jonathan Luna dropped off the face of the earth near Exit 286 of the turnpike, I contacted several former and current reporters and editors associated with the York Dispatch. Why had the sex exposés suddenly stopped? I asked.

J.P. Kurish was one of the reporters who wrote for the York Dispatch at the time of the courthouse sex scandal. Kurish has since left the paper and today works for the state senate in Harrisburg. He's amiable, with an easy-going personality.

The week after Jonathan Luna's death I spoke with Kurish and we reflected on the York courthouse sex scandal. He described almost a comic atmosphere attending the episode, of participants who were none too bright and who seemed to suffer a comic pratfall at every turn.

"These guys weren't the sharpest knives in the drawer," Kurish chuckles. That said, "We spoke often at the newspaper about the implications of all this, and the problems of systemic corruption in York."

J.P. Kurish recounted for me the beginning of the York, Pennsylvania courthouse sex scandal. It began inauspiciously, but soon would drag his newspaper into a black hole from which no light would escape.

Kurish says he was covering a political function when a pol came up to him and asked, "Are you going to do anything about Delp and the prostitute?"

The sexcapades at the courthouse had spread like a contagion to the statehouse, and already was the buzz of political circles. His curiosity aroused, Kurish says he made a few phone calls.

It soon became clear, thanks no less to a threatening letter from

Sen. Delp's attorney, that here was an important story. Someone appeared to be supplying prostitutes out of the York County courthouse, and a senator had used state funds to pay for "a date" with one of the women. (An interesting aspect of local mores, newspaper employees note, was that the public seemed more upset about the misuse of the public money than the existence of the sex clubs.)

The Dispatch found itself sitting on quite a story, but how to proceed?

The principals in the scandal are described by former reporter Kurish as washouts from the gang that couldn't shoot straight. Dicky Parks, one of the two deceased ringleaders, fashioned himself as a gangster-in-training. It was as if Parks was reading from a gangster manual. Even so, always beneath the surface lurked a threat.

"One day in the middle of the whole thing Parks called me up at the paper as if to chat," Kurish recalls. "He says, 'I know where your wife is.'"

Kurish described his impression of Parks and company as goofballs intent on influence peddling. It was always about the money. Parks and associates approached young Senator Delp with offers of women in order to win state contracts and, ultimately, protection. Parks' connections to the DA's office put the young senator at ease. DA Rebert, after all, was Delp's mentor.

As the Pennsylvania sex scandal unfolded in the late 1990s, and the systemic nature of corruption in York County became more evident, the newspaper staff didn't know where to turn, or whom to trust. They noticed that everyone in town seemed to play golf with either the pimps, or the lawyers in the DA's office. They saw that judges, sworn to uphold the law, turned a blind eye.

Even the vice cops seemed to be corrupted. One cop mysteriously paid off his mortgage with cash, Kurish recalls. The sex-crazed nature of the town spilled out onto both sides of the police blotter. Even the cops were getting into The Act.

One of York's primary state police undercover vice cops convinced his supervisor that he had to actually *receive* oral sex before he could make an arrest, Kurish laughs. Court cases include descriptions of the state trooper involved in sex acts. At one sex bust, DA Rebert supposedly watched from a closet, Kurish says.

"We didn't know who the good guys were," Kurish tells me.

South central Pennsylvania seems at times awash in a sea of corruption. The Dispatch didn't have the resources or staff to get to the bottom of things, Kurish says.

Even so, some things were evident. "There's no doubt (deputy DA drug prosecutor) Bill Graff was at the heart of everything that was going on," Kurish smiles, arching his brows. The involvement of the county's chief drug prosecutor and the unaccountable nature of the funds in the DA's office cried out for investigation by appropriate authorities. But the office of Republican state Attorney General Mike Fisher flatly refused to investigate Republican DA Rebert's office. Fisher has since gone on the bench as a federal judge.

The ensuing spectacle of trying to find somebody to do something to investigate the sex club slush fund at times seemed not only futile, but also ridiculous and pathetic. You just can't imagine a Norman Rockwell painting of the public spectacle. Father, hat in hand, speaking up, trying to get somebody to do something about the meatball prostitution ring being run in the courthouse. Down the street from the spot where Thomas Paine once debated the future of democracy. Ultimately it's very disempowering. In Pennsylvania these days good people still bother to complain, but you can't even get someone to stop by and promise to at least look into things. We've gotten to the point where we're complaining about that.

Kurish remembers one low point: Dispatch editor and publisher Jim Sneddon on the phone to the state attorney general's office, pleading with them to look into the case.

The newspaper staff felt particularly powerless to deal with allegations of secret slush funds and organized crime involvement. For that York required a real lawman. But where to find one?

3
Daily newspaper hires private detective, unearths allegations involving turnpike security provider

At times like this, my mind wanders to the story of Diogenes, who's said to have poked around ancient Athens with a lantern in broad daylight, searching for an honest man. When darkness is nigh, I too like to lift my lamp around a community, and search for the good.

The citizens of York luckily had men like Kurish and editor and publisher Jim Sneddon working for their town newspaper. Sneddon, like Kurish, seems to genuinely care about his community, what's going on, and what's *not* going on.

Sneddon sports a white shock of hair, set off by a snowy Mark Twain mustache. He's got a streak of idealism in him, a sense of how things ought to be. Principles make a man dangerous in a town that's gone bad.

Sneddon and his staff early on worried that the limited resources of the Dispatch were no match for the magnitude of the story. Dispatch reporters by and large had no heavy-duty investigative experience. They needed help, which they knew wouldn't be forthcoming from "law enforcement sources" working in the DA's office. So where to turn?

The paper's attorney, Niles S. Benn, took an unusual course of action, Sneddon tells me. Benn in his own right is a stalwart of the York community. His practice represents the town newspaper, and he's a member of the Rotary and other community organizations. Benn has served as chairman of the board of Holy Spirit Health Systems. For five years Benn served as chairman of the board of Holy Spirit Hospital in Camp Hill, in suburban Harrisburg. Holy Spirit is operated by the Catholic order Sisters of Christian Charity, of New Jersey. These are community pillars.

Hoping to expose the courthouse sex ring, Benn hired a private investigator to work for the newspaper. I'm unaware of any other instance of a newspaper hiring a private investigator for editorial purposes.

The newspaper's hiring of a private detective is amazing and dangerous all at once. Reporters and newspapers enjoy immunities not enjoyed by private eyes. Our First Amendment guarantees press freedoms. In Pennsylvania, a shield law also rightly protects writers from revealing sources. None of these protections apply to a private eye. A private investigator is licensed by a court, and can be called to testify before a court at any time. When a newspaper is reporting on political or judicial corruption, such as we see here, the use of a private investigator becomes problematic.

The hiring of a private investigator is a transaction in the public marketplace. When a public institution such as a newspaper hires a licensed private detective to investigate a public official — a senator, or a county district attorney, or their associates, say, a provider of public security — that's a very public act, and the public has a right to know about it. Sometimes there's unseen ramifications for the employer of the investigator. Ralph Nader gained fame by writing an exposé on car safety, *Unsafe at Any Speed,* in the 1960s. Shortly thereafter General Motors hired a private detective to investigate Nader's politics, religion and sex life, an act that backfired on the car company when the public found out. Nader sued the car maker, and won $425,000 in an out-of-court settlement.

When an institution hires a private eye to look into public business, the lines of private and public blur. Sooner or later, the public finds out about it. And why not? The inspector is examining the public's house.

So where's our report?

Sneddon tells me that newspaper attorney Niles Benn contracted a private investigator who Benn claimed to have worked with in the past. Sneddon says his understanding was that the private investigator was based in Harrisburg. He says he met with the detective a few times. The handling and payment of the private eye were administered through Benn, Sneddon says. The idea, Sneddon explains, was to set up some sort of "firewall" between the newspaper staff and the detective. No doubt for some of the aforementioned reasons.

The newspaper-paid detective gathered information and reported back. The plan was for the newspaper reporters to take it from there. Several rather peculiar things happened on the way to publication.

Sneddon says the private eye proved particularly adept at talking with the prostitutes, some who had moved on to Reading, Pennsylvania. Again, not far from where Luna was found.

What did the town newspaper, its staff, and its attorney, who works alongside the good Sisters of Christian Charity, find out with the help of its private investigator?

Much of what I've already described:

- As is the case in Baltimore police HQ, there's a money laundering component to the York, Pennsylvania courthouse prostitution ring. The money laundering, the daily newspaper staff came to believe, played a role in broader criminal activities; loosely accounted public funds administered by deputy DA, and chief drug prosecutor, William Graff, were suspected of finding their way into the money laundering scheme.
- As mentioned, organized crime figures, some possibly based in Baltimore, are believed to have set up shop in sleepy York, and are involved in the supply of women, and other enterprises.
- Russell Wantz, the York car dealer and the owner of the Schaad Detective Agency, was alleged by numerous Yorkers to have involvement with The Reciprocity Club, and its well-heeled sex ring. Wantz started out in the vending machine business in York and over the years has worked in various law enforcement capacities in York County.

The daily newspaper staff grew concerned about the security contractor. Wantz soon moved to the center of its investigation.

All this is remarkable, since Wantz continues to provide security for some of the most sensitive public places in Pennsylvania, including the turnpike.

The Schaad Detective Agency advertises an office in Lancaster County, on Rohrerstown Road, off Rt. 30.

Schaad is also listed on the web page membership roster of the Maryland Investigators and Security Association, which lobbies for security interests in Maryland. (When you click the "Code of Ethics" link on the web page it humorously comes up blank.)

Publisher Sneddon and others wondered what to do. Their civic duty, and pride, seemed to require them to do something. So they sought police help.

4
City police commissioner, seeking help, gets 'File 13'

Newspaper publisher Jim Sneddon took his concerns, and information, to York, Pennsylvania, city police Commissioner Herbert Grofcsik. Grofcsik is an upright law enforcement official. He's regarded in York as an honest, good cop. In this story, he's one of the few in law enforcement who actually did his job. Police Commissioner Grofcsik turned out to be the real lawman everyone was looking for. But he could only go so far in a community gone bad.

Working in his official capacity as police commissioner, Grofcsik says he heard evidence, among other things, that security provider Russell Wantz was allegedly involved in a secret prostitution ring, centered around the York County courthouse, with tentacles spreading throughout central Pennsylvania and its law enforcement circles; that a secret drug fund administered by deputy DA William Graff was allegedly used in connection with the prostitution ring, and was furthermore allegedly used in a money laundering capacity for broader criminal activities; and that a compromised District Attorney Stan Rebert was turning an unlawful blind eye to all this.

Grofcsik says he knew his hands were tied, due to the district attorney office's close ties to the prostitution ring. "The DA's office wouldn't do anything," Grofcsik told me. "And the state attorney general's office was refusing to do anything due to politics. So I moved it on to a higher authority."

Seeking help, York Police Commissioner Grofcsik called in federal investigators. Grofcsik says he arranged a meeting between newspaper publisher Sneddon and an agent of the U. S. Justice Department.

Sneddon met with the federal agent and shared his concerns. He says the agent took his information.

At this writing, in 2004, Sneddon serves as York's city controller, an elected position.

Police Commissioner Grofcsik makes the obvious case that the Pennsylvania sex clubs require thorough federal investigation. All the more so in light of the security risks posed by the allegations involving Russell Wantz and his company's security contracts with Pennsylvania state agencies.

Broader issues become evident. Standard background checks used today for security employment aren't good enough, Grofcsik points out. Background checks currently used on our prospective law enforcement and security contractors are grossly inadequate for those entrusted with public security.

The current "background check" discovers little more than one's arrest record and perhaps credit history, Grofcsik tells me. Even these meager records, Grofcsik points out, can be altered or easily erased by a dishonest law enforcement professional.

Would a background check reveal the type of the allegations like those involving the sex clubs that have been passed on to federal investigators? I asked Grofcsik.

"No," he says matter-of-factly. He says the U.S. Department of Justice must get actively involved by assigning experienced investigators to interview the many people willing or available to talk in York, PA. "They need to put a few men on the ground and on the case."

As it stands today, law enforcement personnel pretty much vouch for each other. Glaring problems in this good-old-boy network are evident. This also helps explain why the FBI is reluctant to turn the looking glass inward when looking for Jonathan Luna's murderer. They all vouch for each other.

A few weeks after Jonathan Luna's death, in December 2003, I spoke with Grofcsik about the status of the Pennsylvania sex club case.

Perhaps the federal investigators were "still working on it," Grofcsik said he hoped. "Or maybe they stuck it in a File 13 someplace."

Here all these pillars of the community are asking for help from the U.S. Justice Department. The police commissioner. The editor and publisher of the daily newspaper. The lawyer who works alongside our good Sisters of Christian Charity. And all the other concerned citizens of central Pennsylvania.

It's tough to think that all these good people have been asking for help all along, yet no one in the United States Justice Department has done a thing. Maybe soon they will.

Agent Jennifer Smith Love, after all, says no stone will be left unturned.

5
Not the sound, but the silence

What happened to the local newspaper coverage of the York courthouse sex ring? It was shut down, newspaper employees say, under pressure from the district attorney caught in the middle of the scandal.

Former Dispatch reporter Kurish remembers that developments were quite sobering, even frightening. They'd already received threats. Two men had died, under mysterious circumstances. It was a critical time.

Editor and publisher Jim Sneddon says he gave York Dispatch reporter Mark Scolforo a list of questions to pursue with the district attorney's office. Scolforo, Sneddon intimates, for some reason dragged his feet and then, insubordinately, outright refused to work on the story.

"Scolforo refused to follow instructions and work on the story," Sneddon bristles.

Meanwhile, Dispatch insiders say they suspect District Attorney Stanley Rebert applied pressure on the newspaper to kill the story, and to fire publisher Sneddon.

"I know for a fact Rebert called (Dispatch president) Joe Zerbe," Sneddon told me, when I asked about reports of pressure to kill the story. "About six weeks later I was fired."

Sneddon's firing at the paper officially has been attributed to an unrelated editing dispute. The Dispatch continues to publish under a U.S. Justice Department-approved anti-trust waiver called a joint operating agreement. The two York daily newspapers share ownership of their printing plant and other properties. Both papers continue to position themselves for ownership by a single company. To do all this they require the anti-trust waiver from the Justice Department.

It all seems to go back to the Justice Department, doesn't it?

Look at the travesty here: a newspaper has a story about the refusal of the Justice Department to investigate a sex ring and slush fund, perhaps with connections to the death of an assistant U.S. attorney, but the newspaper can't publish the story without fear Justice will retaliate by canceling its joint-operating agreement.

It's a troubling public offense when a district attorney pressures a newspaper. It's just as troubling when the newspaper caves in, with such important security matters at stake. Who is looking out for the public interest and trust? Who's looking out for the security of our public places?

The feeling here is that the public trust and safety has been violated by the Justice Department. The police and security personnel must get out of the prostitution business. But for that to happen in central Pennsylvania, the Justice Department must first get out of the newspaper business.

The public, and our Congress, should revisit the workings and wisdom of this and other Justice Department-approved newspaper and media arrangements.

In any event, Sneddon was gone, and Dispatch reporters say their paper acceded to the DA's pressure to drop the story.

Wantz's Schaad Detective Agency, protected by his hometown district attorney, and a chastised daily newspaper, remains uninvestigated. Schaad personnel guard the York County courthouse, and the Pennsylvania Department of Transportation licensing facility in Harrisburg. And now, the turnpike. It's not unusual to see Schaad personnel behind the scenes at these places, as one empties one's pockets to pass through security checkpoints.

For many Pennsylvanians familiar with the ongoing sex ring allegations, the presence of uninvestigated Schaad personnel at these sensitive public places causes a mix of emotions from derision to, at times, even fear and revulsion. Citizens must empty their pockets before Schaad personnel, but nobody bothers to check the guards. *Quis custodiet ipsos custodes?*

So the courthouse sex ring, unimpeded, keeps rolling to this day. I'm told one of the York County sex clubs today exploits a safe harbor in Wrightsville, where a club is run within an easy drive across the river into Lancaster County, not far, as the crow flies, from the isolated spot where prosecutor Jonathan Luna died.

Dispatch reporter Mark Scolforo's role becomes noteworthy. Why had Scolforo disobeyed his editor and refused to pursue the law enforcement sex ring slush fund story? Had he got wind that Sneddon was about to lose his editorship? In the ensuing years, after publisher Sneddon's departure from the Dispatch, reporter Scolforo became at times, well, a mouthpiece for the local DA's office. A stenographer for those in power. A good way to keep one's job at Pravda, I suppose. I've seen Scolforo withhold any amount of information from readers. But these days I've seen lots of reporters do that.

Scolforo's wife also works for the Dispatch. Had some hidden economic interest colored Mark Scolforo's actions or, rather, inactions? Was Scolforo scared, or just playing it safe? Was he frightened or intimidated by reports of mob involvement?

The York Dispatch in the last few years fell into precipitous decline. A mass of firings and an exodus of writers and editors have plagued the paper. Reporter Scolforo left the paper to write with the Associated Press, in the wire service's Harrisburg bureau. In recent years the AP too has had its share of problems.

In December 2003, Scolforo filed stories with the AP about the murder of Jonathan Luna. He handled the Pennsylvania end of many of the wire service stories. The AP, and Scolforo, generally took the tack in most of its dispatches that Luna's murder defied earthly explanation.

Two weeks or so after Jonathan Luna's murder, I visited Scolforo at the AP office in the main capitol building in Harrisburg.

I asked Scolforo about reports that the York Dispatch had learned of the involvement of Baltimore organized crime figures in the York courthouse sex ring.

He acknowledged that was the case. He suddenly looked alarmed, even scared.

I asked whether it might be within the realm of possibility that the Baltimore mob, with help from the sex ring Scolforo refused to expose in York, might have played a hand in the murder of Jonathan

Luna.

"It's conceivable," he allowed.

I mentioned that several people had expressed anger and revulsion about having to pass through security checkpoints at the courthouse and in state buildings, manned as they were by Schaad Detective Agency employees. Didn't it seem to Scolforo like a poor joke? I started to ask. His eyes bugged out at the mention of the Schaad people guarding high-security state buildings. Scolforo darted his eyes. He seemed to be looking off in a corner of his mind, to a place he didn't want to go.

Then, abruptly, he strangely said that he didn't think he'd be following that line of inquiry in his Associated Press reports.

I wasn't making any requests, I replied. I was writing about what had happened to cause the failure of the York Dispatch to publish.

I asked Scolforo why the story was spiked.

He suddenly, and curiously, flashed in anger. That's too mild. He exploded. "That's a matter involving my former employer, and I'm not going to talk about that!" he yelled. Nearby, children were singing Christmas carols. As I say, his wife still works at the Dispatch. Some conflict, economic or otherwise, is at work here, I considered.

The AP no longer has much competition in Pennsylvania from the United Press International, which years ago closed its offices in Harrisburg. In a state which once boasted hundreds of family-owned newspapers, Pennsylvania today is left in the dark by a monopoly press.

The Knight-Ridder-owned Philadelphia Inquirer is only a shadow of its former self. In its muckraking heyday in the 1970s, under the stewardship of Eugene Roberts, the Inquirer was heard. Now the Inky's fallen silent. It's not the sound, but the silence we must worry about, Roberts used to presciently warn. The only other large newspaper in the state, the Pittsburgh Post-Gazette— well, even in the ancient case of mobster John Bazzano, we see the Post-Gazette mysteriously places fig leaves over stories.

After exploding in anger, and expressing displeasure with my proclivity to actually publish a story, Scolforo stormed off. I must be doing something right. We'd been standing off the rotunda in the capitol building. It was nearing Christmas. School children sang carols on the capitol steps. By the door, capitol policemen were opening bags and examining the pockets of the visitors in the capitol rotunda, Pennsylvania's central public place. Having cleared security, Pennsylvanians are required to wear a badge marked "visitor."

Layers of public lies and deceit are at play here. Pennsylvania's news organizations aren't telling the public what they need to know about deficiencies and lawlessness in their police agencies and courts. Shadowy security officers working in our most sensitive public places hold themselves above any security checks.

The visiting public, who after all are the *owners,* not "visitors" in their own public houses, should perhaps more truthfully be issued badges which read "endangered."

6
A failure to communicate: 'Returned to Sender / Unread'

Police Commissioner Grofcsik left office in 2002 with the outgoing administration of Mayor Charles Robertson. While working on this book, I asked former Mayor Robertson whether he was aware that his police commissioner in his official capacity had asked federal authorities to investigate the York courthouse prostitution ring. Robertson expressed surprise.

"I had no idea," Robertson told me. "My policy as mayor was to stay out of the police and the fire department. I let the police commissioner do his job."

We wonder if a threatened District Attorney Rebert charged Mayor Robertson with the murder of Lillie Belle Allen solely to get Police Commissioner Grofcsik out of the way, and to stop the sex investigation of Rebert's office.

Robertson, himself a career policeman in York, volunteered he'd always made it his personal policy to steer a wide berth from Russell Wantz, the owner of Schaad Detective Agency. "Russell Wantz was always throwing parties, and sending me invitations to come," the mayor, who is a bachelor, says. "I never went to any of his parties."

Why not? I asked Robertson.

The mayor explained Wantz always had a bad reputation in the York police force. Wantz used to "practically live in the detective bureau" when he was hanging around his mentor, York police Detective Russell Schaad, the founder of the detective agency. Police Detective Captain Charles McCaffery, "told me to stay away from Wantz," Robertson said.

Quite by accident, early in 2003, I met a close relative of Richard Parks, the deceased escort provider, in a bookstore. This woman shook her head at all that had transpired, before and after the death of Parks. She recalled deputy DA Bill Graff sitting on the family sofa, grinning while Parks and his associates plied their trade.

"Russ Wantz is in the middle of it all," this woman tells me quietly. "But he's protected by the district attorney. No one can do anything about it." She shook her head and walked away.

Russell Wantz, the owner of the Schaad Detective Agency, has not only been given protection by his hometown DA. The Pennsylvania state police, and the FBI, are failing to do their jobs by not conducting a full background check of Wantz and his associates, as demanded by concerned citizens in York.

This was driven home to me one day when I visited Schaad office in the Pennsylvania Department of Transportation headquarters in Harrisburg. The Schaad agency has a small office off the main lobby, where Pennsylvanians stand in line to renew their driver's licenses, and vehicle registrations. Down the hall, applicants pose for their ID photos. Uniformed private guards wearing Schaad badges and insignia drift in and out of the office, patrolling the transportation headquarters and its grounds. One guard drifted out from a closed-to-the-public office where licenses and other documents are processed.

I stopped this Schaad guard to ask about employment prospects at the detective agency. Which state offices do they guard? I asked.

"We're here, the turnpike, the LCB (Liquor Control Board), all over the state," the guard bragged.

I was given a four-page Schaad Detective Agency application for employment. Upon my application for employment, the application advises, the appropriate "investigating" government agencies will be informed. Whatever that means.

"I authorize investigation of all statements contained in this application for employment as may be necessary in arriving at employment decision," the Schaad application reads. "I understand that an investigation may be made.... This inquiry may include information as to my character, general reputation, and personal characteristics, as well as information about my work performance and workplace conduct. I consent to this investigation and to the consideration of any statements or references or former employers that are given in response to the inquiry."

Hmm, I wondered, would the inquiry uncover whether the applicant had been involved in a sex club? What if the applicant worked as a caterer at a Reciprocity Club event?

With the application for employment, the Schaad guard gave me further instructions. To work in sensitive positions like the transportation building and the turnpike, the guard said, "you must get a form 235 from the Pennsylvania State Police. It includes an FBI background check."

Why then, I wondered, has not the owner of the Schaad Detective Agency been subjected to proper examination befitting his responsibility and the public trust, as his hometown police commissioner and newspaper publisher suggested of the U.S. Justice Department?

Wantz did not return a request for comment left at his detective agency.

A hallmark of systemic corruption is that concerned citizens have nowhere to turn with their complaints and concerns. The entire system's gone bad. No one can ring the alarm bell. Time and again, in Pennsylvania, people have come to me not only with stories of outrageous corruption, but complaints that they have no place to go with their concerns.

Citizens, and even officials, have lost faith in the state police and the FBI. Worse, they fear retaliation if they come forward.

Why are they afraid? As we've seen, the FBI is distrusted. Our top federal police force lacks integrity and trustworthiness, and is badly overdue for reform, and reorganization. Our state police forces aren't fairing much better.

In Maryland, top state police officials were caught financing a sex ring with a secret slush fund. On the other end of Jonathan Luna's ride, in Pennsylvania, the Pennsylvania State Police in late 2003 reported that *thirty-four* of its troopers had been *convicted* of crimes in the previous eight years. The convictions stemmed from *eighty-eight* felony and misdemeanor cases ranging from sexual assault, incest, indecent exposure, illegal wiretapping, to drunk driving. Of the thirty-four convictions, eight troopers still remained on the job. Zero tolerance for everyone but them. This, in the police agency once described by Theodore Roosevelt as the finest in the world. It's shameful.

These problems in our state police denote not only a lack of oversight, as has plagued the FBI, but also a lack of public involvement. Americans are being conditioned to be fearful of speaking out against problems or outright corruption in our police forces and our courts.

How bad is it? One day a court expert told me of an influence-peddling scheme involving a York County, Pennsylvania, judge.

This expert it so happened had testified in a prominent case before another judge, York County Common Pleas Judge Sheryl Ann Dorney. It was an important case involving children attacked at school by a mentally ill, machete-wielding man. The attack turns out to have been preventable. Two county agencies neglected to pass along warnings to authorities. As a result, children were hurt. The allegations demand investigation.

I wrote Judge Dorney a registered letter in February 2003, ten months before Jonathan Luna's death, informing her of the new information in her case, and asking for an interview.

In the same letter, as a courtesy, I passed along to Judge Dorney the town newspaper's allegations that security personnel were running a sex ring in her courthouse, and that there was not a mechanism in place to properly review the backgrounds of the guards. By this time, making matters worse, the county sheriff, William Hose, had been accused in open court of helping to instigate the murder of Lillie Belle Allen, the young, black, minister's daughter caught in a police ambush in 1969. It was a year after the mayor of York had been acquitted by a jury for the same murder. Charming town, isn't it?

I wrote Judge Dorney, "In this day of heightened security, do you find it ironic or merely business-as-usual in York County that an alleged pimp and an accused participant in a botched police murder are standing guard at the doorways of our courthouse? What sort of message does this send to our citizens and our youth?"

I concluded by passing along the oft-heard complaint that, "the fear of retaliation and retribution (prevents citizens) from coming forward to report crimes such as these to the appropriate authorities."

Several canon in the Pennsylvania Code of Judicial Conduct, which governs state judges, not only demand, but rightly *require* Dorney to take action. A judge isn't supposed to casually sit around gabbing and corresponding about law breaking, particularly, we might suppose, murder, prostitution and reckless endangerment of children.

One canon reads, "A judge should take or initiate appropriate disciplinary actions against a judge or a or lawyer for unprofessional conduct of which the judge may become aware.... Disciplinary measures may include reporting a judge's or lawyer's misconduct to an appropriate disciplinary body."

Months passed. On May 21, 2003, Judge Dorney returned my letter inside her own envelope, printed with her official court letterhead. Across the bottom of the envelope was marked, in big letters, "Returned to Sender / Unread." My letter had obviously been opened and read. What we had here was a failure to communicate.

Though saddened, I confess I was not surprised. Saddest of all were all those children who were hurt, due to official negligence, who Dorney did nothing to protect. There was only one more place to turn. I reported Judge Dorney to the state Judicial Conduct Board, itself an ethically challenged body.

Months later, on October 29, 2003, I received a strangely unsigned and anonymous letter from the Conduct Board. If Dorney was afraid, so was the Conduct Board.

"The Board has asked me to advise you that it has dismissed the complaint," my unnamed correspondent informed me. "The Judicial Conduct Board appreciates your taking the time to make your complaint known and for your interest in the improvement of our judicial system."

The letter bears no signature or identifying mark of the sender at the Conduct Board.

As far as I know, the York County courthouse sex ring is the only such institution kept open by the courts outside of Nevada.

We can only hope Jonathan Luna did not meet his death, leaving two young children without a father, because Judge Dorney and the Pennsylvania Judicial Conduct Board didn't uphold the rule of law.

On December 10, 2007, Pennsylvania state security contractor Russell Wantz, Jr., owner of the Schaad Detective Agency, was arrested by police in Dauphin County, Pennsylvania, outside of Harrisburg, on charges of soliciting a prostitute.